Rumer Godden is one of Brita... authors, with many justly famous a... both adults and children to her credit, including *Black Narcissus* and *The Greengage Summer*. Both volumes of her autobiography, *A Time to Dance, No Time to Weep* and *A House With Four Rooms* were published by Macmillan in 1987 and 1989 respectively. A collection of short stories with Jon Godden, *Indian Dust*, also appeared in 1989.

She lives in Scotland.

RUMER GODDEN

Coromandel Sea Change

The Greengage Summer

The River

PAN BOOKS

Coromandel Sea Change first published 1991 by Macmillan
and first published by Pan Books 1992
The Greengage Summer first published 1958 by Macmillan
and first published by Pan Books 1961: published with a new preface by Pan Books 1993
The River first published 1946 by Michael Joseph Ltd
and first published by Pan Books 1991 with a new preface

This combined edition published 1995 by Pan Books
an imprint of Macmillan General Books
25 Eccleston Place, London SW1W 9NF

Associated companies throughout the world

ISBN 0 330 34594 X

1 3 5 7 9 10 8 6 4 2

A CIP catalogue record for this book is available from
the British Library

Printed and bound in Great Britain by
Cox & Wyman Ltd, Reading, Berkshire

Coromandel
Sea Change

To Oscar – Sir Owain Jenkins –
my dear old 'enemy', who has done
so much to help me

'They come for the sea change,' said
Auntie Sanni and she might have added . . .
'into something rich and strange.'

Contents

Acknowledgements

My sincere thanks are due to: Alan Maclean for his guidance over the book; my editor, Hazel Orme, for her constant care and patience; Tigger Stack for her expert help on Indian affairs and beliefs, also Shahrukh Husain whose books and advice have been invaluable; to Sir Owain Jenkins for his contribution of precious tidbits and, as always, to Ena Logan Brown and Sheila Anderson who typed and retyped without flagging.

R. G.

List of Characters

Auntie Sanni	Miss Sanni to her servants, owner of Patna Hall
Colonel McIndoe	her husband

Staff at Patna Hall

Samuel	butler and major domo
Hannah	his wife, housekeeper
Kuku	the young hotel manager
Thambi	lifeguard on the beach and general guard
Moses } Somu }	lifeguards on the beach
Ganga	the wine waiter
Mustafa } Abdul } Ahmed }	waiters
Alfredo	the Goanese cook

houseboys, sweepers, a washerman, gardeners, etc.

For the election

Gopal Rau	candidate for the Patriotism Party
Mrs Padmina Retty	candidate for the People's Shelter Party
Krishnan Bhanj	candidate for the Root and Flower Party
Dr Hari Coomaraswamy	leader of the Root and Flower Party's campaign
Mr Srinivasan	his aide
Sharma	their young District Agent

Ravi ⎫	
Anil ⎭	young party workers
the disciples	other young men and women of the Root and Flower Party campaign

Guests at Patna Hall this week

Sir John and Lady (Alicia) Fisher	
Mrs Olga Manning	
Professor Aaron	leader of the International Association of Art, Technology and Culture
Professor Ellen Webster	lecturer to the group
Mrs van den Mar	leader of eighteen American lady archaeologists, professional and amateur
Mrs Glover ⎫	
Mrs Schlumberger ⎪	
Dr Julia Lovat ⎬	archaeologists
Miss Pritt ⎪	
Mr Menzies ⎭	
Blaise St John Browne ⎫	
Mary Browne ⎭	on honeymoon

Others

Kanu	a small fisherboy
Shyama	Thambi's wife
Chief Inspector Anand	police officer
Krishna ⎫	
Radha ⎬	gods and goddesses
Lakshmi ⎭	

Animals

Slippers	a donkey
Birdie	an elephant
Udata	a squirrel
Christabel	Auntie Sanni's mynah bird

Time

any time

Saturday

Saturday was change-over day at Patna Hall.

'Two hundred sheets,' shouted the *vanna* – the old washerman was close to weeping. 'Two hundred pillowcases *and* the towels. That is too much.'

'It is because of the election.' Auntie Sanni was unmoved. 'So many people coming and going besides our own guests.'

Usually guests, as Auntie Sanni liked to call them, stayed at least a week or ten days, two weeks sometimes three, even three months like Mrs Manning. Sheets were changed three times a week and always, of course, when a guest came or went but now, 'Too many,' wailed the *vanna*.

'It is for the good of your country.' Hannah, the Madrassi housekeeper, was always a reconciler; she also happened to be a strong partisan for the new and hopeful Root and Flower Party. 'Don't you care for your country?'

'I care that I can't wash two hundred sheets.'

'A contract is a contract.' Auntie Sanni was unrelenting. 'It does not say how many or how little. Take them and go.'

'And none of your ironing without washing them first,' sharp little Kuku put in.

'Wash them yourself,' said the *vanna* and left the bundles lying on the floor.

* * *

The three women in the linen room took no notice. They knew, as the *vanna* knew, that there were many *vannas* in Shantipur, even more in the port of Ghandara four kilometres away, all with swarming families, all poor; not one of them would let a contract with Patna Hall be taken from him. 'He will soon be back,' Hannah prophesied.

The linen room at Patna Hall was in a small cloistered courtyard built at the side of the main house for administrative offices and linen room, store rooms, a pantry or confectioner's room where Patna Hall's own specialist puddings and desserts were made with, nowadays, a refrigerating room. These were to be expected but Auntie Sanni's office was part business, part conservatory, part menagerie. The convolvulus blue of morning glory tumbled over the window, pots of canna lilies and hibiscus stood in corners; tame birds, cockateels and mynahs, flew round the room. One mynah, Christabel, had learned to call Kuku so cleverly that Kuku never knew if it were Christabel or Auntie Sanni. There were doves; bright green parakeets flew in from the garden and mingled with them all – often they perched on Auntie Sanni's desk, watching her fearlessly, their scarlet-topped heads on one side. It was not only birds: two cats, tabbies, slept stretched on a mat in the sun; a brown spotted goat was tethered outside while her kids wandered in and out, one white, one brown as if the colours had been divided. 'But don't let the monkeys in,' Hannah had warned Kuku, 'they take too many things.'

The monkeys were small, brown and wild; their brown faces and bright eyes peered from the trees. They ran across the courtyard on all fours, their tails lifted, their small skinny hands quickly into anything – 'and everything,' said Hannah – and always, all through rooms and cloister, the soft Indian sea breeze blew bringing the sound of the waves crashing on the beach below.

* * *

2

Auntie Sanni – Miss Sanni to her staff and servants – was called Auntie because, in Eurasian parlance, that is the title given to any grown-up female whether she has nephews and nieces or not. Auntie Sanni had none by blood but, over the years, had acquired many – Auntie of the universe would have fitted her. She dominated the linen room as she dominated Patna Hall. 'Why?' Kuku often wondered. To her Auntie Sanni was only an unattractive massive old woman, nobody knew how old. 'No shape to her at all,' said Kuku, looking at her in one of her usual cotton dresses like a tent reaching to her feet, its voluminous folds patterned with blue flowers; Auntie Sanni called them her 'Mother Hubbards' from the garments missionaries used to hand out to the natives. On her feet were country-made sandals. Auntie Sanni's face looked young because of her head of short curls like a child's, their red still auburn. Her skin was true Eurasian, the pale yellow brown of old ivory against which her eyes looked curiously light, sea-colour eyes, now green, now blue, set wide, again like a child's but Hannah, even Kuku, could have told that Auntie Sanni was no child.

Hannah, almost her bondswoman, began piling the bundles tidily together, her silver bangles slipping up and down her arms. Hannah liked everything to be tidy, clean, exact, as did her husband, Samuel. They, for Auntie Sanni, were the twin pillars of Patna Hall.

Hannah was a big woman – though not beside Auntie Sanni. Kuku, when she was with them, looked wand slim, quick and brilliant as a kingfisher in her electric blue sari with its lurex border. Hannah had eyed that sari. 'Muslin for morning is nice,' she had said, 'and practical.'

'This, too, is practical,' Kuku had retorted. 'It is drip dry.'

Hannah herself wore a crisp white sari edged with red and an old-fashioned red bodice high in the neck, her scant grey hair pinned into a knob. In spite of this simplicity she was laden with silver jewellery: bangles; the lobes of her

3

ears hung down with the weight of earrings; she had finger rings and toe rings on her gnarled bare feet; everyone knew where Hannah was by the sound of clinking. Kuku's *choli* stopped in a curve under breasts that were young and full, it left her midriff bare, supple and brown; her hair which could have made the usual graceful coil was instead frizzed into a mane that reached her shoulders; she had a flower over her left ear. 'Miss Sanni, why let her go about so?' Hannah often said to Auntie Sanni. 'That hair! Those nails! And a sari should be muslin, silk or gauze,' and Auntie Sanni always answered, 'I don't think Kuku has saris like that.'

Kuku was an orphan, brought up in St Perpetua's Home in Madras. 'St Perpetua's, very good,' Hannah had always maintained. She and Samuel were English-speaking Thomist Christians. 'St Thomas, apostle, came to Madras and is buried there,' they said. Kuku, though, was now proudly agnostic. No one knew what Auntie Sanni believed; perhaps all religions met in her as they met peaceably in Patna Hall; the gardeners were Brahmins, the sweeper women, untouchables, the waiters all Muslim while the head bearer, Colonel McIndoe's personal servant from Nepal, was a Buddhist. Nothing seemed to disturb any of them and, 'Yes, St Perpetua's is very good,' Auntie Sanni endorsed Hannah. 'It gives all its girls an excellent education and trains them for work but I don't think they get many saris.'

Kuku had been trained in hotel management. 'I didn't have to be trained,' said Auntie Sanni. 'I knew.'

Auntie Sanni's grandfather had started the hotel in the eighteen nineties but the house was older than that, 'Built by some nabob of the East India Company in the eighteenth century to catch the sea breezes,' she had told Kuku.

'Could they have come so far without cars or the railway?'

'Far from Calcutta but there were plenty of East India Company men in Madras. They would have had horses and palanquins.'

'What are palanquins?' asked Kuku.

'My grandfather made a fortune out of indigo in Bihar,' Auntie Sanni would tell the guests. 'That's why the hotel is called Patna Hall. Patna is the capital of Bihar.' She herself had never seen the acres of the leafy flowering shrub that brought such riches as, processed – 'My grandfather had his own factory' – the flowers turned from olive to orange and finally to the intense blue of indigo. 'All sailors' livery used to be dyed with it, all blue cloth until chemical dyes became rife.' 'Rife' as Auntie Sanni said it was a dirty word. 'My grandfather got out just in time. They were lovely colours, indigo, madder, sepia, those greens and turmeric yellows,' she said softly. 'It is seldom nowadays that you get colours like that.'

Patna Hall was the only substantial house on that stretch of the Coromandel coast; its stucco, as befitted the property of an indigo planter, was painted blue, now faded to paleness; it rose three storeys high to a parapeted roof. The porticoed entrance faced inwards towards the village of Shantipur with its palms and *simile* trees, their cotton flowers scarlet; behind them low hills, where coffee grew, cut off the horizon. There were servants' quarters, the courtyard offices, a gatehouse, a large vegetable garden, a small farm and poultry yard, even a private cemetery.

On the other side of the house facing the sea, a garden of English and Indian flowers sloped to a private beach that had a bungalow annexe. On every side dunes of fine white sand stretched away, planted with feathery casuarina trees; on the right the dunes led to a grove of mango and more *simile* trees; on the left they rose to a knoll that overlooked the demesne. On the foreshore of hard sand, the great rollers of the Coromandel Sea thundered down, giant waves that rose to eight, even ten feet, before they crashed sending a wash far up the sand. Further out, by day, the sea was a deep sapphire blue.

The hotel beach was forbidden to fishermen or their boats; indeed, the sea there was netted to a distance of five hundred yards not only against fishermen but sharks; every night Thambi, the lifeguard, and his assistants, Moses and Somu, unfolded a high strong-meshed fence across the private beach padlocking it so that the beach was cut off from the sea. 'Unless there is bathing by moonlight,' said Thambi.

'Please,' Auntie Sanni would say seriously to each guest, 'please remember it is dangerous to go out alone to bathe. With the force and power of those waves, you must take a guard.'

Women bathers usually had to have a man each side to hold them and bring them up through the wave to ride gloriously back on its crest of surf. Thambi would let no one go into it without wearing one of the fishermen's pointed wicker helmets bound firmly under the chin; the helmet's peak would pierce the waves that otherwise might stun. 'Ours is not a gentle sea,' said Auntie Sanni, 'and please,' she said again to her guests, 'no one must swim unless Thambi is on the beach.'

Patna Hall looked tall from the beach, the blue of its stucco ornamented with decorations of scrolls and flowers like daisies, oddly inconsequential. The flat roof was bounded by its balustraded parapet, which had a wide ledge on which young adventurous guests liked to sit. At night the house lights shone far across the sea; a small glow came, too, from the gatehouse where Thambi and his wife Shyama lived. Thambi was another of Auntie Sanni's right hands, hotel guard as well as beach lifeguard; it was Shyama who was supposed to open and shut the gates but as they were always open she had nothing to

6

do except to cook a little, dry chillies in the sun and wash her hair. 'Lazy little slut,' said Kuku. 'Thambi ought to beat her.'

'I thought you were a feminist.'

'I am but I don't like to see her.'

'I do,' said Auntie Sanni with a vision of the scarlet of the chillies and the blue-black hair.

Overlooking garden and sea, verandahs ran the full length of the house above a basement of cellars and fuel stores that was half buried in sand. The lower verandah was the sitting place for the whole hotel, with cane chairs and tables, cane stools and old-fashioned steamer chairs with extended boards each side on which feet could comfortably be put up. There was a bar at one end; at the other, Auntie Sanni's swing couch had bright chintz covers and cushions; before lunch – which she called tiffin – and before dinner she liked to sit there and reign.

Inside, behind the verandah the rooms were high, floored with dark red stone which Samuel saw was polished; every morning a posse of village women came in to sit on the floor moving slowly forward on their bottoms as they pushed bottles, their ends wrapped in a waxed cloth until the stone shone. The upper air was stirred by *punkahs* – electric flat-bladed fans; when the sea breeze was strong they stirred by themselves. If the wind was too high, sand blew in over the floors to Samuel's grief.

There was a billiard room; though few house guests played billiards, gentlemen, chiefly Indian, came in from Ghandara to play and have drinks – there was a bar in the billiard room as well. The verandah was reserved for resident guests.

The drawing room, away from the sea, was immense, a double room; the stone floor here was green. It was so little used that the electric fans overhead creaked when they were switched on. 'So much empty space,' mourned Kuku.

7

'Which is always useful,' said Auntie Sanni, 'and makes for peace and health, two things that are uncommon in this country which is why people come.'

Hannah reigned over the bedrooms with, under her, not women servants but men, bearers or houseboys in brass-buttoned white tunics, white trousers, black caps, while Samuel was king of the dining room behind the verandah.

Samuel was regal, white-whiskered, white-bearded, his clothes immaculately white and starched, his turban huge with, round it, a red and gold band on which, in brass, was Auntie Sanni's family crest – 'My grandfather's crest.' The waiters wore modest imitations – woe betide any of them who had a spot or smudge on their tunics or trousers.

The food was delectable, the service unhurried; neither Auntie Sanni nor Samuel had heard of unions and, though luncheon was served at one, dinner at eight, the dining room kept no hours. The food was brought in from the cookhouse outside; in the magical way of Indian servants it was kept hot by the old-fashioned use of packing cases lined with zinc in which were gridded shelves with a brazier burning red below.

From the first day she came there had been battles between Kuku and Samuel. 'Always objecting. Never do as she is asked. Why not?' demanded Samuel.

'I suppose an orphan girl without money has to fight,' said Auntie Sanni. 'Poor little Kuku. She hasn't learned that the best way to fight is by not fighting. Also, we are getting old, Samuel, perhaps we need fresh blood,' and, seeing disbelief in his eyes, 'but I think Kuku will soon go on to something else, she won't be satisfied here. Besides St Perpetua's asked me to take her. Kuku needs a chance.'

'I think we are full up,' said Auntie Sanni in her office this Saturday morning.

'Full up! My God!' Kuku had brought the ledger from the reception desk in the hall. 'I don't know where to put them all.'

'Let me see.' Auntie Sanni opened the big register. There were, of course, permanencies, in chief Colonel McIndoe, Auntie Sanni's husband, though no one called her Mrs McIndoe. They had a suite on the first floor overlooking the sea. There was Kuku's small room on the floor above. 'The first room I have ever had of my own,' she had exclaimed in delight when she came. Samuel and Hannah had their own neat house, kept apart from the other servants' quarters by a hedge of poinsettias. 'Let me see,' said Auntie Sanni.

'Sir John and Lady Fisher?' Kuku peered over her shoulder.

'Number one,' said Hannah immediately.

'They are our oldest, dearest guests.' Auntie Sanni's voice dropped into a singsong which, like most Eurasians, she did not recognise as part Indian though it made Kuku wince – Kuku had tried to acquire an American accent. 'Sir John says they can only stay a week this time. You will put flowers in their room and fruit and order a taxi to meet the connection from Delhi.

'Professor Aaron and his ladies . . .'

'Eighteen of them,' added Hannah.

'One tourist professor, eighteen tourist ladies!' Kuku giggled but Hannah looked at her severely. 'This is Patna Hall,' said the look. 'We don't take tourists.'

Auntie Sanni explained, 'It is a cultural group. The International Association of Art, Technology and Culture. Professor Aaron brings a group every year, sometimes for archaeology, sometimes it is botany. Sometimes there are men but all are highly qualified. Last year the group was French, this year they are American.'

'Americans are the worst tourists,' said Kuku.

'You say that because you have heard it.' For once

Auntie Sanni was wrathful. 'What do you know about it? The British can be every bit as bad, also the Germans and you will not call these ladies tourists, do you hear? Some of them themselves are professors.'

'Old?' asked Kuku without interest.

'Usually middle-aged. Young people haven't the time or money – the tours are very expensive.'

'They come from all over,' said Hannah. 'They will bring books, notebooks, maps, binoculars, magnifying glasses, cameras, what all.'

'This time it is archaeology. They will visit the new diggings at Ghorāghat, also the cave paintings in our own hills but, especially, the great Dawn Temple at Ghorāghat, the temple of Usas, the Dawn goddess.' Auntie Sanni, who had never seen the Dawn Temple, still said it reverently, then, 'A single for Professor Aaron,' she said returning to the ledger. 'Nine doubles for the ladies, they will not mind sharing. They are usually not fussy,' she told Kuku.

'Mr R. Menzies,' Kuku read out. 'He does not say when he is arriving.'

'Well, then, we cannot meet him. Give him a first floor back and, later tonight, Dr Coomaraswamy and Mr Srinivasan will be here.'

'What again?'

'Of course.' Hannah at once grew heated. 'Isn't Dr Coomaraswamy the leader of our campaign? Isn't Mr Srinivasan his aide? Isn't this the week of the election? The campaign starts tomorrow. Of course they are all coming back.'

'Except Krishnan Bhanj, your candidate,' said Kuku.

That slowed Hannah. 'I do not know why,' she said, 'so often he has stayed here since he was a little boy, he and his parents, very good high-up people. He was here last month. Why not now?'

'No one knows but Krishnan,' said Auntie Sanni, 'and we can be sure he knows why.'

'God almighty Krishnan!' mocked Kuku. 'He's not going to win you know. It said so on the radio. Padmina Retty has held the seat for so long. Mrs Retty, Mother to the People of Konak.'

'Much good has it done them.' Hannah was fierce.

'Krishnan Bhanj is an upstart. They all say so.'

'Hardly an upstart,' said Auntie Sanni. 'Krishnan has been in politics since the day he was born, but in any case, I could not have had Mrs Retty here with Dr Coomaraswamy. He booked first. Also, with him', Auntie Sanni told them, 'will be at least ten, maybe twenty young electioneering assistants.'

'My God!' but Auntie Sanni was unperturbed. 'They will be out on the campaign all day and they can sleep in Paradise.'

Paradise was a line of cell-like rooms on Patna Hall's roof. Once upon a time European or American chauffeurs were put there, now and again ladies' maids. 'When we had people from the embassies,' said Auntie Sanni and, of the men, 'They are young. They can sleep three or four to a room. Buy *charpoys*,' she ordered Kuku.

'Mrs Manning?' asked Kuku.

There was a pause, then, 'She stays where she is,' said Auntie Sanni.

'Taking up two rooms when we are so full and she hasn't paid for a month!'

'I think she cannot pay at present,' said Auntie Sanni.

'Manning Memsahib is not like a memsahib,' said Hannah. 'She washes her own things in the bathroom to save the *vanna*'s bill.'

That seemed sense to Kuku. 'We were encouraged to do that at St Perpetua's.'

'You are you,' Hannah's look said plainly.

'Mrs Manning still orders whisky, your whisky . . .' Kuku came out against Mrs Manning. 'Olga,' she mocked. 'I thought only Russians were called Olga and showing off with the piano.' If Kuku had admitted to what had hurt and rankled in her with Mrs Manning it was that Olga Manning had called her 'housekeeper'.

'The housekeeper is Hannah. I am hotel manager.'

'Indeed!' The hazel eyes had looked at her amused. 'How long have you been that?' and, 'Six weeks,' Kuku had had to say and now, 'Where is Mr Manning, I should like to know?' she asked.

'Kuku, we do not pry into our guests' affairs.'

'Perhaps better if we did and they are not guests, they are clients and supposed,' Kuku said defiantly, 'supposed to pay.'

Auntie Sanni did not choose to answer that. Instead, 'Mr and Mrs Browne,' she read out. 'They will not arrive until Sunday afternoon. Lady Malcolm recommended them. The girl is freshly out from England. They are, I believe, on honeymoon.'

'Aie!' said Hannah. 'They should have had the bridal suite.'

'Dr Coomaraswamy and Mr Srinivasan have booked the bridal suite long ago for the whole of the campaign.'

'What a bridal pair!' Kuku giggled again.

'Mr and Mrs Browne can have the second half of the bungalow,' said Auntie Sanni. 'So close to the beach and away from other guests, they should be happy there.'

That made Kuku brood again over Mrs Manning in the bungalow's other half, the half that had a sitting room.

'Miss Sanni,' she said, 'you will never make a profit.'

'Profit?' asked Auntie Sanni, as if to say what could she do with a profit. 'Patna Hall pays its way very nicely,' her singsong went on. 'Colonel McIndoe and I, Samuel and Hannah and Thambi have all that we want.'

Kuku's exasperation broke. 'You should put up one of those hotel notices on your gates, "Do Not Disturb".'

'That would be very nice,' said Auntie Sanni.

12

* * *

Professor Aaron and the cultural ladies, as Hannah called them, were the first to arrive, in time for luncheon; eighteen ladies. 'They can match with the young men in Paradise.' Kuku giggled again.

The big red-bearded Professor kissed Auntie Sanni, bowed to Hannah and introduced the group, which was led by Mrs van den Mar from Michigan – not with the waved blue-grey hair, Kuku had automatically expected. Mrs van den Mar wore hers in a plait round her head and, for all her elegance – 'I think she is rich,' whispered Kuku – was plump, comfortable, 'and I think comforting,' Auntie Sanni would have said. 'A good leader.' She introduced the most distinguished archaeologist of them all, Professor Ellen Webster, thin, earnest, brown hair cut in a fringe, spectacles. 'She is a senior professor in the Department of Archaeology at Yale University. She will give us our lectures,' said Professor Aaron. 'And who', he asked, 'is this charming young person?'

'Miss Kuku Vikram, who has come to help me,' said Auntie Sanni.

'You don't need any help,' the Professor said gallantly.

As Hannah had predicted they had much paraphernalia: satchels, shoulder bags full of notebooks, shooting sticks, camp stools, binoculars, cameras, dark glasses. To Kuku they seemed, too, all dressed alike; each carried a light raincoat; they wore cotton short-sleeved shirts, skirts or trousers in neutral colours, one or two in blue denim; some had eyeshades, others cotton-brimmed hats and all were eager, happy, intent. Impressed in spite of herself, Kuku murmured to Hannah, 'They must be very cultured.'

Mrs van den Mar's first eager question to Auntie Sanni, though, was anything but cultural. 'We're looking forward to your famous mulligatawny soup Professor Aaron has told us so much about. We hope it will be for lunch.'

13

'The soup of the day is vichyssoise,' Kuku said with pride.

Their faces fell. 'I can have vichyssoise in Michigan,' said Mrs van den Mar.

'I told you so,' Samuel hissed at Kuku, his moustaches bristling with fury. 'Do you think, after so many years butler at Patna Hall, I do not know what sahibs like to eat? You . . .' If Samuel had known the word 'chit' he would have used it, all he could say was 'upstart'.

'We shall have mulligatawny tomorrow,' and Auntie Sanni softened the blow further, 'Today we have our equally famous prawn curry, prawns fresh from the sea. Now, may Miss Kuku and Hannah show you to your rooms?'

Half an hour later, the ladies gathered on the verandah where Kuku served at the bar. 'Coffee, tea and soft drinks only,' Auntie Sanni had laid down. 'Indian young ladies do not serve hard drinks or wine,' but to Samuel's anger Kuku often transgressed, usurping what belonged to Ganga, the wine waiter. Now she served the cultural ladies with a favourite suggested by Professor Aaron, 'Gin and ginger beer, taken long, with plenty of ice,' but, 'Do you know how to make mint julep?' one of them asked Kuku. 'So refreshing!' Kuku, to her chagrin, had to ask Samuel. Some had iced tea. 'That's a very beautiful sari,' another said to Kuku, seduced by the colour. Samuel sniffed.

'Well, have you settled in?' Professor Aaron went from one to another.

'Indeed,' said a gentle Mrs Glover. 'We are charmed, Professor, truly charmed. We never expected anything like this.'

'I certainly did *not* expect anything like this,' an indignant voice came as a stout lady stumped on to the verandah. 'Have you *seen* the bathrooms?'

'They are primitive,' Mrs Glover had to admit.

'Primitive! Never did I think that to take a bath I should have to sit on a stool and pour water over me with a *pitcher*.' Mrs Schlumberger was the group grumbler. Now she looked up sharply. Kuku had not been able to restrain a giggle.

'Isn't it good to do as the people here do?' pleaded Mrs Glover.

'And it's far more hygienic than lying in a bath using the same water over and over again,' that was Dr Julia Lovat. 'The Indians say that we Westerners with our baths are like buffaloes wallowing in their own dirty water.'

'Julia! How can you?'

'All the same, I shall miss my shower.' Miss Pritt, the only unmarried one and handsome, tried to placate.

'We'll miss far more than that.' Mrs Schlumberger was not to be appeased. 'That sweet little manager agrees with me. Says the lady refuses to modernise.'

'Oh, come! There is air-conditioning . . .'

'No telephone in the rooms . . . no room-service . . . I wouldn't have come if I had known.'

'We can always arrange to send you back,' Mrs van den Mar said sweetly. 'Ah, lunch! I expect you'll feel better after lunch.'

Two large round tables had been set up for them in the dining room, Professor Aaron hosting one, Mrs van den Mar the other. 'For lectures they will use the drawing room,' Auntie Sanni had said, 'so open it properly,' she told Kuku. 'Put flowers.'

When opened the drawing room looked well with its Persian carpets – 'Kerman,' said Auntie Sanni – on the dark green floor. Potted palms stood in polished brass pots, also on the floor; chairs and sofas were covered in a sweet pea chintz. Around the fireplace, which had an enormous grate, a fire seat made a circle; the mantel above held Victorian china and over it was a painting, a portrait

15

of Auntie Sanni as a child with the same short chestnut curls; other paintings of the indigo plantations hung on the walls. There was an upright piano with pleated silk above the keyboard and brass candlesticks; antique as it was, Mrs Manning liked to play it in the evenings, even when the room was shrouded.

'Well, she can't do that while the conference is on,' said Kuku with satisfaction. Then an idea struck her. 'Couldn't she play something catchy for us during dinner? We could move the piano into the dining room. I will ask her.'

'You will *not*.' Auntie Sanni came down on Kuku like the juggernaut at the Dawn Temple which came out on festival days to carry the Goddess and could crush mere humans under its wheels. 'In our dining room people can still enjoy their food in *quiet*.' All the same, Auntie Sanni was uneasy about Mrs Manning's playing in the evenings. 'It sounds so lonely,' she had said more than once to Hannah.

'It is lonely,' said Hannah.

'You have not changed one i-o-ta.' Auntie Sanni greeted Sir John and Lady Fisher.

'Nor you.' Lady Fisher kissed Auntie Sanni. 'You never change.'

Sir John, on the verge of his sixties – 'I retire next year' – was, in Auntie Sanni's canny diagnosis, all that was elegant and excellent: still slim, upright, his voice was quiet and firm; his sun-tanned skin, after years in the tropics, contrasted oddly with his silvered hair, while Lady Fisher had kept a complexion that looked as if it had never felt a rough wind. 'I don't suppose it has,' said Auntie Sanni.

In any case Lady Fisher preferred not to go on the beach or bathe or lie in the sun. 'Then why does she come?' asked Kuku.

'To be with Sir John,' with which Lady Fisher and Sir John would have completely agreed.

16

'Have you never heard', asked Auntie Sanni, 'that men need rest? The more successful they are, the more in the public eye, the more they need it. There was never a more restful and calm person than Lady Fisher or one who listens more,' but now, 'I am sorry,' she told the Fishers as she led them from the hall to the verandah, 'sorry that the election should have come at this time. The house is so full, I am afraid you will have little peace.'

'I don't think it will disturb us,' said Sir John, while, 'Dear Aunt Sanni,' said Lady Fisher – she and Sir John gave her the dignity of 'Aunt' – 'with you there is always peace.'

'They have been coming here for fifteen years,' Auntie Sanni told Kuku. 'I am proud to say they are our friends, Colonel McIndoe's and mine.'

'A tinpot little election, how could it disturb them?' Kuku asked on the verandah that evening and was overheard by Dr Coomaraswamy.

'Tinpot!' He was indignant. 'An election that concerns at least a quarter of a million people?'

'Perhaps a million people,' put in Mr Srinivasan.

'There are too many people.'

Kuku seemed able to flirt even with the ends of her sari; Dr Coomaraswamy's brown eyes, already so prominent that they looked like a fish's or seemed, as a snail's, to have come out on stalks following Kuku's every movement. 'Yes, too many,' Mr Srinivasan was saying. 'If we have a million, soon there will be two million. Not long and there will be four. For-tun-ately one of the most important things in our Root and Flower Party's programme is restriction, the making popular of the use of condoms—'

'Srinivasan! Not in front of Lady Fisher and Miss Kuku,' cried Dr Coomaraswamy.

'I think, dear Doctor, both Kuku and I have heard of birth control,' said Lady Fisher.

Dr Coomaraswamy knew that he was elderly, as his wife Uma was always telling him; elderly and unlovely, he thought. He was bald, over-stout, obviously well to do, well dressed – his suits were made for him in London. He flashed gold, gold-rimmed spectacles, gold pocket watch on a gold watch chain that stretched tightly across his stomach, the diamond in his little golden finger ring. By contrast, Mr Srinivasan was a little man, thin and light as an insect, always anxious, dressed in an ill-fitting European suit and what seemed to be over-large shoes, meticulously polished.

With them had come a cohort of young men. 'No young women?' Auntie Sanni had asked in surprise.

'They are staying at Ghandara in our headquarters. Females', said Dr Coomaraswamy, 'do not mind discomfort so much – they are more dedicated, I think. Besides Krishnan has a special mission for them. At the moment he will not tell me what but they are to go among the women which is good – the women's vote is important to us.'

'Of utmost importance,' said Mr Srinivasan.

The young men were in national dress, 'For this week,' said Dr Coomaraswamy. 'And for our young women, I myself have provided for them saris in green and white edged with yellow, our Party colours. They are to go in sandals, marigolds in their hair. Padmina Retty's women go in trousers! We shall be traditional which, strangely, is nowadays more modern.'

Charming as the young men were, they threatened to overrun Patna Hall until they found Paradise. 'They will be out at Ghandara or in the country most of the day,' soothed Auntie Sanni. Besides providing *charpoys* and cotton quilts she had ordered braziers to be lit on the roof and she told Samuel, 'Send two of the waiters, Mustafa and Ahmed, up with pots and pans so they can cook.'

18

'Kebabs are not on the menu,' Kuku objected.

'They are now,' said Auntie Sanni.

Mr Menzies came late that evening in a small red car, appearing out of the dark. 'From where?' asked Kuku, trying to be friendly, at the reception desk. He did not answer.

It was the first time she had seen, in actual flesh, a gentleman wearing a hair ribbon, his hair tied back in a bow. Sometimes men wore them on television – 'Oh, why, why, won't Auntie Sanni allow television?' had been Kuku's moan – but those men were young; if Mr Menzies had known it he was, for Kuku, too old to be of any interest. She did not either like his over-pink complexion, yellow-pink, like the little crabs on the beach when they are cooked. Kuku could not suppress a giggle, though Auntie Sanni had impressed, 'Best manners only while you are at reception.' Still less did she like the way his eyes – again, as if from the beach, they reminded her of small grey pebbles – looked her over and at once dismissed her. She did not know that Mr Menzies was not interested in girls unless they were in society which would have made them, for him, likely fodder.

He gave a London club as an address. 'Savage Club?' Kuku could not believe it but, 'He must be respectable to have a club,' she said afterwards to Auntie Sanni. 'Club' to Kuku meant exclusiveness.

'For how long will you be staying?' she asked.

'I'll see. Don't bother to come up,' he said. 'The boy can show me.' The 'boy', one of the bearers, picked up his briefcase, typewriter and suitcase.

'I'm afraid there is not a garage for your car.'

'Doesn't matter. It's only borrowed.'

'Most clients not coming by car,' Kuku explained.

At that he smiled. 'Ah! But, then, I am not most clients.'

Sunday

Kuku was never to forget her first sight of the Brownes or, rather, Mr Browne: she hardly noticed the girl.

They arrived in the peace of Sunday's late afternoon when everyone and everything seemed quiet before the stir of dinner; it was as if the little dust of the new guests had settled. 'It always does at Patna Hall,' said Auntie Sanni.

Dr Coomaraswamy, Mr Srinivasan and the cohorts had removed themselves to the Party Headquarters at Ghandara – they had their own hired coach. Mr Menzies had followed them not long after. 'He must be something connected with politics,' Kuku had guessed. The cultural ladies and Professor Aaron had set aside Sunday for resting after their long journey and stayed in their rooms. Sir John and Lady Fisher were on the verandah, she stitching, he reading; they might never have been away. Mrs Manning was walking along the beach. All was quiet when the Shantipur taxi drew up.

'Browne with an e,' the young man instructed as he signed the register at the desk but Kuku hardly heard: she was gazing at his height, his fairness that was to her dazzlingly fair.

The young wife seemed no match for her husband – she was so slight, her over-large spectacles making her look like a schoolgirl – but she too was fair, grey-eyed with mouse-pale brown hair that fell to her shoulders and hid her face as it swung forward like a soft bell.

Both, though, had what Kuku called English complexions. 'Apple blossom,' murmured Kuku in despair.

Kuku was dark-skinned and had been schooled to think that, above all, fairness was desirable, all beauty had to be fair. The marriage advertisements in the newspapers showed that clearly: 'Educated England, returned young barrister seeks fair girl'. Sometimes it was the other way on: 'Highly educated, executive-positioned, fair Brahmin young lady wishes to contact eligible young gentleman in similar employment', or more naïve and old-fashioned: 'Wanted: young man, preferably in Government Service for fair good-looking girl. Knows music and knitting'. There did not seem much hope for the Kukus of this world.

He signed the register 'Blaise St John Browne'. 'Blaise! What an uncommon name!' Kuku dared to say. He looked at her with such surprise that she saw she had transgressed and flushed. The girl saw it too and stepped forward. 'You don't have to sign,' he told her. 'You come under me.'

Auntie Sanni, who had appeared in the doorway, caught the look she gave him; caught too, a sight of a small firm chin, when the hair swung back, as she firmly signed her name, 'Mary Browne'.

There was more to it than that. 'When my husband was born,' the girl told Kuku, 'his parents could not decide on a name uncommon enough for him, so they compromised with Blaise.'

'Mary!' He had turned crimson. 'For God's sake . . .'

But the clear voice went on. 'When I was born the nurses asked my father what I should be called – it had to be the nurses, unfortunately my mother had died. He said the first name that came into his head, "Mary." You can't wonder,' the girl would not stop, 'we were in Rome, you see, and Rome is full of Marys though there they say "Maria".'

'Mary, Reception isn't even remotely interested—'

21

'Oh, but I am, I am,' cried Kuku.

'All those churches: Santa Maria degli Angeli, Santa Maria dell' Assunta, Santa Maria Maggiore, Santa Maria Rotondo . . .'

Now what, wondered Auntie Sanni, could have provoked all that?

Mary could have told her: it was the journey from Madras. It had enchanted her, especially after three weeks spent in Ootacamund, 'Which might have been England,' she had said disappointed. 'It even has a vicar.'

'My dear child, most Indian towns of any size have an Anglican vicar,' Blaise had told her. 'Why not?'

'I . . . just didn't expect it.' Mary knew she sounded naïve.

From Madras the train had gone through forests where sun filtered between tall trees and creepers; villages, golden-thatched, the houses often on stilts, appeared and disappeared. Mary saw elephants, the first elephants she had seen working. 'Bumble, look. Do look' – she had always heard Blaise called Bumble – 'Look,' but he was reading the *Madras Times*.

The elephants pulled logs; the small brown men round them gesticulated as they fastened chains or goaded the huge animals, swaying in their strength to strip trees with their trunks or push against them with their foreheads. In the groves she saw flowers growing along the tree branches in festoons. 'Bumble, could those possibly be wild orchids? Come and look.'

Indulgently he had come but carrying his paper. 'I wouldn't know an orchid from a daisy.'

'You must do.'

'I know those big purple ornate things you buy in florists.'

'These are wild,' but he had gone back to his reading.

On ponds or village tanks, water lilies floated. Often monkeys, small and brown, swung away from the train

22

among the trees. When the railway left the forests to run along the shore, nets seemingly as fine as gossamer were spread on the white sand and there were boats. Mary had sat entranced by the colour and sun but she did not ask Blaise to look again.

Now, at reception, Auntie Sanni thought it time to intervene and sailed into the hall. 'Good evening. Welcome to . . . ' but 'What's this?' Mr Browne was saying to Kuku 'Share a bungalow? An out bungalow! I booked for the main hotel.'

In agitation Kuku began hastily to turn the pages as if she were looking for another room but Auntie Sanni went on as if Blaise Browne had not spoken. 'Welcome to Patna Hall. I am Mrs McIndoe, the proprietor. The main hotel is full but, quite apart from that, we always put our younger guests in the bungalow if we can.' She made it sound like a favour. 'They like to be on the beach and so do away with formalities.'

'Yes, Blaise, it would be much nicer.' The girl's tone was conciliating, almost coaxing; obviously she did not want a scene.

'I booked—'

'I am sure you will find the bungalow most suitable.' Auntie Sanni put an end to the argument. 'Miss Kuku will take you there.'

'How handsome he is!' Kuku whispered to Auntie Sanni as the Brownes collected coats and hand luggage. Thambi picked up suitcases, tennis racquets, a big bag of golf clubs. 'So big and blond, like a young god. Is it Apollo?'

'Apollo?' Auntie Sanni looked sharply at Kuku.

Kuku took them down a small path that wound through what seemed a large garden; a path of white sand that glimmered in India's sudden dusk and was edged with shells and lit by old-fashioned lamp-posts. The sound of the sea grew louder as they came nearer. The bungalow

23

was almost on the beach, only separated by a narrow strip of garden from the foreshore; the roof was of palm thatch. The verandah rails shone white in the lamplight. Wicker chairs and a table stood on the floor of polished red stone. The bedroom had little but a wide bed, 'An *almirah*,' said Kuku opening the cupboard door to show hanging space and shelves, a chest of drawers with a looking glass and two chairs. *Durries* were on the floor.

To Mary it all gave a feeling of lightness and freedom but she could tell Blaise was not pleased, less pleased when he saw the bathroom, a dark little room, divided by a low kerb behind which was a single tap. 'Only cold water,' Kuku had to say in shame. Tall *gharras* were filled each morning from it, 'So that the water stays cool,' Auntie Sanni would have explained. Beside the *gharras* was a stool and an outsize zinc mug 'For pouring water over yourself,' but 'An Indian bathroom!' Blaise was as dismayed as Mrs Schlumberger.

'Our waterman will bring plenty of hot water', Kuku hurried to say, 'if you telephone.'

'At least we have a telephone,' said Blaise.

'Only a line to the house, I'm afraid,' Kuku apologised, but Mary could not think why they needed a telephone or hot water. 'We can bathe in the sea.'

'And there is a bar.' Kuku could show that in its small refrigerated cupboard with pride. 'You can help yourselves. There is ice but anything you want I shall bring.'

Blaise, who had not really looked at Kuku, said, '*Atcha*' as when dismissing a servant. Kuku, hurt, flushed darker, gathered up her sari and went. 'She hasn't even given us a key.'

'Why do we need a key?' asked Mary. 'It's all wide open.' Though the bungalow had heavy full-length wooden shutters to close against a storm, they were left folded back and the doorways had only half-doors set midway; made of light wood and woven palm, they swung slightly in the breeze. Now Mary pushed through them on to the verandah and stood there looking.

From the moment they had driven up to Patna Hall she had known she loved it; it seemed to breathe a new air. In those three weeks at Ootacamund the time had dragged so they had seemed like three years. They had stayed at the club and only met the club people, retired English or else westernised Indians; Blaise had played golf; Mary walked round with him. In the evening there was bridge; she had sat beside him until, desperate, she had wheedled, 'For the last week of your leave couldn't we go somewhere Indian, in India?'

'Little silly. Ooty is in India.'

'No, it's *not*,' but she did not say it, only coaxed, 'Lady Malcolm says there is a hotel further north by the sea, "India unchanged," she says.'

Blaise frowned. 'Lady Malcolm is the only person I have not liked here in Ootacamund.'

Mary had looked at him startled. Lady Malcolm was the only person she had liked.

Now, out on the verandah, she felt the sea breeze which was strong but warm. In India, night falls quickly and now, as the bungalow lights fell on the beach, she could only make out the pale crests of the rollers. Their noise surprised her; as they crashed on the sand the whole bungalow shook. Looking along the beach and the wet sand she could see small lights, lanterns or fires under a darkness of trees. She lifted her face to look up at the stars, at one in particular which shone over the sea, Hesperus, Venus, the evening star. My star, thought Mary. Behind it was the shape of a growing moon. Suddenly, an immense happiness filled her. What does anything matter? thought Mary. I'm here.

'No hangers.' Blaise was walking about, peering into

the cupboard, opening drawers. 'This really is a run-down place.'

'It doesn't feel like that. I like it.' Mary did not say 'love'. 'Funny,' she said, 'I never heard you called Blaise until Bombay. I thought you were Bumble. We were Bumble and Merry.'

'I have always been Blaise.'

'Yes,' and she said sadly, 'I suppose we've gone public.'

'I should hope so. You're my wife.' Blaise came and gave her a swift hug but she sensed that he was stiff as he always was when he was embarrassed – Mary had already learned that. It seemed he did not want to remember a certain little hidden garden hut in Norway, a memory she had clung to all these days. 'They're much nicer before you marry them.' Who had said that? Lady Malcolm . . . But I wanted to marry, thought Mary.

The sadness was interrupted by a clip-clopping sound, like heavy horse hoofs on a hard road but, How can anything clip-clop on sand? thought Mary. Then she saw a small brown shape with a white nose: a donkey had come up on the verandah.

'Bumble, Bumble. There's a donkey on the verandah.'

'A *donkey*! Get it out at once,' but Mary had seen why it clopped: the donkey's hoofs had never been trimmed or cut so that they turned up like Turkish slippers.

'Oh!' cried Mary. 'Oh, poor thing. Bumble, come and look.'

Long ago when in Rome, the small Mary had had an Italian nurse, Giovanna. Darling Giovanna, thought Mary as she remembered now how Giovanna had told her that because Jesus Christ sat on a donkey colt for his entrance into Jerusalem – it was somehow mixed, in Mary's otherwise pagan mind, with palms – 'Ever since,' Giovanna had said, 'all donkeys bear stripes like a cross on their backs.' Mary had not known if the story were true but she had always honoured donkeys and here, on this one's back, was the striped cross, plain to see. 'Bumble, look. Do come and look. Poor little thing.'

A laugh came from behind a white painted wickerwork partition. 'He isn't poor. He's a perfect little pest.'

The laugh, the voice were musical and deep for a woman but it was a woman who appeared on the garden path below the verandah. In the gathering dusk Mary could not see her plainly but had the impression of someone tall, thin as the wrapped skirt of her dress showed – an elegant dress – of dark hair pulled back into a coil at the nape of the neck. Mary could not see her face. 'A pest?' she said. 'He's sweet.'

'He's not at all sweet. No one has ever been able to shoe him or even catch him. Yet he likes people. He's here all the time. He comes up the side steps.'

'That he won't.' Blaise appeared in the doorway but, 'What's his name?' asked Mary.

'He hasn't a name. He's one of Auntie Sanni's pensioners.'

'Auntie Sanni? Do you mean Mrs McIndoe?'

'Auntie Sanni to us. You'll see.' The woman – lady, Mary corrected herself – paused looking at them, taking them in. 'How do you do? I am Mrs Manning, Olga Manning. I have a sitting room. Come round and have a drink and I'll tell you all about everything.'

'Thank you,' Blaise said quickly, 'but we have to change for dinner or we'll be late. Come along, Mary.' Mary gave a defiant little shrug, went down the steps, round the partition to Olga Manning's sitting room. The donkey clopped after her.

'Tonight is the inaugural meeting of our campaign.' Dr Coomaraswamy, Mr Srinivasan behind him, had come out on the house verandah for a drink before the gong sounded for dinner and found Sir John and Lady Fisher already there.

'Our inaugural meeting,' repeated Mr Srinivasan.

'Would you not come, Sir John, and give us your blessing?'

'My dear man,' Sir John laid his hand on the Doctor's shoulder, 'the last thing I feel like is a political meeting.'

'That is a pity. I am to make my inaugural speech.' Dr Coomaraswamy smiled at the thought: he loved oratory. 'I must make it exactly explicit. This is a rural district—'

'The people are extremely rural,' put in Mr Srinivasan.

'So that everything has to be explained, but everything, in Telegu as well as Tamil. Fortunately I, myself, am multilingual.' Dr Coomaraswamy visibly swelled. 'In European languages as well ... I shall begin ...'

'Does Dr Coomaraswamy have to make his inaugural speech twice?' Kuku asked audibly. Fortunately the Doctor was called to the telephone.

'Constantly he is called to the telephone.' Mr Srinivasan scurried after him.

'Same dear old Coomaraswamy,' said Sir John when they had gone. 'But I should have been interested to hear young Krishnan.'

'So would I,' said Lady Fisher.

'Where is your candidate?' Sir John asked when Dr Coomaraswamy and his echo came back. 'Where is Krishnan?'

There was a pause. The Doctor and Mr Srinivasan looked at one another with a slight unease, then, 'Krishnan Bhanj has chosen to remain at our headquarters in Ghandara.'

'In Ghandara,' confirmed Mr Srinivasan and Dr Coomaraswamy gave a sigh, such a sigh that, clearly, it came from the depths of his being. 'I confess to you, Sir John, I am profoundly disturbed. We do not understand at all what Krishnan is doing.'

'Or not doing,' Mr Srinivasan said piteously.

'Yet I have to accede as if there were some mystery

force. For instance, only last week I allowed him, from party funds, to spend ten thousand rupees on umbrellas.'

'*Umbrellas?*'

'Precisely.'

'To be distributed,' explained Mr Srinivasan.

'In Konak?' asked Sir John.

'No, not in Konak. That I could have understood but Krishnan ordered as far away as possible, actually in Bihar. It has something to do with the mission of our young women but now he asks a further twenty-five thousand rupees which he needs to carry this project out. It looks as if', Dr Coomaraswamy was still more glum, 'I myself will have to supply that.'

'But an umbrella', said Sir John, 'is the symbol of Padmina Retty's Shelter Party.'

'I have told Krishnan that. Besides, of course, he knows it perfectly well.'

'Hmm,' said Sir John.

The knoll to the left of Patna Hall was an unexpectedly high mound, topped by palm trees whose fronds rattled in the wind; a small path went up to where, under them, Auntie Sanni had put a seat. Every evening, when she had bathed and washed her hair, she would put on another clean, freshly ironed Mother Hubbard dress, also her pearl necklace, the pearls real and beautifully matched, take her palm leaf fan from Hannah, who had attended her, and then come out on the wide verandah where Colonel McIndoe, dressed too for dinner in linen trousers, a cummerbund and jacket, waited for her. He would make an arm, she would put her hand in it and slowly, because of her weight, they would walk up to the knoll. 'Walk! She lumbers,' said Kuku.

From the knoll they could survey all that was Auntie Sanni's: the hotel, the demesne and the beach – she had to acknowledge she could not own the sea.

On the other side of the hotel, in the grove, the trees were dark against the white sand. The fishermen had shrines under the casuarinas and sometimes lit *dipas* there. They made the pricks of light Mary had seen.

Below, Patna Hall itself was lit into brightness, its lights, like a necklace, going down to the shore. A red light shone from the roof where braziers had been lit to make the barbecue for the cohorts – Sir John had nicknamed them 'the disciples'. Auntie Sanni could see smoke going up, pale in the dimness of the young moon and a sudden flame when the braziers were fanned. An answering glow came from the gatehouse where Shyama was cooking, Thambi keeping watch but, tonight, there was another glow, red and living from the mango grove. 'Someone has lit a fire there,' said Auntie Sanni. She looked towards the village where a drum was being beaten. 'Something is in the air,' said Auntie Sanni.

It was always a proud moment for Samuel when he sounded the gong for dinner.

Though dinner might go on being served until ten or eleven, the gong for the residents was rung punctually at eight. 'That is late for Americans,' Kuku had pointed out. 'In the Taj Hotel they begin serving dinner at half past six.'

'If they come to Patna Hall', said Auntie Sanni, 'they must do as we do.'

At five to eight, Samuel turned on the dining-room lights so that the starched white of the tablecloths was reflected in the polished dark red of the floor, which reflected, too, the white clothes of the waiters with their cummerbunds and turban bands of red and gold. The wine waiter, Ganga, an Ooriyah who served only wine and drinks, not food, was further distinguished by gold buttons and epaulettes. 'We have a wine waiter,' Samuel had told Kuku. 'He will fetch the drinks. There is no need for you to come from the bar.' Kuku still came, the end of her evening sari flowing as she moved between the tables, outdoing Ganga. Like Samuel, this was the best time of the day for Kuku.

At eight, everything was ready, the waiters at their stations, every table set, napkins fluted in the glasses, silver glittering, fresh flowers on every table. Soup was waiting in the hot cases where the small braziers shone red; final touches were being given in the kitchens. A small army of dishwashers was ready to run with hot food between kitchen and pantry. Samuel made a quick round of dining room, pantry, kitchens, pantry, dining room; then he sounded the gong.

The tables began to fill; Dr Coomaraswamy and Mr Srinivasan had darted in as soon as the first gong beat sounded. After them Auntie Sanni and Colonel McIndoe led the way; their table was nearest the verandah, Sir John and Lady Fisher's opposite. Professor Aaron and his ladies took their already familiar places at the two round tables; smaller tables at the back were for Mr Menzies, Mrs Manning and, a little secluded, a honeymoon table for the Brownes. Dr Coomaraswamy's table was midway between the Fishers and Auntie Sanni. 'Too close,' she said to the Colonel, 'I don't like politics in my dining room. Those two hardly waited for the gong!' She frowned: they were not eating, they were gobbling.

'Yes. Yes. We are in a hurry,' Dr Coomaraswamy told Samuel. 'We have to get to Ghandara. Tonight is our inaugural meeting.'

He was excited, talking volubly but, 'Eat. Eat,' begged Mr Srinivasan. Auntie Sanni turned her eyes away.

For the Brownes she had ordered a bottle of white wine; Samuel had it ready in a silver bucket. The flowers on the table were like a bouquet; the head *mali* had sent an underling inland to gather orchids so that even Kuku was satisfied. 'Though, of course, there isn't a florist even in Ghandara,' she had complained. Samuel was eagerly

31

hovering but Blaise Browne came into the dining room alone.

He did not notice the flowers, ignored the white wine and nodded curtly to Samuel. The soup was brought and left to grow cold. It was not until ten minutes later that Auntie Sanni saw him stand up – 'He has good manners,' she said softly to Colonel McIndoe – as the young wife came in, following Mrs Manning. 'Oh dear!' said Auntie Sanni.

The soft brown hair fell forward as the girl bent to look at and touch the flowers. Then she saw the white wine. 'Bumble! You ordered *wine*! How exciting and how sweet of you,' the clear young voice sounded across the room.

'Nothing to do with me. Mary, sit down.'

'Are you cross?' asked Mary.

'Of course I'm cross. Think what it looks like.'

'Looks like?'

'Our first night here, a honeymoon couple, and I have to appear in the dining room alone.'

'You should have come to Mrs Manning.' Mary refused to be upset.

'Sit *down*.'

Lady Fisher looked across the room. 'So that's Rory Scott's Mary.'

'Didn't he call her Merry?' Sir John was looking too. 'I thought she was still at school.'

'Schools,' corrected Lady Fisher. 'I seem to remember there were several – Rory was always moving on so that Mary never settled. No wonder he had trouble. Well, a girl without a mother . . .'

'Yes.' Sir John had seen the tilt of the head beside Blaise, the turned shoulder. 'I can guess she's a handful, a plain little piece.'

'Not when she smiles.' Mary had smiled across at Auntie Sanni. 'Not with those eyes. She has her mother's eyes. Do you remember how Anne's bewitched Rory?'

But Sir John was frowning. 'Surely she's young to be married?'

'She must be . . . let me see . . . eighteen.'

'Still too young. He's old Archie Browne's son, you remember them in Istanbul.'

'Yes. The boy was born there. I remember the fuss. So this is the wonderful Blaise! What a nest of diplomats we are! But, John, you must admit he's very good-looking.'

'So was his mother, in a florid way. Archie's a good chap, if humdrum,' which for Lady Fisher confirmed again what she already knew, that Sir John did not care for Mrs Browne but he was looking again across the room.

'It's what they call a good match,' said Lady Fisher.

'Except that it isn't a match. I can guess that girl isn't ordinary, any more than her father,' by which Lady Fisher knew that Sir John did care for Rory's Mary.

The cultural ladies were looking too. 'Charming, quite charming, though not what you'd call a beauty,' they murmured. 'These English girls have *such* complexions!'

'She looks quite dewy.' Dr Lovat sounded almost dreamy.

'Dewy?'

'As if the dew was still on her,' explained Mrs van den Mar.

'Can't we drink the wine?' Mary was saying, but Samuel had already taken matters in hand. A waiter had removed the cold soup, another slipped hot plates in front of each of them while Samuel proffered a dish from which rose a delectable smell, '*Koftas*, Sahib. Little fish balls of fresh crayfish. Very good. I think Sahib hungry,' he said, deftly serving Blaise, while Ganga filled the wineglasses; the pop when he had opened the wine set off clapping from the other tables. 'From Miss Sanni, best wishes,' said Samuel.

'We should drink to her,' Mary raised her glass,

'and to them all.' Flushed, she stood up and drank to the dining room; Blaise had to follow. A pleased hum answered them. After the *koftas* came partridges, plump, each sitting on its square of toast, with a piquant bread sauce, gravy, fresh vegetables. Blaise began visibly to be appeased. The old butler is right, thought Mary, men are better when they have been fed.

Lady Fisher could have told her that.

At first Olga Manning had watched the Brownes' table with a hint of malicious amusement in her eyes, which changed to a curious sadness. When she had finished — she ate far too quickly and too little — she got up and went out; she went so fast the gauze of her sleeves brushed the backs of chairs and the potted palms. She stopped at the verandah bar, ordered a double whisky and, avoiding any talk with Kuku, took it into the drawing room which was not being used that night as the cultural ladies were going out.

Every year at the outset of his tour, Professor Aaron's group was invited to a reception at the old palace of Konak. 'Not that the Maharajah is there,' Professor Aaron explained. He had stood up to brief the ladies while they still sat at dinner. 'He lives in the South of France now. Here he has to be plain Mr Konak but he keeps his titles abroad. It is his steward who will entertain us.'

The palace, built on a steep slope of the Ghandari Hills, was falling into disrepair, 'But you can still imagine its life.' Professor Aaron tried to conjure it up: 'Though there is a grand staircase, there are ramps between different levels so that the court ladies could be transported in miniature rickshaws. One or two rickshaws are still there. They are inlaid with mother-of-pearl.'

'That sounds utterly romantic,' cried Mrs Glover.

'But we won't be transported in rickshaws.' Mrs

Schlumberger was ready to object. 'Does that mean we'll have to walk? I can't manage uphill.'

'You can always spend a quiet evening here.' Mrs van den Mar stemmed the complaint.

'And there might well be elephants.' Dr Lovat was an experienced traveller.

'True, the gateways were built high to let elephants through,' said Professor Aaron, 'but I'm afraid there are no elephants now.' If the ladies were disappointed they did not show it; they had not come to India to see elephants but Mary, who had been listening, sighed.

'I expect the Raja's private court will be lit for you.' The Professor was still trying to beguile. 'That's where the dancing girls danced for their lord alone.' Mary seemed to hear the strange Indian music, the tinkling of anklet bells. 'The courtyard is so high that at night it is said to be roofed with stars.'

'Oh, I should like to go,' said Mary but, 'Has the palace any architectural interest?' asked Miss Pritt. 'Should we bring our notebooks?'

'Perhaps I wouldn't like to go,' said Mary.

In the big empty drawing room next door, Olga Manning began to play.

'Now what's happening?' asked Sir John.

A young man in flowing white had come hurriedly into the dining room.

'Who's he?' Lady Fisher wondered.

'A boy called Sharma. Coomaraswamy introduced him to me. The Party's district agent.'

'He doesn't look like a district agent,' said Lady Fisher. 'More like a dusky angel.'

'A messenger from the gods,' Sir John suggested. 'But I think he has only come to tell them the Party's coach is ready.'

Dr Coomaraswamy reluctantly put down his knife

and fork. Mr Srinivasan took a last mouthful; he was still chewing as he went after the Doctor and Sharma.

In a moment or two, Mr Menzies followed them. 'He must be in politics,' said Lady Fisher.

'Or journalism.' Sir John did not seem quite at ease. 'I can't imagine that a journalist of any prominence would find this campaign of importance. Yet I seem to have heard . . .'

'I don't like middle-aged men who try to look like girls.' Lady Fisher had noted the hair ribbon.

She and Sir John were used to long-haired men. Their own son, Timothy, 'Looks like one of the apostles,' said Sir John.

'But he's young and the beard fits it.' Lady Fisher smiled. 'But this . . .'

'Not very attractive, certainly, and − bold,' was the word that came to Sir John from the way Mr Menzies had given orders to the waiters and spoke across the room to the cultural ladies. He was a short man, barely reaching to Sir John's shoulder yet, 'I can guess he's potent.' Sir John still felt an unease.

'They haven't waited for the trifle.' Samuel was grieved for Dr Coomaraswamy and Mr Srinivasan.

'No, I don't like politics in my dining room,' Auntie Sanni said. She did not like quarrelling either.

Dinner at Patna Hall always ended with dessert, home-made sweets, crystallised fruit, fresh nuts, on especially fine porcelain plates, each with a finger bowl filled with warm water and floating flower petals. 'No one has finger bowls nowadays,' Kuku had said, 'and these are silver. They have to be *cleaned*.'

'Kashmiri silver,' said Samuel. 'Old Master Sahib brought them from Srinagar.' The silver was chased with a design of chenar leaves and iris, lined on the inner side with gilt.

'Of course they must be cleaned and polished,' said Samuel. Generations of polishing had worn them thin but, 'No one in my dining room', said Samuel, 'has a dessert plate without a finger bowl.'

He placed them himself in front of Blaise and Mary. 'How pretty,' said Mary of the finger bowls and Samuel smiled.

'Samuel likes that girl,' Auntie Sanni said to Colonel McIndoe as Mary looked up at the old butler.

'Do you think I could have a few carrots and sugar lumps for my donkey?'

'Of course, Miss Baba.'

Miss Baba had slipped out and Blaise's displeasure was back. He said to Mary, 'Miss Baba! You're not a child. It's not your donkey and you're not going to adopt it,' and, to Samuel, '*Memsahib* doesn't want any carrots,' and then, 'Talking of which, I would rather you wouldn't be so friendly with this Mrs Manning.'

'Why not?'

'There's something about her, Mary. I'm a good judge of character,' said Blaise with satisfaction. 'You must let me know best.'

'Even when I don't think you do?'

'They don't look very happy over there.' Lady Fisher had been watching. 'Rory's an old friend, John, and we knew Archie Browne.'

'Slightly.'

'Slightly or not, go and ask those young people to have coffee with us on the verandah.'

Mary had not wanted to have coffee on the verandah; she wanted to be out in the night but Blaise was flattered at being asked by Sir John Fisher. 'He's really my chief – by remote control,' he had whispered to Mary. Blaise had completely recovered himself and now, as he stood talking, the lights showed off his fair hair. Kuku, her vivid sari showing off the brown plumpness below the tight gold of her bodice, brought his coffee, fluttering her eyelashes as she served him; he took the cup without noticing her and went on talking to Sir John. Blaise was palpably enjoying talking to Sir John – Because he is Sir John, thought Mary, which was captious but she knew it was true. Well, why not? she told herself and, It's you who are cross now. We're both tired. Yet she did not feel tired, it was only . . . I didn't want to spend my first real Indian night in chit-chat.

She was sitting on a low stool beside Lady Fisher who, in courtesy, was asking her about her father – 'It's a long time since we saw Rory' – about England and the wedding in Bombay . . . Just what I don't want to talk about.

If only I could get up and walk away, thought Mary, be back on that other verandah where I can watch those waves coming in roller after roller, sending their wash far up the sand. If I could look over them and see how the sky comes down over the sea to meet the horizon, a great bowl of stars. If I held up mý hand against it, all round my fingers would be nothing but air, emptiness. I don't want to say Rory is well – as far as I know; that Bumble and I were married in Bombay's cathedral. I don't want to say I like India. *Like!* When I'm . . . what *is* the right word? Yes, enthralled. Then she looked at Lady Fisher, who had discreetly returned to her embroidery and was listening to her husband and Blaise – or thinking her own thoughts? And what must she be thinking of me? thought Mary uncomfortably. Why, tonight, am I not able . . . ? Oh, I wish something would happen, or somebody come to rescue me.

A sudden hubbub filled the verandah. Dr Coomaraswamy had come back surrounded by some of the young men but, 'Go. Go,' he cried to them. 'Go now. I must think,' and mopping his bald head he came along the verandah giving small moans.

38

'My dear fellow!' Sir John helped him to a chair. 'Let me get you a drink. Brandy?'

'Iced water. Please. Please.'

'And for me,' Mr Srinivasan was even more dishevelled and distressed, 'if you would be so kind. Water.'

'I'll get it,' said Blaise but Kuku had already gone.

'What has happened?'

'*Catastrophe!*' Dr Coomaraswamy sank into the wicker chair, his head in his hands, while Mr Srinivasan beat his together. 'Catastrophe? Utter catastrophe.'

'What kind of catastrophe?'

'Krishnan . . . Krishnan Bhanj . . .' Dr Coomaraswamy could hardly speak. 'Candidate in the state of Konak for the Root and Flower Party, our Party, our candidate—'

'Was our candidate,' moaned Mr Srinivasan.

'Was?' Sir John was startled. 'Is he dead?'

'No. No.'

'He has withdrawn?'

'No. Oh, no! No. No!'

'Better if he had,' wailed Mr Srinivasan.

'Then?'

'Worse than that,' and Dr Coomaraswamy said in a voice hoarse with shock, '*Krishnan Bhanj has taken a vow of silence.*'

Silence. How lovely, thought Mary as a torrent of talk broke out above her. Auntie Sanni and Colonel McIndoe had joined the group; Kuku came with tumblers of iced water as Dr Coomaraswamy began to tell the tale.

'We were all on the platform. Every influential person. All such important people. I, the chairman of the Root and Flower Party—'

'And Krishnan?' asked Lady Fisher.

'Nat-u-ral-ly. Krishnan – on the platform. I myself was speaking, only to introduce him, you understand – I myself—'

'For long?' asked Lady Fisher.

39

'Oh no, not at all. Perhaps ten minutes.'

'Ten minutes *is* long for an introduction,' said Sir John.

'It was the inaugural speech.' For a moment Dr Coomaraswamy had dignity, then the injury welled up. 'Speaking – on the platform when Krishnan got up and – and—'

'And?'

'He walked out.'

'Well, Indian politicians often do walk out,' said Lady Fisher.

'Yes, Lady Sahib, but he left a note.'

'It was I who picked it up,' Mr Srinivasan moaned again.

'What did it say?'

'It said,' came the unfailing voice of Mr Srinivasan, '"This is enough. I am not speaking tonight. I am not speaking throughout the campaign. I have taken a vow of silence."'

A sound, quickly smothered, came from Sir John, a sound that made Dr Coomaraswamy look at him sharply.

'This Krishnan Bhanj,' Mary, in a low voice, asked Lady Fisher, 'what is he like?'

'Blue-black,' said Kuku derisively.

'Kuku! I know he's dark—' Lady Fisher protested.

'Blue-black,' Kuku insisted. 'Which doesn't suit his name.'

'"Krishnan" comes from the Hindu god Krishna', Lady Fisher explained, 'one of the avators or manifestations of Vishnu, second god of the Hindu Trinity – Brahma the Creator, Vishnu the Preserver and Shiva, Death, who is also Resurrection. Whenever there is trouble on earth Vishnu comes down; at first he was a fish, then an animal, later as a man or god like Krishna, who is usually shown with a blue skin.'

'Blue? A *blue* skin?' asked Mary.

'Pale blue,' said Lady Fisher. 'Krishnan is dark but he

is a man and he can't help his colour. After all, he isn't Krishna. The god is blue because he drank poison in the milk of his wet nurse. She was a demon in disguise but the milk did not harm him, only her. He sucked so fiercely that he emptied her body of all energy and she fell dead. That's what they say.'

'Old folk tales,' said Kuku in contempt.

'They're not exactly folk tales,' and Lady Fisher smiled. 'When Krishna came down on earth, he was, of course, a baby. He had to be abandoned by his royal parents but was found by a cowherd who brought him up, like Perdita in *The Winter's Tale*.'

'William Shakespeare,' said Kuku, proud to know.

'Yes.' Lady Fisher's needle went in and out with a gentle plucking sound that made this, to Mary, fantastic conversation of gods and demons mixed up with cowherds and poison, everyday.

She looked up at Auntie Sanni who had come to sit with them, towering among them; Mary was reminded of a mountain with small towns, villages and farms and their innumerable occupations and preoccupations held safely in its folds. Auntie Sanni obviously loved to hear Lady Fisher talk, and Mary guessed that Auntie Sanni would be indulgent to any belief – as long as it is belief, thought Mary. And why am I so interested? she wondered. Usually I hate being told things, but now she wanted to know more about these strange immortal beings and, 'Go on, please,' she said to Lady Fisher.

'As Krishna grew older he sported', Lady Fisher chose the word carefully, 'with his foster father's *gopis*.'

'*Gopis*?'

'Milkmaids.'

'Sported!' Kuku was indignant. 'Imagine, Mrs Browne, the *gopis* were so much in love with him they longed to be his flute so that his lips would perpetually caress them. Silly girls! Like all men, he was heartless.'

41

'All men?' Lady Fisher laughed. 'Certainly not all men. Take Krishnan Bhanj.'

'Like all men.' Of course! As Lady Fisher said, this Krishnan Bhanj is a man. That thought gave Mary a slight shock and, looking at Kuku, she wondered if perhaps he had 'sported', that exact word, with her. 'You know Mr Bhanj?'

'He was staying here when I first came.' Kuku gave a still indignant little snort. 'He called me Didi – sister. I am not his sister.'

'I'm sure he said that as he would have said Bhai – to a young man.' Lady Fisher defended him. 'Bhai means brother,' she told Mary.

'Exactly,' said Kuku with venom and, I can guess it was you who tried to sport with Krishnan, thought Mary with a sudden astuteness, which was confirmed when Kuku said, 'Krishnan. Krishna. What is the difference? All Krishna did was to play tricks on poor girls.'

'Not always,' said Lady Fisher. 'Remember, there was Radha.'

'Radha?' asked Mary.

'Krishna met his match with Radha in more ways than one. She seemed to be a *gopi* but Radha was a god as well.'

'Goddess. She shone among the *gopis*.' Though she was contemptuous Kuku had seen pictures from the Hindu scriptures. 'Anyway, Krishnan Bhanj may think he is a god but he's not Krishna.'

'That's not what the villagers think.' Mr Menzies had come up the verandah and was standing beside them.

'Krishnan Bhanj was so good, so excellent,' Mr Srinivasan lamented. 'A barrister, he is particularly versed in law, England returned.' Mr Srinivasan's English belonged to the thirties and forties. They talk differently, thought Mary. They don't take short cuts – is not instead of isn't; will not instead of won't; they break up syllables . . . 'Par-tic-u-lar-ly' 'Krishnan also speaks English per-fect-ly,' Mr Srinivasan was going on. 'Also his great advantage to us is that he speaks Tamil as well as Telegu.'

'What advantage is that if he will not speak at all?' Dr Coomaraswamy was in despair.

'Where is Krishnan now?' asked Sir John.

'We do not know. We do not know *anything*.' Once more Mr Srinivasan beat his hands together.

'I, myself,' said Dr Coomaraswamy, 'am going now to look for him. He was at Ghandara where, for the election, as I have told you, he preferred to stay.'

'One little room,' Mr Srinivasan went on, 'a *charpoy*, table and chair, not even a fan when he might have stayed here. He cannot be in his right mind. To go off and leave us in this fixation.'

'We went straight to headquarters. He was not there,' explained Dr Coomaraswamy. 'He left his clothes, his suit, shirt, tie— '

'Even his shoes, his socks!'

'So what is he wearing?'

'I suppose national dress. Maybe only a *lunghi*. It would not be past him, our candidate!' Dr Coomaraswamy cried bitterly. 'What has come over him? Where is he?'

'Have you asked in the village?'

'Nat-u-rally. They are a wall.'

'You mean, they stonewalled?'

'Yes, walls of stone!'

'They knew in the village before you knew.' It was the first time Auntie Sanni had spoken.

'But why should he have come here, except to Patna Hall? What is there for him here in Shantipur?'

With quiet footsteps, the young Sharma came along the verandah, made a graceful *namaskar* to the company and handed the Doctor a note.

'I ab-so-lute-ly do not understand,' Dr Coomaraswamy

cried when he had read it. 'Why? What use?' and he read it aloud. '"Tomorrow, by first dawn, you will get a lorry and in it set up a small *pandal*..."'

'What is a *pandal*?' Mary whispered to Lady Fisher.

'A sort of tabernacle. The people make them on festival days for an image of one of the gods. They are usually bamboo, decorated with banana tree stems and garlands of lucky mango leaves and marigolds.'

'"A pandal,"' read Dr Coomaraswamy, '"as for a god. I will sit in it. The people will see me." But this is idiotic!' he cried. 'This is i-di-o-tic.'

'It is brilliant,' said Mr Menzies.

'Surely,' Blaise said to Sir John when the Indians had gone, 'it can't be serious. This Krishnan must be some sort of jumped-up play actor who has taken them all in?'

'On the contrary, Krishnan Bhanj has not only been canvassing for weeks throughout Konak, for the past five years, he has been steadily and culminatively working towards this election in his own way here in Konak and doing untold good, how good we shall not know for perhaps decades. Besides, his father is perhaps the most respected politician in all India, of absolute integrity,' said Sir John. 'I know of no one who would not trust him.'

'And extraordinarily good-looking, with a great presence,' came from Lady Fisher. 'Krishnan is very much his son.'

'Vijay Bhanj has been Ambassador in Washington and has represented India in conferences everywhere from Sri Lanka to Moscow. No young man could have a better background.'

'Partly because', said Lady Fisher, 'his mother, Leila, is a deeply spiritual woman, some of which, I think, is in Krishnan too. She comes from near here, from South India which perhaps has the deepest roots. I love Leila,' and Lady Fisher told Mary, 'When I came out to Delhi, as a

44

new bride, she would not let me be the usual English wife, blind to the country. She taught me Hindi and about Hinduism for which I shall be eternally grateful. I hope, Mary, someone will do the same for you.'

'Sir John laughed. He laughed. I am sure of it.' Dr Coomaraswamy was standing by the window of the first floor room in the party's headquarters at Ghandara. The room, usually used as his office and usually buzzing with activity, was silent; the whole of the two-storey stucco-faced house, important in this town of bazaar shanties, corrugated iron, cheap concrete blocks, was empty. Every helper had been sent far and wide, some to look for Krishnan, some in search of the required lorry.

On the outside, the house, verandah and balconies were swathed with muslin draperies in the Root and Flower Party's colours, green, saffron yellow and white: 'Green for hope, saffron for holiness, white for pure intention,' Dr Coomaraswamy liked to explain. Over them hung the party's posters; for weeks the disciples had been putting them up all over the state – it was a point of honour between all parties not to tear down each other's posters. They were pictures with a symbol. 'You must remember most of our people cannot read, so the party symbol is of utmost importance.' Dr Coomaraswamy always emphasised, 'And it must be recognisable instantly.' Krishnan's symbol was of three wise-looking cows lying among flowers; they would be on the voting papers too and instantly identifiable with Krishnan. 'There is', Dr Coomaraswamy said in satisfaction, 'not one man, woman or child who does not know the Krishna story.' At Headquarters every poster was garlanded with fresh lucky mango leaves; their very freshness seemed a mockery to Dr Coomaraswamy.

He was not even sure now about his inaugural speech. He heard Sir John's voice, 'Ten minutes is long for an

45

introduction.' 'But I like to speak,' said Dr Coomaraswamy piteously to the empty room. 'Also, what I had to say, was it not important?'

'Yes, but it still depends on the way you say it,' Krishnan had cautioned and, 'He knows me,' Dr Coomaraswamy had to admit. Krishnan had also forbidden any expletives: 'No foul words or abuse.'

'But Gopal Rau has denounced you as "cheat", "liar", "hypocrite"; Mrs Retty as "dirty humbug", "ignorant swine"—'

'And in return you will call them "gentleman", "lady", "benefactor", "mother", even, "prince".'

'But those are kindly.'

'It depends on how you say them.' Krishnan had smiled.

'Yes, but,' Dr Coomaraswamy had been sad, 'my words were so beautifully foul!'

He had opened his speech with what he thought was simple directness – and in the current fashion: 'Friends,' and then went on, as Mr Srinivasan told him afterwards, to spoil it by 'people of Konak, men, women and our beloved children: accustomed as I am to public speaking, tonight when I come to open this, the final week, of our Root and Flower Party's campaign for which we owe so much to so many of you, my heart is so full that I can hardly speak . . .'

'Speak. Speak,' hissed Mr Srinivasan who, as always, had been close beside him.

'The few words I have to say to you tonight are of such import, such freshness, newness of approach that they awe me and make my very lips to tremble . . .'

'Don't tremble. Go *on*!' mouthed Mr Srinivasan.

'We shall begin with the root. The root goes on to flower, the flower will bring you fruit, much fruit. For you, for all Konak, perhaps for millions, our new manifesto offers this hope. Men and women, for you, at this very moment, hope is hovering with bright wings . . .'

Dr Coomaraswamy had particularly liked 'bright wings' but Mr Srinivasan was making frantic accelerating gestures and Dr Coomaraswamy had gathered momentum – too much momentum. 'You must think before you speak,' Uma, his wife, had always urged but at speed, 'Friends,' he had cried, 'you are aware that for decades, if not generations, our beloved country, through the corruption, avarice, greed, exploitation of the few in power, has been standing on the edge of the precipice of utter disaster. Let us,' and here he had raised his fist in exaltation as his voice rang out, 'let us take the first step forward.'

Too late he saw Mr Srinivasan collapse; too late knew what he had said but the most bitter mortification of all had been that no one had noticed. They had not been listening, Dr Coomaraswamy thought now in anguish. My words might have been hot air. Perhaps they were hot air but he had not lacked courage; he had continued but then Krishnan had walked out.

Yes, he has made me a laughing stock, Dr Coomaraswamy thought bitterly now of Krishnan: umbrellas, a lorry, a *pandal* as for a god. 'I will sit in it,' Krishnan had said. 'You will not,' Dr Coomaraswamy had vowed but then Sir John had laughed – he, Dr Coomaraswamy, was certain it had been a laugh. Not only that, there were other cryptic things that had been said. 'What did they *mean?*' asked the Doctor.

'Krishnan is bats. Bats,' Mr Srinivasan had been moaning.

'Bats hang upside down, which seems topsy-turvy to us but it's their way.' Sir John had been perfectly grave.

'So he should have been.' Dr Coomaraswamy was momentarily incensed. 'It is no laughing matter. I, myself, have invested two *crores* at least in this campaign . . .' – 'And did I not tell you not to?' Uma had said, over and over again, thought Dr Coomaraswamy wearily.

'And why care so much about Sir John?' Uma had said

that too, also over and over again. 'You are a Doctor of Medicine, MA, MRCS, Edinburgh,' she said this continually. 'Also, I do not care, at all, for Lady Fisher.'

'You mean she does not care for you.' Dr Coomaraswamy had not said that; Uma was formidable, bigger than he. 'Lady Fisher is an inveterate snob,' said Uma but, I believed Sir John and I were friends, Dr Coomaraswamy thought now. He calls me Coomaraswamy, I say, Sir John . . . He winced, remembering the terrible time when he had said, 'Sir Fisher'. 'Solecism! Solecism!' he could have cried aloud to the unresponsive walls of Headquarters.

He had taken off his jacket to ease the tiredness of his shoulders, had let his braces hang down. My God, my belly! thought Dr Coomaraswamy – he could not see his feet and could feel the rolls of fat around his neck and face; to add to his misery he knew sweat was glistening on the baldness of his scalp. I am thoroughly unlovely, no girl would look at me, thought Dr Coomaraswamy.

'Girl? What girl?' Uma seemed to pounce even on his thoughts. 'What is this I hear about a girl?'

'My angel, you know there is no one else but you,' and at once, as if in reality he had said it, there came into Dr Coomaraswamy's mind a vision of Kuku as she had been this night: the sweet scent of her hair, the enticing girl flesh between *choli* and sari – he could have put his hands around her waist – the shadow of the long eyelashes on her cheeks. 'Those eyelashes did not flutter for you,' he told himself cruelly. 'They were for that young Blaise Browne, you old fool.' Still he found he was listening for the soft swish of a sari – Uma wore hers kilted up to show thick ankles and sensible nurse's white canvas shoes, which made her feet look larger than ever, whereas Dr Coomaraswamy could not help having, in his eye, the sight of little feet with slender bones, the nails painted red, delicate sandals held by a thong between the toes. Each time he saw them a quiver of delight had run through Dr Coomaraswamy. No one has ever written a poem to toes, he thought. He had a mind to try, but again, 'Old fool, keep to what is your business,' he told himself and his thoughts returned to the deserted Party, the lost *crores* of rupees – worst, the loss of face. He could have wailed aloud, 'What to do now? What, in heaven or earth, to do?'

It was late, almost on midnight, when Dr Coomaraswamy came back to Patna Hall. The breeze was soft, benign, as he left his taxi and crossed the courtyard. The house slept; the moon had gone. Then, as he came out on the verandah, he saw a figure sitting quietly in a chair.

'At last,' said Sir John.

'You . . . you have been waiting for me?'

'I was getting worried. You look all in. You need a stiff drink.'

'Whisky peg, Srinivasan still calls it,' Dr Coomaraswamy tried to joke.

When they had their glasses, 'Well, have you found him?' asked Sir John.

'Nowhere. Not anywhere.'

'Hari, what are you going to do?'

'I don't know. I *do not* know. John' – Sir John had said Hari – 'John, you tell me.'

'There's only one thing you can do. You haven't time to get another candidate. In any case, Krishnan Bhanj has not withdrawn, so—' Sir John interrupted himself, 'Are you sure it's not nerves? Young candidates often have a case of nerves.'

'Krishnan has no nerves. I wish he had, it might make him more amenable. Nervous? On the contrary . . .'

'Then', said Sir John, 'you can only do as he says.'

'This antic? You mean the lorry, the *pandal* and all? This nonsense?'

'I mean the lorry, the *pandal*, this nonsense – to the

letter – and now, Hari, my friend, go to bed and try and get some sleep.'

'Hari. My friend.' It was as if all the sore places had miraculously healed. Tears came into Dr Coomaraswamy's eyes. 'John— ' he began.

'Hallo,' said Sir John, 'who's that?'

He had gone to the verandah rail. Dr Coomaraswamy joined him. Someone was running along the beach, a slim someone in a pale blue dress, hair flying. 'That is Mr Browne's young wife,' said Dr Coomaraswamy, 'and alone.'

'Alone?' Sir John scanned the beach. 'So it seems.'

'She should not be out alone this time of night.'

'She should not,' said Sir John, 'but she is.'

Sunday–Monday:
Midnight Hour

'I should have said no in Bombay.'

Sunday's evening had grown better as it went on; Blaise, unusual for him, had joined the women: Auntie Sanni, Lady Fisher – and me, thought Mary. Kuku had gone to bed. Sir John was talking to Professor Aaron who, having brought his ladies safely home from the palace, had come on to the verandah to say goodnight. 'Professor Webster and I have our lectures ready.' He stretched and yawned. 'Tomorrow we go to see the cave paintings in the hills.'

Mr Menzies had disappeared to do some telephoning. 'Always he is telephoning,' Kuku had said as she watched him go.

Sitting in a chair by Auntie Sanni, Blaise had drawn Mary, on her stool, to lean against his knee. He was listening, not talking, and every now and again he ran his fingers through her hair – he might have been Bumble again. Auntie Sanni's voice was soothing too in its quiet singsong; she was telling Blaise the history of Patna Hall and of her grandfather's estate in Bihar, his factory and indigo fields. Indigo. Indigo: Mary seemed to see acres of a strange plant brilliantly blue – but it's Krishna who is blue, or is it Vishnu? Vishna? Krishu? The names began to merge into a maze. 'Mary, you're half asleep,' said Blaise. 'Come, I'll take you to bed.'

'It's very late, almost midnight.' Lady Fisher folded her embroidery. As Blaise pulled Mary to her feet and

51

steadied her, she bent and kissed Lady Fisher and Auntie Sanni.

Outside in the garden it was magical, the air balmy, the sky a dome of stars. The long flowerbeds were spangled with fireflies. Fireflies and stars, which are which? wondered sleepy Mary, while there was a scent of such sweetness that it made her more sleepy still. Then, at the foot of the steps, they heard the piano. 'She's still playing,' said Mary. It made her uneasy and as she listened, 'Chopin,' she whispered. The nocturne ended; Olga Manning began the little A major prelude with its pleading and, 'I should go and say goodnight to her.' Mary moved towards the steps.

'You should not,' said Blaise and caught her back. 'Don't you see, she's desperate for friendship.'

The music seemed an echo of that; it made Mary say, 'Haven't you ever felt desperate?' but Blaise was in a peaceful mood. 'I'm desperate to go to bed.'

A waiter on late duty came down the steps. 'Memsahib,' he called, and handed Mary a basket of carrots and sugar lumps. 'Samuel say for donkey.'

'Throw them away,' said Blaise but, forgetting Mrs Manning and the playing, Mary had run down the bungalow path. 'How do you call a donkey if you don't know its name?' She tried a whistle. There was an answering whicker and when Blaise caught up with her most of the carrots and sugar were gone. 'I don't believe anyone has been kind to him before,' she told Blaise. 'I'm going to call him Slippers.'

'Call him gumboots, if you like,' Blaise said yawning, 'as long as he stays in the garden and doesn't come on the verandah.'

While Blaise undressed in the bathroom, Mary went out to look at the sea. The thundering of the waves seemed to have a lulling sound now; the breeze, gentle tonight, blew through the room. 'That's why,' Auntie

Sanni had told Blaise when, among other things, he had asked for a mosquito net, 'at Patna Hall we do not need them. We do not have mosquitoes which is a boon.' The big double bed, without a net, had its sheet and light quilt turned back – Patna Hall had thin Indian cotton quilts, 'Not proper blankets or eiderdowns,' Kuku had lamented. Mary's short nightdress had been laid out; she looked at it and felt a sudden distaste.

'Where did you meet that outrageously handsome husband of yours?' Mrs Manning – Olga – had asked.

'In Norway. Rory, my father, has a lodge there, like a chalet above one of the fiords. He likes fishing, when he can.'

'Your father's a diplomat?'

'Yes. Bumble – Blaise was his Second Secretary in Kuala Lumpur. When they came on leave, Rory asked Blaise to Norway to fish. I joined them. I had just left school, my last, thank God.'

'So . . . Blaise is in the service too?'

'Yes,' and now, It has not really dawned on me, thought Mary looking at the nightdress, how important to Blaise his work is yet he jeopardised it, or thought he did, for me. Well, he had been out of England for a year, perhaps he was starved. She knew now that, when in any foreign posting, Blaise would never have considered any of the native girls. And I? thought Mary. I had not been really close to a young man before – she could see that schoolgirl Mary – and I suppose I was feeling emancipated, grown up . . .

There was a little hut where we put overflow guests . . . she had not, of course, told Olga Manning this – never, never anybody, thought Mary. Blaise and I used to go there, mostly at night. Nobody knew. It was fun, thought Mary, with longing. We made love – and it was love. There was only a single bed; once Bumble fell on the floor. He just laughed. It was good. It never seemed

53

wrong, but . . . Mary's nails dug into the flesh of her palms. In these double beds, I can't.

'Merry, are you coming?'

'Don't call me Merry.'

'Does it matter what I call you?' Blaise had come amiably out of the bathroom; he was wearing only a *lunghi* – many young Western men new to India had taken to sleeping in them – it wrapped his loins and stalwart legs. His torso still shone from the ladling of water from the mug; as he bent his knees to look in the looking glass, his hair glistened too. He was young, fresh, powerful, but Mary asked, 'Blaise, in Norway, what made you tell Rory about us and the hut?'

'It was the only honourable thing to do.'

'Wouldn't it have been more honourable to ask me first?'

He ignored that and went on, 'Besides I had to, you weren't like other girls.'

'I was exactly like other girls.'

'Not for me.' For a moment Mary thought it was Bumble speaking, her Bumble, but then, 'Rory was my chief,' Blaise explained. 'In my very first posting which was vital. If I hadn't told him and he had found out, he might have wrecked my career before it really started.'

'I see.' Mary said it slowly and, 'You haven't told me that before.' She swallowed trying to keep down her dismay. Then she blazed, 'Rory wouldn't have done that. Even if he had minded – and I think he did mind – he would never have done that. He's not that sort of man. Don't you know *anything* about people?' and Save me, save me, beat in her every nerve.

An answer came, a clip-clopping and Slippers appeared on the verandah. He gave a whicker when he saw Mary, came confidently through the doorway and began nosing round the chest of drawers, clopped to the bed, nuzzling the pillows. 'He's looking for more carrots and sugar!' Mary's laugh was cut short.

'Get out! Out, you little beast,' yelled the already angry Blaise. 'In our *bedroom*!' and, as the little donkey looked at him in surprise, a shoe came hurtling across the room. Slippers shied in fright, slipping and slithering on the stone floor; hampered by his hoofs, he could not get his balance and half fell across the bed. Blaise took up the other shoe.

'Blaise, don't! Don't!'

'I'm only trying to get him out.'

'You needn't *hurt* him,' but, 'Get off the bed,' Blaise shouted at the donkey. 'Get *off*!'

Slippers righted himself and stood trembling. 'Don't. *Don't!*' wailed Mary again but, holding the shoe by the toe, Blaise advanced on Slippers and beat him with the heel on his rump and sides. Blaise had not meant it but the shoe flew out of his hand and caught the soft nose. 'He's bleeding!' screamed Mary.

Blood had begun to ooze from one nostril; the ears went back as with terrified brays, stumbling over his distorted hoofs, Slippers fled to the verandah. Slipping and sliding again, they heard him crash down the steps. 'He may have broken his legs!' and Mary shouted at Blaise, 'I'll never like you again! Never!' as she ran down the steps. 'I'm going,' she shouted 'and I'm not coming back!'

Slippers had not broken his legs. He was stumbling along the beach. She ran after him.

'Mary, don't be silly. Come back. Come back at once.' Blaise's words floated back to him on the breeze.

Mary ran along the beach past fishing boats drawn up, nets stretched to dry, until she caught up with Slippers. For a while he would not come to her but at last the bruised and bloodied nose touched her hand. Taking off her shoes, holding him by the rope around his neck, she

led him into the sea, hoping the water would ease his legs
— they must be bruised. With her free hand, she patted
him, talking to him; the trembling eased to a quivering.
Then she led him back to dry land.

There, her arms round his neck, Mary began to cry,
cry as she had never done before. I should have said no
in Bombay, gone with Rory to Peru . . . Peru, London, the
North Pole, anywhere. She sobbed against Slippers's rough
neck as the donkey stood quietly, holding her weight. I
should have been warned, thought Mary. Hadn't Blaise
said that very first time when he got up from the ridiculous
bed, 'I shall never forgive myself, never. I must see your
father at once.' She had only pulled him down, 'Don't you
dare,' and kissed him. And there was magic, she insisted
now, a sort of magic, in the long Norwegian summer
days, hardly any night. Then how had it come to this?
She did not know. I suppose in Ootacamund I kept my
eyes shut tight. Now they were painfully open and, 'Oh,
Rory, Rory, I wish you were here.'

Far out to sea there was a steamer, its lights making a
chain of pinprick reflections across the water; the steamer
looked as small and lonely in that vastness as Mary felt.
She turned to go back but behind the beach was a line
of what seemed to be small trees, soft and feathery with,
behind them again, taller trees; though Mary did not know
it, this was the casuarina and mango grove. As she looked,
she saw a glow that flickered. A fire, thought Mary.

Her shoes in her hand, her bare feet making no
noise on the sand, she walked up slowly through the
fuzzy trees, their feathery branches brushing her face.
Vaguely she could see, among them, bushes of what
seemed to be scarlet flowers, hibiscus; holding the bell
of one of them, she stood at the edge of a clearing among
the taller trees.

There was a roof of palm matting stretched between
two slender trunks of trees; below it, animal skins, deer

and goat, lay on the sand before a seat or a couch – or was it a throne? To the side was a big earthenware pitcher for water, a brass *lota*, a few brass platters and long-handled spoons – Mary had come out without her spectacles yet every detail seemed printed on her eyes. A washing line was stretched, too, between two trees – a line hung with loincloths and, incongruously, a sweater. Behind the washing was a pile of brushwood and green brown stems – could they be sugar cane? wondered Mary.

The fire was in front, a fire of wood; tending it was a young man, blue-black – Mary felt as if she recognised him. He was wearing a loincloth with another cloth across his shoulders. His hair looked oddly white; then, as the fire flared up, Mary saw his hair was full of ashes. On his face, two arched eyebrows were drawn in white with, between them, a white U-shape that Lady Fisher had said was the sign of the god Vishnu; the lips were scarlet.

He stood up. At that moment, Slippers, who had followed Mary, gave her such a sudden shove with his nose that she dropped her shoes.

At the sound, quick as a cat, the young man had leapt to the couch and was sitting in the lotus position – legs crossed, each foot up to rest on the opposite knee, looking exactly, thought Mary, like one of the gods in the pictures she had seen in the bazaar.

'Come,' a voice called, a mellifluous voice that had an echo of a flute. 'Come.'

Her arm around the donkey's neck, Mary came. 'Oh, it's you,' the young man said and got off the throne.

Mary had stepped into the circle of light; there was a small lantern set on the sand. He picked it up, holding it to see her. Mary knew her face was tear-stained, her eyes red from crying, her hair in tangles, her skirt soaked with salt water from washing Slippers and that she smelled of donkey. 'Never mind. Please sit down,' he said, as if he had read her thoughts, and then, not a question but a statement, 'You are from Auntie Sanni's.'

'Yes.'

'Mrs Blaise Browne.'

'Yes.' Mary was reluctant to say it.

'On honeymoon.'

'Yes.'

'Not much honey, I think.' He was holding the lantern closer. 'Too much moon?'

'Yes.' That was like a sob.

'Moons wane,' he said, 'not like ours tonight which will grow bigger. That is propitious. If you start anything new always do it on a waxing moon. Perhaps your husband would say that is superstitious?'

'Yes.'

'It is not superstitious to take notice of seasons, tides, sun and moon. So, you ran away to be with the donkey instead?'

'Yes.'

'If you can only say one word,' he laughed, 'undoubtedly "yes" is better than "no".'

Was he mocking her? No. His voice was tender – and, You could trust him to be tender, she thought, instinctively. She was beginning to unwind from the hard little ball she had made of herself. There was something about the gaiety that was irresistible; she found she was responding. 'They are looking everywhere for you,' she told him.

He laughed. 'Looking far and wide. They will not think of looking close.'

'But why are you talking to me?' she said. 'I thought you had taken a vow of silence.'

'A public vow. This is private. The make-up is public too; underneath it, I assure you, I am a most presentable person.'

More than that, Mary could have said. There was

something magnificent about him – a curious word to use for a young man. She found she was looking at him with an again curious minuteness; he was not tall but was so slim he looked taller. She could see, in the firelight, how the muscles moved with rippling ease, almost like a great cat's, under the dark skin – Yes, blue-black, thought Mary. The shoulders were broad, the head well set, his face fine-boned, a straight nose with sensitive nostrils; his eyes were brown not black as with many Indians – they looked light in the darkness of his skin.

'You ask me why – the vow, I mean.' He bent down and scooped a little of the sand and let it trickle through his fingers. 'I think you know', he said, 'what it is to be out of love?'

'Yes.' That was so fervent that they both laughed, happy, easy laughter.

He threw more wood on the fire which leapt up, sending sparks high in the air. Sparks, fireflies, stars. Mary felt dizzy; the sand though, warm and dry, was firm under her as she sat, her wet skirt spread around her; he was opposite, sitting Indian fashion on his heels.

'Your name is Krishnan from Krishna?'

'That is so.'

'Do you play the flute?'

'No, only the fool,' he laughed, then conceded, 'well, I play a little but not as well as Krishna, who could? And your name is?'

'Mary.'

'Mary Browne.' He tried it over.

'Browne with an e,' Mary mocked which she knew was disloyal.

'Then, Mary Browne, how did you come here?'

'Blaise, my husband, was posted to India. I followed him.'

'He wasn't your husband then?'

'No, not until Bombay.'

Blaise had insisted, 'It must be properly arranged.'

'Properly?' She had laughed but to her surprise, Rory, who had always allowed her to do as she wanted – almost, she had to admit, there had been those schools – and who did not care a fig what his world thought about him, took the same view but, 'I . . . I'm not ready to be married yet,' Mary, even in her ardency, had said.

'Exactly what I think,' and Rory had urged, 'Merry, come with me to Peru.' Rory, too, had a new and even more senior posting. 'Then if in two or three years' time you still . . .'

'Two or three years!' the young Mary had cried in anguish, at eighteen that seemed aeons, and, 'So I came,' she said now to Krishnan.

'*Atcha!*' He accepted that with the ambiguous Hindustani word.

There was a sound of crashing: something heavy was coming through the trees. Slippers, who – contributing to the peacefulness – was lying near on the sand, his legs bent under him, his ears still, pricked them and gave a whicker as, behind the shanty shelter, a big hulk appeared. 'An elephant!' cried Mary.

'My elephant,' said Krishnan. 'At least she belongs to the Maharajah but as he is absent she has been lent to me for the campaign.'

'I didn't know there was a Maharajah.'

'His Highness Tirupatha Deva Raja of Konak. He has other titles but not as lovely for instance as, best of all, the Seem of Swat. The Maharajah used to own the state. He had palaces, three forts, an army, foot and horse.'

'And elephants?'

'Yes, especially one elephant, very fierce, the Maharajah kept for trampling people. In those days that was the usual punishment and every now and then the fierce elephant was sent into towns and villages to trample a few peasants and officials to remind them the Maharajah was the Maharajah.'

'That can't be true.'

'I do not always speak the truth,' said Krishnan. 'Who does? But this is true. Now the current Maharajah is plain Mr Konak, the treasury is forfeit, most of the palaces are colleges or hospitals, the forts and armies gone. He has only this one small elephant – she is small because her mother discarded her. She has become a pet.'

'Where is her – is it a *mahout*? – the man who drives her?'

'Drunk, I expect,' said Krishnan. 'She wanders at night.'

'But is she safe?'

'She wouldn't trample a chicken, she's far too wise. The villagers give her sweets.'

'Will she come if you call?'

'If I have sugar cane. Fortunately I have,' and in his fluting voice he called, 'Come, come, Birdie.'

'*Birdie*? That's not a name for an elephant.'

'It is in remembrance,' said Krishnan. 'When I was a little boy I had an English governess, Miss Birdwood. We called her Birdie. She, too, was an orphan.'

'Is that why you speak English so well?'

'Well, I was at school in England, then went to Oxford.'

He let these small details about himself fall into the conversation. Is he showing off? thought Mary. Yes, he is, to me. It made her feel pleasingly important. She tried to see the small dark boy he must have been with the governess, Birdie; he would have had the same brown eyes, probably mischievous, the haughty face. Miss Birdie could not have had an easy time except that, Mary was sure, he was affectionate. At Oxford he must have worn a suit, at least a jersey and trousers, which seemed incredible, and at once, as if she had spoken aloud, Krishnan said, 'I assure you, I was perfectly proper.'

Mary blushed but the elephant had come, standing,

swaying on the other side of the fire from the donkey who stayed in quiet comradeship.

Krishnan had said Birdie was small but to Mary she loomed large. She looked at the width of her back with its grey, wrinkled skin, the ridiculously small tail, the outsize toenails on the big feet, half buried in the sand, and lifted her eyes to the head with its curious dome – again, she was looking in detail. The ears were not as big as the elephants she had seen in Africa. 'Indian elephants are more elegant,' said Krishnan. 'Perhaps because they are used for state occasions and for walking in processions.' Birdie's ears were shapely, mottled pink and brown on the underside. The eyes looked – tiny, Mary thought in surprise, yet elephants' eyes are supposed to have a hundred facets. More surprising were the eyelashes – 'I never knew elephants had eyelashes!'

'Like a film star's,' said Krishnan. The trunk was reaching towards him, its tip lifted to show small pink divisions. A stem of sugar cane came, was accepted whole with leaves; the trunk stuffed it into the mouth with its absurd underlip, came back again while Krishnan crooned words in Telugu. How gentle he is, thought Mary.

'You give her some,' said Krishnan.

'Would she take it from me? Would she?'

'Don't be so doubting, try.'

The trunk came towards Mary, accepted, then suddenly slapped the ground, sending a shower of sand over her. *'Ayyo!'* cried Krishnan. 'That's enough. That was play,' he explained. 'She's the only elephant I know who amuses herself. The palace uses her to fetch marketing and firewood. For that she has to go inland, across a river, wide and shallow. To while away the time, she puts her trunk just under the water and blows bubbles but she would much rather walk in processions – they hire her out for weddings,' and he sang:

'With rings on her fingers
[though they would have to be earrings]
And bells on her toes,
She shall have music
Wherever she goes.'

His voice was full and sweet; it filled Mary with
a happiness as light as the bubbles Birdie blew. What
did it matter if they broke and disappeared? 'It seems
so strange,' she said. 'Nursery rhymes and bubbles. To
be at Oxford you have to be clever.'

'Naturally. I got a first.'

'Then politics – and you know about elephants?'

'At the moment I know everything,' said Krishnan.
'My father says when I am older I shall know that I
don't know anything but I haven't reached as far as
that yet.'

'My father says', Mary was not to be outdone, 'that
you should always pretend to know less than you do about
things. With me, that isn't difficult. I don't know anything.
One of my headmistresses wrote in my report, "Mary has
a marvellous capacity for sitting in a class and absorbing
absolutely nothing." But I can speak French and Italian –
servants' French and Italian.'

'You talk to the servants, you won't talk to our
friends,' Rory used to reproach her.

'Your friends,' even as a child, Mary had retorted
that. 'We move about so much, I don't have time to
make any.'

'I don't think', she told Krishnan now, 'I ever had a
friend but the servants stayed with us. They took me to
market. Markets are much more interesting than drawing
rooms. I suppose there have to be drawing rooms.'

'For you, yes,' said Krishnan. 'You see, I know your
father's name: Roderick Frobisher Sinclair Scott.'

'That's not half as grand as it sounds. It's only

because in Scotland, if you inherit land, for instance from your mother or grandmother—'

'On the maternal side?'

'Yes, you add her surname to your own. You could end with four but Rory's only a younger son.'

'They are proud old names, yet you would rather be Mary Browne?'

'That's what I thought,' and Mary quickly turned the talk away from herself. 'Sing something again,' she said, 'something Indian.'

He sang in Tamil first, then in English:

> 'A cradle of *chaudan*
> A cord of silk.
> Come, little moon bird
> I'll rock the cradle,
> Rock you to sleep
> Sleep.'

'That,' said Krishnan 'is one of the lullabies *ayahs* sing to children when they are in bed.' He stood up. 'Now, before you go to sleep, moonbird, or they send out a search party and raise a sensation, I must take you back.'

'I'll leave you here,' he said when they came near the bungalow. 'I don't want to be shot.'

Mary watched him go. Suddenly he began to dance in and out of the waves, taking long leaps over the stretched-out nets and the prows of boats. Slippers and Birdie had come out of the grove to watch, standing one behind the other at the foot of the dunes; as he turned to join them, he looked along the beach and raised his hand.

Mary raised hers in return.

Monday

'Rory's family couldn't be bettered,' Lady Fisher said in satisfaction. Sir John had told her about seeing Mary on the beach late last night. 'Her mother was a Foljambe, a Devon Foljambe. That ought to be all right.'

'Alicia, you are a constant joy to me.' Sir John in his dressing gown was standing at the window. 'You never change.'

'I see no reason to change.' Lady Fisher was as placid as ever. 'I believe in good breeding – at any level – and it's a comfort to know people's backgrounds . . . it helps one to understand why they behave as they do.'

It was a perfect morning. Early mornings in India are not like mornings anywhere else; they have a purity, 'Perhaps', Sir John often said, 'because they begin with ritual washings and prayer.' In every town and village the people were making their morning ablutions, going down into the rivers or village tanks or pools, standing waist high in the water, pouring it over themselves, lifting their hands in prayer. In Shantipur the villagers did not go into the sea like the fishermen – the waves were too strong – but all were at prayer, purifying themselves.

There were smells: of dew on leaves and grass, of smoke from small fires of dung, of cooking in mustard oil; sudden whiffs of sweetness came from flowers opening in the first sun and, oddly mingling, European smells of toast for the early morning teas being made in the pantry at Patna Hall.

The wind was only a breeze. Along the beach, the waves were almost gentle; black dots of fishing boats were out on a calm sea. 'They must have gone out early,' said Sir John.

Auntie Sanni's doves were calling from the dovecote in the courtyard while parakeets swung and chattered in the jacaranda and acacia trees; monkeys were industriously searching one another for fleas. There was a tumble of bougainvillaea and of morning glory along the walls, their convolvulus-shaped flowers brilliantly blue. As Sir John looked, Hannah came down the upstairs verandah, bringing their morning tea with toast and plantains, small bananas, extra sweet. 'Who could want breakfast after this?' asked Lady Fisher.

'I do,' said Sir John, 'at Patna Hall.'

Hannah, in a clean white sari, her bracelets clinking, put down the tray and made *namaskar*. Lesser guests had their trays brought by the houseboys.

'Thank you, Hannah.' As Lady Fisher poured, she began again where she had left off. 'Anne, Mary's mother, Anne Foljambe remember, would never have countenanced this marriage. Mary should have stayed at that excellent convent in Brussels. She had seemed settled. Do you remember we took her out while we were there?'

'Rory always let her do what she liked.'

'Yes, but to marry so young.'

'Probably couldn't stop her,' said Sir John. 'Pity the young man's not up to her.'

'Most people would say the other way round. He's an only son, there's plenty of money but . . . How does he stand with you, John?'

'Steady, therefore dependable. Completely honest, of course. Excellently briefed – up to a point – but I detect', Sir John winced, 'a certain arrogance, or is it pretentiousness?'

'That's from Mother,' Lady Fisher said at once.

'Yes. Old Archie Browne's a good chap though, invaluable in secondary places where, I can guess, Master Blaise will follow him.'

'Poor Mrs Browne.'

'But, Alicia, that girl! She's quicksilver. I was watching her last night when you were telling the Krishna story, response in every line.'

'Probably too much response.' Lady Fisher sighed. 'Well, she married him, she'll have to conform, though it seems a pity to clip her wings.'

'I don't think she'll let them be clipped,' said Sir John.

Dr Coomaraswamy, in his shirtsleeves, without a tie, his fringe of hair ruffled, was on the telephone. 'Since six a.m. have I been on the telephone,' he told Samuel, who was supervising the tables for breakfast, while Mr Srinivasan frantically looked up numbers. 'Hallo. Hallo.' Another stream of Telegu then the Doctor hung up. 'No contractor has a lorry free. Not one.'

'And what, anyway, are we doing with a lorry?' Mr Srinivasan seemed to beseech heaven.

'Only what we have to do,' said Dr Coomaraswamy — 'Gloomaraswamy', as Krishnan often called him.

'What we have to do? And what will that be?'

Gloomaraswamy lost his temper. 'I only know if this fool antic has to be done at all, it must be done properly.'

'*Pandal*, garlands and all?'

'*Pandal*, garlands, posters, loudspeakers, bloody well all.'

'We cannot do it without a lorry,' said Mr Srinivasan in despair.

'I have a lorry.' Fresh as the morning, his white clothes immaculate, his ringleted hair oiled, came Sharma, once more a messenger for good. 'A beautiful lorry.'

'Who got it?'

'I,' said Sharma. 'Am I not District Agent?'

'Whose is it?'

'Surijlal Chand's.'

'Surijlal's? But he's Opposition.'

'No longer,' said Sharma with his angelic smile. 'No longer.'

'But . . . how?'

'I took him to see Krishnan. Surijlal is a highly religious man. He was up at dawn saying his prayers. Do you know where he is now?'

'How could I know?' said Dr Coomaraswamy crossly. 'I am not Surijlal's keeper.'

'He is taking *darshan*,' said Sharma. '*Darshan* of Krishnan . . . sitting, not saying a word, filled with joy and we have his lorry.'

'But . . . what is it costing?'

'Nothing. He has given it.'

'Surijlal has *given* it? And he a *bania*. I do not believe . . .'

'There it is,' said Sharma, leading them through the hall, and there, by the portico, stood a full-size lorry, almost new and already decorated with tassels, beads and paper flowers.

'But this is excellent.' Mr Srinivasan was hopping up and down in excitement.

'Call everyone!' a recovered Dr Coomaraswamy shouted. 'Srinivasan, go up to Paradise and gather everybody at once. Tell them to hurry.'

Auntie Sanni heard the lorry drive up, then, later, Coomaraswamy's voice shrilly exhorting as the young men came hurrying down the outside staircase with a hubbub of excited voices as orders were shouted from under the portico. The other side of the house was in peace and, as Auntie Sanni on her swing couch was sipping her tea, Hannah, in full clinking, massaged her legs.

'Kuku not up yet?' asked Auntie Sanni. 'She should be.'

'Let her sleep,' said Hannah, 'for all the good she is.'

Mary wanted to sleep too but, 'Wake up,' came Blaise's voice. 'Tea. We're going to have a swim before breakfast.'

Their tray had been set down on the verandah table; rolling over, Mary could see the teapot in its cosy, the pile of toast, bananas, and thought of the bedside Teasmaid of the hotel in Ootacamund and smiled. She was too lazy to get up and lay blinking in the light – Blaise had opened the half doors, sunshine lay on the stone floors and Blaise, holding his cup of tea, was in his bathing shorts. 'Come and swim.' Generously he made no allusion to the night before. 'Come on.'

'No, thank you,' said Mary. She was lying on the far side of the bed, the furthest she had been able to get from him but, by his friendliness, he seemed to have forgotten everything or decided to put it out of his mind – he had been asleep when she came in.

Now, as she lay, she was still filled with the happiness and ease of the grove and, 'Krishnan, Krishnan,' she whispered into the pillow.

'Mary, a good swim . . .'

'No, I don't want to have this buffeted out of me,' but she could not tell that to Blaise and, 'You go,' she said, trying to sound half asleep.

'Right, I will.'

Beyond the partition, Olga Manning had been listening to the news. She clicked the transistor off and, standing in the doorway, looked at the waves. She could not see them though; her eyes were blind with tears. As if she had to prevent them spilling down her cheeks, she clenched her hands hard.

* * *

69

A furious altercation broke out on the beach.

'Sahib wish to swim?' Thambi had come up to Blaise. 'I call Somu.'

'Somu?'

'Lifeguard. Very good young man. He swim with you.'

'For what?'

'At Patna Hall,' said Thambi, 'no guest swim in our sea alone and must wear helmet, Sahib.' He showed the pointed, strong wickerwork cap. 'For break waveforce. Necessary, Sahib.'

'Absolute bull! Don't be silly, man. The sea's perfectly calm.'

'Look calm,' said Thambi, 'but deep, has currents, waves in one minute get too strong. Sahib, please to wait while Somu come.'

'Why should I wait? I swim when and how I want.'

'No, Sahib.' Thambi stood firm. 'It is rule. No guest swim alone. I call Somu.'

'Damned impudent cheek!'

Blaise was back in the bedroom putting on his towelling bathrobe.

'Where are you going?'

'To have this out with Mrs McIndoe.'

'Auntie Sanni?' Mary had been listening, willy-nilly: Blaise had been shouting. 'Blaise,' she tried, 'why not just do as they say? Wouldn't it be more simple? When they see what a strong swimmer you are, of course they'll let you be alone.'

'I won't take this from anyone,' declared Blaise.

Mary had to sympathise. His swimming was the thing of which Blaise was most proud and with reason; she remembered him in Norway and how impressed she and Rory had been. 'Blaise,' she began again but was not surprised to find that he had gone.

'Mr Browne, my grandfather kept the rule and so do I,' said Auntie Sanni. 'Each bather takes a man,

70

sometimes two, and wears the helmet. It is wise.'

'Quite, for most people. I don't want to boast, Mrs McIndoe,' said Blaise, 'but I was chosen for training to swim the English Channel.'

'The English Channel is not the Coromandel coast, Mr Browne.' Auntie Sanni was unimpressed. 'I am sorry to disappoint you but no visitor swims alone from our beach.'

'Then I'll go further up the beach.'

'If you like.' Auntie Sanni's singsong was calm. 'Patna Hall beach is netted and enclosed far out to sea. Elsewhere there are sharks. That is why the fishermen go out four at a time,' and seeing Blaise look like a small boy balked, echoing Mary she coaxed, 'Mr Browne, why not, this first time at any rate, go in with Somu? I expect you swim like a man but he swims like a fish, in-stinc-tive-ly. Try him this morning, Mr Browne, then if he and Thambi think— '

'How kind!' said Blaise, which irony was lost on Auntie Sanni. 'I prefer not to swim at all.'

The lorry could not have been better: like all Surijlal Chand's possessions it was flashy, painted bright yellow, 'For-tun-ate-ly one of our party's colours,' crooned Mr Srinivasan. Green was provided by mango leaf garlands, the white by the background of the posters, of Krishnan's symbolic three cows among stylised flowers.

'It could not be more eyecatching,' Dr Coomaraswamy had to admit both of the lorry and symbol. Two loud-speakers were connected to a battery; in case it failed, there was a megaphone. Dr Coomaraswamy was to stand on the tail of the lorry. 'Yes, I myself must speak all day, since Krishnan . . .'

The *pandal*'s throne seat was raised, 'So everyone can see him,' said Sharma, and was handsomely set off by whole banana trees, their wide long leaves fresh; their stems were swathed in yellow and green. When Krishnan took his seat, naked except for a small loincloth, his skin shining blue-black – Sharma had used plenty of oil – his face painted, the U mark of Vishnu on his forehead, the garlands round his neck – white mogra flowers that had a heady jasmine scent – he looked a veritable god.

He sat in the lotus position. 'You will get cramp,' Mr Srinivasan predicted.

'I never get cramp,' wrote Krishnan. He had a pad and ball pen beside him on which he put down his orders.

Everyone was ready. 'But will the people take it?' the Doctor worried – 'buts' were flying about like vicious small brickbats.

'Surijlal took it,' said Sharma.

With a sense of occasion he had found a conch; as the lorry swept out on the sandy road outside the grove, followed by a small fleet of jeeps, motor bikes and Ambassador cars filled and spilling over with the disciples. 'Ulla, ulla, ullulah.' The conch sounded its holiness as the cortège drove past Patna Hall, then slowly through the village. 'Through all villages we must be slow, then away to Ghandara, slow through the bazaar, then other villages, other towns,' cried Sharma. 'Ulla, ulla, ullulah. Ulla.'

'What shall we do?' asked Blaise after breakfast.

'It was a glorious breakfast,' said Mary. She had eaten papaya, a luscious fruit, large as a melon but golden-fleshed, black-seeded, then kedgeree and, at Samuel's insistence, bacon, sausages – 'At Patna Hall we make our own' – with scrambled eggs, which Auntie Sanni called 'rumble-tumble'. Finally, toast and marmalade, all with large cups of coffee.

'I've never seen you eat like this,' said Blaise.

'I've never eaten like this.'

'Are you sure you've had enough?' he teased as she laid down her napkin. 'Well, what can we do today?'

'I'm too full to do anything,' and not only with

breakfast she could have said. 'I'm going to lie on the beach in the sun like a lizard.' These dear little Indian lizards, thought Mary . . . There was one now, climbing up the dining-room wall – she had heard that if anyone touched their tails, the tails would fall off . . . I don't want anyone to touch me, thought Mary.

Back at the bungalow, she took a towel, spread it on the beach and lay face down, basking.

'I think I'll play golf.' Blaise's bag of clubs was bigger than Mary. 'The brochure says there is a golf course.'

He was soon back, disgruntled. 'Call that a golf course. Absolute con! All on sand! Not even nine holes.'

'Better than nothing.' Mary was half asleep.

'Anyhow I can't play alone.' Blaise sounded lost. 'Sir John won't come out. I tried Menzies but he's at his bloody typewriter. Mary, I'll give you a lesson.'

'No.'

'Merry . . .'

'I can't.' Mary shut her eyes and her ears. 'I can't.'

Blaise was reduced to putting on the flattest sand-green he could find.

Mary lay idly watching the small crabs that scuttled down the beach to meet the highest ripple of each wave; each crab threw up a minute flurry of sand. Crabs, lizards, the elephant Birdie, the sea and the sky seemed to merge and come into one, be 'cosmi', thought Mary. That was a big claim yet true. I am cosmic, she thought, so is a crab or a lizard. If she shut her eyes she seemed to see circles of light that moved, changed and fused. Cosmos, thought Mary, or is the plural 'cosmi'? But 'cosmos' can't have a plural, you silly. She went back to being a lizard and was soon asleep.

Mary was woken by Hannah planting a beach umbrella beside her in the sand. 'Not good, *baba*, to lie in sun too long. You have sunstroke, brain fever. Too hot.' She opened the umbrella. It was true, Mary was too hot and was grateful for the shade. 'And you drink,' commanded Hannah. Besides the umbrella, she had brought a jug of still lemon. 'We make our own lemonade . . . drink, *baba*.'

It was plain that Hannah, Samuel and now Thambi, who had come up too and was smiling down at her, had a conspiracy to look after her but '*baba*', thought Mary sitting up, her arms round her bare knees. *Baba*, child. Yes, I am behaving like a child. She put a lock of hair behind her ear; her hair felt soft, like a child's but, 'You must try to be older,' she told herself sternly. 'You're a married woman. Be generous.' That was a word she had not used before and as Thambi asked, 'Missy swim?' she said, 'I must go and tell my Sahib,' got up and went to look for Blaise.

They swam. 'Sahib strong swimmer,' Thambi said in admiration but Mary noticed the young Somu swimming beside Blaise.

Moses and another fisherman held Mary, diving with her under a towering wave. For a moment she felt her feet standing on a floor of sand – the sea floor? – then they swept her up through the wave; it fell like a weight of thunder on her head but the point of the wicker helmet pierced it and she was up; deftly they turned her, their brown hands strong and quick, then, with them, she was riding in on the crest. On the shore they let her go as, gasping, laughing in exhilaration, the wave trundled her up the beach. 'I've never felt anything like this,' she called to Blaise.

'I must say the bathing *is* marvellous,' he shouted back above the noise of the surf. For the first time at Patna Hall he looked happy . . . as a sandboy, thought Mary – he was covered in sand. 'Let's go in again.'

'Yes,' called Mary. He dived back into a wave, followed at once by Somu while Mary held out her hands to Moses and the fisherman.

Towels round their necks, she and Blaise walked

back to the bungalow, then up to the house for lunch in friendliness.

They played tennis all afternoon.

'Isn't there something very dear about this place?' Mrs Glover asked the other ladies, stretching her feet luxuriously as she sat in the comfortable verandah chair. 'Unlike the other hotels we've stayed at, coming back here in the evening is like coming home.'

The group had spent the day driving out into the hills to see the newly discovered cave paintings; now they were resting on the verandah and, 'Yes,' said Mrs van den Mar in content, 'it is like coming home! Such a welcome.'

'That nice Hannah made me sit down, took off my shoes and massaged my feet,' said Mrs Glover, 'pressing them, pulling out the toes. Exquisite.'

Mrs Schlumberger shuddered. 'I can't stand her bangles, rattle, clink, chink. Anyway, she never came near *me*.'

'I'm not surprised,' but Mrs van den Mar refrained from saying it.

'And my feet are more swollen than Mrs Glover's. There was far, far too much walking.' Mrs Schlumberger glared at Professor Webster.

'But those cave paintings, those colours still there after all these centuries.' Miss Pritt was rapt. 'The old true colours, crimson and brown madder and turmeric, indigo – those violets and greens.'

'They looked very dirty to me.' Mrs Schlumberger was still cross. 'Shabby and old.'

'Old! I should say! Two thousand seven hundred years!' Dr Lovat had been as moved as Miss Pritt.

'Maybe later, second century BC,' Professor Webster had to caution.

'Before Christ! Think of it! And as your eyes get accustomed, the faces seem to speak to you, so expressive, witty

75

and eloquent. Those *apsaras*! The heavenly dancing girls, the verses in their honour scratched on the walls.' Professor Webster had translated them and Dr Lovat quoted: 'The lily-coloured ones. The doe-eyed beauties . . . Mystical!'

'Mystical! Utterly disgusting. Obscene! That multiple sexual intercourse!' Mrs Schlumberger said in outrage. 'How dare Professor Aaron expose us to such things?'

'Multiple intercourse was supposed to be the paradigm of ultimate bliss.' Dr Lovat was deliberately taunting Mrs Schlumberger. 'It's an allegory for the way sex is revered in Indian culture. That's why the girls are enchanting,' and she quoted, 'If the senses are not captivated the lure will not work.'

'Lure! I'm surprised at you, Julia.'

'But did you see those student workers?' Mrs van den Mar skilfully changed the conversation. 'Students cleaning those wonderful murals with acetone. *By order!*'

'Yes,' Professor Webster was wrathful, 'the colours will be ruined. I shall write to the Department of Archaeology.'

But Miss Pritt was not concerned with departments. 'Those paintings seemed to distil all these centuries of art as if they had been five minutes.'

'Centuries in which, by comparison, we have gained nothing, nothing,' said Mrs Glover.

'Something happened to painting,' said Dr Lovat, 'when it came off the walls. With murals and frescoes it was pure.'

'You mean, as soon as it turned into pictures, buying and selling came in and something went out,' said Ellen Webster.

'Joy and, yes, awe, you're right,' said Dr Lovat.

'Just as something happened to men's minds when they built office blocks higher than a spire . . .'

Kuku gave an enormous yawn.

* * *

It was towards dusk when Mary and Blaise were leaving the tennis court that they heard the soft beating of drums and with them a chanting; looking up, Mary saw lights moving, people carrying lit torches. A procession was coming down the hill beyond the village. She could make out men in white – they carried the flares – and, less distinct because of their coloured clothes, women who seemed to be carrying round baskets on their heads heaped, she saw when the torchlight fell on them, with fruit and flowers. The light fell, too, on chests carried on poles laid each side of them and painted scarlet. 'Marriage chests,' said Olga Manning.

She had come out in the late afternoon to watch them play. 'Uninvited,' Blaise had muttered. As soon as they came off the court she had come up to them whereupon he had picked up the racquets and presses and left.

Olga had taken no notice. 'It's for a wedding,' she explained to Mary. 'There must be one near, in some village. This is the bride's dowry being brought down to the bridegroom's house. She must be a hill girl. Poor little thing, probably married to a man she doesn't know,' and Mary, startled, thought, I'm married to a man I don't know. Almost she said it aloud but, as if she had, Olga said with curious passion, 'None of us should marry, unless we love a man so much we would go through hell for him, which we shall probably have to do.'

'Well, Hari, how did it go?' Sir John asked on the verandah that evening.

'It did not go. Not at all. Not at all.' Dr Coomaraswamy again was in despair. 'Everywhere we went Padmina Retty was before us, so skilfully she had arranged it. She is eloquent, so eloquent.' Dr Coomaraswamy had tears in his eyes. 'They tell me one speech lasted over an hour, while Krishnan— '

'A contrast indeed!'

'Everyone was so much astonished,' came Mr Srinivasan's moan.

'Good,' said Sir John, 'good.'

'What good?' Dr Coomaraswamy had become angry. 'What if they are astonished into inertia? Inertia! I myself spoke and spoke but I am no match for Padmina. They did not listen, only looked.'

'Isn't that what they were supposed to do?' asked Sir John.

Lady Fisher, changed for dinner, came out and sat by Sir John. She was smiling. 'Kuku', she told him quietly, 'asked me if there were really a man's club in London called the Savage.'

'How did she come to hear of it?'

'Apparently Mr Menzies gave it as his London address. I think she had a vision of men in skins, tearing meat with their hands and teeth.'

As if she had fathomed Kuku's dearest longings, Lady Fisher had given her, to Hannah's intense disapproval, a pure silk sari. 'Even sent to Ghandara for it. Sharma bought it,' Hannah told Samuel.

'That was dear of you, Alicia,' Auntie Sanni had said. 'I am most glad.' In consequence Lady Fisher now was Kuku's confidante.

'The Savage Club is real enough.' Sir John was thoughtful. 'I'm not as sure about Menzies.'

'Mr Menzies has been at least half an hour on the telephone,' an indignant Kuku told Auntie Sanni. One of Patna Hall's two telephones was in a kiosk that stood in the hall; the other in Auntie Sanni's office was available only to her and Colonel McIndoe. 'I needed urgently to order a few stores. Twice I came back. He was still there. When I stood to show I was waiting, he shut the door.'

'I expect he had some business to do.' Auntie Sanni was not disturbed.

The International Association of Art, Technology and Culture was having a lecture that night given by Professor Webster. 'And they have been out in the hills since eight this morning. Where do they get the appetite?' Auntie Sanni marvelled as she marvelled each year. 'Kuku, you must warn Mrs Manning – I'm afraid she can't have the drawing room tonight but tell her that, though the lecture is for the group, anyone who cares to is welcome to come.'

'No, thank you,' was Olga's answer, 'and, Kuku, will you tell Auntie Sanni I have to go to Calcutta in the morning and, please, order a taxi for the station.'

'Another of those mysterious trips,' Kuku told Mary, who had come with Blaise to wait for dinner.

'Why mysterious?'

'She keeps on going, coming back. Why so often? She tells no one.'

'Why should she?'

That to Mary was one of the best things at Patna Hall. Except for Kuku, no one asked that perpetual why? why? why? No one asked you why you wanted to lie alone in the sun, only brought you a beach umbrella and a drink of lemon but Kuku's eyes were bright as a little snake's. 'She travels second class,' said Kuku.

Kuku's spite was partly born of a sense of hopelessness; Blaise was wearing white linen trousers, a primrose-coloured silk shirt, a deeper yellow and grey striped tie. They set off his hair, his fresh tanned skin and his height. 'Not Apollo, Adonis,' murmured Kuku. She could have scratched Mary's eyes out, especially when, as if purposely, Mary stopped at Mrs Manning's table in the dining room and asked her to have coffee with them after dinner.

'Mary, you've forgotten,' came the inevitable from Blaise. 'The Fishers have already asked us. I'm sorry, Mrs Manning,' and after he had steered Mary away, 'I told you to stay clear of her. She's a leech.'

On any other night, when after dinner they came back to the verandah, Mary would have gone defiantly and sat down by Olga but, I must keep Blaise in a good mood tonight, she thought. Then he'll sleep – she had not known she could be so guileful. He must sleep because I'm going to see Krishnan.

Krishnan. Krishnan. All day the thought of him had come back to her. Krishnan – happiness. There was a poem she had learnt at one of those schools, a poem she loved:

> 'My heart is like a singing bird
> whose nest is in a watered shoot' . . .

It had sung in her mind all day. Am I in love? wondered Mary. No, I've been in love. I don't want that again, thank you. This is different, unimaginable, like the waves here that are quite different from anywhere else on earth. Outwardly, on Patna Hall's verandah, the young wife of this eminently suitable young man appeared to be listening to the talk that was going on around her while all the time she only heard 'My heart is like a singing bird . . .' and, 'Soon it will be time,' she told herself. 'Soon.'

It was Sir John who broke up the talk early. Mary had already seen him go quietly down the verandah to Olga Manning – To ask her to join us. Mary was grateful but Olga, though she smiled, shook her head. Soon after she had left and now, 'I must drop in on this lecture,' said Sir John.

'The culture lecture?' Blaise was surprised. 'I thought the group . . .'

'Were a bit comical?' asked Sir John. 'What those who knew no better used to call culture vultures?' Blaise blushed. 'In actuality, they are giving India the compliment of trying to understand her art and civilisation.' Oh, I like Sir John, I like him, thought Mary. 'I think we should honour that and I suggest, Coomaraswamy, you come with me and', said Sir John, 'you might invite Professor Aaron's ladies to come to one of your rallies and see how you run your election. Take them round with you.'

'With things as they are?' cried Dr Coomaraswamy in acute pain. 'Also you have forgotten, Sir John, tonight Padmina Retty's inaugural rally is going on with great display, *She* knows how it should be done. I should have been there already to watch, God help me. So – no lecture for me.'

As he and Mr Srinivasan went, Lady Fisher left her embroidery. 'I'll come, John,' but, 'Miss Sanni, Colonel Sahib, Lady Sahib,' Samuel burst out of the dining room in excitement. 'It is the radio. I have been listening to the radio. Come. Come quickly. They say Padmina Retty's rally in utter discredit.'

The voice was going on. 'Poor Mrs Retty. A huge audience was sitting, many on the grass – the rally is being held in Ghandara's botanical park. Bands had been playing as the decorated platform was filled with dignitaries while, over it, was suspended Padmina Retty's symbol, a giant open umbrella which slowly turned showing the party's name, the People's Shelter Party and the slogan promise: "I will shelter you." Mrs Retty, a commanding figure in a billowing blue and silver sari – blue for promise – standing at the microphone was in full eloquence. Certainly she can hold her audience. "I, Padmina Retty . . ." when suddenly, among the audience one figure after the other stood up, men, women, many women and, yes, children, each holding an umbrella which they opened and held up, ancient umbrellas, stained, tattered, torn, some showing only ribs, some with ribs broken, all palpably useless. As their bearers stood steadily it was more eloquent than words!

'Mrs Retty's own words faltered, in any case they would not have been heard because a ripple of laughter began which spread to a gale, the whole audience laughing in complete glee . . . but under the glee old resentments flared. There were catcalls, shouts – something Mrs Retty had not encountered before. I must add that, prominent among the umbrella holders were young women dressed in green, yellow and white, colours, as we know, of another party. It was fortunate that they were protected by their fellow males because, as could have been predicted, fighting broke out. It could have become a riot but the police were prepared and quelled it swiftly . . .

'Mrs Retty had left the platform. There was, of course, no sign of Krishnan Bhanj.'

Samuel so far forgot himself that he clapped. Hannah clapped too, Lady Fisher clapped with her as did Mary, and even Colonel McIndoe. Mary was laughing with delight until Blaise spoke. 'Wasn't that rather an antic in a serious election?' asked Blaise.

'Yes, you see, our young women had been all over,' Dr Coomaraswamy told later when he and his supporters came back. He was still shaking with laughter. His young men, some of them with black eyes, bruises and cuts, were being tended in Paradise by Mr Srinivasan, Samuel and Hannah. 'Krishnan planned it so well,' the Doctor went on. 'A month ago to Bihar he had sent them. By jeep, car, motorcycle, bullock cart they had travelled among the villages to carry out this trading, new umbrellas for old – what you used to call, I think, in England gamps. It took time to persuade the people – they could not believe a new umbrella for old. It also took time to persuade our Konak people tonight. Did I not tell you, just to stand up and open their old umbrellas, five rupees for each we had to give,' but Dr Coomaraswamy said it happily. 'Once they understood how they enjoyed! Our young men and women started the laughter but almost immediately everyone was laughing of themselves.' Dr Coomaraswamy laughed too.

'Just because I hit the donkey.'

'It's nothing to do with the donkey.'

The sound of the hard young voices came through the partition to Olga Manning.

'You might at least try.' That was Blaise. Then Mary, 'It's no use if you have to try.' The voices rose as, 'No!' shrieked Mary. 'No!' and, 'God,' shouted Blaise, 'anyone would think I was trying to *rape* you. You are my *wife*.'

'Do you think you could desist', Olga Manning's voice came from her side of the bungalow, 'and let me get some sleep?'

A guilty silence. Then, 'I apologise', called Blaise, 'for my wife.'

'Apologise for yourself!' shouted Mary.

'Very well. Goodnight.' Blaise flung himself on the bed. Then, seeing Mary dressing, 'Where are you going?'

'Out, if you don't mind.'

'Go where you like. I don't care a damn,' said Blaise.

Auntie Sanni, as if her thumbs had pricked her, had come out on the top verandah, looked down across the garden to the beach and saw Mary fling out of the bungalow and down the steps to the shore.

'*Ayyo!*' said Auntie Sanni.

'Well, Doctor. What will you do tomorrow?' Sir John, Dr Coomaraswamy with Professor Aaron were having a nightcap on the deserted verandah.

'You should not say, "What will you do?" What can I do? God knows! God knows! Tomorrow Padmina Retty is holding a second rally. There will be thousands—'

'This Krishnan Bhanj,' Professor Aaron ventured to say. 'Have you, forgive me, but have you, shall we say, been mistaken, taken in by his charm – I hear he is charming – and perhaps his position? Vijay Bhanj's son?' and the

Doctor seemed to hear Uma's voice, 'You see, Hari' – Uma was emancipated enough to call her husband firmly by his given name – 'you see how you have been carried away by this Krishnan. It is always the same: if they are beautiful, sweet-mannered, you are over the moon. Isn't it the old call of the flesh?' Uma had said 'flesh' with distaste.

'Krishnan Bhanj is a most gifted politician,' Dr Coomaraswamy said aloud, adding silently to Uma, 'Flesh has nothing to do with it,' and at once had a vision of Kuku. 'Please, please,' he cried silently. 'Please, Kuku, get out of my mind.'

She had glided between the tables at dinner, bending to set glasses down on his.

'We have a wine waiter,' Samuel had growled.

'The Doctor asked me to bring.'

That was true. 'What is that perfume you put on your hair?' It had almost touched him.

'Jasmine.'

'I will send you a bottle.'

'Do. It will be costly.' Was there a touch of malice in that?

He had watched her as she went back to the bar, his fork half-way to his lips. 'A great booby you must have looked,' Uma would have told him but the walk was so smooth, sinuous, the hips undulating. 'Is it my fault our candidate has good looks?' he cried now to invisible Uma, yet he could not rebut Professor Aaron and said bitterly to Sir John, 'The campaign is dead loss. Dead loss.'

A car drew up. Then Mr Menzies came along the verandah.

'Where have you sprung from?'

'Madras.'

'That's a long drive.'

'Yes.' He looked tired but his eyes were alert. 'You've had a bad day,' he said to the Doctor as he poured himself a whisky.

84

'Desperate. Dead loss!' moaned Dr Coomaraswamy.
'I should cheer up, if I were you,' said Mr Menzies.

Mary had to wait on the beach to let her anger die down – instinctively, I can't bring anger into the grove, she thought – waited, too, in case Blaise had, after all, followed her. There was a sound but it was only Slippers. After his tidbit, he had waited hopefully outside the bungalow; now he had plodded after her until he came close enough for her to pat him and pull his ears.

Suddenly he lifted his nose and brayed. At the same time, Mary heard an excited chattering and laughing. A group of boys was standing round one boy who was holding something; their dark skins, black heads, tattered clothes told Mary they were fisherboys. More excited laughter broke out; above it she heard a piercing shriek, than another, a small animal's shriek, and she started to run, Slippers lumbering after her. 'What have you got there? What are you doing?' She cried it in English, scattering the boys. 'Devils! *Shaitan!*' she screamed, because the boy in the middle held a small grey squirrel, one of the squirrels that abound in India.

They had tied a rag over its head to prevent it biting; it cried and squirmed as they poked it with slivers of pointed bamboo, fine and sharp as skewers. Blood was over the boy's hands. 'Give it to me,' stormed Mary. She snatched the squirrel, rag and all, as, with the flat of her other hand, she hit the boy hard across the face, then slapped the other boys. '*Jao!* Go! *Chelo* – ' the first words she had learnt of Hindustani. '*Chelo . . . Hut jao! Shaitan!*'

But these were fisherboys, not town boys easily quelled. She was one among seven or eight of them, not little boys but ten-, eleven-year-olds. Caught by surprise, at first they had stood dumb; the slaps roused them. With an outbreak of furious voices they closed in round her. Holding the squirrel close, Mary stood as hands and fists came out to hit, scratch, pinch, claw. Then Krishnan was beside her. He did not speak but took the squirrel from her. The frantic squirming stopped instantly and it was still as he raised his hand over the boys, only raised it; as one, they bent, scooped up sand and poured it over his feet, touching them with their heads. 'Kanu,' he said to the ringleader boy. 'Lady,' and unwillingly Kanu did the same to Mary who, as he lifted his head, gently laid her hand on it. He shook it off at once and with the others ran away through the trees.

'Is it badly hurt?'

'We'll see.'

He led, the way to the fire. Mary's knees seemed to give way and she sank down on the sand. 'How could they? How could anyone be so cruel?' She hid her face so long that Slippers poked her with his nose.

'Look,' said Krishnan. He was sitting cross-legged on his goatskin throne and on one folded knee was the squirrel, sitting upright. Its wounds showed red in the firelight but it was nibbling a nut held in its small claws, its head cocked on one side, its black eyes brilliant. 'We call squirrels *udata* in Telegu,' he said. 'She has had some milk. Now this little *udata* will get well, thanks to you.'

'Not me. Thanks to you. They would have taken her back. Oh, why must people be so cruel? Even children!'

'Particularly children.' He spoke gently. 'They don't know any better,' and now Mary did not see the evil, pointed sticks but the small heads bent to touch Krishnan's feet.

Her angry trembling ceased. 'What are those marks on her back?' she asked.

'Long long ago,' said Krishnan, 'the young god, Prince Rama – another incarnation of Vishnu – had a beautiful wife, Sita. Indian girls, when they are married, are told to be a "little Sita", she was so perfect. But Sita was stolen by a powerful demon – he had ten heads – who carried her off in his terrible claws to Sri Lanka.

'Rama was in despair as to how he could get her back. How could he take his army across that wide sea? But Hanuman, who is the Monkey God, called all the monkeys of India to build Rama a bridge. Thousands of great powerful apes and strong quick monkeys carried stones, rocks, boulders from the mountains to the shore. Quarries were dug, mighty rocks brought down to the sea, great boulders hewn into blocks. It was such a gigantic task that the very gods of heaven marvelled while Rama himself watched amazed.

'As he watched he saw a great monkey almost trip over a squirrel who was on the beach too. From his height, the monkey looked down a long, long way at the tiny squirrel and saw she had a pebble in her mouth.

'"What are you doing?"

'The little squirrel looked up. "I am helping to build the bridge to Lanka so that Rama may bring back his beloved wife, Sita."

'"Helping to build the bridge!" The monkey burst into a roar of laughter and called all the other monkeys. "Did you hear that? The squirrel says she is helping to build our bridge. Did you ever hear anything so funny in your life?" The others laughed too, then all of them said, "Shoo. We've no time for play and the likes of you."

'But the squirrel would not shoo. Again and again the monkeys picked her up and put her out of the way; she always came back with the pebbles until one of the monkeys grew angry and not only picked her up but flung her hard across the beach. She fell into Rama's hands where he stood.

'Rama held the squirrel close – just as you did – and said to the monkeys, "How dare you despise her? This little squirrel with her pebbles has love in her heart that would move heaven and earth with its power." And, lo!'

said Krishnan dramatically, 'Rama was transformed back into his origin, the great god Vishnu, the Preserver. Vishnu stroked the squirrel's back and as he put her down the monkeys saw, on her grey fur, these white lines that were the marks of the great God's fingers. Since when, Udata, you have those marks on your back, haven't you?'

Mary put out a hand and touched the stripes; the squirrel allowed her. 'It's the same as Christ riding on the donkey,' she said. 'All donkeys have the mark of the cross, even Slippers far away in India. It's the same.'

'All the same.'

'Will she come to me?'

'I'll ask her.'

He talks to her as if he were a squirrel, thought Mary.

'How do you know I wasn't?' Krishnan said with his strange power of following her thoughts. 'I could have been a squirrel, couldn't I?' he asked the squirrel. 'But', he said to Slippers, 'I do not seriously think I could have been a donkey.'

'You're conceited,' said Mary.

'If I am, why not? A peacock struts and spreads his tail because he is a peacock. That would have suited me. Peacocks are sacred in India and I am about to become sacred. I could have been a peacock. That is what we Hindus believe,' and he mocked, 'Don't tread on that cockroach, it might have been your grandfather. Don't tread on a cockroach but let children starve because you have put chalk in flour, given short weight, foreclosed on a peasant's one little field before he has time to pay off the debt.' His eyes blazed with indignation.

'Is that what your Party is about?'

'Of course. Why do you think I'm doing this?'

'I don't know. I only know I like what you are doing.'

'Not always. You couldn't. Remember all is fair in love and war. Politics now are a war, a bitter, greedy war and I have to fight Padmina Retty in every way I can. You don't know, Mary, thank God you have had no need to know, but Indian politics are corrupt, venal as never before. If Padmina Retty's manifesto had been truthful, it would have said: (a) The People's Shelter Party totally believes that, in the state of Konak, one family, the Rettys, should have total rule and that in perpetuity; (b) every member of the People's Shelter Party will give full material and emotional help to its leader in misappropriating funds; (c) the People's Shelter Party will support only those people who believe in hooliganism and slander.'

'That's terribly damning.'

'Not damning enough. The same goes for Gopal Rau, though he has not a chance. I tell you,' said Krishnan, 'no one from a family of integrity would dream of going into politics except a mopus like me. Even a mope, though, knows that no one can get into Parliament without so much wheeling and dealing that it disgusts. Not to mention spending money, floods of money, which is where our Dr Coomaraswamy comes in.'

'That funny old fat man?'

'That funny old fat man is a visionary. No one but a visionary would back me. I do not think', said Krishnan, 'poor Coomaraswamy will get his money back. A candidate can only be elected for five years, but he or she can retrieve his money, even make a fortune, by way of taking bribes, cheating, pulling strings, dispensing patronage, which must be paid for. The people know very well, if a village helps to get a candidate elected, it will be the first to get electricity or a well. If it resists, no electricity, no well. Patronage! I couldn't patronise a bee, yet the dear Doctor has worked with me and my ideals for years.'

'Years?'

'Yes, you don't think I came to this in five minutes? And all the time he has had to put up with a barrage from his terrible wife.' Krishnan mocked again, '"So easilee you are bamboozled, Hari" — Hari is Dr

Coomaraswamy's name.' Krishnan, whose English was smoother, more rounded than most Englishmen's, caught the wife's accent to perfection. '"And you are like a child with sweets so easily parted from your mon-ee." But Uma is right,' said Krishnan. 'I am using Coomaraswamy but that is a good man, Mary. How he has helped us.' Krishnan brooded again. 'The fisherpeople should be all right, but they are, in fact, the very poorest, virtually bonded in debt to the middle men and victims of the powerful fish-market Mafia. Mary,' he asked, 'what do you think the village people most need?'

'Water,' Mary said at once.

'Indeed, yes, and the wells will come faster if they work with us. I will not promise what I cannot do. What else?'

'Trees. Seed.'

'Yes, but not first.' His eyes darkened. 'Outside people coming in, would-do-goods, could plant a million trees – a million million – and change nothing because it would all begin again, but someone who plants ideas, knowledge, respect for our earth', Krishnan was deeply in earnest, '*might* just succeed.' Now his eyes seemed alight.

'Mary, I have been trying to do that for the last five years and I know it works, otherwise I would never have presumed – yes, *presumed* – to be a people's candidate. Let me tell you: I got one villager to let us use his piece of land that was bare – he would have said, of no use. He and his wife and children built mud walls and channels so that we could irrigate from quite far away. Then we came with saplings and seedlings. Now on his scruffy land he has an orchard, with pineapples and tea growing under the trees and enough grass to feed his cow and buffalo.'

'If,' said Krishnan, himself visionary, 'if we can teach one or two villages to feed themselves and their animals, that may spread and save the whole continent. If not,' the light went out of his eyes and he shrugged, 'at least a few less villages have less hungry children.'

'Lady Fisher told me', said Mary, 'that when there is great trouble in the world, Vishnu comes down in one form or another. I wish he would come now.'

'It is a belief,' said Krishnan. 'Some people would call it a delusion but I believe it is a good belief.'

'Love and war,' said Mary. 'Can politics be love?'

'They can, thank God.'

Mary watched his hand stroking the contented squirrel.

'I think you love everyone, everything,' she said.

He laughed. 'That wouldn't be possible.' Then he was serious again. 'It is that I am everyone, everything, just as everything, everyone is me.'

'Even the hateful ones?'

'Particularly the hateful ones because I am very hateful, very often.'

'But I . . . I like people and things – or dislike them – violently.'

'That is because you are thinking of yourself, not them,' which was true. 'See, now,' he said, 'here is a creature' – he says creatures, created things, not animals, thought Mary – 'a creature who does like you. Birdie has brought you a bouquet.'

The little elephant – how can an elephant be little? thought Mary, but Birdie is – held in her trunk a whole stem of plantains, at least thirty small bananas on a stem. 'I think you have stolen that,' Krishnan told her. 'Bad girl!' but he patted her trunk. He broke off the plantains, gave two to Mary, took three for himself, bit off a small end for the squirrel, gave ten to Slippers, the rest back to Birdie. The stem he threw on the fire so that the flames leapt up. They munched in companionship. Mary liked the way Birdie ate, picking up a plantain in her trunk and delicately putting it in her mouth; Udata nibbled; Slippers's bananas went round and round in his mouth – he would keep his the longest.

'This is the last time I can speak with you,' Krishnan

said. 'Tomorrow the vow must be absolute. I shall not know who might be listening.'

He sighed. '*Ayyo!* How my legs ache with all that sitting.'

'I ache too, inside me,' but Mary did not say it. She must not think back over the day, 'But the sea was wonderful,' she said. 'Those waves!'

'The sea. Yes. Let's go and get clean.' He jumped up and held out his hand to Mary.

On the beach he unwound his loin and shoulder cloths, leaving him with only a clout. Mary pulled her dress off over her head.

A pile of fishermen's helmets had been left by a boat. 'Put this on.' He put on his own. 'Don't be afraid,' he said. 'Thambi and I have been swimming here since we were five years old.' He took Mary straight through the waves, far out where he let her go. On the shore, Slippers, Birdie and a dot that was Udata had come out to watch. Mary could hear the thunder of the waves on the beach, here it was still; the water, warm and balmy, was dark blue. They swam, floated.

When Mary was tired, Krishnan came behind her, took her shoulders and let her rest. 'Let's stay here for ever,' she said.

'If only we could.'

Back on the beach, dressed, he and the animals walked her back but, before they reached the bungalow, Mary stopped. 'Don't come any nearer,' she said, 'it might be broken.'

Krishnan did not ask her what 'it' was.

Tuesday

'Would anyone object', Mr Menzies asked the whole dining room at breakfast, 'if, because of the election, we put on the morning news?' Without waiting for an answer he switched on the big verandah radio.

'This is the English Programme of All India Radio. Here is the news.'

The news was always read in Tamil, Telegu and English.

Now the voice, speaking in English, was reading the headlines: 'The drought is beginning to be felt in the Gamjam district. In Sri Kakylam there have been riots . . .' The breakfasters listened with half an ear if they listened at all. 'The bodies of two children, both boys, have been found in a field near the village of Palangaon. The trial, under Mr Justice Rajan, of the Englishman, Colin Armstrong, charged with fraud, embezzlement and trafficking in drugs, is drawing to a close . . . and now, the election in Konak.'

'Aie!' cried Dr Coomaraswamy and silence fell as everybody listened.

'The débâcle that befell Mrs Padmina Retty's People's Shelter Party last night could not help but leave traces this morning. For one thing, the symbol of the umbrella has disappeared. All posters have been hastily torn down and there has been some hand-fighting in the square where these two rival Parties' headquarters face one another. Mrs Retty, as befits a professional and long-accustomed campaigner, is cool and unperturbed. Her headquarters is buzzing with activity while the opposite building is strangely quiet and, except for two secretaries, empty. Again, there is no sign of Krishnan Bhanj.

'"I am not surprised," says Mrs Retty. "After that antic last night"' – she used the same word as Blaise who smiled in self-congratulation. '"After that antic, Krishnan dare not face me . . ."

'But', asked the voice on the radio, 'could he outface her? Mrs Retty, it seems, has not heard of a lorry that, since dawn, has been driving through the countryside.'

'I, myself, sent him out,' Dr Coomaraswamy interrupted, he had a ray of hope. 'But' – once again 'buts' were flying like brickbats – 'but was I wise?' he sighed.

'You couldn't have stopped him,' said Sir John.

'Have you seen the morning papers?' asked Mr Menzies.

Patna Hall's Goanese cook, Alfredo, collected them when he went to do the marketing at Ghandara, as he did every morning. In time-honoured fashion, the papers were ironed and then Kuku laid them out on the verandah tables for the guests; Colonel McIndoe's were taken by his bearer to his study. 'Ah! The *Madras Times*. The *Nilgiri Herald. All India Universal.*' Sir John picked up the *Madras Times*. 'It's the leading article.'

'Read it. Read it,' begged Dr Coomaraswamy.

Sir John read: '"Is it disrespectful to ask if Krishnan Bhanj, candidate for the new Root and Flower Party, has taken his startling vow of silence in response to a direct commandment from the gods – in which case who dare say him 'nay'?" That's a tongue-in-cheek remark if ever I heard one,' said Sir John. '"Or is this rising young politician playing a wily game of cards? If so, he is playing it well. Mrs Retty was routed last night and without violence, simply by a superior display of that insidious and most deadly of weapons, ridicule, making a story that will be told as long as politics exist. Already a ripple is spreading through Konak, a ripple from town to town, village to village. It may be only curiosity, maybe it is

94

reverence, but one can forecast that soon, Mrs Padmina Retty's audience will have gone elsewhere, waiting for a garlanded lorry that has on it a *pandal* and, in the *pandal*, a young god silently blessing." That', said Sir John, 'was written, I'm sure, by Ajax.'

'Ah!' Dr Coomaraswamy gave a very different sigh.

'Who is Ajax?' asked Mr Srinivasan.

'Probably the best political correspondent in India and the Far East. If he is covering this election, you are in luck but he is best known for his gossip columns which spread on occasions to London and Europe. He is adept at dirt.'

'*Ayyo!*' Dr Coomaraswamy was well pleased.

'Looking to see if anything has been cut?'

Coming out from breakfast, Sir John had found Mr Menzies at one of the verandah tables, studying the article in the *Madras Times* and, as he looked up startled, 'You are, of course, Ajax,' said Sir John.

'I am.' There was something more than self-satisfaction, insolence, in the way Mr Menzies said that. 'And I don't let them cut my stuff. Clever of you to guess,' he told Sir John.

'Not at all. It was quite transparent,' and with a nod Sir John went on down the verandah leaving Mr Menzies slightly taken aback.

It is going to be a lovely empty day, thought Mary. They are all going away.

'I am taking Mrs Manning to the train,' Kuku told Mary. Her eyes were bright with the same brightness, Mary could not help thinking, that had been in the boys' eyes when they were tormenting the squirrel. 'I think she will be meeting someone.'

You want me to ask, 'What sort of someone?' thought Mary. Well, I won't.

Kuku's look said, 'Prig.'

* * *

95

Professor Aaron was taking his group to see the famous Dawn Temple at Gorāghat, fifty miles along the coast.

Sir John, Lady Fisher and Blaise were going too.

'I'd much rather be swimming or playing tennis,' Blaise grumbled as he picked up his packed lunch, binoculars and hat.

'Then why don't you?' asked Mary.

'If Sir John goes, I must.'

'Why?'

'You're always asking why.' Blaise was irritable. 'He's a big noise, that's why.'

'I think he'll know if you're pretending.'

'Pretend what? The Dawn Temple is very fine, even from the point of view of history. It's marvellous how they carried those enormous blocks of stone to build it. It's one of those things one should see.'

'Even if you don't want to? And it isn't only history, it's beauty,' said Mary, 'old, old beauty. Lady Fisher says it faces East and just at dawn, as the sun rises, the whole temple turns gold and rose-coloured.'

'If it makes you so lyrical, why don't you come?' But Mary shook her head. 'I'd like to go there early, early in the morning before dawn, all by myself, not in a coach full of people with cameras and binoculars and notebooks.'

Mary's day turned out not to be empty, not at all: it was filled with Patna Hall. 'Samuel is taking me to the bazaar,' she had told Blaise.

'You mean you would rather go with a servant to see an ordinary squalid bazaar than a splendid excursion like this, with Sir John, Professor Aaron, his group – and me?'

'Much rather,' said Mary.

'I find you utterly incomprehensible.'

'I know you do,' said Mary sadly. 'And I you,' but she did not add that.

Blaise hated all bazaars. 'All those rows of shanty huts and booths, corrugated iron, stucco houses blotched with damp! Even the temples are tawdry. Their silver roofs are made of beaten-out kerosene tins.'

'I think that's clever if you can't afford silver,' said Mary.

'And the *smells*! Cess in the gutters . . . men squatting down to relieve themselves even while you pass. Rancid *ghee* from the cookshops and that horrible mustard oil they cook in. Rotting fruit and meat hung too long and flies, flies, flies. If you walk on the pavements – if they can be called pavements – you tread on phlegm and red betel where people have spat. Ugh! And all those beggars and children with swollen stomachs and sore eyes. Once, perhaps, one could find good things in the bazaar, muslins, pottery, but now it's all machine-made, plastic, ugly. Mary, I hate you to go there. I know there are wonderful things to see in India but there are some things it's better for you not to see.'

'I want to see it whole.'

But Blaise had made up his mind. 'You're not to go,' he said as authoritatively as Rory. 'You're not to go.'

'I'm going,' said Mary.

Auntie Sanni had overheard. 'You're not very kind to that husband of yours,' she said.

'He shouldn't order me about. I'm not his child.'

'Come. Come. He only wants to protect you,' said Auntie Sanni. 'If your husband is a real man, that is in-nate.'

'I don't want to be protected. Don't you see?' Mary was hot-cheeked. 'I've never been anywhere, seen anything . . .'

'Except, as I understand, Italy, Paris, Norway, Brussels . . .'

'I meant India. Besides in those countries Rory always sent me to *school*.' Mary said it as if it were the ultimate betrayal. 'You don't know, Auntie Sanni, what girls' boarding schools are like, so – so little. I was – choked.' Mary could not find the right word. 'There was one,' she had to admit, 'a convent in Brussels which was part of something bigger. The nuns had something else to concern themselves with apart from girls.' She said that word in scorn. 'Even at home, Rory never let me be really free to do things – or thought he didn't. Now Blaise thinks he won't allow me either. Well, he has another think coming.'

'It's early days yet,' said Auntie Sanni.

'I knew you'd say that.'

'I do say it,' Auntie Sanni spoke sternly. 'Mary, child, be careful. You may cause more damage than you mean.'

'I'd like to go to the bazaar every day and do my own shopping,' Mary was to tell Blaise. It was an every day she had not glimpsed before yet perhaps had sensed. Everything Blaise had said of the bazaar was true: the stench, the shanty huts and booths, the flies . . . but the first shop she and Samuel came to was the shop where kites were made and sold costing a few *annas*, kites of thinnest paper, in colours of pink, green, white, red, with a wicker spool to fly them from, wound with a pound of thread. The thread had been run through ground glass so that the boys – Samuel told Mary that kite-fliers were always boys – could challenge other kites, cross strings with them, cut them adrift and proudly tie another bob of paper on their own kite's tail.

The front of the moneychanger and jeweller's shop was barred; he sat behind the bars on a red cushion, quilted with black and white flowers. Though this was South India he was a Marwari from Marwar in Rajasthan, known for businessmen and financiers. He had a small black cap on his head, steel spectacles and many ledgers.

There was nothing in his shop but a safe, a pair of scales and a table a few inches high. In India jewellery is sold by weight, jewellery made of silver threads woven into patterns and flowers. Mary, watching fascinated, saw a man buying a ring – which the Marwari took out of his safe – and paying for it. The moneylender took the money and reckoned it by weighing.

'Miss Baba like something – a nice brooch, nice ring?' asked Samuel but Mary did not want to buy, only watch.

A little black goat came by with twin kids; they butted their mother in vain because her udders were covered by a neat white bag.

'Goat milk very precious,' said Samuel.

There was a bangle shop with most of the bangles made of glass in clear goblin fruit colours of green, blue, amber and red. 'Miss Baba not buy,' Samuel cautioned. 'They break and cut very bad.'

The sari shop had the shimmering colours of heavy silk. 'They expensive,' said Samuel with feeling, remembering Lady Fisher's gift to Kuku: cotton saris like Hannah's had plain borders. Children's dresses with low waists, cut square and flat, like paper-doll dresses, hung outside in the street. The grain shops had grain set out in different colours in black wicker baskets and with them were sold great purple roots and knots of ginger, chillies and spice. There was a stall devoted to selling only drinking coconuts which could be split there and then if the customer wanted. 'Coconut milk very refresh,' said Samuel.

'I'd like to taste them,' said Mary.

'Not in the bazaar,' said Samuel.

A tassel shop had silk tassels in vivid colours of scarlet, brilliant pink or blue, orange, violent yellow, and, 'What are those for?' Mary saw small velvet and gold thread balls.

'For missies to tie on end of pigtail, very pretty.'

To Mary the temple was interesting and, Yes, clever, thought Mary, its outside walls and floors tessellated with broken pieces of china, countless pieces. The temple's gods were two big Western jointed dolls with eyes that opened and shut. They were dressed in gaudy muslin and tinsel and wreathed with paper flowers. 'Priest puts them to bed every night, morning gets them up. Hindu worship,' said Samuel with contempt but Mary saw that in front of them was a low table with offerings of sweets and flowers. A woman came to pray; on the brass tray she put a little powdered sugar and with her thumb she made on it the pattern of the sun for luck.

She looked up at Mary and smiled.

A sound like a murmur began to run through the bazaar: it grew louder and, with it, music and the ululation of a conch blown in jubilation. A lorry was coming down the road, heralded by motorcyclists, carrying between each pair of them long scarves of green, yellow and white. One held aloft on a pole a poster like a banner – the poster of 'The Three Wise Cows', as Mary had begun to call them.

She had seen them last night in the grove when Krishnan had shown a copy to her, three stylised cows, bells hung round their necks – clearly they were cherished – lying at peace among equally stylised flowers and looking out at the people with wise kind eyes. 'Is the script Telegu?' Mary had asked.

'Yes. Telegu script is decorative for posters. It goes oodle, oodle, oodle.' It certainly looked it.

'You speak Telegu?'

'I speak everything,' Krishnan had said. 'As required – Tamil, Telegu, Hindi, English, French, even a little Russian.'

'Don't boast,' Mary had said in pretended severity. Then 'Why did you choose cows?'

'Because they symbolise me,' and, as she had looked

100

puzzled, he had said like Dr Coomaraswamy, 'Symbols are crucially important in an Indian election. Every party has one. You must remember that most of the men and women in Konak cannot read so that written names and slogans mean nothing to them and, when they come to vote, how can they tell which is the candidate they want? Only if the symbol is at once identifiable. You have heard Padmina Retty had an umbrella, signifying "shelter". Well, we put an end to that. Now she has a star, which is not very wise for voters. Our third candidate, Gopal Rau, has a flower . . . so . . . "The star," they'll say, "might be Padmina . . ." yet equally the flower might be Padmina but my cows . . . There is no one,' said Krishnan, 'in towns or villages, near or far, who does not know the story of Krishna, the cowherds who adopted him, the *gopis*, so, as soon as they see my cows, three for prosperity, "Ah!" they will say, "That's Krishnan," and, notice, under the cows there is a flute.'

Now, in the bazaar, Mary heard it.

All the people began to look, pressing nearer. Shop-keepers stood up on their stalls; small boys wriggled through the crowd to the front; other urchins ran to meet the sound. The murmuring was loud now and grew to a shout as the lorry came close and paused. On a throne Krishnan was sitting – How his legs will ache tonight, thought Mary. The blue-black of his skin shone – with sweat? she wondered. Or oil? – against the *pandal*'s bright green leaves that fluttered as the lorry drove. It was the first time Mary had seen Krishnan in daylight and, with a shock, saw, even with the make-up, the Vishnu horseshoe shape in white on his forehead, eyes outlined in black, reddened lips, how beautiful he was. Not handsome or good-looking, beautiful, thought Mary.

Dr Coomaraswamy, sweating and stout, stood on the tailboard of the lorry bellowing through a microphone; when he paused, out of breath, Indian music invisibly played while behind the lorry followed jeeps and cars, one behind the other, overflowing with young men and women who immediately jumped down and came through the crowd to give out small pictures of the god Krishna. Sharma, in his flowing white, stood on the roof of the lorry's cab. A man beside Mary gave a shout, 'Ayyo.' The crowd took it up. 'Ayyo, ayyo-yo. Jai, Krishna. Jai, Krishna.'

Krishnan's eyes looked. Has he seen me? wondered Mary. She hoped he had.

Everyone was shouting now. Dr Coomaraswamy put down his microphone, he could not be heard, but Sharma's conch sounded over the noise. Still Krishnan did not move except to raise his hand, palm towards the people, fingers pointing upwards in benediction, blessing them while he smiled his extraordinary sweet smile.

The lorry passed on, Dr Coomaraswamy talking again through his microphone in a strident torrent of words. The jeeps crowded after and after them, bicycles, bullock carts, the bullocks being urged on, the driver whacking them and twisting their tails so that Mary hid her eyes. 'Miss Baba, better you come home,' Samuel said in her ear.

All that morning, 'It is too early to say,' Dr Coomaraswamy had told himself, 'always you are too optimistic,' as Uma had said over and over again 'Always you are carried away, either despair or huzzahs,' but the Doctor could not help seeing how, as the lorry approached, people stopped at once on the road; men shut their umbrellas in respect – it could be reverence; one or two prostrated themselves in the dust; women bent low as they peeped behind their saris.

'I am not huzzahing.' In his mind, Dr Coomaraswamy was telling Uma that. 'But, my darling, I begin to think . . .'

* * *

As Mary came up on the bungalow verandah on her way to wash and change for lunch, she saw Kuku coming out of Olga Manning's rooms. 'Just checking to see everything is clean,' Kuku explained, but there was an elation about her that made Mary pause. As if that showed she was curious, Kuku came closer. 'I was right,' Kuku whispered, 'she has a lover.'

'She's too old,' was Mary's instant young reaction, then remembered what Blaise had said of Olga's desperation and, 'How do you know?' she felt compelled to ask.

'Looking in her drawers, I found gentlemen's handkerchiefs,' said Kuku with relish. 'Not only that, gold cufflinks, a gentleman's gold watch.'

'She is keeping them for someone.' The whole of Mary was drawn together in repellance. 'Why were you looking in someone else's drawers? I have a good mind to tell Auntie Sanni,' she said.

At lunch time Mary found it strange to be in an almost empty dining room. Only she, Colonel McIndoe and Auntie Sanni were there. 'Come over and join us,' called Auntie Sanni.

Mary enjoyed being with them; little was said except of quiet domestic things, which brought a feeling of well-being, of goodwill – towards everyone, thought Mary. It seemed, as with Krishnan, that if Auntie Sanni disliked anyone – Mary had fathomed she had a reserve towards Blaise – she managed to see beyond the dislike. I wish I could, thought Mary, but I can't.

'The stores have come from Spencer's,' Auntie Sanni was telling the Colonel. 'Once a month,' she explained to Mary, 'stores of things one cannot get locally' – Mary was charmed by the way she said 'lo-cal-ly' with a lilt up and down – 'not in the village or Ghandara, come from a big shop in Madras. Samuel has unpacked them. Now Kuku and I must check them, make a list and put them away. Would you like to come and help?'

Mary loved it; the stores seemed to bring an intimacy with Patna Hall that gave her an odd satisfaction. Why should it make her happy to call out to Auntie Sanni, 'Twelve dozen tins of butter'? and, 'I never knew butter could be tinned.'

'Here we can only get ghee,' said Kuku in contempt. 'Butter made with buffalo milk and clarified so it is oily.' She shuddered. 'Horrid!' Twelve dozen tins, that is a gross, thought Mary. The quantities were immense: 'Two hundredweight of brown sugar, white sugar, caster sugar, icing sugar.' Kuku's voice became singsong too as she enumerated: 'Tea, coffee, chocolate. Tinned apricots, prunes.'

Strawberries came from Ootacamund, as did cheeses. Few wines. There was Golconda wine from Hyderabad, liqueurs from Sikkim.

Auntie Sanni checked. Mustafa, the head waiter, Abdul, the next, put sacks, bottles, tins away in cupboards and on shelves. 'Goodness,' said Mary, 'I never dreamed what it takes to run a hotel. Kuku, I would like your job.'

'Like my job?' Kuku was amazed. That anyone should want to work when obviously they did not have to was beyond her. She was particularly out of love with her work at the moment because she knew, when the last tin or bottle had been checked and the store room securely locked, the keys would be given to Samuel. 'I ought to have them,' she said each time; each time Auntie Sanni seemed not to hear.

When at last Mary went down to the bungalow she found that Blaise had come back from the Dawn Temple, plainly anything but exalted. He was asleep on the bed; camera and binoculars had been flung down, he had not taken off his shoes and, even in his sleep, his face was cross, over-pink with sunburn. Mary quietly changed into her swimming things, tiptoed out and was soon laughing and playing in the exhilaration of the waves, Moses and Somu each side of her. When they had finished, Mary beaten by the rollers – 'all over' she would have said – her hair dripping, Somu shyly produced a bracelet of shells threaded on a silk string. Each shell was different: brown speckled ones, pink fingernail-sized ones, almost transparent, brown ones curled into a miniscule horn and fragments of coral, apricot red. She tied the bracelet on while Moses and Thambi applauded. 'I shall keep this for ever,' said Mary, and Somu, when Thambi translated, blushed dark brown with pleasure.

She looked up and saw Blaise, awake now, watching them from the verandah. She waved, showing her arm with the bracelet. 'Look,' she called, 'a present from the sea,' but Blaise had gone into the bedroom.

'You don't want to get familiar with those chaps,' he told Mary when she followed him. 'They might misunderstand.'

'Misunderstand what?'

'I believe that part of the tourist attractions in foreign countries are the, shall we call them, "attentions of the locals"?'

'You mean fucking?'

'That's not a word I would use – and I wish you wouldn't – but yes, it's supposed to be part of the adventure, even for the elderly, or especially the elderly, women.'

'In a group like Professor Aaron's?' Mary did not believe it for a moment. 'Mrs van den Mar. Professor Webster. Dear Mrs Glover. Dr Lovat.' Mary laughed. 'I can't believe it.'

'It wouldn't surprise me,' said Blaise. 'That Miss – is it Pritt?'

'Miss Pritt is in love with India, not Indians.' You spoil

things, she wanted to say, then saw that, fortunately now, for her Blaise could not spoil anything. You don't disturb me one iota, thought Mary. These are my friends.

'. . . This is the news.' It was the middle of dinner and Auntie Sanni looked up and frowned but the voice went on. 'The Government has taken measures to bring relief to the effects of the Gamjam drought . . . Tons of grain, rice, fodder and medical supplies are being flown in . . . Troops have been sent in to reinforce police in quelling the outbreak of riots and violence in Sri Kakylam. The two boys found dead in the village of Palangaon have been identified as Pradeep and Bimal, twin sons of Birendranath Hazarika, a local landowner. Police are treating it as a case of murder.'

'In the trial of the Englishman, Colin Armstrong, charged with fraud, embezzlement and trafficking in drugs, Mr Justice Rajan has today begun his summing up and hopes to finish it tomorrow.

'In Konak, the candidate of the fancifully named Root and Flower Party, Mr Krishnan Bhanj, has been touring the state today. It is said that his strange vow of silence is arousing great interest in towns and villages; his symbol of the three wise cows is everywhere, while the people flock to see him.'

'"I am not afraid," his chief opponent, Mrs Padmina Retty says. She has a new symbol – the defeated umbrella has disappeared – it is now a star. "My star is rising, not setting," she laughed. "The people of Konak are my people. They look to me. They will not let me lose. I shall win."'

'And she well may.' Dr Coomaraswamy was Gloomaraswamy again. 'She is the mother figure, so potent in India.'

'Mother is very dangerous,' Mr Srinivasan, too, was in gloom. 'We must talk very ser-i-ous-ly to Krishnan.'

* * *

106

Professor Webster's lecture was to begin at nine o'clock.

'Dear, are you coming to join us?' kind Mrs Glover asked Mary.

'I'm afraid I can't. Auntie Sanni is going to introduce me to the cook.'

'The *cook*?' Mrs Glover's expression plainly said, 'A cook, when you could listen to Professor Webster!' while Miss Pritt said gravely, 'My dear, Professor Webster is world famous as a lecturer. It's a privilege to hear her.'

'I – I promised,' Mary stammered, and escaped. She had noticed that Auntie Sanni did not come on the verandah after dinner for coffee. 'No, it's my time then to see Alfredo, our cook. We plan the menus and orders for the next day.'

'I thought Kuku . . .'

'Kuku is not capable,' Auntie Sanni said shortly. 'She thinks she knows better.' It was the nearest thing to condemnation Mary had heard her say. Then she asked, 'But would you like to come sometime and listen?' Now Mary caught her just as she was going, like a ship in full sail, into her office.

Every evening when he had finished cooking, Alfredo from Goa left the kitchen to his underlings; he would come back later to see that it was spotless. He bathed, changed into a clean white tunic and trousers, a black waistcoat with red spots, a silver watch chain and a silver turnip watch far bigger than Dr Coomaraswamy's. In the cookhouse it was kept on a shelf in its case with a steady ticking; in all Alfredo's now ten years at Patna Hall it had never lost time. With his lists he presented himself to Auntie Sanni.

They discussed food as two connoisseurs. For luncheon Alfredo suggested fish kebabs.

'*Fish* kebabs?' Mary was surprised.

'Yes, any kind of firm fish, made into cubes, marinated with ground onion, yoghurt and spices, then threaded on

107

skewers and grilled. Very good,' said Auntie Sanni.

'Then, as some sahibs liking English food,' said Alfredo, 'young roast lamb, new potatoes and *brinjals*.'

Auntie Sanni rejected the *brinjals*. Peas would be better.

'What are *brinjals*?' asked Mary, as she continuously asked 'What are . . . ?'

'Missy taste tomorrow.' Alfredo smiled. Missy, Miss Baba, not even Miss Sahib, none of them calls me Memsahib, thought Mary, a little startled.

Dinner was to be carrot and orange soup – again, something of which she had not heard. 'It is delicious,' and Auntie Sanni laughed seeing her doubtful face. 'Refreshing and light, which it needs to be because we are having tandoori chicken.'

'Tandoori?'

'*Tandoor* means an oven, a large long earthenware pot which is buried in clay and earth – fortunately we have one. We put charcoal inside and when it is red hot the coals are raked out; the chicken, spiced and ready, is put inside and sealed and it cooks with an un-im-ag-in-able taste.' Auntie Sanni sounded almost rhapsodical. 'People try and cook it as a barbecue or on a spit. Of course, it is *not* the same! And we shall finish', she told Alfredo, 'with lemon curd tart . . . as an alternative, peppermint ice-cream.'

'I'm going to have both,' said Mary.

When the menus were settled, to Mary's surprise, Auntie Sanni opened the bag she always carried and counted out notes, notes for a hundred rupees not the usual twenties, tens, fives and ones. 'Do you give Alfredo money every night?'

'Every night,' said Auntie Sanni. 'He has to shop in the bazaar, here and in Ghandara, and must pay cash. In the morning he will give me his account. Then there will be a great argument, eh, Alfredo?' Alfredo smiled and nodded. 'He himself will have bargained and so he has to have his "tea money" — the little extra on everything where he has cheated me, but not too much,' said Auntie Sanni in pretended severity. 'He understands and I understand.'

'How nice!' said Mary.

'Would you like to see the baskets of what he will bring?'

'Oh, I would.'

'You will have to get up early.'

'I will' — again there was that happiness. Is it, Mary asked herself as she went back to the verandah, because all this is something I haven't known anything about, making other people happy and comfortable? Then that was lost as, Soon, somehow, I will see Krishnan again, thought Mary. We might — we might swim, but she could not go until Blaise was asleep and Blaise was playing bridge with the Fishers and Colonel McIndoe, their four heads bent over the green baize of the table Kuku had set up. The cards gleamed in the electric light.

'Two hearts.'

'Three no trumps.'

'Four clubs . . .'

Bridge! thought Mary, while outside the night waited, the waves sounding on the beach, the moon, bigger now, shedding light on sea, sand and on the trees in the grove. Is Krishnan waiting there? wondered Mary.

She knew, of course, he was not waiting for her — no one could be more self-contained — but, 'Krishnan, Krishnan,' all of Mary sent that call out silently over the verandah rails, to the sea, the sky and the grove until, 'What are you looking at?' Blaise asked from the table.

'I was wondering where Slippers was.'

'Mary's like Titania,' said Sir John.

'Titania?' asked Blaise, momentarily puzzled.

'Methinks I am enamoured of an ass!'

'Don't be silly, John.' Lady Fisher spoke with unwonted asperity. 'She's simply sorry for that poor donkey. I do not understand how Auntie Sanni let him get like that.'

'He belonged to the washerman.' Mary had learned that from Hannah. 'He has never been broken. When they tried to make him carry the washing, he kicked and bolted so the washerman let him go wild. By the time Auntie Sanni knew, his hoofs were like that because no one could get near enough to cut them. I shall have them cut one day,' said Mary with certainty.

Lady Fisher looked at her over the cards.

The lecture was over. Professor Aaron and the ladies came out on the verandah – 'For the cool air,' called Mrs Glover – but, seeing the bridge players, they hushed their voices as they collected around the bar for a goodnight drink and soft discussion. Professor Webster came to Auntie Sanni.

'We have finished.'

'And I'm sure successfully.'

'Yes, I'm glad to say.' Professor Webster's cheeks were flushed from her efforts; her eyes shone.

'And what was your subject?'

'After today, at Gorāghat and the Temple, it was about Usas, goddess of the Dawn, one of the Shining Ones, the old nature gods.' Mary was listening: It's these old gods, true gods, I believe in, she thought. 'Usas is the daughter of the sky,' Professor Webster went on, 'sister of night and married to Surya, the sun god. She travels in a chariot drawn by seven cows; its huge wheels are carved in stone, the cows are there too. The temple faces the east so that when the sun rises its first rays touch the cows and they turn rose red. I have slides to show this and there is a path of gold to the sea.'

'Oh!' breathed Mary. 'Oh!'

But Lady Fisher broke the enchantment. 'Dear,' she called to Mary, 'I feel a little chilly. Would you run upstairs and fetch me my wrap? It's on a chair, just a light shawl. Thank you, dear child.'

As, noiselessly, Mary came up the stairs, she saw a small black figure sidling along the corridor towards one of the rooms. It was the boy on the beach, the squirrel boy. What is he doing here? wondered Mary. Next moment the same question came ringing down the corridor. 'Kanu! Why you here?' and a stream of scolding Telegu. It was Hannah, come from turning down the guests' beds for the night. She strode down the corridor, her jewellery clinking, one hand uplifted ready to slap but the boy ducked and escaped down the stairs.

'That boy very bad, little devil. Evil!' and, 'How dared he?' cried Hannah, her nostrils snorting. 'Dare come into Patna Hall at all, then come upstairs. *Upstairs!*'

It was past midnight when Mary got to the grove.

'God, I'm tired,' Blaise had said in the bungalow bedroom.

'I'm not,' said Mary, 'but then I didn't go all that way to the temple. I think, for a little while, I'll go along the beach.' Perhaps she had sounded breathless because Blaise was suddenly alert. 'Out? At this time?'

'Just to stretch my legs.'

He accepted that, perhaps too tired to bother. 'Don't be long,' was all he said.

Slippers came as he always came but as Mary turned from the beach towards the grove, where the fire should have been leaping there was only a dull red glow.

She stepped nearer. The grove was as she had always seen it: the fire, the roof of matting between the trees, the seat with its goatskins, the brass *lota* and pans shining as if someone had cleaned them, the pitcher of water, the line of white washing, the cut sugar cane, all there the same but the grove was empty.

She stood, sick with disappointment, balked. Then there was a sound, light as the wind, and a young man appeared . . . The same young man who came with

111

a message into the dining room our first night, thought Mary. Swiftly he began to mend the fire, kicking the wood together with his bare feet until the branches flamed. He jumped when Mary came into the firelight, then stood holding a branch as if he were brandishing it.

'I think you are . . .?'

'Sharma,' he said, still on guard.

'I am Mary Browne, staying at Patna Hall. Do you speak English?'

'A little.'

'Where is . . . Mr Krishnan?'

'Krishnan Bhanj is holding *dhashan* at Ghandara.'

'*Dhashan*?'

'Many peoples coming to see him. He will be there all night.'

'All night?'

'Yes. I must hurry,' said Sharma. 'We get ready for tomorrow.' He paused. 'I think I see you in the bazaar?'

'Yes,' said Mary. 'Yes.'

He was gone. Mary waited but it did not seem as if even Birdie would come; there was no sign of Udata. Perhaps Krishnan had taken the squirrel to Ghandara and Mary had turned to go when she heard voices, light young voices. Another fire was burning beyond the trees, the voices were singing in a gentle contented chant. Followed by Slippers, Mary went to see.

It was the boys, the same boys who had tormented Udata but now were squatting on their heels in a circle, faces illumined by the firelight, black polls bent, their hands busy making garlands, and, at once, Of course, thought Mary, garlands for the lorry. They are helping Krishnan. As she stepped nearer they looked up but without animosity; their eyes, bright in their dark faces, were merry, their hands did not stop and, 'Show me,' said Mary. As if they understood, the smallest handed up a garland. It was made of mango leaves, fresh, pungent and surprisingly heavy.

'*Shabash*!' said Mary, another word she had learned. 'I'll help you,' and she knelt to sit down as they made room for her. She looked round the circle. 'Where's the big boy? Where's Shaitan, Kanu?'

'Kanu?' For a moment they stared at her, then they collapsed into laughter as if she had made a good joke. 'Kanu!' The name went from lip to lip. 'Kanu! Kanu!' they cried. 'Kanu! *Ayyo! Ayyo! Ayyo-yo.*'

Mystified, Mary picked up a garland to see how it was knotted.

'Mary,' came a voice. 'Mary.'

Quickly, still holding the garland, Mary stood up, like a nymph surprised.

'What the hell are you doing?' asked Blaise.

'Why did you come after me?' In the bungalow bedroom Mary turned on Blaise.

'Isn't it reasonable,' asked Blaise who was being extraordinarily patient, 'reasonable for a husband, if his wife goes wandering night after night—'

'Only two nights,' Mary interrupted.

'Three,' said Blaise. 'Tonight's the third.'

'Why? Can't I do what I like?'

'Making garlands with fisherboys as if you were one of them seems a strange thing to like.'

'I happen to be interested in the Root and Flower Party.'

'How can you be?' Blaise asked. 'You haven't been here long enough. Nor do you know anything about India.'

'I knew more about India in five minutes than you would if you stayed five years,' Mary wanted to fling at him. Yet, of course, what he said was true and, What do I know? she thought hopelessly.

'Anyway, I don't want you to be involved with any of this damned masquerade.'

'If it's a masquerade I'm sure it's for a good cause.'

113

'I doubt it and I don't want you to be involved.'

'I would give anything to be involved,' she told him flatly, but had to add, 'I don't see how I can be.' Had Krishnan not said, 'This is the last time I can speak with you.'

In Ghandara after the *dhashan*, 'We must find ourselves a mother figure,' Dr Coomaraswamy told Krishnan.

'Copycat' wrote Krishnan on his pad. For a moment he sat, wrapped in thought, then wrote, 'Not a mother. Allure.'

'*Allure?*'

'Yes. Goddesses. Two goddesses, Lakshmi for good fortune, Radha for love; both young, beautiful.'

'Who?'

'Kuku,' wrote Krishnan. 'Kuku in the most brilliant most vulgar of her saris so that she looks like the *bania*'s glossy catalogue pictures of Lakshmi. Lots of jewellery, you'll have to hire. Auntie Sanni will give her leave, I'm sure. Yes, Kuku for Lakshmi.'

'And Radha?'

Krishnan smiled. 'Little Radha?' and he wrote, 'Mrs Blaise Browne.'

'But she is English! It would not be popular at all if Radha was a Western goddess.'

'Dress her up,' wrote Krishnan.

'We could, and hide her hair. She is sunburned.' Mr Srinivasan liked the idea. 'She could pass for fair wheaten complexion which a goddess should have.'

'But it's impossible,' Dr Coomaraswamy almost spluttered. 'Can't you imagine? Sir John and Lady Fisher, they would never approve. Sir Professor Aaron, the ladies, Hannah, Samuel, and that young man, Mr Blaise!' Dr Coomaraswamy did not like Blaise. 'He's her *husband*. He would never consent.'

But Krishnan wrote, 'Don't ask him. Ask her.'

Wednesday

'Dr Coomaraswamy Sahib coming,' said Thambi.

Thambi, who was alert to everything that happened in Konak to its very borders, was Krishnan's loyal supporter and knew exactly why Dr Coomaraswamy was coming. Blaise and Mary had come out early for a morning swim; Blaise had already gone in, Moses after him. 'Can't I once, even once, swim without these water rats?' Blaise had exploded.

'Sea can change any minute,' Thambi had answered as always, 'Moses knows this sea,' and, 'Wait, Miss Baba,' he said as Dr Coomaraswamy came puffing down the sandy path – Even walking downhill, he gets out of breath, thought Mary. It was not that; Dr Coomaraswamy was agitated.

'Mrs Browne, forgive me for intruding at this early hour. I hope I have not disturbed you.'

'Of course not. I was just going to swim.'

'No. No. Not now. Please not now, Mrs Browne. I have an ex-tra-or-din-ary favour to ask you. Please do not take offence.'

He mopped his forehead. Does he always have to mop? thought Mary as, 'What favour?' she asked.

'One that I myself would never have asked, but Krishnan—'

'Krishnan?' Now Mary was surprised.

'As, at present, Krishnan Bhanj himself will not go into society, you do not know him . . .' Mary did not contradict the Doctor, 'but in India's mysterious way he knows of you . . .'

'The ways of India are even more mysterious than you think,' Mary would have told him, but again did not say it. Instead, 'What does Mr Bhanj want?'

Dr Coomaraswamy cleared his throat – if Mary had not been there he would have spat the phlegm out on the sand. 'It has happened that Mrs Padmina Retty, candidate for the People's Shelter Party, Krishnan's opponent, has come out as the Mother Figure for the state, that is the Mother Goddess. Padmina is a very clever woman, Mrs Browne. Also, in all religions, the "mother" is, I think, potent but in India you do not know how potent.'

'You mean, like the Virgin Mary?'

'Indian goddesses are not virgin, Mrs Browne, not at all and, so, more potent. We shall have to combat. We, the Root and Flower Party, need for Krishnan a feminine counterpart. Not a mother, that would be copycat.' Dr Coomaraswamy quoted Krishnan with as much satisfaction as if he had thought of this himself. 'We must be different, also challenging. So we shall import goddesses. Mrs Browne, will you come with us on our lorry to be the goddess Radha? *Please*. We so need this allure.'

'I'm not alluring.'

'Indeed you are, but it is the female element that is more important, gentle, supportive, as are the Hindu goddesses.'

'I thought they were fierce.'

'Some, not others. Supportive, also beautiful.'

'I am not beautiful, Dr Coomaraswamy.'

He did not think so either but, 'As Radha you will be. We shall dress you. All the clothes I have ready.'

'What would I have to do?'

'Nothing but sit and smile most graciously. Hold your hand so, Krishnan will show you. You will have a small throne on the lorry. With bamboo and leaves we shall shade you. Please.'

Mary did not waver any more. Go with Krishnan, she thought. Be near him all day. See the villages and little towns and, 'What can I say but "Yes".' She smiled happily on Dr Coomaraswamy. 'Goddesses don't wear spectacles though. Give me a minute to put in my contact lenses and I'll come.'

When she came back Blaise was far out to sea and, 'Tell Sahib I have gone out for the day. I'll see him this evening,' Mary told Thambi.

'Not for all the tea in China,' said Kuku.

'I am not talking about tea, I am talking about cash.'

'How much?' asked Kuku.

'She'll not consent,' Dr Coomaraswamy had told Krishnan.

'She will if you offer enough. Try three hundred rupees.'

'*Three hundred?*'

'Kukus are expensive and we don't want to fail.'

'We shall give you a hundred rupees. *One hundred,*' the Doctor told her now.

Kuku gave a snort. 'How much do Krishnan's girls at Ghandara get?'

'Our young women do it for love.'

'I'm sure they do. Krishnan's *gopis!*'

'Miss Kuku, you may not sneer at our candidate. Three hundred.'

Kuku settled for five – And I, myself, shall extort every *anna* of that, Dr Coomaraswamy had peculiar pleasure in promising himself this. Yet, 'If you had known,' he told Kuku silently, 'I would have given you a thousand rupees, two thousand. For you, I am weakness itself.' Instead, he was able to say, 'You will stand throughout.'

'I shall faint.'

'That will be ten rupees off. You will wear green with

117

yellow and white or yellow with green and white – Party colours.'

'I will wear yellow and green, India's colours.'

'You will wear what I say,' said Dr Coomaraswamy, 'and you will not ogle Krishnan Bhanj.'

'Ogle? What is ogle?'

'You know very well,' and Kuku laughed.

She did not laugh when the lorry came and she saw Radha.

'Who is that?'

'Don't you know?' Dr Coomaraswamy was delighted but Kuku had seen the grey eyes.

'Mrs *Browne*!' she cried.

'Kindly, Mrs Browne has consented to be the Radha goddess, your companion,' said Dr Coomaraswamy.

'For kindness, not for cash,' Mr Srinivasan put in.

Kuku said at once, 'She is far better dressed than I am.' It was Shyama who had dressed Mary in the gatehouse. The sari was green gauze patterned with gold thread stars, the *choli* gold tissue – Mary was titillated to feel her midriff bare; fortunately, from wearing her bikini, it was sunburnt too. Her hair was hidden by a black silk cap gathered at the back into flowers, a pigtail hanging ended by one of the little velvet and gold thread balls she had seen in the bazaar. Below the cap her forehead had been painted white which made her skin look darker, the white edged with red dots; her arms were painted with patterns too, the soles of her feet and the palms of her hands red. There were strings of white flowers, a gold necklace and bangles. Shyama had outlined Mary's eyes with kohl, painted the lids blue and reddened her lips vividly red. 'She says you must take this make-up with you, to freshen in the heat,' Dr Coomaraswamy had said, and, 'She says to tell you now you are most beautiful.'

Then, by the lorry, 'Far better dressed than I am. I'm not coming,' cried Kuku.

Sharma picked her up and put her in the lorry. 'You have come,' he said.

'Thambi, that was a bad thing to do.' Auntie Sanni had sent for Thambi immediately when, as was inevitable, she heard about the dressing up in the gatehouse. She spoke in English to be more severe. 'Very bad.'

'Bad?' Thambi was astonished. 'It was for the Party.'

'I suppose that was what Krishnan felt,' Auntie Sanni said when she told the Fishers. 'Better you hear this from me than from Samuel or Hannah.'

'All the same, I am surprised at Krishnan,' said Sir John.

'I think Krishnan', said Lady Fisher, 'is not averse to a little play. Think how mischievous the god Krishna was.'

'But Mary must have known this was *not* right,' Sir John was fulminating. 'All those years with Rory . . .'

'She did not know,' said Auntie Sanni, 'because she did not give herself time to think. Nor would I – or you – have done at eighteen.'

The decorated lorry made its way from small town to small town, village to village, a slow way because it was stopped again and again by the crowds. Soon each stop seemed joined to the other by the people along the roads as Sharma blew his conch, drums beat from the jeeps and cars behind with the shrill whine of Indian music and Dr Coomaraswamy bellowing from the microphone. Every time they stopped, a throng pressed forward.

'Where do they all come from?' asked Dr Coomaraswamy.

'I think from everywhere.' Mr Srinivasan was almost cheerful.

It was a reverent crowd. Again men shut the umbrellas that had shielded them from the sun and made *namaskar*; women, usually shy, hiding themselves behind their sari ends, now threw flowers, garlands, jostled forward to touch. 'You *must not shrink*,' Dr Coomaraswamy said angrily to Kuku. 'Stand up or else . . .'

He glanced at Mary who sat so still he thought she was asleep – but no; she bent a little to the crowd, let the women touch her, received the homage, dutifully kept the other hand in blessing. He saw her, now and again, look at Krishnan and Krishnan looked back with that irradiating smile but once Dr Coomaraswamy saw what he could hardly believe: Krishnan gave young Mrs Browne a . . . wink? wondered Dr Coomaraswamy. Could it have been a wink? There was no time to think further. He had to go back to his microphone. 'People of the State of Konak, men and women, friends . . .'

'*Jai* – Krishnan. *Jai* – Krishnan,' and as the crowd swelled the cry grew into a roar.

'Stand up,' he commanded Kuku.

'I want to blow my nose.'

'That will be five rupees off.'

'Out for the day!' On the beach Blaise had been incredulous.

'She say,' Thambi could not help enjoying this – he had heard 'water rats' – 'she say she see you this evening,' and he volunteered, 'She quite safe. Sahib.'

'But where has she gone?'

And Thambi had pleasure in saying, 'On Krishnan Bhanj's lorry.'

'That young Blaise!' Sir John had said in wrath. 'Not a word or, I can guess, a thought as to what is going on between him and Mary, only what people might think.'

Blaise had come up to breakfast but had contained himself until the Fishers had finished. He followed them on to the verandah. 'Gone on this fool lorry. Not a word to me only a message from that far too cocky fellow Thambi,' and, 'Suppose it gets into the papers?' Blaise said in agony.

'Well, it's bound to be on the news. They seem to be following this election step by step. The papers will, of course, copy.'

'I meant the British papers.'

'My dear boy, to the average Britisher, if they know where it is at all, Konak is a little patch, perhaps the size of a postage stamp on the map of India and about as interesting.'

'Not if there's something unusual. This chap Ajax seems to be able to make anything unusual.'

'It is unusual, one can't gainsay that.'

'She is dressed up. They may not know it is Mary.'

'In this blasted country everyone knows everything. 'No.' Blaise set his teeth. 'This time Mary has gone over the edge.'

'Many people are bewitched on their first encounter with India.' Lady Fisher tried to be soothing. 'Bewitched or repelled.'

'I'd far rather she was repelled.'

'Still, if you're wise you'll take no notice.'

'Notice!' Blaise had exploded again. 'She's my *wife*.'

'Blaise have you thought', said Lady Fisher, 'that the effect of this could be the reverse of scandal? If Krishnan Bhanj wins— '

'He can't win, surely?'

'Suppose he does, wouldn't it be a commendation – what Dr Coomaraswamy would call a feather – for a rising young diplomat to have a wife with such understanding of Indian affairs, so percipient that she personally backed this election and went campaigning?'

Blaise looked at her dumbfounded, shook his head bewildered and left.

Mr Menzies was again going through the newspapers and Sir John deliberately voiced what he had said to Lady Fisher. 'I'm surprised that a journalist of your reputation should take such an interest in what, after all, is not a big or important election.'

Mr Menzies looked up. 'To me all elections are important.' There was a distinct swagger. 'Not because of the politics. They're not really my game.'

'Game?' asked Sir John. 'In India they are vitally serious.'

'Exactly. That is why, in my case, it's not the politics, it's the politicians at election times. They are so beautifully vulnerable.' Mr Menzies chortled.

'For your filthy column?' Sir John managed to keep his voice pleasant.

'Exactly,' Mr Menzies said with delight.

'So? I don't think you'll find much in the way of titillation in Padmina Retty, or poor old Gopal Rau – or Krishnan Bhanj.'

Sir John added Krishnan deliberately and kept his voice mild.

'We'll see,' said Mr Menzies, highly pleased. 'We'll see.'

'John,' Auntie Sanni called from her swing couch where she had come to sit quietly before going on with the day's round – 'I like to take this time to consider my guests', she had told Mary, 'and their needs.' This morning the needs were troubling her and, 'John, have you time to come and talk a little?'

'All the time in the world.'

'For the first week in years,' said Auntie Sanni, 'I'm troubled, very troubled, about my guests – some of them.'

122

'Such as?'

'Obviously, Olga Manning.'

'With reason,' said Sir John.

'Someone must help her,' and Auntie Sanni looked at him, the sea-green blue eyes as trustful as a trusting child's. 'You will, John.' It was not a question; it was a fact.

'If I can. I'll try and talk to her when she comes back from Calcutta – if she comes back.'

'She owes me money, so she will.' Auntie Sanni said it with certainty. 'Then there's Kuku.'

'She is meant to be a help not a worry.'

Auntie Sanni smiled. 'I know – and she *is* a help, she works hard but . . .'

'But?'

'When she left St Perpetua's she was sweet. Now she's so knowing. We haven't done her any good, and I foresee pain. She hasn't a chance, and I can't give her one, not of the kind she would thank me for.'

'I hope you're wrong. Who besides? Mary?'

'No. Mary can look after herself.'

'Which is why you like her!'

'She is likeable,' was as far as Auntie Sanni would go. 'No, John, it's the young man, Mr Browne.' Sir John noticed he was still Mr Browne. 'Oh, John, why can't we all be born with wit?' She looked far across the sea, sparkling in the morning, an increasing frown on her face. 'John, I'm afraid. Mary doesn't know, doesn't dream . . . This isn't England or even Europe. It's such a violent place.'

Sir John got up, went to the railing and looked down at the out-bungalow, whistling as he pondered. Suddenly he broke off. 'That young fool!'

Two men in bathing shorts were strolling along the beach. 'He's talking to Menzies,' said Sir John.

'No! Oh, no,' said Auntie Sanni.

* * *

It was the coconut water that woke Mary out of her trance.

'Where have I been?'

'Only four hours on that damned lorry.' Kuku had collapsed on the sand.

To Mary it had seemed like five minutes. Now the lorry and its following jeeps and cars had pulled off the dust road into a small oasis of trees in the midst of what had seemed to be a desert wasteland without villages. There were no people, only birds: cranes, wading in a stagnant pool, small wild brown birds she recognised as partridges wandering in coteries, mynahs and, of course, crows. Mats were being spread. 'You must rest and eat,' Dr Coomaraswamy told Mary. 'Drink a little, not too much,' and Sharma had sent a boy shinning up a coconut palm – there seemed to be innumerable small boys. Some had ridden on the car roofs or hung on to their backs. Mary tried not to think of the abominable Kanu.

The boy up the palm tree threw the nuts down to the ground where Sharma took the tops off them with a *panga*, splitting each so skilfully that none of the water was lost. 'Drink. You must drink,' Dr Coomaraswamy told Mary again as she sat; she still seemed dazed.

'It has been too much for her,' said Mr Srinivasan but Krishnan took the nut and held it to her lips. Even here he could not speak. 'In India even the trees have ears,' Dr Coomaraswamy would have told her but Krishnan's eyes commanded her; she felt the rough wood of the nut edge, the coolness of the water, as, obediently, she drank.

It was Krishnan, too, who had lifted her down from the lorry; Kuku had had to jump only helped by Sharma's hand. Now she stood up to wring out her sari. 'My God! The sweat. You'll have to get me fresh clothes.'

124

'They will dry in the sun,' Sharma soothed her.

Mary, oddly enough, was untouched, her sari still fresh, and, never, thought Dr Coomaraswamy, had he seen anything as shining as her grey eyes. He was unused to light eyes; his ideal was for brown eyes, lustrous, deeply lashed — Not like Uma's he thought with a pang of guilt, though Uma, when she was young, had been handsome. Kuku's eyes were black, small and, he had to admit, malicious. Then why am I so much seduced? He did not know but now, 'This blue-grey,' he murmured to Mr Srinivasan, 'we do not have this colour of eyes in India, sometimes violet or green but not this.' Mary Browne's eyes today were like diamonds, he thought, brilliant in a way that alarmed him. Has she fever? and, 'Eat a little,' he urged her. 'See we will bring food to you. Then, on this mat, you must stretch out and sleep!'

Krishnan himself had had to be helped off the lorry; now two of the young men were pummelling him and rubbing his legs. 'He has been im-mo-bile all those hours.' Mr Srinivasan hopped like an agitated bird. 'How can he keep it up?'

Krishnan did say one word. '*Chūp.*' Then, while Mary watched, he clasped his hands behind his neck, using his elbows to support him until he stood on the crown of his head, his feet high in the air, his powerful body erect as a pillar, 'So that the blood can run the other way,' Dr Coomaraswamy explained to Mary, 'which is good for the body — and the brain.'

'I could not have done those hours on the lorry without yoga,' Krishnan told Mary afterwards as he stretched, bent, leapt, ran.

Food was brought on banana leaves for Kuku and Mary to eat in the Indian way with their fingers and apart from the men, 'Usually *after* the men,' Kuku said with acerbity, 'with their left-overs,' but Mary found it restful – no fuss with talk or plates, knives, forks, spoons. The food was hot and good; it had travelled in aluminium pans that fitted together into a carrier, the bottom pan filled with live coals. There were rice, curry, spicy little *koftas* of prawns, *puris*, vegetables but Mary only nibbled. 'I don't want to be disturbed,' she could have said. Soon she lay down and was asleep.

Dr Coomaraswamy had to wake her. It was the first time he had seen an Englishwoman asleep. He looked at the shadow her eyelashes made on her cheeks; the skin below them was . . . like petals, he thought – why did Mary Browne continually make him think of flowers? It's because she's so young, he thought – and pure. He hesitated to touch her.

Kuku laughed as she watched. 'Go on, wake her with a kiss.'

Dr Coomaraswamy was shocked. To him Mary, like Krishnan, was in a different category – she was Blaise Browne's wife but Dr Coomaraswamy felt she belonged to Krishnan, he did not know how or why but he had seen Krishnan not only look at her and give her the especially tender smile he gave to most women and children – 'and to a little goat or a squirrel,' the Doctor had to say – but he, Dr Coomaraswamy, had seen that wink. The wink immediately put her on a level he could not reach.

'Go on, kiss her. You like young women.'

'Kuku, you are most lewd. I shall fine you fifty rupees.'

'We misjudged Menzies,' Blaise told the Fishers at lunch time. 'Thought he was just a journalist who likes to make a mystery. Actually, he's a sympathetic type.'.

'Type's the right word for him.' Sir John almost said it but stopped himself, only saying, 'I hope you didn't talk to him about Mary.'

'Of course not.' Blaise, Sir John was sure, lived by a code which laid down that one did not talk about one's wife to other men. 'Of course not, at least I hope not,' and Blaise defended himself. 'If I did a little, what's the harm? He's on holiday. Apparently he has a hell of a life in Delhi and in London. It seems that to write a newspaper gossip column means continual parties and pressures from people wanting to get into the news. He's here for quiet. He's taking me to Ghandara this afternoon so we can get a decent round of golf but the course wouldn't be grass, would it?'

'Sand,' said Sir John. 'For grass you would probably have to go to Madras. . . . Pity you couldn't – out of the way,' he wanted to add.

'Why should Mary Browne?' Kuku was asking. 'Why should she sit when I have to stand?'

'I'll stand,' said Mary. 'Let Kuku sit.'

'That is not the plan.'

'She has stood for four hours.'

'So she should at that price.'

'Price?' Mary was puzzled.

'Do you think I would do this for nothing? Or do you call it love?' sneered Kuku.

'I don't call it anything. I just want to do it.'

'For love?' Kuku insisted.

Dr Coomaraswamy intervened. 'It will not be long now,' he soothed. 'As we get towards evening it will be cooler, it will not seem so long.'

'I like it long,' said Mary.

'This seems a roundabout way to get to Ghandara,' Blaise said in the car.

'So it is. I'm sorry. I must have taken the wrong turning. Hallo!' said Mr Menzies. 'Here they are!'

'You promised.' Blaise was furious.

'I'm sorry but how was I to know where they would be?'

Mr Menzies had to stop, the crowds round the lorry were so thick. He opened the sun-roof and stood on the seat. *'Golly!'* he said. Reluctantly, Blaise stood up beside him.

Surrounded by the surging mass of people the lorry looked small, the figures on it even smaller, but Blaise recognised Kuku, then looked from her to the smaller throne and, 'Is that Mary?' he asked dazed.

'Cleverly disguised at any rate,' Mr Menzies comforted him. 'But yes, it undoubtedly is.'

Kuku, Lakshmi, in her green and white patterned gold-edged sari, gold bodice, seemed to melt into the lorry's decorations as did Krishnan, though his blue-blackness could be seen, while Mary, Radha, shone in all the wheaten fairness Mr Srinivasan had hoped.

'Couldn't be more conspicuous,' Blaise agonised. 'And she must be recognised as she's the only Western person there.'

'She wouldn't have been the only one if you had gone with her,' Mr Menzies pointed out.

Blaise stared at him. 'I? With that rabble?'

Mr Menzies gave a soft whistle. 'So you *are* at odds!' He sounded amused. 'I thought you were.'

'Why?' Blaise was cold, trying to fend him off.

'From what I have seen. No one can say I am not interested in my fellow men – and women,' said Mr Menzies sweetly. 'Your wife is so transparently young.'

'You make me sound like a child-stealer. It was she who wanted us to be married.'

'And now she doesn't.'

'Who said so? Good God! We haven't been married a month.'

'That *is* quick.' Unerringly, the insidious drops of poison fell. 'But India does go to people's heads and Mr

Krishnan Bhanj knows very well how to make himself – shall we say – attractive?'

'Don't!' Blaise cried out before he could stop himself, then tried to recover. 'I don't think I feel like playing golf. Would you be kind enough to drive me back to the hotel?'

Kuku had seen Blaise at once and began to redrape her sari more gracefully, then waved the peacock fan Sharma had given her to help against the heat.

Dr Coomaraswamy, for a moment released from his megaphone – the microphone had failed – followed her eyes. 'Menzies, young Browne! You will not plume,' he said furiously to Kuku. 'You are here for the crowd. Also put that fan down or you will get nothing at all.'

'It is I who have bought you for today,' he wanted to cry, 'so no tricks.' The plain fact that Kuku liked Blaise inflamed his own longing. The bodice she wore showed the cleavage between her breasts; her sweat had stained the silk under her arms and, where the bodice ended, her midriff glistened with it; he could imagine the glistening between her thighs and delight carried him away. Besides, it was sweet to torment her. What fun, thought Dr Coomaraswamy, if I could whip Kuku. If I could have – is it a *sjambok*? – that long whip that hisses in the air as its lash comes down. He saw himself wielding it, then had to say, as Uma would have, 'And how silly you would look,' and 'Stand up, girl,' he shouted. 'Smile!' It was no use saying, 'I'll fine you,' he knew he never would.

Mary had not seen Blaise, she was too interested; in contrast to the morning when she had been entranced, everything now was vivid. As the lorry drove and stopped – stopped every few minutes, it seemed to her – she had never imagined such crowds or smelled them, the peculiar smell of an Indian crowd: not dirt, Indians are personally clean,

but of sweat, the *coconut* oil men and women used on their
bodies and hair and an intrinsic spicy yet musty smell of
clothes washed too often and seldom properly dried; of the
spat phlegm, cess and dust everywhere trodden in and, over
it in the lorry, the strong heady scent of crushed flowers
and the withering leaves of garlands.

Dark hands reached out to touch her, voices and eyes
pleaded; babies, their eyes rimmed with kohl, were held
up to see and for her to see and bless. The voices chanted:
'Jai Krishnan.'

'Jai Krishnan.'

'Jai Shri Krishnan.'

'Jai Krishnan Hari.'

Dr Coomaraswamy's voice boomed on through the
megaphone with words Mary could not understand. Mr
Srinivasan took his place but his voice was reedy after
the Doctor's rounded mellifluent tones, 'Which could
coax a bee off a flower,' Krishnan used to joke but,
as if the bee had stung, It can't coax Kuku, thought
Dr Coomaraswamy.

As soon as the megaphone paused, music and songs
from the jeeps and cars took over,

> 'O Krishnakumar, the one who steals butter,
> The one with red eyes,
> The one who brings bliss,
> O Krishna . . .'

sung with drums, cymbals and the sound of the conch,
though now, Mary noticed, it was not Sharma who blew
it but a disciple called Ravi.

Over it all was Krishnan enthroned, not moving only
smiling, holding up that benevolent hand. I don't care what
anyone says, thought Mary, there *is* something mystical
about this. Perhaps it comes from the people, their faith,
yet it is through Krishnan.

130

One outside moment did break through: towards late afternoon she became conscious that a red car, its sun-roof open, had drawn alongside the lorry with – on its back seat – a photographer, his camera pointing through the window, first directly at her, next at Krishnan; then, as the car drew a little away, it took in both of them. The driver was Mr Menzies and standing on the passenger seat beside him was Kanu, his eyeballs, as they rolled in excitement, showing white in his dark face as, with one hand in easy familiarity, he steadied himself on Mr Menzies' shoulder. A moment Mary had put out of her mind came back, giving a feeling of dismay: that early morning, when she came through Patna Hall on the way to the gatehouse and had run up to the top verandah to look down on the beach to see if Blaise was still swimming, there, along the corridor, was Kanu again, sitting cross-legged on the floor outside a door. This time he was dressed in clean white shorts, a yellow shirt – silk, Mary had thought – a red flower jauntily behind his ear. As he gave her a salaam without getting up, which she knew was impertinent, she had seen on his wrist a new watch. The door was Mr Menzies'.

Why should I have minded that? wondered Mary – and why should she, who hated tell-tales, have said to Samuel, who had come – solicitous as always – to see the lorry off, 'Samuel, that boy Kanu is upstairs again.'

'Kanu?' and, '*Ayyo,*' Samuel said with distaste. 'Miss Baba, I will see to it.'

Now as she saw the new watch gleam on the thin dark wrist, Mary did not like it. She did not like the camera either.

'Mrs Browne,' Dr Coomaraswamy whispered to prompt her. With a start of guilt, Mary went back to Krishnan's afternoon.

Offerings were laid at her feet as well as his, flowers thrown in her lap: marigolds, flaunting scarlet cotton-tree

131

flowers, white mogra buds. Coins were thrown too – they hurt like little flints: *annas*, *pice*, even cowries – those little shells, used as the smallest possible coins; sometimes whole rupees were recklessly thrown from hard-earned savings. Kuku grew angry. '*Ari!* They hurt!' But Mary was touched almost to tears. 'Scoop them up and give them back,' she wanted to say but knew she must only smile and accept.

'How was it?' Sir John asked when at last the lorry drove into Patna Hall to drop off Mary, Kuku and the disciples before taking Krishnan, Dr Coomaraswamy, Mr Srinivasan and the young women back to Ghandara for Krishnan to rest before the evening *dhashan* he would hold that night. Sir John came to meet them, jumping Mary down among the admiring disciples.

'How was it?'

'Exaltation!' said Mary.

'Mary,' Sir John was grave, 'I want to speak to you and so does Alicia.'

'You're angry! You mustn't be. Oh, Sir John, not tonight. Don't be angry tonight when everything's so wonderful.'

'What could I do?' he asked Lady Fisher.

'You must be tired.' Lady Fisher had come into the hall.

'I'm not in the least bit tired,' and suddenly Mary clasped her in a tight hug, gave her a resounding kiss, kissed Sir John then whirled through the hall on to the verandah where she hugged Auntie Sanni, dared to kiss Colonel McIndoe and a few of Professor Aaron's ladies, Mrs van den Mar, Professor Webster, Miss Pritt and Dr Lovat who had come back from a second expedition to the Dawn Temple. She left them slightly startled, met Hannah and threw her arms round her, darted into the dining room to shake Samuel's hands and the waiters', even the stately

Ganga's. 'Where's Bumble?' she called. 'Oh, I expect down at the bungalow. I'll call him. It would be nice to play a silly game. Come on,' she called to the disciples. 'Come down to the beach. Give me ten minutes to get out of these beautiful clothes in the gatehouse and we'll show you how to play rounders. Come!'

Released, too, for the moment, the disciples came with whoops of joy. Soon the beach was full of running white figures with Mary's blue shorts and shirt flashing among them.

'She's over-excited,' said Auntie Sanni, watching from the verandah, where Lady Fisher had come out to join her.

'Violently over-excited,' said Lady Fisher. 'Oh dear!'

'It looks rather fun,' said Dr Lovat. 'Let's go down and join in.'

'I'm not talking to you,' Blaise had said.

'I don't want you to talk. We want you to play.' Changed back into her morning clothes, her face and arms clean where Shyama had reluctantly washed off the kohl, henna and colours – 'She say you much more pretty with,' Thambi had told Mary – she had run into the bungalow bedroom to fetch Blaise.

'Play?'

'Yes, with me and the young men, Dr Coomaraswamy's young men, and I guess some of the ladies.'

'And, I suppose, Krishnan Bhanj.' It was meant to be withering – Mr Menzies' insinuations had rankled – but Mary's, 'Oh, Krishnan has gone back to Ghandara,' was so careless that Blaise felt slightly reassured.

'Play what?'

'Rounders.' Mary had cast off her shoes.

'That's a kid's game.'

'All the better.' Already she was outside and showing

the disciples how to mark out the round – 'With my golf clubs!' Blaise, who had followed her, was outraged.

'It won't hurt them. They make good posts.'

'You haven't a bat.'

'This'll do.' She had picked up a flat-faced piece of driftwood. 'Anil. Ravi,' she called to two of the disciples whose names she knew, 'Blaise and I will go first to show you.'

Blaise came portentously forward. 'I'll tell you the rules—'

'We don't need rules,' Mary interrupted. 'We've chosen our sides. They'll pick it up as we go. You'll see. Come on. You bowl, I'll bat. See,' she called to the young men and ladies – five of the cultural ladies had come – 'you have to catch the ball to get me out or catch it and throw it to hit me when I'm between posts and I'll be out. Are you ready? Blaise, throw!'

'You're not playing properly.'

'Don't be such a pomp. Throw!'

They were, Blaise had to admit, quick – he had not yet met India's barefoot quicksilver hockey players – and now two more ladies came. 'Can we join, Mr Browne?'

Mollified by their presence, 'Of course,' said Blaise. 'Join the team. I'll be umpire,' and he threw the ball to Anil.

'We don't need an umpire,' called Mary.

Nor did they. 'Out!' shouted Blaise when Ravi fell headlong by a golf club post a moment before he was caught.

'I'm not out, my head is in,' cried Ravi.

'Out.'

'In,' they chorused, laughing.

'Of course, if you're going to cheat . . .'

You do not, Mary sensed, even in her daredevil mood, accuse Indians of cheating: it is like holding explosives to flame and hastily she intervened. 'Of course we're going to cheat. All of us will cheat. It's part of the fun. I'll cheat. You'll cheat.'

'I don't call that fun and I don't cheat.' Blaise stalked off into the bungalow.

Mrs Glover went after him. 'Mr Browne, do play. You make us feel badly.'

'In England we play games properly. We keep the rules.'

'Well, I don't know about properly and rules but this is real fun and what we needed. We've all been at a high pitch of emotion all day.' Reluctantly Blaise came out but only stood watching.

'Letters for you, Doctor.'

'Not now. Not now.' Dr Coomaraswamy said it irritably. 'Not when I have a thousand, thousand worries.' Then he saw that it was Kuku.

There was no one else on the verandah; except for Auntie Sanni and Colonel McIndoe who had gone to the knoll, everyone else was in their room or on the beach. 'It looks a nice romp,' said Dr Coomaraswamy.

'I do not romp,' said Kuku. 'Besides I have work to do.'

'Unfortunately I, too . . .' Dr Coomaraswamy passed his hand over his eyes as if to shut out doings with which he could no longer cope. Then, 'Kuku, where are you going?'

'To bath and change.'

'I myself must bath and change.'

'But first,' said Kuku, 'I should like my five hundred rupees,' and seeing his face grow immediately stern, came closer with what she knew was a winning smile – the smile he had asked for all day – as she murmured, 'You are not going to fine me, are you?'

She had never been as close; he could smell, not her scent, that had faded in the sun, but, far more tantalising again, her warmth, her girl sweat. Her hair dishevelled, almost brushed his temples – she was taller than he. All thought of Uma faded from Dr Coomaraswamy's mind. 'Kuku, first come to my room.'

'Your room?' Kuku laughed. 'Don't be a silly old man.'

'You are so beautiful. I'll give—' he swallowed, 'I'll give you another five hundred rupees.'

For a moment a glint came into Kuku's eyes; he thought it a promising glint that made him quiver but she looked down to the beach where, among the dark figures, a blond head stood out as the last rays of the sun going down over the sea, touched the blond to gold.

'Not for ten thousand rupees,' said Kuku, her whole face softened, illumined and, when she spoke next, her voice was soft. 'You see, Dr Coomaraswamy, I too am in love.'

It was beginning to be dusk on the beach; they could no longer see the ball; the play, the running ebbed. At the same time the flames of braziers showed on the roof of Patna Hall while lanterns shone along the parapet. Some time before Anil and Ravi had slipped away; now they came back washed and changed. They stood together and Ravi cried, 'You are invited to Paradise. Auntie Sanni has agreed. Tonight is the end of our campaign so the Root and Flower Party invite you to a barbecue, Indian fashion – on the roof. Please, everyone, yes everyone, come. Sir John. Lady Fisher. Professor Aaron. Mrs van den Mar. Professor Webster. Ladies. Mr and Mrs Browne – par-tic-u-lar-ly Mrs Browne – please to accept.'

'What could be better?' It was Mrs van den Mar's voice.

'Well, I must say,' said Mrs Glover, 'that was the best time I've had in months. Who would have thought my old legs could run as fast!'

'Who would have thought', Miss Pritt was aglow, 'that an archaeological tour could have ended in a children's ball game then being invited to a party by those delightful young men?'

'Charmers all of them,' said Dr Lovat.

'Julia! Beware.'

'They're far too busy,' Dr Lovat said calmly, 'and too committed. Later tonight we, too, shall be truly serious.'

'Yes.' Professor Webster spoke to Mrs van den Mar as they walked up to Patna Hall. 'We mustn't be late for the *dhashan*.'

'We shan't. They'll all be needed for it, the young men,' said Mrs van den Mar.

'But which *dhashan*?' Professor Aaron had come to meet them. 'I've just been listening to the radio news and it seems there will be two, so where do we go?'

'To Krishnan Bhanj's *dhashan*.'

'Both are Krishnan's.'

'That can't be. He can't be in two places at once,' Dr Lovat objected.

'It appears he can.'

It had been in that noon break in the oasis that the news had come to Dr Coomaraswamy. One of the disciples had taken the opportunity of listening to the mid-day radio and had run to get the Doctor to come to his jeep in time for the repeat of the news in English. First the headlines, 'Padmina Retty outwits – and out-distances – Krishnan Bhanj . . .' Then, 'On this, the final day of the campaign, dismayed perhaps by Krishnan Bhanj's, shall we say, "divine progress" through Konak's towns and villages, Mrs Retty has gone into space. She has hired an aeroplane and so today, this final day, she has covered far more of Konak than he. "His poor little lorry is slow," says Padmina. "Ignorant puppy, the very crowds impede

137

it! I shall be swift, able to appear in outlying places he cannot hope to reach . . ." '

'Damn Padmina Retty to hell!' swore Dr Coomaraswamy. He rushed to alert Krishnan who was peacefully eating. 'She will go by air. Do we now have to hire a plane?'

'Copycat,' wrote Krishnan again. 'Aeroplane will utterly destroy image so carefully built up,' he wrote and continued eating, crunching the still crisp *dosas* between his white teeth.

'Then what to do?'

Krishnan licked his fingers and wrote, 'Duplicate.'

'Duplicate?'

'Yes, immediately.'

As one who was now part of the campaign, though only like Vishnu's squirrel helping to build the great bridge by bringing pebbles, Dr Coomaraswamy told Mary about this latest move. 'Fort-un-ate-ly, our benefactor Mr Surijlal Chand has an identical lorry, same make, same colour. It is to be decorated i-den-tic-ally – I have detached some of our young men to see to this – same *pandal*, same garlands, colours and posters and Sharma is so like Krishnan that, i-den-tic-al in dress and make-up, few will tell the difference.'

'He's not nearly as dark,' objected Mary.

'All the better. Krishnan should be fair.'

'Nor as big.'

'We shall seat him higher. We shall be touring until the early hours.'

'What happens', asked Mary, 'if they meet or the people see them both?'

'No matter.' Dr Coomaraswamy spoke almost cheerfully as he echoed what Krishnan had written, 'Hindu gods can duplicate themselves, indeed multiply themselves. Did not Krishna become twenty-four Krishnas to please the *gopis*, the milkmaids?'

'My goodness,' said Professor Webster on the path up from the beach. 'How I'd like to go to both *dhashan*s.'

I only want to go to one, thought Mary.

On the knoll, looking down on the empty beach, the blaze of light on the roof, 'I feel there is a tide,' Auntie Sanni said to Colonel McIndoe. 'Listen to the drums.'

When Blaise came up from the bungalow, Patna Hall's big verandah was deserted.

He had avoided Mary, going into the bathroom as she came out of it, staying there until she had gone, coming out changed into slacks, a thin jersey, then strolling along the beach until he was sure she was at the roof barbecue. He had heard the invitation; at the bar there was no one, he poured himself a drink, then another. He could hear sounds of people going up and down the outside stairs, of American voices, Indian voices, laughter; they came down too from the roof. He turned his back.

Fireflies flickered in the garden and down the path. A garden boy came out to switch on the lanterns down the path sending the bats away where before they had flown and swooped almost brushing Blaise's hair. 'Yuk!' he had cried out in horror; they seemed part, to him, of this horrible night. He had another whisky. 'That girl should have been at the bar,' he muttered but Kuku, too, was up on the roof – though treating the barbecue with disdain, making a point of talking to Professor Aaron and the ladies, not to the disciples, except in their role as waiters.

'Why is the dining room closed?' Blaise had finally come in from the bar to find the dining room empty, the tables bare. Only the youngest waiter, Ahmed, was there fetching glasses from a cupboard. 'Why is the dining room closed?'

'No dinner in dining room tonight.' The boy picked up his tray obviously wanting to get away from this inexplicably angry sahib.

'No dinner! In Christ's name, why not? This is supposed to be an hotel.'

'Plenty of dinner.'

To Ahmed's relief, Samuel appeared. 'Plenty but tonight served up on the roof. Miss Sanni's orders. Come, Sahib, I show you the way.'

'No, thanks.'

'Excellent dinner,' crooned Samuel. 'It is our Root and Flower Party's invitation. Miss Sanni say we all accept.'

'Does she?' Blaise sounded dangerous.

'Indian fashion barbecue. Western as well. I and Ahmed cook that. Sahib enjoy it very much.'

A voice interrupted; in the pantry Ahmed had turned on the radio and the voice of the reader in English came through: 'This is All India Radio. Here is the news. The trial of Colin Armstrong closed today. Mr Justice Rajan . . .' A clatter of plates drowned the rest. Then, 'In the state of Konak, the election has entered an impressive stage . . .'

'Turn that damn thing off!' Blaise almost screamed. Samuel was more than perturbed. That a sahib, one of Auntie Sanni's sahibs, should misbehave — Samuel could not bring himself to say 'offend' — seemed unbelievable. Yet not half an hour ago he had had another such encounter, worse, a confrontation he had to admit. He had caught Mr Menzies in the hall as he went out. Mr Menzies had not been invited to the barbecue but did not seem to mind.

'Menzies, Sahib.'

'What is it? I'm in a hurry.' He had been in a hurry all day, the red car whizzing in and out. 'Well?'

'Sahib, that boy Kanu, he may not come into Patna Hall,' and before Mr Menzies could object, 'If Sahib is needing a body servant— '

'Body servant! That's rich.' Mr Menzies was laughing — it sounded to Samuel like demon laughter. 'Ho! Ho!' He clapped Samuel on the shoulder. 'You say more than you know, old man,' but Samuel shook off the hand as if it had been a snake and drew himself up to look Mr Menzies in the face.

'I am knowing' – Samuel deliberately left out the 'sahib' – 'I know very well, which is why I have to speak.'

The laughter ceased. 'And I suppose you will tell your Auntie Sanni?'

'Miss Sanni,' Samuel corrected him. 'I do not tell such to a lady. I am telling *my* Sahib, Colonel McIndoe.'

For a moment Samuel had thought he had disconcerted Mr Menzies. Then Mr Menzies shrugged and went off whistling to his car. Now Samuel's grave eyes took in Blaise's flushed face, over-bright eyes, the smell of whisky and, 'Sahib must eat,' said Samuel. 'If Sahib too tired to come upstairs, I bring some good things down.' He spoke a few quick words to Ahmed. 'Ahmed is laying you a table.'

'Don't bother. I don't want anything.'

'Sahib must eat.'

'Shut up, you,' shouted Blaise and went back to the bar.

'Miss Baba, come down,' Samuel whispered to Mary up on the roof. 'Ask Sahib to come to the barbecue. Missy, come down, please.'

No, thought Mary, please no.

She had been utterly content, sitting in the firelight on a *durrie* by Auntie Sanni. The disciples had provided stools and benches for their older guests; the rest sat on mats or *durries* while a few of the young men, more adventurous, dared to sit on the parapet, their backs to the sixty-foot drop below, while they ate and dangled their legs. Samuel and his staff had carried up china, glasses and cutlery but Mary had been delighted to see there were also banana leaves and the small metal tumblers used for drinking. The disciples, sniffing success, were overflowing with hospitality and affectionate happiness.

'Eat, please eat.'

'Here is drink.'

141

'Please, Auntie Sanni.'

'Professor.'

'Lady.'

'Lady.'

'Mrs Browne.'

'Call me Mary.'

'Not Mary, Radha. We think you are true goddess, Radha.'

Up on the roof is nearer to the stars, Mary had been thinking. The sky seemed like a spangled bowl meeting the horizon far out to sea and, as she had seen when she had looked over the back parapet, was met by the tall palms and cotton trees of the village with, behind them, the hills, holders of the cave paintings that had so thrilled the ladies. To the east was Auntie Sanni's knoll, to the west, the sand-dunes lit tonight by a chain of shrine lights, though the grove itself was, at the moment, dark and still. On the lit roof, plied by the disciples, she was contentedly eating the delicious food with her fingers.

'Ugh!' said Mrs Schlumberger and, peering, 'What is it?'

'Delectable!' said Dr Lovat.

'But I like to know what I am eating. It smells.'

'Of course. It's spicy.'

'Memsahib rather have western? Hamburger? French fries?' Anil was anxious to please but when he brought them, 'Not on a *leaf*, boy. I'm not a barbarian.'

'I am, I'll eat them,' Mary offered. 'I'm ravenous,' but Anil had spirited up plate, knife, fork, napkin, while Ravi emptied a pyramid of saffron rice on a fresh banana leaf for Mary. Then Samuel was at her elbow.

'Missy. Miss Baba.'

'Oh, all right.' Like Krishnan, Mary licked her fingers, one by one, laughing. She stood up, shook out her skirt — she had changed into a dress for the *dhashan* — and went downstairs.

* * *

142

'A pretty poor show,' said Blaise, 'a hotel not serving dinner.'

'Blaise, don't you see, it's an exceptional night? Everyone has election fever and there's such good food. I've never tasted real Indian food before. Bumble, do come. Everyone's up there, Sir John, Lady Fisher, Professor Aaron and all the ladies. Auntie Sanni— '

'She's *not* your aunt.'

Mary was too happy to quarrel. 'It won't be long. We will all be going on to the *dhashan*. Bumble, why won't you join in?'

'I did try to join in there, down on the beach and a bloody fool you made me look.'

'I'm sorry. I suppose I was excited.'

'If anyone knows how a game should be played,' the whisky was beginning to work on Blaise's resentment, 'how it ought to be played . . .'

'It wasn't an ought sort of game.'

'Then it ought to be.'

'Ought! Ought!' Mary was near to losing her temper. 'Ought is a bully word. Blaise, why? Why do you have to spoil everything?'

'*I* spoil?'

'Yes,' but Mary felt an odd pang of pity. 'Bumble, please. This is an . . . an enchanted night. Look at the fireflies, the stars. Everyone's so happy, so affectionate. Krishnan— '

'Don't talk to me about that black cheat. Don't dare to say his name. Go on,' shouted Blaise, 'go upstairs to him and his like,' and he slapped Mary hard across her face. 'And you can take that with you.'

The sound of the slap seemed to reverberate through Patna Hall. In the pantry Samuel dropped a dish.

For a moment Mary stood still with shock, the red mark spreading on her cheek. Her hand came up to feel it as if she could not believe it. Then she said, in a whisper, 'You won't do that again. I'm going.'

It was late when Sir John went down to the bungalow. He had left Lady Fisher and Auntie Sanni on the verandah. Kuku had gone to bed. Paradise was dark now, its bonfires sunk to embers; along the beach, the noise of the surf was broken by drums beating from the grove where Sir John could see lights, flares, behind the lights of the shrines as he came down the path. The drums quickened; he could hear the high notes of a flute, then chanting, a slow rhythmic chant. Slippers, driven away by the crowd, was standing looking wistfully at the bungalow. He turned to follow Sir John. 'Better not, old fellow,' Sir John told him and with a pat turned him round.

Blaise, it seemed, had had more whisky – the room's own small bar stood open, its whisky bottle three-quarters empty. Samuel, though his legs were tired, his feet sore from climbing up the steep stairs to Paradise, had come bringing a plate of sandwiches and a basket of fruit; they were on the table untouched while Blaise sat staring out to sea, his head on his hands. When Sir John came in he looked up, glowering, 'I wanted to be left alone.'

'So I gathered but I have come', said Sir John, 'to take you to the *dhashan*.'

'The bloody *dhashan*? That's the last thing . . .' The words were slurred.

'I think you should come, for your own sake,' said Sir John and, peremptorily, 'Stand *up*, boy.'

At first Blaise could not walk beside Sir John but wove an unsteady way, veering down almost to the waves, back up the sand; then slowly the cooler air and the breeze revived him. Soon, too, the size of the gathering began to dawn on him; it reached far wider than the grove, overflowing through the dunes and the fluffy casuarina trees and along the beach. Blaise had seen the crowds that afternoon but here were, 'A thousand? Two thousand?' he murmured, dazed.

'More,' said Sir John. 'Far more.'

The music and chanting had stopped for a breathing space and they heard the stirrings, the undertone murmuring of a reverent multitude, men and women packed close sitting on the sand, the women with flowers in the coils of their hair; some men were bareheaded, most had small turbans – the pale cloth shone in the glow of lanterns hung in the trees and on poles, stretching away as far as they could see. Boys were everywhere, some up the trees; girls, small and older, sat with their mothers.

Among them, like vigilantes in white – again Sir John was reminded of angels – the disciples stood sentinel or moved silently offering *chattis* of hot coffee or pepper water, *biris*, fruit or pān – betel nut. Though the people took them, their heads never moved, their gaze was too fixed on where, in a clear space, a fire burned sending up sparks, while behind it, on a high throne heaped with flowers, sat Krishnan, blue-black as usual, his skin shining with oil, his eyes outlined with kohl, his lips vermilion, the white U mark of Vishnu on his forehead. He looked outsize as he smiled gently, tenderly, on his people. Behind was an elephant Sir John had often seen in the village; now it was unattended, content. On Krishnan's knee sat a squirrel, its grey fur ruddy in the firelight, its tail plumed up. As they watched, Krishnan absently gave it a nut; it nibbled, holding the nut in its paws, its beady eyes giving a quick look at the crowds, then trustingly up at Krishnan.

'I must say he is magnificent,' said Sir John.

Blaise stood staring, a little of the implications reaching him at last – until he saw Mary.

The cultural ladies were here and there among the people; most of them had brought camp stools but Mary sat on a deerskin almost at Krishnan's feet. She was stringing a garland as were the boys squatting round her; as she looked down to pick up a flower her hair swung its bell round her face and fell back as she looked up again to thread the flower; her white dress seemed, like the squirrel, to be stained with red light from the fire. As Blaise looked, she held up the garland towards Krishnan.

'Lady Fisher said she was bewitched.' Blaise's voice was far too loud.

'Hush!'

'She's not bewitched. She's besotted. Sotted.'

'That's an ugly word.' Sir John spoke quietly, firmly, hoping to calm him.

'Ugly! Look at *that*!' Blaise shouted the words out. Krishnan had smiled on the flowers. '*It*'s bloody ugly.'

'*Chūp!*' Sir John used the Hindi word and, at the same time, slapped his hand over Blaise's mouth. 'How dare you disturb everyone? What is ugly in this? The fire, flowers, animals – even the monkeys behave – these children and humble people?' Then, by luck, Sir John saw Thambi standing with Moses and beckoned them with a quick jerk of his head. 'Take Browne Sahib back to the bungalow. *Take* him,' ordered Sir John.

'Jai Krishnan. Jai Krishnan,' and as even greater reverence broke through, 'Jai Shri Krishnan,' then, 'Jai Shri Krishnan Hari.'

Chanting. Music. Silence. Silence, chanting, music; even in the silence the piercing yet sweet call of the flute seemed to go on as Krishnan now and again put it to his lips to play. 'I didn't know how well Krishnan played the flute,' Mary murmured to Ravi when he paused beside her.

'He has to play but, then, Krishnan can do anything,' whispered ecstatic Ravi.

Can Sharma? wondered Mary.

The moon rose higher, began to go down so that it hung lower over the sea. In twos and threes, the cultural ladies began unostentatiously to leave; Professor Aaron followed them. Sir John made his way to Mary. 'That's enough, young Mary. This will go on all night.'

'I *should* have liked to go to the other *dhashan* to see Sharma Krishnan,' said Professor Webster who had lingered.

'That will go on all night too.'

'Yes.' Dr Coomaraswamy had joined them. 'Also, I myself have been back and forth every hour. That *dhashan* is at Mudalier, not far from Ghandara on the inland side, exactly the replica of this. The effect is ex-tra-or-din-ary!' His eyes shone. 'Believe me, some of these people will walk the twelve miles to see the duplication.'

'They believe im-pli-cit-ly.' Mr Srinivasan, too, was in euphoria.

'An extremely successful political trick.' Mr Menzies, in his now almost familiar way, had appeared from nowhere.

'Trick!' Mr Srinivasan's voice was shrill from the affront. 'It is to save the people. They must be saved,' the little man said earnestly. 'Krishnan has made no false promises – unlike other candidates – only the truth, simple truth of what he can do with this holy help, what, we pray, he will do.'

'Well! Well! Well!' said Mr Menzies. 'Be as it may, I am going to look at Number Two. Mrs Browne, can I take you?'

Mr Menzies did not ask Professor Webster and Sir John moved closer to Mary but she had instinctively drawn back. In any case, Sharma after Krishnan, no, she thought, and aloud, 'I think I'd rather not.'

'Good girl,' said Sir John. 'I will take you back.'

'Back?' Startled out of her happiness, panic set in. The slap Mary had forgotten seemed to tingle on her cheek. 'I can't go back. I don't know where to go but I can't sleep in the bungalow with Blaise. I can't.'

'Of course you can't.' Sir John put his arm round her. 'Blaise has had enough, too, for tonight. You are to sleep in our dressing room. Auntie Sanni has arranged it. Come.'

Thursday

When the first beginnings of daylight filtered through the dressing room curtains, Mary still had not slept. Too tired? Too excited? Too dismayed? But she did not feel dismayed, even though she knew the dismay was serious, nor was she tired or excited, only awake and waiting. Waiting for what?

Then it came; the sound of a flute played softly. She flung off the sheet, went to the window and looked behind the curtains. Yes, it was Krishnan standing under the window and with him, in the dim light, she saw the big shape of Birdie.

Krishnan wore no make-up, no garlands, only a clean white tunic and loose trousers, his hair brushed back. As he saw her, he put a finger to his lips, hushing her, then beckoned.

Mary had gone to bed in her slip; now she pulled last night's dress on, brushed her hair with one of Sir John's hairbrushes and, taking her sandals, stole out in her bare feet and ran downstairs.

'Krishnan.'

'Ssh! Mary, would you, will you, come with me?'

Krishnan seemed suddenly young and – not unhappy – troubled.

'Come where?'

'To the temple.'

'The Dawn Temple?'

'No, no. There's a little temple. It's so hidden in the

hills hardly anyone knows it. I call it mine. I'm going there to make my *puja*.'

'*Puja*?'

'Prayer. Before the voting. I promised my mother.' He took Mary's hand, twining his fingers in hers. 'Perhaps, Mary, thinking of her, I find myself very lonely. Well . . .' For a moment he was proud again, 'I have to be lonely but sometimes everyone needs . . .' It seemed to be difficult for eloquent Krishnan to find words. Then, 'Mary, will you come with me?' and, rapidly, 'Birdie will take us, it's not far into the hills, as she's always coming and going no one will notice us. I won't be long. You'll be back in bed before anyone is up to see you gone. You— '

'Ssh!' said Mary in her turn. 'Of course I'll come.'

Birdie knelt down to let them climb on to the pad Krishnan had fastened on her back; he swung up and reached down a hand to help Mary. 'Lie down behind me,' he whispered as he settled himself on the elephant's neck.

'I thought no one could drive an elephant except its *mahout*,' said Mary as they went along.

'Perhaps in another time I was a *mahout*.'

Mary had ridden elephants before, short rides in a *howdah* but not in this free, ordinary way; she could feel Birdie's great body through the pad, her shoulders moving, her powerful, comfortable, half-rolling half-swaying gait. Birdie had been well trained: if a branch overhung – this roundabout way to the hills led through patches of jungle – to a command from Krishnan, her trunk came up to break it off in case it hit her passengers. When they came to a swamp she tested the ground with a cautious forefoot before she would venture on it. Presently they began to climb; Mary felt a cooler air and, as she lay, lulled by the rhythmical swaying, she went, at last, to sleep.

* * *

149

The temple was inset into the hills, higher hills fold on fold around it so that it looked out across vistas to the sea; it was walled with small bricks made of native earth turned by centuries of sun to dark gold, as was its courtyard floor of smooth, old stone. There was a stoop for water in one wall and a small pillared pavilion in which hung a bell. 'What a funny smell,' whispered Mary. 'What is it?'

'Bats,' said Krishnan, wrinkling his nose. '*Ghee* gone rancid and, I should guess, crushed marigolds.' She could smell their pungency.

Krishnan set the bell lightly ringing; the sound carried over the gulf all around. Behind the pavilion Mary could see an inner temple, empty under its dome though in the centre of the floor, on a low plinth, burnt a fire with a steady flame. 'It never goes out,' Krishnan told her.

She had woken when Birdie stopped and knelt. Krishnan had lifted her down and she had stood, rubbing her eyes awake, blinking at the sunlight while he brought down from Birdie's back the bundle of sugar cane he had brought as feed, untied it and scattered the canes. '*Kachiyundu*,' he told her in Telegu, as she got to her feet. The little eyes blinked as Mary's had, the mottled ears flapped and Birdie did as she was told.

'Come.'

'Why the fire?' asked Mary.

'This temple belongs to another of the old, old elemental gods like Surya, the Sun God, Indra, God of Storm, Thunder and Rain. This is for Agni, God of Fire. We all love Agni because though he is the son of heaven he lives on earth and in all our homes because he warms them and cooks our food. Perhaps that is why I love to come here when I miss home. Agni can never die because he is born each time we make a marriage by rubbing two pieces of dry wood together or strike a flint or match and he, like us, has to be fed.'

150

Krishnan laughed. 'See, I have brought him an offering of *ghee*.'

As Krishnan poured the butter on the fire and the flame shot up, the priest appeared: not old, a young man wearing only a *lunghi*, his hair oiled back and the Brahmin sacred thread, three-stranded across his chest from his shoulder to his waist.

'Krishna-ji,' he greeted Krishnan as an old and revered friend, making *namaskar*. '*Anandum*. Peace.' He gave a deep *salaam* to Mary, then silently opened a slit of a door behind the fire, motioning them to go in.

Mary had taken off her shoes but still she hesitated, looking up at Krishnan. 'You can go in,' he said, 'but, Mary, it is the innermost sanctuary, infinitely holy. It is in all our temples but you have to find it. You will only find it if you come there to take *darshan* which is simply to be with, behold, God, not kneel or pray, only look ... look ... and not with cameras and notebooks ... People who bring those, cut themselves off, they cannot come in. We call it the womb-house because, as only God is there, in it you can, as it were, be born again.'

'Even I, an outsider?' she whispered.

'There are no outsiders here. Go in.'

Mary went in: the little room, windowless, smelled of incense, the oldest symbol of prayer. It was lit by the flickering of the butter-fed fire and on the wall was a painting, very old, thought Mary, painted directly on to the stone, not of a god or goddess but of a sun rising, its rays still showing traces of pigment, red and yellow; below it, storm clouds were dark and swollen with rain falling. At the base, rising to meet them, as if challenging the storm, rose Agni's flames, coloured red with deep yellow. 'Sun – Storm – Fire – Surya – Indra – Agni,' whispered Mary and, as if he would say that too, Krishnan took her hand again. They stood together, looking as he had said she should look, only looking while, behind them, the young priest took a shallow brass bowl with, in it, five *dipas* burning in oil and, quietly chanting his mantra, waved it before the fire, walking round it.

As they came out, he handed the bowl to Krishnan who waved it too, his lips moving, as the light of the small flames shot high up into the dome. Krishnan handed the bowl to Mary and, as she waved the flames, 'O God, Gods, please, for Krishnan,' she urged in a mantra of her own. 'For Krishnan, please.'

It was late when she woke in the dressing room. 'I shan't go to sleep,' she had told Krishnan. 'I can't after this.'

'At least lie down,' he had said and yawned himself. 'I shall sleep now. I haven't for two nights, it hasn't been possible but, you see, for twenty-four hours before voting all parties have to stop campaigning, not a move, not a step, not a speech. Of course, we are all busy behind the scenes getting ready for tomorrow but dear Coomaraswamy will do that. I shall sleep, sleep, sleep and I am not homesick any more. Thank you, Mary.'

Though Patna Hall had been stirring, no one had seen her go and come; undisturbed she had slipped into bed and, before she could tell it all over again in her mind as she had meant to, she was asleep.

Now as she lay in bright sunlight, for a moment she wondered where she was until she saw Sir John's hairbrushes, ivory-backed and crested on the dressing table, his ties hanging over the looking glass. Someone had hung her dress over a chair, put the shoes she had cast off neatly together; they were a reminder that, 'People expect me to do everyday things . . . I shall have to do them,' she told herself. 'To begin with, go down to the bungalow, wash and get into clean clothes.' She could have asked Hannah to bring her things but, 'You'll have to go some-time,' she told herself. 'With luck, Blaise will be asleep.'

'I'm afraid Blaise will have a massive hangover,' Sir John had said but, of course, sometime he'll have to wake. What then? thought Mary. The mark of the slap was still on her cheek, and it had stung more deeply. 'I'll never speak to him again!' she had vowed. Now, 'Don't be childish,' said what seemed to be an older, steadier Mary. Then, 'What am I to do?' she asked and, as if Krishnan had answered, 'You can try being kind.'

Two days ago, she would have been in revolt against that. Why should I be kind when Blaise...? But now she seemed to see, in the temple, the little flames in the bowl as Krishnan waved it, sending the light high into the dome. 'I couldn't send it as high as that,' she whispered. 'But, yes, I can try.'

Slowly, she got out of bed.

'Hannah,' said Auntie Sanni when, on the upper verandah, Hannah brought her morning tea. 'I should like you to go down to the bungalow this morning and see if Manning Memsahib's things are ready to be packed.'

'Packed?' Kuku looked up from where, at Auntie Sanni's dictation, she had been writing out the day's menus. 'You think she won't come back?'

'She may not be able to,' and Auntie Sanni went on to Hannah, 'Do any washing that is needed and Kuku, in any case, put flowers in her room.'

'She owes you so much money, she will probably stay away,' said Kuku.

'That is the one thing that may bring her back,' said Auntie Sanni.

'I'll go to the bungalow,' Kuku offered.

'I asked Hannah,' said Auntie Sanni.

Blaise, a long mound in the wide bed, stayed inert while Mary washed and dressed. He was breathing heavily and, He reeks! she wrinkled up her nose in disgust

153

then, unexpectedly, Poor Blaise! She left the shutters wide open for the sea breeze to blow in, salty, cleansing, and went up the path for breakfast; again, she was ravenously hungry.

After it she lingered on Patna Hall's verandah, trying to will herself to go down to the bungalow. If I want to swim, and I do, I must get my things. She had some sugar lumps for Slippers. He's waiting for me but I'll walk along the beach first, she decided, putting off the moment of going back to Blaise.

As, carrying her shoes, she walked, in and out of the ripples of the waves, the water cold on her feet, the sun warm on her neck, How I love this place, thought Mary. It isn't only Krishnan. She lifted her face to the sun, the breeze and shut her eyes, standing to feel the sun through her eyelids but, 'You can't stay here all day with your eyes shut,' she told herself. 'You have to go back. But what can I say?' she asked. 'What can either of us say after that slap?' Then, 'Be patient. Something will come,' and suddenly, That might be a little splinter of Auntie Sanni's wisdom, she conceded smiling.

The fishing boats were coming in; it must have been a good morning because they had been out twice. Mary could hear the men chanting as they pulled in the heavy nets, long lines of them along the beach. As usual, the best of the catch was being taken either to the refrigerated lorry vans drawn up ready or to the drying sheds; the rest was spilled out on the sand for the fisherwomen to take, either to use or to sell in the villages. A little group was standing looking at something on the sand, something boys were racing up to see.

Mary went closer.

'Bumble! Bumble! Wake up. *Please*.'
Mary was calling that from the verandah but Blaise

was already awake, sitting up in bed holding his throbbing head as she came hurtling in. All Mary's serenity was gone: half sobbing, her eyes wide with horror, she begged, 'Blaise, don't ever, *ever* even think of going swimming further along the beach away from our own. Don't, *please*.'

'What *are* you talking about?'

'You've said you would from the beginning. Remember how cross you were with Thambi and Moses but, Blaise, don't. Don't.'

He saw her shorts were soaked and stained red, her legs too, her arms and hands. 'Is that blood?'

'Yes . . . Yes.'

'Come here,' said Blaise. He was still wearing the shirt of the night before, his hair rumpled; he still stank but Mary came. Gently he pulled her nearer, she was shaking. He put his arm round her and took her to the bathroom.

'Please . . . get the blood off my hands.' Her lips were trembling.

He washed her hands over a *gharra*, washed her face, too, and gave her a glass of water. 'Rinse and spit it out,' then he brought her back to the bed. 'What is all this about? Tell me.'

'The catch was on the beach, the part left for the people to take, fish, flapping and slipping, starfish, crabs. There was a baby shark.' Mary began to tremble again. 'Not longer than three, four feet. They had turned it on its back; it was white and hard though it was a baby. When its tail flailed it knocked over a small boy. Its mouth came down almost to its middle, hideous,' she shuddered, 'almost a half hoop with teeth. Cruel teeth. An old woman bent down to look and touched it and it snapped . . . took . . . took off her hand.' Blaise held Mary fast. 'The other women made a great noise but kept back. Thambi came and clubbed it. I had to help him hold the stump in the sea until the men came and took the old woman away. Blaise, promise me you won't swim anywhere, *anywhere* outside our nets.'

'I thought you didn't care what I did.'

'Of course I care.' How could I help caring about that for anyone? but this different Mary did not say that. A new thought had struck her. That night when I swam with Krishnan, there weren't any sharks – or were there?

But Blaise was speaking urgently. 'Mary, let's go away. There's a mid-day train. Let's go now.'

'Now?' She pulled away from him. Sat up. 'Before the election?'

'Damn the election. It's nothing to do with us.'

'It is. It is to do with me,' she said the words slowly. 'I'm bound up in it,' and, more quickly, 'I couldn't possibly go now.'

'Mary, please. Since we came here everything's been wrong.'

She looked at him in amazement. 'For me everything's been right.'

'It's this Krishnan. You're under a spell.' Blaise was choosing his words carefully. 'Mary, you don't realise it but you are. I'm not going to blame you,' he said magnanimously. 'Lots of girls go in at the deep end when they first meet Indians.'

'In at the deep end?' Mary looked at him, incredulous. 'I'm up. Up where I have never been before.'

'He's using you— '

'That's what's so wonderful and I never dreamed until this morning he could need . . .' again she did not say it as, 'Tell me something,' Blaise went on, 'did you go to him or he to you?'

'I didn't go. I . . . came across him. In the grove our first night. The night you drove me out over Slippers. I sat by Krishnan's fire. We talked,' said Mary, half dreaming.

156

'Was that all?'

'That was all.' All! It was everything.

'Did he ask you to come back?'

'No.'

'Who asked you to go on the lorry?'

'Dr Coomaraswamy.'

'Not Krishnan?'

'Krishnan told him to. I asked the young men to play rounders.'

'You went to the *dhashan*.'

'We all went.'

'Did he ask you to?'

'He never asks.' That had been true – until this morning – and Mary had to pause.

Blaise noticed that and, at once, 'Mary, I want a straight answer to a straight question. Tell me the truth.'

'Krishnan doesn't need to ask.' It was the best evasion she could think of. 'People come to him. They give.'

'More fools they.'

'Don't be horrid.'

'I'm not horrid. I'm worried.' Blaise took her firmly by the shoulders and swung her round to look at him. 'Mary, I have to ask you, have you done anything wrong?'

'Wrong?' She was startled. '*Wrong?*' How could it be wrong? Then she looked at Blaise's face, perplexed as it was honest and miserable. 'You mean . . .'

'Yes. You wouldn't be afraid to tell me, would you?' He was still gentle. 'I'd rather know.'

At that moment Mary liked Blaise more than she had liked him since Bombay and, 'If I haven't told you everything,' she said, 'it's only because you wouldn't have understood but I know I haven't done anything – wrong.'

'I believe you,' said Blaise. 'But promise me one thing.'

'What?'

'That you won't go to the grove or near any of them, unless you are asked.'

Mary thought she owed Blaise that and, 'I won't go unless I am asked,' she said resolutely, at once, perversely remembering under her window at dawn the sound of the flute.

There were footsteps on the verandah. Hannah had come to look after Mrs Manning's things.

'Ayah,' called Blaise. 'Ayah.'

Hannah was not used to being called Ayah but came. 'Will you help the little Memsahib? She has had a shock.'

'Thambi told me.' Hannah clicked her tongue when she saw the blood on Mary. 'Come, Baba.'

'If you don't mind I'll sleep some more,' Blaise said when Hannah had gone. 'Mary, I'm sorry about last night.' He had realised his state. 'Then I'll have a swim, from our beach.' He smiled at her but, It won't do, thought Mary as, leaving him, she went up to the house. 'I want a straight answer to a straight question. Tell me the truth.' That rang in her ears but, 'How can you answer when you are only just finding out?' asked Mary. No one had told her of the Indian concept of truth, that it is like water poured into your hand but you can only catch a few drops.

Professor Aaron and the cultural ladies were leaving.

Their coach was drawn up under the portico which was crowded with luggage while they gathered in the hall; all had their raincoats, cameras, binoculars, shooting sticks, camp stools and satchels of notebooks. 'Far more full than when we came,' they said in satisfaction. Last snapshots were being taken of Auntie Sanni, Kuku, Samuel, Hannah, Thambi; Professor Aaron was counting heads and trying to placate Mrs Schlumberger. 'We should have had a discount for sharing a room and you should tell Mrs

McIndoe about the disgrace of the bathrooms,' but, from the others, 'We've had a wonderful, wonderful time,' was said over and over again. 'We never expected anything like this.'

Miss Pritt was almost in tears. Mrs van den Mar had the recipe for mulligatawny soup, Mrs Glover a collection of flowers Hannah had helped her to press. Professor Webster declared she was coming back next year, 'If you will have me, dear Auntie Sanni.'

'And me,' cried Dr Lovat.

Kuku was dazzled, though at first she had been offended, by large tips. 'No. No, nothing. I cannot take this. I cannot possibly take this.'

'Of course you can, my dear, you deserve it.'

Mary appeared panting. In her distress over the shark she had forgotten the ladies were leaving until Hannah reminded her; she had had to run up the path.

A chorus broke out. 'We thought you weren't coming to say goodbye.'

'Of course I was.'

'I should have hated to go without seeing you.'

They gathered round her, gave her their addresses. 'If you come to the States again be sure to let us know,' and, 'We'd love you to stay awhile with us.'

'My apartment's so small,' Mrs Schlumberger hastened to say, 'I can't offer a guest room.'

'I can offer you three,' Mrs Glover laughed, 'any time.' They thanked her for last night. 'It was real fun,' and, 'You're no ordinary girl,' they told her. 'We didn't know English girls could be like you,' and Mrs van den Mar called, 'Say goodbye for us to that lord of creation of yours.'

'Lord of creation?'

'More than a mite dictatorial,' said Mrs van den Mar. 'My dear, you shouldn't let him.'

'And don't *you* get dictatorial,' said Dr Lovat.

When the coach had gone, Patna Hall was extraordinarily quiet. Are the disciples all asleep? wondered Mary, Or are they away working behind the scenes as Krishnan had said? Dr Coomaraswamy and Mr Srinivasan had breakfasted in the bridal suite, though Mr Srinivasan had been out early to Ghandara. He had come back disturbed. 'Hari, do you know who made all the arrangements for Padmina Retty's aeroplane?'

'Who? Not Surijlal?'

'Surijlal is most loyal adherent. It was that Menzies.'

'Mr Menzies! I thought he was on our side.'

'I think he is playing loose and fast. Hari, I fear trouble.'

'There can't be trouble now,' said Dr Coomaraswamy.

Mary did not want to go back to the bungalow and Blaise. Anyway, he's sleeping it off. Then, Shall I swim? But a shudder came. I'd rather swim with him. Sleep in the sun? She had had little sleep yet was filled with a curious energy. What can I do?

'Mary.'

'It is strange,' Auntie Sanni had said to Colonel McIndoe. 'This girl I have never set eyes on before, nor she on me, seems to feel much as I do about Patna Hall,' and did not all the servants call her Missy, Miss Baba? While Christabel, the pet mynah bird, had begun to call 'Mary' in Auntie Sanni's voice.

Colonel McIndoe had patted Auntie Sanni's hand.

Now Auntie Sanni, wearing a huge white apron and drying her hands on a towel came to call Mary. 'Thursday is the day', said Auntie Sanni, 'when we make what Hannah calls "dainties" – desserts and sweets for the week. These cannot be trusted to Alfredo. Always I make them myself.'

'Yourself! Only Hannah, me, two boys and a washer-up

woman to wait on her,' Kuku was to say in an aside to Mary.

'Also, today, we are crystallising cherries. They have been flown in from Kulu in the north where it is almost the cherry season. These are early. I thought you might like to come and help. Would you?'

'Would I!' If a life belt had been thrown to Mary in a choppy sea she could not have caught it more thankfully.

It was, Mary saw at once, a ritual, 'Every Thursday,' as Auntie Sanni had told her. The confectionery pantry, as it was known at Patna Hall, was separate from the kitchen, in fact in the courtyard annexe, next to the linen room, store rooms and near Auntie Sanni's office. The same flowers were there but no cats, goat or kids were allowed; no birds could fly in; doors and windows were screened with fine mesh.

The room had a tiled floor and walls that could be washed; counters were fitted with surfaces of wood that could be scrubbed and on them were slabs of marble of different sizes. Shelves of copper saucepans, moulds – 'Best French ones,' said Auntie Sanni – were in easy reach, all sparklingly clean and polished with ashes, 'Our washer-up women earn their pay.' The calor gas cooker was large, the refrigerator larger, a vast old-fashioned one run on kerosene; its whirring filled the room punctuated by the cooing of Auntie Sanni's doves outside, the only birds bold enough to come near. Monkeys had thieved some handfuls of cherries as they had been carried in but Hannah had scolded them back into the trees.

The cherries from Kulu, in finely woven travelling baskets, were on the floor; two boys, well scrubbed, wearing white shorts and tunics were carefully de-stalking them under Hannah's watchful eyes. 'To stay fresh, cherries must be picked on their stalks,' Auntie Sanni told Mary.

They were carefully de-stoned, too, the boys using small silver picks, the stones thrown into a bucket, while the cherries were put, carefully again in case they bruised, into large bowls. When enough were ready they were taken to Hannah who was stirring hot syrup, heavy with sugar and tinged with rosewater. 'They must not boil or they won't stay firm,' said Auntie Sanni. 'Then, when they're cooled they will be rolled in fine sugar.'

As Hannah worked her bangles clinked. 'It's not hygienic. You ought to take them off,' Kuku told her.

'They will not come off,' said Hannah serenely. 'My hands are grown too big.'

The crystallised cherries were not only for the week but to last the whole year. 'These are the second batch. Hannah is just finishing off the first – it has taken twelve days.'

'Twelve days!' Mary looked with awe at the racks of cherries drying, plump and tender.

'Fresh syrup has to be boiled every day, then poured over the fruit, then they are drained. On the sixth day the fruit is simmered for three or four minutes – this helps to keep the cherries plump; they are left to soak for four more days. Then you carefully take the cherries out, put them on racks to drain, next in a cool oven to dry until they are no longer sticky to handle. Now Hannah will give them the crystallised finish.'

Kuku gave a yawn but Mary, enchanted by this minutiae, watched how skilfully Hannah dipped each cherry in a pan of boiling water, then rolled it in sugar that had been spread on clean paper.

'Come,' said Auntie Sanni, 'I will teach you to make *rasgula*, a Bengali recipe. See, we take two pints of milk, lemons, semolina . . .'

'Semolina?' Mary was surprised.

'Here it is called *sooji* and we shall need green

cardamom seeds for spice.' The spices, dozens of them, were in a special glass-fronted cabinet.

'They are very costly,' said Kuku. Hot and cross, she pushed her hair back with sticky fingers. 'We could buy these sweetmeats far more cheaply in Ghandara. There are good Bengali sweetmeat sellers there.'

'It wouldn't be the same.'

Of course it wouldn't be the same, Mary felt, almost fiercely. This – this is home, what makes a home, which is why I love Patna Hall so much. She remembered what Krishnan had told her that very morning – her secret morning – of Agni who warms our homes and cooks our food and, 'How can you say it would be the same?' she upbraided Kuku.

'Besides, they haven't the good milk,' said more practical Auntie Sanni. Her desserts were made with rich milk from the Jersey cows she had imported. Their faces look like Krishnan's wise cows, Mary had thought. They were kept in Patna Hall's small homestead behind the knoll where, too, was the poultry yard so that eggs were fresh every day, chickens and ducks provided plump for the table instead of the usual Indian scrawny ones. 'Besides,' Auntie Sanni went on, 'bought Indian sweetmeats are too sweet for Western tastes. But don't think we do all Indian,' she said to Mary. 'We have *hereditary* recipes, some, I think, unique. There is a velvet cream that came from my English grandmother, perhaps from her grandmother, rich cream, lemon, a little leaf gelatine, wine . . .'

'In the recipe it should be raisin wine. We have to use Golconda,' Kuku was spiteful, 'and the cream can curdle as you put it in.'

'Only if you are impatient,' said Auntie Sanni.

'Costs a fortune but that doesn't matter,' said Kuku, but Auntie Sanni only said, 'Put on this apron, Mary, and I'll show you.'

The time went more quickly than Mary could have

believed, they were so busy. Samuel brought cold cucumber soup – 'Delicious,' she said – rolls and butter, fruit.

Later, 'Why don't you take this into the dining room,' Auntie Sanni said of the latest confection, 'and let them taste what you have made?'

Only Sir John, Lady Fisher and Blaise were in the dining room, sitting together. Blaise had swum then sluiced himself in the bathroom, put on fresh clothes but his face was pinker than usual. His eyes look as if they had been boiled, thought Mary, which was not kind, I must have cooking on the brain, but how can you help what leaps into your mind?

'This is Mrs Beeton's "Pretty Orange Pudding",' she said putting the dish down in front of them. 'Auntie Sanni has one of the earliest editions of the cookbook, eighteen sixty-one. It says, "Take six oranges", though we took sixty to make ten puddings, for dinner tonight. Mrs Beeton calls it, "A pretty dish of oranges, exceedingly ornamental", and isn't it? I made it.'

She was wearing one of Auntie Sanni's capacious aprons, wrapped and kilted around her; her cheeks were flushed, her hair dark with sweat; her spectacles were askew – 'It's too hot for contact lenses,' she had said – she had a dab of powdered sugar on her nose but to Sir John she looked almost pretty; the grey of her eyes lit almost to blue. 'Thank you, hussy,' he said.

'It is a pretty pudding,' said Lady Fisher.

'Mary seems to have been adopted as the child of the house,' said Lady Fisher.

'She isn't a child. She happens to be a married woman.' Blaise was stiff again. 'Something Mrs McIndoe chooses to forget.'

'Auntie Sanni?'

'I prefer to call her Mrs McIndoe. I'm afraid I don't share your high opinion of her.'

'It's not only high,' said Lady Fisher, 'it's loving. We've been coming here for years, haven't we, John, and we know how wise she is.'

'I don't subscribe to that either. In any case, I am taking Mary away tomorrow, a day early.'

'Will she go?' asked Lady Fisher, which Blaise ignored.

'When she is through with this nonsensical cooking, I'll tell her *and* she has promised me not to go near this Krishnan creature again.'

They looked at him, both incredulous. 'Mary promised that?'

'I'm glad to say she did.'

'I'm not glad,' said Lady Fisher and, 'Blaise,' began Sir John, 'Mary is having an experience—'

'Which I don't choose to let her have—'

'You have just said she isn't a child. Don't you see,' Lady Fisher pleaded, 'how Mary longs to be part of something, to be needed, be of help . . .?'

'She can help me. That's what she married me for, didn't she?' He got up, leaving the pudding. 'If you'll excuse me, I'll go and get some more sleep. I still have a bit of a head and, of course, I apologise about last night.'

When he had gone, 'Insufferable young dolt,' said Sir John, but Lady Fisher only said, 'Poor silly boy.'

The confectionery was over by two o'clock. Hot, sticky all over even to her hair, but happy, Mary ran down the path to the bungalow and came quietly into the bedroom, thinking Blaise might be asleep. He was not; looking considerably ruffled, he was writing a letter.

'Who is that to?'

'Mrs McIndoe.'

'Auntie Sanni. Why?'

Instead of answering he looked at her. 'God, you look a mess. You'd better go and wash.'

'Not before you've told me why you are writing to Auntie Sanni.'

'To tell her we are leaving tomorrow.'

'No!'

'Yes.' Blaise held up a hand. 'Please, I don't want a fuss. Besides, what is there to stay for? You've promised to have no more to do with the election.'

'I didn't say that.'

But Blaise had risen. 'I'm taking this up to the house now.'

How dared he? Left in the bedroom Mary felt choked. Without asking or consulting! She walked up and down in helpless anger, then, I'll go for a swim. It was either that or tears.

Thambi came to help her. Somu too but Thambi, as if he sensed something was more than wrong, took Mary himself, Somu swimming alongside, but there was none of the exhilaration and joy of riding in on the waves. Afterwards they brought a beach umbrella as Mary spread her towel and lay down; only then could she give way.

No tears came though, only indignation. Without even consulting. I can't go now, not before the election, yet how can I stay? Blaise has all our money. She could not be sure where Rory was. Peru – or it could be Washington or London.

Then, suddenly, I know, thought Mary, I'll go to Auntie Sanni. She'll find a way. I'll talk to her tonight after she has seen Alfredo.

It was a comfortable thought; the anger ebbed. Mary gave a great yawn and was soon asleep.

When Mary had gone to sleep, the sun had been hot on her legs so that she had been careful to keep her head in the shade of the umbrella. When she woke she was chill.

As she sat up, rubbing her eyes, she saw that the men had left; the foreshore was empty and the sun was going down, its rays sending a path almost to her feet. She could still feel the battering of the waves on her body; they still crashed down but beyond their white crests the sea was calm, deep blue. Then the sun went behind the horizon, the gold lingered and was gone. The heat haze from the water rose in a mist over the waves; by contrast, a chill little wind blew over the sand.

It was twilight, the Indian short twilight, 'cow-dust time' Krishnan had called it, and Mary remembered what she had seen from the train, cattle being driven home, dust rising from their hoofs, patient cows, lumbering oxen and buffaloes while smoke rose from the cooking fires among the huts of the villages. As she looked now at the bungalow, lights were up on the verandah: Thambi must have switched them on as he went to his gatehouse, as he had the lanterns along the path.

Why is twilight always a melancholy time? wondered Mary. She listened, there was no sound of a drum. Along the beach no small lamps burned before the shrines. Paradise was dark, everything was in abeyance though probably the disciples were in Ghandara or in other countless voting places getting ready for tomorrow. Probably Krishnan too. That's why the grove is dark and the thought dawned poignantly, I shan't see Krishnan again and, in desolation, I suppose I must – *must* go in and dress, have some dinner – though she wanted neither. She got up and picked up her towel. Thambi or Moses would put down the umbrella when they drew out the fencing along the foreshore. As, reluctantly, she walked towards the bungalow, more lights came on in the other half and she saw Thambi putting down luggage, Hannah drawing the curtains. Olga Manning was there.

'You *have* come back,' Mary said in the doorway and before she could stop herself, 'Auntie Sanni and Hannah thought you mightn't.'

'There was nowhere else to go.'

At once Mary's own unhappiness dwindled into an ordinary everyday trouble, this was tragic. Olga's usually erect figure was bowed. Still in her travelling clothes she was making no effort to unpack or change but sat at the room's solitary table looking out at the darkening sea. Under the electric light her skin looked bruised; her hair had come undone, its coil was tumbling down her back; her hands were dirty.

'Olga, is there anything I can do?'

'Please, Mary, I can't talk to you now.' The deep voice was a hoarse whisper.

Mary went next door. Blaise was in the bathroom. Fresh whisky had been put in their bar. She measured a large one, added more, took the tumbler round the partition and put it quietly on the table.

'Bless you.'

'Would you like . . .' Mary ventured, 'like me to get Samuel to send your dinner down here?'

'My dinner!' Olga laughed. 'I don't think I can say "my dinner" any longer but I suppose one must eat while one can,' and seeing Mary's concern, 'No, Mary darling. I shall change and come up as usual.'

For dinner the dining room was full. Dr Coomaraswamy and Mr Srinivasan were eating less hurriedly than usual. 'I have only two speeches to write,' Dr Coomaraswamy had said and Mr Srinivasan, 'A success speech and a loss speech – just in case.' 'Victory! Victory!' Dr Coomaraswamy had let himself write but, 'Victory is not yet,' said cautious Mr Srinivasan.

Auntie Sanni and the Colonel and Mr Menzies were at their accustomed tables. Olga Manning had appeared, groomed, clean, changed, to Mary's relief and had gone unobtrusively to hers, only nodding to Auntie Sanni; Blaise and Mary were dining with the Fishers, 'As it's our last night.' Mary did not contradict him. At least it means I needn't talk to him.

The diners were augmented by a dinner party of men. 'From Ghandara,' Sir John told them. 'Here for some kind of conference.' It seemed to be a festive meeting; there was laughter, even cheers as Kuku, in the beautiful violet-coloured silk sari Lady Fisher had given her, flitted round them. Dr Coomaraswamy kept his eye on his plate as the banter filled the room.

Suddenly it ceased. 'This is All India Radio. Here is the news.' There was absolute attention. 'I expect there'll be something about their meeting,' whispered Blaise as the news began but first was the election.

'In Konak, expectancy is tense on this day before voting as interest mounts in the struggle between the long-established Mrs Padmina Retty and Krishnan Bhanj's new Root and Flower Party. In spite of Mrs Retty's helicopter, all yesterday it was Krishnan Bhanj who drew the crowds. In fact today he has had to hide himself to avoid the charge of illegally campaigning. "He campaigns in spite of himself," said Dr Coomaraswamy, leader of this brilliant concept. Here are a few words from Dr Coomaraswamy himself . . .'

As his words boomed out, Dr Coomaraswamy kept his head bowed while the whole room listened. Samuel had interrupted the serving; he and the waiters stood respectfully still. Only Kuku moved and flaunted. When the voice finished everybody clapped.

The news, though, was not finished: 'Today in Calcutta, Mr Justice Rajan sentenced the Englishman, Colin Armstrong, to twelve years' imprisonment. Mr Armstrong was convicted of fraud, smuggling and trafficking in drugs.'

At an imperative nod from Colonel McIndoe, Samuel switched off the radio. At the same moment Mr Menzies got up and crossed the dining room to Olga Manning's table. 'Good evening, Mrs Armstrong,' he said.

A gasp went from table to table. The whole dinner party had turned to look. Mary sprang up but Blaise pulled her down as Auntie Sanni rose to her massive height. Her dress billowing, she, too, crossed the room. 'Mr Menzies,' she said, 'you will leave my hotel, *now*.'

'Of course you knew he was Ajax?'

'I'm afraid I didn't.' Blaise blushed.

'No? I should have thought those recordings, those articles were unmistakable.'

'Auntie Sanni knew from the beginning,' Lady Fisher had pleasure in saying.

'Then why didn't she turn him out before?'

'He was being very useful,' said Sir John, 'bolstering our election. Auntie Sanni, remember, is a dear friend of the Bhanj family and Menzies could hardly have been more helpful but tonight . . . Swine!' said Sir John.

'After all this distress and unpleasantness,' Blaise said a little later, 'what I feel like is a game of bridge.'

'Sensible idea,' Sir John stopped walking up and down. 'But we haven't a four.'

'Mary,' said Blaise, 'it's time you learnt to play.'

'You know I hate cards.' She was seething with – she sensed unreasonable – anger and indignation. 'If you're uncomfortable about anything, play cards!'

'There is nothing we can do for Mrs Manning,' Sir John told her gently, 'She has gone with Auntie Sanni so she's in good hands.'

That was part of the dismay. There would be no chance now of talking to Auntie Sanni. So I'm trapped, thought Mary, trapped.

'McIndoe might play,' Sir John was saying. 'He sometimes does. I'll ask him.'

The Colonel got up, willingly Mary thought. I expect he, too, wants to put this out of his mind. Kuku brought the card table, fresh packs of cards, score pads and stood by while they sat down, her eyes fixed on Blaise as Lady Fisher dealt.

Mary had thought of asking Sir John to intercede with Blaise; now she remembered vividly how once Lady Fisher had – gently, it was true – remonstrated with her when she, Mary, had gone to the bazaar instead of the Dawn Temple, 'As Blaise so wanted you to do,' and she had retorted, 'I've been doing what Blaise wanted for three whole weeks. Can't I have anything for myself?'

No sympathy, instead, 'Diplomats have to keep a certain position,' Lady Fisher had not said 'prestige'. 'Their wives, in a way, have to be diplomats too, even if it means tremendous self-sacrifice. I did it, your mother did it, so why not you?'

It would be no use talking to either Fisher – and a surge of frustration filled Mary, made worse when, 'Mary,' said Lady Fisher, 'come and talk to us when one of us is dummy.' 'Good God, *no*!' Mary wanted to scream but succeeded in only shaking her head. She stood up and put on Blaise's jacket. 'I think I'll go to bed. I'm chilly and tired.' Yes, go to bed, put her head under the sheet and shut out everything, everyone and never care about anything ever again.

As she stood up on the path, the shadowed garden seemed dark and empty, the lanterns on the path dim. Only the lights on Patna Hall's verandah were bright, shining down on the four heads bent over the green table. Bridge! thought Mary furiously.

A waft of sweetness came to her. Who was it who had once told her that flowers can send you a message? The scent was queen of the night, with its small scented flowers. Carnations? Roses? I know what I can do, thought Mary. I'll pick a bunch of flowers to put in Olga's room, with some more whisky. That will show her at least *someone* cares about her. In the pocket of Blaise's jacket was a small mother-of-pearl-handled penknife; she took it out. Cutting stems along the borders was soothing, laying one flower against another, sniffing the fragrance; the storm in her mind began to lull, and, though she could not exactly remember the words, she began to hum that Hindi lullaby . . .

> 'A cradle of . . .
> A cord of silk . . .
> Come, little moonbird . . .'

When she had cut enough she went, softly singing, down the path. 'All right, Slippers,' she called, 'I'm coming.' She had his sugar and carrots in her handkerchief.

He whickered back.

'Tsst.'

A small boy stepped out of the shadows. Mary knew him; he was one of the boys she had made garlands with. True, he had tormented the squirrel but he was smaller than the others and had attached himself to her, hanging all day yesterday around the lorry. Now he held out a paper to her, thin Indian paper folded. She recognised Krishnan's writing and her heart began to beat quickly as she took the paper to the nearest lantern to read.

'Mary, can you come and help me? I am alone.'

'Krishnan Sahib. Where is Krishnan Sahib?'

The boy pointed along the beach.

He's here! In the grove! A surge of happiness rose in Mary but she looked towards the verandah.

'*Kachiyundu*,' she said to the boy as Krishnan had said at the temple to Birdie, '*kachiyundu*. Wait,' and gestured that she would give him money.

Forsaking Slippers she ran to the bungalow, left his sugar on the chest of drawers, quickly arranged the flowers in a vase, carried them and a glass of whisky to Olga's room then wrote on the back of the paper 'For Blaise. You see I *have* been asked!' In the pocket of his jacket she found some change and, taking a rupee, she hung the jacket on the back of a chair – she was no longer chill. Tingling with warmth, she ran back to the boy. 'Take this,' she gave him the paper, 'take,' she pointed to the lit verandah. 'For Sahib.' She held up the rupee.

The boy's eyes gleamed as he saw it. He nodded, took the rupee and the note and set off up the path. Mary watched him then, 'Stay,' she said to the disappointed Slippers, 'I can't stop now,' and ran to the beach.

She did not see a bigger boy, wearing a yellow shirt, leap out of the bushes and jump on the smaller one, screwing the rupee out of his hand and beating him until he fled.

For a moment the boy in the yellow shirt scrutinised the note, crumpled it and let it drop as he set off after Mary.

The note lay on the side of the path.

Mary did not have to go as far as the grove. From a distance, across the stretch of moonlit sand, she saw what first seemed to be a dark rock in the froth and whiteness of the waves' edges. It can't be a rock, she thought, this beach doesn't have rocks. Then, as she came nearer, she could see a figure standing on it, a dark-skinned figure wearing only a loincloth. As she looked, something like a thick snake came up – A sea monster, thought Mary for a horrified moment, or no, a hose, as a spray of water was sent up into the air then fell, deluging the figure. '*Ayyo!*' came a furious voice. '*Mösāgadu! Pishācha mu!* Bad girl! Devil!'

It was Krishnan. He saw Mary and came to meet her, streaming with water, his hair in wet streaks.

'I thought you were hidden at Ghandara, or are you your double?'

173

'In a way, yes. Sharma is there. But come, we are wasting time.'

As he spoke the rock stood up – an elephant, Birdie.

Mary stared. 'What *has* happened to her?'

'You may well ask. Idiots! Idiots!' It was the first time Mary had seen Krishnan angry.

Birdie had been painted – Decorated? thought Mary – her forehead and trunk, her sides and legs bedizened with patterns in yellow, vermilion, indigo, black and white; her ears were patterned as was the length of her trunk. 'Idiots!' cried Krishnan again. 'They have spoiled everything.'

'Spoiled what?' Mary had to ask.

'Tomorrow, election day is crucial – you know that.' She nodded. 'All parties will go each in their procession through Ghandara ending at the town hall; the candidate from Madras, Gopal Rau, of whom no one seems to have heard, Mrs Retty and us. Gopal Rau will not have much, Padmina will have everything, a great *tamasha* – razzmatazz, bands, military, maybe even a tank, loudspeakers. She has a white jeep but probably she'll arrive in her aeroplane.'

'And you?'

'We shall have nothing.'

'*Nothing?*'

'Let Padmina have the blare, we shall be dulcet.' Krishnan lingered on the word; he had recovered himself. 'Fortunately, she has chosen to go first, then poor Rau, so we shall be last which is propitious. The last will be first.' He laughed. 'In front will walk our young men and women, the men all in white, feet bare – they will be making *namaskar* – the girls in our colours, muslin saris, simple, hair coiled with flowers, they will be leading garlanded cows—'

'The *gopis*,' said Mary.

'Exactly. For weeks we have been fattening them and grooming them – the cows not the girls. Then will come

174

children; we have chosen the healthiest, again a little plump. The boys will have garlands and carry paper kites, again in our colours; the little girls will have baskets of flowers to scatter, constantly replenished,' he sounded as if he were Dr Coomaraswamy. 'They will sing. For other music there will be only the conch, drums, a single flute. I think there will be silence to hear it. We must leave room for reverence.

'Then will come my friend the priest from Agni's temple, wearing a saffron robe with his beads, his staff – he is of height but not the height of me. He will lead a sacred bull. Then I shall come, not in regalia or paint as the god Krishna but as I, myself' – and he said, 'I sound like Coomaraswamy – not wearing a best English suit but, like my people, a loincloth, walking in the dust . . . little Udata on my shoulder.'

'If she'll stay.'

'She'll stay. I, not riding on an elephant but humbly leading her, she to be carrying her fodder on her own back.' The fury returned. 'To decorate an elephant takes two, three days and we must wash it off tonight – the *mahout* is too drunk to help. To call the village or fishermen would be publicity, take away surprise. Look, I am scrubbing Birdie's sides, legs and feet with sand and a brick. That is too heavy work for you but could you do her face and ears? I went to the Hall and borrowed scrubbing brushes – but be careful, her ears may flap you.'

'Won't Birdie mind?'

'She adores it, all elephants love their bath and she is accustomed. She does, though, get playful – watch her trunk. When you come to do her trunk stand astride it so that if she lifts it you will only tumble into the wash of the sea, but you will be soaked as I am. Better take off your dress,' and, suddenly formal, he said, 'Mrs Browne, it is most good of you to come.'

'Browne with an e.' Mary felt suddenly impish.

'Browne with an e,' said Krishnan and laughed again. 'Oh, how I like you, Mary. I like you very much. See, my temper has gone.' Suddenly, too, he leapt and danced across the beach, did handstands, then, 'That's enough. Come to work.'

'Is Mary with you?' Blaise was standing at Olga Manning's door.

The game of bridge had petered out as soon as Auntie Sanni came out alone on the verandah. Colonel McIndoe immediately laid down his cards with an apology, got up, went with her to the swing couch and sat down beside her. Sir John and Lady Fisher followed them, leaving Blaise at the table; he shuffled the cards, put them into neat packs, stood a moment looking over to the now moonlit beach. Then, 'I had better go down to Mary,' he said, and to Auntie Sanni, he began, 'I know I booked for a week but . . .'

'You will not be charged for the extra day.' Auntie Sanni cut him short.

'Well, goodnight.'

Talking in low tones, their faces grave, they hardly noticed him go.

At the bungalow steps Slippers was patiently waiting, he was missing Mary and, 'Where is my ritual of carrots and sugar?' he was patently saying. He whickered at Blaise who only said, 'Shoo,' then waved his arms, advancing so threateningly that the little donkey shied away.

'Merry, where are you?'

No answer.

'Mary.'

The room was empty, the shutters wide open, the bathroom empty too; the bedsheets were folded back, his *lunghi* and Mary's short nightdress laid out in Hannah's way.

'Is Mary with you?'

176

Olga Manning came to her door. She was wearing a faded kimono, her hair hanging down her back; even Blaise noticed the tiredness of her face and was moved to say, 'Rotten about your husband.'

She flared. 'It isn't rotten. It never was. Colin did not do that. He was framed.' She put her hand to her throat as if it choked her to speak. 'Better not talk about it. No, I haven't seen Mary.'

'Didn't she come to the bungalow?'

'Not that I know of,' and Olga offered, 'She goes to the grove.'

'I know but they're all at Ghandara.'

'Krishnan Bhanj isn't. I met him in the hotel garden as I came down.'

'Krishnan Bhanj?'

'Yes,' and innocently Olga said, 'Perhaps she has gone to see him.'

It was Blaise's turn to flare. 'Then she has broken her promise.' He stopped and his own innate honesty made him say, 'Yet I'm sure Mary wouldn't do that.' Then the seeds Mr Menzies had sown began to grow. 'Or would she? It seems she will do anything,' and bitterness burst out. 'We haven't been married a month. You'd think she could be faithful for just a month, and with an *Indian*. All right,' he shouted. 'All right!'

He strode across the verandah on to the beach.

'Phew!' Krishnan stood up, wiping the sweat and salt water off his face with his hand. 'There seems to be a mighty lot of elephant.'

The paint had lodged in the cracks of the coarse grained scaly skin. 'They must have put oil in the tempera,' said Krishnan. Both he and Mary were stained with the yellow, vermilion and blue; the black had got under Mary's nails; only the white came off in flakes.

'I should have thought the fisherboys would have loved

177

to help.' She rested: after a fierce bout of scrubbing her arms ached.

'They would but they would have talked.'

'How did you get rid of them?'

'Told them to go.' His look seemed to say, 'How else?'

'It's odd,' Mary put back a wet strand of her hair, staining it red, 'when you tell someone to do something, they obey and want to do it.' She was thinking aloud. 'When Blaise tells them, they don't – and won't. Why?'

'Because Blaise Sahib is Blaise Sahib and Krishnan is Krishnan. There is no other explanation. There never is,' said Krishnan.

A voice came from the beach. 'Mary. Mary. Where are you? Come back at once.'

Blaise!

He came bearing down on them, with a splat of wood – the piece of flotsam they had used in rounders last night – in his hand. 'Mary!' The shout was so loud that Birdie surged to her feet. Blaise stopped and gaped. 'What in hell are you doing?'

'As you see, giving an elephant a bath,' Krishnan said equably.

'Giving an elephant a bath? What tomfoolery is this?'

'It is anything but tomfoolery. For reasons I have no time to explain, it is imperative she is bathed,' and, 'Ūrakundu,' Krishnan ordered Birdie, 'ūrakundu – Lie down.'

'In any case I was not speaking to you,' said angry Blaise. 'I have come to fetch my wife. Do you hear?'

'Then you are speaking to me.'

'Yes.'

'Ask her if she wants to go,' Krishnan said between scouring – Birdie was recumbent again. 'Better stand back if you, too, don't want to be soaked.'

'Mary, *will* you come?'

'I can't. An elephant has two ears, and I have only finished one.'

Blaise turned on Krishnan. 'I also came to have this out with you. Come on.' He brandished the splat of wood.

'My dear man, I'm far too busy to fight with you just now,' said Krishnan. 'Why not forget it, get a brick – there's a pile over there – and help us?'

The hand holding the wood dropped as if Blaise were bemused. Mary again felt that pang of pity. 'Yes, Bumble, be a sport' – she knew that word would appeal to him. 'Join in. There's nothing to be cross about.'

'Nothing to be cross about! I'm not a fool. Do you think I don't know what's been going on?' Astonished they stood up though Krishnan kept a quiescent hand on Birdie. 'Look at you,' screamed Blaise, 'both half naked and soon you'll be more naked from what I hear. I'm not going to have it,' and he advanced on Mary with his splat.

'Don't do that,' Krishnan warned him. 'You won't want to have done that.'

'Out of my way,' and Blaise came on.

With one leap Krishnan was off Birdie, caught Blaise and, with a twist, sent him spinning down on to his back on the sand; next moment Krishnan had lifted him and set him on his feet. 'Go back to the Hall,' Krishnan said sternly. 'Mary will doubtless come when we are finished.'

'*We!* You impertinent bastard.'

'I am not impertinent and I am not a bastard and I don t want to have to knock you down again,' said Krishnan. 'Please go so that we can get on with the work – the little elephant is getting tired and hungry.'

'I'm not one of your sycophants', ranted Blaise, 'to do what I'm told. Do you think I don't know all about you pseudo Krishnas? We have them in England too. You with your young girls and boys, your slaves.'

Krishnan took no notice but worked on with his brick.

'Mary!' It was a bellow now. 'I'll give you one more

179

chance. Come now or don't come at all. Which? *Which?*'
Mary did not answer; she, too, went on scrubbing, this
time on Birdie's second ear.

For a moment Blaise stood irresolute in his anger,
then before turning, he spat.

'*Blaise* spat!' Mary sat back on her heels amazed.

'Being an Indian I can spit further than you,' Krishnan
called after him. 'Naturally. We have had centuries of
practice.'

Even Krishnan did not see a small yellow-clad figure
come out from behind the nearest casuarina tree and take
itself quickly to the road where a red car was waiting.

Blaise heard the noise before he came into the bedroom,
heavy hoofs clopping about on stone. Seeing him gone,
Slippers had dared to come into the bedroom, seeking the
sugar he thought was his due. He had knocked over the
photograph of Blaise's mother that stood on the dressing
table, breaking the glass; nuzzled brushes, combs, creams
and lotions off on to the floor and now, having found
on the chest of drawers the sugar Mary had left, was
munching contentedly when Blaise switched on the light.
At the sight of him, Slippers gave the equivalent of a
donkey scream, a bray.

'What are you doing here, you little brute?' and, seeing
the devastation, all Blaise's thwarted anger broke. 'Take
that and that,' the splat of wood came down again and
again. '*Chelo. Jao.* Go. Go. *Hut jao.* Go at once. *Chelo.
Chelo.* Hurry up.' But Slippers could not go. In panic,
slithering on the floor, trying to get away, he had penned
himself behind the bed. The little donkey's ears were laid
back, his eyes rolled but he could not move. '*Hut jao!*'
There was a sudden stench: a flux of liquid dung spattered
on to the floor. 'Christ! Phewgh!' screamed Blaise.

'He couldn't help it.' Olga Manning had come in.

'You drove him behind the bed. Here, help me push it and let him out,' and, to the miserable donkey, 'Here, boy, gently, boy. Come. Come.' Trembling, guided by her hand, Slippers back-clopped out and fled. They heard him slipping on the verandah then crash down the steps.

'You deserved that,' Olga said to Blaise. 'I'm glad he did it. Just because you can't juggernaut over your very nice wife, you take it out on an animal. You big bully.'

'Go away and mind your own business!' Blaise exploded. 'A dirty business it is from what I hear, dirty, no matter what you say. Go!'

'With pleasure,' said Olga. 'You can clear up the mess.'

Kuku answered the house telephone – she had an extension in her room. 'What? *What?* My God, how disgusting! I am coming down. Go on to the verandah and we shall come. I am bringing the sweeper women, hot water, disinfectants.'

The explosions had done good and Blaise was calmer now. 'I'm sorry to have disturbed you.'

'You didn't disturb me in the least,' but Kuku was in a thin wrapper dressing gown; the two sweepers, roused from sleep for the second time that day, were grumbling under their breaths.

'I'm afraid I did disturb you but donkey shit is no joke.'

'Certainly it is not. I shall speak firmly to Miss Sanni in the morning. As for disturbing, that is what I am here for. Now, while the women are finishing, let me straighten the bed.'

As she bent forward, the dark hair brushed the side of the bed where Blaise's *lunghi* was laid; as she carefully smoothed it, her wrapper swung open showing the rounded brown body, the perfect small breasts, rose-tipped nipples. Modestly Kuku caught the wrapper together, glanced up at Blaise and laughed.

Blaise had not looked, really looked, at Kuku before, taking her almost as part of the hotel furniture and not far removed from Samuel and Hannah though he had thought her saris a little flaunting. 'Showing off,' he would have said.

Now he was struck with her beauty, provocative beauty: the small roguish face set in the mane of black hair, eyes brilliant – and knowing – below expressive eyebrows and, when she looked down, as she met his gaze, he saw the long lashes that had so entranced Dr Coomaraswamy. Kuku's mouth was slightly pouted, she had a small tip-tilted nose, small pretty teeth. When she stood up, supple in every movement, and tightened the wrapper round her, Blaise could see through it even to the fuzz of hair between her thighs; it was dark brown not black; at once he felt an answering movement in himself. 'I suppose I've been starved,' he almost said aloud, pitying himself.

'Now that the sweepers have gone, let me get you a drink.' With her gliding undulating walk, Kuku went to the small bar. 'You were so-o distressed,' she crooned.

'Well, donkey shit on your bedroom floor.' Blaise tried to be normal.

'Disgusting!' She brought him the glass. 'I have put ice in it.'

'You deserve one.'

Kuku's eyes shone but, 'Auntie Sanni doesn't let me drink.'

'Just for me,' said Blaise and she poured a small one.

'And give me another,' he said.

She brought it. Now she was so close he could smell her scent and sweat, as the Doctor had done; as he took the glass her fingers touched his; he let them tighten.

'Kuku is a beautiful name.'

She shrugged. 'One gets tired of it. "Kuku do this.

182

Kuku do that." Day in, day out. I am an orphan, you know. I cannot do what I want.'

'What do you want, Kuku?'

She looked up at him. 'You,' breathed Kuku. The worship in her eyes was balm to his soreness. 'I have loved you from the first moment I saw you,' she whispered. 'These people are all blind. They do not know what you are.' This was balm too. 'Your little silly Mary thinks she has found a god in that Krishnan. I know when I have found mine.'

The two heads, black and gold were together on one pillow; the sheet, thrown back, showed brown and pale legs closely entwined. Kuku's hand again and again caressed while his played with a strand of her hair. 'Kiss me, a long, long kiss,' and, 'Love me again,' pleaded Kuku.

'No more.' Blaise was sleepy.

'One more.' She bit him on the ear, raising a spot of blood. 'I'm a tiger.' A shrill squeal of laughter.

'You're a mosquito.' Another shriek as he rolled over on her again.

'No! No!' squealed Kuku.

'You asked for it . . .'

'Well. Well. Well.' Once again it was Olga Manning. 'You'd think', she mocked, 'he could be faithful for one month – and with an Indian.'

An outraged shriek came from Kuku as, startled, she snatched her wrapper and ran to the bathroom. Blaise, caught mid-way in the act, looked up as dampness spread round him.

'I'm sorry I interrupted you', Olga was contemptuous, 'but I couldn't think what the noise was. Well,' she said again, 'you've done it now.'

'Have I? Did I?' He sounded dazed. Then, as he looked round the room, the floor still wet where the sweepers had washed it, his clothes flung down on it, and smelled disinfectant mingled with the jasmine scent on his pillow, realisation came back, realisation and disgust. 'To hell with all women,' shouted Blaise. He caught up a towel, pushed past Olga in the doorway and out on to the beach.

'That was the last I saw of him,' Olga Armstrong was to say.

It was beginning to be dawn, the sky paling over the sea as Krishnan at last led a clean and shining Birdie out of the waves; not a speck of paint was left on her as she stood, flapping her ears to dry them, lifting her trunk in happiness to spray herself again. 'She did not like the paint either,' said Krishnan as he took her up the beach. 'Now she must have a good feed. I have sugar cane, *gram* and *jaggery* balls which she loves.' Mary followed them wringing the water out of her slip. She was so tired she staggered.

'For us I will make some tea. You must take off your wet things. Here, dry yourself with this.' He threw her a towel.

As Birdie contentedly ate, breaking up the cane with her foot and trunk, picking up the balls and stuffing them into her mouth, Krishnan put the remains of the fire together, poking it with a stick, throwing on pieces of wood. He had lit a small methylated stove, incongruous in that setting, but soon a pan of water was boiling and he threw in tea leaves. Mary, unaccountably shivering, was glad of the fire, even more glad when Krishnan handed her a bowl of strong sweet tea. She had pulled on her dress, hung her slip and briefs on a bush to dry.

'A little rice?'

She shook her head. 'I had dinner.'

'More than I had.' The rice had been left cold. Krishnan warmed it, mixed it with dried fish, and soon was scooping it up with his fingers. Again she saw how white and even his teeth were.

'I think,' he said, 'it would be better if you did not go back to your husband tonight.'

184

'I don't think I could.'

'The question is, what to do with you? All Patna Hall will be asleep and we don't want to cause a stir. If I made you comfortable, here in the grove, would you be afraid?'

'I'm too tired to be afraid.'

'True. You're half asleep,' but, 'Where will you be?' she asked, all at once awake.

'Udata and I have to ride Birdie to Ghandara. I dare not trust Birdie to her *mahout* and his people. They might try to paint her all over again.' He laughed.

'Krishnan, are you ever tired?'

'Not when I cannot be.' He got up. 'Here is a clean *lunghi*. Sleep in that.'

He arranged a bed for her on the deerskins, taking quilts and pillows from the throne. Mary lay down, the *lunghi* round her. Krishnan tucked its end in, Indian fashion. 'Your hair will dry. Sleep.'

But, 'Krishnan, what about Blaise?' she asked. 'Is it my fault? Why is there all this trouble?' and Krishnan answered as he had answered before, 'Because you are you and Blaise is Blaise. The two don't mix.'

'Then what am I to do? How can we live together?'

'You will get older,' said Krishnan. 'So will he. I don't think he can change but you will learn how to live with him – and not mix – as many wives do, the wise ones. Indian women, I think, are particularly wise in this: they know how not to mix yet never let their husbands guess it.'

'Must I?' asked Mary.

His hand closed over hers; she could have stayed with that warm clasp for ever.

'There are destinies,' Krishnan said. 'Yours and mine. But don't think of that tonight. Go to sleep.'

He took his hand away, touched her hair and left. She heard him call to Birdie, then a rustling as they went through the trees.

Friday

Mary was woken by the parakeets. A pair was quarrelling in a tree overhead, their bright green flashing between the dark-leaved mango branches, their red beaks chattering as they made their raucous cries. Perhaps they're husband and wife, thought Mary smiling – Blaise and me – then ceased to smile as she remembered the angry words on the beach. Krishnan did his best, even when he had to interfere. Mary thought Blaise would really have hit her; He slapped me before. She shut her eyes trying to keep thoughts of Blaise out of the way. This is Krishnan's day, his vital day. She thought of him riding Birdie away last night, through the dark – with Udata, of course; Birdie would be docile. Docile, dulcet, there was a sweetness about those words; with Krishnan everything, everyone became docile – even me, thought Mary and, Yes, I must go back.

When she sat up she found she had been showered with scarlet petals, the *simile* trees were dropping their cotton flowers. In one week they are going over, thought Mary and realisation came to her – Today we go away too. She could not believe it, the very thought brought such a feeling of emptiness that she hurriedly put it out of her mind. 'Don't think about it yet,' she told herself. Instead, 'Today is the election.'

Krishnan will win, thought Mary. He couldn't not, yet the sceptical voices intervened: 'Of all the way-out notions.' 'The man's mad!' 'Masquerading as a god.' Krishnan himself had told her, 'It will be tricky.' Mary

186

picked up a cotton flower that had fallen without breaking and began to pick off the petals. 'He will win. He won't. He will. He won't.' Yet knowing, as the scarlet petals fell over her feet, they would end, 'He will.'

'But I', she whispered, 'have to go back to Blaise.'

'Must I?' she had asked Krishnan.

'I think you must.'

If I can, thought Mary. I . . . I have to get over myself first. I can. She picked up another flower. 'You can. You can't. You can.' Mary sat looking at the sepals of the flower, bare now that the brilliantly coloured petals had gone all but one. She pulled it. 'You can't,' it said.

'The elephant was decorated especially and at great cost for the pomp,' pleaded Dr Coomaraswamy.

'I had told you, *ordered* you.' The campaign was over. Krishnan could speak. 'There will be no pomp.'

A bitter scene was going on in the Ghandara headquarters between Krishnan and Dr Coomaraswamy.

'You have undone the elephant,' the Doctor almost screamed. 'After such work! Such cost!'

'Against express orders.' When Krishnan was cool, it meant he was angry.

'*I* am the director of this campaign,' Dr Coomaraswamy blustered.

'He is the director,' Mr Srinivasan echoed.

'And I am the campaign.'

'True. True,' said Mr Srinivasan, 'but— '

'There is no but. Everything is to be carried out exactly as I said.'

'Krishnan, think. I beg you to think. This is *the* day. The crucial day.'

'Then this is all the more crucial.'

'Surely it is time for a little display? True, you have brought the people out marvellously . . .'

'Most marvellously,' piped faithful Srinivasan.

'They will be disappointed.'

'Far more disappointed if I renege.'

'Renege?'

'Destroy my image, which is what you would have me do. *Stupidity!*' cried Krishnan.

'I do not like stupidity.' Dr Coomaraswamy drew himself up.

'Then don't be it. Can't you *see*?' asked Krishnan.

'I see that Padmina Retty will come with a great splash, aeroplane, bands, decorations – maybe *decorated* elephants – horses, parade.'

'Yes, and you will ask her, demand of her, to tell you, in public, then and there, what it cost. You will say to the crowd, "Ask your Mother Padmina what it cost" – "Mother" will be mockery. "Ask her what it cost and who will pay."' Krishnan stood up, his eyes flashing. ' "Who pays? Not your mother. Not any Retty. Oh, no! Then who? You," ' stormed Krishnan. ' "You, the people. Ask her how many of the *pice* you have been allowed to earn with your toil, your poor tools, have gone into her pocket. Or the pockets of her aides who talk to you so sweetly. Oh, yes! They hold out a hand to you, sweetly, sweetly, while the other hand is robbing you." '

'Then ask, "What is the cost of Krishnan Bhanj? Nothing. He asks nothing. Not one *pice* do you have to pay. He himself takes nothing. His followers take nothing. He gives and so people give gladly to him. Brothers and sisters, give him your votes." That is what you will say,' said Krishnan.

'But . . . I have already ordered two bands.'

'Then you can pay them yourself or tell them to go away.'

'I have hired horses. Already they are caparisoned.'

'Then uncaparison them.'

'Boy and girl scouts.'

'Boy and girl scouts I don't mind.'

'He doesn't mind boy and girl scouts.' Mr Srinivasan was thankful.

'Yes, that is a good idea – but – scouts? *Are* there any in Konak?'

'In truth, no,' and Dr Coomaraswamy had to admit, 'I have had to buy uniforms.'

'The children can keep the uniforms. They will be delighted but wear them they will not, *will not*,' repeated Krishnan severely, 'for the procession. If anything is not in truth, then no. This political campaign, unlike all other political campaigns, must be in truth. Absolute truth. Nothing else will I have.'

'Then it will be disaster.'

'Then it will be success.'

Mary sang as she went along the shore. Singing! I oughtn't to be singing. I have to make peace, at least a sort of peace, with Blaise. I'll try – though it seems unlikely, thought Mary. Yet still she sang:

> 'Early one morning,
> Just as the sun was rising,
> I heard a pretty maiden in the valley below:
> Oh, never leave me,
> Oh, don't deceive me.
> How could you use a poor maiden so?'

She laughed as she picked up a piece of seaweed with her toes and cast it back into the sea.

There were no boats on the shore; the fishermen must have gone out early; it was, as well, too early for people to come down to the beach. The dawn was rosy – she thought of Usas the Dawn Goddess, daughter of the sky, sister of night. There was a pink light over the sea, pale tender pink, giving no inkling of the heat that was to come. Yes, it will be hot, thought Mary, hard for the people who have to walk in the processions.

She would have liked to have gone up to the Hall to see if she could find Hannah and ask her for some earlier-than-normal early tea but first she had to make herself respectable. I need a bath. The stains of colour would be difficult to wash off. I wonder if it's too early to ring the house for hot water. I could telephone quietly so as not to wake Blaise. I must look an apparition. I need to wash my hair too.

Her bare feet made no sound on the verandah; the shutters were open; a half door swung in the sea breeze. Mary stepped inside and stood puzzled.

There was no one in the room; the bed was oddly rumpled, its pillows cast aside. There was, too, an odd smell; strong disinfectant but with it, or under it, a stink, thought Mary, wrinkling up her nose . . . something that reminded her of the smell that hung about stables.

Coming further in, she saw Blaise's clothes lying in a crumpled heap at the foot of the bed. Perhaps he had wanted a swim to cool himself off after the quarrel . . . but his bathing trunks, put to dry, still hung on the verandah rail.

Did he change to go up to the Hall? But why change? He didn't get wet. Was he so angry that he had determined to leave Patna Hall at once and gone up to order a taxi? She looked through his clothes; they were all there. He wouldn't have gone up to the Hall naked. Besides, wouldn't he have packed? She couldn't imagine Blaise leaving his possessions behind. Then where is he? wondered Mary.

She looked at the partition. Shall I ask Olga? But there was no sound from her rooms. She looked so tired and unhappy last night she should sleep, and Mary quietly went out. 'Blaise, Blaise,' she called along the beach. 'Blaise.' The sound came back to her from emptiness.

It was then that she heard a whickering, not a pleased sound but a whickering of distress: Slippers came out of the bushes and with him the stench she had smelled in the bedroom but stronger. He was limping, worse than limping, lurching as he tried to move; one foot was dragging and Mary saw the fetlock was swollen, the pitiable hoof was on its side. Slippers was shaking in violent spasms. His sides were smeared with dung and there were marks on his neck – Blaise with the heel of his shoe again! Mary, too, was shaking but with fury. He had hit Slippers on the eyes as well: one was swollen and bleeding; there was blood on his nose. 'Horrible,' cried Mary aloud. 'Horrible! Blaise must have found you in the bedroom again,' she cried to Slippers. 'Oh, why did you go in?' and then she knew. 'You were looking for your sugar because I forgot to give it to you. It's *I* who am horrible.' She buried her face in Slippers's furry neck. 'He drove you off the verandah too quickly and you have broken your poor foot. Stay there,' Mary ordered him. 'Don't try to move. Stay.'

She tore up the path; the house was silent, shuttered. How odd! People come for the sea breezes and sleep with their shutters closed, but at the gatehouse she found Thambi, squatting on his haunches, beginning to blow up a small fire for the lazy Shyama.

'Thambi! Thambi!'

Thambi rose to his feet at this frantic apparition.

'Thambi – Slippers – donkey – hurt, very hurt. Get vet. Vet-er-in-a-rian animal doctor. Animal hurt. Doctor. Quick.'

Thambi, always intelligent, understood. 'Animal hurt,' but doctor seemed to him strange. Donkeys, to Thambi, were neither here nor there, a means of transport, bearers of burdens. He, Samuel and Hannah had often deplored Auntie Sanni's keeping of Slippers. The donkey did not matter but Mary's distress did. 'I come,' said Thambi. 'First I call Miss Sanni.'

191

'The vet. The vet,' Mary was still saying it hysterically as she stood by Slippers.

'There is no use for the vet,' and Auntie Sanni said words in Telegu to Thambi who ran to the house.

Auntie Sanni's nightclothes looked no different from her dresses; she had come down the path billowing and calm. Gently she spoke to Slippers, touching the bloody marks on his head and eye, only her mouth had tightened, the sea-green of her eyes grown dark. Gently she had felt down his leg to the broken fetlock and had shaken her head. 'The bone is fragmented. See, bits are through the skin. He has made it worse by dragging it. Besides the hoof is too heavy for it to mend. Poor donkey,' she said. 'Why wouldn't you let us . . . ?' Then to Mary, 'Colonel McIndoe will come.'

'Colonel McIndoe!'

'He is firm and quick,' said Auntie Sanni. 'Mary, go inside.'

White to the lips, Mary said, 'I'm not a child, Auntie Sanni, I'll stay.'

The shot rang out to the hills and echoed back. 'Better go to Mr Browne,' Auntie Sanni told Mary. 'This will startle him.'

Mary stood up from where she had knelt by Slippers, stretched prone now on the sand. Her tears had fallen on his fur.

'No more pain,' said Auntie Sanni. 'No more blows. Poor little donkey.'

'Just because I forgot his sugar.' Then, 'Blaise!' Recollection came flooding back. 'Auntie Sanni, Blaise isn't there. He isn't – anywhere.'

Quietly, methodically, Auntie Sanni went through the room, questioning Mary as quietly. 'If he had come up to the Hall, I should have known – our nightwatchman would have called me and,' Auntie Sanni sniffed, 'Mary, someone else has been in this room.'

'Who?'

Auntie Sanni did not answer that. Instead, 'You are sure he has taken nothing?'

'Nothing,' and, out on the beach again, Mary said, 'He must have gone swimming but what – ' she felt as if she asked the sky, the sea itself, 'what's the harm in that? Blaise is a strong, strong swimmer.'

'Miss Baba, look,' and Mary saw what she had not noticed before, the long mesh screen with its barbed top and hinges was still stretched between its iron posts across the Patna Hall beach. 'Is not open,' said Thambi – he had not unlocked it. 'Ten foot high,' said Thambi. 'No sahib, even athlete, get over that.'

'Then . . . ?' Mary looked with rising horror along the beach. 'No. Oh, no!'

'I think yes,' said Thambi. Scanning the wash of the waves, he saw something, darted along the sand, lifted a small object, white, limp and brought it to them. It was an hotel towel.

'*Ayyo!*'

'*Ayyo! Ay-ayyo!*' Thambi cried in horror. '*Ay-yo-ma!*'

Up in their room, the Fishers heard the shot. Sir John put on his dressing gown and went out on the upper verandah to look. 'As far as I can see,' he called back to Lady Fisher, 'something has happened to the donkey. Colonel McIndoe is there.'

'The Colonel? Then it's serious.'

'Yes. The poor beast is down.'

'Mary will be upset. Poor child.'

Then came running footsteps, a voice, 'Sir John! Sir John!'

It was a Mary they had not seen before, her dress limp,

193

stained with odd colours as was she, colour-stains from
Birdie's paint and blood – that had been from Slippers's
eye. Her feet were bare, her hair stiff with dried salt, her
face tear-stained, the eyes wide with panic.

'The poor donkey's been put down,' Sir John began
but, 'Worse – than Slippers.' Mary was out of breath.
'Worse.'

'What is worse?'

'Blaise,' stammered Mary. 'Blaise. He went for a swim.'

'Is that all?' their looks seemed to say when a sound
like another shot but a muffled shot came from over their
heads. The next moment, across the verandah, they saw
a shower of coloured stars descending over the sea. 'A
rocket,' said Sir John.

Next moment came another, then another. 'It's Patna
Hall's own alarm signal,' said Sir John. 'Thambi is letting
rockets off from the roof to alert the fishing boats, maybe
the coastguards.'

'Great God in heaven!' said Lady Fisher.

Out on the verandah, carrying the Fishers' morning
tea tray, Hannah heard the rockets. As if in echo of Lady
Fisher, putting the tray carefully down on a table, Hannah
knelt, made the sign of the cross and she, too, whispered,
'God in heaven. Merciful God. Mother of God. Blessed
Virgin.'

Kuku was woken by the shot.

From the window she saw the gathering on the beach
and drew a sharp breath. Like Sir John, 'Colonel McIndoe
is there,' she whispered. 'My God!'

She dressed as fast as she could but her fingers were
trembling so much that she could hardly knot her sari;
when she tried to brush out her hair, she dropped the
brush. Managing to slip through the house without being
seen by any of the servants she ran, not down the path
but by a side track through the bushes to the bungalow,

194

coming round its far end. No one was near as she knocked on Olga Manning's door.

'Olga. Olga. Please may I come in? It's Kuku.'

There was no answer.

'Olga, I *must* come in.' The door was not locked. Kuku pushed it open.

Drugged by tiredness and the whisky Mary and Auntie Sanni had given her, Olga had slept through the shot, the voices, the rockets. Now Kuku shook her awake. 'Olga, *please.* Try and wake. It is *urgent.* Olga.'

Slowly, struggling through waves of weariness and heaviness, Olga sat up. 'It's morning.' She blinked at the light.

'Of course it's morning. Olga.'

'Who . . . who is it?'

'Kuku. Kuku.'

'What d'you want?'

'Promise,' cried Kuku, 'promise you won't tell.'

'Tell what?'

'What you saw last night.'

'Last night?'

'Yes. Blaise – Mr Browne – and me. Please, Olga. They're all out there now. They can't find Blaise and Mary is making a great fuss. Nobody knows but you. It all depends on you. Auntie Sanni would send me away.'

'I don't think she would.' Olga Manning was struggling to be awake, to remember. 'Not Auntie Sanni.'

'She might. Hannah, Samuel, they'll sneer. Always they have hated me. Olga, I was virgin. I am not a girl like that. Blaise was the first and I love him. Olga, don't injure him or me. Give me your word. Promise you won't tell.'

'I promise I won't tell. In any case, it's not my concern, nothing to do with me. Now go away and let me sleep.'

* * *

195

'I can't drink brandy before breakfast.' Mary said it with a tremulous laugh. 'I can't.'

'You are going to,' said Lady Fisher.

'I not understand English memsahibs,' Thambi had told Auntie Sanni. 'Miss Baba, she cry for donkey, no tear for husband.'

Mary was too appalled to cry. 'I told Blaise about the baby shark,' she had said that over and over again. 'I told him. I thought he had listened but he was so angry. Why was he so angry? I don't understand. I don't. I don't. I don't.'

'Mary, tell me something,' said Lady Fisher. She had not attempted to hold Mary close as she would have liked to do or try to comfort her. 'She would have cast me off,' she told Sir John.

'Tell me something,' she said again to Mary, 'did you promise Blaise you would not see Krishnan Bhanj again? Did you?'

That arrested the frenzy. Mary looked at Lady Fisher in astonishment. 'I didn't. I wouldn't have. I promised Blaise I wouldn't go near any of them — unless I was asked.'

'You were asked?'

'Of course. Krishnan asked me. I left you playing bridge. I hated you for playing bridge when poor Olga . . .'

'Yes, yes, but go on,' said Lady Fisher.

'There was a boy waiting on the path. He had a note, a piece of paper really, from Krishnan.' Mary's voice trembled. 'It asked me to come and help him in the grove.'

'But he was at Ghandara.'

'He wasn't. He was with the elephant.'

'*Elephant?*'

'Yes. We had to wash the paint off Birdie. It was *imperative.*' In her distraction Mary quoted Krishnan to Lady Fisher's bewilderment.

'I don't understand a word you are saying.'

'No I don't suppose you do, nobody does but it's true. There's to be no grand decorations in Krishnan's procession so we had to wash the paint off the elephant. Krishnan couldn't do it all so he asked me to help him and I went. I don't care if you don't believe me, but first I made the boy wait and wrote a note on the back of the paper – so Blaise knew where I was. The boy took it.'

'No note came.'

'I gave the boy a rupee.'

'No note came . . .' but light broke on Mary. 'I see! Blaise thought I had broken my word. *That*'s why he was so angry but I did send the note, I did.'

'Yes, you did.'

Sir John had come on to the verandah. 'I found this on the path.' He had undone the crumpled ball of paper, wet and limp but decipherable. 'For Blaise,' read out Sir John, and, ' "You see, I have been asked." '

'Yes.' There was a slithering sound. To her surprise Mary slumped to the floor.

'But what are they *doing*?' That was Mary's first frantic question.

She had come round to find herself lying on her dressing-room bed with Hannah mopping her face with cold water, pouring more over her hands while Lady Fisher held her. Impatiently Mary shook her head but Hannah persisted. 'Baba, lie still. In a moment better,' and, strangely, Mary let her. Hannah dried her face and hands, sat her up and Sir John held the glass of brandy to her lips. 'Not a word until you've drunk this . . .'

Then, 'Something. We must do *something* – at least *try*,' begged Mary.

'Look,' said Sir John and took her to the verandah rail.

The fishing boats had come back but not to the beach. Thambi and Moses had taken Patna Hall's own motorboat out, '. . . and a battering they got as they went through the waves,' said Sir John. Now the other boats had closed in to make a flotilla; through Sir John's binoculars Mary could see Thambi conferring. Then, as the gazers on the verandah watched, the flotilla broke up, the boats going in different directions.

A few minutes later, a speedboat from the coastguard station came into sight and soon was circling round them. 'I should be on that,' Mary cried. 'Sir John, I ought to be looking. I must go out. I will.'

'You would only be a hindrance,' said Sir John. 'You must trust them, Mary. No one knows this coast better than these men. If anyone can find Blaise they will.'

'And if they can't?' Mary stared across the sea. 'Give him back. Oh, please, give him back,' she was pleading.

'Mary, *baba*. Come with Hannah. You must change that dress, wash, eat. Many sahibs will be needing you,' but, 'Leave me alone,' cried Mary. 'Just for one minute, leave me alone.' She tore herself from Hannah and ran down into the hall.

'Let her go,' said Sir John. 'Samuel and I will see she doesn't go down to the beach. Let her go.' He followed her downstairs.

'Sanni, is there any chance?' Sir John asked as Auntie Sanni came to join him.

'If there were, the fishing boats would have picked him up long ago – they went out first at midnight. The coastguards say there has been no other boat near.' Auntie Sanni seemed heavier than ever.

'Blaise was a strong swimmer.'

'Even so, our strongest young men don't go out alone into this sea, John, it is infested. If they find him,' said Auntie Sanni, 'God knows what they will find.'

* * *

198

'Mrs Browne.'

Mary spun round. She had gone into the hall. No one was there and holding on to the reception desk she had been trying to still her turmoil. Now she saw that a familiar small red car was drawn up under the portico.

'Mr Menzies!' Mary recoiled. 'I don't want to talk to you.'

'But you will,' Mr Menzies smiled. 'I have come to bring you good news of your friend Krishnan Bhanj. He is your friend, isn't he?'

'I . . . I have been working for his party.' Mary's instinct told her to be cautious.

'Very laudable,' said Mr Menzies. 'So you will be very glad. Voting began at dawn this morning. Konak is usually politically apathetic. Krishnan has roused it. I have never seen such a turnout. In my opinion Padmina Retty might as well pack up and go home.'

'You mean Krishnan might win?' Mary, off her guard, came nearer. 'He will win?'

'I believe overwhelmingly. There! At least that has made you happy,' and Mary felt she had to say, 'Thank you for coming to tell me.'

'And now you tell me,' said Mr Menzies. 'Mrs Browne, when did you last see your husband?'

Mary flinched but firmly shut her lips and turned to go.

'You won't tell me? I have just been to see Mrs Armstrong. She won't tell me either. Pity. You ladies are making a mistake. If you won't tell me, I shall have to make it up or rely on other people – as perhaps I have done already – perhaps someone who doesn't like you so well. They are apt to distort. So am I.' Mr Menzies laughed but he was serious. 'Of course, this *isn't* gossip, in which I specialise, yet it soon could be. You wouldn't want this catastrophe—'

'It isn't catastrophe—'

'Yet,' he finished for her. 'You wouldn't want it

199

turned into sensationalism, would you? Wouldn't it be better to talk to me? When did you last see your husband?'

'He was – playing bridge.'

'And where were you? That is the question, isn't it?'

Mary, unfailingly transparent, was looking round the hall this way and that, trying to escape but Mr Menzies came nearer.

'Mrs Browne, tell me. I think your father is a well-to-do man, isn't he? Very well to do.'

'Rory?' Mary could not think what Rory had to do with this. 'I . . . suppose so.'

'And the parents of poor Blaise . . . more than well to do. Wealthy?'

'Why are you asking me these questions?'

'Well, you see,' said Mr Menzies, 'I know what happened later that night on the beach.'

For a moment Mary looked at him wide-eyed, then she followed his glance to the portico and the red car and saw the now familiar curly black head, though the yellow shirt had been changed for a red one and, 'I see,' said Mary. 'Kanu!'

'Kanu is an excellent small informer – and helps me in more ways than one.'

You really are repulsive, thought Mary, with your horrible ribbon scruff hair and crab pink face and horrid plumpness.

'Still there are ways', he was saying, 'of keeping things out of the papers.'

'Certainly there are.' Sir John had appeared in the Hall. 'Ways and means you probably have not taken into account but, Menzies,' said Sir John, 'Miss Sanni ordered you out of her hotel. Will you go or shall I have you put out?'

'I have a reason to be here, Sir John.'

'I am sure you have. In fact, I know you had a hand

in this mischief, if tragedy or near tragedy can be called that. I hope it will rest on your conscience.'

'My conscience is perfectly at ease, thank you, Sir John. I am a newsman and news is news.'

'Not all news. We have a police injunction.'

'Injunction!'

'The police insist that nothing is released until the full facts are known. They are thinking of our Office and of Mr Browne's family — which is more than you have done — also of Patna Hall which you will leave at once and take your scurrility with you.'

'Sir John, did you say, "the police"?'

He had brought Mary back to the verandah, holding her, trying to stop her quivering. 'You and Hannah are the only people she would let touch her,' Lady Fisher was to say and soon, 'Sir John,' Mary managed to whisper, 'did you say the police?'

'It has to be the police, Mary. Chief Inspector Anand has sent a message — he cannot leave Ghandara while the voting is on, he hasn't that many men though he has sent to Madras. He asks that you, Mrs Manning — I mean Mrs Armstrong — and Kuku will come to him.'

'Olga and Kuku?' Mary was puzzled.

'Also Thambi and the sweeper women who cleaned up the mess in the bungalow last night.'

'Slippers's mess?'

'Yes, he fouled the floor.'

'*That* was the smell and Blaise hit him, hit him with the heel of his shoe like he did before and it's all my fault. Oh, I can't bear it. I can't bear it.' She was shuddering from head to foot.

Sir John held her but Auntie Sanni had come out. 'Stand up,' said Auntie Sanni to Mary. 'We have Kuku in hysterics. That's enough. Go and get yourself ready and be of help.'

'Oh, Aunt Sanni,' Lady Fisher demurred but it acted like a charm. Mary stood erect, tossed back her hair, tried to give them a smile and obeyed.

'That is my girl,' said Auntie Sanni.

Krishnan had told Mary that election days in India were joyous events but she had not known it would be like this. 'It's a *mela* – a fair,' said Sir John. All along the roads on the way to Ghandara, men, women and children, in what they had as best clothes, had come on foot, singing. 'All over Konak they have been out since dawn,' said Sir John. They came, too, in bullock carts, the bullocks garlanded, the carts decorated with flowers and scraps of bright cloth. Lorries wearing jewellery and tassels swept by, while cars and jeeps, sent by the parties to ferry voters, had drapes in party colours, the blue of Padmina Retty, red for Gopal Rau, green, yellow, and white for Krishnan Bhanj. Bicycles were decorated too, as were the rickshaws; some of the rickshaws had loudspeakers.

The square by Ghandara's town hall was packed and, as in every town in the State, entertainers had come: men who danced on stilts, conjurors, puppet theatres – those whose puppets told the story of the God Krishna were especially popular, as were his storytellers. There were sweetmeat sellers; rival teahouses were free, paid for by their parties. 'One bowl of tea or coffee with one biscuit only,' Dr Coomaraswamy had specified, 'and that will cost me a *lakh* of rupees.' Toysellers came through the crowds carrying poles wound in straw, stuck with paper windmills in bright colours, paper dolls, long paper whistles which made piercing squeals.

Coming from a side road, hooting as they inched through the crammed roads, the Patna Hall cars had to wait while the processions passed. Gopal Rau had decided not to process at all which, under the circumstances, was wise but they saw the tail end of Padmina

202

Retty's display: mounted soldiers in full dress, their lances fluttering pennants; foot soldiers wearing the dress of the Maharajah's late army. Behind them Padmina rode, not in her famous white jeep but in the blue *howdah* of a decorated elephant much larger than Birdie. 'They must have had to send away for that one,' said Sir John. All round her marched her men in brocaded *achkans*, gauze turbans or English suits; her women helpers in glittering saris carried peacock feather fans. Behind them came brass bands blaring Indian and English music, new tunes and old favourites, the 'Dambuster's March' and 'Colonel Bogey', while overhead circled her aeroplane, pulling a banner, bright blue with a star. The rear was brought up by horsemen and boys running almost between their hoofs.

It was impressive. 'Very well done,' said Sir John.

'Horrendously well done,' Dr Coomaraswamy had said.

Then came a silence, all the more striking after the fanfare and tantara that had gone before, until an old and reverend priest with a white beard and saffron robe appeared on a white horse without saddle or bridle. The priest held up his hand for quiet. Even the rickshaws hushed as the ululation of a conch sounded and Krishnan's procession came into sight.

It was exactly as he had said with, after the deafening bands, that soft undulating ululation introducing the drums beating to keep time with the seductive melody of a flute piercing through the crowds – 'Yes, dulcet,' murmured Mary. Then came the disciples, young vigorous men barefoot in spotless white, their hair flowing, their hands held in *namaskar*.

Behind them, on a lorry, bare and plain, Dr Coomaraswamy spoke through a microphone. 'I cannot walk and speak,' he had told Krishnan. 'I am too aged. Besides, on the ground no one will hear me.'

'All the better,' said Sharma, the irrepressible.

When the Doctor paused to draw breath, the young men sang.

Then came a space in which another priest, young – 'From Agni's temple,' Mary whispered – dressed in saffron, led a huge sacred bull, the cap on its hump worked in beads, its neck garlanded. It placidly chewed its cud as it walked, veering from side to side when the crowd offered it tidbits.

Next walked the children, healthy pretty boys and girls. They drew 'ahs' and 'aies' from the people as the little girls scattered flower petals while the boys carried their kites and garlands. They too sang, their voices shrill:

'Lord Krishna, Lord of All,
We put you in your cradle.
We bind you with a chain of gold,
Your hands are red with henna.
We gave you milk, we gave you kisses.
Little Lord Krishna.'

Last came Krishnan, magnificently tall, his skin oiled so that once again it shone but with its own darkness, still almost blue-black – Perhaps Krishna blue is intrinsic, thought Mary, and even in her misery that strange happiness swelled. He wore only a loincloth; the squirrel was on his shoulder as he led Birdie on a saffron-coloured rope, the elephant shining too with cleanliness, her trunk every now and then touching Krishnan. He did not look at the crowd, only straight forward as waves of reverence and, yes, love, thought Mary, came on all sides and a murmured, 'Jai Krishnan. Jai Krishnan,' then 'Jai Shri Krishnan. Jai Shri Krishnan Hari.' It swelled louder and louder as the crowd took it up. Behind him, which drew delighted laughter, three of the most good-looking girl disciples led the three cows of the Root and Flower symbol.

For a moment Mary forgot the terrible present. 'Jai Krishnan,' she breathed. 'Jai Shri Krishnan.'

The crowds had surged around the bull so that the procession had to halt while the young men ran to persuade the people to move back. 'No police. No force,' Krishnan had laid down so that it took a little time. Meanwhile, the lorry was on a level with the first Patna Hall car which held Sir John and, in the back seat, Mary, Olga and Kuku – Thambi and the sweepers were behind. Dr Coomaraswamy, who was not sweltering in a suit – he had to wear national dress: 'Though I am not habituated' – saw that Kuku, nearest the window was weeping.

Weeping! Immediately Dr Coomaraswamy was transported into a dream ... 'Uma, here is a girl in trouble' – he did not know what trouble but never mind – 'Let us take her into our home and befriend her. Always she has been treated as a nobody – we will set her on her feet. You, Uma, will teach her in your wonderful ways. I ...' He did not know quite what he would do but he saw a grateful Kuku, sweet, emollient, 'I am so grateful, so grateful,' and he would say, paternalistically, of course, 'Kuku, come here.' At that the dream broke. 'For what', Uma would, of course, ask, 'are you befriending this girl? Tell me the truth.' Dr Coomaraswamy had to admit he knew another truth. 'I too am in love.' He saw Kuku's face illumined, softened as she had said that and he knew, no matter what her grief, there was no place in it for him. It was as well that the lorry was able to move a few paces. The cars succeeded in getting by and Kuku was borne away, as far as Dr Coomaraswamy was concerned, for ever.

The police station, undecorated, was a sturdier building than the town hall, made, too, of stucco. 'It will be cool,' Olga said thankfully.

Two policemen stood on the steps in regulation khaki shorts, tunics, puttees, boots and red-banded turbans; brass shone on their belt buckles and shoulder straps. 'Chief Inspector Anand keeps his men in trim,' Sir John approved.

The Chief Inspector came out to meet them: a plump, dapper little man, his uniform, too, was impeccable. He had a moustache so fine it looked as if it had been pencilled in dandy fashion but his eyes were kind as he took them into a waiting room, apologising for bringing them out in the heat.

'May I see you first, Mrs Armstrong, since you were the last person to see Mr Browne . . .' He did not add, 'alive.'

Olga Manning Armstrong did not lie; she simply told the truth but not the whole truth, giving her testimony with a quiet steadfastness that impressed the Chief Inspector.

'Well, I am used to courts,' she told Mary afterwards.

'Mr Browne came to your door.'

'Yes, to ask if I had seen Mary, his wife.'

'And you had not?'

'No. I was going to bed.'

'It must be painful for you', said sympathetic Chief Inspector Anand, 'to have me question you just now when there is so much tragedy but you can be of utmost help. What made you, Mrs Armstrong, go in later?'

'He, Mr Browne, was hurting the donkey – of course, I didn't know then how badly it was hurt but I heard the blows. I couldn't stand that.'

'He was angry?'

'Very. Then I heard Kuku – Miss Vikram. She had come down with the sweepers.'

'And later?'

'I thought I had better look in to see if there was anything I could do – really for Mary's sake.'

'She was not there?'

'No. I didn't do any good. Mr Browne pushed past me and rushed out.'

'Why do you think he rushed out?'

'He did not like what I said.'

'About the donkey?'

Olga bowed her head.

'You did not see him again?'

'How could I? I went back to bed.'

'Thank you, Mrs Armstrong.'

To Kuku lies were second nature but she did not dare to tell them now. 'Mr Browne telephoned the house. You answered?'

'Nat-u-rally. I am hotel manager.' Kuku did not say it with pride, she was terrified. 'I called two of our women sweepers. We cleaned up the room. It was – disgusting. Blaise – Mr Browne – was right to be angry. He was right,' pleaded Kuku.

'When the sweepers had gone?'

'I tidied the room. The donkey had smashed a photograph – glass . . .'

'Then?'

'I went back.' There had been only an infinitesimal pause.

'You did not see Mr Browne go out?'

'No. I had gone myself,' said Kuku with truth.

'Thank you, Miss Vikram.'

'Do I have to tell the Inspector everything?' Mary asked Sir John, still shuddering.

'Strictly speaking, you don't have to tell him anything. It is simply that we and they are trying to find out what has happened to Blaise. We must find out so that it will help if you tell them what is relevant.'

'That I was with Krishnan?'

'It is relevant. I'll be with you, Mary. Tell the Chief Inspector openly how you helped Krishnan with the elephant, how, from the time you came to Konak, you have helped with the Party's plans, made friends with all of them, believed in them,' but the Chief Inspector was to ask, 'Your husband, did he share in this belief?'

'No.'

'Do you know why?'

Mary was too honest to prevaricate. 'He did not like me having anything away from him.'

'Ah!' said the Chief Inspector. 'Perhaps last night he came after you?'

'Yes.'

'Has he done that before?'

'Yes,' and, 'I know what you mean,' flashed Mary, 'but he saw nothing because there was nothing to see.'

'Last night? To be fair, Mrs Browne, most men would not be pleased to find their wife, a newly married wife, Mrs Browne, out on the beach at night with someone who was to him . . .' the Chief Inspector did not say 'outsider', instead he said, 'a stranger,' and he asked, 'Was there a quarrel?'

'Not a quarrel. We were only teasing him. I wish we hadn't.'

Chief Inspector Anand was acute. 'Because your husband did not understand you were only teasing?'

'Yes,' and Mary had to say, 'I'm afraid he took it seriously.'

'Seriously enough to make him take his own life?'

'Take his own life?' The aghast astonishment was genuine. '*Blaise*,' and involuntarily it came out, 'Blaise would never have done that. I was the one who was always wrong.'

'Yet he must have gone deliberately into that dangerous sea.'

'He was angry, too angry to think what he was doing.

Oh, don't you see?' cried Mary. 'He was angry with us. He went back to the bungalow and found Slippers – the donkey. That was my fault. I had forgotten the sugar.' Tears came into her eyes. 'Slippers made that mess. It must have made Blaise furious. I'm sure he didn't know what he was doing. He probably felt filthied. He was always very particular. I'm sure he just wanted to get clean.' Into her mind came Krishnan saying, 'The sea washes everything away,' and suddenly, 'Don't. Don't,' cried Mary. 'Don't ask me any more.'

There was the sound of a motor scooter, the Indian put-putti. A policeman came into the room and whispered to the Chief Inspector. 'Excuse me for a moment, Mrs Browne, Sir John.'

They heard a murmured colloquy but not the words. Then quick orders. Sir John got up. The Chief Inspector came back and with him a middle-aged policewoman, the first Mary had seen. I didn't know India had them, she thought. This one wore, Mary was always to remember, khaki trousers, tunic and cap like the Chief Inspector's, with a red border. She moved quietly to stand behind Mary's chair.

Chief Inspector Anand cleared his throat. 'A messenger has just come from the beach at Shantipur. Mrs Browne, I do not want to distress you but I must ask you, do you recognise this ring?'

A heavy gold ring with a crest, a stag's head and a motto, '*Loyauté et vérité*'. 'Yes,' Mary said with stiff lips. 'It's his. It is – his signet ring. He always wears it on his left hand.'

'Mrs Browne, a fisherman found it. Diving, he saw on the sea bed a small shine of gold. It was on . . . on . . .' The Inspector hesitated to go on. The policewoman moved to Mary. 'On – a finger, Mrs Browne.'

'Only a finger?' Mary whispered.

'I'm afraid it is only a finger. The – the shark must

209

have dropped it. Maybe there were two sharks and they had a fight. That can happen . . .'

'I told him about the baby shark!' Mary screamed it so loudly that the policewoman put her hands on the quivering shoulders. Mary shook her off. 'I told him. I begged him. He wouldn't listen. I told him.' She suddenly stood up. 'I think I'm going to be sick.'

They had been a long time at the police station. Mary had vomited until she thought she had brought up the dregs of her being. The Chief Inspector had wanted to call a doctor but 'She'll be better after this,' said Olga, whom Sir John had called in; strong and capable, she had held Mary steadily, not sympathising but encouraging her. When at last they drove back through the town it was in the afternoon sun; the processions had long ended, the crowd was milling round the town hall though voting was still going on, the queues, seemingly endless, moving step by step towards the polling booths.

Voters made their cross or mark opposite the symbol, many of the women holding a baby on their hip while a toddler clutched their sari, but all eyes were alight with interest and awe.

Krishnan, though, was standing alone on the town-hall steps. 'Good!' Sir John could not help saying, 'Good!'

Mary opened her eyes and looked.

Krishnan was no longer wearing his loincloth; he was dressed like the disciples, all in white, but stood head and shoulders above them as they gathered jubilantly round him. He stood making *namaskar* over and over again to the crowd. There was no sign of Padmina Retty.

'Is he winning?' asked Mary.

'Counting will go on all through the night,' said Sir John, 'but it looks as if he has already won.'

Of course he doesn't know, thought Mary. How

could he? As she thought that, Krishnan looked up.

He saw the car, the police – Chief Inspector Anand had given them outriders. Krishnan looked, a long look. Then he bent and whispered to Sharma who ran down the steps, wriggled and squeezed his way through the mass of people. He could not get to the cars but reached a police outrider.

'Get me a car,' ordered Krishnan.

'A car? Why a car? You can't go anywhere now,' cried Dr Coomaraswamy.

'I must. I shall be back as soon as I can.'

'But, *Krishnan*! How can you go? Look at the multitude. You cannot leave them.'

'I must. You must talk to them until I come back.'

'That will not satisfy them. Krishnan, wouldn't someone else do? Sharma . . .'

'No one else will do.' Krishnan was violent. 'I have a debt to pay. Sharma, get me a car – or better, a motorbike and a helmet and gloves to disguise me.'

As evening came on a hush lay over Patna Hall, a tense hush. Hannah, Samuel and the servants did their work quietly with shocked faces, Hannah's lips moving constantly in prayer. Kuku was prostrate in her room. 'Why should she take on so?' Hannah said to Samuel. 'We go on with our work, why cannot she? What was Browne Sahib to her?' asked Hannah indignantly, 'While little Memsahib, poor little Memsahib . . .'

For the second time Hannah had helped Mary to clean herself. Auntie Sanni had moved her out of the bungalow into the room next to the Fishers. There Hannah had put her almost bodily into bed. Mary had gone into a deep sleep with Lady Fisher watchful in the next room. 'Eighteen and a widow,' she had said in grief.

Olga Manning – it was still difficult for Patna Hall

to think of her as Olga Armstrong – had tactfully gone down to the bungalow. 'Do you mind being there alone?' asked Sir John.

'I think I am past minding anything.'

Now Sir John was on the telephone trying to get calls through to England and New York. 'Mary,' he had said, 'you must tell Rory.'

'Rory? What is this to do with Rory?' her look seemed to say. 'Rory may be in New York, Washington, Peru.'

'It's quite easy to telephone any of them.'

'I know. At school I used to have to call all kinds of places but if I did, what could he do?'

'Look after you,' but Sir John refrained from saying it. 'And Blaise's people. His poor mother . . .'

'Mrs Browne? Yes,' said Mary. 'I know I must speak to Mrs Browne.'

'Perhaps tomorrow,' said Sir John. 'For now, better let me.'

'If you would.'

The telephone system at Konak was antiquated. 'It takes time to get through,' Auntie Sanni always told her guests. 'You need to have patience,' and now, 'Kuku should have got through for you.' For the first time that day Auntie Sanni was exasperated.

The beach was empty now. All the fishing boats had come back, the coastguard speedboat had gone. There was no more they could do. Thambi had let them go and sorrowfully made his way back to the gatehouse where, for once, Shyama had made him an evening meal. 'Is my fault,' he had said miserably again and again. 'I am guard,'

'Not all night as well as all day.' Auntie Sanni had tried to comfort him. 'Besides, Browne Sahib was headstrong.'

The villagers, too, had gone back to the village –

212

those who had not gone to Ghandara to vote or had come back. A drum was beating but mournfully, though, as usual, smoke from the cooking fires had begun to go up. 'Life has to go on,' said Auntie Sanni.

At Patna Hall the cookhouse was already lit; Samuel, in the dining room, was beginning his ritual. 'They must have dinner,' though who would come he did not know. Not, of course, Dr Coomaraswamy or Mr Srinivasan – Samuel had not thought it respectful to switch on the news. Not, he was glad to think, Mr Menzies. Mrs Manning, perhaps. Sir John and Lady Fisher. Miss Sanni, Colonel Sahib – that evening the Hall was closed to outsiders. 'Attend to the bar,' he told Ganga, 'that good-for-nothing will not come down.'

Auntie Sanni herself had bathed and changed; Colonel McIndoe had dressed and, as usual walking together, they went up to the knoll where they sat on the bench. Every now and then Colonel McIndoe's hand patted Auntie Sanni's knee.

'It looks all just the same,' she said at last. Patna Hall and its domain, its private beach where the net was up and locked; today no one had wanted to go swimming. The palm trees in the village stirred quietly in the breeze, the hills behind were darkening; the grove was still darker. 'But I think they will light the lamps at the shrines tonight,' said Auntie Sanni. There was a little break in her voice; Colonel McIndoe patted her knee.

Suddenly she stiffened, stood up, shading her eyes from the rays of the setting sun as she looked.

'Aie!' said Auntie Sanni. 'Aie! Look, Colonel. Look.'

A lone figure was coming down the beach. Straining her eyes, Auntie Sanni saw the height and size, its blue-blackness.

'Krishnan,' she whispered. 'It's Krishnan.'

As they watched he dived into the sea.

* * *

213

'Mary. Mary, dear. You must wake up.' Lady Fisher, usually so gentle, was shaking her firmly. Mary sat up, dazed. 'Here, put on your dress.' Hannah had put one ready and Lady Fisher brought it. 'Wash your face.' She led Mary to the washbasin, splashed cold water, dried her, brushed her hair. 'You're needed downstairs.'

Lady Fisher was grave, portentous. She took Mary's hand. 'You know, dear, that Blaise is dead.'

'Worse than dead.' The shudder came back.

'No,' said Lady Fisher, 'Krishnan has brought him.'

'*Krishnan?*'

'Yes, brought his body,' and, as Mary did not move, 'It's not frightening, Mary. It's touching. Come and see.'

It was in the courtyard. There was no sign of Krishnan – Of course, he has to be at Ghandara, thought Mary. The servants had respectfully kept out of the way but Samuel and Hannah, as privileged, moved to stand protectively by her.

Thambi, Moses and Somu were with a circle of fishermen and villagers. They had made a bier. 'It was the only way they could carry him,' said Sir John who stood beside it as it lay where they had put it down on the courtyard ground. It was a simple Indian bier of bamboo poles, laced together like a hammock with coconut fibre string, a bier the fishermen would have used for themselves though – as probably they would not have done for themselves – it was garlanded with leaves and flowers, hibiscus, marigolds, a tribute to Auntie Sanni: Blaise had been her guest.

His body was covered with a clean white sheet but Indian fashion his head, left bare, rested on the flowers. His hair had dried and looked strangely fair against their brilliance; his eyes were shut as if he were asleep. The healthy sunburn of his skin had gone: it had a blue tinge as did the lips; there were dark bruises, too, but the face was peaceful. Blaise was handsome even in death.

214

'He was a wonderful swimmer,' said Sir John. 'Instinctively he must have dived deep down and the currents wedged him between two rocks. There are caves down there but it's a miracle the sharks left him and that Krishnan found him.'

'Krishnan is his father's and mother's son,' said Lady Fisher. 'He risked his life going into that sea.'

'He always does,' Mary said it almost absently. 'He and Thambi have been swimming there since they were little boys. I've been in that sea with him.'

'With Krishnan?' Sir John and Lady Fisher looked at one another.

'With him it was quite safe,' explained Mary. 'He knows the currents and crevices and the sharks don't touch him but Blaise . . .' Shudders shook her again.

'He went in without a helmet,' said Sir John. 'They were all locked up. Thambi thinks he would have been at least half stunned by the waves – mercifully.'

There was the sound of frantic cries. Kuku rushed into the courtyard, her sari dragging, her hair half over her eyes. She cast herself down by the bier, tears flooding as she pulled the cloth back to kiss Blaise's feet. When she saw them mangled, her shrieks filled the courtyard.

'Kuku! Stop that.'

'What are you doing here?'

'How dare you interfere?'

'You should show more respect.'

Hannah, Samuel, even Sir John were trying to drag her away. 'Come away at once,' Lady Fisher commanded but Kuku took no notice, only clung.

'I loved him. You never did,' she flung at Mary. 'I loved him.'

'Mary, don't speak to her.'

Kuku crouched over the bier, her sobbing went on. 'I loved him.'

'I'm glad you did,' said Mary and put her hand on

215

Kuku's shoulder. 'I'm glad.' She looked at the others. 'Help her, please, please,' and Auntie Sanni came, lifted Kuku gently and led her away.

Mary bent down, touched the flowers, not Blaise. She stood up and, 'Thank you,' she said to the men. 'It's beautiful.' As Thambi translated, she made them a *namaskar*.

They, too, turned away.

'Bumble,' Mary whispered as she stood looking down at the bier. 'Blaise. The sad thing is', she whispered, 'that you would so much rather have had a proper coffin. I'm sorry. I'm sorry.'

Saturday

Blaise was buried early in the morning next day. 'There is nothing else to be done in this heat,' Sir John had said on the telephone to Mr and Mrs Browne. 'Even if you flew out tonight, you couldn't be in time.'

It was so early that, as Mary had seen the morning before – Only yesterday, she thought – the waves breaking on the beach were pink, the sands rosy, too, in the first light. Auntie Sanni had suggested that the burial should be in Patna Hall's own small private cemetery set behind the knoll and securely walled against jackals and roving animals. In its centre was a gūl-mohr tree, now in blossom, a riot of orange and yellow. 'My grandfather, grandmother, father and mother are all buried here,' said Auntie Sanni, 'as Colonel McIndoe and I shall be in our turn.' She did not mention a little grave, with an even smaller cross that had only a name, 'Mary McIndoe', the daughter who had lived only one day. 'We will put Blaise here,' Auntie Sanni had said to this second Mary. 'They can move him later if they like.'

Auntie Sanni did not say 'you'. It was as if she knew that, in her mind, Mary had handed Blaise back to the Brownes.

Overnight he had lain in the chapel Samuel and Hannah had hastily improvised. They knew what had to be done. A coffin was produced – 'It was to have been mine,' said Auntie Sanni. 'The Colonel and I have always kept ours handy. Coffins do not exist in Shantipur, not even in Ghandara.'

217

It was put on trestles in the centre of the room, a wreath laid on it – Hannah would have liked a cross; candles in tall candlesticks were lit on each side to burn all night; there were cushions to kneel on and, 'I'll watch with you,' Hannah told Mary.

'Watch whom?' said Mary's puzzled look.

'I shall watch,' said Kuku who had stolen in to look.

'That Miss Sanni will never allow.'

'Kuku shall do as she likes,' Mary was firm, 'but if it had been me . . .' she looked at the candles, the shut room, 'I should have liked to be burned on my bier on the beach.'

Kuku was shocked. 'English people do not do such things.'

'Shelley did,' said Mary.

'Shelley?'

'But he was a poet,' Mary went on, 'Blaise wasn't.'

No Episcopalian priest was near enough. 'He would have had to come from Madras.' There was a priest at Ghandara, Father Sebastian Gonzalives was chaplain at the convent but, 'Roman Catholic,' said Sir John. 'Better not. The Brownes might not like it.'

'Why do religions have to have edges?' asked Mary.

Surprisingly, Colonel McIndoe, not Sir John, read the burial service and led the prayers. All Patna Hall's staff was there except Kuku: 'I couldn't bear it. I couldn't,' she had wept. Olga Armstrong, as she was beginning to be called, was beside the Fishers. The servants stood in a circle, Christian, Muslim, Hindu, every one of them from Samuel down to the sweepers including the two women who had cleaned up Slippers's ordure but, as untouchables, they had to stand apart, especially from the gardeners who were Brahmins – More edges, thought Mary.

I suppose Slippers has been taken away. Do they have knackers in India? She shivered. I wonder, she thought dizzily, if he and Blaise will ever meet – would it be in heaven? The next world? Another world? Or would it be in what, I think, they call limbo? And what would they say to one another? You're supposed to forgive and the thought struck her, How surprised Blaise will be to find a donkey in heaven. To me, it wouldn't be heaven without them. She came back to the funeral and listened as Colonel McIndoe's voice, modulated and clear went on, '. . . We therefore commit his body to the ground, dust to dust . . .' But here it shouldn't be dust, she thought, it should be sand. If it had been the sea – this time she did not shudder.

> Of his bones are coral made,
> Those are pearls which were his eyes . . .

That would be right for Krishnan. Krishnan had had to go back, after all, thought Mary, there is still an election. She looked up at the spreading gūl-mohr tree; Blaise would have liked an apple tree or a rose bush. The sound of the waves was too loud now. He was stunned by the waves – mercifully. 'Oh, God, stun me,' prayed Mary.

'Mary. Mary, dear. They want you to sprinkle a little earth on the coffin. You have to be the first.' All of them sprinkled, the servants *salaam*ing when they had done it. Samuel and Hannah made the sign of the cross. Then the grave was closed.

'Kuku, you will get up im-med-iat-ely.' It was after the funeral breakfast which Samuel, to fit the occasion, had served at one large table, a breakfast even more lavish than usual though nobody ate more than a little. Kuku had still not appeared. 'Now, get up. Dress yourself properly and come and do what you are here to do.' Auntie Sanni was stern.

'I can't.'

'There is much work. Everyone is leaving after lunch. Sir

John will want his account, also Dr Coomaraswamy. That will be large because of all the young people in Paradise. Let the Brownes' bill rest. I expect Mr Browne Senior will settle that.'

'The Brownes' bill? Blaise's! How can you be so heartless?'

'We are running an hotel. The accounts must be done. We must go through the register and allot rooms. Other guests will be arriving.'

'Other guests.' Kuku sat up. 'Haven't you any *feeling*?' she demanded. 'If not any respect? Out of respect, surely, we should close for tonight.'

'And inconvenience and disappoint several people who are coming, maybe have already left home, hoping for a little rest and peace? I will give you half an hour,' but in the doorway Auntie Sanni stopped and said more kindly, 'It is time to stop crying, Kuku. I have been running this hotel for fifty years. In that time, of course, all kinds of things have happened, small things, big ones, bad and good, happy and tragic, but Patna Hall has never closed,' said Auntie Sanni.

'Mary, would you like me to help you pack?' asked Olga.

'Pack?' It had obviously not occurred to Mary.

'Yes. Say if you would rather I didn't but today is Saturday, change-over day. Hannah is too busy to do it for you. I don't know if your room in the bungalow is let or not but in any case I thought packing might be painful for you, especially Blaise's things, and being in the bungalow alone.'

'I don't want to be in the bungalow at all.'

'These things have to be done.' Olga was kind. 'If you let me help you, it can be very quick.' As Mary still did not answer, 'I assume you will be going away like the rest of us.'

'You?' asked Mary.

'Yes. I can't trespass on Auntie Sanni's kindness any longer.'

'Where will you go?'

Olga shrugged. 'Somewhere, probably in Calcutta. I have been offered work – of a sort.'

'I was going to tell Blaise I would stay on here with Auntie Sanni without him,' said Mary. 'Now that I'm without him, I can't stay.'

Samuel had not thought it respectful to put on the radio during the funeral breakfast so that Dr Coomaraswamy and Mr Srinivasan had to follow the news in the papers.

'Krishnan Bhanj triumphs in Konak.' 'A landslide victory for Krishnan Bhanj.' 'Though counting is still going on, Krishnan Bhanj and the Root and Flower Party already have a majority of some hundred and forty thousand votes over the other candidates, a near record for any candidate in elections anywhere in India.' Dr Coomaraswamy, marvelled 'A hundred and forty thousand plus! Even the great Aditya family landowners have forsaken Gopal Rau and come over to Krishnan.'

'Mrs Padmina Retty, eighty-nine thousand.'

'Gopal Rau, fifty.'

Every fresh paragraph was balm to Dr Coomaraswamy – Uma cannot say now I should not meddle in politics.

There were, of course, other headlines. 'Young English diplomat drowned . . .'

Dr Coomaraswamy hastily folded the papers.

Though he and Mr Srinivasan had been up all night they had come from Ghandara for the funeral. 'When we have so much to do,' complained Mr Srinivasan.

'It is only seemly. We have been, after all, staying in the same hotel, Mrs Browne has taken part in the campaign. Above all, Sir John Fisher would expect it. In any case we have to leave. There is packing up, accounts to settle – I must leave you to do that and we must prepare

221

for this afternoon. We are holding a victory celebration,' he had told Sir John. 'But before anything else,' he said to Mr Srinivasan now, 'we must pay condolence respects to Mrs Browne.'

'Is she able?' asked Mr Srinivasan.

'Probably she will be lying down but still . . .'

'When my daughter had the measles,' Mr Srinivasan was filled with concern, 'we caused her to lie on a mat on the floor, a mat woven of grasses and dampened for coolness — to cool the fever,' he explained. 'Also, we surrounded her with fresh neem leaves. Neem is so very soothing.'

'Mrs Browne has no fever,' but, Dr Coomaraswamy was distressed, 'She is so young to be widowed. I do not know what to say.'

To put off the moment, they lingered on the verandah and leafed through the papers again until, at last, 'Speak from the heart,' suggested Mr Srinivasan, 'then you cannot be wrong,' but Dr Coomaraswamy's heart was elsewhere.

He had not lingered only from embarrassment; in spite of all resolutions he had been waiting, hoping — A last glimpse, he told himself, though to Sir John, 'I, myself, must go straight to Delhi and make my report,' he had said, 'also see Krishnan's father. I expect he and Mrs Bhanj will come here. Then I must return to my neglected work and, of course, to my beloved wife, Uma,' but, as he said it, the heart Mr Srinivasan had spoken of felt like lead. He saw his clinic — he had been so proud of it — with its spacious grounds, its chalets, communal lounges and dining room, the big medical building, and it all seemed sterile; even the corridors were sterile, everything arranged according to Uma. Outside the clinic windows would be neat gravel walks, no vista of green lawns, white sands, blue sea, colours of flowers; no blooms of jasmine to put in someone's hair. There would not be the teasing voice, the laughter, even if the laughter, the teasing were not for him.

'It's getting late,' Mr Srinivasan reminded him and Dr Coomaraswamy was forced to ask Samuel, 'Where is the little Memsahib?'

'She helping Miss Sanni with the accountings.'

That shocked both the Doctor and Mr Srinivasan.

'Surely she should be weeping?'

'A widow should weep.'

'She is in the office,' Samuel assured them.

Mary had never seen Auntie Sanni as pressed – Come to that, I have never seen her pressed at all. Now she was busy in her office, busy at reception, in the linen and store rooms.

Olga had been right: the packing had not taken long, the luggage was soon ready, Mary's separate from Blaise's, '. . . which will go to England if his father and mother want it.' Mary looked at the golf clubs in their heavy bag, the tennis rackets in their presses, the camera, and turned away. His watch had gone; the signet ring she had put in the pocket of her shorts. Then, going to find Auntie Sanni in the office, seeing her desk littered with papers, account sheets, stacks of small signed chits on different spikes, 'Can I help?' asked Mary. 'I'm quite good at accounts.'

'That's more than I am.' Auntie Sanni laid down her pen. 'Kuku says we should have a computer but who of us knows how to work one? There is a calculator but I don't know how to use that either,' she sounded in near despair, 'and there are all the flowers to do. I can*not* arrange flowers.'

'Where is Kuku?'

'Lachrymosing.' Mary had not heard Auntie Sanni be as cross.

'If that one takes on so much over what is nothing

223

to do with her,' Hannah with two houseboys, their arms full of folded sheets, pillow cases and towels had brought the key of the linen room to Auntie Sanni, 'what she do', demanded Hannah, 'when she have real sorrow?'

'Perhaps it is real sorrow,' said Mary.

'Pah!' Hannah sounded as if she spat.

'If you really could do these accounts,' Auntie Sanni wavered, 'but it doesn't seem fitting.'

'It is. It is,' urged Mary. 'I should be better with something to do. *Please.*'

'Well, then. Here are the account forms. You see they are divided – hotel accommodation and board, telephone, laundry, drinks – each room has its chits. You check them and enclose them with the account. For Dr Coomaraswamy there is another account for the young people in Paradise, they only had half board and then,' Auntie Sanni said of what evidently defeated her, 'you have to add them all up to a total.'

'I think I can do that.'

'You enclose them neatly in an envelope, *sealed,*' Auntie Sanni specified. 'Kuku wanted to add ten per cent for service charge but no, we would not do that. Guests give or not give as they choose.'

It was peaceful working in the office; the doves' cooing seemed gently healing. The stack of envelopes – sealed, thought Mary with a smile for Auntie Sanni – grew steadily. By noon she had almost finished. 'Perhaps I can do the flowers as well?'

When Sir John had seen Mary come up to the Hall and go in to Auntie Sanni, he went down to the bungalow. Olga, dressed to travel, was sitting on the little verandah. 'May I join you for a moment?'

'Of course.'

'Mrs Armstrong, Olga, would it be an intrusion if I asked you what you are planning to do?'

'I must do what I can.'

'Alone in Calcutta?'

'Well, I don't see people now or expect them to see me. I shall have to earn, of course, some kind of living. Colin, naturally, has had no salary these past two years. There is a clinic I worked for in Calcutta, a poor one, not like Dr Coomaraswamy's,' she smiled, 'in the slums. They will take me back and provide a room but, at the moment, we're penniless.'

'Then I suggest you let me give you this.'

Startled, she said, 'Oh, no!'

'Oh, yes! Alicia and I have worried about you.'

'Worried about *me*?'

'Is that so unusual?'

'Most unusual, I have found . . .' She could not go on.

'Then . . .' and Sir John put a folder on the table.

'What is it?'

'An air ticket to London – London's a good starting ground – and a little wherewithal to help while you find your feet. We, Alicia and I, want you to take it. Will you?'

She was silent, looking at the folder, struggling, then, 'I can't find any words,' she said.

'It doesn't need words. Take it.'

'Colin would tell me to accept.'

'Well, then?'

'I can't, Sir John.' The eyes lifted to his were full of tears. 'There are no thanks good enough, grateful enough to you and Lady Fisher but I can't. I must stay as close to him as I can.'

'For twelve years?'

'It may not be twelve years. He may get remission but, if need be, for ever.'

'They will only let you see him once a month.'

'I shall still see him once a month.'

Sir John put his hand on hers. 'And I thought . . .'

he said, 'I thought I knew something about loyalty and love.'

'It makes one do silly things, doesn't it? Like staying in abominable Calcutta. Never mind.' With a smile, she gave the folder back to him. He had not seen her smile before; it transformed the ravaged face and lit her eyes to a luminous brown. 'Please don't feel badly. One day, even if it's not for twelve years, I may come and ask you for other air tickets – for two.'

'I go to my beloved wife.' Dr Coomaraswamy had repeated that when he had made his farewell speeches, flowery to Auntie Sanni, more flowery to Mary, 'My beloved wife,' but could not stop himself saying, 'Miss Kuku, I think, is not appearing ... No?' asked wistful Dr Coomaraswamy.

'Our Doctor,' said Auntie Sanni when Mr Srinivasan had escorted him away, 'our dear Doctor, fancies Kuku. I say "fancies" because he will never get as much as a glance from her, poor man. His wife is a gorgon. Yes. Poor man.' Auntie Sanni sighed.

Poor Kuku, Mary wanted to say but instead, 'Auntie Sanni, may I go up and see her?'

Auntie Sanni gave Mary a long and penetrating look. 'I'm sure you will be kind,' she said.

'Kuku?' Mary knocked again.

'Kuku?'

'Go away. I don't want any of you to come in,' cried a hysterical voice.

'I'm not "any of you",' said Mary and pushed – the door had no lock.

Kuku was lying on the bed as dishevelled as when Mary had last seen her at the foot of the bier. Her sari was half off and rumpled, her face so swollen with tiredness and crying that she looked almost ugly. Has she watched all

226

night? wondered Mary, who had not gone near the chapel but stayed, watching, in her room.

'And of them all,' snarled Kuku, 'the last person I want is you.'

'I know.'

'Then why force yourself on me? What do you want?'

'To give you this.'

Mary took the signet ring out of her pocket and held it out. 'It was his.'

'His?'

'Yes. Didn't you notice? He always wore it on the little finger of his left hand.'

'The finger that the shark . . .'

'Yes.' Mary hurried on. 'Look. This is his crest, a stag's head. He was proud of that.'

'Most people not having a crest?' Kuku whispered.

'Exactly.'

Kuku seemed stunned by wonder. She held the ring close, turning it, turning it; her own little finger traced the stag head. 'He should have been proud. His ring – and you want me to have it.'

'Yes. I think you should.'

'What do the words mean?'

'They're French. Loyalty and truth. You should have it. You were more loyal than I and you loved him.'

Kuku was driven to be honest. 'Mary, he didn't love me. He . . .' she brought herself to say it, 'for him, I didn't exist . . . until the end.'

'That doesn't matter. You loved him.' Mary closed Kuku's fingers over the ring.

'Mees.' As Mary came out of Kuku's room, an apparition startled her, as did the urgent voice. 'Mees.'

Kanu, in his haste to reach her, was scrambling on all fours to the door opening on to what had been Mr Menzies' room. His red shirt was as rumpled as Kuku's

227

sari had been; his face, too, was swollen with tears. He has been hiding under the bed, thought Mary. Behind him, the room was empty, clean, swept, dusted, the bed freshly made up; towels, drinking water, flowers, ready for an incoming guest.

'Kanu. If Hannah—'

'Hannah!' He spat, got up on his knees, entreating Mary.

'Menzies, Menzies Sahib. Mees. Please.'

'Menzies Sahib has left hotel. Gone.' Mary tried to free herself but the small black hands held her.

'Gone car,' sobbed Kanu, 'no take Kanu. "Get out car. Get *out!*"' he mimicked Mr Menzies. '"Out!"' Then sobs overtook him. 'No take Kanu. No take.' Terrible sobs. Kanu was suddenly a small boy woefully bereft. A gabble of Telegu followed – Mary guessed he was saying, 'Where is he?' and, 'I don't know where. Not know.' She shook her head. 'Ghandara? Madras? I don't know.'

'Kanu go too. Please. Mees.'

Mary shook her head again. 'Kanu, I can't help.'

They heard Hannah's bangles, her tread: with a cry of despair, Kanu vanished down the stairs.

'*Chota* Memsahib' Mary had been promoted: 'Little Memsahib.' It was Samuel. 'The telephone. Master's father and mother. They wish speak with you.'

'Oh, no.' Mary visibly shrank.

'They waiting,' Samuel said severely.

The line was not good but Mary could hear the grief and concern in their voices – they were speaking on party lines – 'Dear, dear Mary. Are you better? Sir John said . . .'

'Much better now.'

'He says you are being very brave. Poor little girl.'

Mary winced. 'Not brave. Not little girl.'

'Can't hear. Never mind. Just to tell you we are

228

bringing darling Blaise home from that horrible place.'

'*Horrible* place?' From the open telephone kiosk Mary could catch a glimpse of the garden, gūl-mohr trees and pink and white acacias, parakeets flying in them. She could hear Auntie Sanni's doves and, distantly, the sound of the waves, feel the sea breeze, warm, scented. She tried to come back to the telephone. 'Take Blaise?'

The voices seemed to go on in a meaningless babble. 'I don't understand,' said Mary.

'Never mind. We don't want to distress you, dear child, Sir John will explain,' and, 'Mary, darling,' came Mrs Browne's voice, 'the moment you are home, you must come straight to us.'

'Home?' asked Mary, bewildered.

'Yes, Archie has been trying to get in touch with Rory.'

'I don't know exactly where Rory is,' said Mary.

'Your own father?' – faint disapproval.

'I often don't know where he is.'

'Can't hear. Never mind, get Sir John. Don't worry. We'll take care of you.'

I can take care of myself – but this new and learning-to-be-more-gracious Mary did not say it, only, 'Thank you . . . thank . . .' Unexpected sobs overtook her. Sir John quietly put her out of the way.

'They said, "Take Blaise home." '

'They mean back to England.'

'How?' The telephone call, its jerk into reality, had amazed Mary.

'A special coffin is made, then they fly him home by air.'

'You mean dig him up and bury him again?'

'Dear Mary! I hope you didn't say that to his mother?'

'That's what it is, isn't it?'

Like Mrs Browne, Lady Fisher wanted to be tender. 'Don't distress yourself,' she said. 'It will all be seen to. You needn't know anything about it,' but, 'I think it's the best thing,' said Mary, 'Blaise never liked it here. I think it's what he would have wanted.' Her face lit. 'And it means I can come back here to Auntie Sanni. She says I can come whenever I like.'

'Mary,' Lady Fisher knew she had to be practical, 'you're leaving here with us, of course, coming to Delhi?'

'Delhi?'

'John,' called Lady Fisher, 'John.'

'You'll stay with us in Delhi, won't you?' Sir John used tact. 'At least until we get in touch with Rory. If he's in New York I'm sure he'll fly over to fetch you.'

Come straight to us. You're leaving here with us. Fly over to fetch you. 'No,' said Mary. 'Thank you both and everyone, especially you,' she said to Lady Fisher, 'and Sir John for all you've done but I'm going by myself.'

'Where?'

'To Calcutta. That's the worst place, isn't it? I want the worst. To Calcutta like Olga.'

'To do what?'

'To try and do what Krishnan has taught me.'

There was a silence then, 'Mary,' said Lady Fisher, 'you seem to have known Krishnan Bhanj well, far more well than we thought.'

'It *was* well.' Mary smiled, a happy confident smile. 'Dear Lady Fisher, don't worry. I'll find work in a hostel, a poor people's or children's home.'

'Mary, you don't have to. There'll be plenty of money.'

'I do have to. I need to do something difficult, dreadful. Don't you see I have to try and ... and make up.'

'Expiate,' said Sir John and touched her cheek but, 'Isn't that a little exaggerated?' asked Lady Fisher.

'No it's *not*. Olga understands. She'll help me.'

'How can she, in her situation?'

'That makes her the very person.'

'At least try and tell us this: what did Krishnan teach you?'

'To love,' said Mary simply.

Again the Fishers looked at one another in some consternation.

'Mary, do you know what you are saying?'

'For the first time I do.'

'You and Krishnan Bhanj!'

'Not just Krishnan.' Mary's eyes were dreamy. 'Everyone. Anyone.'

'Mary!' For a moment they were shocked, but afterwards 'We ought to have trusted her,' Lady Fisher said to Sir John. 'Besides, we knew that Krishnan as a true Hindu would not in any way traduce another man's wife. While Mary . . .'

'It's not what you think.' Mary had said that at once. 'It's . . . it's that . . .' she had picked up a shell from one of the bowls of shells kept on the verandah tables. And suddenly she found words – I only had thoughts, could never say them – but now, 'Most of us, almost all of us,' said this newly eloquent Mary, 'are shut in a shell and because it's so filled with ourselves, there's no room to let anyone or anything in, nothing outside ourselves when, if we only knew, there's the whole of . . . well everything . . .'

'Creation?' suggested Sir John.

'Yes. We don't know it but we are part of everyone, everything.' Mary saw Krishnan's hand stroking Udata's grey squirrel back, saw her stripes from Vishnu's hand. 'It's all there only we're too shut in our shell to see it or feel it. Krishnan opened my shell and let me out. It's perfectly logical because', she held the shell to her ear and listened, 'it's only in an empty shell,' said Mary, 'that you hear the sound of the sea.'

'All the same,' Lady Fisher told Sir John with certainty when Mary had gone, 'it's Krishnan that girl really loves.'

* * *

231

'Mrs Browne, please to excuse me', it was a flustered Mr Srinivasan, 'but I have looked in reception and there is no one there. Not Miss Kuku. Not Miss Sanni. It is the last thing I have to do and urgent as I have to go to Ghandara for the parade. You were in the office, Mrs Browne. Can you help me?'

'If I can,' and 'If you will come to reception.' Mary followed him and, 'What is it you have to do?'

'Book a room, a permanent room, for Mr Krishnan Bhanj.'

'Here? At Patna Hall?'

'Where else?' asked Mr Srinivasan. 'He will have to come so often to his constituency. Not like other members, he will be continually among his people, working with them,' and seeing her startled face, he said again, 'Where else? Always he has been coming here, first as a little boy with father and mother.'

'Of course,' said Mary slowly, 'that's when he made friends with Thambi.'

'He will need to be much at Konak. He must be with his constituents.'

The words were like small hammers driving reality in. 'Here, not in the grove?'

'The grove, I think, is over.'

When Mr Srinivasan had gone and she had made a note for Auntie Sanni and entered the booking in the register, 'Mr Krishnan Bhanj, MP', which looked strange, almost foreign, Mary put her elbows on the cool teak wood of the reception counter, her hands over her ears to shut out the sound of the sea, her eyes closed to keep out the sunshine outside. 'Understand,' said Mary to Mary, 'Krishnan will come and you will not be here. It is probable you will never see Krishnan again.'

'Then you are not looking,' said a voice.

Mary's eyes seemed to fly open, her hands to fall. It was Krishnan's uncanny way of knowing her thoughts

232

but who was this elegant young man standing in the hall, tall, exceedingly good-looking, exceedingly dark? He wore a well-cut European suit of fine linen, a shirt of palest blue that set off his good looks, a public-school tie – Harrow? wondered Mary – pale socks and polished shoes; his hair was cut and brushed back. 'Ready for the victory parade,' said Krishnan.

Then he came closer. 'Mary, I am sorry. Deeply, deeply sorry. I wish I hadn't taunted Blaise,' said Krishnan.

'So do I. We both did.'

'We are birds of one feather.'

'We always have been,' said Mary and, unsteadily, 'Except . . . Krishnan, I can't forgive Blaise for Slippers. The rest I can manage but that . . .'

'It is still raw,' said Krishnan. 'Still sore.'

'But for us, it's over.' 'Over' seemed a desolate word.

'Not at all,' said Krishnan. 'When something is over, something else begins. Therefore' – Krishnan still kept some tags of old-fashioned English – 'we shall see one another again.'

'I don't think so. I shall be, I hope, working in a slum in Calcutta. You will be in Delhi in Parliament. Don't they call it the Round House?'

'The Monkey House,' said Krishnan. 'I am still not there yet. Also, I may not stay there just as you may not stay in your slum. Perhaps one day, when we are old, Auntie Sanni might ask us to run Patna Hall for her. That would be fun.'

'Yes,' said Mary fervently.

'And, Mary, I should very much like you to meet my father and mother. And now,' said Krishnan, 'let's go and have a drink.'

Mary came round the reception desk counter. 'I have never known you drink anything but coconut water and that out of a coconut shell.'

'Monkeys can change their ways,' said Krishnan.

233

* * *

'Krishnan. Sir John. Krishnan. Sir John.' The frantic voice reached the drawing room where they were all gathered; a sudden squall of rain had driven them from the verandah where Kuku, dressed and groomed, only her face still marked with tearstains, her eyelids red, had been serving coffee after luncheon – a special luncheon that Samuel had been allowed to plan as if to show that Patna Hall was still Patna Hall, 'no matter what,' as Auntie Sanni said. The luncheon had included mulligatawny soup.

It was also a farewell to which the drawing room lent a certain stateliness. Everyone was ready to go; the luggage was in the cars. When Kuku finished serving, she began taking round the visitors' book for signing when Dr Coomaraswamy, his bald head and coat shoulders wet with rain, came in panting, Mr Srinivasan at his heels. 'Sir John! Sir John!'

'Doctor! What is it?'

'It is that –' Dr Coomaraswamy almost choked, 'it is that in two hours we should be holding the victory parade, ju-bi-lant-ly. We were— ' Dr Coomaraswamy really did choke.

'We were dry and home,' Mr Srinivasan helped him. 'Krishnan has won by a hundred and sixty-nine thousand votes, far over Padmina Retty. A record! A hundred and sixty-nine thousand.'

'I myself was so jubilant. Now look at this. *Look* at this!' Dr Coomaraswamy had a typewritten sheet in his hand. 'Scandal!' cried Dr Coomaraswamy in an extreme of horror. 'We cannot have scandal now.'

'But we have,' cried Mr Srinivasan.

'No Member of Parliament can afford scandal. Oh, why didn't you tell me, Krishnan? You could have confided. We could have prevented. Sir John, you have influence in London, more influence here but even you, I think, cannot avert this.'

234

'But it must be stopped.' Mr Srinivasan was wringing his hands.

'Stopped! It must be blown sky high but who is to blow it? How can we block this?'

'You can't.'

Mr Menzies, as cool as Dr Coomaraswamy was hot, sauntered into the room. 'Coomaraswamy is right,' he said, 'not even you, Sir John, can stop it. The injunction is over. This is public news now. News.'

'What news?' Krishnan stood up.

'Ah! The successful candidate, God Krishnan!' Mr Menzies made a mock bow.

'Tell us what news.' Krishnan was unperturbed.

'I suggest you read it,' said Mr Menzies. 'Read it aloud. As the Doctor seems upset, for which he has every reason as you shall hear – perhaps you, Sir John?'

Sir John took the sheets with disdain. ' "The gods amuse themselves," ' he read aloud. 'Indeed they do! Who was the dressed-up girl who travelled Konak with Krishnan Bhanj on his lorry? Was she Radha the goddess, conveniently come to life, or was she, in fact, the young bride of Mr Blaise Browne who has so mysteriously drowned? What was Mrs Browne doing alone with Krishnan in the grove at Shantipur where he had made his ashram? An ashram for two?

' "Is it surprising that there was a midnight quarrel on the sands? A quarrel that ended in Mr Browne's being knocked down after which a certain lady did not come back to her hotel all night, the night on which Mr Browne took an unaccountable swim in a sea he knew to be dangerous, so dangerous he might not come back. One has to ask, 'Did he want to come back?'

' "Krishnan Bhanj has won his election in a landslide of triumph. Could it not turn into an avalanche to bury him?

' "Krishnan Bhanj took the vow of silence we have

heard so much about; it would seem he took no vow of anything else. How ironic if his – shall we call it appetite? – and his temper, will silence him for ever." '

The appalled stillness was broken by a shriek of joy. 'Menzies Sahib! Menzies Sahib!' A scurry of small feet and into the drawing room hurtled Kanu in his red shirt, his face bright with happiness as he flung himself on Mr Menzies. 'Sahib back. Come back for Kanu. Sahib! Sahib!'

'Well,' said Krishnan, 'your little spy.'

Kanu clung to Mr Menzies, the curly head rubbing against him, his face upturned in rapture. 'Sahib. Kanu's Sahib.'

'*Chūp!* Get out!' Mr Menzies wrenched the thin arms away. There was a slap, a piteous cry. 'Haven't I told you? Go!'

He was holding Kanu by the back of his shirt, shaking him, when Auntie Sanni spoke. 'Let that boy go. How dare you hurt a child in my drawing room?' She said a few words in Telegu to Kanu as he stood whimpering and cowering, then clapped her hands.

Samuel appeared as if by magic – 'Or not magic,' Krishnan murmured to Mary, 'he has been listening.'

'Samuel take Kanu away,' Auntie Sanni said in English. 'Keep him. Don't let him out of your sight and send for his father and mother. We shall be needing them.'

When Samuel had taken Kanu, 'That boy', said Mr Menzies in bravado, 'has been pestering me all this week.'

'So you pestered him with silk shirts, a watch, car rides, sweets,' said Krishnan. 'Or should we say paid him?'

'Krishnan, please,' Dr Coomaraswamy interrupted in misery, 'the boy is not important—'

'He is very important,' said Auntie Sanni.

'But, Miss Sanni, time is running fast. Can we not return to our business?'

'Certainly,' said Mr Menzies.

Sir John came back to the paper. 'I take it,' he said with disdain, 'this will go out tonight?'

'To every Indian newspaper. It is my own, shall we say, scoop? It will be on the evening news, radio and television. It may make the evening papers. London will follow suit, press and all the media, unless . . . ' said Mr Menzies.

'Unless?'

'It is always possible to buy things,' said Mr Menzies to the air.

'He is asking' – Dr Coomaraswamy could hardly bring himself to say it – 'asking eighty *lakhs* of rupees.'

'Five hundred thousand pounds,' moaned Mr Srinivasan.

'Almost a *crore*.'

'You are lucky it isn't a *crore*,' said Mr Menzies.

'Eighty *lakhs* is not possible. I have not got it. The Party has not got it. All that I have is already staked in this election.'

'Pity,' said Mr Menzies. 'Would the Brownes not help since they would be, shall we say, distressed?' Mr Menzies was smooth. 'They, I think, have plenty stashed away – or your father, Mrs Browne? The redoubtable Rory, Roderick Frobisher Sinclair Scott,' he mocked.

'Blackmail is, may I remind you,' Sir John had even more disdain, 'a criminal offence.'

'So it is. The trouble with blackmail', Mr Menzies seated himself on the arm of one of Auntie Sanni's sofas and lit a cigarette, 'is that to prove it all the allegations have to come out, be made public and you wouldn't want that, would you?' He turned to Krishnan. 'Or you, Mr Bhanj. Your parents are very wealthy. What is this worth to them and you?'

'Nothing,' said Krishnan. 'To them or to me. Publish your filth.' He looked at his watch. 'In precisely one hour I shall be facing my people. I shall face them and – Sir John, would you give me that paper – I shall read to them, but in their own language, yes, over the loudspeakers, what Sir John has just read to us here. Every word,' said Krishnan. 'Then I shall ask them what I am to do with my victory – forfeit it or use it to serve them? The Root and Flower Party is founded on the people, for the people. It is for them to decide but not one *anna* will you get from any Bhanj.'

'And Delhi?' asked Mr Menzies. 'What will they think in Delhi?'

'What they think in Konak.' Krishnan was steady. 'My father is there.'

'And London? I think I can say I am certain of London. They will be extremely interested in . . . shall we call it the personal side?'

'London is very far away,' quavered Mr Srinivasan.

'Not for the Brownes,' said Lady Fisher.

'Not for Blaise.' Mary, who had sat proudly up after Krishnan's words, hid her face in her hands.

There was a movement. Auntie Sanni, majestically massive among them, held up her hand, then said what they had all heard her say many times, 'That is enough.'

'You must all have wondered', said Auntie Sanni, 'what Mr Menzies was doing here at Patna Hall. Now we know – almost in full. As Ajax, a clever journalist, it seemed he was attracted to Konak by the scent of an unusual story, Krishnan's vow of silence, but he found more. In elections there is usually something more, which can be very rewarding in a different way. That is perhaps why Mr Menzies is so assiduous in attending them.

'I am not concerned with politics,' said Auntie Sanni. 'They pass but some things do not pass. Though I wish Krishnan Bhanj's Party well, this attempted blackmail is not so important.' Dr Coomaraswamy gave an indignant gasp. 'What is of utmost concern is the damage you, Mr

238

Menzies, have done or are trying to do to other people's lives: to a rising politician who has dedicated his life to his cause; to a young woman who, no matter how you make it seem, is innocent. Worse, a young man on whom your insinuations worked to such a pitch that it ended in his death.'

'You can't accuse me of that.'

'In part.' Auntie Sanni did not falter. 'And, perhaps worst of all, a child. Kanu may not seem of much importance to any of you as Dr Coomaraswamy has said, but he is significant, very significant.

'I must remind you, Mr Menzies, that under Indian law, homosexuality, even with consenting adults, is a criminal offence. Seduction of a child is an even worse offence and Kanu is only ten.'

'What has he been telling you?' Mr Menzies' tongue came out to moisten his lips which seemed to have gone dry; his pink was now a curious grey. 'What?'

'Nothing as yet but he will. As you heard, Samuel has sent for his father and mother. Also we can call Chief Inspector Anand.'

'The police!'

'Yes.' Colonel McIndoe got up and stood by Auntie Sanni's chair. 'We shall give you one chance, Menzies. You will not only leave this hotel, you will leave the state of Konak today. I and two of Dr Coomaraswamy's aides – if you will allow them, Doctor – will have much pleasure in escorting you to Madras, Delhi, Calcutta, wherever you prefer to go, but the moment you publish one word of your allegations we shall inform the police – as you said of London, they will be much interested in the personal side.'

Mr Menzies looked at him with hate.

'Well?' said Colonel McIndoe. 'Yes or no?'

'Why do you ask me? You know I have to say yes.'

'Very well, we'll go now. We'll arrange about your

car. My wife will take care of Kanu. Doctor, please call your young men.'

'Not yet.' Krishnan, too, was up. 'I have a few things to settle with Mr Menzies.' He took Mr Menzies by the coat collar almost lifting him off his feet and, as Mr Menzies cried out, 'I'm not going to hit you,' said Krishnan. 'Unfortunately, you are as much protected by the law as we innocents are. I shall not leave a mark on you, I promise. It will be a little wrestling match, except that I do not think you are a match for me.'

'No. No.' Mr Menzies' cry was almost a shriek but Krishnan only said, 'Come outside.'

'Congratulations on your victory, Doctor, and to you, Mr Srinivasan,' Auntie Sanni was saying as she stood making farewells. 'I don't suppose we shall see you again for a time. Let us hope Konak will not need another election for some years.'

'Miss Sanni, madam, Colonel McIndoe,' Dr Coomaraswamy cleared his throat, 'we can never express our gratitude. This momentous victory . . .'

'Most momentous,' said Mr Srinivasan.

'is entirely owing . . .'

'Don't let him make a speech,' Sir John whispered in her ear. 'We shall miss our train,' and, 'Goodbye, dear Doctor,' Auntie Sanni said firmly, 'Goodbye, Mr Srinivasan. You must leave, I know, for Ghandara. Your victory parade,' and she went on to the Fishers. 'John. Alicia. Next year and I hope more peacefully.'

Kuku had drawn Mary aside. 'Will you tell Miss Sanni you have given me the ring? They will think I stole it else.'

'Kuku, they would never— '

'Hannah and Samuel would,' and Mary had to admit she could hear their voices, 'Give poor young master's ring to that good-for-nothing girl.'

'I'll tell her.'

Kuku gave Mary a kiss.

'Mary, come to us and Patna Hall whenever you can and bring Olga.'

'I shall. I . . . can't begin to say thank you.'

'Then don't. You will be my girl always.'

'Always.'

Mary had been down to the beach to say goodbye to Thambi, Moses and especially Somu. They were gathering up the helmets to clean them, shaking out the umbrellas, raking over the sand, getting ready for the incoming guests. The umbrellas, like the sand, were wet from the rain.

They came to greet her. Mary had brought Blaise's splendid pair of binoculars to give to Thambi who took them with deep respect. 'Memsahib come back soon,' said Thambi. 'Memsahib not be afraid. Sahib, he rest now.'

'They are taking him to England,' Thambi inclined his dignified head – the ways of Westerners were unfathomable to him – 'but Memsahib stay India.'

'I hope so.' Yet Mary could not help a sense of a knell sounding in her: The scarlet cotton flowers are dropping. Well, all flowers lose their petals, the brilliance fades. Slippers has gone. Udata and Birdie will come looking for Krishnan. It is over, thought Mary, then stopped. Hadn't Krishnan said, 'When something is over, something else begins'?

At the same moment, 'Look,' said Thambi.

Over the sea, still dark from the storm, far out away from waves made angry by wind and rain, their crests a strange grey as they crashed on the shore, was a rainbow, a perfect rainbow, its arc in all its colours, meeting the sea on either side. '*Indradhanassu.*' Thambi gave its Telegu name. 'Is bow of Indra.' Indra, God of Storm and Mary remembered the painting in the hill temple: he sets his bow to show that every storm has an end.

'Mr and Mrs Prendergast,' Kuku read from the register.

'Number one,' said Hannah.

'They are old friends,' explained Auntie Sanni.

'The Right Honourable Viscount Normington and Viscountess Normington,' Kuku read with relish.

'They have booked the bridal suite. Their servant can go in Paradise.'

'Mr and Mrs Arjit Roy and three children.'

'They will have the whole bungalow.' Kuku gave a little gasp; if Auntie Sanni and Hannah heard they made no sign.

'Mr and Mrs Banerjee . . .'

'Two hundred *and fifty* sheets this week. Five hundred pillowcases,' shouted the *vanna* in the linen room. 'Worse than last week. It is *too* much.'

'It was because of the election.' Hannah tried to soothe him. 'The election is over. This week will be more peaceful. There will not be so many. Come, brother,' she crooned. 'Take them and wash them.'

'Wash them yourself.' The *vanna* left them on the floor.

All the clamour had died away. Everything was . . . 'normal,' said Auntie Sanni. The fishing boats had gone out, come back; the catch was on the shore. The grove was silent, the village went about its daily chores. The *mahout* had taken Birdie back to the palace. A small grey squirrel, plump now and agile, played in the trees. 'I wish you could have had a more peaceful time,' she had told the Fishers as they said goodbye.

'Oddly enough, no matter what happens, here there is peace,' said Lady Fisher.

'Yes,' said Auntie Sanni. 'Sometimes there is upset, this week a deep upset, but slowly . . .' she dropped into her singsong voice, 'it is like the sea, the waves — they beat in such thunder, the wash surges up the beach but cannot help spreading into ripples. Then they ebb. Everything goes with them, in a short while there is not even a mark left on the sand. No. There may be a little mark,' conceded Auntie Sanni.

Epilogue

January

Dear Mr and Mrs Browne,

[wrote Auntie Sanni who still kept her careful school-girl script — she remembered the 'e'.]

I am writing to you at the request of Miss Kuku Vikram recently in my employ. She has gone now to better herself at an hotel in Bombay. She wishes me to tell you that a little boy was born to her here at Patna Hall on Christmas Eve, the son of your late son, Mr Blaise Browne. There is no mistaking; the resemblance is extraordinary. The child is fair, with his father's blue eyes and shows promise of the same . . . [Auntie Sanni was not sure how to spell physique so wrote] physic. A lovely healthy child. He has been baptised as Blaise.

Kuku, who is now only twenty-one, is unable to support him, she is an orphan and has to make her way. She will make no claim on him if you will take him as your own. He is presently at Patna Hall with me.

I await your instructions.

Yours truly,

Sanita McIndoe
Proprietress

Underneath she wrote 'Auntie Sanni'.

244

Glossary

NB Telegin words are spelt phonetically.

achkan	tunic coat, high-collared and buttoned as worn by Nehru
almirah	wardrobe
anna	small coinage equivalent to a penny but sixteen to the rupee
apsara	celestial dancing girls dedicated to the gods
Ari!	'Oh!' but stronger. Frequently a remonstrance
Atcha	agreed, good
ayah	children's nurse or female servant in the service of women
Ayyo!	as for *Ari* (Telegu)
bania	merchant, money-lender, shopkeeper
biri	type of cigarette made from raw dried leaves
brinjals	egg plant/aubergine
charpoy	simple Indian bed with wooden frame and legs laced across with string, usually coconut string
chatti	earthenware bowl; for a tea chatti, small – and smashed when it has been drunk from
Chelo	Get going. Go!
choli	tight-fitting bodice
Chŭp	Hush. Shut up
crore	100,000,000 rupees. Ten million. Ten lakhs
darshan	an audience, as for a king or holyman, but also, for the person attending, gaining grace by the simple act of 'beholding', looking without speaking or trying to make any sort of contact – certainly not taking photographs
dipa	small earthenware lamp, heart-shaped with a little wick floating in oil

dosa	pancake, sometimes stuffed, made from slightly fermented gram flour
durbar	state or court formal reception
durrie	cotton, woven, striped rug or carpet
gharra	large earthenware vessel
ghee	clarified butter
gopi	milkmaid
gram	grain
Hut jao	Go at once. Swiftly [but stronger]
jaggery	a kind of molasses but thicker, almost like fudge
Jai!	(pronounced Jy) Hail!
Jao!	Go!
Kachiyundu	Wait (Telegu)
kofta	ball of minced fish or meat
lakh	100,000 rupees
lota	small pot, usually of brass
lunghi	sarong
mali	gardener
namaskar	a greeting made with the hands held together as in prayer
pandal	a form of awning, usually connected with a religious feast day or a wedding. Can be made of silk or cotton, brightly coloured, or leaves such as banana leaves on their stems
panga	a long blunt-ended blade with one sharp side
pice	a quarter of an anna
punkah	overhead fan, now usually electric-bladed
puri	deep-fried small round of puffy flat bread, sometimes stuffed
Shabash	Fine. Good. Well done
shaitan	devil
simile	cotton trees
tamasha	a great show; something done lavishly
vanna	washerman (Telegu)

The Greengage
Summer

PREFACE TO THE THIRD EDITION

The Greengage Summer is true, or partly true: when I was fifteen, my elder sister Jon seventeen going on eighteen, two totally self-involved adolescents, our mother, Mam, driven by despair over us, made an announcement: "We are going," she said, "to the Battlefields of France" – those words were in capitals – "and perhaps when you see the rows and rows of crosses for those young men who gave their lives for you, it might make you stop and think of your selfishness."

Mam had never been to France or anywhere on the Continent. She spoke no French but this was a crusade; her cheeks were flushed, her blue eyes determined. "We have to change trains at Rouen and have two hours to wait so I shall take you to the market place to see where Joan of Arc was burnt" – she had read it all up thoroughly – "St Joan, too, might make you think. And," she added, "you are not to tell Aunt Mary. She thinks we are going to the seaside."

We did not see where Joan of Arc was burnt; all I remember of the time in Rouen were the first French strawberry tarts we ate – Rose our youngest sister in heaven – she and the next sister, Nancy, were with us. We spent the whole two hours in a patisserie opposite the station because Mam could go no further. She had not absolutely deceived Aunt Mary; we had been at the seaside in Varengeville in Normandy for three weeks and there Mam had been bitten on the leg by a horsefly. On the train her leg began to swell with agonizing pain. Jon and I knew enough about fevers to know she had high fever; by the time we arrived in Paris she was helpless.

I can see us now, the four of us on the platform of the Gare de l'Est, grouped around Mam who sits on our suitcases. "Children you . . . Jon . . . Rumer . . . you must . . ." is all she can say, but though Jon and I were, to our minds, quite old, not children at all, we were oddly inexperienced and tongue-tied into shyness and dismay.

Mam had asked a clergyman friend for advice and he had told her that Château Thierry, a town on the Marne, had been the American Headquarters in the war. "If you want to see the battlefields there can be no better place," he had said and recommended a small pension, the Hôtel des Violettes. As with Joan of Arc, we failed to see the battlefields but we did reach Château Thierry.

Not without a private battle. "Jon, you must get a porter and ask him," I said.

"You speak better French. You ask him."

"I don't speak better French."

"You do."

"Girls," said Mam feebly, and, "Go on," commanded Jon.

I had to beard a horrible and extortionate porter like a bear in a blue blouse and station cap; at first, he could not understand a word I said – which was not surprising – until at last, "Château Thierry," he shouted; it sounded as if he were swearing and we wondered what was wrong with Château Thierry. Mercifully the train left from the same Gare de l'Est. He shouldered and swung some of our suitcases, we carried the rest, another porter almost carried Mam and, after parting with far too many francs, we found ourselves in a second-class compartment, bumping slowly through a flat countryside.

It is difficult, with the novel I was to write about those two months in Château Thierry and the film that followed it, to know what I remember as happening, what is transposed in the novel, and what is overlaid by the film; each seems to shimmer through the others. I do not know if we really had to walk from the station, Jon and I one on each side of Mam holding her up, a boy pushing our luggage in a handcart, Nancy and Rose trailing behind as, "Hôtel des Violettes," we said over and over again.

"*Si*," said the boy, "*si*," and nodded ahead to where trees, iron railings, and tall scrolled iron gates showed, behind them, a big house with lights. "Hôtel des Violettes." We felt a tingle of anticipation.

In the book and film, the hotel was called the Hôtel des

Oeillets-carnations, but, as I write, I smell the "Violettes" smell of warm dust and cool plaster, of jessamine and of box hedges in the sun, of dew on the long grass – the smell fills the garden – and, in the house, it is of Gaston the chef's cooking; of furniture polish, damp linen, and always a little of drains. There are sounds that seem to belong only to des Violettes: the patter of the poplar-tree leaves along the courtyard walk, a tap running in the kitchen with a clatter of pans and china, mixed with the sound of high French voices, especially of the chamber-maids as they call to one another out of the bedroom windows; the thump of someone washing clothes in the river sounds close and barges puff up-stream; a faint noise comes from the town and near, the plop of a fish; a greengage falls.

The river was the Marne; and beyond the hotel's formal garden of gravel paths, statues, small flower beds edged with box, an orchard stretched to a wall in which a blue door opened on to the river bank. The orchard seemed to us immense; there were seven alleys of greengage trees alone; they were ripe and in the dining room, Toinette, the waitress, built them, on dessert plates, into pyramids. "Reines Claudes," she would say, to teach us their names; always afterward we called this time the greengage summer.

Madame – I will call her Madame Chenal – was kind; few hotel keepers would have accepted a critically ill foreign woman with four children. The doctor was there that night and she comforted and reassured us, calling in an Englishwoman, a Mrs Martin staying in the hotel who, herself, had a small girl. Mrs Martin coaxed Nancy and Rose to eat supper and put them to bed; meanwhile Jon and I were almost overcome by the hotel.

The Hôtel des Violettes had been a château; it had elegant rooms, a great hall from which a painted panelled staircase led up to a first and second floor of bedrooms – there were attic bedrooms above with mansard windows. The salon was panelled too, with sofas and chairs in gilt and brocade; the dining room had – what particularly impressed me – blue satin wallpaper. Our bedrooms were large with four-poster beds – it seemed at first that there was only a hard bolster, no pillows;

we were surprised when we found them in the vast armoires. The windows had shutters too heavy for us to close; we could see lanterns lit along the drive and, even in that night of distress, we lingered, breathing the warm fragrance and, again, felt the tingle of anticipation.

Mam had septicaemia, acutely dangerous in the days before penicillin.

"Are there no relatives we could send for?" asked poor Madame Chenal and before I could open my mouth, "None," said Jon firmly.

Poor Mam! How could she have known it would all turn out the opposite of her innocent plan. To begin with, Château Thierry was in the champagne country, a luxury town to which the buyers came for the vintage. It was, too, famous for its liqueur chocolates – Jon was to be given boxes of them. We gorged ourselves, and on the delectable food, especially the ripe fruit in the orchard. Perhaps part of the feeling of being in a dream was because we ate so much; we were, too, out of ourselves from being so suddenly immersed in France.

There was shock after shock. "Do you know," asked Nancy who managed to discover everything, "Madame Chenal has a lover. What's a lover?"

Jean Pierre, a French Canadian, was big, handsome with heavy-lidded eyes, astonishingly blue, and a mass of wiry dark hair. He smelled of sweat and drink – he was often drunk. Years afterwards, I discovered he was a spy who was trading on Madame's bounty. He fell in love with Jon, at first furtively. He used to get a ladder and climb up to our window as we undressed for bed. The first time I froze with terror and let out a scream but Jon's hand came like a clamp on my lips.

"Be quiet!" and, "You're not to tell – ever."

"Suppose he comes in?"

"He won't."

"Why?"

"Because he knows that I don't like him. He keeps on bothering me," said Jon, "so I asked Toinette what to say and I said it. *Salaud*," said Jon with relish . . .

"Weren't you afraid?"

"No. Why should I be?" She gave a shrug. "Men do what you want them to," said this new Jon. I was speechless.

It was not only Jean Pierre. There was Mr Martin, husband of the kind Englishwoman; he was English too, young, slim, with lazy good manners and perfectly dressed.

They had a four-year-old daughter, Betsy, and to our relief, took charge of Nancy and Rose. Mr Martin, Madame told us, worked in a bank in Paris; he left every morning before we were up and came back late but during weekends he was there and, in his magnificent car, drove us out into the green and gold countryside, its white roads winding between vineyards, where the grapes were heavy. He took us to a restaurant overlooking the river and let us order as we liked. "*Comme il est gentil*," said Madame Chenal, but I saw him looking at Jon, not as Jean Pierre looked, avidly, but with a half-unwilling tenderness and this time Jon looked back.

The weeks passed, the vintage began, and everything, the hotel, the whole town, was filled with bubbling life. I saw men and women drunk; I remember a gutter running with wine from a broken cask and children scooping it up to drink. The young men were rowdy and no longer stared at us but sometimes would not let us pass. I knew enough to know they would not have given even a wolf whistle for me – it was Jon.

That August she was eighteen and, for her birthday, Mam let her choose herself a dress which is imprinted on my memory as are many of Jon's dresses. This was strawberry-pink French voile piped with white, and chic – which none of our dresses had been.

The hotel guests clapped when she came in to dinner wearing it. There were murmurs of "*Ravissante*" . . . "*Charmante*" . . . "*Adorable*" and "*Heureuse anniversaire!*" – Madame had told them it was her birthday – "*Heureuse anniversaire!*" they called and raised their glasses. It was the first time I saw Jon blush.

One of the buyers, Monsieur Bosanquet, sent a bottle of champagne over to our table. Jon and I sipped it reverently. We took the bottle up to Mam who could sit up now and walk a little; as she drank her wan face took on a little colour, her eyes had an echo of her sparkle. "I had forgotten how it tasted. Nectar!" she said and looked at Jon with love and pride, but that was the last night of our dreams.

Next morning we woke to find the hotel in chaos and full of police, the gates guarded by gendarmes, even the blue door in the orchard. Mr and Mrs Martin and Betsy had gone in the night and a Paris bank had been robbed, "Of millions and millions," said Toinette. Mr Martin was a well-known international thief; Mrs Martin was not his wife but an accomplice and Betsy was not their child, she was borrowed or hired to add to the illusion of their being an ordinary English family.

We were interviewed by the police, even Rose. When Mr Martin took us out, where did we go? Did he meet anyone? Did he leave us in the car and go anywhere? Had we heard Mr and Mrs Martin talking? Jon was stiff and as non-committal as if she hated them but I felt like a heroine, shielding Mr Martin and talked willingly until, out of the corner of her mouth, Jon hissed, "Stop, stop."

"But I'm only trying to help him. Don't you mind about Mr Martin?"

"Mr Martin!" Jon made a sound like "p'fui".

It was over. Mam was soon able to travel, though painfully, and took us home.

There was an unexpected – and touching – sequel. One day of Mr Martin's last week at the Hôtel des Violettes, as he was leaving for work, the handle of his attaché case had come off – it would have been called a briefcase now – and Jon had lent him hers, a small case but made of crocodile leather from a crocodile Fa had shot. Jon treasured it but it had disappeared with Mr Martin.

He was not caught but three months later the case came back, posted to Eastbourne from the South of France – he must have taken a considerable risk to send it. When Jon opened the wrapping and saw the case she burst into tears.

CHAPTER 1

ON AND off, all that hot French August, we made ourselves ill from eating the greengages. Joss and I felt guilty; we were still at the age when we thought being greedy was a childish fault, and this gave our guilt a tinge of hopelessness because, up to then, we had believed that as we grew older our faults would disappear, and none of them did. Hester of course was quite unabashed; Will—though he was called Willmouse then—Willmouse and Vicky were too small to reach any but the lowest branches, but they found fruit fallen in the grass; we were all strictly forbidden to climb the trees.

The garden at Les Oeillets was divided into three: first the terrace and gravelled garden round the house; then, separated by a low box hedge, the wilderness with its statues and old paths; and, between the wilderness and the river, the orchard with its high walls. In the end wall a blue door led to the river bank.

The orchard seemed to us immense, and perhaps it was, for there were seven alleys of greengage trees alone; between them, even in that blazing summer, dew lay all day in the long grass. The trees were old, twisted, covered in lichen and moss, but I shall never forget the fruit. In the hotel dining-room Mauricette built it into marvellous pyramids on dessert plates laid with vine leaves. 'Reines Claudes,' she would say to teach us its name as she put our particular plate down, but we were too full to eat. In the orchard we had not even to pick fruit—it fell off the trees into our hands.

The greengages had a pale-blue bloom, especially in the shade, but in the sun the flesh showed amber through the

5

clear-green skin; if it were cracked the juice was doubly warm and sweet. Coming from the streets and small front gardens of Southstone, we had not been let loose in an orchard before; it was no wonder we ate too much.

"Summer sickness," said Mademoiselle Zizi.

"Indigestion," said Madame Corbet.

I do not know which it was, but ever afterwards, in our family, we called that the greengage summer.

.   .   .   .   .   .

"You are the one who should write this," I told Joss, "it happened chiefly to you"; but Joss shut that out, as she always shuts out things, or shuts them in so that no one can guess.

"You are the one who likes words," said Joss. "Besides . . ." and she paused. "It happened as much to you."

I did not answer that. I am grown up now—or almost grown up—"and we still can't get over it!" said Joss.

"Most people don't have . . . that . . . in thirty or forty years," I said in defence.

"Most people don't have it at all," said Joss.

If I stop what I am doing for a moment, or in any time when I am quiet, in those cracks in the night that have been with me ever since when I cannot sleep and thoughts seep in, I am back; I can smell the Les Oeillets smells of hot dust and cool plaster walls, of jessamine and box leaves in the sun, of dew in the long grass; the smell that filled house and garden of Monsieur Armand's cooking and the house's own smell of damp linen, or furniture polish, and always, a little, of drains. I can hear the sounds that seem to belong only to Les Oeillets: the patter of the poplar trees along the courtyard wall, of a tap running in the kitchen mixed with the sound of high French voices, of the thump of Rex's tail and another thump of someone washing clothes on the river bank; of barges puffing upstream and Mauricette's toneless singing—she always sang through her nose; of Toinette and Nicole's quick loud French as they talked to one another out of the upstairs windows; of the faint noise of the town and, near, the plop of a fish or of a greengage falling.

"But you were glad enough to come back," said Uncle William.

"*We* never came back," said Joss.

. . . . .

The odd thing was, when that time was over, we, Joss and I, were still sixteen and thirteen, the ages we had been when we arrived on that stifling hot evening at the beginning of August. We were Mother, Joss, I—Cecil—Hester and the Littles, Willmouse and Vicky. It must have been nine o'clock.

"Why were you so late?" asked Mademoiselle Zizi. "There are plenty of trains in the day."

"We were waiting in the Gare de l'Est for Mother to get better."

"And she didn't get better," said Willmouse.

"And we had nothing to eat all day," said Vicky, "but some horrid sausage and bread."

"And the oranges we had with us," said Hester, who was always accurate, "twelve oranges. We ate them in the train."

Mademoiselle Zizi shuddered, and I burned to think that now she must know we were the kind of family that ate oranges in trains.

There had been no taxis at the station, but after a stress that I do not like to remember—the whole day had been like a bad dream—we found a porter who would take our suitcases on a handcart.

It was beginning to be dusk when our little procession left the station; men were coming back from fishing, women were talking in doorways and in their stiff gardens where gladioli and zinnias seemed to float, oddly coloured in the twilight, behind iron railings. 'French people don't have gardens,' Uncle William was to say, 'they grow flowers.' Children were playing in the streets; Willmouse and Vicky stared at them; I think they had thought they were the only children in the world kept up to this late hour.

All round us was the confusion of the strange town, strange houses, strange streets. The people stared at us too, but we did not feel it. We did not feel anything; our bodies seemed not to belong to us but to be walking apart while we floated, as the flowers did, in the dusk. Perhaps we were too tired to feel.

The handcart bumped over cobbles that, even though we had not walked on cobbles before, we knew were unmistakably French. Mother gave a small moan each time the porter turned into another street. It seemed a long way, and by the time we came to the hotel gates lamplight was showing in the houses and most of the doors were shut. At Les Oeillets every night after dark the dogs were let loose and the outer gates closed, leaving only a wicket-gate unlocked; the handcart would not go through that and we had to wait—still apart from ourselves—while the porter rang the bell.

It clanged. There was a deep barking. We did not know Rex and Rita then but could tell it was a big dog's bark; two voices commanded it to stop, a woman's, shrill, and a man's—or a boy's talking like a man; that was a good guess, for it was a large boy who appeared. He had on a white apron; we saw it glimmering towards us. His apron flapped, his shoes flapped too, and a lock of hair fell into his eyes as he bent forward to pull the bolt; he held the gate open to let us pass, and we smelled his smell of sweat and cigarettes and . . . "Is it onions?" I whispered.

"Not onion, garlic," Hester whispered back. "Don't you remember the sausage in the Gare de l'Est?" He was dirty and untidy and he did not smile.

Then we went into the hotel and—"Good God! An orphanage!" said Eliot.

.   .   .   .   .

Afterwards he apologised for that. "But you were all wearing grey flannel," he said, and he asked, "Why were you wearing grey flannel?"

8

Hester looked at him. "Perhaps you haven't been in England for a long time," she said gently. "Those were our school clothes."

In England we—except Joss—had been proud of them. There are two sorts of families; for one a school uniform is a step down, the feeling of being like everybody else; for the other that feeling is an achievement, the uniform a better, more complete set of clothes than any worn before. We belonged to the second category, and Willmouse's grey shorts and jacket, our St Helena's coats and skirts and hats, were our best clothes, the only ones suitable for travelling.

'Other girls have other clothes,' Joss said often.

'Not when an Uncle William pays for them,' said Mother.

Now Joss's eyes threw darts of hate at Eliot though he could not have been expected to know who she was. Our school hats were soup-plate shaped; Vicky in hers looked like a mushroom on two legs, but Joss's was small on her mass of dark hair and showed her forehead. She looked almost ugly in that hat, and the pleated skirt of her suit was too short.

Of course a great many things happened before Eliot said that about the orphanage; he did not even come in until later; but it was Eliot whom we remember of that first evening. He was its ace.

"When he came there was no more dreadfulness," said Hester, but I had to add, "Except *the* dreadfulness."

CHAPTER 2

"WHAT! ONLY two passports?" said Mademoiselle Zizi when I took ours to the office next morning.

"Joss, my sister, has hers; the rest of us are on my mother's." I hated to have to say that. The hotel boy who had let us in was listening—his name, we knew now, was

Paul; he was scornfully polishing the brass grille and could squint down at the passports. His look said plainly that he would not go about with a mother.

I had fought about that passport. "Why should Joss have one and not I?"

"She is sixteen," said Mother, and added, "You forget how young you are."

Three years separated each of us children—Father's expeditions usually lasted three years—but Joss and I had always been the Big Ones, as Willmouse and Vicky were the Littles, with Hester in a no-man's-land between. Joss and Cecil, it had been one word though it had meant I had sometimes to be older than I conveniently could; now I was relegated to a no-man's-land myself. I could see it was inevitable—thirteen is not child, not woman, not ... declared, I thought, as Joss was now—but it hurt. The separate passport was a public confirmation of the status Joss had taken for herself; she had moved into it quite naturally, leaving me behind as she had moved from the bedroom we had always shared into one of her own. "There are things," said Mother, purposely vague though she knew I knew perfectly well what those things were, and she had let Joss change with Willmouse, moving him in to me.

Hester would have been a more natural companion, but she could not be separated from Vicky. "I have to sleep with my foot in her bed, you see," said Hester.

"Your foot *out*, in *her* bed?" I asked.

"Yes, or she won't go to sleep."

"But isn't it cold?"

"Sometimes." Hester added I was not to tell Mother. A great deal of the peace in our house was kept by Hester, but I was shocked. I spoke to Vicky. "But that is how I know she is there," said Vicky as if that justified it.

"But it's naughty."

"I don't mind being naughty," said Vicky.

A line might have been run through our family dividing it, with Hester, Vicky and me on one side, Joss and Willmouse on the other. Our surname was Grey; I wished it had been Shelmerdine or de Courcy, ffrench with two small 'ff''s, or double-barrelled like Stuyvesant-Knox, but it was, simply, Grey. "Better than Bullock," said Joss. We had not quite escaped that; Uncle William was a Bullock, William John Bullock, and Vicky, Hester and I were as unmistakably Bullock as he, short, bluff, pink-faced, with eyes as blue as larkspurs.

It was not as bad for Hester and Vicky, because the Bullocks made pretty children; Vicky, fair-haired, with pearly flesh, was enchanting, and Hester, with her ringlets and rosiness, had kept her appeal; but in me, as in Uncle William, the plumpness had become a solid shortness, the fair hair was mouse, the rosy cheeks a fresh pinkness. No one ever looked as normal as Uncle William, and I wanted to look startling. Why could I not have been born to look like Joss, to be Joss? Joss and Willmouse were dark and slim, with such an ivory skin that their lashes and hair looked darker. "Like Snow White," said Hester with the only trace of envy I ever heard in her. They were, too, delicately unusual; Willmouse had the peaked look of an elf while Joss's eyes had the almond shape that had given her her nickname. "Because Chinese people have slant eyes," said Joss.

"Are supposed to have them," Father had corrected her on one of his times at home. "Most of them have eyes as straight as anyone."

"They have them in paintings," said Joss, who knew all about painting. She and Willmouse were equally vain—and clever; Joss was a serious painter and Willmouse had what we called his 'dressage'. It was years before we found out that that had to do with horses not clothes. Willmouse's scrapbooks and workbox and the dolls that so distressed Uncle William—'Dolls! Gordon's ghost!'—were part of it; the books held a collection of fashion prints, designs, and patterns of stuffs; Willmouse needed his scissors and pins for draping his designs—'I don't *sew*,' he said; 'that will be done in my workrooms'—while the dolls, his models, Miss Dawn and Dolores, were not dolls but artist's lay figures carved in wood with articulated joints. They had been given to Joss by Uncle William to help her in her painting, but to Mother's bewilderment she would not touch them, while Willmouse had annexed them. Mother could deal with us little Bullocks. Though we were often rude or obstinate, 'That is normal,' said Mother, but with Joss and Willmouse it was as if, in our quiet farmyard, she had hatched two cygnets and, 'Everything I do is wrong,' said poor Mother.

It seemed to be; for instance, when Joss complained that the art mistress at St. Helena's was no use Mother enrolled Joss in a London correspondence art course, but that had led to difficulties. 'Dear Mr A . . .' Joss wrote in the second lesson to her far-off master, 'I send you the design you asked for using a flower, St John's Wort, and the drawing of the woman—my mother—I am sorry I cannot find a naked man anywhere.'

With Joss and Willmouse even the Grey in their names took on an elegance; Joanna Grey, William Grey, had a good sound while Cecil or Victoria Grey were nothing, though Hester Grey suited Hester.

It had never been fair, but now, I thought, it was growing more unfair, for Joss had blossomed; that was what people said of young girls and I saw it was the right word; she was like a tree or a branch where every bud was breaking into flower.

She would not undress with me any more, and I was glad because my pinkness was still distressingly straight up and down while she had a waist now, slim and so supple I could not help watching it, and curves that tapered to long slim legs, while her breasts had swelled. I knew how soft these were and that they were tender, for once, out of curiosity, I touched them and she had jumped and sworn at me. As Joss grew, she grew more irritable, with flashes of temper that were sometimes cruel; she was restless too, as if she were always excited, which was odd because her face was serene and withdrawn, almost secret, I thought, with only the palest pink flush on her cheeks to tell of the excitement inside. "Is Joss beautiful?" I asked with a pang.

"Just now," said Mother, "just now."

I tried desperately to keep up with Joss. Cecil de Courcy, de Haviland, Cecil du Guesclin, Winnington-Withers . . . Winter. That was a beautiful name, and I thought, I shall use it when I am a writer, or a nun; Cecil Winter, Sister Cecilia Winter; but I was not yet a writer, or a nun, nor did I know that I should ever be either. At the moment I was more like a chameleon, coloured by other people's business, and now I burned as I had burned about us eating oranges in the train when I saw Mademoiselle Zizi's lips twitch as she read out our names from Mother's passport. There was barely room for us all in the space.

"You went chasing across France with that gaggle of children?" Uncle William said afterwards.

"We didn't chase," said Mother, "we went quite slowly by train." Sometimes Mother was no older than Hester and that passport with its single stamp, in spite of all the names, looked like a child's.

"Et votre père?" asked Madame Corbet.

"Yes. Where is your father?" asked Mademoiselle Zizi.

"In Tibet," said Hester.

"Ti-*bet*?"

I should have done better without Hester, who could never learn to temper anything. It was odd—and annoying—that I always wanted us not to be ordinary, but when we were a little extraordinary I blushed.

"Juste ciel! What is he doing in Tibet?" asked Mademoiselle Zizi.

"Picking flowers," said Hester.

"*Picking flowers!*" Mademoiselle Zizi repeated it in French, and Paul gave a short guffaw which made me rap out what was almost a French sentence: "Il est botaniste." I added, in English, that he was on an expedition. "He usually is," said Hester.

Mademoiselle Zizi and Madame Corbet looked at one another. "Mon Dieu! Mon Dieu! Eh quoi?" said Madame Corbet. "Il n'y a personne pour s'occuper de tout ce monde-là?"

They began to talk about us in French as if we were not there. "They have not been in France before," said Mademoiselle Zizi, looking at the passports.

"They have not been anywhere," said Madame Corbet.

"We have," I began hotly. "My sister Joss was born in India. Mother's old passport expired, that's all . . ." but they did not listen.

"And they don't speak French."

That was wounding, because up to that moment I had believed that Joss and I, particularly I, spoke French very well. "You ought to," said Joss, "you learned enough." That was not kind, for learning French poetry was a punishment at St Helena's.

"Never mind," whispered Hester. "Look how it has helped you, being bad." Certainly it was the only thing at which I ever beat Joss and the hours I had spent over 'Le temps a laissé son manteau, De vent, de froideur et de pluie,' 'Mignonne, allons voir si la rose' and the Verlaines I had grown to love, and stood me in good stead; I had been able to understand, all that nightmare day, what people had said, and really it was I, more than Joss, who had piloted us all here. I *did* speak French, but, as if he knew what I was thinking, Paul sniffed and drew his finger across his nose and wiped it on the back of his trousers, which looked rude.

"We cannot be expected to look after them," Madame Corbet was saying.

"We can look after ourselves," I said with dignity. "We are not little children."

Mademoiselle Zizi picked up Joss's passport and then threw it down on the desk. "Sixteen," she said, "a child," and asked me in English, "Have you no relative, no one at all who could come?"

Before I could stop her Hester had answered. "Uncle William."

.   .   .   .   .

Uncle William was Mother's brother, ten years older than she . . . "though it might have been a hundred," said Joss. Most grown people are like icebergs, three-tenths showing, seven-tenths submerged—that is why a collision with one of them is unexpectedly hurtful—but Mother was like a child transparently above board and open, "To any scallywag," said Uncle William.

I sometimes wondered if he ranked Father as a scallywag, but he did not say it and Uncle William said most things. "If you had listened to me," was his favourite. I do not think Mother had listened to him when she married, but, all the same, when she brought Joss back from India—babies cannot go on expeditions—he had met them and brought them to Southstone, "And Belmont Road," said Joss bitterly.

"How did we know enough to hate it?" she asked afterwards, "when it was all we could remember?" We disliked and were ashamed of the ugly cheap little house with its pebbledash, its imitation Tudor gables and leaded windows. "Silly to cut glass up into all those bits," said Willmouse, but it was one of Uncle William's houses—he owned several in Southstone—and he kindly let us live in it. "He *is* so kind!" Mother said and sighed.

Uncle William spent money and time and effort on us children, "and words," said Hester, "heaps and heaps of words," while Father came only at long intervals and, when he did come, hardly lifted his eyes from his collections of ferns or orchids to look at his wife and children. I think he could scarcely tell the Littles apart, yet we loved him and longed for him to come home; we ran our legs off on his errands and were proud of belonging to him. "Oh well," said Hester, "I will look after Uncle William when he is old."

Did we need Uncle William? I could never make up my mind, just as I could never make out if Mother were very silly or very wise. Take her dealings with Willmouse. "He says he won't wear it," she had said, handing back his new school cap at his school.

"Then he must leave," said the headmaster.

Mother consulted with Willmouse and, "He would rather leave," said Mother, and Willmouse left, until Uncle William heard.

"Why can't I go to a girls' school?" asked Willmouse. "They don't have caps and perhaps I could wear my muff."

"Gordon's ghost!" said Uncle William.

The muff was white fur lined with satin; Willmouse had bought it with the money Uncle William gave him for his fifth birthday.

"What did you buy, boy? A cricket bat? A train?"

"A muff," said Willmouse.

"Gordon's ghost!" said Uncle William. We never discovered who the ghost was, but Willmouse often made Uncle William say things like 'Gordon's ghost!' and 'The only boy amongst them and he isn't a boy!'

Willmouse was little then, but I think we, ourselves, sometimes wished we had a proper boy. "He is Willmouse," said Mother. That was what she understood about him, about us all, even Joss, in our different ways. Perhaps if she had been left to deal with us alone there would not have been the discontent and rudeness.

I think now that the discontent was because we were never quite comfortable in Southstone and the rudeness came from the discontent; it was as if a pattern-mould were being pressed down on us into which we could not fit. For one thing we were much poorer than the people we knew, poor to be Uncle William's sister, nieces and nephew; and we had this curiously absent father while other girls' fathers went to offices and caught trains and belonged to the Sussex Club. Mother too was not like other mothers, nor like a grown-up at all; she patently preferred being with Vicky or Willmouse or any of us than playing bridge, or organising bazaars, or having coffee or luncheon or tea with the select

Southstone ladies. When any of us—except Hester, who was at home anywhere—went out to tea in one of the big red-brick houses, with lawns and laurel bushes and meticulously gravelled driveways, we felt interlopers. We were odd, belonging and not belonging, and odd is an uncomfortable thing to be; we did not want to belong but were humiliated that we did not. I know now it was not good for us to live in Southstone. We should not have been as odd somewhere bigger, in London perhaps.

"In London," said Joss dreamily, "you can be anyone. You never know whom you are sitting next to. He might be a beggar or a duke."

"Or a thief," said Uncle William, who had decided views on London.

"Southstone . . ." I began.

"Is where you live," said Uncle William.

"It's all middle, middle, middle," I said. It was. No beggars and no dukes. "Just middle."

"My dear child, that is the world."

"The world is *not* all middle," said Joss.

"Most of it is. Why should you be different?"

We could not think of any reason, yet we knew we were; every heart-beat told us that. "How shall we ever get out of Southstone?" I asked Joss in despair.

Then we were rude to Mother again and she took us to Vieux-Moutiers—Vieux-Moutiers and Les Oeillets.

.   .   .   .   .

I do not know what it was that drove her to it. Probably Joss and I had been more than usually difficult and unkind, for I had followed Joss in this new bullying of Mother, of being horrid to Hester and snapping at the Littles, of criticising; I joined in from habit and from principle.

"Oh, Mother! You are so slow!"

"Do we have to have that *disgusting* old tea cosy?"

"*Must* you wear that hat?"

I think at that time, she was only happy when she was

with Willmouse and Vicky; she and Hester were too alike to know if they were happy together or not; it would have been like trying to know if one were happy in one's own skin.

"*Why* do you have to have a shopping bag?" Joss would say.

"To put the shopping in," said Mother, astonished.

"*Why* must Hester wear plimsolls in the street?"

"She is going on the beach."

It was on the beach that it happened.

We did not go away for the summer holidays—"Or any holidays," said Joss discontentedly—but spent long days on the beach, picnicking. "Must we?" asked Joss.

"I thought you liked it," said Mother, but Joss shuddered.

Our picnics were even more family ones than most; we had baskets and bags bulging with bathing towels and Thermos flasks, and a dreadful aluminium food container, brought home by Father from India, that was always coming apart in the street. We had buckets and spades and shrimping-nets, jerseys and paper bags. "Like a bank holiday," said Joss; "and must Hester talk to *everyone*? She's such a blatant child."

We had to wear what we called our scarecrows, old faded-out patched cottons. "I can't help it," said Mother. "I can't let your good clothes get covered with salt and oil."

"We haven't any good clothes," said Joss.

Mother was gentle, but that day we went too far. I do not remember what we did, but she lost her temper. "You are abominably selfish," she said.

When she was angry she did not go white as Joss did—she went pink. "You never think of anyone but yourselves."

We stared. Whom else should we think of?

"Everyone tells me you are badly brought up and it's true."

"You brought us up," said Joss.

"It's true," repeated Mother.

"What are you going to do about it?" I asked as insolently as I could, and Hester stole a hand into hers.

"I shall do something."

"What?"

Mother took a deep breath. "I shall take you to the battle-fields of France."

"The *battlefields of France*!"

We were still speaking rudely, but it was feeble, the last intermittent gunfire before surrender. "Why?"

"So that you can see what other people have given," said Mother, "given for your sakes; and what other people will do in sacrifice. Perhaps that will make you ashamed and make you think. And Saint Joan," said Mother, "Saint Joan at the stake. We shall stop at wherever it was and see where she was burned."

"Oh, *Mother*! Not in the middle of the summer holidays!"

"Holidays or not," said Mother, and shut her lips.

"Pooh! You haven't enough money," said Joss, but she sounded a little frightened.

"I shall use the legacy."

"The legacy is for college," said Joss.

"This is college," said Mother. "It is education. You need to learn ... what I cannot teach you," said Mother, her voice quivering.

She did not ask Uncle William's advice. She went to Mr Stillbotham.

Mr Stillbotham was an elderly Theosophist, who lived in Belmont Road and was the only person in it, as far as we knew, who travelled. Father, of course, could not be said to live in Belmont Road. Mr Stillbotham spent his winters in the South of France; we admired him for that and thought him distinguished with his silver hair, pince-nez, blue-and-white-striped shirts and bow-ties. We also liked his manner to us which was full of courtesy and admiration—particularly for Joss.

> "*Standing with reluctant feet,*
> *Where the brook and river meet,*"

Mr Stillbotham would say when he saw her. Altogether he seemed a suitable person to advise us, and we approved.

"You wish to visit your dead?" he asked when Mother told him about the battlefields. "They are not dead but liv . . ." but for the purposes of our visit Mother needed them dead and she cut him short. "Can you tell us of an hotel, not too expensive, and near the cemeteries?" she said.

"Les Oeillets at Vieux-Moutiers." That was the first time we heard its name. "You will find plenty of motors at the station."

Saint Joan had been burned, it seemed, at Rouen. "But you can break your journey there if you go by Newhaven-Dieppe, which will be cheaper," said Mr Stillbotham; "or if you preferred it you could spend the afternoon in Paris."

Spend the afternoon in Paris! Saint Joan had not the slightest chance after that. "I shall see the Louvre," said Joss. "Mona Lisa. The Winged Victory."

"I shall see the shops," said Willmouse and, as always when he was stirred, his face went white.

"Do you remember those strawberry tarts, little strawberries in syrup, that Father once brought back?" asked Vicky. "They came from Paris," she said reverently.

Hester and I, as usual, were far more ordinary; she would be happy buying postcards and taking snapshots with her Brownie camera, while I, the chameleon, would be with them all in turns. "Well, you enjoy it more in that way," said Mother. We were all equally excited.

"If you listen to me . . ." said Uncle William, but nobody listened.

"Very well," said Uncle William. "When you get into trouble don't ask me for help."

"We shall not need help," said Mother, dignified; but the day before we left she was bitten on the leg by a horse-fly. "A little fly," said Hester, "to do all that!"

When Mother took down her stocking in the train from Dieppe, the leg was swollen and the skin looked purple, green and blue. "Like a bruise," said Hester. "Did you bruise it? All over?" she finished uncertainly.

Mother shook her head. She fumbled with her handbag

as if she could not control her hands and she shivered although she was hot.

"You are ill," said Joss accusingly, and Mother could not deny it.

It was altogether a disappointing as well as a dismaying day. From the train France did not look very different from England; it had the Constable, Peter Rabbit colours we had grown up with, and in Paris we did not see the Louvre, nor the shops, nor eat strawberry tarts. We did not buy a single postcard, nor take a photograph; we waited in the waiting-room for Mother to get well. The attendant in a dark-blue overall with a black crochet shawl came and looked at us, but we were too shy to speak to her. "Why didn't you go to Cook's? Lunn's? The American Express? Any of them would have helped you." Uncle William has asked us that often, but Joss and I had then only one idea: to get Mother, the Littles, Hester, ourselves and our suit-cases to Vieux-Moutiers and Les Oeillets.

There was a train at seven. I remember I went to a food wagon and bought rolls and sausage. I did not know what else to buy and Joss would not go. "But you are the eldest," I said.

"You are the best at French," said Joss cruelly.

Like a herd we drew together and sniffed the sausage; we had not smelled garlic before and we gave it to the attendant; we ate the rolls.

I remember when Vicky touched Mother's leg, Mother gave a little scream and quickly bit her lips. "Don't worry," she said in a moment, "one is not sent anything one can't bear," but she had to bite her lips again. I remember, too, that Willmouse disappeared. "Il est parti voir les locos," said the attendant, but there was a new *Vogue* on a kiosk and he had gone to look at that.

I do not remember the train, only that Mr Stillbotham had been wrong and there were no taxis at the station. "Mais c'est pas bien loin," said the porter, and we took the handcart.

"But Mother can't walk," said Hester.

"She must." A terrible hardness had come upon us. We took her by her arms. She moaned and stumbled, and Hester wept. At last we came to the gates.

As we waited after the porter rang the bell I moved away from the others. I had had the sudden sense of a garden, sharp because it cut me from them. Through the gates I could see a courtyard with gravel round a square of grass in front of the house. To the side, paths led away into the trees; the light was almost gone now and trees showed dimly, grey-green along the wall, while the garden was black in the depth of the shadows. There was a steady light pattering sound—I did not know then that French sound of poplar leaves. A bird gave a sleepy call; an owl answered it, that strange night noise that I recognised though I had not heard it before.

I could smell a summer smell of cut grass and, near me, some flower scent that was heady and sweet; a white flower, I thought, jessamine or syringa. After the city and train my skin was cinder-dry and the air was gratefully cool against my face. I was filled with a sense of peace; all the fears and ignorance of the day seemed to drop away. This was the Hotel des Oeillets, real, not the mirage we had held in front of us through the travelling; we had arrived.

•   •   •   •   •

"L'hôtel n'acccepte pas les malades," said Madame Corbet.

"Does that mean she won't take sick people?" I asked Joss.

"I think it does."

The office at Les Oeillets was off the stairs, it was not big enough to be called a room; steps led up from the hall to an entresol with a landing and doors; the office was an annexe to this landing, separated from it by a counter and brass grille. There was just room behind the counter for a safe, a keyboard with pigeon-holes for letters, and Madame

Corbet's desk with its telephone and account books. Now we, Joss, Hester, Willmouse, Vicky and I, stood in front of the grille; Willmouse's eyes were just level with the counter; only the top of Vicky's hat showed.

The staircase was panelled in pale green, riddled with curious holes, but the holes did not take away from its elegance. The hall was elegant too. It was odd that we, who had never seen elegance before—though it was our favourite word—immediately recognised it—except Hester. "It isn't like the Metropole or Cavendish,"she said regretfully. They were the big hotels on Southstone's grand parade, but instinctively I liked this better. The staircase made a graceful shape as it led up to the floor above. The banister-rail was dark polished wood, the banisters thin and white; halfway up was a round window that showed a glimpse of trees, and in the wall were crystal wall lamps that matched the chandelier in the hall. We looked at that, amazed, for we had never seen a chandelier in a house. The hall had a squared marble floor; its chairs were gilt with faded brocade cushions; four small tables stood against the walls. "But they are only halves," said Willmouse in surprise. We had never seen console tables either.

In that hall our fibre suitcases looked cheap. We had other luggage even more vulgar; a basket, the bag that had held the oranges, a brown-paper parcel of the Littles' Wellington boots, an untidy heap of raincoats with their belts hanging; and we all carried treasures. Joss's, of course, were neat, a drawing-board strapped to her wooden paintbox. Hester had her camera, Willmouse his scrapbooks and workbox packed up with Miss Dawn and Dolores, while Vicky had Nebuchadnezzar in a basket. Nebuchadnezzar was a pig made out of a potato, with matchstick eyes and legs; she had made him at school and carried him about ever since, though he was beginning to shrivel a little. "When he is quite shrivelled I shall eat him," said Vicky. Mother sitting on a chair had her hat on one side and the coat of her good suit wrongly buttoned; she leaned her head against the chair back and shut her eyes, and her face seemed as mottled now as her leg. As for us, we were crumpled, untidy, and dirty, Hester's and Vicky's faces were streaked with dirt and tears, their socks had come down, and all our shoes were dusty. I could see that we were not at all the kind of family that would be an ornament to any hotel.

"I expect a doctor will come and take our mother to hospital," Joss said in English.

"L'hôtel n'accepte pas les enfants seuls."

"She won't take children by themselves."

"But if we *are* by ourselves?" said Hester.

Madame Corbet sat behind the grille with the hotel books spread out round her. On this hot evening she was wearing a black high-necked blouse; a black crochet shawl with bobbles was crossed on her shoulders. She wore a finger-guard of stained celluloid and her face looked stained too with sallow marks; her hair was in two black snakes coiled in a knot on the top of her head and she had a moustache of heavy black down on which Willmouse, straining to look over the counter, had instantly fixed his eyes. All the time we were talking I saw him examining it.

Joss was desperate. I knew that by her white face and the bigness of her eyes. She had taken over Mother's capacious old handbag, which looked oddly big on her. "S'il vous plaît, aidez-nous," she said. I knew how difficult it was for her to humble herself, but Madame Corbet only shrugged so that the topknot and the bobbles of her shawl danced. "Et qu'est-ce que je peux y faire, moi? Je ne suis pas la patronne. Je suis Madame Corbet, c'est tout." She said that as if to be Madame Corbet was something derogatory.

"If it is not your hotel, where is . . ." Joss consulted the paper Mr Stillbotham had given us. "Where is Mademoiselle de Presle?"

"Mademoiselle Zizi? Elle va dîner au château de Méry."

Joss and I looked at one another. Did she say *going* out to dinner. In Southstone we had supper at seven o'clock; now it was nearly ten.

24

"Au château de Méry," repeated Madame Corbet impressively.

The maid who had helped with our luggage and who was now waiting on the stairs rolled up her eyes and crossed herself; she was pert and Madame Corbet spoke sharply.

"Y sont des amis . . ." "Amis means friends," I told Hester. "Mademoiselle de Presle is going to a big house, a château, that might mean a castle, to friends."

"Des amis à Monsieur Eliot . . ." said the maid. Why did she say "Mr Eliot's friends" so meaningly?

Madame Corbet ignored her. To us she said, "They say the President of the Board of Trade is to be there," and I thought, So, she can speak English.

"Then we can't see Mademoiselle de Presle?" asked Joss.

"Naturally not."

"But what can we do?"

Madame Corbet shrugged. "Vous feriez bien d'aller au commissariat. Oui, allez au commissariat."

"Commissariat?" What was that? We looked at one another mystified. "Police," said the hotel boy Paul from his place on the landing. "Go police."

Joss's face flamed as though Madame Corbet had slapped it. "Come," she said to us.

We left the counter and followed Joss across the hall, walking round the two big Alsatian dogs who lifted their dark-furred faces. One wagged its tail; it was the first sign of friendliness Les Oeillets had given us. Perhaps it was that that made Madame Corbet feel ashamed.

"Vous pouvez laisser les bagages," she said.

"No thank you," said Joss.

This was proud but not very practical. The porter had gone and I do not know how we should have managed with Mother and the Littles, but at that moment the dogs stood up, wagging their tails more violently and looking towards a white door on the entresol landing. It opened and Mademoiselle Zizi and Eliot came out.

It was the first time we had seen anyone in 'tails'. Uncle

William had a dinner-jacket, of course, but our vision had gone no further than that. I say 'tails' because it was at Eliot we looked. It seems strange now that, seeing a man and a woman both in full evening dress, we looked at the man first, but there was no question about it. Hester gave a little gasp.

"Were you ever a sailor?" Joss asked Eliot afterwards. I knew what she meant; he was tall and brown and lean, as were sailors in magazine pictures. His eyes even had lines at the sides as if he had wrinkled them looking at the sun. "Were you a sailor?"

"Probably," said Eliot.

"Don't you know?" asked Hester incredulous.

"I know I was a soldier," said Eliot. "Tinker, tailor, soldier, sailor, richman, poorman . . ." but Hester interrupted him.

"You can't have been everything," she said.

"I pretty well was," said Eliot.

We took it for granted that his eyes were blue. His hair was brown, a little grizzled. His face had curious high cheekbones. "From my Chinese grandmother," he told us solemnly. We believed him, and it still seems to me now that his hands and feet were so small as to be oriental. "I am descended from Genghis Khan," he was to tell us, and Hester asked, "Who was Genghis Khan?"

"A fearful Tartar," said Eliot, smoothing her hair.

His clothes were so impeccable—that was a word I liked and had taught to Willmouse—that they looked as if he had just bought them.

"Well, he had." Hester said that later. "Poor Eliot. He could never keep his clothes long."

"What do you mean?"

"He said so. He said, 'Pity, I like this coat. I hate to leave it.' That was his checked one; of course, he was thinking aloud. He did not know I was there. Toinette is always saying that his shirts and pyjamas are new."

That night he wore medals. "His?" Uncle William always

said he doubted it but "Of course they were his," we said indignantly.

He had a carnation in his buttonhole, a dark-red one, and it seemed to symbolise Eliot for us. Why are flowers bought by men so much more notable than those bought by women? I do not know, but they are. Father brought flowers into the house but they were dried, pressed brown, the life gone out of them; with Eliot the flower was alive.

Behind him came Mademoiselle Zizi. When we looked at her we were struck dumb with shyness because Mademoiselle Zizi was ... "Bare," whispered Hester. Arms, neck and shoulders, "and back and front," said Hester reluctantly. We did not know what little puritans we were until we saw Mademoiselle Zizi.

Privately I thought her very beautiful, with her heavy dark-red hair and eyes that seemed almost too enormous— like a sunflower's. They were blued ... "on the *lids*," said Hester, surprised, and her mouth was very, very red. What there was of her dress was gauze, black.

I saw Willmouse looking at the dress critically at first, then satisfied. "That is a real dress," whispered Willmouse, "and what a smell!"

"Is the smell the lady?" asked Vicky. It had filled the hall as Mademoiselle Zizi came in.

They came down the steps from the landing, stopped at the sight of us, and it was then that Eliot said, "Good God! An orphanage!"

Joss was too angry to notice that he spoke in English.

"Don't worry," she said bitingly, "we are not staying." To us she said sharply, "Come on. We will take the luggage first and come back for Mother."

She walked past Eliot to the door, her painting things under her arm; she had picked up two suitcases; Vicky, carrying Nebuchadnezzar's basket, was holding to one of them. The rest of us followed, loyally staggering too. Paul went to open the door, but Eliot stepped forward.

"Where are you going this time of night?"

"To the police." Joss's nostrils were pinched with temper.

"The police? Why?"

"Because of you *French*," said Joss furiously.

"I'm not French, I'm English," said Eliot.

Mother must have heard that. She gave a moan and said, "Please." Eliot looked past us to her, and his face changed. "Zizi," he said, "she's ill."

He went quickly to Mother, bent down and took her hand, feeling it as he questioned her, but after that 'Please' Mother did not speak again, and her head rolled against the chair.

"She's very ill, Zizi," he said. "We must help."

"But . . . our dinner." Her English was pretty and clipped.

"All the same."

"But we shall be late!"

"All the same." It sounded like a command. "Irène," he called to Madame Corbet, "ring Doctor Giroux"; and to Mauricette, "Open the rooms."

I heard Madame Corbet pick up the telephone, the maid shrugged and went to the keyboard. Paul took the suitcases from Joss, but Mademoiselle Zizi stayed where she had been, at the foot of the steps, her beautiful dress held up.

CHAPTER 3

To WAKE for the first time in a new place can be like another birth. I think that to me it was perhaps more startling than to most people because for as long as I could remember I had woken each morning in the same bedroom in Belmont Road, that essentially English bedroom with its wallpaper faded to a grey-blue pattern; to the same white curtains and blue linoleum, the brown rug worn in places so that the white showed through the brown; to the same white-enamelled iron beds, paisley eiderdowns, and the pictures that were framed prints from old supplements to the *Illustrated London News*. Uncle William and Mother had had those pictures when they were children, but Joss had taken them down and put up a Chinese painting instead; she took that with her to Willmouse's room, and I brought the prints back. 'Cecil is sentimental,' said Joss.

There, in the early mornings, lying between sleeping and waking, I could hear and identify all the so ordinary early morning sounds: the milkman's pony, the paperboy's quick steps, the thud as the paper dropped through the letter-box into the hall, the postman——though there was not often anything for us——the cheeping of sparrows, the clock on the town hall with its chimes, Mother's squirrel-quick little foot-steps as she went downstairs to pull the damper out so that the water would be hot for our baths.

This morning my ears were filled with a high clear sound broken into small sharp edges; it was a little while before I knew it was from birds. The room was filled with dim light; the ceiling was high and the walls far away, for it was a big room. I made out the top of a green shutter and then saw that the shutters ran from the ceiling to a floor of plain polished boards without a rug. I was in an immense bed and beside me lay Willmouse.

We had slept without pillows; mysteriously there had been none on the beds and we were too shy to ask; besides, 'oreiller' was a difficult word to pronounce. I remember how surprised we were when we found the pillows in the wardrobe. I never knew why Toinette kept them there.

The sheets felt dry and hot as if their cotton were brittle. I swung my legs over the edge of the bed and slipped down; the boards were cool under my feet as I walked to the win-dow. After a few moments I found how the shutters opened and threw them back.

I was looking into the tops of the trees; at first I thought the house was ringed with them, then I saw that it was only a poplar in front of the window, filling the room with its sound, and beyond it a single great tree that I thought was a willow, though I had not known willows could grow as tall; through its hanging branches I could see, further away, serried rows of fruit trees, some of them heavy with fruit. Perhaps it was this first sight that made me always think of the garden at Les Oeillets as green, green and gold as was that whole countryside of the Marne where, beyond the town, the champagne vineyards stretched for miles along the river, vineyards and cherry orchards, for this was cherry country too, famous for cherries in liqueur. Mother had been thinking of the battlefields; she had not thought to enquire about the country itself; I am sure she had not meant to bring us to a luxury corner of France where the trees and the vines changed almost symbolically in the autumn to gold.

We were not to see that, nor did I know anything about it as I stood by the open window, yet, from the garden, I had a foretaste of that green and amber time and a sense of the countryside in the haze that lay around the town. I could not see the town behind the trees, only a glimpse of houses climbing a hill that had a building on it, a ruined castle or château with ramparts and a tower. The houses were yellow-white, jumbled below the ramparts. I guessed they spread down to what must be a river, for there was the chugging sound of a boat. The chugging was near; the river, I thought, must be on the other side of the orchard.

Our rooms were on the second floor, and if I looked directly down I could see a flight of iron steps with a scrolled iron railing leading from a terrace along the house into a garden that seemed to be made of gravel and small flower-beds. I was to learn that Robert, the silent, cross gardener, spent all his time raking the gravel smooth, tidying the beds. There was a round bed in the middle which held an iron urn planted with geraniums and smaller plots along the sides were bedded with flowers that even in that early light had violent colours. It looked a garden from one of our French grammar books, hideous and formal, but beyond it a low box hedge bounded a wilderness of grass and shrubs and trees, bamboos, a monkey puzzle smothered in creepers, and tangles of roses. Overgrown paths wound among them where white statues glimmered; some of the statues were broken, their arms and legs hacked off; one was lying on its side. Beyond the wilderness was what seemed to be an orchard, and in its high wall a blue door. As I looked at the door a barge hooted from the river.

The garden was light, but it was a young light without sun, clear and stained green by the shrubs and trees. The peace I had felt at the gates of Les Oeillets filled me again and I could have whistled like the birds for well-being and joy. Then, as I stood there in my pyjamas looking down, a man came down the iron steps. He was an old man with white hair and a small white beard; from above he looked nearly square. He wore blue cotton trousers, a white coat and a beret—men wearing berets still looked strange to me. He was carrying many things: something that looked like an easel with long legs, a camp stool, a case, and a bulging white cotton umbrella, the kind of umbrella people put up outside their bathing chalets on the beach at Southstone. He seemed in a hurry; I watched him scurry across the gravel, disappear in the wilderness, and caught a glimpse of him among the fruit trees. Then he was at the far blue door, where he had to put everything down to open it.

"That was Monsieur Joubert," said Eliot when I asked him. "Monsieur Joubert going out to catch the first light."

"Who is Monsieur Joubert?"

"A painter."

A painter! Joss would like to hear that.

"A very famous painter," said Mademoiselle Zizi. "Even an ignorant little English girl should have heard of Marc Joubert."

"He didn't look famous," I said in defence. "He was wearing funny clothes and he looked . . ." I tried to think how to express his scurrying haste. ". . . anxious."

"He probably was," said Eliot. "It's only for a short

while that the light stays like that. I have a belief," and I remember Eliot sounded defiant, as if a belief were a strange thing to have, "that as soon as a human goes out into the morning it is spoilt . . . except a Monsieur Joubert or," and his eyes looked at us thoughtfully, "perhaps children."

"Do you like children so much?" asked Mademoiselle Zizi.

"I don't know any," said Eliot.

Now I watched Monsieur Joubert without knowing his name. The blue door shut with a distant bang and I heard another sound close beside me, in the next room, and I knew what had wakened me. It was Joss in the little room off our bedroom—she had chosen it though they had meant it for Willmouse; the sound was Joss having an attack.

'Nerves,' Mother used to say of these, but Uncle William said they were bilious. Probably both were right. The attacks came at the most inconvenient times and, as I listened, the day began to foreclose on me; it must, I knew, be a difficult day, frightening, probably humiliating, and now Joss was useless. I went in, and she was as I knew I should find her, retching, her skin a curious green-yellow, her eyes looking as though they were bursting with pain. Now she would have to be in a darkened room for days, and I would have to be responsible for everything.

"Perhaps it was the soup," I said as I held her head.

"I—didn't—eat the soup." Though she was being sick as she said it I knew she was offended. That made me remember I was offended too. The maid Mauricette had brought up the soup in bowls on a tray after we had been bundled off to bed, Joss and I with Hester and Willmouse and Vicky . . . "and we are not Hester and Willmouse and Vicky," said Joss.

"I'm sorry. I made a mistake," Eliot said when I pointed this out to him—Joss refused to mention it. "You must remember we were all a bit confused." Eliot could be very charming; he smiled at Joss and put his hand on hers. "You won't forgive me?"

32

"No," said Joss and took her hand away.

Now, "Shall I get Mother?" I asked Joss.

"Don't be silly. There is a nun in her room."

"A *nun?*" Prickles of superstition swept over me. "Then . . . is she dying?"

"Don't be si-lly," but Joss's voice was fainter. "Lots of hospital nurses are nuns—especially in France."

"How do you know?"

"The Madame told me . . . I went in last night," but she had sunk from the washing-stand on to the bed and could not talk any more. In a moment she had to struggle up again. I helped her, and when it was over she lay back, her skin clammy, her eyes closed. The washing stand had only a heavy china basin and jug; there seemed to be no slop pail, only a strange object like an enamelled footbath or a doll's bath, on legs—we had not met a bidet before—and it was too shallow. "If you could get a basin or a bucket," Joss whispered, "I could manage in bed."

"From where?" I said, appalled.

"Downstairs. There must be one. Go and look."

"In someone else's house?"

"It isn't a house. It's an hotel."

"Supposing I meet someone . . ."

"You could ask them."

I shrank from it, but I had to go. "What is the French for bucket?" I asked.

. . . . .

The stairs creaked as I came down, though I crept carefully. I remember the surprise of the bullet-holes; in the daylight I saw that the pale green paint was pocked with them. "Of course," Mademoiselle Zizi often explained. "They machine-gunned the stairs."

"And the marks are still there!" the visitors used to say in wonder.

"As you see," and Mademoiselle Zizi would smile with pride.

"If it were my house," Joss said, "I should have filled them up at once."

Now I came down cautiously because of the two dogs, but when I saw them I felt a coward. They were in the hall, chained each on a low bed; they knew I had been accepted the night before and they lifted their faces and moved their tails.

I had had another timid idea that Madame Corbet would be in the office, but the grille was locked, the counter bare, and the hall was empty. Next to it on the right was a large open room with a bar and, at the garden end, what must have been a conservatory, leading through glassed doors to the terrace. The big room had small iron tables, and chairs painted green, coat stands, tubs bound with brass and filled with sand for cigarette ends. The bar was covered with white dustsheets. On the left of the hall were doors and a sign that said 'Restaurant'. At the back was a baize-covered door that must, I thought, lead to the kitchen.

When I had pushed it open I did not have far to go. At the end of a short passage was a table stacked with flower vases and bowls. I took a bowl and, almost before the door had stopped swinging, was back into the hall, where I patted the dogs. I had turned upstairs, when the white door on the landing opened and a man came out. He was wearing a silk patterned dressing-gown—like an actor's, I thought—leather slippers, and was smoking a cigarette. It was Eliot.

We both stopped abruptly. I knew how I must look, my raincoat bundled round me, blue-and-white-striped pyjamas showing, bare feet, and my hair tied back with a blue ribbon like a baby's. Then I forgot about myself, staring at him. This was another Eliot than the kind Englishman of last night; someone cold and . . . ruthless, I thought. That was a strange word to come into my head when I did not know the meaning of 'ruth'. 'Eliot's eyes are not blue,' Hester was to say. 'They are green-grey, like pebbles.' Now, close to him on the stairs, I saw they were grey and coldly angry. "What are you doing down here?"

I showed the bowl. "Joss, my sister, is ill."

"God! Children!" he said. He put his hand behind him and closed the door, leaning against it. Then he was more kind. "Eaten too much?" he asked, but I, remembering Joss's offendedness, was stiff.

"She is not that sort of sister," I said and went on upstairs.

It was a day or two afterwards that, when for some reason we wanted Eliot, I said, "I shall fetch him," and crossed the hall to the landing and the white door.

"Where are you going?" asked Hester.

"To his room."

"That is not Eliot's room," said Hester. "That is Mademoiselle Zizi's."

CHAPTER 4

"Who let that man into my room?" asked Joss.

It was after tea on that first strange day—"Only there wasn't any tea," said Vicky; we had not learned about the French children's goûter yet—it was what should have been after tea, that Eliot looked at us sitting forlornly round a table in the bar and asked, "Shouldn't there be one more of you?" Then he had asked me to take him upstairs to see Joss.

She lay stiff and flat in the bed while he was in the room; her hair was spread on the pillow and in the gloom of the closed shutters her sick face looked small as a turnip-goblin's. She might have been any age, and he was as familiar as he would have been with someone as young as Vicky.

"Are you a better girl?"

She answered him in monosyllables. "Yes."

35

"Cheer up. You will be well soon."

"Yes."

"Is there anything you want? You can have it, you know."

"No."

I think Eliot did not know quite what to do. "You are not worrying too much about your mother? We are taking care of her." No answer. Presently he went out and Joss reared up on her pillow.

"Who let him in?"

"I . . . did."

"How dared you?"

"But . . . he is in charge of us."

"Cha . . ." She looked at me in astonishment. "Who said so?"

"Mother. She asked him."

"She always was an *idiot*!" said Joss.

The sickness had started again. I waited while she retched miserably into the bowl by the bed. At last she lay back exhausted and, wearily accustomed, I brought her face flannel and wiped the sweat off her face and hands, and dried them. I knew her skin hurt by the way she winced, but as soon as she could speak she croaked, "You must . . . tell Mother."

I stood by the bed holding the towel and cleared my throat. It seemed to have a frog in it too. "I can't tell Mother," I said. "Joss, they . . . they have taken her to the hospital."

Joss had been too ill to know, but it had been a split day, split between Les Oeillets and Belmont Road.

As soon as I was dressed I had gone and knocked softly on Mother's door. It had opened and Joss had been right—the nun was there. She was dressed in white, with a black veil, girdle and crucifix. I had not been close to a nun before and gazed at her startled. She put her finger to her lip and shook her head. Pinpricked all over with fear, I tiptoed away.

Then Hester and Vicky came in asking for breakfast. "There isn't any," I said, quailing, but they insisted there was plenty downstairs, and in the end I had to take them and find the dining-room. Willmouse had gone there already. In the big room I tried to be as travelled and self-contained as even Joss could have wished, but there was Hester's clear unabashed voice and Vicky's obstinacy about food; she was as stubbornly British as John Bull. "I want breakfast," she said. I gave her coffee and a croissant. "This isn't breakfast," said Vicky, "I want a n'egg."

"You can't have eggs for breakfast in France."

"Of course you can," Eliot was to say. "Lots of people ask for them." He added that I was not to be a travel snob, but I was a travel snob and an age snob too. Vicky was, of course, too much for me; as usual, she got her own way, and I had to ask not only for an egg but for babyish milk and jam.

It was Paul who brought them—I soon learned that Mauricette would seldom bother herself to wait on us. Paul deliberately put the milk and jam at my place. "Essuie-toi l'bec avec ta bavette," he said. I did not guess he had said 'Wipe your mouth on your bib' until I got upstairs and looked up 'bavette' in our pocket Larousse, but I knew it was something derogatory and I looked sternly at this Paul.

He was a tall, thin, dirty and greasy boy dressed in blue cotton trousers and a ragged shirt. He wore the white apron and the grey-white canvas shoes—we had not learned yet to call them espandrilles—he had worn last night. His shirt had the sleeves rolled up; his elbows looked as sharp as knives, and when he turned his back the shoulderblades stuck out. He had lank, yellow hair, with a lock falling over his forehead, and his face had hollows in the cheeks. I did not know about Paul in those days, but even then, in my carelessness and ignorance, I was worried by his face. We had come to see the battlefields and, though we did not know it, this face was a part of them.

Who was Paul? Nobody knew. Even his name might

have belonged to almost any nationality; it was one of the few that hardly change in pronunciation from one country to another. Paul could have been English, German, French, Austrian, Russian. His mother, Madame Corbet said contemptuously, had 'gone with the soldiers'.

"Gone where?" asked Hester, but nobody answered that. "Our father's a botanist," Hester told Paul. "What's yours?"

"Un troufion," said Paul, and when we looked mystified he pretended to march and salute.

"Oh, a soldier!" I said.

"What was his name?" asked Hester, but the father did not seem to have had a name. One day Paul said, "J'avais une p'tite soeur."

"A little sister?" By then Hester was beginning to understand.

"Une mulâtre," said Paul carelessly, and, seeing we did not understand that either, he said, "Une négresse," and showed half on his finger.

"Negro? But you are not mulat . . . what you called it," we said, puzzled, and asked, "Where is she, your sister?"

Paul shrugged.

"Don't you know?"

He shook his head. "Elle a disparu."

Hester looked enquiringly at me. "She disappeared," I said.

"Does he mean dead?" asked Hester.

I tried him with that. "Morte?" I asked sympathetically.

"Perdue," said Paul. "Pssts," and he made as if to throw something away.

"But you don't lose *sisters*." Paul's silence said clearly that you did. We felt dizzy.

He had been found in the American camp when it was broken up; the soldiers themselves had found him and been kind. When they went home to America he was taken to the almshouse, the Hôtel-Dieu. "God's hotel?" asked Hester. "That should have been good." But Madame Corbet said it was where they put old people waiting to die, and lunatics and badly treated children from the courts. "That doesn't *sound* good," said Hester doubtfully.

Madame Corbet did not seem disturbed. "Where are they to go in a little town like this?" she asked. She added that Paul was bad and ran away, the police brought him back, and—"Mademoiselle Zizi, out of her kindness, let him work here."

It did not seem very kind. As we were to find out, Paul worked from six in the morning—or before, if there were a party for breakfast—until midnight—or after if there were dinners. He had plenty to eat—everyone near Monsieur Armand, the chef, had that—but Paul's sleeping place was in a cupboard under the stairs, and had not even a window; the bed was planks with a straw mattress, there was a dirty pillow and the kind of blanket given to dogs.

"But all that was no reason to make a set at me," I said afterwards, but it seemed it was. I think now our coming, so unaware, so pink and protected, gave Paul a smart he had not known before, and particularly when Joss was near him, every spot of grease, each broken black nail stood out, and the smell of him, in which he lived unnoticing, stank.

The first morning we knew none of this and I looked at him, my chin high, then coldly turned my eyes away. It was not done as Joss would have done it, but it was the best I could do. I spread Vicky's croissant with jam and poured out her cup of milk; then, copying a big Frenchman in the corner, I dipped my own croissant in the dark bitter coffee and ate it like that. It tasted nasty, but at least it was French.

After breakfast I sent Hester, Willmouse and Vicky out to explore. I watched them as they scampered down the alleys of the orchard, and my legs itched to run too; still, in spite of my teens, that urge to run and scamper and roll like a colt would rise in me, but Paul was watching; besides, with Mother and Joss ill I felt as weighted with cares as Uncle William. I went out on to the terrace and stood at the top of the iron steps holding the rail that was already warm from the sun.

I could not feel an Uncle William for long. All around me rose the sounds of this, my first real French morning. Overhead the voices of two women talked. From Joss's window that, unlike ours, faced the road, I had seen them earlier come in through the gate. They were the daily maids and now they flung mattresses over the sills upstairs, shook dusters and brooms. One called from her window to the other, 'Toinette, la clé du quatorze,' and the other shrilled back, 'En bas, Nicole, sur le tableau.' Why should that have ravished me? I do not know, but it did. Water was running in what I guessed was the kitchen because of the clatter of china and a man's big voice shouting orders. Mauricette was singing in the dining-room a nasal little song:

> "*Je l'ai tellement dans le peau,*
> *C'est mon homme.*
> *Que j'en suis marteau,*
> *C'est . . . mon . . . homme.*"

A typewriter clacked in the office. I looked over the garden to the green dew of the wilderness and orchard, the sun haze beyond, and I could stay in no longer; slowly I went down the steps, across the gravel, past the flower-beds and through a gap in the box hedge. Stepping in dew, my head in the sun, I walked into the orchard and, before I knew what I had done, reached up to touch a greengage. It came off, warm and smooth, into my hand. I looked quickly round, but no one came, no voice scolded and, after a moment, I bit into the the ripe golden flesh. Then I ate another, and another until replete with fruit and ecstasy, I went back to my post.

There was no sign of Mademoiselle Zizi, but presently Eliot came out. He was aloof and unapproachable. How did I know then that he had these times? I do not know, but, as if the first greengage had been an Eden apple, I was suddenly older and wiser and did not try to speak to him. He passed me as if I did not exist and went out into the sun.

He was wearing linen trousers, a dark-blue open-necked shirt. Mauricette ran out with a deckchair for him, but he was curt with her. How wonderful to be as curt in French as in English! The ecstasy faded. I was suddenly depressed again. How inferior we were; our family had never been anywhere at all and did not know anything.

Then Paul came out and jerked his thumb over his shoulder for me to go to the office. Madame Corbet sent me to fetch our passports, and Hester bobbed up and told about Uncle William.

Monsieur William John Bullock, wrote Mademoiselle Zizi on a slip of paper; then she opened the grille and the flap of the counter and came out. She ran upstairs, and her heels sounded very determined as she crossed the landing to Mother's room. My heart sank, and I pushed Hester away in disgust and went up too.

Mother was a prisoner in the bed; a cage had been put over the bad leg and she lay on her back, her eyes looking this way and that, past Mademoiselle Zizi, past the nun; then she saw me in the doorway and beckoned me. I slipped past the foot of the bed and knelt down. Mother clutched me and whispered, but the whisper was so thick and blurred that I could hardly understand it. "Get the Englishman," whispered Mother, "that man who was English."

Mademoiselle Zizi's ears were sharp. "No! You are not to!" she cried, but I had slipped out.

When Eliot came I knew how good he was. "Not good," said Hester, who was exact. "A good person would not have done it. Not good—kind," which was nearer our hearts.

He came in looking tall in that room of women.

"Mais Eliot, je t'en prie . . ."

"Wait, Zizi." He bent down and Mother caught his hand. I knew how hot hers were from when she had held me, and her eyes were full of pain. "Is there anything I can do for you?" asked Eliot.

"Don't let them." It was the same thick whisper. "Don't let them."

"Eliot, this is nothing to do with you."

"Please, Zizi." He bent down lower. "Don't let them what?"

Mother could look very like Hester. "Don't let them send for William."

I saw his lips twitch. "But . . ."

"He will say 'I told you so'," whispered Mother.

"I see," said Eliot. "Yes. I understand."

"But she has to go to hospital," cried Mademoiselle Zizi. "Bon Dieu! Et si elle allait mourir?" She went on so fast that I could not keep up, but Eliot, while the stream of French went on, kept Mother's hand.

"Why did he consent? A fellow like that?" Uncle William said afterwards. "It wasn't in keeping."

"Perhaps," said Joss privately to me, "Eliot once had an Uncle William."

.   .   .   .   .

"But what can I tell Irène?" said Mademoiselle Zizi.

I think she and Eliot spoke in English sometimes because they did not want the servants to understand, but they mixed it; sometimes one would ask a question in English, the other answer it in French, or the other way round. "What can I tell Irène?"

"That you can put two into a single room and charge for both."

"Eliot, you are laughing at me."

"Not laughing, predicting."

"But can they pay?" asked Mademoiselle Zizi. "They do not look as if they had much."

"If they can't I will."

"Have you so much money, Eliot?"

He did not tell her. "It comes and goes," he said and there was the sound of a kiss; but Eliot said something else, something odd and . . . not pleasant, I thought, "Those children can be useful."

"How useful?"

42

"Stop people talking."

"Let them talk," said Mademoiselle Zizi.

"Don't be silly, Zizi. This is a little town and you have to live in it. The children will give me a reason for being here. After all, now I'm their guardian. They can be camouflage."

I did not like us being camouflage, and he was right about the rooms. Hester and Vicky slept one each end of a single bed, and Joss was in our dressing-room, which was not really a bedroom at all. We were not allowed to use the bathrooms, and our only lavatory was the one we called the Hole, because it was in a cubbyhole opening off the stairs; there was no pedestal or seat, only a pan in the floor and two places to put one's feet—'à la turque,' Paul called it, but it was awkward for someone as small as Vicky and ignominious for big girls. "And it smells the stairs," said Hester. Madame Corbet charged us for towels and soap; when I went that first morning to the desk to ask for some lemon water for Joss, Madame Corbet already had two pages on the ledger marked 15, 16 and 16ᵃ, and there were several entries in her spider-fine writing. The lemon would be written in at once.

Paul kept the bar in the afternoons and Madame Corbet called to him to get it. "Alors vous restez?" he asked, looking me over.

"Yes, we are staying," I said coldly. I added sarcastically in French—I was determined to speak French to Paul—that I hoped it would not derange him.

He shrugged and Paul's shrug was indescribably rude. "Les enfants trouvés, y faut b'en s'en occuper, hein?" he said, and turned to take the slip for the lemon to the desk before he gave the glass to me.

I had caught 'found children', that means ,'strays', I thought . . . strays! And as he went he pulled my hair.

There was no one in the hall but ourselves, no one to remind me I was big, almost grown up. Suddenly I had had enough of Paul. I ran after him and hit him as hard as I could on the jaw.

He was so surprised that he almost fell; the lemon water went spinning across the hall, his long legs slithered and his apron slipped as he clutched at the newel-post on the steps leading to the landing; then, holding to the post, he bent forward and looked at me; the lock of hair had fallen farther over his eyes and they gleamed through it like an animal's. "So," said Paul. "So."

"Yes. So," I said.

He came at me, but I was waiting. Paul was tall but he was gangling, while I was a Bullock and all Bullocks were solid and strong. I got one more hit in on his chest, then his arms were like a flail hitting me, and he knocked me over; in a moment we were both on the ground, rolling and scratching. I remember him pounding my head on the marble, then Madame Corbet screamed and people came running. I saw Mauricette's legs, black skirt and frilled apron, before my own blood blinded me as I dug my thumbs into Paul's throat until we were taken like kittens by the scruffs of our necks and shaken apart.

It was the chef. I could smell the grease on his white clothes and had a startling view of his fat cheeks, polished black moustache and high white cap seen through the tears that were stupidly pouring from my eyes.

Eliot's voice came. "Let them go," he said, and the chef dropped us—again like kittens—and we stood in the middle of them all, breathing hard and glaring at one another. Mauricette held a table napkin to my nose; it was not her table napkin and Madame Corbet snatched it away. Eliot looked at us amused and passed me his handkerchief; I was very much ashamed.

I thought he would say something about my being a girl, even a young lady, but he did not. I suppose that to him we were two young animals. "Next time," he said, "fight in the garden. This is a lady's house," and he said it in French for Paul, "Vous êtes ici chez une dame comme il faut." Paul made a rude noise. "Chez une dame comme il faut," repeated Eliot—his voice was so peremptory that

Paul stood up straight—"et vous vous tiendrez comme il faut."

Late that evening I met Paul again. At dusk the garden greenness took on a richer light as if the rays of the sunset stayed there prisoned by the walls; the leaves glimmered and the grass; the broken statues that were chill and white in the morning turned almost to gold. Robert had ceased his raking and gone home. The dogs lay out on the warm gravel, voices came more gently from the house, everything was filled with peace. I was still in the habits of Belmont Road and, sore as I was, with my swelled nose, I had come to find Vicky—I guessed she was with Monsieur Armand, whom she had instantly adopted—to put her to bed.

Paul was sitting on a stone step outside the kitchen. I did not know whether to pass him or go back through the house; that would have looked a retreat and I decided to pass him, though I was trembling. As I came nearer he stood up.

All right. If you want to fight, I thought, but ... "Please, Mees," he said and pulled out a crumpled paper packet of the horrible-smelling cigarettes he smoked and held them out to me.

I expect I blushed—no one had ever offered me a cigarette before—then I saw it was not condescension; he was offering them as to an equal. I took one. I did not know at all how I should smoke it, but was immensely flattered. Paul struck a match for me; I took my first puff and choked; he patted me on the back, and then we were sitting down together on the steps.

Vicky was hours late going to bed. "Well, she is in France; she must do as French children do," I said. Belmont Road was disappearing fast.

When I went up to Joss she drew away across the bed and said, "Whew!"

"It's a Gauloise, a French cigarette." I tried to sound careless, but Joss's look remained cold and she said icily, "You seem to have settled in here very quickly."

CHAPTER 5

WE HAD settled. After that first disrupted day we might have been in Vieux-Moutiers all our lives. Why did we like it so much? "Because it was not Southstone," said Uncle William testily. There was truth in that; after Southstone this old French town, drenched that year in sun, seemed especially beautiful. Southstone had not grown; it had been built in a few years as a watering place. Its red-brick houses with slated roofs stood in well-ordered asphalt roads, planted neatly with laburnum and bright-pink may trees, each cased in a stand of wire-netting; it had a Winter Garden for concerts, a skating rink, covered tennis courts, swimming baths, tea rooms and large shops. Its cliffs were cut up into municipal gardens, its foreshore into a parade with a bandstand and pier, a Round Tower, clock-golf course and an aquarium. Vieux-Moutiers, beside its wide peaceful river, was centuries old; its upper and lower town had grown slowly, haphazardly, or crumbled away with disuse. It was so small that one could not get lost, though it had a maze of tiny cobbled lanes around the Place, where the market was held twice a week in front of the Hôtel de Ville, as we learned to call the town hall.

The Hôtel de Ville was sixteenth-century, and the upper town was crowned by the monastery whose ramparts I had seen from my window; besides a monastery, it was a prison and held the old Donjon St Pierre. There was a gate through which Saint Joan had ridden with Charles VII, and I heard an American visitor read out from his guide-book ... "She had probably heard Mass in the chapel, and the horse-block from which she mounted her horse still stands in the courtyard."

"Saint Joan? Then was she a person?" I asked. "I thought she was a saint."

"A saint is a person, you little silly," said Eliot; "that is the whole point."

Nobody told us about Vieux-Moutiers. Its history dawned on us as we overheard the visitors talking, or wandered by ourselves in the streets. The hospital, for instance. There was a notice over the stairs that we saw when we went to leave the bunches of wild flowers we picked for Mother. *Essuyez vos pieds, SVP.* said the notice, and we carefully wiped our feet while we spelled out the rest: 'Erigée en 1304 par la grâce de Jeanne de Navarre, épouse de Philippe le Bel.' Our mother, *our* mother, was in a hospital built by a queen. I wished I were married to Philip the Beautiful.

In the upper town there was a cream-washed house with marigold-coloured, patched stains on its walls; by its front door was a plaque. A poet had lived there, a famous one, and when we read his name the classrooms at St Helena's came back, my punishments, Hester reciting at the school concert. '*That* poet lived *here*.' I did not think a poet had ever lived in Southstone; it would be almost better to be married to a poet than to Philippe le Bel, and I took a flake from the cream-crusted walls to keep for ever.

It was altogether a poet's town. Monsieur Joubert made us see that; he was working on two canvases, a morning one and one that he began after four o'clock when the light turned more gold. Looking at those paintings, watching as they slowly came to life, we saw the colours of the houses along the river bank and up the hill, the faint varyings of the shabby plaster, the pink and grey-green of the paint as it blistered on doors and shutters; I do not think there was a newly painted house in the whole town. We saw the shadows of the river, the black, white and scarlet reflections of a barge eddying in the water, reflections of houses, trees, fishermen, children. Up above were the ruins of the monastery walls, their old stone turned a honey-yellow; the air was hazed with the town smoke against the sky. There were other colours: grains of grey and white that were pigeons and cats, the unexpected pink of an apron, a man's blue overalls, a jug, a cask, a child's toy; and there were sounds: the sound of the bells, of hammering from the boat-yards, the hoot of a barge, the land hooter of the Brass Instruments Factory behind the town and, nearer, the cries of children bathing in the Plage des Saules.

In Vieux-Moutiers we were foreigners, which was more comfortable than being odd; the town was accustomed to tourists and nobody stared at us; we had achieved an obscurity that was strangely restful.

In Southstone our family circle had been five children alone with Mother. Our importance had receded only on Father's rare visits; Uncle William and his friends were as uninteresting as the dead to us, and children's doings, problems, ideas and jokes had filled all our horizons. At Les Oeillets we were as insignificant as grass under trees, under the light and shadow of the grown-ups.

We had, too, been chiefly with girls and women, and had been ruled by Mother, who made a private child's world for us; now suddenly we were surrounded by a public and almost rude life. Madame Corbet told us not to go beyond the gates at night because on the bridge into the town and along the canal behind the Plage sometimes there were drunken men; we often heard their uncertain singing. Monsieur Joubert was painting a picture—a picture to hang in a public gallery—of Robert's wife, suckling her baby. In the kitchen we saw Paul pull Mauricette down on his lap and run his hand up under her skirt; then Monsieur Armand would turn round and give Paul a box on the ear and pull Mauricette to him and kiss her himself. "With those moustaches it must prick," said Hester, which was a little girl's view, while I had become as stretched and as sensitive as an Indian with his ear to the ground, or as an insect's feeler or the needle in a compass to these doings. The sound of those loud kisses seemed to go on and on in my ears; but that was nothing to the way I watched how Mademoiselle Zizi would catch at Eliot as he went by, and how he would kiss her hand or her arm or her neck, sometimes her mouth. Eliot and Mademoiselle Zizi—and Madame Corbet—made an intense drama for me.

It was Paul who told us about the drama. We could speak little French; he had no more than a word or two of American English and yet Paul, as he sat with us on the kitchen steps those summer evenings, was like a floodlamp, illuminating everyone at Les Oeillets in the most garish possible colours.

When I say us I mean Hester and me. Hester seemed to have moved up to become to me what I had been to Joss, a second self, a substantial shadow. Willmouse and Vicky had other interests. France and Mademoiselle Zizi had given Willmouse new ideas, and he was busily making a new collection; his atelier was a grass bank in the orchard under a cherry tree. Vicky had attached herself to Monsieur Armand, who gave her tidbits from morning to night. If Joss had not still been ill we should not have seen so much of Paul—"I do not talk to kitchen boys," she said, which explained why she was so ignorant—but her bout of sickness would not stop. "It is the shock," said the doctor. It was more than shock; she had one of her womanly times— 'Eve's curse' we called it. It was as if she were being changed, sloughing off the old Joss like a skin. The doctor, whom we had learned to call Monsieur le Directeur from our visits to the hospital, came to see her twice and talked of moving her to be with Mother; in French hospitals, it seemed, there was a bed for a relation in private rooms. "But your mother is too ill," said Madame Corbet. She added that we were all a great nuisance.

There was little we could do for Joss. I made her bed and brought her barley drinks; Toinette took her cups of thin soup called 'bouillon', Eliot looked in on her every night for a moment; for the rest she lay in the darkened room and told us to leave her alone. It was an odd world without Joss or Mother; every day Hester and I wrote notes to Mother, and the Littles collected bunches of flowers which we all carried over the bridge to the hospital, passing a café called the Giraffe where Eliot often went for a drink. I do not know if Mother read our notes, but not much of ourselves went into them; it was not that we did not care—at moments ever

49

day we cared abominably and were often frightened and lost
—but Mother seemed to have become remote from us. That
was just as well; sometimes I was a little uneasy and thought:
If Mother knew what we talk about ... but she did not
know and I crushed the uneasiness down.

Hester asked Paul most of the questions. "Why does
Madame Corbet hate us?"

She did hate us. She even wrote the figures into our
account as if the pen could poison the paper; we watched in
dread for her topknot to bob up over the grille and a reproof
to be rapped out. Not even Vicky escaped. 'Pourquoi est-ce
qu'elle nous déteste?"

"Parce-qu' c'est Eliot qui a tout arrangé."

"Not Eliot?"

"Si."

"Then doesn't she hate Eliot?"

"Si."

Paul's 'Si' seemed to steal into my bones and stay there; it
was sinister but exciting.

"*Hates* Eliot? Elle déteste Eliot?" I said while Hester's
calm, little-girl voice went on, "Why does she hate Eliot?"

The answer came back, "Parce qu'elle en tient pour
Mademoiselle Zizi"; and seeing I did not understand, "She
love Mademoiselle Zizi."

"A lady love a *lady*?"

We did not believe it, but "Si" said Paul.

Now we had been told we saw it for ourselves. The
topknot did not only come up to watch us; it spied on every
movement of Mademoiselle Zizi.

Every evening we sat there on the steps—Paul with his
Gauloise, his thin knees pointed under his apron—and from
the garden, where twilight was falling, came that flower-
sweet scent. I had always meant to go and look for its bush,
find the flower, and instinctively I knew it was a better idea
than to sit listening to this. The kitchen dustbins stood by
the steps, the smell of their refuse filled our nostrils. That
seemed symbolic and often I half rose, then sat down again

on the warm stone. If Paul had the end of a bottle of wine, he would pass it to Hester, who would tip it up, take a mouthful and pass it on to me; I would take one and hand it to Paul. "How disgusting!" said Joss when I told her.

"It isn't. We wipe the top on Paul's apron."

"Ouch!" said Joss and looked as if she would be sick again.

Once, after I had taken such a drink, with the dark vinegar taste of the wine in my mouth, I had said, "I think Mademoiselle Zizi is in love with Eliot."

There were empty bottles by the dustbin; one of them had gold foil on its neck. Paul stripped the foil off, shaped it into a round and handed it to me. "Tu ne l'as pas volée," he had said gravely as he gave it to me for a medal.

Evening after evening Hester took up the saga. "Does Eliot love—aime—Mademoiselle Zizi?"

"Pas lui," said Paul and laughed. "Not him."

If his 'Si' had stolen into my bones, the laughing woke them up. 'They should never have let you talk to that boy!' Everyone said that afterwards; it was not Paul who was at fault but my own thoughts. Coming from our Eden world of Belmont Road I was like a young novice horse who jumps too high, while Paul had been born an imp of the world, the real world. To him all this was entirely natural; that was what women were for. "J'avais quatorze ans quand j'ai fait l'amour la première fois," he told me. At fourteen! I looked at him suspiciously, but he was not boasting. He was·far more interested in lorries. "Renault, Berliet, Willème," he said as if they were unimaginably beautiful names, and looked away across the garden, his face soft with his dream. He could not know that when he told me small prickles seemed to be breaking out all over me and the back of my knees felt hot. I had to persist. "You mean . . . you made love? When you were *fourteen*?"

He laughed and put his arm round my neck, his hand under my dress. I jumped as, quite casually and calmly, he felt my breasts, but he took his hand away. "Deux petits

51

citrons," he said and laughed. Citrons! Lemons! He laughed again at the outraged look on my face and, with his finger, tapped my nose as one would a little animal if it were too eager. There was no doubt about it. It was I, not Paul, who was bad.

I could not help it; it was a stain spreading through my bones. I began to wonder about bones; Vicky's, I thought, must be like a chicken's, pearly-pink and blue with a little clear red. Monsieur Joubert's, for some reason, seemed to me the same as Vicky's—perhaps they would not take a stain. "Well, he is busy," said Joss when I expounded this to her. Paul's and Hester's seemed red too, clean and honest; Joss's I did not know about and would not have dared to enquire. I wondered guiltily about mine and passed hastily on. "Mademoiselle Zizi's are purple," I said.

"No, mauve," said Joss.

Madame Corbet's bones I saw as black and green, gangrenous with wicked thoughts. "And Eliot's?" asked Joss.

We were both silent. We had not the faintest idea what Eliot's would be.

CHAPTER 6

"Eliot est un vrai mystère," said Paul. Yes, a great mystery, I thought, and sighed.

One of the oddest things about Eliot was that he had nothing that helped us to understand what kind of a person he was. Everyone else had things, "toi et moi, moi qui parle," said Paul. That was true. Mademoiselle Zizi had her bottles and jars, her scents and dresses; Madame Corbet had her crucifix and beads, I had seen them on her chest of drawers; Paul had his pictures of lorries, Berliet and Willème, pasted up in his cupboard, just as we had our treasures. "Mais Monsieur Eliot, il n'a rien," Paul said, not even a photograph or a paper, and even in Eliot's drawers, Paul told us, were only clothes folded up.

"You mean you look in other people's drawers?" we said, shocked.

"Si," said Paul cheerfully. Eliot had nothing, nothing to tell about himself.

"He has books," I objected. "I cut them for him." I liked doing it, it was a labour of love to cut the interminable pages of those paper-bound French novels. "But when he has finished them he throws them away," I had to admit.

"I cut them too," said Hester, and she added, "but he has something, his beautiful paper-knife."

I had never seen a paper-knife like Eliot's. We thought it was silver, but I suppose now it was steel, thin, about twelve inches long. "Thirteen," said Eliot, "my lucky number." Its blade was sharp-pointed, with bevelled edges. "Be careful," said Eliot when we cut the pages; "don't let the Littles have it, it's sharp." It was. I remember once I dropped it point down on the grass, it went in and stayed upright.

It had a ring at the top with strange lettering. "Chinese," said Eliot.

"Where did you get it?" asked Hester, and Eliot said dramatically, "From my ancestor, Genghis Khan."

When we were with Eliot all that Paul told us disappeared—or was confirmed, confirmed as a part of life; we no more thought and wondered about it than we should have wondered about Eliot brushing his teeth.

He had us in excellent order, even Vicky. Though we were often a chorus, following him, we kept our distance when told. The hotel had its own bathing place, a cove in an inlet of the river made by a small island a few hundred yards along the bank; it was screened by bulrushes and hazels and shaded by big willow trees; when Eliot had lunched in the hotel he would sunbathe in the cove afterwards, lying on its sand; 'imported sand,' he told us. "The

Marne has only gravel." He would not strip but let the sun soak through his clothes, his head and eyes shielded by an old yachting cap.

Then we stayed respectfully at a distance, which is what he meant us to do. He would seldom pick himself up until we had gone in for the goûter we owed to Paul. Paul gave us our food and at four o'clock had taken to coming to the kitchen door and whistling; I think we should have heard that whistle for miles. The goûter was delicious, though I do not know how we held it as well as all the other food; we were beginning to eat as much as the French themselves. Paul would take one of the long thin loaves called 'baguettes', chop eight or ten inches off it, split that, spread the split with butter and clap in ham or jam or a slab of chocolate from the showcase in the hall.

"But won't Madame Corbet . . .?"

Paul made a rude noise and pretended to write with his hand; it was true, Madame Corbet behind the grille was entering the chocolate in the ledger.

Even for Eliot we would not have missed our goûter, but it was a long-drawn-out time, for Monsieur Armand had taken to making us pay for it. "Il faut payer," he would say gravely. "Little dogs must sing for their supper." He used to make Vicky, who sometimes lisped, say an old tongue-twister, "Combien sont ces six saucissons? Ces six saucissons sont six sous. Six sous, ces six saucissons? Mais ces six saucissons sont trop chers."

Four o'clock was Monsieur Armand's rest time; the lunches were finished, the kitchen was tidy and it was not time yet to begin dinners. Then he sat at the table by the window, where the light was made green by the vine, and he read the newspaper, and drank a bottle of wine. He was very comfortable, his shoes off, his cap on the dresser; Vicky sat on the table by him, and the kitchen cat, Minette, curled herself in the patch of sun at his feet. It always amused Monsieur Armand to hear us talk—he thought English an excruciatingly funny language—and he had taken to making me, every day, translate some passage in the newspaper. I learned more French in the kitchen at Les Oeillets than even in the punishments at St Helena's.

That kitchen was a pleasant place; its whitewashed walls were made green near the window by the vine, and orange-gold near the fire; the light caught reflections in the rows of copper pans that hung down the middle of the room. Below them were the working tables, with hot shelves above them from which Mauricette took the dishes on the dining-room side as Monsieur Armand and Paul put them in from the other.

Behind the tables was the great stove of iron with polished steel handles and hinges. There were two sinks, a big one and a smaller for washing up silver and glass and petits déjeuners. In the next room was the machine for ice-cream, the marble slabs for making pâtisserie and the small store of vegetables; beyond that was the big store, where meat, poultry, fish and oysters were kept; Monsieur Armand took out what was needed once each day. The fish were in tanks outside. There was a spit over an open fire at the end of the room, a red-bricked floor, and always a good smell of cooking onions, new bread, coffee and wine. In the afternoons Toinette and Nicole would be talking gently in the scullery as they peeled potatoes or cut beans, or else there would be a smell of singeing and hot linen as they ironed in the linen-room along the passage. Mauricette would wander in and out from the garden, her apron off, and take a sip from Monsieur Armand's glass, while Paul would pause in his work to tease her, or they would both listen gravely to my reading. I do not know what newspaper Monsieur Armand read, but the bits he gave me were always sensational. "Que veut dire 'belle-mère'?" I would ask.

"Wife mother," said Monsieur Armand, making a face.

"Oh, mother-in-law!" and I would read, 'Mother-in-law hits husband with hatchet', or 'Baby girl found dead in trunk in . . . "grenier", qu'est-ce que c'est?' but they could not make me understand and I had to look it up; the baby girl had been found in the attic.

Monsieur Armand seemed to think these horrors were good for me, which was odd because he was very particular what Paul said when we were neat—he did not know what we talked of on the steps—and if Paul used swearwords Monsieur Armand would smack his head. When Vicky's rosy little mouth said, 'Merde!' and 'Ordure' he washed it out with a piece of kitchen soap, but when I read, 'Thieves entice young wife while accomplice takes twenty thousand francs'-worth of rings and brooches' or 'Soldiers tie schoolgirl on bed', he would chuckle with delight.

Sometimes we chafed because we knew when we raced back to the cove Eliot would be gone. He liked to walk along the bank undisturbed—perhaps to get away for a little while from his female admirers—sometimes he would walk downstream into the town and cross the bridge to the Giraffe. We would go back to the house and wait faithfully to see if he wanted us when he came in.

"I like that man," said Vicky, which was surprising because Eliot never gave her anything to eat and she was allowed to trot round after Monsieur Armand, who gave her plenty; in her time at Les Oeillets Vicky grew very fat. She did not trot round after Eliot—none of us would have dared to do that—but when he noticed us, as he did quite often in an absent-minded way, she would give up the kitchen, the slivers of chicken and spoonfuls of cream, and stay where he was likely to be.

"And I like him," said Willmouse. "He is the only person I know except Mother who has never laughed at me."

That was the first time I knew Willmouse minded being laughed at. Then he was brave, this odd little brother of mine; it was strange how having a stranger added to the family had made one look at its members with different eyes.

Eliot treated Willmouse with particular seriousness. He would look at Miss Dawn's and Dolores' new dresses, examining them and criticising carefully. He bought Willmouse a book from Paris, not a fashion magazine but a big book of old masters. "Study them," he told Willmouse, "especially the primitives; they will give you a sense of drapery and colour." Willmouse only nodded, but his eyes kindled.

"But books like that cost a fortune!" cried Madame Corbet.

"Not a fortune, just a bit," said Eliot.

"But for a child!"

"This child needs it."

Hester did not say what she felt, but she had used up the last film in her Brownie on Eliot. Too shy to ask, she had crept up on tiptoe and taken a snapshot of him as he slept in his deck-chair and spent the last of her travelling francs on having it developed at La Maison Kodak. She had shown the photograph to no one but stuck it on cardboard, with a cardboard stand, and made a frame of the dried white shells we found along the river; it stood on her chest of drawers, though she hid it while Toinette cleaned the room, and, in a chipped liqueur glass begged from Mauricette, a tiny bouquet of flowers was always put in front of it. I was too old to show what I felt or even to say it . . . and I would not have dared to ask Joss.

With Eliot, as if under a spell, we accepted everything, trusted everything, but when he went to Paris, as he often did, we became suspicious and very critical indeed.

If Mademoiselle Zizi had known that gallery of hard young eyes was watching her I wonder if she would have been different. From morning to night at Les Oeillets we sat in judgment on her, and the judgments were severe. "Well, none of it is *true*," said Hester.

That was not quite fair. In everything there was a grain of truth.

Take her name: Zizi, we knew now from Paul, was a little girl's name, "And she is not a little girl," said Hester. She told lies about Les Oeillets too. "It was my father's house, my grandfather's and great-great-great-grand-father's," Mademoiselle Zizi used to tell the visitors, "The de Presles have lived here since 1731."

"Is it as old as *that*?" asked the visitors.

"It has seen ten wars," said Mademoiselle Zizi. It had been the headquarters of the American Army; the holes in the staircase were from machine-gun bullets; in the cupboard in my room was a stain on the floor; the stain was blood, from the American soldier who had been shot there. On our second day Rita and Rex dug up a skull in the garden.

"Poor house!" Mademoiselle Zizi would say pathetically. "After each war it has healed, but now I am the only one left. I never thought to see my home an hotel!" She looked at the conservatory bar with its tables and chairs. "When I was a little girl it was full of carnations, such carnations, with a vine across the roof."

When she said this, if Paul were near, he spat. He beckoned me and showed me a date under the wistaria above the front door. The date said 1885. "M'sieur Presle était boucher," said Paul.

"Un boucher?" I said, disappointed. It did not seem possible that Mademoiselle Zizi was the daughter of a butcher but Paul went on, prodding me with his finger as if he would push the words into me, and reluctantly I relayed what he said to Hester. "The butcher bought Les Oeillets as an hotel with money he got from selling bad meat to the soldiers."

The bulletholes were real, but when the staircase was painted they were not closed up but picked out again; the stain in the cupboard was made freshly every now and then by Paul with blood from the kitchen; and one day, when a char-à-bancs party was coming, he beckoned me out into the garden and showed me what he had in his hand, the skull. It was gruesome, with its eye-sockets and long cheekbones. Paul laughed and made the broken jaw move so that it looked as if it were talking. He had to shut Rita and Rex in the kennel or they would have dug it up at once; he buried it under the urn in the middle flowerbed and with it put a piece of raw liver. "Le pourboire," he said and laughed again.

I did not laugh. I was thinking how impressed we had been the first day, how war and death had seemed so close that we had felt almost as Mother had wanted us to feel—ashamed and . . . holy? I thought. Now I felt a fool and I did not like Mademoiselle Zizi or Madame Corbet or Paul; they made Les Oeillets horrid, I thought; but the skull was a man's skull, probably a soldier's, that had been found in the garden. There was a grain of truth.

It was, oddly, Madame Corbet who came best out of our scrutiny, "Because she doesn't pretend," said Hester. She was always Madame Corbet, uncompromising, with her black blouse and skirt, stifling shawl, heavy skin, moustache, hard black beady eyes, topknot and all. There was no mistaking Madame Corbet; the sound of her voice, perpetually raised in scolding, haggling, objecting, had at least the sound of honesty; with Mademoiselle Zizi, even more than with the house, nothing was what it seemed.

She had a habit when Eliot was away of leaving the door of her room open and talking across the landing to Madame Corbet in the office while she, Mademoiselle Zizi, was dressing. We could see in and, "Her face is mostly powder," said Hester.

"And do you know," said Vicky in astonishment, "Mademoiselle Zizi's eyelashes take off!" We did not believe that was possible until, spying, we saw it with our own eyes.

"She does that with her bosoms too," said Willmouse.

"Bosoms? Do you call them bosoms?" asked Hester doubtfully.

"I saw them lying across a chair," said Willmouse. He was calm, but the rest of us were shocked. "I have made bosoms for Miss Dawn and Dolores," he said: "I never thought of that before."

It was all very odd; Les Oeillets was Mademoiselle Zizi's hotel, yet she asked Madame Corbet for money. "Mais il faut que je m'achète une chemisette," Hester might have pleaded like that, "une petite chemisette."

I translated that for Hester, who nodded, full of sympathy;

she was always on the side of the oppressed. But who was the oppressed one here? "A little blouse."

"Pour lui," Madame Corbet spat out the word. We had long since learned that "lui" was always Eliot.

'I wonder why he chose that hotel.' Uncle William wondered that afterwards, 'It seems so unsuitable.' Then he answered himself, as he often did, 'But was it? Comfortable, unostentatious, enough foreigners to make him inconspicuous, midway between Paris and the border, and a silly woman who would do anything for him.'

"He is ruining the business," Madame Corbett often said that to Mademoiselle Zizi. "Always you tell every client we are full up."

"Not always," said Mademoiselle Zizi.

"And this is the season. All those empty rooms!"

"I do not want to have strangers here with us."

"You are mad."

"Because I do not want to have talk?"

"Talk! The whole town is talking. Someone will report us. In the end we shall lose our star."

I knew what star she meant, the star before Les Oeillets in the guide-book. It seemed to be very important, but Mademoiselle Zizi only shrugged.

"Ten years," said Madame Corbet in a low, thick voice as if it were choked with anger or tears. "Ten years I could have been a nun, but no, I have worked here, to get that star, to pull this hotel up, put myself aside for you. And you will not listen. You throw it all away."

Once we saw Madame Corbet slap Mademoiselle Zizi. The sound of it rang across the hall. It was a slap in the face and Mademoiselle Zizi stumbled against the desk, holding her cheek with her hand.

It was very quiet in the hall after the slap and we held our breath; presently there was a new sound, of sobbing, but it was not Mademoiselle Zizi who sobbed; it was Madame Corbet.

Mademoiselle Zizi took her hand down and knelt by

Madame Corbet, holding her, rocking her. Little words, in French, broken, reached us, whispered words, "Chérie... Jamais, jamais... Oubliez ça... N'y pensez plus... Chérie..." We tiptoed away.

It was not often we went away; in fact I do not think we should have left the house at all if we had not been turned out.

That was Eliot's doing. "It's very well for you," I heard Mademoiselle Zizi say to him. "You go off to Paris. I had fifty-eight people for lunch today and these children to see to as well."

"Don't see to them," said Eliot. "Give them some food and turn them out."

"Can I?"

"Of course you can. Children like picnics."

We should have liked it, even preferred it, had it not been for what we missed.

"What did you miss?" asked Uncle William. "A lot of trippers."

"Were they trippers?" asked Hester dazed. "But... we have trippers in Southstone."

The Les Oeillets ones, we were sure, were quite quite different. They came almost every day. It was the season, 'la grande saison,' said Mauricette. They came in cars and chars-à-bancs. "Then it isn't so queer to visit battlefields," I said. There were no battlefields now, only fields where corn and grass grew, and thousands of poppies and marguerites. We saw pictures of them in the guidebooks. "Do the soldiers come up in the corn?" asked Hester, but of course the soldiers were not there, except those who had been blown to pieces or rotted where they fell, "like the soldier in the garden," said Hester. They were laid in neat rows in the war cemeteries, with crosses for Christians and stars for Jews. There were pictures in the guidebooks of these too. Hester studied them and said, "I would rather have a star, they are prettier." Paul looked over her shoulder and made his rude noise. "Mr. Stillbotham says the cemeteries are beautiful, like gardens," Hester reproved him. "Comme les jardins," she said.

"Jardins!" said Paul, and in English he piped mockingly, "Be good boy, get killed in war, Papa and Mama come see you in pretty garden."

There were papas and mamas, sisters, brothers, uncles, aunts, even a few grandparents; they all seemed to be having a good time, but I could not help thinking of the skull, and the bulletholes; I wondered what it was like to be buried and not to be sitting in this pretty satin-papered dining-room, eating the things the visitors ate, hors-d'œuvres and pâté, poulet à l'estragon, veal and steaks, salads and green-gages, and I hoped I need never be dead.

Most of the visitors were American; we became used to seeing the far-away place names in the desk book, Illinois, Wisconsin, California, but there were Canadians, Austra-lians, people from South Africa, New Zealand, and some, not many, from England. In the few times we met any of them, on the landing or on the stairs, they would ask us in French the way to the lavatory; they took it for granted we were French, which flattered us, and in their efforts to speak to us called the lavatory many strange things. We would listen and ask gravely, "Le pissoir?" and watch their faces as we showed them the Hole.

"But we have modern cloakrooms downstairs!" Mademoi-selle Zizi would cry when she heard the chain go. She guessed that it was we who had shown them and made our going out more strict.

Just when things were getting interesting, and at Les Oeillets they were interesting indeed, we were sent away. In the mornings everyone was busy. Madame Corbet would put on a black apron; if Eliot were in Paris Mademoiselle Zizi would attend to the bar, but if he were with us Madame Corbet had to do that as well; Mauricette would be in the dining-room spreading clean tablecloths, polishing glass and silver; Paul would wipe the little tables under the vine arbour outside and open the umbrellas on the terrace. Monsieur

Armand would call him away all the time, and Madame Corbet would call him back. Madame Corbet gave out stores
and unlocked the fish tank that stood in the shade of the
arbour outside the kitchen and would let Monsieur Armand
choose the fish that were swimming in it alive—Hester
shuddered when she saw them. "And the snails," cried
Hester in agony. We could not bear the snails. "Except
to eat," said Vicky. They were supposed to come from
Burgundy, but Monsieur Armand would take the hotel car,
go out in the fields and gather them in a sack. When he
brought them in he would put them in a great tin box full
of salt which made them spew and gradually they seasoned
themselves ready for eating. It was cruel, but Vicky was
right; when they came bubbling in their shells on their
especial silver dishes, with the smell of garlic we were
learning to like, we forgot the box of salt. Vicky had had
more of them than we, but Paul slipped one or two on to our
plates when someone ordered them and showed us how to
dig them out with the small snail fork. We ate the fish from
the tank, the snails . . . 'and the chickens,' Vicky was to tell
Uncle William. The chickens were cruel too; they were left
in a cage so that they would not walk and spoil the tenderness of their flesh.

As the morning went on Monsieur Armand would grow
more loud and more red; beads of sweat ran along the ends
of his moustache and dripped off, though he wiped them
with the end of the cloth he wore tied round his neck. Paul
worked like a machine, and the dining-room began to look
elegant, with its flowers and tables gleaming with linen and
silver. Mauricette shouted to Madame Corbet to come and
see, Madame Corbet shouted back that she was coming.
'Un instant!' she would shout. Everyone shouted. Monsieur
Armand shouted to Nicole and Toinette to hurry up and
finish the rooms, Mademoiselle Zizi shouted to Monsieur
Armand not to shout, while Nicole and Toinette shouted
downstairs that they could not do everything, that they had
only two arms each and two legs. Sometimes Mauricette, if

she were in a good mood, let us count out rolls or pleat napkins or snip the brown edges off the carnations so that they looked like fresh ones; but when the first people were almost due to come Madame Corbet would march out of the office and into the kitchen, come back and set out, on a table in the hall, the packages Paul had made ready after breakfast. If we were not there she would send him to fetch us, and would needle looks at us if we did not collect our picnics at once and go towards the door.

It was strangely ignominious; we had to keep out of sight; Willmouse and I were not allowed into our bedroom because the bloodstain was on show and we had to tidy away all our things. Every day it was a feeling of soreness and neglect. "And will they remember to give Joss anything?" asked Hester. "I don't want anything," Joss said each day, but I felt she should have been asked. This was the time when we missed Mother most and hated Madame Corbet, Mademoiselle Zizi, Les Oeillets, hated them all. "But not Eliot," said Hester.

"He does not know what it's like," I said. "He isn't here."

Though we were sore, I think now it was those hours by ourselves that kept us sane; they restored us. All the hectic kaleidoscopic bits of this new life, broken up vividly by Paul, came together again in those hours when we had, willy-nilly, to be alone.

I was often quite alone except for Hester, whom I did not count. Vicky slipped back to Monsieur Armand; there was no need to give her luncheon, she had plenty in the kitchen. Willmouse took his package to the cherry tree where his materials were spread out. "I only have time to snatch a sandwich and a cup of coffee," we would hear him murmur and know he was being interviewed by *Vogue* or *Le Jardin des Modes* or *l'Elégance*; Miss Dawn and Dolores were on a diet and ate nothing for lunch except fruit juice, "greengage juice," said Willmouse, and we would give him greengages for them and for himself, putting some in our own handkerchiefs to take away.

We were told not to come back until four o'clock and the boundary we were set was the box hedge. On one side lay the house and its happenings, a shifting and changing pattern of Eliot, Mademoiselle Zizi, Madame Corbet, Paul, Monsieur Armand, Mauricette, the carloads and chars-à-bancs of visitors; when we were away from it, it was as unreal as the cocktails they all drank or as the top garden with its cut-up flowerbeds of plants Robert brought in boxes, its gravel, its iron urn, the skull buried every day.

On the wilderness and orchard side was an older, more truthful world; every day, as we passed into it, I caught its older, simpler scents: the smell of box, of mint, syringa, roses, dew on the grass, warm ripe fruit, smells of every summer. There was peace in the overgrown grass walks and heavy bushes, in the long orchard alleys where the greengages ripened in their own time and were neither forced nor pruned; here everything was itself, exactly as it seemed.

When we went through the blue door we were on the margin of the river and here we would sometimes encounter Monsieur Joubert, though soon he would get up and go in to lunch because the light had grown too hard and brilliant. His stool and umbrella were left for the afternoon, but I like to think we did not dream of shading ourselves or sitting down. We went to the cove or farther along, where the inlet joined the main bank by a plank bridge, and the towing-path ran between the river and the fields. Here and there there was a willow tree, as big as the ones in the garden, its leaves blown silver by the wind; bulrushes grew along the water verges here, great, hot, black-headed, taller than we, and everywhere hung wreaths and cascades of white convolvulus; skiffs were moored to poles dug in the bank, and now and again there was a barge tied up. Other barges passed all through the day and we stood still to look at them; some were towing still more barges behind them, and whole families lived on board, with washing, hens, firewood, and sometimes a garden planted in pots. When a barge

the bank to let the wash splash up on
knees, wetting our scarecrows. There were
working in the cabbages or vines, but we did
to them or they to us.

a kilometre downstream from Les Oeillets was the
own; every evening, after goûter, Hester and I would walk
there, crossing the bridge by the Giraffe to leave our notes
for Mother. Downstream was for the evening; this empty
time of lunch and early afternoon belonged upstream, to the
country and the bare river, as we called this long stretch with
its empty banks.

In a way, then, we were bare too; the cocoon of excitement into which we spun ourselves seemed left behind; we
went back to being children and that was restful.

A simplicity had descended on us. Coming to France for
only a short time, we had few clothes with us; our coats
and skirts hung in the wardrobe with our more respectable
dresses. We wore our scarecrows which Mother had brought
in case we went picnicking or on a beach, and because we
could not be bothered to clean our shoes we went barefoot.

I do not suppose it occurred to Eliot that we had no money
or that we needed any. Madame Corbet had taken Mother's
travellers' cheques and cash and our finances had been lifted
into a region far over our heads; we could not even read the
spiky figures in Madame Corbet's books. "And you are not
to bother your mother with anything," said Eliot; "just
write and send your love." Being unable to have anything,
mysteriously we did not need anything, except, "How I wish
we could bathe at the Plage," Hester said often.

The Plage was the Plage des Saules between Les Oeillets
and the bridge where another island made a narrow reach
of water that was almost a canal. A white wooden bridge
crossed it to the Plage, which was shut off by a railing on
which a notice said: 'Interdit aux enfants de moins de dix
ans qui ne sont pas accompagnés par une grande personne.'

The Plage had three swimming enclosures, divided from
the main river by painted wooden rods; the green water

66

looked cool and inviting, and there were diving-boards and chutes; red and white cabins were let for dressing-rooms, and there was a kiosk that sold ices and sirops. On hot thirsty days we could read the painted letters on its boards: 'Glaces—Fraise, Vanille, Citron, Moka et Chocolat.' "Oh well!" said Hester.

There was nowhere else to bathe except the Plage and the cove. The Marne had dangerous currents, and at the cove a notice said: 'Interdit aux baigneurs qui ne sont pas forts nageurs.' Neither of us were the strong swimmers required and all we dared do was to undress in the hotel bathing hut, put on our old salt-stained bathing dresses and lie in the shallows.

When the clock on the Hôtel de Ville struck one we would come out and open our food. It was a moment to wait for. Paul put up our picnics, and he, being on the side of the downtrodden, would filch things we were not supposed to have.

Monsieur Armand told him to put aside yesterday's dinner rolls for us, last night's meat, now cold, sardines and eggs out of the hors-d'œuvres, but Paul would switch the rolls with fresh ones just carried into the kitchen in the baker's wooden trays, and steal chicken legs, éclairs or jam tarts and, in the kindness of his heart, pâté, even caviare, which Hester would throw in the river. To us who were used to picnics of hard-boiled eggs, potted-meat sandwiches, apples and milk chocolate, Les Oeillets picnics were banquets; to add to their wonder we were always given bottles of wine and water to drink.

Every day I asked Hester, "Where shall we go?"

"Nowhere," Hester would say, and we would lie in the cove or on the bank and watch the fish, the sun on our backs and heads; in this short time our hair had begun to look bleached, our scarecrows more faded. We watched the fish, or a barge, or a distant peasant family bending and raking, as we listened to the willow leaves or dozed, scarcely talking; there was nothing to listen to but these simple things, no one to look at, no one who was anyone, no questions, and the time would pass until at last from the Hôtel de Ville the clock would strike four and we would sit up and sigh.

The odd part was that, though we chafed at being sent out, when the time came we did not want to go in. Seen at a distance and in perspective, I flinched from it. Mademoiselle Zizi, Madame Corbet, Eliot, Paul, they seemed too much, but at least, I thought comfortably, they are nothing to do with us. We are just watching.

Then on the eighth day—it might have been the seventh or the ninth, I had lost count—when we went in and upstairs to see Joss, her shutters were open and she was sitting by her window dressed in a respectable cotton; she had washed her hair and was drying and brushing it over a towel in the sun.

"Are you better?"

"Quite better," said Joss. "Mauricette brought me up some lunch."

"*Mauricette!*"

"She is the maid, isn't she?"

We did not now think of that haughty queen, Mauricette, as a maid.

"Did you ask her?"

"I rang," said Joss simply.

We stared at our sister. Even Vicky seemed to come out of her private shell to take in Joss's unperturbed face with its cool paleness.

"You have washed your hair," I said.

"Yes." She looked at us. "You must wash yours." She did not say what she thought of our dirt and we were silent. At Les Oeillets washing seemed left out of calculations for children, and beside us Joss looked as delicate and fresh as a flower.

Vicky said suddenly, "Mademoiselle Zizi's hair isn't red. They make it red in a shop."

"I know," said Joss.

"You *know?*" Hester and I said that together.

"I knew the first time I saw her," said Joss, leaning forward to look at herself in the looking-glass; she had moved to the dressing-table.

"How did you know?"

"Because it was a little bit black at the roots."

"It looks like a bundle," said Vicky. I knew what she meant. Mademoiselle Zizi's hair looked dry and heavy.

Joss did not answer. Watching herself, she picked up her brush and began to brush out her own hair that was soft and impeccably its own black.

CHAPTER 7

THAT WAS one of the evenings when Eliot came home.

"He likes to get out of the heat and dust of Paris," said Mademoiselle Zizi.

"Ninety kilometres!" said Paul caustically. Ninety kilometres. Eliot had taught us to put them into miles: "Divide by eight, multiply by five." Fifty-five miles was as near as I could get and that certainly seemed a long way to come, but, "He comes for her," I said.

"Quatre-vingt-dix kilomètres!" said Paul and spat.

When Eliot came the house was completely changed. Every evening, towards five o'clock, Mademoiselle Zizi dressed herself in one of her pretty dresses; "Not pretty, elegant," corrected Willmouse. She redid her hair, rouged and powdered, put her eyelashes in and blue-shadowed her eyes. "Then she takes a pencil and draws her eyebrows." said Hester. "How funny to pull them out and have pencil ones instead." Mademoiselle Zizi put scent on her upper lip and behind her ears and—Hester sank her voice to a whisper —even Hester was learning that some things should not be openly spoken of—"she puts scent between her bosoms."

If the telephone rang Mademoiselle Zizi would fly into the office but usually she would go and wait in the little salon, which was behind the bar. It too was elegant. We were not allowed to go into it but could look through the glass panels of its door; we admired the little room with its pale carpet that had loops of flowers, its walls that were inlaid with panels of blue brocade, its table in the middle with paintings in the wood, and the gilt chairs with backs and seats of yellow satin that were arranged stiffly round the walls.

Mademoiselle Zizi should have been working in the bar, but she sat in the little salon, we knew, because from it she could watch the courtyard gates and the drive for the first glimpse of Eliot's car.

No one else had a car like Eliot's. It was a Rolls-Royce, old, a little battered, but its blue and silver length always looked handsome among the French and American cars. "Why choose one that stood out?" Uncle William asked that. "Unless he wanted to stand out," said Uncle William.

Eliot sometimes changed his plans. Then towards dinner-time—and dinner was late at Les Oeillets, often not till ten o'clock—the waiting would begin to end. Mademoiselle Zizi would leave the little salon and come slowly back to the bar, and presently she would follow Madame Corbet into the dining-room and to their table by the private screen. Mademoiselle Zizi wilted in her chair, crumbling bread in her fingers, while Madame Corbet sat upright. On the nights when Eliot was there he often sat at their table, and then, we noticed, Madame Corbet always ate very quickly, cutting sharply with her knife—as if she would like to cut Eliot, we thought—not speaking. She would have dark spots of colour in her sallow cheeks, and she would always finish and get up while they were still at the second course. Eliot stood up for her as she went, but she never gave him a glance, and in a minute we would hear the typewriter keys rattling in the office as if she were typing very fast.

When she and Mademoiselle Zizi were alone, Madame

Corbet stayed in the dining-room until after everyone had finished. A quiet would be over everything. Monsieur Armand, unless special visitors were there, left the cooking to Paul. Mauricette waited on the tables in her slippers; even the dogs stayed out in the hall, their heads on their paws; no one but Eliot dared give them scraps.

We, of course, had finished long ago; we had our dinner when the staff had theirs, but we stayed on at our table, playing cards with old packs from the bar, Racing Demon or Pelmanism or Snap, and we would watch Mademoiselle Zizi's head with its coils of red hair sink lower and lower as she listened to Madame Corbet; then she would go into the bar and begin to drink.

"Oh well, we might as well go out," said Hester.

Out meant hanging about in the orchard and the garden eating greengages, until Paul was free to come out on the steps. Then we sat and smoked with him—even Hester would have a puff. Once Eliot had come home unexpectedly and found us there. We were afraid he might be cross, but he only ruffled Hester's hair and said, "You little gossips."

Usually he came for dinner. The dogs would hear his car; they knew long before we did that he was coming and they would stand up, shaking themselves and wagging their great tails. I think we did much the same thing. Hester and Vicky would rush to clasp his legs, while Willmouse stood and smiled, which for him was the equivalent of rushing. "You see," Mademoiselle Zizi said once to Madame Corbet. "See how children and dogs love him. That is the test of a good man." Madame Corbet sniffed.

With a flounce of her apron Mauricette would take Eliot's cap and gloves; Monsieur Armand would peer through the kitchen door and start something sizzling on the spit or stove; Paul, if he were there, would mutter under his breath about the extra washing-up, and in the office, Madame Corbet would be still, her topknot craned to watch Mademoiselle Zizi meet Eliot.

On his side there was nothing that anyone might not see.

Because of the visitors, if there were any, or for us, he would say something quiet, 'Bonjour, mademoiselle' or 'Ça va?', but she seemed not to care for anyone, the visitors, or us, or Madame Corbet; she would run to him and hang on his arm; it was as if she could not help it, even though, I thought, it annoyed him; when she looked at him, after he had been away, her eyes were so alight with happiness that even I, silly and romantic as I was, thought it would have been better not to let us all see she loved him as much as that. Sometimes Eliot seemed extraordinarily tired; then he had a strained look on his face, a nerve twitching by his mouth. "Well, I expect," said Hester afterwards, "he had often been up all night." Then Mademoiselle Zizi fussed. "You must have a drink," she would say, her eyes searching his face. "I will get you a drink. Have a comfortable chair, not that one. Let Mauricette get you some other shoes." Until he would say, 'For God's sake, Zizi!' Then those wide, constantly hurt eyes would fill with tears and her face would quiver. It was surprising a grown person could be so stupid; even I knew that the best thing was to leave him alone until he had been quiet for a while, had one or two drinks, and then say something casual, even rude. That would make him smile and say, 'You little tyke!'

That night of Joss's being better there were visitors: a young American with a red sunburned face, three American ladies, and a French colonel with his wife and child; before dinner we all sat at different tables in the bar.

When anyone was speaking French directly to me I could understand, but when they spoke to one another I could not be sure. Now I knew the French family were talking about us, I saw the wife gesticulate admiringly at Willmouse—women always found Willmouse charming while men were doubtful—at Vicky's fall of flaxen hair, at Hester's eyes and curls. These were the family good points and we were used to them being noticed, but I thought I heard Eliot say something that surprised me. "Soeur is sister, isn't it?" I asked Joss afterwards. "It couldn't be anything else?"

72

"How could it?" asked Joss.

"Then Eliot said Mother was his sister."

"He couldn't have because she isn't."

"No, but . . . He said he was our guardian."

"I suppose for the moment he is."

"Yes, but . . . He said he always took us to the seaside, but this year he had left it too late. He could not get away to see us in England and so he brought us here."

"Was this in French?" asked Joss.

"Yes."

"Then you got muddled."

I was sure I had not. Those sentences kept coming back in my mind and, "They were lies," I said.

Eliot talked from our table to the French people, he did not join them. We were all round him; Hester and I were playing Racing Demon at the next table with automatic silent swiftness, our eyes and ears really on him; Willmouse was hunched up in the chair beside him, his nose in his big book. "That boy needs spectacles," Uncle William often said, but, "If you get them I won't wear them," Willmouse told Mother. Vicky was on the floor by Eliot's feet, where Nebuchadnezzar was grazing in a field fenced with Eliot's matches.

We did not usually cluster round him when he came home but kept a respectful distance, but this evening we were on a different plane. "What is the matter with you?" he had said, looking at us. He looked more carefully and then said, "You are clean."

With Joss up we had changed for dinner. The scarecrows were on our chairs upstairs, we were in our respectable cottons. That was not all. Usually at this time we went into the dining-room to dine before the visitors came in; Paul would get up from the staff table to serve us, probably from a saucepan or a pan, his mouth still full. This evening we waited for Joss. Mademoiselle Zizi was not there; she was in the office with Madame Corbet waiting for a telephone call from Marseilles.

At Les Oeillets we had adopted certain places for our own; each one of us had chosen one or two. Willmouse had the bank under the cherry tree, of course, but he also owned the little salon; though he had never been in it, it was his. Hester liked the conservatory and a certain small bed of picotees because its warm clove smell reminded her of the carnation Eliot had worn on our first night that seemed now ages ago. Vicky had the vine arbour, perhaps because it was near the kitchen, and she said she liked the bidets—"They are like dear little baths for dolls," said Vicky. I loved the wilderness; it was poetical with its white statues and the white jessamine, and, for some reason, I loved the staircase, which was why I so much resented the machine-gun holes.

At that time of day the sun sinking behind the trees struck through the landing window and turned the staircase into a funnel of light; even the treads of the stairs seemed barred with gold and, through the round window, came the sound of trills and flutings, the birds singing their evening song in the garden, before it dropped to silence. The staircase might have been Jacob's ladder, stairs to heaven.

. I had been looking at it, no, not looking, almost melting into it, Racing Demon forgotten, and had turned my eyes away because of the brightness when I became aware of Eliot's stillness.

"Go on," said Hester, a card ready to slam down, but I did not move.

Eliot had been going to drink, but his glass was quite still in his hand; the Colonel was wrinkling up his eyes, the young American leaning forward. They were all looking.

They were looking at my staircase. Then I saw they were not, or not exactly. They were looking at Joss coming down.

As if those days of sickness and shock had made her clean and delicate, she looked pale and . . . pure, I thought, as a snowflake or white blossom, while I was my ordinary brown and pink. She had on the twin of the cotton dress I wore, but it was graceful on her; she was wearing the sandals she had bought with her birthday money, white, open-toed, while I wore our clumsy brown school sandals. She seemed to have grown more dignified, taller, and her dress was a little too tight; the shape of her bosoms—for ever after I was to think of them as bosoms—showed and the sun gave points of light to the darkness of her newly washed hair.

When I was jealous of Joss, Mother used to say, 'Jealousy is ugly. It hurts no one but yourself. Don't be jealous', but if one is, how does one help it? It is wrong to be jealous, but . . .

"It isn't wrong," said Eliot when afterwards I asked him this in despair.

"Not wrong to be jealous?" That was against everything I had heard.

"No," said Eliot firmly. "It's what you do with jealousy that can be wrong."

I think I knew that for myself. That night I could have said cruel, unkind things to Joss, wished her any harm; the cards seemed to swim in front of my eyes and I felt bitter and angry as she came quite naturally up to us.

Willmouse went on reading, Hester piled cards on my aces, Vicky grazed Nebuchadnezzar, but Eliot stood up.

That surprised me and made me more bitter than ever. 'It's only Joss', I wanted to cry. There was a pause and it dawned upon me that Eliot did not know who she was. "It's only Joss." This time I said it aloud and, as he still looked puzzled, "Joss, the one who was ill."

"One of *you*?" It was an unflattering disbelief. I had to remember he had only seen her before as a schoolgirl with a big forehead in an ugly hat and, in bed, as a tousled sick child; it was mysterious that these were Joss as well.

"Et c'est votre nièce, cette ravissante jeune personne?" said the Colonel from the next table, "Adorable! Adorable!" Eliot's face looked hot with embarrassment. Did Joss know, I wondered, that she had been called his niece? And ravishing, adorable, I thought, smarting, but she did not seem to have heard and took the chair Eliot pulled out for her and sat down. As he did not speak she said, "I'm better, but you must think we are a most unhealthy family."

She spoke so calmly that, unwilling though I was, admiration filled me. I knew she was shy, for there was pink now in her cheeks, and that telltale front of her dress moved quickly up and down. Eliot did not answer, which was difficult for Joss. The pink deepened and she tried again, "I hope the children haven't been bothering you."

That was too much. I said loudly, "We don't bother," and Eliot started as if I had . . . wakened him up, I thought.

"Will you have a drink?" he asked Joss.

"Could I have a still lemon?" she said with that false calm.

"He never asked us to have a lemon," whispered Hester as Willmouse was told to go and order one.

"I?" asked Willmouse, deep in his book.

"Yes, you," said Eliot so curtly that Willmouse went.

It was Mademoiselle Zizi, her telephone call finished, who brought the drink. She was puzzled. "Eliot, Willmouse says you want a citron? Is that true?"

As she came Joss stood up. She need not have, under the circumstances, but her schoolgirl habits were strong upon her. She stood up and Mademoiselle Zizi looked at her, as surprised as Eliot had been . . . but, I thought, not at all in the same way.

She and Joss were standing side by side and now I saw Eliot look down; his glance stayed down for a moment as if it were arrested, and I moved my chair to see what he saw. He was looking at their feet. Mademoiselle Zizi was wearing sandals too, open-toed black ones with high heels; they showed her toenails painted deep red, but the toes were brown and twisted, thickened with corn marks, the big toes turned inwards with an ugly bump. If I had been Mademoiselle Zizi I should have hidden them, and once again her stupidity gave me a pang, for beside her Joss's feet seemed to rest lightly under the white cross straps of her sandals, pretty slim feet, straight-toed, unblemished, the nails pearl pink. Mademoiselle Zizi had followed Eliot's eyes too. Abruptly she put the lemon down and walked round the table to the other side.

"Merci bien, Mademoiselle," said Joss and hesitated. "I have to say 'good evening'," she said uncertainly.

Mademoiselle Zizi did not answer at once; she only looked at Joss. Then, "I had not understood," she said.

"Understood?" asked Joss.

"That any of you were . . . so big," said Mademoiselle Zizi.

CHAPTER 8

DINNER WAS not comfortable that night. If anyone French came to the hotel, Eliot dined alone, not at the table by the screen, and tonight, all through dinner, his eyes kept coming to Joss, still with that amazed look, and from her table Mademoiselle Zizi's eyes followed his. At last she got up and left the dining-room. I do not think he noticed her going.

We, at our table, had long waits because Paul did not come to us at all. He had on the white coat he wore when help was needed in the dining-room, but he only brought dishes to the service door for Mauricette and took the dirty plates from her. I heard her order him, in angry whispers, to come in and help her, but he would not. Joss, of course, did not know it was different; she sat innocently well mannered and patient, but Vicky began to nod with sleep and Willmouse yawned and even fidgeted. It was absurdly late for them, but for a long time now their bedtime had been forgotten. I had given up worrying about it after that first day and Joss must have been bemused, because she did not say anything. "I never went to bed before eleven, not once," Vicky told Uncle William afterwards.

77

Hester beckoned to Paul to bring us the dish he was holding in the doorway, but he scowled and turned his back. There was celery soup, stuffed tomatoes, veal with potatoes, flageolet beans served separately as they did here, cheese and fruit. We had only reached the veal when Mademoiselle Zizi called Eliot from the office. He threw his napkin down impatiently and went out. Soon the visitors finished and left too, but Mauricette still walked past us, putting things away instead of bringing our fruit. We, who were familiar, began to be annoyed, but Joss said, "Naturally they have to attend to the more important visitors first."

She seemed not to know that Mauricette was taking it out on us, that Paul was shunning us. How could she? When Mauricette at last planked down our plate of greengages, the cut-glass bowl of water for our fingers and the clean plates, Joss said, "Merci," as if Mauricette had been normally polite. "Mademoiselle Zizi vous attend dans le bureau," said Mauricette, "si des fois vous auriez fini," she added sarcastically.

Joss looked enquiringly at me; she was not used to Mauricette's quick talking. "Mademoiselle Zizi wants us in the office," I said. "Oh, Joss!"

She was a little startled, and we others looked at one another. The table, with us round it, seemed suddenly small and the dining-room big and foreign.

.   .   .   .   .

"Who gave you permission to change your time for dinner?" asked Mademoiselle Zizi.

Joss looked at me in surprise. "We have been having it when Monsieur Armand and the others have theirs," I explained to her.

"What others?"

"Mauricette, Paul, Toinette, Nicole." I was beginning to regret this childish helter-skelter week; it was partly regret that it was over, our happy obscurity was lost; Joss was dragging us into the limelight.

"Who said you could change?"

Joss turned her eyes on Mademoiselle Zizi. Her voice was still gentle as she asked, "You want us to eat with your servants?"

Mademoiselle Zizi's neck went red. "Mauricette cannot manage with so many in the dining-room."

I should have accepted that, but Joss answered, "But Cecil says you often have sixty people for luncheon. Tonight we were only fifteen."

"I do not wish"—Mademoiselle Zizi floundered a little—"to have children with adults."

Joss's soft answer came relentlessly. "But Monsieur le Colonel and Madame . . . I don't know their name . . . had their little girl with them tonight."

"Do not argue with Mademoiselle Zizi," said Madame Corbet to Joss with such venom that Joss was surprised again.

"I—I'm sorry," said Joss, "but our mother would not like it."

"Your mother left you in my charge," said Mademoiselle Zizi.

Joss could have taken refuge in being small, a child, but, "Could I?" asked Joss afterwards. "I am as big as I am." I suppose she had to be, but I see now that what she said was like a stone thrown into a pool; it spread ripples.

"Your mother left you in my charge," Mademoiselle Zizi said.

"She left us in Mr. Eliot's," said Joss. "Shall we ask him what he thinks?"

I thought Mademoiselle Zizi was going to slap Joss, but she controlled herself and, after a moment, "You may have your dinner with the guests," she said, "but I forbid you, absolutely forbid you, to trouble Monsieur Eliot."

.   .   .   .   .

After a while Hester and I went to the back steps. We did not want Paul to think we had deserted him, but, though he saw us and knew that we knew that he saw us, he did not

79

come. He worked ostentatiously in the kitchen, and each time Monsieur Armand passed him he said, "Bougre de gâte-sauce! Marmiton miteux! Expèce de mitron de merde! Va donc, eh! Ordure!" I knew they were swear words, but what they meant I fortunately did not know; and I did not know, either, why he should be out of temper with Monsieur Armand.

"What *is* the matter with Paul?" asked Hester.

CHAPTER 9

THEN CAME the three days. "I had rather you did not write about those," Joss said after I had put that down.

"I must. They were part of it."

"They were—the only part." When she said that she looked away from me, and neither of us spoke.

The next morning Mademoiselle Zizi had met Eliot in the hall; he had on his linen trousers and dark-blue shirt, the canvas shoes that we now knew were espadrilles, his old cap, and was carrying dark glasses. "But you said you were going to Paris," she said and seemed troubled.

He laughed and put his hands on Hester's and Will-mouse's heads. "I must see to my family, Zizi." When he saw her face he went to her and, holding her arms, swayed her gently backwards and forwards. "Can't a man have a day or two off?"

In the wilderness he picked a bunch of roses and took Joss and me to see Mother. The doctor, Monsieur le Directeur, met us and, as if we were grown ladies, took us over the hospital. In the men's ward we bowed, as Eliot did, and said, 'Bonjour, messieurs'; in the women's and maternity wards, 'Bonjour, mesdames', and felt as if we were royalty.

"A French hospital is not different from English ones," said Joss, determined to be sophisticated, but I was too uplifted to care if I were sophisticated or not. "*English* hospitals are not called the Hotel of God," I said. "They don't have nuns with their nurses; they were not built in 1304 by the Queen of Philip the Beautiful. There has never been a Philip the Beautiful in England. *And* the patients don't have wine with their lunch"—we had seen the noonday food trolleys coming up—"and their relations can't come in and out when they like. French hospitals are more interesting and more friendly."

"She is observant, this young Mademoiselle," said Monsieur le Directeur when Eliot had translated for him, and I was flattered.

Eliot talked in the passage with the nun in charge of the private wing while a nurse took us in to see Mother. "For two minutes," said the nun through the open door. I was glad it was only two minutes, for I must admit that seeing Mother dashed the day. The private rooms were blue-and-white cubicles that seemed shut in another world of hushed quietness. A strange smell hung round Mother— "They had to open her leg again yesterday," Eliot had warned us—and tears ran out from under her lids while she held our hands. I could never have imagined Mother pale, but she was yellow-white like wax. We were frightened.

She asked us, "Are you quite . . . all right?" It was a faraway whisper.

"Quite all right." I said it absently for, though I was frightened and full of pity, I could not help listening to Eliot in the passage outside. He can talk to anyone in French or English, I thought with a pang. I listened to his easy voice and heard the agitation of pleasure in the little nun's answers, and wondered if a woman could ever be like Eliot; and, if she could, could I be she? I was suddenly more grateful for my punishments at St Helena's, and to Monsieur Armand and his newspaper lessons, and decided to stop being shy and practise my French on everyone from that day.

"I have been . . . so worried," breathed Mother.

I do not know how Eliot caught that, but he broke off what he was saying and came to her. "You are forbidden to worry," he said. When he was there Mother opened her eyes and smiled at him; she seemed to quieten, not to want to talk any more, and he motioned us to go away. Presently he stood up and came out too, leaving the bunch of roses on the bed.

As we walked back through the town many people greeted him; he was continually stopping and shaking hands with someone. "In France you must always shake hands," he told us. "Watch the children." There were scores of children. If it had been term time, Eliot said, they would have been in black overalls, carrying satchels that were like brief-cases while the ones from far off would have square luncheon baskets as well; we watched and saw, sure enough, that as soon as the children met anyone they knew they gave their hands. The streets were full of people; there were women in slippers, wearing shawls like Madame Corbet's and carrying heavy shopping bags; there were men in blue overalls, patched and faded, with berets like Monsieur Joubert. There were business men in heavy suits, lorry men and carters, nuns, boys and girls, children all dressed in pinafores, and I said, "Children don't wear pinafores in England."

The town was always gay, with its café tables and chairs under striped awnings along the pavements. I had always liked the shop names. 'Aux Joyeux Carillons', a happy ring of bells was fitting for toys and games. 'A la Fourmi', dresses. Why an ant for dresses? "Ants are industrious," said Eliot. "I expect they sew with little tiny stitches." 'Graines potagères, Graines de Fleurs'; I had wondered what that meant. "A seed shop, juggins. Vegetable and flower seeds." 'Anne Maria Ferrière. Modes Transformations'; 'Crémerie Centrale, en Gros et demi-Gros'; 'Les Meubles Tulin'; 'J. Binet. Bonneterie Lingerie. Spécialité de Bas.'

We had often longed to buy flowers for Mother at l'Eglantine: roses, carnations and glowing spikes of gladioli, and in the hardware shop there was a set of twin cups and saucers in green china lettered 'Toi' and 'Moi'. "Thou and Me," whispered Hester; we thought that touching and meant one day to buy them for Father and Mother. "If we *ever* have any money," sighed Hester. "And we must take something back for Uncle William. Perhaps one of those pipes with crests and pictures on it or perhaps a vase of those *beautiful* wax flowers."

Now Eliot let us linger at the sweet and cake shop that Joss had not seen; he explained the different kinds of cakes to us: éclairs, rum babas, meringues with crème chantilly, pears and apples crystallised whole in sugar. He did not make the mistake of offering us any but took us inside to buy a carton of chocolates to take back to Hester and the Littles. There was a rich smell in the shop from the chocolates, and of liqueur from the brandied cherries for which Vieux-Moutiers was famous. There were sugared almonds, marrons glacés, and crystallised violets, rose leaves and mimosa balls. "But are there no ordinary sweets?" I asked.

"You buy those at a grocer's," said Eliot, "but here they have sucettes." Sucettes were lollipops, and, "I don't think Mademoiselle Zizi would like us to have those," I said.

We watched while the mademoiselle did the carton up in white paper, tying it with golden thread and sealing it with a golden seal. It seemed inexpressibly elegant to us. "Don't you get tired of using that word?" asked Eliot when I said this to him, but we did not.

"They don't do boxes up like that in Southstone," said Joss.

"In London they might," said Eliot.

"This isn't London. This is a little town, smaller than Southstone."

"The French understand living," said Eliot, and I longed to be French.

Then he took us to the Giraffe. Dazzled, we sat at one

of the small marble-topped tables I had passed so often. The waiter poured wine and water for me but filled up a glass for Joss; Joss tried not to glow but she glowed. When Monsieur Gérard, the proprietor, came and talked to us she sat very erect, holding the glass of pale golden wine, her eyes going from Monsieur Gérard to Eliot and back again as she tried to keep up with the quick French. I remember that her hair caught the sun again as it struck down through the awning, and from the heat, or perhaps the wine, tiny beads of sweat came out on her forehead and neck. Eliot put out a finger and touched one. "Dew of Joss," he said, and Joss sat oddly still.

"Does it taste of salt?" I asked.

"Sugar and spice," said Eliot and once again his eyes stayed on Joss and he seemed to listen half absently to Monsieur Gérard.

Then we went back to Les Oeillets and on the hall table were our packages laid out.

"What are those?" asked Eliot.

"Our picnics," and I explained to Joss, "We have to go out now."

Eliot looked at the packages, at Joss, and then out to the orchard shimmering green in the sun. A noise of people came from the bar, loud voices and laughter, the sound of glasses, hearty tones, and, "I will have a picnic too," said Eliot.

"A picnic! For you?" asked Madame Corbet.

"For me," said Eliot. Madame Corbet seemed not to know whether to be shocked or pleased, but she went to get another package ready.

"What was he thinking of?" asked Uncle William afterwards.

"He wasn't thinking," I said. "Just for once he forgot to think." I believe now I hit on the truth. I am still haunted by Eliot's voice saying, "Can't a man have a day or two off?"

We went to the cove, "All six of us," said Hester. Willmouse left his sewing and came, Vicky deserted Monsieur Armand though there was going to be oeufs à la neige for lunch. "Alone, with that man!" Uncle William said afterwards of Joss, but they were never alone. We were always with them, a chorus and, though we did not know it then, a guard.

At the blue door we met Monsieur Joubert coming in. When he saw Joss he took off his hat—he changed the beret, when the sun grew hot, for a panama. He smiled and stood back to let us pass, and stood looking after us, the hat in his hand. Joss walked one side of Eliot, her head level with his shoulder. Vicky was on the other, swinging on his hand. Willmouse and Hester were in front, Hester walking backwards and talking all the time, and I came behind. When I looked back Monsieur Joubert was still gazing thoughtfully after us.

It was a gay picnic. We felt more as if we had escaped than as if we were shut out. After luncheon Vicky fell asleep, her head on Joss's lap; Hester and Willmouse paddled, and I lay, as Eliot liked to do, flat, face downwards on the sand. Joss's and Eliot's voices were a low murmur; they seemed to have a great deal to talk about, but I was too peaceful to be jealous; everything—and everybody—was at peace.

Then, "Come along, all you lazybones," said Eliot; "I have to go to Soissons. Who would like a drive?"

I sat up, and, "In your Rolls-Royce?" breathed Willmouse, coming out of the water.

"Yes. We can look at the cathedral."

In the Rolls-Royce! We looked at one another, excitement spilling out of our faces. "But . . . won't Mademoiselle Zizi mind?" I said.

"Why should she mind?" Eliot's voice had the coldness that only I knew and I was quiet, but none of us went into the house; we washed our faces and hands in the river and left our packages on the back steps.

As we drove along the road to Soissons the stooks were

piled in the fields, stooks of dark-coloured corn, darker than in England. In the woods the wood-cutters had stacked cut logs to dry. "Think of having *fires*!" said Hester. The heat was shimmering between the trees, and hot air fanned our cheeks. It was unmistakably France not England; we passed a statue of the Virgin standing above the cornfields, a cart laden with casks of wine, a French military cemetery with a crop of the small wooden crosses we had seen in the guidebooks. At last we drove into Soissons, with the twin towers of its ruined Abbey, its thick-walled houses, honey-coloured plaster wash and wide cathedral square.

Outside the cathedral, "Put something on your heads," said Eliot to Joss and me, "the people like it," but neither of us had anything.

Eliot lent me his handkerchief, but there was nothing for Joss; then a woman coming out paused to admire us—it was part of the warm happy day to be admired; she had been in the cathedral and in her hand had a black lace veil. I had seen women with them in Vieux-Moutiers; they wore them to go into the churches, and she came up and put it gently over Joss's hair. "Voilà ce qu'il vous faut, Mademoiselle," she said and showed Eliot a door in one of the houses opposite where we could bring back the veil.

The meshes of the veil made Joss's hair look even finer and shadowed her face so that it seemed mysterious; her skin looked more ivory than ever, and Eliot kept glancing at her. I went and walked by myself, trying not to feel the hot sharpness in my heart.

Inside, the cathedral, with its wide doors opening on the sunlit square, was light, not dim. The long nave was of pale stone cut like huge bricks; the floor was stone, too, and worn. Why was it so worn?

"This is the old floor. The walls are newer. Soissons cathedral was knocked down in the war. They built it up," said Eliot.

"What! This great thing?"

We had to tilt our heads back to look up at the vaulted

roof with its flutings of stone, at the huge rose window in the transept, the long windows below with their amber and red and brilliant blues that sent coloured light down to the floor stones. It was all vast, sealed in quiet. "This great thing," said Eliot softly.

'Il est interdit de circuler dans la cathédrale durant les offices,' said notices on the walls, and "What offices?" we asked, looking round for desks and telephones.

"Divine Offices: Lauds, Vespers, Compline," said Eliot. We still looked blank and he laughed and said, "You little English ignoramuses."

Madame Corbet said often, "The English have no religion," and with Eliot and us as the only English people at Les Oeillets she might have been pardoned for thinking that. "What, no church?" she had asked us on our first Sunday; and on the second, "Do you never go to church?"

"At Christmas and at Easter," I told her.

"And when we were christened, of course," said Hester.

"The English have no religion," decided Madame Corbet.

We had not been in a Catholic church; it was interesting, from the massive stone pillars to the gilt stations of the Cross along the walls. We looked at the rows of chairs. "Do all those people come?" "They come," said Eliot. There was a smell of incense that made us sniff, and we liked the candles that gave a warm light to the small side chapels. "Who puts them there?"

"People," said Eliot. "Watch." People were coming in and out all the time though there was no service. They came and prayed on their own, some of them with beads; some brought flowers and some lit candles. They were not dressed up. Some even had shopping bags or tools; one of the women was wearing slippers as if she were at home; indeed, they all seemed comfortably at home. I had not imagined one could feel at home in a church.

In the Chapel of the Resurrection the flowers and candles were white, but, to our intense astonishment, the Virgin was black. "Isn't she beautiful?" said Eliot.

Can a black person be beautiful? Such an idea had not occurred to our insular little minds. "Why is she black?"

"She often has a black statue in France," said Eliot.

"The guidebooks say the very first sacred statues were carved from bog oak, which is black," said Joss and she asked, "Would this one be as old as that?"

"I don't know," said Eliot, "but she is very, very old."

"How old?" asked Hester.

"Hundreds of years, I expect," said Eliot; "and she is supposed to be miraculous."

"Miraculous?" Hester was puzzled.

"She can work miracles."

"*Really?*" We all gazed at the statue.

"They say so," said Eliot, "and so thousands and thousands of candles have burnt in front of her and the smoke has turned her even blacker."

"Her cloak is beautiful," said Willmouse in a whisper. It was white brocade with a pattern of blue keys, and he put up a finger to touch it. Both she and the Holy Child had on small crowns set with jewels. "Rubies and turquoise," said Eliot.

"Real?" breathed Willmouse and gazed at them, rapt, as Eliot nodded. Hester, who always wanted to test things, held her hand over a candle flame and, sure enough, it made a black mark. Vicky tugged at Joss's arm. "Let me see the rubies," she whispered and Joss lifted her up.

As she held Vicky up to see the crown, Joss's face was lit by the candles so that it was gilded, framed by the black lace. Mother had said Joss was beautiful 'just now', but in this moment I knew it was more than that; my sister's beauty was real, for always . . . like a painting, I thought, marked out, and then Eliot's hands gripped my shoulders. They hurt and I craned my head back to look at him and saw what I had guessed from the hardness of his hands; he did not even know he had touched me; he was looking at Joss as Willmouse had looked at the jewels.

A few minutes earlier I should have jerked away, hurt and

angry, but now I stood quietly, letting myself be used. Perhaps the Black Virgin had worked another of her small miracles, because I did not struggle any more: Joss was beautiful and I was not; she, not I, was marked; Eliot looked at her and did not even notice me and yet I was not jealous. I was sad, but it was a contained, secret sadness and I was not jealous.

When we came out of the cathedral it was good to feel the sun again, warm on our arms and heads. Hester and Willmouse went back with the veil, and Eliot made them rehearse what they would say: 'Mille remerciements, Madame', and 'Merci pour votre bonté'. When they came back he took us all into a pâtisserie for coffee, chocolate and cakes. Since the shop in Vieux-Moutiers that morning Joss and I had been haunted by visions of babas and meringues, 'And those pears', Joss had said longingly, and we took a long while to choose; for Vicky it was the most earnest moment of the day, but Eliot was patient. He ordered chocolate for us, and for himself and Joss iced coffee, which came in tall glasses with thick straws and long silver spoons. The pâtisserie was, if anything, more elegant than the one in Vieux-Moutiers, and Joss must have been feeling what I felt, for presently she said to Eliot, "I am sorry about our clothes."

"Your clothes?"

"Yes," said Joss briefly.

"I like your clothes," said Eliot.

"You couldn't possibly." I could tell by the way she said it, her nostrils pinched in, that she was suffering.

"I like them," said Eliot and put his hands over hers on her knee, "I like everything about you."

Again that momentary stillness; then she took her hand away.

. . . . . .

The colour of that day was gold, but the next was green, for Eliot took us and our picnics to the forest of Compiègne. All day we wandered and walked in the long avenues and glades of beech trees. In that high summer the forest was intensely green, laced under the trees by green-white cow parsley, with sturdier shapes of bracken and, underfoot, white shamrock-leafed wood sorrel. We found honeysuckle, and Hester twined it into wreaths for the Littles. "Willmouse looks like a faun," said Eliot, pointing at Willmouse running in the bracken with his shirt off, the wreath of flowers on his head. Hardly anybody was in the forest. We came upon two deserted lakes, reflecting the green and the stretches of blue from the sky where there was not a cloud; white water lilies rocked a little when Hester and Vicky splashed sticks in the water, making ripples; that and the clucking of a disturbed moorhen were the only sounds. "People forget about Compiègne," said Eliot.

When we were tired we got back in the car and drove; the Rolls seemed to go soundlessly down the long avenues, and everywhere was the same filtering green, sunrays coming through branches, flickering gently on the ground. We came to a village, grey in the trees, and it had a château, a castle with turrets and walls. "Like the Sleeping Beauty's," said Hester.

I said prettily, "It's a fairytale day."

"It isn't. It's true," said Joss. She said it vehemently, and vehemence was so unlike Joss that we all looked at her.

"It is true," said Eliot. He drew her arm through his, but I could see it was not possible for Joss to walk arm in arm with him, and as soon as she could she took her arm away.

I do not know what time we ate our luncheon, perhaps three o'clock, and afterwards we lay in the warm grass and slept. Then we met a French family picnicking too; the children were Raoul, Elisabeth who was called Babette, and Jeanne; their names belong for ever to that enchanted day. I remember they were playing pat-ball, but we taught them rounders, playing England against France. They gave us lemonade, and we drank their health before we drove away.

Towards evening we got out of the car and walked again. The sun was lower now, and the light slanting down the glades and through the trees was deeper, richer . . . and heavier, I thought. We were heavy too, surfeited with happiness. Vicky dragged her feet, Joss looked pale. "I think we had better have some dinner," said Eliot.

"Dinner?"

"Yes. Do you remember that little restaurant on the lake? Let's go and dine there."

"In a *restaurant*?" Joss and I said it together. We had forgotten about trying to be sophisticated.

"Why not?" asked Eliot, and Hester promptly exposed us.

"We have never been in a restaurant," she explained. "Only in Violet Tearooms or the Oriental Café."

"Would you like to go in one?"

"But . . . can we?"

"Of course we can," said Eliot.

Joss looked at her watch. "It's nine o'clock!" She sounded a little alarmed.

"All the more reason to dine."

"Won't . . ." I could see Joss did not want to mention Mademoiselle Zizi, ". . . they be cross?"

"We shall telephone," said Eliot; but when we came to the chalet restaurant, La Grenouille, its walls painted with frogs, other real frogs sounding from the marsh, there was no telephone. "They will guess," said Eliot. "Come along."

At first we were disappointed. The word 'restaurant' for us meant places like the glimpses we had taken into hotel dining-rooms as we walked along the promenade at Southstone, the hotels Hester admired. We had thought of waiters, white table-cloths, shaded lights, silver, flowers, napkins cocked into shapes better even than Mauricette made them. La Grenouille was a holiday restaurant, a chalet in a garden where a notice board said, 'Jeux divers', and there were croquet hoops, see-saws and swings. The dining-room was pitchpine wood, with glassed-in side walls. It was used for shooting parties in the autumn, the patron told us, and on the wooden walls, above the frog paintings, were stuffed heads, a boar, foxes and chamois, while antlers were made into electric lights. The tables had paper tablecloths in green and red plaid—"Paper?" whispered Hester unwilling to believe it—and the chairs were folding wooden ones. The patron came to meet us in his shirt-sleeves and wearing checked cotton trousers and old espadrilles; nor had he shaved. Our eyes examined him disapprovingly while he and Eliot talked. "He can give us soup," said Eliot, "fillet steaks, tarte and cheese. Will that do?" Distantly, because we did not want to show we were disappointed, we said of course it would do. "Thank you," added Joss, and we chorused, "Thank you."

The soup and the yard-long bread from which we broke off pieces as we needed them were good, and as the patron cooked our steaks in front of us and dusk came down, shutting the little glass-sided restaurant into a world of its own, the disappointment went. Eliot gave us vin rosé, and the rose-coloured wine, the réchaud flame, the lights were reflected in the windows over and over again, shutting us into a warm lit world. Eliot talked to the patron and his wife, and we began to talk too; then we were laughing, and soon our laughter could have been heard the other side of the lake. Everything made us laugh, for this was better, happier than anything we had imagined.

As we waited for the steaks we read aloud the menu and all the dishes on it, "that are not there," said Eliot, and we bantered the patron about that.

"Is andouillette a lark?" I asked.

"That's alouette, duffer. Andouillette is a kind of sausage," said Eliot and translated for the patron. I felt I had been witty as they laughed again. The steaks were cooked with field mushrooms and served with fried potatoes; after them was a salad, and when the great tarte was brought, its apple filling glazed with apricot jam, even Vicky thought the dinner complete.

Eliot's face looked calm and happy. He is happy with us, I thought, and when at last we got up to go it was nearly eleven. "We shan't get back till twelve o'clock," said Joss.

"Well, what of it?" asked Eliot. He sounded a little defiant and we looked at one another, our faces scared.

The evening before, when we came back from Soissons, Mademoiselle Zizi had joined us for drinks; we had the pink grenadine sirop we liked while she and Eliot drank martinis. We had told her about the cathedral, the cakes, of all we had done and seen. She had sat next to Eliot, with Willmouse on the arm of her chair; Joss, on the far side of Eliot, mending a rent in Vicky's scarecrow, had been so quiet that she was almost outside the circle; it had all been pleasant and easy, but we guessed it would be different tonight.

Mademoiselle Zizi was waiting when we got in. Eliot had taken Vicky asleep from the car and, as he carried her in, she still slept soundly against his shoulder, while his other hand held up the stumbling Willmouse. The honeysuckle wreaths were crooked now, Hester and Joss and I had our hands full of flowers and ferns, our dresses were crumpled, our hair had leaves in it, and our faces were flushed. "So! You had a good time!" said Mademoiselle Zizi.

"Thank you, a very good time," said Eliot. Mauricette was peeping; he beckoned her and gave Vicky into her arms. "Take Monsieur Willmouse as well," he said. Mauricette would always do anything for Eliot and she obediently took them. "Zizi," he said, "give me a drink."

"You look as if you had had a drink already."

"I have had a little vine rosé," said Eliot. "I want a real drink." He looked at her face that had strange pouches under the eyes, patches of red on her cheek and neck. "So do you."

I did not think she did; she looked as if it were she who had had one already . . . or two or three or half a dozen, I thought. I know now it is children who accept life; grown people cover it up and pretend it is different with drinks, and as Eliot turned her towards the bar he whispered over his shoulder, "Go up to bed." It was not an order, but said as if in a conspiracy. We silently disappeared and he led Mademoiselle Zizi away.

"But it was spoilt," Hester said, and I think she was right. Nothing had that pure happiness again. I wish we had stopped after Compiègne, but the next day Eliot said he must take us to the caves at Dormans. "And it was very spoilt," said Hester.

It began with trouble over Paul. Eliot had gone down to the Giraffe for cigarettes after breakfast. When he came back he found Paul in his room.

"Stealing?" asked Mademoiselle Zizi, frightened.

"I don't think so," said Eliot. "He was just nosing around, but you can't have that. He must go. At once."

"In the middle of our season?" said Madame Corbet dryly.

"Yes. You can't employ a boy like that."

"Mais, Eliot . . ." pleaded Mademoiselle Zizi, but Eliot would not relent. "I said he must go."

Hester tugged at Joss. "Ask Eliot not to," she said urgently. "Please, Joss. If Paul has to go now he will lose his summer bonus and he will never get his lorry. Ask Eliot, Joss."

Perhaps Joss was not unwilling to try where Mademoiselle Zizi had failed. She went to Eliot and put her hand on his arm, looking up at him, and presently we heard him say, "Very well . . . if you will come out with me again today."

"Can you spare the time?" said Joss doubtfully.

"Of course I can. We will go to the caves."

"What caves?" we said. It was pronounced 'carve' not 'cave'.

"The champagne cellars. You can't be in the champagne country and not see those."

"Are we in the champagne country?" asked Joss, startled.

"I shall show you," said Eliot.

In our bones we knew it was better not to go—perhaps our bones were getting wiser as they grew stained—but

Eliot was queerly determined that morning ... as obstinate, I thought, as Vicky. When one came to know them it was surprising how childish grown people could be. I think, too, he did not mean to take the rest of us. He began by trying to get rid of the Littles.

"But I *need* to go," Willmouse pointed out to him. "I must know about champagne."

"We shall leave Vicky, then," said Eliot, but he did not know Vicky as we did.

"We are going where we have to walk a long way in the dark," he told her.

"I like the dark," said Vicky.

"You wouldn't like this."

"I would."

"You stay with Monsieur Armand and I will bring you back a doll."

"I don't want a doll. I have Nebuchadnezzar."

"If you come to France," said Eliot, "you must have a French doll."

"All right," said Vicky placidly, but when we were ready in the hall she came downstairs; she had on a respectable cotton, clean socks, her soup-plate hat, and carried Nebuchadnezzar in his basket. "I will help you choose the doll," she said to Eliot and put her hand in his. "And it was odd," said Hester. "If he had not taken Vicky he must have been seen."

For us champagne will always have a ghost; it can never be a wine for feasts but one for mourning. "Because it made the first crack," said Hester.

When we drove in through the important-looking iron and gilded gates at Dormans we had no inkling. It was more magnificent than any place we had seen. There was a lodge by the gates, then a great courtyard laid out with lawns and hot-coloured flowers, red and yellow, and facing the courtyard what looked to us like a palace but Eliot said were packing rooms and offices. As we got out of the car we stopped, not believing our eyes, for wide baskets seemed to be walking slowly past the palace by themselves. "They are bottle baskets on wheels," said Eliot, laughing at our faces, "running along their own little railway line."

An entrance with turrets led into the cellars, "But you must not call them cellars," said Eliot. "They are caves, ten miles of galleries, like the Catacombs."

"Tours go over all day long in summer," Eliot had told us and, sure enough, a tourist party was there. It was French, but we were allowed to join it and Eliot interpreted for us. The tour of the caves was as quick as going over the cathedral had been slow, and we had no time to say 'Why?', which must have been a relief for him.

We went down into the darkness and coldness of the galleries. "But it is warmer than above ground in winter," said the guide, "because the temperature never changes." First we saw the enormous casks in which the wine waited until it was bottled, then we walked after the French party down the long cellar lanes where the bottles were racked, neck downwards in the pupitres, as the stands were called, and the bottle-twisters moved with their jets of light among the racks, twisting, twisting the bottles with a rattling rhythm that echoed in the vaulted roof.

"Every bottle gets a twist every two days," said Eliot.

"Why?" We did manage to get one in then.

"To bring the sediment down on the cork, and this is an art," said Eliot. "The remueur—bottle-twister—is a devoted person, all his thoughts are for the cuvée he is working on. You see," he said to Hester, "*he* doesn't talk. The whole racking place must be quiet and still; even the currents of air we make as we walk by disturb the wine."

We had not heard of wine being disturbed before and the Littles looked solemn and walked on tiptoe.

We heard pops. "What are they doing?" asked Vicky, enchanted.

"That's where they change the corks," said Eliot. "When the wine is needed the cork is changed." We saw a team of men working together at small machines; they froze the bottle necks, drew the corks—"Which is what makes the pop!" said Hester, watching—and the sediment with it, smelt the wine, recorked it, muzzled it—"With a tiny wire muzzle," said Hester admiringly—then the bottles were stored—"Upside-down again," said Hester—until they were despatched or used, perhaps years later.

We saw magnums and jeroboams and half bottles, and some 1893 champagne draped in the strange webbed fungus that always comes in the caves from the wetness of the chalk. We saw pink champagne—"For the English," said the guide contemptuously, and the whole party turned to look at us—and we were shown the rare red wine of the champagne country. Then we came up into the daylight again, to the packing-room, where women worked at unbelievable speed putting on the gold-foil tops, the scarlet seal, the label, and giving each bottle the final wrapping in pink paper.

When we were out in the sunlight again, still surrounded by the party, the guide asked if we would like to visit the museum, in the office opposite. "Would you?" asked Eliot. Hester and I wanted to, but Vicky and Willmouse were tired, and as we stood debating a man, dressed as Willmouse hoped to be dressed one day, in a black coat, striped trousers, white shirt, silver-and-black tie and a red carnation, came from the office doorway. Like the woman at Soissons cathedral, he had been admiring us.

In Southstone, I thought, if anyone looked at us our spirits immediately curled up in shame and we withered; with Eliot it was suddenly different. It was partly the Rolls, his height and his clothes, but that did not explain it all; we were the same, dressed the same, yet we were quite different, at ease, confidently good-looking and poised.

The man spoke to us in English. "You are English, Monsieur?"

"Yes."

"May I say you have a fine family?"

"We like being called a fine family, don't we?" Eliot asked us, and in this junketing mood we did.

"Perhaps you would care to take a glass of our champagne with us, Monsieur; you . . ." I noticed he was looking especially at Joss, "and Mademoiselle and the demoiselles?"

"*Champagne?*" We were dumbfounded.

"Would you like to?" asked Eliot.

"Champagne, for *us?*" I could not believe it, and even Joss was shaken out of her calm. She put her hand on Eliot's arm and said, "Oh, could we?"

"Can I taste a little, a little?" pleaded Willmouse.

"And I," whispered Hester.

"I don't want champagne, I want a sirop," said Vicky.

"If you would step into our little museum you could look at the pictures until it comes," said the man.

He led us to the door, opened it, then closed it again. From inside we had heard the sound of voices, men's voices speaking French, and footsteps coming near. "A moment," said our man. "They are just coming out. There has been a luncheon in the directors' room." As we looked impressed he said, "It is the Annual Convocation of Le Brochet de la Marne. That is a fishing club," he explained. "It is a hundred years old and famous. No, not only local, it has members as far away as Paris. Every year they come here for four days—it's a competition, you understand—and on the last day every year the directors of Dormans entertain them at luncheon. We have some famous members," he said; "doctors, lawyers, artists, even a bishop. This year the guest of honour is what in your country you would call your Sherlock Holmes, one of the greatest detectives in France. If you wait a moment you will see him coming out, Inspector Jules Cailleux."

"Cailleux!" I suppose it was Eliot who said that, but it did not sound like Eliot, and I saw he had picked Vicky up and was holding her in front of him on his arm.

"Put me down!" She was mortally offended. She slapped Eliot, but he did not put her down.

"We have forgotten your doll," he said and looked at his watch. "Nous vous remercions infiniment, Monsieur, mais nous n'avons vraiment pas le temps d'attendre. Merci mille fois," and—what was he saying?—"I had forgotten. I have an appointment in Rheims."

"Mais, Monsieur. . . ."

"Je regrette . . ." and he turned to us. "Come along."

"But . . ."

"Eliot!"

"You said . . ."

"Come *along*!" Eliot's voice was as I had heard it once before, cold and clipped. "Come, if you don't want to walk home. Encore mille fois merci," he said again to the man; "un autre jour."

He went towards the car holding Vicky, who hid his face from us. We were following, amazed, when a group of men came out of the door, three of them dressed like our man, the rest in suits or flannels and tweed jackets; there were two priests, and in the middle a little man in a suit of mixed sand- and olive-coloured cloth that went well with his sand-coloured hair and clipped moustache. "That must be the Inspector . . . did he say Cailleux?" asked Joss. The men's faces were red and they all looked jovial, but, great detective or not, we were given no time to look. Eliot had started the Rolls and we had to run across the courtyard and scramble in, even Joss. It was the first time he had treated her in this undignified way—he might have been Uncle William—and her cheeks looked as if they burned.

He drove swiftly round the courtyard and through the gates, and before the men had left the office steps we were out on the road and speeding down it.

We drove in dead silence until at last Hester spoke. "This is the road to Soissons, Eliot."

"I know."

"You said you had an appointment in Rheims."

"I know."

After a moment Hester asked, "Do you tell lies, Eliot?"

"Yes."

He drove fast into Soissons and stopped at a toyshop, got

99

out and helped Vicky from the back seat; he glanced at Joss and said, "Cecil, you come."

In the shop he was not as he usually was with people. "Une poupée? Mais oui, Monsieur. Voulez-vous une belle petite poupée ou une originale?" the shop-girl asked. I did not know what 'une originale' meant, but Eliot did not answer and I had to say, "Une belle petite poupée, that means a pretty little doll," I told Vicky.

Vicky took a long while to choose, but when we were back with the others and heading for Vieux-Moutiers the silence was still unbroken.

At last Eliot stopped the car. "I'm sorry I had to do that," he said.

"Then why did you?" asked Joss.

"I had a reason," said Eliot, "that you would not understand."

"Then you can't expect us to understand, can you?" asked Joss. Her voice was cold but it trembled a little.

"All right. I tell lies," said Eliot violently. It was the first time he had come up against a family opinion. "I tell lies, and so do you and you and you, all of you."

"For you to tell them is different," said Hester.

"I didn't ask to be a hero."

"They mean you are grown up," said Joss coldly.

"I see," said Eliot. "You expect yourselves to be comfortably riddled with faults. . . ."

"We are."

"And you think you will lose them when you grow up."

"I hope so," I said firmly.

"You poor little fools!"

Joss put her hand on Eliot's knee. "Eliot, what has made you so unhappy?"

He looked down at her hand and I shall always remember his answer. "What has made you so unhappy?" Joss asked, and he answered, "Being perfectly happy for two days."

After a moment he turned to look at us in the back seat. "Has none of you ever tasted champagne?"

"Don't be *silly*," said Joss exasperated. "How could we?"
And I said sorrowfully, "We have never even seen it."

"It is not as exciting as all that," said Eliot. "You soon
get tired of it." Silence. "I suppose, to you, that is another
silly thing to say."

"Yes."

He did not say anything more but started the car. When
we got back to the hotel we separated; it seemed by mutual
consent.

⋅   ⋅   ⋅   ⋅   ⋅

There were roses on our table that night. Usually ours
was the only one without flowers. Nobody else was dining
but Monsieur Joubert and Eliot; Madame Corbet's and
Mademoiselle Zizi's places had not been used. Besides the
roses we had a clean starched cloth—often ours was left
on dirty—clean napkins made into cocked hats, and by
each place was a new kind of glass, high, with a three-inch
stem, cut into patterns. "What are these?" we asked.

"Flûtes de champagne," said Mauricette and laughed.

"Glasses for drinking champagne," said Monsieur Joubert
in careful English. He had never spoken to us before except
to say 'Bonjour'. Now he was as interested as Mauricette.
"They have a hollow stem and help the wine to sparkle," he
explained.

Mauricette served our soup. She was friendly that night
and did not slam things down on the table nor lean across us.
After the soup there was chicken, not the perpetual veal
and flageolets. Then Mauricette, with a smile at the corners
of her mouth, brought in one of the silver wine buckets we
had often helped to fill with ice; she stood it by our table.
In it was a dark-green gold-topped bottle. It might have
been one of those we had seen that day. Eliot left his table,
came to ours, and drew the cork, making us jump. It was
the same popping we had heard at Dormans, but it sounded
louder in the dining-room. Then Mauricette wrapped the
bottle in a napkin, carried it to Eliot's table and poured a
little into his glass and gave it to him to taste. He sipped

it and nodded, and went back to his table. For one moment we had thought it might all be for him, but she filled Joss's glass, and went round the table. After Hester, she hesitated, but Eliot said, "Monsieur Willmouse will take a little. Bring a grenadine for Mademoiselle Vicky."

We sat in amazed silence, looking at the glasses and the pale sparkling wine. I think our eyes must have been quite round, our faces awed, but I admired Joss. No matter how moved she did not lose her manners. She got up, went to the bucket, reverently lifted the bottle from the ice, copied Mauricette by wrapping it in a napkin, took it to Eliot and filled his glass up. "May I offer some to Monsieur Joubert?" she asked.

"It's your wine," said Eliot. "Say, 'Vous prendrez bien un verre, Monsieur?'"

She took it to Monsieur Joubert. "Vous prendrez bien un verre, Monsieur?" Mauricette ran with a glass and Joss poured. "Thank you, Mademoiselle Hebe," said Monsieur Joubert.

When Joss was back in her place he lifted his glass and called, "Santé!"

"Santé."

"Santé."

"Santé."

"Santé."

"Santé."

Willmouse was white, Hester approached her lips as if she were afraid champagne might bite, Joss looked over her glass at Eliot and quickly lowered her lids, and we drank. "It goes up your nose," said Willmouse. "I like it going up my nose."

"Monsieur Eliot," called Monsieur Joubert, "you must take the bouchon—the cork—wet it and touch it behind Mademoiselle's ears," and to Joss, "Always with the first bottle of champagne you taste that must be done."

Eliot came over to us. Mauricette gave him the cork, he wetted it and we watched, as in a ritual, while he lifted

Joss's hair and touched it behind her ear. I do not know why, but we all clapped. "Now you must keep it for ever," said Monsieur Joubert to Joss.

"Eliot! *E-liot!*"

Mademoiselle Zizi's voice rang through the hall. The next moment she appeared in the dining-room. "Eliot!"

I thought that, quite deliberately, he touched the cork to Joss's other ear before he answered, "I am here, Zizi."

"Irène says you ordered champagne, Dormans . . . for those children."

"Yes."

"Are you mad?"

"It was for a reason, Zizi."

Had Mademoiselle Zizi forgotten her rouge? She was curiously white; her eyes had dark, purple-coloured stains under them as if she had spilt the eye-shadow, only it was darker than that. "I know your reason!" said Mademoiselle Zizi.

Those haunted-looking eyes took in the table, the roses, the chicken. "Who said you could do this?"

"Pauv' p'tits choux!" said Mauricette. 'Y sont si mignons, ces enfants." She had often called us the reverse of cabbages or sweet. "Armand et moi leur avons préparé une petite surprise."

"With my things?"

Joss got up. She did what she thought was the best thing. Taking Vicky's flûte de champagne from where it stood unused beside the glass of grenadine, she filled it from the bottle and brought it to Mademoiselle Zizi. "Mademoiselle, vous voudrez bien prendre un verre?"

I thought she would not, but Mademoiselle Zizi took the glass. Her eyes turned from Eliot to Joss and back to Eliot. "Santé," said Eliot pleasantly.

Mademoiselle Zizi went even whiter; her mouth made an ugly grimace, and she threw the champagne back at Joss.

．　　　．　　　．　　　．　　　．

We knew from newspapers and books that grown people quarrelled but we had never heard them.

After Mademoiselle Zizi had thrown the champagne no one moved or spoke though Mauricette gave a loud gasp; the glass had fallen with a tinkling crash and the tinkle seemed to go on and on. Then Monsieur Joubert got to his feet and walked out of the dining-room and Vicky began to cry. "I want Mother! I want Mother!" she wailed. Joss's dress was wet with champagne, it trickled down the front of her skirt; she shook her hair back as if she were dazed, then ran out of the room and through the hall. We heard the terrace door bang, and Eliot said to Mademoiselle Zizi, "I want to see you alone."

They did not wait to reach the office before they began; their angry loud voices rang through the hall. They spoke English when they remembered because of Mauricette and the rest who were listening with all their ears, but they kept breaking into French.

"I should never have let them be there at dinner," cried Mademoiselle Zizi. "That girl!"

"She was quite right," said Eliot. "The small ones could eat with the servants, but she and Cecil are big."

"Of course you take her part."

"I don't."

"You do. For three days I have scarcely seen you."

"For Christ's sake, Zizi! I happened to have a little time and amused the poor brats."

"Brats. Qu'est-ce que c'est 'brats'?"

"Children, then."

"You don't think of them as children."

"Don't be ridiculous."

"Ridiculous! For three days . . ." Mademoiselle Zizi was crying.

"*Don't keep on saying that!*" Then Eliot's voice altered. "Zizi, you're not jealous of a little girl?"

"First she is big, then she is little. Remarkable!" That was Madame Corbet, who had come out of the office.

"Is it too much to ask," said Eliot, his voice like ice again, "that we might occasionally talk without Irène?"

"And why may I not remain?"

"Because this is not your business."

"Zizi is my business. I gave up my vocation to look after her."

"Then it was not a vocation."

"Irène, please go." That was Mademoiselle Zizi.

"And leave him to talk you down?"

"Go! Go! Go!" Mademoiselle Zizi's voice was a scream.

"Let *us* go," said Hester and her voice quivered. "Let's go in the garden and get some greengages." But before we could move Madame Corbet came through the dining-room. Her neck was patched with crimson, her topknot shook and the bobbles on her shawl danced up and down. "Ah, le vaurien! Canaille! Fripouille!" said Madame Corbet as she passed. We shrank down in our chairs.

"Eliot, écoute. Écoute-moi . . ." Mademoiselle Zizi's voice was soft and I guessed she had gone close to Eliot. I stood up to see, and yes, she had; she was standing in front of him pleading. "It is too much responsibility, Eliot. Please! Please let us send for this uncle and get them away."

"Dear Zizi, because of a child . . ."

"She isn't a child."

"Of course she is, to me . . . to us."

"I saw you look at her."

"She happens to be pretty."

Mademoiselle Zizi shook her head. "You looked at her because you like her."

"Don't be absurd."

"Then send for the uncle."

"Zizi." Eliot had taken her hands. "I gave my word; besides . . ." I had the feeling he was choosing the words very carefully. "I can't have the uncle, an Englishman, here now."

"Because he is English?" She sounded scornful.

"I explained to you, Zizi. I can't have talk yet."

"But a man in Southstone. That is in Sussex—it is far away from London."

"Not so far. I can't afford to risk it."

"But if I don't mind."

"I mind for you, and if there were talk it might spoil everything."

"But Sussex and London," pleaded Mademoiselle Zizi.

I did not know what they were talking of. I could have told them that Uncle William never went to London, but Eliot sounded as if he were . . . making excuses, I thought. He said now, "You never know."

"N-no," said Mademoiselle Zizi slowly and . . . she is coming to heel, I thought. "Zizi, promise. Promise me you won't do anything."

"Irène says . . ."

"You know Irène would do anything to separate us. Promise." Without looking I knew he had put his arm round Mademoiselle Zizi. I looked at the floor, the blood thrummed in my ears, and my little lemons throbbed. "Zizi."

"Let's go out," whispered Mademoiselle Zizi. "Let's go away from here. Somewhere. Anywhere."

"But why?"

"Because."

"Because?"

"I can't bear it," cried Mademoiselle Zizi. "The house, Irène, them. All of them."

"Get a coat then," said Eliot. He sounded as if he had given up. Why should he sound like that when it was Mademoiselle Zizi who had been defeated? I tiptoed out into the hall. He was there alone, but Mademoiselle Zizi was only fetching her coat; and she soon came back. He said as if he were very tired, "Come through the garden. We will go to the Giraffe."

As they reached the glass door it opened and Joss stood there. Behind her the garden was twilit now; she must have been alone in the dusk . . . in the orchard, I thought, looking at her drenched sandals; her feet and the hem of her dress were soaked, and it was only in the orchard that the dew lay like that. I did not think Joss knew where she had been. Her eyes still looked shocked.

For a moment Mademoiselle Zizi and Eliot stopped. Then Mademoiselle Zizi walked past, her head high.

Joss's eyes went to Eliot. There was no appeal in them, she simply looked. There was a pause, like a breath. Then Eliot squared his shoulders as if he had made up his mind. He went after Mademoiselle Zizi and passed Joss as if she were not there.

CHAPTER 10

When someone has been slapped in the face it is polite not to look at them. I went to a table in the bar, picked up a magazine and turned the pages over while Hester quietly gathered Vicky and Willmouse and took them to bed; I heard them go one after the other into the Hole, then the bedroom doors shut.

The house had never seemed as big. I could hear Madame Corbet scolding Paul; I knew it was Paul because he did not answer as Mauricette did, then I remembered that Mauricette was not there. She had gone to the cinema with Monsieur Armand; soon after the quarrel began we had seen them cross the courtyard and go out arm in arm.

Madame Corbet came from the kitchen and went into the office. I heard her lock up, take the keys and go out. Would she go to the Giraffe and spy on the others or to the convent which was where Paul said she went, though the convent would hardly be open at this hour. I could not guess, but soon after all the lights went off. That was one of Madame Corbet's economies; if she wanted to go out and the house were empty of people—we and Paul did not count as people—she would turn off the electricity at the main; she would be back, the lights suitably burning, before Mademoiselle Zizi and Eliot came in.

Though it was only dusk outside, the house was immediately dark, which made it more desolate. At other times when Madame Corbet had done this Hester and I had been in the garden with Paul, 'talking gossip,' said Joss scornfully, but quite often, 'Not gossip, dreams,' I could have said. We talked about what we should do when we were grown; I was to be a writer or a nun, a nun as Madame Corbet had wanted to be; Hester thought she might keep a tea-shop or an hotel like Mademoiselle Zizi; Paul talked about his lorries. "If I stay the summer," he said, "I shall get the bonus," and he told us again how, at the end of the season, Madame Corbet shared out the tips. "It makes a lot," said Paul; he had seen a good secondhand Berliet at the garage; but now Joss and I were inside; even the dogs were away, they had gone with Eliot and Mademoiselle Zizi, and the house was eerie; it seemed to creak with invisible footsteps; a breeze in the garden sounded like rustling, a curtain flapped. There was a waxing moon, and the early moonlight, mixed with dusk, fell in at the windows and made the light more eerie still. Joss must have felt it, for she came and sat at the table by me. I could just see the pale oval of her face, the whiteness of her arms.

"Shall we go to bed?" I asked.

"I . . . can't." There was a pause. Our voices in the emptiness seemed small, then, "They have even kept our passports," said Joss.

"Our passports?" I asked.

"Yes. How dared they!"

"But . . . what should they have done?"

"They are *ours*," said Joss fiercely.

"But why do you want them?"

"I'm going home," she snapped, "and one can't travel without them."

"But . . ." Every sentence I said seemed to begin with 'but'. "But how can you go?"

"By myself if I must," and she thrust at me, "You were quite happy without me when I was ill. You were happier."

The way in which she said it made it a guilty thing to have been, but I had to admit it. "But it is far more interesting now," I blurted out.

"You call it interesting!"

"Yes. Oh, Joss! Don't—don't spoil it."

"*Spoil* it!" She bent her head.

"I know it is sometimes difficult . . ." I began.

"Difficult!" All she seemed able to do was echo my words, spitting them out as if they tasted bitter.

"Yes, I know, but we are *alive*," I argued. "Think how alive we are. It isn't like Southstone, where we just went on and on and nothing ever happened. Here I can feel us living. Don't you feel as if you were being stretched?"

"It hurts to be stretched," said Joss.

There was a flapping sound that was oddly cheerful, not the flapping curtain but a flap of slippers, and a glimmer of light appeared that grew larger. Joss raised her head as Paul came through the kitchen doorway carrying two lighted candles in bottles. "Vieille guenon!" he said of Madame Corbet. "Carne!" The bad words sounded matter-of-fact and cheerful too. Paul put the bottles down on our table. "V'là ce que j'ai trouvé!" he said, felt in his pocket and brought out the champagne cork. He put it beside Joss.

"Merci," said Joss dully.

"Vous n'en voulez pas?"

Joss shook her head. "It doesn't seem very lucky," she said and, laboriously, "Pas bonne chance."

"C'est la vie," said Paul without rancour. "Les gens." People! I thought, and winced.

"Psst!" Paul spat the people out on the floor. Joss did not even flinch. In fact, she looked better. Perhaps it was the chili in the elephant's eye. Father had told us about that;

in India, when an elephant has a wound that hurts so that the pain cannot be borne the mahout squirts chili juice into its eye for the smarting to distract it.

I guessed that Joss would have liked to have spat too; then the anger faded; she rolled the cork forlornly on the table.

Paul looked at it and her, then he whispered to me. "He kept the champagne," I told Joss.

"I don't want it."

"Le champagne c'est toujours du champagne," said Paul. He added that he was not going to let that she-cat have it.

"The she-cat is Mauricette," I explained to Joss.

"What can we do with it?" asked Joss.

"We could . . . drink it," I said timidly.

"Out of other people's glasses!"

"Only ours. Monsieur Joubert drank his. Ours and . . . Eliot's." Joss turned her head away.

Paul came back with a round tray. He had tactfully poured all the glassfuls back into the bottle so that no one could know which was which. There were two clean glasses. "Where is yours?" and I asked clumsily, "Et pour vous?"

A pleased look came into his face, but he looked at Joss. "Certainement," said Joss.

He fetched another glass and I filled it.

"Ça fait du bien par où ça passe," said Paul, drinking. His eyes seemed eager.

"Santé!" I said, but Paul would not drink to that.

He spat again, then lifted his glass, "Encore un que les salauds n'auront pas. Qu'ils aillent au diable, les cassepieds."

"Les cassepieds," I said.

"Les cassepieds!" said Joss, her eyes dark.

We drank. I tried not to grimace at the strange feeling in my nose, but my eyelids flickered so that Paul laughed. Joss managed to hide everything but one long shudder.

"Vous vous y ferez vite," said Paul, but I did not think we should soon get used to it. He and Joss finished the bottle, then he looked at the empty glasses and asked, "Encore un coup, hein?"

"Encore?" Paul tapped the bottle and pretended he was opening another. "But it's all locked up," I said.

"Si," said Paul mockingly.

Joss thought he had not understood. "Madame Corbet a emporté—has taken the keys—les clefs," she said.

"Si," said Paul and laughed. Then he flapped across the hall and went into Mademoiselle Zizi's room. In a moment he was back holding up a bunch of keys.

"Zizi, where are your keys? You had better give them to me." How many times had I heard Madame Corbet say that and, "You are not fit to have them." It seemed Madame Corbet was right.

Paul turned towards the kitchen door. Behind it stone steps went down to the cellar.

"But, Paul . . ."

Joss cut across me. "Go on," said Joss. "Allez-y." She was not despairing now but sitting up straight. "Go on," she said to Paul, and I knew that the hurt was really angry now. That made me afraid; when Joss was angry she did not care what she did.

"Joss. He shouldn't . . ."

"Shut up," said Joss.

Paul came back with two tall bottles. "Vous en boirez pas du comme ça à l'étranger," he said. "C'est moi qui vous le dis."

I was proud that I could understand him when Joss could not. "You won't drink this away . . . outside France."

"Why?" asked Joss. "What is it? Qu'est-ce que c'est?"

"Champagne nature," and seeing we did not understand he said, "Blanc de blanc."

When I think of that evening it seems to run together into that name. 'Blanc de blanc.' It sounded like the name of a fairy prince—I think the bubbles in the champagne were mounting to my head—blanc de blanc de blanc de blanc . . .

"We mustn't drink it," I said, but the words seemed to burst in the air and disappear.

"We drank the other," said Joss.

"Our wine . . . given to us." Now I seemed to have lost some words.

"Shut up."

Paul caught that. "Shut up," he said amiably to me and poured the wine. Joss lifted her glass to me and drank; she emptied the glass straight off. "Mazette!" said Paul in admiration. He filled it again and she laid her hand on his. "Thank you, Paul," she said. "It was s-sweet of you to get this for us." She had drunk too quickly. The 's-sweet' was a tiny hiccup, but it was not that that sobered me. It was Paul's face. Paul had not understood what she said, but his face had flooded with crimson and that pleased look was in his eyes.

"Joss, don't. He will think you mean it."

"W-what if he does?" She leant towards Paul and said, "You give cigarettes to Cecil. Why not to me?"

"Cigarette?" Paul sounded dazed, but he brought out his packet. Joss took one and he tossed her the matches. It was not that he meant to be rude, but he did not know how to treat girls. Joss tried to light the cigarette, but the smoke got into her eyes. Paul laughed at her and, taking the cigarette, lit it himself, then he put it into her lips. For some reason I did not like to see that. "Joss, don't."

"Why not?"

I would not say 'Why not?' I said instead, "You will hurt him."

Her eyes narrowed into small glints. "I am g-going to hurt him." This time the hiccup was loud.

"You are getting drunk," I said disagreeably.

"I want to. I am going to get d-drunk." She lifted her glass. "I am g-going to do all the d-disgusting things they do." She drank the wine off and held out her glass while I was doubtfully sipping mine. I do not know how many Paul had had, but when he had poured for her the bottle of Blanc de blanc was empty. "L'autre," commanded Joss.

Paul picked up the other and showed it to me. "Bouzy Rouge," he said.

"Bouzy? Bouzy. Bouzy." Joss started to laugh, and the laugh turned into giggles like the bubbles coming up. "C-Cecil. B-Bouzy!" but I was still with Blanc de blanc. It was a mountain, a pudding, shoe polish, a white poodle.

"Boozy," said Joss.

"Blanc de blanc de blanc."

Paul looked at us gravely. He was swaying a little as he stood and said solemnly, "Il faut se mettre à genoux pour déguster celui-là."

I did not understand. "On our knees to drink this? Why?"

He put his hands together and rolled up his eyes.

I collapsed into more giggles; Joss giggled too. "What does Boozy say?"

"He says we should . . . pray."

"Let's pray." She put her hands together, but I took violent exception to that. "Joss, you are not to. *You . . . are . . . not . . . to!*" I banged the table with the empty bottle.

"P-pious p-prig!"

"N-not a p-prig!" and I burst into tears. Joss looked as if she might cry too. She put her arm round my neck. "Don't," she begged. "Don't!"

"Then you don't," I said, still angry, and she pulled away, offended. "Cry then," she said. "Howl. I don't c-care. Tell Paul to open the wine."

Paul was having difficulty with the corkscrew. He located the cork, but as soon as he tried to spiral the screw in it slipped sideways. Now he tried again and seared his thumb. "Aïe! Merde!" said Paul. "Hit it," said Joss, "tapez dessus," and he hit the bottle against one of the console tables. The neck smashed off on the floor with a gush of red wine that spattered his apron and hand. There was an ugly great gash across the table.

I was horrified. "Paul. *Paul!*"

He swore at me with his new word. "Shut up!" and poured the wine.

"I don't want any," I said, but he picked up my glass, drank the white and filled it with the red. It seemed to my bleared eyes that the whole hall was spread with red wine—the glasses were red and the pool on the floor. Paul and Joss's hands seemed to come nearer and go away again, as did the candle flames in the bottles. When I looked at the walls they moved inwards a little, while the stairs went sideways. It was no longer blanc de blanc, that happy time; the red was terrible, and I began to cry again.

Joss had drunk her glass already. I do not know why she was not sick. "Another cigarette. Encore une Gauloise," she said.

Paul looked at her. His eyes seemed to squint so that he looked hideous and he said, "Viens la prendre."

He was sitting back from the table, his knees apart, his apron dangling between them, a cigarette stuck to his lower lip. Now he pulled open his shirt and showed where the cigarettes were crumpled inside. "Viens-y," he said. Joss went pale and stood uncertainly up.

I knew what he would do. I had seen him with Mauricette too often. Mauricette could look after herself, but, "Joss, you are not to" I screamed. "You are not to!" I pushed her down and screamed at Paul, "Ne la touchez pas!"

He turned on me and ordered me to bed. "Toi, va faire dodo! Au pieu!"

"I won't. Joss! Joss!"

Paul picked up the bottle. I do not know what would have happened if Joss had not settled it herself. She had been sitting where I had pushed her; now, quite softly, with a sigh, she fell forward on the table, knocking over my un-touched glass. Her head rolled a little, her hair tumbled forward into the wine and began to soak it up.

We heard footsteps. The garden door opened, Monsieur Joubert and Mademoiselle Zizi came in and stopped, with Eliot close behind them. At the same moment the lights went on and there was a scurry of steps in the kitchen passage; Madame Corbet had stayed too late and the others had beaten her; she came running in breathless and stopped too. "Grands Dieux!" said Madame Corbet. The others said nothing, they simply stood.

It must have looked an orgy with the bottles and glasses, the candles burnt down in the bottles, the wine on the table, the cigarette-ends where we had thrown them down on the floor with more wine and broken glass. "Grands Dieux!" said Madame Corbet again.

Then I saw the rat in Paul. "C'est pas moi! C'est pas moi!" His voice was shrill with fear. "C'est elle"—he pointed at Joss; "elle et Mademoiselle Cecil. Elles m'ont forcé!"

"La ferme!" said Eliot, which was the rudest way I had heard of saying 'Shut up'.

Mademoiselle Zizi had stayed in the doorway; it was as if she kept her skirts held back. Eliot crossed at once to Joss, but before he reached her Monsieur Joubert came up behind and stood with his hands on her chair. It was as if he kept Eliot off. Monsieur Joubert bent and straightened Joss up, but she could not sit; her head fell forward again. "She is drunk," said Monsieur Joubert to Eliot as if it were an accusation, and he said, in English too, "I do not know what has been going on here but it is not good." He was not looking at us but at Eliot and Mademoiselle Zizi.

"*Good!*" Mademoiselle Zizi was defensive. "To be drunk at their age! On my wine!"

"And look at the table!" cried Madame Corbet.

"Ma petite table! My little table! Ah!" Mademoiselle Zizi's voice was agonised.

Madame Corbet darted forward and picked up the bottles. "Zizi! The Villers Marmery and Bouzy Rouge!"

Paul had been picking up the broken glass. Now he

rolled it in his apron and slipped adroitly through the kitchen door. Joss was insensible; there was only I, Cecil, to face them. I was standing unsteadily where I had risen by the table and Madame Corbet turned on me and slapped my cheeks. "Petite canaille . . . Je m'en vais te flanquer une correction. Drôlesse! Oh! Cette petite crapule!"

"Stop that, Irène," said Eliot. "Stop. Hush!" he said more loudly as the stream of names went on.

"Hush! And who is to pay for it?"

"You can put it on my bill," said Monsieur Joubert and there was silence. He bent and picked Joss up. "Mademoiselle Cecil, can you walk upstairs to your room?"

My ears were singing with Madame Corbet's slaps, but I managed to leave the table and zigzag to the stairs; there the banister-rail came unexpectedly into my hand. Monsieur Joubert followed, carrying Joss.

"Let me take her," said Eliot.

"I think you have done enough," said Monsieur Joubert. He carried Joss up. I followed, missing some steps but holding by the banister-rail. Eliot was left standing at the foot of the stairs.

CHAPTER 11

"IF THIS is how grown people feel," said Joss, "they are even worse pigs than I thought."

I said, perhaps tactlessly, "They know when to stop."

"Do they!" said Joss. "Look at Mademoiselle Zizi." But I had to be fair.

"Of all the grown-ups she is the only one who doesn't seem to know," and I sighed. "I suppose one has to learn even to drink."

I did not remember getting into bed, but I had woken

to find myself under the clothes though dressed. "Dressed in bed!" said Willmouse. "Cecil, *what* have you been doing?" It was not often Willmouse asked questions, and when he had seen how unwell I was he had slipped on his vest and shorts, brushed his hair and gone out. I think he kept Hester and Vicky away.

When I had gone in to Joss she too was in bed, the covers tucked carefully round her, her sandals placed neatly side by side on the rug, but she also was dressed. I felt so miserable that I woke her and she was cross. Then, sitting up, she had taken in where she was, her crumpled dress, the smell on her hair and she gave a sound like a moan and shut her eyes.

We felt our bones were stained now indeed and, too shamed to go down to breakfast, we stayed in Joss's room. "But it wasn't our fault," I argued and used a phrase I had read in Monsieur Armand's newspapers, "They drove us to it," but Joss was more truthful than I.

"It was our fault," she said wearily, "and we shall have to learn."

"Learn what?"

"To manage."

"Manage what?"

"Manage what happens to us better than this. I smell," said Joss.

"I smell too," I said.

"Not as badly as I do," and once more she covered her eyes with her hand. It was only to shut out the light, but it looked tragic and I felt torn.

When something is badly needed it is amazing how an answer will come. I was moved to tell Joss about Monsieur Joubert. She was quiet as she listened, then she took her hand down. "You mean he said, 'Put it on my bill', just like that?" she asked.

"Just like that."

"He wasn't angry?"

"Not with us."

"And I was drunk."

"Very."

"Like those men by the canal."

"Yes. He carried you up to bed."

"Not . . . Eliot?"

"Eliot wanted to but Monsieur Joubert would not let him."

Joss thought for a moment, then got out of bed, went to the washstand, poured water into the basin and began to splash her face. She did not speak while she dried her face and hands, then stripped off her crumpled dress; I knew she was thinking very deeply or she would have told me to go away. At last, as she was putting on a clean dress I asked, "What are you going to do?"

"Give Monsieur Joubert one of my paintings," she said.

"But, Joss! He is famous. He gets hundreds of pounds for a portrait. He has paintings in big galleries like the Salon and the Academy."

"Not the Academy. The Uffizi in Florence. They have just bought some of his," said Joss calmly, putting on her shoes.

"He is to have an exhibition in London this year," I argued; "Madame Corbet said so. He . . . he won't be bothered with a girl, Joss. He is Marc Joubert. Madame Corbet says he is one of the best painters in the world."

"Then he will know when a painting is good," said Joss.

She was, of course, right. Monsieur Joubert did not send her away; he held the little painting at arm's length, looked at it again, put it up on a chair and went away from it. Nor was he play-acting—I do not think Monsieur Joubert ever acted. We all stood round in a chorus while a familiar catechism began. "You did this yourself?"

"Yes," said Joss, and we nodded.

"No one helped you?"

"No," and we shook our heads.

"Then what are you doing mixing yourself up with other things?" asked Monsieur Joubert.

Joss said uncertainly, "There *are* other things."

The answer came back, "Not for you."

"I am going to an art school soon," said Joss.

"When?"

"Perhaps when the holidays are over."

"Painters don't have holidays," said Monsieur Joubert. "They don't know how. Why an art school?"

"I need to learn to draw," said Joss meekly.

I thought he would say 'Nonsense' but he nodded. "That won't spoil you. When Madame your mother is better I will speak with her," and he said to me, "Does she talk?"

"Mother?" I asked, startled.

"Mademoiselle." He pointed at Joss.

"Oh! She! Sometimes."

He pounced. "Not all times?"

"Oh no! That's Hester."

"Then," said Monsieur Joubert, "Mademoiselle Joss can come and paint with me. Not near but near enough, but no other child must come," and he said fiercely to the rest of us, "Keep away!"

We nodded again, our eyes wide with respect. This, we knew, was something different from Eliot.

Eliot made one approach to Joss. Before dinner she stayed out on the terrace so that she need not meet him in the bar. Mademoiselle Zizi was talking to some American arrivals and he went out.

"Joss."

"Yes."

"I'm sorry. Joss, I had to do that."

Joss said nothing.

"You won't talk to me?" asked Eliot.

"No," said Joss.

"Tomorrow I'm not going to Paris and . . ."

"I will be busy tomorrow," and it was true, not an excuse.

From that day we were split as we had been . . . before Eliot, I thought. Vicky went back to Monsieur Armand, Willmouse stayed in his cherry bank atelier, Hester and I rambled alone. Joss got up in the mornings now as early as Monsieur Joubert; almost before it was light she was out on the bank—she too was painting two pictures—and she went early to bed. "There is no light then. I might as well go to bed," she said. The other people in the house hardly saw her at all.

As Hester and I dawdled at the cove we would watch her. She had none of the trappings Monsieur Joubert had, not even a camp stool; she sat on an upturned wooden box and held her board on her knee. She had not any proper canvas, only a piece of linen stretched on the board, but Monsieur Joubert showed her a way of washing it over with two or three coats of white—"not paint, tempera," said Joss —to make it smooth. He had given her a flat tin box filled with jars of tempera and, "One day, he will help me with oils," she said. Worst of all she had no umbrella and she had to sit out in the heat with only her old straw hat to shade her and that had been bent when it was packed so that the straw had split; I could not imagine Joss consenting under any other circumstances to wear it. Every now and then she climbed down the bank and wetted her handkerchief to spread on the crown; even so, she was sickly pale at the end of the day.

"Monsieur Joubert ought to send you in."

"He doesn't notice me," said Joss with pride. She knew how to please him and she only interrupted her work to join us when we went to pay our evening visit to Mother. We were allowed to go and see Mother every day now and, "I'm painting," Joss told her and Mother looked relieved.

"And what are you doing, Cecil?"

"Nothing."

"But you are looking after the Littles?"

"Yes," I said grudgingly. I had to. Joss was as good an elder sister as any, but, when she was painting, Vicky or Willmouse could have fallen into the Marne and she would not have known.

"Only they wouldn't," said Hester.

"No, but Willmouse goes off every evening alone and he shouldn't."

Every evening when he had finished his work Willmouse put his things away: his box of scraps, his sewing-box, Miss Dawn and Dolores, and their new confections; then he tidied himself, which was only a form because he was always tidy— even his scarecrows managed to be neat; he would wash his face and hands, sleek down his hair with his private bottle of eau-de-Cologne and, like any old gentleman, go for a little walk. A new barge, the *Marie France* 47, had anchored above the cove; he liked to walk up and look at that.

"Why don't you go when we go?"

"I like to go by myself."

"You can't always do what you like."

"I can," said Willmouse.

I let him. It was too hot, everything was too strained, to bother.

Before Eliot. We were back to that time, yet we were not back. It was the same, and it was not the same. A curious tenseness was in the house. Eliot when he came from Paris looked bone tired and haggard, and he was so curt with Mademoiselle Zizi that her eyes looked bigger than ever with perpetual tears. She was very silly. She kept searching his face, beseeching him with those big eyes instead of leaving him alone; we scurried out of his way as soon as we saw that tiredness in his face.

For three days he did not come at all. Mademoiselle Zizi went to the telephone four or five times. We heard her ask for the same Paris number, then wait, listening, while that far-off bell rang and rang. There was never any answer. If the office telephone went she would leap out of her chair; then she would sink back again as she heard Madame Corbet's, "Hôtel des Oeillets. Oui, madame. Oui. Certainement."

Then there was Paul. I could bear his having tried to make Joss come to him, that was to be expected of Paul;

if he had hit me that night, as I think he meant to with the bottle, I could have expected that too; but he had sneaked out and left me. In our code that was mean.

"Mauricette says you were drunk," said Hester.

"So that was what was the matter with you," said Will-mouse.

"She says you shouldn't be with Paul." Hester was troubled.

"He is a horrid boy," said Vicky. "He gave me a bit of frog to eat and said it was chicken."

"Did you eat it?"

"You *can* eat them," said Vicky, as if that settled it.

Neither of the Littles liked Paul. Hester, of course, took a more lenient view. "But you were not there," I said. "You don't know how awful he was," I said.

"More awful than you and Joss?"

"Yes," and then, thinking of what Paul had been through, the camps and the Hôtel-Dieu, the half-negro sister, I had to say, "I don't know."

I did not want to see all these things in Paul, but since coming to Les Oeillets I seemed to see a long way into people, even when I did not wish it. "You think of no one but yourselves," Mother had said on that long-ago day on the beach, and how much more comfortable that had been. I seemed to see into everyone and, "There isn't anybody good," I said in misery.

"Yes, there is," said Hester; "Monsieur Joubert."

Perhaps even he was not completely good but he was . . . kept good, I thought; we could see him now, with Joss faithfully behind him, both of them busy. "I wish I had painting or dressage or something," I said, and asked, "How can you be good if you are just lying about?"

"Mother says not everyone can have things."

"Then they can't be good," I said firmly.

Hester was looking at the river, at the water eddying down. There was a long silence, then, "Cecil, is Eliot good?" she asked.

The question seemed to fall with a plop into the peaceful water.

"We love him," I said uncertainly. Can one love someone who is not good? That was as much a reversal of our ideas as that the Black Virgin was beautiful.

Is Eliot good? It was a question I would rather not have answered and I was glad when the water-whirls took it away.

CHAPTER 12

IT WAS the third week of August, and the same high summer weather; even in the cove it was hot; hardly a breeze disturbed the willows so that they hung dustily green, not showing their silver; the grass was dusty and untidy, filled with the litter left by Sunday walkers and picnickers; the bulrushes were untidy too; they were ripe and powdering, and if we accidentally brushed a spear-rod a stain of brown was left on our skin and clothes. In the orchard the greengages were almost over and at dinner small white grapes appeared on the table. "Are they champagne grapes?" we asked—we had become most conscious of champagne—but Mauricette shook her head. "These are from the Midi. Ours are not ripe till the end of September," and she said, "But you will be here for the vintage, of course."

We did not dispute that. It seemed to us we were here for ever. Mother was better but still not out of bed, not even sitting up. Next month the holidays would be over, but there were still three and a half weeks to go and at Les Oeillets each day was like a year. Twenty-three days; twenty-three years. Who bothers what will happen in twenty-three years?

I remember thinking that as I was lying on my stomach in the sun at the edge of the cove, looking down into the water where hundreds of tiny fish were nibbling at nothing that I could see. If I threw in a crumb they would all dart round it, taking bites, as something sensational would divert us. I supposed a fish's only sensation was food . . . food and death, I thought, watching a big fish hovering over them. Sometimes someone from the town or the hotel would bring a fine net and scoop these little fish up, a hundred or so of them, to fry crisp and season with salt and lemon, and eat with slices of brown bread and butter. I had eaten dozens; now I, part of their fate, hung over them and they did not even see me. Ugh! I thought.

My back seemed to be melting with heat, but suddenly I felt cold as if my blood had chilled. There was nothing one could do; at any moment the big fish, the net, might come to any of us, to me. I looked at the nibbling shoal again. If there were a crumb they darted, but even if the shadow of a very big fish went over them they did not move from the crumb. They were too busy living.

Well then, I thought; and slowly the cold ebbed away and again I could feel the heat beating through my dress on to my skin, but I could not forget that cold. "Funny, I was never afraid of death before," I told Hester.

"You never thought about it," said Hester and she comforted me. "It was only the fish." I had put death firmly out of my mind when she said thoughtfully, "I don't know why but I don't like these days."

I did not like them either, but there seemed nothing wrong; in fact there was a new friendliness in the house. We had put Paul out of bounds so that we heard no scandal; Mademoiselle Zizi and Joss kept truce under Monsieur Joubert; Madame Corbet, perhaps because she wished she had not slapped me, was less sharp; and for us it was as if we had taken a step or two backwards; we were children again, and that was a relief.

Joss finished her first painting and took it to Mother. Vicky had her fifth birthday; Monsieur Armand made her a cake and we had a French birthday party. We were to remember it always. "Because it was from then," said Hester afterwards. "That was the day," she said, "when Eliot began to be where he wasn't."

"And wasn't where he was."

It was a queer birthday party. A table was carried out in the garden, Mauricette covered it with a white cloth and decorated it with vine leaves from the arbour. In the middle was the cake, covered with cream icing and nuts, and round it Mauricette put a ring of wine-glasses filled with grenadine. "No tea?" asked Vicky puzzled, but there was no tea. Mademoiselle Zizi came and Madame Corbet, Mauricette, Monsieur Armand, Toinette and Nicole, Robert the gardener and his wife and baby; Monsieur Joubert and Joss left their painting, Willmouse his sewing. Paul curtly refused to come out of the kitchen, and Eliot, though he had known about the party, had gone to Paris. That made it more amiable but less exciting.

It did not last long; there were no presents, Mother could not be reminded and we could not buy them without any money, but Vicky, with so few birthdays behind her, was not in the habit of presents and did not know what she was missing. We drank her health, cut the cake, and after eating and drinking, broke up. Joss, Hester and I went to the hospital, Willmouse took his walk, and Vicky had more cake in the kitchen.

When Willmouse came in he said, "Who told you Eliot was in Paris?"

"He is."

"He isn't. He's here."

"How do you know?"

"I saw him," but Willmouse seemed perplexed.

"What's the matter?" I asked him.

"It was Eliot, not in Eliot's clothes."

"You must have made a mistake."

"I don't make mistakes about clothes," said Willmouse.

He had been walking home along the bank—"You know the bit along the path where the cove is hidden in the bulrushes?"—when Eliot had appeared, walking in front of him. "And he was wearing blue, like the overalls here but trousers and one of those striped jersey shirts."

"Eliot doesn't wear those sort of clothes," said Hester.

"I *know*," said Willmouse exasperated. "That's why."

"Why?"

"Why it seems funny when he does."

"Are you *sure*?" asked Hester.

"Don't I know about clothes?" said Willmouse in a terrible voice, and Hester subsided.

"He went off the path just above the bulrushes where it has a side path into the wood." Willmouse wrinkled his forehead again. "Do you know, it looked—I thought—but he couldn't have . . ."

"Couldn't have what?"

"Come off the new barge." Willmouse sounded oddly positive, but what would Eliot have been doing on the *Marie France*?

We liked barges with their black hulls and clean scrubbed decks, and had all been up to look at this one. We often looked into barge cabins to see their shining brass, their curtains and pots of flowers; often there was a cat or a bird in a cage, a mother and lots of children, but the *Marie France* did not seem to have a woman aboard. Her brass was not polished, there were no curtains or flowers. She was a dingy barge and we saw only two men, in the cotton trousers Willmouse had described, but they did not wear jerseys, even cotton ones; they were naked above the waist, with black sailor caps.

"It wasn't Eliot," I said, and that seemed positive when Eliot came back at nine o'clock that night.

"Did you have a good day?" Mademoiselle Zizi asked anxiously.

"Damnably hot," said Eliot. He looked exhausted.

He had brought Vicky a box of chocolates such as we had never seen or imagined; it was a pink satin box painted with roses and tied with wide velvet ribbon, and inside, where most boxes have paper-lace edgings, it had real lace. It was marked Dorat. "One of the most expensive chocolate shops in Paris," exclaimed Madame Corbet.

"You see he was in Paris," I told Willmouse.

"Yes," said Willmouse, but he did not sound convinced.

Eliot stayed at Les Oeillets next day, but he did not sit, as he usually did, reading in the garden. First he took the Littles to see Mother; when he came back he asked Hester and me if we would like to go with him into the town. We passed Joss on the river bank, but she did not turn her head, nor did Eliot say anything. In the town he bought postcards, giving them to us, and then some grapes for Mother, which we took to the hospital, calling on Monsieur le Directeur, who called out, "À ce soir," when we left.

"Why à ce soir?" I asked.

"He is coming tonight. There's a big dinner," said Eliot. "Didn't you know?"

"We are not told things," I said.

As soon as we got in Eliot coaxed Mademoiselle Zizi out to the Giraffe. "That's three times," said Hester.

"That Eliot has gone into the town?"

"Yes. Isn't he fidgety?" said Hester.

He could not have had very much lunch, for just after twelve he came to the cove where Hester and I had taken our picnics and turned us out. "Keep away," he said. "I want to sleep."

"But we haven't eaten our picnics."

"Well, go and eat them somewhere else."

There was no one about. Monsieur Joubert had gone in, he lunched at twelve. Joss could not accompany him; she ate her picnic humbly in the orchard; after that they both went to their rooms to sleep. Willmouse too, after his picnic, would take a nap under his cherry tree; like the little old gentleman he was he would cover his face with his handkerchief. Vicky was still at the age when she was put to rest and was collected by Joss on her own way up. Monsieur Armand, when the luncheons were over, would read the newspaper on the kitchen table, Mauricette lazed in the kitchen or garden, Mademoiselle Zizi lay in a long chair on the terrace, and I think even Madame Corbet nodded in the office. Hester and I had meant to bathe, immersing ourselves, coming out now and again in the sun, going back; the water would have been cool, but now we could not bathe.

Eliot must have divined this, for he asked, "Did you want to bathe?" and he suggested, "Go to the Plage for once."

"We should have to pay," said Hester.

Eliot laughed. "You little skinflints."

That hurt us. "Ever since we have been here," I said in a muffled voice, "we haven't had any money."

"Why not?" asked Eliot.

"Nobody has given us any." Hester's voice was muffled too. It was from the remembrance of the times we had looked over at the Plage, read the list of ices, gazed in at the sweetshops in the town, at those wonderfully coloured sucettes and, in l'Eglantine, at the gladioli we had wanted for Mother; it was the remembrance of Vicky not having any birthday presents, of wanting to buy 'Moi et Toi' and something for Uncle William that made us sound choked.

"Usually we have pocket money every week," I explained.

"Good Lord! I'm sorry," said Eliot. "Why didn't you ask? Look. Have three weeks, now," and he took out his wallet, fat with French notes, and peeled off seven. "One for Hester, one between Vicky and Willmouse, two for Cecil and three for Joss."

We looked at them stunned and neither of us moved. "Take them," said Eliot; he sounded impatient, but we shook our heads. "What's the matter now?"

"It's too much," said Hester, and I added, "More than a pound each."

"If I say you can have it."

"We can't," said Hester, shocked. "You see, Vicky has sixpence, Willmouse has ninepence, I have a shilling, Cecil has two, and Joss has another arrangement." I would not have told all this, but Hester never minded exposing the family. "She has ten shillings, but she has to pay her bus fares and buy her own stamps and soap and toothpaste and handkerchiefs and stockings."

"Don't. You make me giddy," said Eliot. "Well, have this for now." But we still shook our heads.

"Must you be so appallingly honest?" He said it so harshly that we stared.

"I suppose," said Hester, wavering, "that Mother would pay for us to bathe."

"Look," said Eliot, "I'm tired." He did not seem tired but . . . was it excited? Why? I wondered. Why should he be excited on this hot sleepy afternoon? "Take this." He gave us a note. "Go and bathe and we will settle the rest this evening." We still hesitated and he shouted, "Go! If anyone comes near me before five o'clock I shall skin them alive."

In fairness we ought to have gone and fetched the others when we had finished our picnics, but, "They are probably asleep," said Hester. "They can go afterwards. There's heaps of money." And so we went to the Plage we had looked at and yearned after so often. We walked over the white bridge, past the railing with the life-belt, in at the gate, and took our tickets from the sleepy caretaker; we rented one of the red-and-white cabins and used all three pools and the low-, the middle-, but not the high-diving boards. I could dive, though sometimes I hit the water with a slap; Hester simply jumped off, holding her nose. It was blissfully cool and for an hour or two we were like a pair of porpoises playing. At last we came out, and after we had dressed we bought strawberry ices from the kiosk and ate them at one of the white tables. "Eliot *is* good!" said Hester reverently as she licked her cardboard spoon.

The ices were spun out as long as we could. "We had better not have another one, had we?" asked Hester, but in the end we had another between us. We spun that one out as well. Four o'clock struck, but, "I don't want any goûter," she said; nor did I.

We left the Plage and walked back along the bank; it was then that Hester said, "Let's creep up on Eliot."

"For what?"

"Just to love him," said Hester. Another Eastern idea of which Father had told us was the taking of 'darshan', that even to look on anyone good or great would feed the soul.

"He told us not to."

"How will be know?" asked Hester.

Les Oeillets had taught us to be as adept as Red Indians in stealing up on what we wanted to see and we came up to the cove without a sound. Eliot was lying, as he always lay, face downwards on the sand, his length pressed into it, his head pillowed on his arms, the old cap tilted over his eyes. Behind the bulrushes we crept up on him. He was lying with his head towards us. "Fast asleep," breathed Hester.

That must have made a sound, for he stirred, stirred and lifted his head and . . . it was not Eliot.

In Eliot's clothes, under Eliot's cap, we were looking into the face of a dark unknown man. I do not know why it was so frightening, but, for the long moment he looked, we froze as rabbits do and the river seemed to be running in my ears. When his head went down again we retreated backwards through the bulrushes so fast that we were covered in bulrush dust. Then we ran. We reached Joss's box and I sank down on it while Hester fell on the grass. My neck and the backs of my knees were clammy and cold; her chin was shaking.

We sat there a long while without speaking and the sun did not make us any warmer.

At last, "Do you think it could be us . . . after the ices?" asked Hester.

"No."

"It was another m . . ."

"Yes."

130

"Then . . . ?" The question seemed to go on and on.

It was some time later that Hester said, "Hullo! Monsieur Joubert's things have gone." There was no umbrella, no easle or stool, and Joss's box, alone on the river bank, looked small and lonely.

The light grew deeper, swallows were beginning to skim the river as they did when the insects flew down; five o'clock struck from the Hôtel de Ville and we got up to go in. As we reached the blue door it opened and Mademoiselle Zizi came out.

She was in white and carried a deep mauve sunshade, the colour of heliotrope. She was freshly powdered and made up and her scent came to us in waves. "Are you going out?" we asked stupidly.

"Only to the cove, to meet Eliot."

We looked at one another, opened our lips, and shut them.

"Why didn't you tell her?" said Hester after she had gone.

"Why didn't you?"

We did not go in but stayed in the orchard. We talked to Willmouse, admired Miss Dawn's new hat, and played with the dogs. We did not say it to one another but we were waiting to see, and after what seemed a long while the blue door opened again. Mademoiselle Zizi came through, and behind her was Eliot.

CHAPTER 13

As soon as we came into the house we knew that Madame Corbet had sent Mademoiselle Zizi to meet Eliot because she wanted her out of the way.

Madame Corbet was efficient; when anything had to be

arranged at Les Oeillets, a dinner, two or three chars-à-bancs of tourists for luncheon or an early breakfast, it was made ready quietly and swiftly. "But not if Mademoiselle Zizi is there," said Hester. Mademoiselle Zizi gave contradictory orders to Mauricette, upset Monsieur Armand by suggesting last-minute changes in the food, took Paul away from his work, and quarrelled with Madame Corbet. It was wiser to send Mademoiselle Zizi away and now the house was being quickly transformed; we could see it was for a much bigger occasion than any since we had come.

"Is it a *banquet*?" asked Willmouse.

The tables in the dining-room had been moved to make one large T, the whole covered with white cloths and laid with silver and glass. "Ninety-four places," whispered Hester when she had finished counting. The flowers were not being done as usual by Mauricette; Madame from l'Eglantine and her two Mademoiselles in green overalls were arranging them—carnations, asparagus ferns and white flowers like small lilies on one stem; they had a strong, sweet smell. "Mauricette says they are tuber roses," I said.

"I have heard of them," said Willmouse gravely.

In the bar a platform had been made; we knew it was only of boxes, but, laid with a carpet and palms, it looked impressive. There were more flowers in the hall and bar, and a carpet had been put down from the front door to the foot of the stairs, "Because the Sous-Préfet and Monsieur le Maire are coming," said Vicky, who had joined us from the kitchen.

We had seen the Mayor of Southstone at the Armistice parade; he had worn a red-caped cloak, a cocked hat and a great chain. "But I did not know one had mayors to dinner," I said in awe.

"It *is* a banquet," said Willmouse certainly.

"It's the Brass Instruments Ball," said Vicky, who had been in the kitchen most of the day and knew everything.

Not quite everything. It was the Brass Instrument Factory's centenary dinner, but it remained for ever in our minds as the Brass Instruments Ball.

We had often passed the factory when we were exploring across the river and spelled out the lettering on the long notice-board along its wall. 'Emile Perrichaut, fabricant d'instruments de fanfare. Trompettes. Clairons. Médaille de l'Exposition de 1895. Fournisseur de l'Armée.' Now all the thirty workers, with their wives—and husbands, for some of the workers were women—their grown-up sons and daughters were coming and, as well as the Sous-Préfet and the Mayor, the Town Clerk, the Commissaire of Police, the Lieutenant of Gendarmerie, the Chief of the Municipal Band, "Et le Capitaine des Pompiers," said Mauricette, which meant the head of the Fire Brigade. Mauricette said that the doctor, Monsieur le Directeur, was coming because he was the brother-in-law of Monsieur Perrichaut, and that Eliot and Mademoiselle Zizi were invited. There would be no room at Les Oeillets for any visitors that night—the whole hotel was taken up with the Brass Instruments.

"What will they do?" asked Vicky, and I saw she was trying to think of the most exciting things she had heard of people doing. "Drink cider and play cards?" she asked.

"They will eat a lot, drink quite a lot, and make long speeches," said Eliot, who had come up behind us. Hester and I shrank a little from him, but he did not notice. "And then perhaps they will dance."

"To the Brass Instruments Band?" asked Hester.

The Brass Instruments had their own band. We had heard it on Sundays and feast days in the town and guessed that the platform was for them.

"Look what they are to *eat*!" said Vicky.

She had brought us the menu:

> Hors-d'œuvre variés
> Homard à la mayonnaise

"That's lobster," I told Vicky.

"I know, I ate some," she said.

> Poulet Chasseur
> Filet de boeuf rôti jardinière
> Salade de saison
> Fromages variés
> Pièce Montée
> Fruits

"And the pièce has a whole band on top of it," said Vicky. "Monsieur Armand has been four days making it. He said I wasn't to tell you."

She took us to look at it. It was on a silver slab, a great cake with trellises and scrolls of icing and, on top, a sugar band, the bandsmen made of meringue and coloured, the tiny brass instruments of yellow sugar. We could not believe it had been made here in the kitchen. "I am Marc Joubert of the icing sugar," said Monsieur Armand. He seemed radiantly pleased as he chivvied us out of the kitchen, but I had caught sight of Paul, his back turned to us, at the sink with a huge pile of saucepans. When he reached for a cloth the lock of hair fell back and we saw his face looking thinner than ever and as dirtily white as his apron. How I wish now I had gone and spoken to him, but I was afraid he would only have sworn at me.

No one told us what was to happen to us, and we stayed watching in the dining-room while Madame Eglantine and her Mademoiselles put the last flower in the last vase, then we went upstairs and dressed. We put on our best frocks, that we had not worn yet; they were not very grand, crinkled white seersuckers with small rose spots. Mother had made them out of a length she had bought at the sales; Joss had grown out of hers, and they had been handed down so that I wore Joss's, Hester wore mine and Vicky Hester's; with two more to come down, it seemed Vicky would have to wear rose-spotted seersucker for years. Willmouse put on a clean shirt, his silk tie, clean shorts. "What will Joss wear?" asked Hester.

"She will see when she comes in."

"Isn't she in?" asked Hester, but there was no sound from her room.

We cleaned our nails and brushed our hair; Vicky and Hester put on clean white socks—Joss had arranged for our washing to be done, and at last we had clean clothes—I unrolled my one pair of thin stockings and we cleaned our sandals. When we were finished there still had not been a rustle from Joss's room. "If she had been to see Mother she would have been back long ago. Perhaps she went out with Monsieur Joubert," said Hester.

"Someone would have told us."

I knocked. No answer. I went in and Joss was there, lying face downwards on her bed.

"Joss! Are you having an attack?"

No answer.

I went timidly closer. Hester and the Littles stayed at the door.

"Joss. It's Cecil. Speak to me, Joss."

She raised her head but she did not speak to me. "I hate her. I hate her," she said. It sounded as if she were speaking to the whole world.

"Hate whom?" but I knew and, "What happened?" I asked apprehensively.

"She has ended the painting," said Joss.

"Ended the . . ."

"Yes." Joss sat up and beat the pillow with her fist. "Yes! Yes! Yes!"

"But . . . how?"

"He asked me to have lunch with him."

I hesitated. We knew who 'she' was but 'he' might have been . . . "Eliot?" I hazarded.

"Idiot! Monsieur Joubert. It was so hot outside—I think he did it because of that—and I said Yes. There was no one in the dining-room but us and . . . them."

"Mademoiselle Zizi and Eliot?"

"Yes. Madame Corbet was too busy to come in to lunch.

Perhaps we—Monsieur Joubert and I—laughed too much."
She lifted her chin. "I wanted to laugh . . . Eliot . . ." She
broke off.

I had to prompt her. "Eliot?"

"Kept looking," said Joss. "Then, when he had gone—
he went quite soon as if he didn't like it—Mademoiselle
Zizi came to our table and said . . ." She stopped again.

"Said?"

"It was in French but I understood. I wish I hadn't," said
Joss. She looked round and saw the others. "Shut the door,
Cecil."

I slowly crossed the little room and shut the door.
Whether because of the long bathing that afternoon or the
shock in the cove, I seemed to be filled with pains, in my legs
and back and head, pains that hurt, and I did not want to
hear any more . . . ugliness, I thought—I could sense this
was something ugly—and I wished I were with Hester and
the Littles on the other side of the door.

I came back to the bed and Joss whispered, "She told him
she could not have it in her hotel, an old man and a young
girl. That I had . . ."

"Had?"

"Bothered Eliot," said Joss in a whisper. Two tears fell
on the pillow, only two; it was as if she were bleeding, not
crying.

"What happened then?"

"Monsieur Joubert got up and bowed, not to her but to
me."

"*Bowed* to *you?*"

"Yes," said Joss impatiently. "He said, 'When you are a
little older and in another place, and your mother is with
you, we shall meet again. I shall write to her,' and he
left . . ."

"For good?"

"Yes. I saw Paul carry out his luggage and painting
things and a taxi came. I don't think Mademoiselle Zizi
meant Monsieur Joubert to do that—I heard Madame Corbet

being cross—but when she sees me Mademoiselle Zizi can't help what she does. She won't let me have anything. Not anything."

"Why does she hate Joss so terribly?" I asked Hester afterwards. "It seems more than because Eliot likes her."

"It isn't Eliot," said Hester, "not only Eliot," and she added, "You know how, when you have been awful to anyone, you can't bear them."

Now I felt miserably tired, too tired to cope with this hotbed of feelings; it seemed to me the house was filled with them, with hate and love, and the love seemed as bad as the hate. Something bad will happen, I thought, and again those prickles of fear ran over me.

"Joss . . ."

I meant to tell her about the man in the cove but she was not listening—at least she was listening to something else. She asked, "What is happening downstairs?"

I told her about the Brass Instruments Ball; the glory had gone out of it for me, but she got up from the bed. She looked so determined that I asked, "What are you going to do?"

"Go to the party," said Joss.

"But we haven't been asked."

She did not answer that. She looked over my head and said, "I tried to be nice. I found my own thing and kept out of the way. Now I won't."

"Suppose they don't ask you?"

"I shall make them. I can make people do what I like." By 'people' I knew she meant men.

"But, Joss"—I produced this hesitantly—"if you make them won't it seem that you might . . . might be what Mademoiselle Zizi says you are?"

Joss's chin went even higher. "She thinks I am what she is," she said with disdain. "All right. I shall be, only worse." Perhaps she saw the doubt on my face, for she asked, "What else am I to do?"

That sounded like Joss, not Joss cased in this proud hardness, and I said, "Go on painting."

"Without Monsieur Joubert?"

"That's what he would have done."

I thought I had won, but when I looked at her I saw it was no use saying anything more. She had on that look again, her mask look, her eyes almost like slits as if she were calculating, her nostrils pinched and her lips set. "I shall go to this party," said Joss, "and I shall wear Sin."

It was called Sin because she had had no right to buy it. A year before Uncle William had given Joss money to buy a new raincoat; her old one was up to her knees and showed inches of wrist, but she had gone into a dress shop and bought a dress. That was in the sales too, "and it had been marked down from ten guineas," said Joss.

"Ten guineas for a dress!" That seemed fabulous to us—except Willmouse.

"A dress can cost a hundred pounds," said Willmouse.

"But . . . when will you wear it?" Mother had asked, bewildered.

"Perhaps never," said Joss, "but I had to have it." It was ivory silk, stamped with roses. "Not many roses," Hester had said critically, "and not much silk." There did not seem much of anything to cost all that money; it left Joss's neck and arms bare and the skirt was narrow. "It's the cut," Willmouse had explained and examined it carefully. "It is influenced by the Chinese," he pronounced, "which is why it suits her."

For a year it had hung in Joss's cupboard. Now, after she had washed her face and brushed her hair, she took it out of the wardrobe. I had opened the door into my room to let the others come and we watched while she put it on. Beside Sin our seersuckers looked very ordinary and homemade, and, in spite of the Black Virgin, the old envy came back. "It's too tight," I said spitefully. "You *show*."

Joss looked at herself in the looking-glass and smiled. "All the better," she said and laughed at my scandalised face.

I had noticed while she washed that the dark tufts of hair under her arms were gone. "I have a little razor," said Joss. She had a lipstick and powder too. When she had bought these things I did not know, but watched, divided between marvelling and fright while she made up her face. "Don't put on too much," said Willmouse.

"I'm not Mademoiselle Zizi," said Joss witheringly.

When she was ready her glance fell again on me. "What's the matter with you, Cecil?" she asked.

"I have pains."

"Where?"

"In my arms and legs—everywhere."

"Growing pains," said Joss.

.   .   .   .   .

I suppose now it was only an ordinary bourgeois party such as would be held anywhere in the provinces of France, but to us it seemed resplendent and exciting, though we had to admit the guests were not as elegant as the flowers and food. "I think I shall go for my evening walk," said Willmouse after we had seen the first few people arrive. I could tell he was disappointed. We had not taken it into account that they were working people not quite at home in their Sunday best. The men were in dark suits, too heavy for the hot evening, and they wore thick-soled shoes; they all seemed to show a great deal of gold watch-chain and cuff-links. Their wives had meticulously clean blouses, coats and skirts, and wore high-heeled shoes instead of their usual slippers.

We watched from the stairs, not daring to risk going down until there were so many people that Mademoiselle Zizi or Madame Corbet would not notice us.

"Is that Monsieur le Maire?" asked Hester. Everyone bowed politely as they greeted him, but though his beard was imposing he was wearing a plain black suit and had only a little ribbon in his buttonhole to show he was important, no scarlet cloak, cocked hat or chain. The Sous-Préfet, more important than he, had not even a ribbon, but Monsieur Perrichaut was impressive; we knew it must be Monsieur Perrichaut because he was receiving with his wife. He was taller than anyone else—"Except Eliot," said Hester— white-haired, with an important-looking paunch. "Let me look at him," said Joss and gazed as if she were spying out the land. Monsieur Perrichaut seemed fitted to be the owner of the Brass Instruments Factory; his voice was like a saxophone, and when he blew his nose the noise was like a trumpet. He had a young man at his elbow who made introductions in a reedy voice. "Like a piccolo," I whispered, but Joss did not laugh. She was very grave. "Tell me when the doctor comes," she said.

"Monsieur le Directeur?"

"Yes."

"He is here," said Vicky presently.

"Go down," Joss told us. "Go one by one, slip in among them and start shaking hands with everyone. Then they can't send you away. And don't tag on to me," she said severely.

Hester and Vicky disappeared, but I hung back. Joss hummed a little tune—which told me she was nervous— twitched the skirt of her dress straight, frowned at it, shook her hair more loosely on her shoulders, and went down. I watched her as she went straight to the doctor, holding out her hand; then I followed, keeping behind the crowd.

The doctor kept Joss's hand. "Mais . . . c'est la petite Anglaise!" he said. I edged round to see her better.

She was making a comical face—a moue, I thought wisely. "Not so little," she said, and appealed to Monsieur Perrichaut. "I am not very little, pas si petite, am I, monsieur?" Hester had crept up beside me. "She sounds silly . . . like a *lady*," said Hester disapprovingly.

Silly or no, Monsieur Perrichaut seemed to like it. Soon he was asking her, "Vous dînez avec nous, Mademoiselle?" "He *is* asking her to dinner," I told Hester.

"I—I have not been invited," said Joss. She sounded as if

she were pretending to be shy and Hester and I both frowned.

"Je vous invite," and the piccolo was sent to tell Madame Corbet to set another place. "A côté de moi," said the doctor gallantly.

"Monsieur le Directeur s'y connaît," said Monsieur Perrichaut. The most important people were standing round him and now Joss was in the centre of them. Everyone was whispering about her. Mademoiselle Zizi had seen her, but she could not very well send her out.

"Permettez-moi de vous faire mes compliments, Mademoiselle." That was the Sous-Préfet.

"Ah! La jeunesse! La jeunesse!" said Monsieur Perrichaut and they gazed at Joss.

"Absolument ravissante," said Monsieur le Maire. He was standing just in front of me and began to discuss Joss's looks with the man beside him; I could not catch it all but I heard, "Ce teint lumineux!"

"What are they saying?" hissed Hester.

"Compliments," I hissed back.

Eliot was by the bar talking to the young Town Clerk whom Mauricette pointed out to me because she admired him. The Town Clerk was dark and good-looking, but Eliot could look over his head and the heads of most of the others. Joss must have seen him at once, but she appeared not to see him nor did he look at her. I did not like this any more than I liked her pretending to be shy. Things had gone . . . out of truthfulness, I thought. Before we had been unhappy but it was truthful, now we seemed to be playing a game, and I walked away from them all out on to the terrace, where it was cool and quiet. Presently it would be moonlight, a scented, moonlit, summer night, but that seemed to me to make this playing worse, expose it more. I put my elbows on the warm iron rail and leaned my head on my hands, hiding my eyes as if I did not want to see, to look or think, but I was not left in peace for long. Fairy lights had been strung between the trees, and now they came on, red and blue and yellow. "Ah! C'est joli!" cried a woman, and people came out on to the terrace to see. Eliot was with them, and it was then that the next odd thing happened.

I heard my name called; Willmouse was running across the garden. He did not usually run, but now gravel spurted up behind him, his socks were falling down—*Willmouse's* socks. I ran down the steps to meet him. "Cecil, a most e'straordinary thing."

As soon as he reached me he began to tell it though he was half out of breath. "I was having my walk along the river when I saw a man . . ."

I stiffened. "A . . . dark man?"

"Like Madame Corbet," said Willmouse and I knew he meant swarthily dark . . . as ours had been, I thought. "He came out of the bushes," said Willmouse, "and he had a motor-bike; it was a big new red one—at least it looked new. He wheeled it along the bank and then on to the plank bridge to the barge. . . ."

His voice, shrill with wonder and speaking English, must have carried to the terrace. I saw Eliot come to the rail and look down.

"On to the *Marie France*?" I asked Willmouse.

"Yes. The man looked up and down the river as if he wanted to see if anyone was there. He couldn't see me . . ."

"Why not?"

"Because the bulrushes are so tall. Then do you know what he did?" Willmouse paused. He was always dramatic. "He-wheeled-the-bike-across-the-deck-and-dropped-it-over-the-other-side," said Willmouse.

"Into the *river*?"

"Yes."

"Don't be silly."

"He did. Cecil, it was a new . . ."

"And what are you doing out so late?"

Eliot's voice cut across me, and it was the voice he had used that first morning when he came out of Mademoiselle

Zizi's room; I had heard it again in the courtyard at Dormans. He had left the terrace and come down the steps. "Where have you been?" he said to Willmouse.

"F-for my walk." Willmouse was so startled that the words would hardly come.

"Willmouse always goes for a walk," I said defensively.

"You be quiet," said Eliot, and to Willmouse, "You know quite well you are not allowed out so late." Willmouse opened his lips again, but, "Not a word," said Eliot. "I will *not* have disobedience. You can go to bed at once," and he wheeled Willmouse round, a hand on his shoulder.

"But *Eliot!* You *never* . . ." I think I wailed it. It was terrible to see Eliot taking Willmouse up the steps and marching him away like a prisoner. As for Willmouse, he looked grey with shock.

"Mais, Monsieur Eliot"—that was one of a group of men —"vous êtes trop dur."

"In England we discipline boys," said Eliot crisply; to Willmouse he said loudly, "How often have I told you . . ." and at once I knew that Eliot was acting.

Acting on Willmouse! I pushed my way after them to the foot of the stairs. "You have *never* told him," I cried passionately.

"Cecil, stay where you are," said Eliot. His face made me quail, but I only stayed there until he came down, then, challenging him with a look that I hoped was hate, I walked straight up, but the door of our room was locked. I went into Joss's room and tried the door there; it was locked as well. I rattled the handle. "Willmouse, it's Cecil. It's Cecil." There was no answer. I was not surprised. Willmouse was always still and silent if he were offended.

I went back to the landing, where I had another pain, and with it such a sense of desolation that I could hardly bear it. If this were growing—Joss had said that was what the pains were—I did not like it. Down below the party must have been going in to dinner; I heard chairs scraped back, more bursts of laughter, voices. I wondered if Joss were sitting next to the doctor, if Hester and Vicky were there.

There is nothing more melancholy than listening to a party from which one is shut out. I could hear the noise of knives and forks now with the talk and laughter, while on the landing it was growing dark; the stairs were lit only by the light coming up from the hall; smells of food drifted up with the scent of flowers and I thought of Willmouse's banquet and gave a little sob. He was locked in by this inexplicable Eliot and only I cared, mounting guard beside him, but a guard with a bad pain and half in tears. "Willmouse. Willmouse." Still no answer. I could imagine him rigid with shock. "I *hate* Eliot," I said. Then I jumped. In his cat-quiet way he had come up the stairs and was laughing at me.

When he saw the tears he stopped laughing. He said, "I'm sorry. I had to do that."

"Willmouse is *little*. He wanted to see a banquet."

He said, "I know," and then, "I am not as bad as you think." He was carrying a tray; on it was the chicken chasseur from the menu keeping warm under a small glass cloche, gaufrette potatoes, some of what we called 'party toast', toast melba, butter, a meringue and a glass of grenadine; it was a bit of the banquet, but I was not going to relent.

"He won't eat it," I said distantly.

"We shall see," said Eliot. He unlocked the door but kept me out. "Leave him to me," he said.

I went into the Hole because something had happened to my pain; there, in that smelly little cupboard, I found out.

Even there wonder overcame me. Wonder and fear. I shivered. ". . . with reluctant feet, Where the brook and river meet," Mr Stillbotham had said; no matter how reluctant, one was pushed into the full tide. Dazed, I came out of the Hole and went into Joss's room and found what I needed in her drawer. It was no use trying to reach her, she was at dinner . . . and so is Mademoiselle Zizi, I

144

thought. Madame Corbet, Mauricette were busy. I had to manage for myself with those strange first necessities of being a woman, and it was unexpressibly lonely. When I was comfortable I began to cry with excitement and self-pity. I was still crying when I went back on the landing.

I could hear Eliot's voice inside our room; then I thought I heard Willmouse give a tiny laugh like a crow. Eliot was even more of a magician than I thought. Always if Will-mouse were punished he did not speak for at least two days. I listened and, yes, I heard him laugh again. Then Eliot came out. "Still here?"

"Yes," I said, muffled.

"I think he will eat it all," said Eliot. "He liked the drink."

"You needn't lock the door!" That came out like a cry.

"I said I would and I must," said Eliot. "I will come up later." Then he looked at me. "You are in a state, Cecil. What is the matter?"

He should not have asked that; the tears came flooding.

"Is it Willmouse still?"

I shook my head.

"What is it then?" He put his arm round me, bending down. "Tell?"

Who could resist Eliot when he was Eliot? Eliot, not that other cold stranger. "Never talk to anyone about these times," Mother had said when she told us, "especially not to a man. Women should be private." In Southstone I think I should have shrunk suitably from telling Eliot, but Les Oeillets was different and it came out with a rush. "I . . . have turned into a woman."

I did not know how else to put it—Mother had not taught us any of the words—but Eliot did not laugh. He asked, "Just now?"

"Just now," and the tears flowed.

"That isn't anything to cry about," said Eliot gently.

"It . . . hurts."

"Not when you consider how exciting it is."

"Exciting?" That was unexpected.

"Of course."

"But . . . how?"

"Because now you are ready for love."

Love! Probably nothing in the world that Eliot could have said at that moment could have helped me more. Love! Like Mademoiselle Zizi, Juliet, Cleopatra, Eve, like . . . Joss, level with Joss. "I, Cecil," I whispered, dazzled.

"You."

"But . . ." The tears came back. "I am not pretty like Joss."

"You are not pretty like Joss. You are pretty like Cecil."

With my Bullock sturdiness, my pinkness and mouse hair? "I, pretty?"

"Very," said Eliot, and he kissed me on the mouth.

"That scoundrel," Uncle William called him. I only know that night he seemed like an angel to me.

He had to go to dinner, but he took me downstairs and put me to sit in the office which was empty; somehow, in the rush and hubbub, he got Toinette, who was motherly, to make me some tea. How did he know there were only two things in the world I could have swallowed, things English and familiar, bread and butter and tea. I had not known tea could be had in France, though it was tea such as we had not seen, served in a glass, the leaves in a little paper bag tied with a string and soaking in hot water. It was weak, but it was hot, and I made it sweet and ate four slices of bread and butter. The pain had the edge taken off it now and Toinette patted me and called me 'pauvre gosse'. Soon I felt much better.

It was a long peaceful wait until people began to come from dinner to dance or sit at the tables in the bar. I stole out on the stairs to watch. Nobody noticed me and I was glad. Then Hester came to sit beside me; she had been dancing and was excited. "Joss is the belle of the ball, isn't she?" she said.

Everyone wanted to dance with Joss. When the men

tapped one another on the shoulder, taking one another's partner, she changed partners all the time; she was flushed, far more excited than Hester, but that game was going on. Eliot danced with Mademoiselle Zizi, with some of the wives and daughters, with Vicky and Mauricette, but he never seemed to see Joss nor Joss him; she carefully looked away when they passed; she smiled at her partner and tossed her hair back and fluttered her lashes up and down. "Is that flirting?" asked Hester, but I was beginning to see there was another kind of growing pain. I knew Joss was miserable and I ached for her.

"Qui a laissé ces trucs-là dans mon bureau?" Madame Corbet had found the tray with my plate and tea glass. "Is the whole house to be a nursery?" she scolded, and I had to take them to the kitchen. On the way back I had to wait at the service door. They were dancing the carpet dance, the danse du tapis, when the men make a circle and a woman takes a little square of carpet and stands in the centre. When the music stops she kneels down on the carpet in front of the man she chooses, who kisses her and dances with her while everybody claps. He takes her into the circle and this goes on till all the women are in the circle. The crowd had moved back against the wall to watch the dance and I could not get past. As I stood, there was a loud sound of eating in my ear, a smell of sweat and garlic, Paul, and I had another glimpse of what it was like to be Paul. His face and neck were glistening with sweat, his hair hung limply, his apron and shirt were soaked and covered with stains. He must have been washing-up for hours and had taken a moment to eat; he had a piece of sausage clamped in a length of split bread, as he used to make our goûter.

We shouldn't have sent him to Coventry, I thought, and this time was going to make myself speak to him when I saw he had not noticed me; he was watching Joss. When people are watching they forget to pretend and there was something in Paul's face that made me afraid; it was wild, like a wild animal that does not think of itself or any other animal but only of what it wants. Then I learned part of the explanation of why he looked like that; Monsieur Armand called impatiently and Paul turned to go but left the door open and I saw him take a bottle from the shelf behind the door; he tilted it right up before he drank so that I knew it was almost empty. When he put it back he nearly missed the shelf and a moment after I heard a crash of plates.

He came back. Three or four times I noticed him in that door, and then I saw that Joss was smiling at him. She only smiled because she was smiling at everyone, but, "It *is* flirting," Hester said disapprovingly when I got back to the stairs.

It grew late. Some of the people were going home. Vicky had fallen asleep on a sofa; Madame Corbet looked at her two or three times, then picked her up and carried her to bed. The Brass Instruments Band had finished, but a pianist and violin had taken its place. The music sounded very quiet after the band, and the notes of the violin came softly across the floor, sweet with a faint throbbing that made it sound tender.

Joss was standing just below us, and for the moment she was without a partner. I think she hoped she would be left without one, for she turned this way and that and I was sure she was looking for Eliot. Then she saw him, and for the first time that night they looked at one another. She stood still and I knew her eyes would not plead, only look, unmistakably look. She had had to humble herself to do that, but Eliot walked away to the bar. I clenched my fists. Was Eliot quite impervious? To the throbbing music that seemed to us so beautiful? To Joss? Eliot, who had kissed me upstairs? It was only a moment; the next, Joss was smiling at the piccolo, at the Town Clerk; then she smiled and waved at someone else. I looked to see and it was Paul. The wave was too much. He gave a tug at his apron that broke its string, wrenched it from his neck and threw it away, combed his hair with his fingers and reached her before the piccolo, who was weaving through the dancers. "Mademoiselle Joss," said Paul and bowed.

If he had been clean it might have been different. Mauricette had danced and Monsieur Armand, "but not Toinette or Nicole," said Hester. Monsieur Perrichaut called out sharply and a gentleman, who Mauricette told us was Monsieur Dufour of the Commissariat, came up and said to Paul as he stood just below us, "Et toi, mon gaillard, rentre chez toi et restes-y." Monsieur Dufour was, I suppose, in charge of Paul, but Paul had emptied all of that bottle and he shouted so that the words were heard through all the rooms above the music, "Galeux! Gros dégueulasse!" to Monsieur Dufour.

Other men came up; the older ones talked soothingly, but the Town Clerk took hold of Paul, who shook him off.

"Paul! Fais-pas l'imbécile," cried Mauricette and ran for Madame Corbet.

"Rentre," said Monsieur Dufour curtly. "C'est ce que tu as de mieux à faire," but Paul had Joss by the hand.

Joss did not know what to do. Gently she tried to take her hand away. "Dance me," said Paul in his poor English.

"They don't want me to," said Joss.

"Foutez-nouse la paix!" Paul shouted at them. "Elle n'est pas une sacrée snob."

Without his apron Paul looked tall and, in his untidiness and dirt, almost savage among those Sunday clothes. Joss shrank from him though she was trying not to shrink. "Attendez, Paul," she said, "wait," but he was putting his arm round her, when suddenly between them was Eliot.

He had cut in front of Paul so quickly that no one had seen him come up and almost from inside Paul's arm he took Joss and danced with her away down the room. At the same moment Monsieur Dufour caught Paul by the shoulder, the Town Clerk took his other side, and between them they marched him to the door where Madame Corbet and Monsieur Armand were waiting. "Tordu!" shouted Paul as they took him away. "Pelé! Galeux! Fumier!" The words died away along the passage. Hester was crying, "Poor Paul! Poor Paul!" I felt too miserable to speak.

Joss and Eliot did not speak either as they danced. She kept her eyelids down so that her face looked closed; Eliot's was set.

The music stopped when they were by Mademoiselle Zizi, who had come to the foot of the stairs and was watching. Eliot slowly took his arm away but kept Joss's hand. Joss's chin began to shake. For a moment I thought they would have made it up, that he would take her into the garden in the moonlight among the fair lights, but Eliot did another of his incomprehensible things—"He was trying to look after her," said Hester; "he always did look after us,"—he held out his free hand to Mademoiselle Zizi, who gave him her hand wonderingly. He put Joss's into it. "Take her to bed, Zizi," he said.

"No!" They said it together. Joss's was a curt refusal, while Mademoiselle Zizi sounded as if she were being stifled. "No!"

"Yes," said Eliot gently and inexorably. "The party is over now." He turned away abruptly and said, "Good night."

"Eliot, where are you going?" It was a cry from Mademoiselle Zizi.

"Into the garden to smoke," he said, still gently, and stepped outside.

CHAPTER 14

"Cecil. Cecil."

I had been asleep . . . one minute, I thought, and Joss was standing by my bed. She had put her cold hand under the bedclothes and was clutching me. "Cecil."

My eyelids seemed to have weights of sleep on them. I could not open them.

"Cecil."

"Wh-what is it?"

"Ssh! Don't wake Willmouse."

"What is it?" but I had sunk my voice lower, jerked awake now by her cold and shivering.

"It's Paul."

"Paul?"

"On a ladder, looking in at my window."

"*Paul* is?"

"Yes. He is coming in."

"What for?" I said stupidly, but Joss only shivered and said, "Oh, Cecil!"

Then I knew it was true and fear started up as I remembered that look on his face at the dance, but some wisdom saved me from telling Joss. "He has been drinking," was all that I said.

"What can we do?" she asked. Her teeth was chattering.

There was only one thing to do and I sat up. "I will get Eliot."

"No!" She sounded outraged.

"But . . ."

"Don't you *dare*!"

"Then . . . ?"

Joss reluctantly said, "I will go and call Madame Corbet."

"You can't do that."

"Why?"

"She will send Paul away." We were whispering like conspirators. "He will lose his summer bonus and not get his lorry."

"I don't care about his lorry. I must get Madame Corbet or he will come in." She was shaking and I made up my mind. I know now it was one of those moments when one is more noble than one is capable of being. I turned back the bed-clothes. "Get in," I said; "I will go and talk to Paul."

"But . . ."

"I'm not afraid of Paul." But as I said it, that was not true; I was afraid of that look in him, of the words he had shouted as he was taken away, but Joss was horridly easy to convince—it seems to me now she was astoundingly selfish; she agreed at once. "You are sure you don't mind? It isn't you he has come for," she said, "so you will be all right."

Slowly, fearfully, I opened the door, but Paul was not in Joss's room. There was no sign of him, and I slid along the wall and into her bed with a feeling half of relief and half of flatness. Then, with a thrill of fear, I saw that, though no one was there, the two ends of the ladder were against the sill.

I knew then a little of what it must have been to be a sacrifice, a maiden, for instance, bound on the faggots— or, perhaps not as noble as that, one of the goats Father had told us about, tied up as bait for a tiger. Paul was a little like a tiger, and tigers have no pity. What would he do when he found I was not Joss? Would he do what he wanted to do to her? Besides being frightened I was filled with a dreadful curiosity. I had Eve's Curse, that meant I could have a baby although my breasts were only like lemons; they were tingling and I remembered Paul's hand on them, and my thighs tingled too.

Faint and far, I heard the Hôtel de Ville clock strike three times. I remembered that afterwards, three o'clock, and then I heard the ladder creak as somebody came up. I gripped the clothes round me and lay as flat as I could in the bed, my heart beating so that I could hardly breathe but, oddly, in the top of my head. My cheeks were hot, and my eyes stretched to see what they must see. It was not Paul coming up the ladder—it was an animal thing, the tiger. A head and shoulders rose black outside the window, dark with a white patch of face—I had almost expected to see it striped. A hand shook the catch loose so that it fell; the window slowly opened.

I screamed, though without a sound. Nothing hurts as much as a scream in silence. Eliot! Eliot! Eliot! It was a

152

scream, a wild prayer, and I heard footsteps running on the gravel.

The ladder and its figure lifted backwards into the air. Paul gave a cry, half muffled, an animal's cry, as he disappeared, and there was a thud. The ladder had fallen backwards on to the courtyard grass.

I slid out of bed and crept to the window to look. I remember I was so clammy with fear that the night air struck icily on me, and I shivered as Joss had as I looked down.

The ladder lay on the grass; it must have spun as it fell and fallen hard, for it was still quivering, but Paul was standing up, miraculously jumped clear or fallen off. He was standing, though rubbing his elbow and knees, and facing him was Eliot.

Then Eliot had come; but how? How had he heard me? His room was not on this side, nobody's was except Joss's and the visitors' rooms on the first floor, which were empty now. Then my sense woke up. How could Eliot have heard me when I had not made a sound? And what was he doing in the garden in the middle of the night—or not the middle, three o'clock in the morning?

Paul was still without his apron, and again I saw that without the long white limp garment he looked a man; all at once it seemed possible, even fitting, that he should drive a lorry. It was no longer like Willmouse's atelier, half a child's dream. Eliot was not as usual, either; he was wearing . . . and I stopped.

Was he Eliot? What made me so sure he was? This man was in what Willmouse had said Eliot once wore, 'Not Eliot's clothes', cotton trousers, a striped jersey, the cap. The sight of the cap brought back the fear when that face had looked at us, the dark man's face. In the moonlight I strained to see who it was, and yes, it was Eliot. Yet that made me more afraid. I saw the glint of his eyes as he lifted his head and . . . what was he *doing*? As I asked that I saw what I had not noticed before, a small case on the grass.

He must have dropped it when he ran to the ladder. Then was Eliot going away? The case was too small to count as luggage but suddenly I knew Eliot was going away.

I think Paul knew that too. I thought I heard him say, "Vous partez, hein?" with some swear words, though it was too far for me to catch the whole of the quick French.

"Ssst!" That came from Eliot like a whipcrack, a warning, but Paul was drunk, drunk and angry, I thought, and ... 'balked' was the animal-sounding word that came into my mind, as he had been balked from dancing with Joss. Now he was daring to bait Eliot. "Vous partez, hein?"

He went nearer. Out of my small experience I could have told him not to go near Eliot when Eliot was that cold stranger, but Paul made a sudden sideways lunge at the case.

I could not see what happened then, who hit whom. Paul's arms went as they had done when he battered me, but Eliot was fighting as ... one must not fight, I thought appalled. 'Never hit in the stomach or kick,' Uncle William had taught us, but I saw Eliot's knee come up into Paul and Paul let out a sound as if he were torn; then he doubled over, took two or three steps bent across the grass, made a noise like a gurgle and fell on his knees and was sick, his hands beating at his chest, his head wagging.

Eliot waited. I can see him waiting now, nothing seemed as cruel as that, and then he was ... unfair again, but it was worse than unfair, it was cowardly and—a word from school plays came back to me—dastardly. 'Never hit anyone who is down', that was Uncle William too, but, as Paul's head bent lower, Eliot struck down at his back. It was so quick I could hardly believe I saw it, like lightning. What made it truly like lightning was that, in the moonlight, I thought I saw a long thin thing flash in Eliot's hand. For an odd moment I thought it was his paper-knife ... but he would not carry a paper-knife in the garden.

Paul slid gently forward on to the grass, face downward. His legs kicked once or twice, then there were only quivers, like the ladder.

Eliot looked towards the house, along the windows. I shrank behind the curtains. I could not bring myself to look at his face below the cap; I think I expected it to change into that other man . . . the third Eliot. There was our Eliot and the cold unkind one, and him. When I looked again he had lifted Paul; he stood a moment, put Paul down and moved the case, putting it under the bushes. Then he came back to Paul, lifted him again and carried him away round the house.

What had I seen? I did not know. I remember only that heart beating in the top of my head and I seemed to have turned to ice against the window. I could not even shiver. I looked out into the garden where there was nothing but the garden and the moonlight, a few marks on the grass, and the ladder. I could not believe there had been anything else, been that . . . But what was that? What had Eliot done to Paul? As I asked the question I seemed to hear Eliot's voice saying, "I'm sorry. I had to do that." Then . . . ? Then . . . ?

I do not know how long I stood there by the curtain, my hands on the sill. It might have been a few minutes, it might have been half an hour, but suddenly as I looked down I saw Eliot was back.

He was alone. I do not know why that frightened me, but I could not bear it that he was alone.

He came to the ladder, at which he looked down consideringly. It had left marks on the grass, two long sears. I thought he was wondering if he should take the ladder away when, through the night, came a sound that might have been a low hoot from the river or an owl. Eliot turned and picked up the small case.

Once again he scanned the house and again I shrank back against the curtain. Then he was gone.

When I took my hands from the sill the marks of them were there, soaking wet.

CHAPTER 15

IT WAS a morning filled with absences. That sounds contradictory, but it was the absences that made themselves felt. There were two chars-à-bancs parties for breakfast, Americans on their way from Germany to Paris, and we saw once again how hard hotel people worked. Mauricette told us that when the Brass Instruments Ball had finished it had been past one o'clock, but she, Madame Corbet and Paul had had to set to work, sweep out the dining-room and hall and lay sixty places for breakfast . . . "And they will not have coffee and rolls," Vicky told us. "They will have grapefruit, bacon and eggs, hot rolls, jam, coffee and tea and milk." Monsieur Armand, Madame Corbet and Mauricette had to get up at half past six; we knew that because we were woken by cries for Paul.

A long time had gone by last night before I had taken myself out of that room and got into my own bed with Joss and Willmouse. All I could think of was how heavenly warm she was.

"Well?" She had been wide awake.

Why did I not tell her what I had seen? 'I have seen nothing, nothing at all', that was what I was saying over and over again in my head, and aloud I said briefly, "He has gone."

"Are you sure?"

"Quite sure."

I had imagined myself lying awake, seeing it over and over again, but at once I had fallen asleep.

"Paul. Pa-ul. *Paul!*" That was Mauricette. Then came Madame Corbet's steps and she flung open our door, 'without knocking', as Joss observed. Madame Corbet was too hurried to see we were three in the bed together and she did not scold us. "Have any of you children seen Paul . . . Paul Brendel?" She always spoke as if we did not know him.

It was a relief to see Madame Corbet. If she wanted Paul I could not believe he would not come. "When did you see him?" she asked.

"At the party last night," said Joss.

"Tscha!" and Madame Corbet shut the door.

Wakened by the noise Hester and Vicky came in. We were all awake now, in spite of our late night, wide awake except Willmouse, who was fast asleep on the far side of our bed. Nor would he wake.

"Madame Corbet, Willmouse, our little brother, hasn't woken."

"Then wake him."

"We . . . we can't."

Everyone was out of temper that morning and Madame Corbet snapped, "What is wrong with him?"

Nothing was wrong with him except that he was asleep, fast asleep, pale, but he was often pale. When we shook him his head rolled, when we opened his eyelids his eyes showed the whites. "I don't like that," said Hester. It certainly looked alarming. We sat him up, but he sagged back on the pillow. He was cold and breathing a little strangely. "Is he ill or asleep?" I asked.

"I don't think you sleep when you are ill," said Joss. "He is just . . . too asleep."

That was what we told Madame Corbet. "Grands Dieux!" she said. "Why worry me for that? Let him sleep."

When ten o'clock came and he had not stirred we began to worry more. The house was swarming with the Americans; they were taking snapshots of the staircase, of the place under the urn where Rita and Rex had found the skull—as it was so early and Paul had not been found, the bloodstain was left out—and there was no hope of getting anyone to look at Willmouse. Joss made up her mind. "I'm going to the hospital," she said.

"To tell Mother?" I spoke out of my yearning; inexpressibly that morning I was longing for Mother.

"Don't be an idiot," said Joss. "I am going to ask Monsieur le Directeur if Willmouse is all right."

"You could telephone."

"I can't in French. I don't know how to get the number," and Hester said, "I *wish* Eliot were here."

Eliot's was the third absence. He had gone to Paris, Mademoiselle Zizi told the Monsieur from the Police, Monsieur Dufour, who came asking questions.

I had come into the hall on my way upstairs; the chars-à-bancs had driven away, Les Oeillets was quiet again, but in the hall was Monsieur Dufour sitting on a chair, rubbing his chin with the end of his cane, his hat on one of the console tables. I was examining him out of the corner of my eye when Mademoiselle Zizi came from her room. She was in a pale-green dressing-gown, her hair twisted up, her face just as it was without rouge; she suddenly looked to me most beautiful.

"I regret I kept you waiting, Monsieur."

"Une demi-heure," said Monsieur Dufour, but he did not sound angry. His eyes were brown and very kind. He kept them on Mademoiselle Zizi.

They spoke in French, but I could follow them. "I wanted to see Monsieur Eliot," said Monsieur Dufour, "but Irène says he is not here."

"He has gone to Paris, Monsieur."

"At three o'clock in the morning." I wondered what effect it would have on them if I had said that.

"He has a business there?"

"So I understand."

I began to think there was some deep feeling between these two; Monsieur was warmer to Mademoiselle Zizi than she to him; she still distantly called him 'Monsieur'.

"How did he go to Paris if his car is here?"

Now I came to think of it the Rolls was on the drive outside. It had not been there last night, but Mademoiselle Zizi was explaining. "Since yesterday Fouret's have had it for graissage. Today Monsieur Eliot drove up with friends.

Look, Fouret's tag is on the windscreen if you wish to see it, Monsieur."

She minds his questions about Eliot, I thought, and he does not like asking them. It makes him feel awkward. "This is a routine check on all strangers in the town, Zizi," he said. "We have nothing against Monsieur Eliot."

"What could you have?" asked Mademoiselle Zizi, more cold than ever, but he went quietly on with his questions.

"He stays here?"

"Is that a fault?"

"Zizi. I *have* to ask. Please understand."

"You know he stays here. The whole town knows."

"Yes," said Monsieur Dufour. He sounded sorrowful but he went on. "He was here at the dinner yesterday evening?"

"You saw him," said Mademoiselle Zizi.

"But he went to Paris in the day?"

"No."

"No?" asked Monsieur Dufour.

"He was here all day," and she flashed, "He was here in the bar writing letters. Then he took an early lunch and spent the afternoon in the cove." Her eyes fell on me trying to make myself small. "If you do not believe me, ask this child," said Mademoiselle Zizi.

My stomach gave a sudden unexpected heave. I thought I was going to be sick. Monsieur Dufour turned those kind brown eyes on me. "Did you see Monsieur Eliot in the cove?"

"Yes, Monsieur."

His eyes dwelt on me a moment . . . did he guess there was something else? Then I felt a soft little touch on my elbow; it was Hester, as usual. Monsieur Dufour passed to her.

"And did you see Monsieur Eliot in the cove?"

"Yes, Monsieur." It came out patly. I do not know how we agreed silently not to tell what else we had seen. Hester added, "He gave us money to go bathing."

"You see!" cried Mademoiselle Zizi, then she burst out

indignantly, "But why should you ask questions? You *know* Eliot."

"I know him," said Monsieur Dufour, and again he sounded sad, "but I have to make my report."

He had picked up his hat, when Madame Corbet came out of the office. "Have you said anything about Paul?" she asked Mademoiselle Zizi.

"Paul. Ah yes!" and Mademoiselle Zizi turned to Monsieur Dufour again. "I suppose it is you we have to tell. It is Paul . . . Paul Brendel, the boy you sent me."

"He was troublesome last night. What now?"

"Only that he seems to have gone," said Madame Corbet.

. . . . .

The strange morning went on. I remember I was cold, though it was the same brilliant heat, so that even Madame Corbet, sitting in the office, had beads of sweat caught in her moustache and patches of wet on her blouse. As the day went on the coldness seemed confirmed, inexorably, as if hope were slowly frozen out.

The doctor came to see Willmouse. Madame Corbet brought him upstairs. "Sixty people to breakfast, the dinner last night, and now they imagine illness," she said. "These children think they own the whole hotel."

She stood at the bedroom door while Monsieur le Directeur bent over Willmouse and listened to his breathing; he felt his pulse and then raised one of Willmouse's eyelids and looked into his eye that still looked horrible with its rolled-up white. "He is tired out with excitement," said Madame Corbet, "so he sleeps."

"Il a été drogué," said Monsieur le Directeur.

"Drogué? What is drogué?" asked Joss.

It was Madame Corbet who answered in a bewildered voice, "Drugged."

"*Willmouse?*"

Monsieur le Directeur was asking if there were any sleeping tablets in the house that Willmouse could have found. "Coloured ones like sweets," he suggested in French. "Yours?" he asked Madame Corbet. "No, you would not leave them about. Mademoiselle Zizi's?"

"I keep Zizi's," said Madame Corbet. She added that it was impossible.

Impossible, but it had happened. Standing at the foot of the bed with Joss I knew it was not impossible. Unwillingly I knew more. While they had been talking I had seen that supper tray again and the grenadine and heard Eliot's voice saying smoothly, "He liked the drink." But why? I thought giddily, why? Then I remembered how Eliot had suddenly and inexplicably ordered Willmouse to bed when Willmouse had done nothing to deserve it. But ... and I remembered. Willmouse had been talking ... about the motor-bike. I almost said it and clapped my hand to my mouth.

That must have been noticeable, for they all saw it.

"What now?" groaned Madame Corbet. "Truly, these children!"

I had to pretend it was toothache. "She looks pale," said Monsieur le Directeur wearily. "Open your mouth." He looked along my teeth. "She had better go and see Dupont," he said to Madame Corbet. "These," and he tapped two teeth, "look to me as if they should come out."

As the day went on it grew heavier; by 'it' I mean this thing I was trying not to know. I was behaving like an ostrich with its head in the sand, but every now and then the head would be pulled out; I hastily burrowed it back into the sand again.

Willmouse woke in the afternoon, but he was drowsy and stupid and his voice was thick. Joss telephoned the hospital, Madame Corbet getting through for her, and Willmouse was given hot tea. He immediately fell asleep again, but he was warmer.

Joss stayed with him, and Hester and I wandered out along the river. We tacitly agreed we should not go and see Mother; I could not have trusted myself near her. We avoided the cove and between us was a weight of silence. Even to Hester I could not speak of what was in me, and as if she felt a barrier she did not speak either, which was remarkable for Hester, until we came out on the towing-path, when—"Look," she said, "the *Marie France* is gone."

"It had to go sometime," I said. It did not seem important, but there seemed a curious blankness on the river where the little barge had been.

We went in to goûter, getting it ourselves. Mauricette was leaning on Monsieur Armand, reading the paper over his shoulder. "That is why Monsieur Dufour came asking about Monsieur Eliot," she said in French, but I was beginning not to notice if people spoke in French or English. I had been cutting a piece from a baguette and I stopped with the bread in my hand. "Why?" I asked.

"Vol de diamants, à Paris," read out Monsieur Armand. "Coup de main audacieux dans le quartier de l'Etoile. Le malfaiteur s'enfuit avec cent millions de francs de diamants."

"Diamonds?" I asked, and, "What does it mean?" asked Hester.

"Only that there has been a robbery," I said.

"Tell her," said Monsieur Armand, giving the paper to me to do my translation. "Now, nicely, for your sister."

Painfully I began: "An armed . . . Qu'est-ce que c'est 'malfaiteur'?" I asked Monsieur Armand.

"Gangster," said Monsieur Armand, who went to the cinema.

"Armed gangster steals one hundred . . . million . . . it *is* million?" I asked.

"Million," confirmed Monsieur Armand.

"One hundred million francs'-worth of jewels and escapes. Once a month Mademoiselle Yvonne Lebègue, secretary to Monsieur Roger Dixonne, a diamond . . . merchant," I read, stumbling over the unfamiliar words, "whose offices are in the Rue La Fayette, ninth ar . . . what is that?"

"Neuvième arrondissement," explained Monsieur Armand, which left me none the wiser.

"Collects pierres précieuses ... precious stones, chiefly diamonds, from a colleague in the Place du Trocadéro. On Friday, towards three-fifteen, Mademoiselle Lebègue was being driven on her way to the Rue La Fayette through the Rue Dumont d'Urville by Jean Sagan, Monsieur Dixonne's chauffeur. She had with her ... un lot spécial ... special lot of ... qu'est-ce que c'est 'pierres taillées'?" Mauricette pretended to cut sharply with a knife. "Oh, cut stones! ... valued at about one hundred million francs in a small ... qu'est-ce que c'est 'une mallette d'aluminium'?"

Mauricette seized a saucepan and tapped it to show me. "Oh, aluminium case." I had not known cases could be of aluminium. "... which she placed under her feet in the car, a large Mercédès. When the Mercédès was almost ... à la hauteur de la rue ... at the top of the street near the PTT, a small light-blue car, parked on the right side of the road, drew out suddenly and stopped ... in a cross? Oh, crosswise! ... across the road, forcing the Mercédès to stop. At the same time a man appeared by the car, swung open the door by Mademoiselle Lebègue, seized the case, slammed the door and was gone. It was so quickly and quietly done that the chauffeur did not see him at all and, though there were many people on the pavement, no one realised what had happened until Monsieur Sagan jumped out ... aux cris de 'Arrêtez cet homme! Arrêtez-le!' ... crying 'Stop that man! Stop him!', and they heard Mademoiselle Lebègue's cries. Meanwhile the small car had driven off. Monsieur Sagan ran through the crowd, but there was no sign of the thief, who must have ... very well known ..." I translated literally, "known Monsieur Dixonne's habits to be able to organise this attack in less than two minutes."

"Ah ça! Par exemple!" cried Monsieur Armand, full of admiration. "C'est un peu fort!" He added wisely, "La femme était dans l'coup."

"What woman was in it?"

"La secrétaire," said Monsieur Armand and nodded.

Mauricette said they would catch the thief, the police had the number of the small car. Monsieur Armand said the driver was probably just an accomplice and the car was surely stolen; they would find it presently. "On verra bien, you will see," he said, and I went on reading, "This is the third time there has been one of these . . ." I stumbled.

"Hold-ups," said Monsieur Armand.

". . . in this quarter. Paris police are looking for a man of thirty-five or thereabouts, tall, slim, dressed in thin trousers and a green jacket. The swiftness and . . . au . . . audacity lead them to think it is the work of an experienced thief, perhaps the international bandit Allen, who was behind the jewel raids in Cannes last year, whom all efforts by the police failed to catch." I read on, "What is . . . une grand enquête?" I asked.

"Cherchant partout," said Mauricette.

"Oh! Searching everywhere," and Mauricette said, "Même Monsieur Eliot." She laughed as she said it but I did not laugh. Searching everywhere. Even for Eliot! My mind seemed to give a sharp click.

The newspaper said they were checking all foreign people in a radius of Paris and Mauricette was teasing us. "Vous deux, Mademoiselle Cecil et Mademoiselle Hester, et ma p'tite Vicky, ma p'tite reine," and she picked up Vicky and danced with her. Then she stopped and pointed out a picture in the newspaper to me.

We were in the kitchen where everything was familiar—Monsieur Armand, Mauricette, the pots and pans; even the flies crawling on Monsieur Armand's forehead seemed homely, almost dear; but now everything seemed to slide together into a blur behind the picture of a man, and I spelled out the headline above it: " 'I have seen him and shall know him again,' says Inspector Jules Cailleux of the Sûreté Générale, who is handling the case. 'This time we shall get him.' "

I took the newspaper up to Joss. "Inspector Cailleux? He was the one at Dormans," said Joss.

"Yes, on that day . . ." I broke off. I still did not like to mention that day to Joss, but Hester said, "When Eliot was queer."

There was a silence. Then I brought out huskily, "Perhaps he was queer because he did not want Inspector Cailleux to see him."

"Don't imagine things," said Joss sharply, but the sharpness told me she was imagining too.

.   .   .   .   .   .

"Willmouse, wake *up*. Wake *up*! *Willmouse!*"

It was next morning. Late the night before Willmouse had stirred, smiled and woken again. Madame Corbet must have been worried because she came straight up to him and he had had hot soup, some bread and butter, had smiled at us and gone back to sleep. In the night I had heard him rustling. He wanted to go to the Hole and I had taken him. Surely now he must be awake enough to talk . . . or not to talk, I thought desperately.

All night I had pondered, conning over these difficult bits and pieces. Why I? I thought, why should it be I? People are not sent what they cannot bear; Mother had said that in the train, but that was about pain. I could have borne a pain, but this, this horrible knowledge that was in me I could not bear. It's imagination, I said, pushing it out of sight. At all costs, I thought, that was what I must do, refuse it, keep it down, be silent, not talk not let Hester talk, or anyone else. "Willmouse, wake *up*!"

He opened his eyes. "Have I been asleep?" asked Willmouse.

"Can you understand me?" I said.

"Why not?" He was astonished.

"I want you to promise me something." My tone must have been very solemn, for his eyes were as big as an owl's as he looked at me.

"Is it important?"

"Very important. Willmouse, if they—anyone—ask you if you saw anything, say nothing. Promise."

"Did I see anything?" he asked.

.   .   .   .

Two parties were coming for lunch. "You must tidy your room," Madame Corbet told me.

"Shall I make the bloodstain for you, as Paul isn't here?" I asked. I had meant to be sarcastic, to show Madame Corbet we knew what frauds they were, but she only nodded. To her it was normal hotel business and she said, "You could bury the skull as well, but first put Rita and Rex in the kennel or they will dig it up now."

"Where are Rita and Rex?"

They were not on the house-step in their usual place, nor inside the house, nor in the garden; then I heard barks from the orchard, barking and whining. I remember that as I went to see what had excited them I passed the box hedge, rubbing a leaf in my hands to catch the hot bruised smell, and dawdled in the orchard to see if any greengages were left. There were a few, on the trees, overripe in the sun, but still firm under the leaves; I ate both kinds and they added to the chaotic feeling in my stomach. Then, with the dog leashes in my hand, I went down the first long alley.

At the end of the alley there was a pit under the wall; it was filled with loose earth and rotting leaves, grass mowings and weeds; everything was thrown there to make a compost heap for Robert's beloved bedding plants in the top garden.

In this heap Rita was digging; her excited whines and barks sent quivers through Rex, who was sitting upright on the grass, his ears pricked. He was holding something in his mouth and his tail thumped proudly at the sight of me; though Rita found it, it was always Rex who brought the skull and he got up now and came to me and put the thing into my hand.

166

It was an espadrille, grey-white and sodden, with the tapes still knotted. I flinched and dropped it on the ground while Rex looked up at my face and thumped his tail.

"Wait, boy," I said. It was a sound like a croak and I took three steps to see what it was that Rita was digging.

In the brown-yellow of the leaves was something pale. I took another step and the whole orchard seemed to tilt and run into a blur as the kitchen had done when I saw Inspector Cailleux's picture, but now the orchard ran into the sky. The pale thing was a foot, a foot and ankle lying downwards; the rest was under the leaves. There was an edge of blue cotton trouser, but the ankle was bare; its skin looked white and tender as the back of Vicky's neck, a young skin. There was a leaf stuck to it, a little bright-yellow leaf; not knowing what I was doing, I bent down to take it off.

It was stuck; almost absently I scraped it with my nail and my finger touched the skin, and it was cold.

I had been cold for two days, but this cold was different; it was a chill all its own. Shivers went over me and my lips began to shake. The foot was cold and stiff with a dreadful stiffness. The smell of decay that rose up from the leaves and rotting weeds filled my mouth and nose and seemed to me the smell of death. There was no escape now. My head had come out of the sand and I had to know. The foot had worn the espadrille, Paul's espadrille . . . and this was Paul.

CHAPTER 16

"Greengage indigestion!" said Madame Corbet.

She had come upon me sick on the garden path. "Too many greengages," she said, and her topknot shook not with pity but with indignation.

I did not contradict her. I could not, I could only gasp

167

and moan; and she was right, it was as if I were trying to fling out Paul, Eliot, Les Oeillets, all of it; a sudden rising of my stomach to my mouth in the same way that the orchard had run up into the sky.

"Too big a girl to eat so many," scolded Madame Corbet.

"I'm not big. I'm little, too little," I wanted to cry, but I could not speak; she had to help me, unwilling as she was, until at last I could lean against her and get my breath. "Are . . . Rita and Rex shut up?"

"I put them in the kennel," said Madame Corbet, annoyed. "I even have to do that. I have everything to see to. Everything! Have you finished?" she asked sharply.

"I—I think so."

"Then go and lie down. You will not have any lunch."

Thankfully I escaped and went upstairs. In our room I went to the washing-stand which had not been emptied and cleaned. If it had, we were not allowed to touch it until the visitors were gone. I washed and washed my hands; I think I was trying to wash away the feeling of that cold and the smell of the dead leaves. I remember I was trembling, and the beating was back in my head. "You know what you have seen," said that beating. "You know. There is no shadow of doubt. You will have to do something now. What are you going to do?" I should have liked to have crept into the unmade bed and pulled the clothes over my head, but Toinette was at the door. I escaped from her and went into Vicky and Hester's room.

Toinette had finished in here, it was tidy and clean; Nebuchadnezzar, getting very withered now, was in his basket on a chair by Vicky's side of the bed; there were fresh flowers, pimpernels, daisies and wild geranium in Hester's liqueur glass. As I noticed it I had an overwhelming desire to look at Eliot—Eliot who had done . . . that. I opened the drawer where she hid her photograph from Toinette. The little frame was lying on its face. I picked it up, and it was empty.

I was still staring at the empty frame when Joss came in.

"Madame Corbet says . . ." she broke off. Then, "I took it," said Joss.

"The photograph?" She nodded. "So that they shouldn't . . ." I do not know why I asked her that. She could not know who 'they' were, but as if she did know she shook her head. "I told Hester I wanted to copy it . . . make a portrait." Her face was so set and hard it looked like a stone carving of Joss. "But you didn't," I said and asked, "What did you do with it?" She did not answer and I said, "You gave it to Monsieur Dufour."

"No."

"Then what?"

"I sent it to Inspector Cailleux."

"The Dormans man?"

"Yes."

"*Joss!*"

"Eliot shouldn't play fast and loose." She was not stone now. "That is what they call it and that is what it is; keep you, then push you away, take you and push you away. It's cruel. It's not only me; he has done it to Mademoiselle Zizi, and Monsieur Armand says the diamond merchant's secretary woman as well. He played with us, like . . . like chess, she and Mademoiselle Zizi and me."

"He wasn't playing with you."

"Shut up," blazed Joss. "Shut up!" but I was steady.

"He didn't play with any of us," I said. "We were the only people he didn't play with."

Joss went to the window and stood with her back to me.

"When did you do it?" I asked.

"Yesterday. As soon as I knew, after you had brought me the paper, I wrote and went down to the office and asked for a stamp. Madame Corbet gave it to me. I went out to the corner and posted it. It caught the post."

"You don't know it was he."

"If it isn't they won't come," said Joss, but we were both waiting for them to come. "I knew it as soon as I saw the paper," said Joss.

169

"Just from Inspector Cailleux?" I said, marvelling.

"Not from him. From Eliot," and she cried, "That was what made him so unhappy."

"They will get it this morning," I said slowly.

"And Paris isn't very far," said Joss.

There was a silence. We were both listening. Then, "What will they do to him, Cecil?" asked Joss. "Will they put him in prison?"

"They have to catch him first." That was ripped out of me, a hope. Then I knew that I ought not to hope. I said, "Joss . . ."

She had sat down on the bed; she was still listening for sounds outside and, almost absent-mindedly, she raised her eyes to me. "They won't put him in prison," I said.

Her eyes came alive. She rapped out, "Why not?"

"Because if they catch him I think he will have to be hanged." Holding to the bedpost I told her what I had found. When I began she put out her hand and caught my wrist as if she would stop me; it was a stranglehold and my hand went limp and white; when I had finished and she let me go the blood rushing back into it hurt excruciatingly. There was another silence, then, "They don't hang people in France," she said. "They guillotine them."

.   .   .   .   .

"It's the visitors for lunch," I said that quickly when we heard the car slow at the gates.

"It's too early," said Joss.

We were in her room and had only to go to the window to see what car it was, but we stayed huddled together on the bed. The car drove in and stopped. Joss laid her cold hand on my cold one. "Cecil, you look."

"I can't."

"You can. You didn't send for them."

I did not go to the window but went downstairs just as Monsieur Dufour walked in. "What, again?" said Madame Corbet, who was crossing the hall.

"Again," said Monsieur Dufour; his voice did not sound kind but curt and angry. Behind him were two other men; one was big, in a tweed jacket, and carried a despatch case; the other was small, and I held to the banisters as I recognised him. Yes, it was the Dormans man with the sandy hair and moustache, even the sand-and-olive-coloured suit; he had been in the newspaper, now he was here. Inspector Cailleux had come. A curious little sound came from me and seemed to float out into the hall.

As Monsieur Dufour talked rapidly and angrily to Madame Corbet she caught sight of me. "Go into the garden and call Mademoiselle Zizi," she commanded in French.

Mademoiselle Zizi must have been lying in the long chair on the terrace, but I think she too had heard the car because as I came to her she was standing and as still as Joss had been. Did she have some sixth-sense warning? I reached her and she gripped me. "Who is it?"

"The police."

"Police!" Her face looked suddenly older but her eyes were like a child's, filled with fear, looking far over my head.

"Where is Irène?"

"With them. They want you." I paused. "Mademoiselle Zizi . . ."

No answer, only the fingers gripping me, kneading my arm.

"Mademoiselle Zizi." I said it more loudly. Her eyes came back to me, but they looked quite senseless. With my free hand I gave her fingers a sharp slap, but she did not seem to feel it.

"Zizi!" Madame Corbet came down the terrace, "Zizi. Vas-y."

Then Mademoiselle Zizi did let me go. She looked at Madame Corbet and backed away from her. "You!" she said, her voice ugly. "You sent for them."

"I? Why should I?" Madame Corbet put out her hands, but Mademoiselle Zizi still backed away from her.

"It was you."

"Zizi. Qu'est-ce que tu nous racontes?"

"It was you."

"Hush," I said like a grown-up. "Listen. *Listen!*" and I stamped my foot. They stared. "There is something you should see before you go in. It . . . he . . ." I thought I was going to be sick again and tumbled the words out, "It's in the orchard."

"What 'it'?" but I could not tell them.

"Look, quickly, in the heap where the leaves are thrown."

"Et maintenant qu'est-ce que *tu* nous racontes?"

"Quickly."

"What *is* it?" but I had taken refuge in being a child and had begun to cry. "Something . . . I think . . . I found. Oh, look! Look quickly. I will go in and say you are coming, but go. Go."

The policemen were in the bar where Mauricette was bringing them drinks on a tray. Monsieur Dufour was walking up and down, looking miserable and angry; the other two were sitting calmly at a table; Inspector Cailleux was looking round him with what I imagined was a detective look, taking every detail in. I could see Joss on the stairs, her hand holding the rail.

"Et Mademoiselle de Presle? Elle vient?" barked Monsieur Dufour at me.

With Joss watching I was dignified in spite of my red eyes. "Dans un petit moment," I said, closing the garden door behind me; but Monsieur Dufour sprang forward and wrenched it open, for, just then, down in the orchard Mademoiselle Zizi began to scream.

CHAPTER 17

WHEN ANYTHING happens in a house the children are treated like cattle. We were rounded up, herded upstairs and into our rooms; as we went up we could hear Mademoiselle Zizi having hysterics, and Monsieur Dufour trying to calm her. Madame Corbet had to leave her to him, for as usual she had everything to do: control Mauricette, Toinette and Nicole, who seemed to want to have hysterics too, enlist Monsieur Armand's help, telephone the doctor, install Inspector Cailleux in the little salon and allow his assistant to use the telephone in the office. I have always wondered what happened to the parties for lunch.

After Mademoiselle Zizi stopped screaming a horrible calm lay over the house, the house not the garden; the garden was full of police, and Rita and Rex bayed frantically in the kennel. Each time their noise rose it meant a fresh batch of police had arrived. Monsieur Armand saw us looking out of the windows and came up and shuttered them. "Better not to look," he said gently, but we could not help looking through the cracks, all except Joss, who sat as if she had been frozen on the bed.

A dark-blue van drove up.

"What's that?" asked Willmouse fearfully.

"I expect it's some stores for the kitchen," I said, trying to soothe him, "only some stores."

"It's the dead car," said Vicky, who was not supposed to know anything. "It has come for Paul."

The truth spoken so flatly shocked us and we stayed perfectly still listening to the tramp of feet. "He's on a stretcher," said Vicky, peering, "all covered up."

I had a hiccough that shook me from my heels to my head. Hester began to cry. "Paul saved up for his lorry," she said. "Why? Why did God do it?"

173

"God didn't," said Vicky, "it was Eliot. Monsieur Armand said so."

"It was all my fault," said Joss. Sitting on the bed, she twisted her hands together. "If I had gone on painting. Cecil told me to but I would go to the party."

"We went to the party too," said Hester loyally.

"If I hadn't smiled at him . . ."

"Well, if we had never talked to him . . ." I could say that.

". . . he would never have come up the ladder," said Joss, not listening.

"Did he come up a ladder?" Hester and the Littles asked. "Why?" they asked round-eyed.

"To . . . look at Joss."

"Why?"

"Men do at women," said Willmouse.

I told them how Eliot came. "He needn't have come. It was because he thought we were in trouble. He could have gone," I said. "He shook the ladder and Paul fell."

"Nobody meant it, it happened," said Hester; she added mournfully, "And now Eliot has gone."

"I saw him go." They all turned to me, listening carefully as I told them.

"That was how he was dressed," said Willmouse, nodding when I described the clothes. "But . . . I can't believe it," said Willmouse. He looked stunned.

"I can," said Hester, and, feeling our surprise, she explained, "Eliot always said, 'I'm sorry. I had to do that.' If you are all right really, really all right, you don't do things that are sorry."

Presently Madame Corbet appeared. "He wants to see you."

"Who?"

"Inspector Cailleux."

"In our scarecrows?"

"It doesn't matter," said Madame Corbet as one who says, 'Nothing matters now.'

174

She drove us downstairs, all except Joss, who was not to be ordered. "I shall come when I'm ready," she said.

Inspector Cailleux was in the little salon. We had never been allowed to enter it; now we were to go in, in our scarecrows, and sit on the yellow satin chairs, but first we had to wait. The door was open; we could see Monsieur Dufour and the tweed-coated man. When we peeped round we saw that Inspector Cailleux, in his funny-coloured suit, was sitting at the pretty centre table with its painting of Cupids and ribbons; it seemed terrible it should be used for this. Another man was at a table carried in from the bar and put in the window. He was writing, but the other three were talking; by straining every sense I could just keep up.

"I can*not* believe it," Monsieur Dufour was saying. He was walking up and down. "Everyone knew Monsieur Eliot. Why, he was here, dining at this big dinner with us all that night. He must have a nerve of iron."

"He has," said the clipped soft voice of Inspector Cailleux.

"What does he say?" whispered Willmouse.

They must have heard Willmouse whisper, for Inspector Cailleux asked, "Can those children understand French?"

"Very little," said Monsieur Dufour, "except the big one perhaps." He came to the door and glanced at us. "She is not here yet," and he asked, "Shall I close the door?"

"No, leave it. It's too hot," said Inspector Cailleux.

The talk went on. "But how?" Monsieur Dufour was saying. "How? Monsieur Eliot was here all afternoon. You have heard."

"I have heard. That does not mean to say he was."

"But he was. We have evidence. Here all afternoon. Then how was he in Paris, in the Rue Dumont d'Urville, at three o'clock. If this were his work he had an accomplice."

"He had no accomplice," Inspector Cailleux's voice sounded tired. "He works alone, or practically alone; there may be a man hired to drive a car or to telephone, but then he is discarded. We have caught them, Dufour, and they know nothing. Often they don't know who he is. He's too clever to have accomplices; sooner or later one of them would give him away. No, never accomplices, only tools, simple people; especially women."

"Especially women." I knew Monsieur Dufour was thinking of Mademoiselle Zizi; I was thinking of the simple people, of us.

"But how? How?" said Monsieur Dufour again. "I don't understand."

"If we could understand, it would not be Allen."

"What are they talking about?" asked Willmouse, and I lost the rest until Inspector Cailleux said slowly, "I know that man's work as if it were my own."

"Tell us," Willmouse commanded me urgently and I translated sentence by sentence as best I could, but it was hard work listening and telling.

"But . . . right under our noses!" said Monsieur Dufour.

"Under your noses," said Inspector Cailleux. Then he threw down his pen. "What's the good? He has had thirty-six hours. He is hundreds of miles away by now."

"I don't think he is," said Willmouse when I had translated.

"What do you mean?"

"I know where Eliot is."

"Where?"

"On the barge," said Willmouse, "the *Marie France*." The *Marie France* had gone and I remembered that soft strange hoot in the night.

I gazed at my little brother. "But how did you know?"

"He was dressed for it," said Willmouse simply. He added, "Barges go very slowly, but I don't suppose they will think of looking for him there."

"Cecil!" said Hester urgently.

I looked up. Mademoiselle Zizi had come into the bar. I had seen her once without her make-up, but now her face seemed to have come through it. She was a strange grey-white colour and her face was knotted as if it had cords in it, and her hair was tumbled half down on her shoulders. She looked at us, then into the little salon and pointed to it enquiringly and then at us again.

We shook our heads.

Her eyes turned from one to another of us; they seemed to be asking us, and she put her fingers to her lips. Slowly, solemnly, we nodded.

Madame Corbet's quick voice was heard in the hall and Mademoiselle Zizi turned almost in a panic to go. In the doorway she met Joss.

Joss stopped when she saw Mademoiselle Zizi. For a moment they faced one another. Then Mademoiselle Zizi spoke.

"They have told me. So! It was you who sent the photograph."

"Of course." Joss crossed in front of her and said, "Let me sit down, Hester."

In the little salon the voices grew louder. We listened and I said, "They're talking about us."

"We have seen everyone now," Monsieur Dufour had said.

"Except the children." That was Inspector Cailleux.

"They cannot be very important. At least, only the big girl."

"They may be very important. Call them in. I shall take the small ones first; and remember," ordered Inspector Cailleux, "don't speak to the big one. Ignore her."

"It will make her nervous."

"I want her nervous," said Inspector Cailleux.

Monsieur Dufour came to the salon door and beckoned us in. He started when he saw Mademoiselle Zizi. "Zizi," he said, "you should be resting."

"Resting!"

"Well, something. Don't stay here. Please," and he said, "Irène, take her." Madame Corbet put her arm round Mademoiselle Zizi and led her away as we filed in.

"Asseyez-vous, mes enfants."

Because we knew our scarecrows were very dirty we sat

on the edge of the yellow chairs. Last of all Joss, her chin high, spots of red in her cheeks, took a chair by the door.

"Must the little children be in this?" asked Monsieur Dufour in French.

Inspector Cailleux did not raise his head. "They are in it," he said.

He wrote for a few minutes, then suddenly he sat up and looked at us, one after the other. I felt myself go hot, then cold. I think we all had blanched faces. Hester looked like ... like a peeled nut, I thought; as for Joss, it seemed she had put on her mask painted with those two bright spots.

"Which of you took this photograph?"

It was said so casually, and in English, that we started. I do not know what we had expected—to be bullied, asked our names and ages, or have our thumbs twisted—but he was simply holding the snapshot up.

"I did," said Hester with modest pleasure.

"And you are ..." he looked at a paper, "Hester?" She nodded. "Ten years old?" Hester's curls bobbed again. "Ten years old," said Inspector Cailleux in French to Monsieur Dufour, "and she has succeeded in doing what no one else has ever done, getting a photograph of Allen." Then in English, "I must congratulate you, ma p'tite. It is most valuable."

"Valuable?" The pleasure was wiped from Hester's face. "You mean ... my photograph *helped* you?"

"Helped me! It brought me straight here," and to Monsieur Dufour again he said, "I am one of the few, the very few, who have seen Allen. I had him once ... for an hour."

"He got away?" Monsieur Dufour sounded almost pleased.

"He got away." Inspector Cailleux's voice forbade any more questions and I remembered how the newspaper had said: '... whom the police failed to catch.'

"I must ask you for the negative"—Inspector Cailleux was speaking to Hester again—"but we shall give you something very pretty in exchange. A doll. You would like a doll?"

"No," said Hester, her eyes horrified.

"Eliot gave me a doll," said Vicky. "We don't want yours."

"Listen," said Inspector Cailleux, "I am going to speak to you as if you were not children but grown up. You know this man Allen?"

We shook our heads.

"You know Monsieur Eliot?"

We nodded. "He's our friend," said Willmouse.

"Your friend is a thief," said Inspector Cailleux. Hester and the Littles were listening to him solemnly and he warmed. "A thief who stole in many countries, deceived people, took their money and was often cruel to them. I must tell you that sometimes he killed them."

"Like he did Paul?" asked Vicky, interested.

"Vicky, you are not to say things like that," Joss cut in from where she sat by the door.

"If you please, Mademoiselle . . ." said Inspector Cailleux.

"But . . ." began Joss hotly.

"I must ask you to be quiet. I shall come to you . . . later." He made that sound so frightening that I had to press myself down on my chair not to gasp.

Inspector Cailleux returned to the Littles. "He killed Paul," he said. "Are you going to like him after that?"

Hester, Willmouse and Vicky said instantly, "Yes."

Inspector Cailleux looked nonplussed and perhaps a little angry. When he spoke again his voice was sharp. "Like him or not, you have a duty. You know what duty is?"

We all nodded. Eliot was our friend . . . but when a friend kills a friend? And with a paperknife. I felt sure now it was the paperknife, or what we had thought was a paperknife. A rift was being torn between us and Eliot; each word that Inspector Cailleux said made that rift more.

"If you know anything, have seen anything strange or

out of place, about this man Allen or Eliot," he was saying, "it is your duty to tell me."

Dead silence.

"Your duty," said Inspector Cailleux and his eyes went over each of us again. I dared not put my hands down on my chair in case they left marks as they had left them on the windowsill.

Hester was the most honest of us and the most easily worked upon. I had guessed she would feel she had to say something and in the silence she put up her hand.

"Well?"

"He . . ." said Hester as if her throat were dry, "he . . ."

"Yes?" said Inspector Cailleux encouragingly. "He?"

"He lay in the cove . . ." said Hester.

"Yes?" said Inspector Cailleux again, but I had pinched her and she shut her lips.

Again there was silence, but this, of course, could not go on; they were the police. I thought Inspector Cailleux had seen that pinch; detectives saw everything or they would not be detectives. He was looking at me without appearing to look, and it was borne in on me afresh that I was the only one who knew . . . everything, I thought. I could not help another little gasp, and this time his eyes looked straight at me for a second. They looked away at once, but I knew I was marked; quite rightly, not even Joss, who had been so quick to guess, knew all the pieces that fitted together. Each of them knew something, but I knew it all. What was I to do? Here in front of Inspector Cailleux all dreams and wishes fled. These were the police. Soon I should have to tell.

It was beginning to come out.

"You were the one who had the sleeping dose." Inspector Cailleux had turned to Willmouse and he asked Monsieur Dufour, "You think Allen gave the dose to him?"

"The chef, Monsieur Armand, says Monsieur . . . Allen took up a tray for the boy. We think, but we do not know."

"We can guess," said Inspector Cailleux, and to Willmouse, "What was on the tray you were brought?"

"Food," said Willmouse, "banquet food; chicken and party toast and a meringue. A beautiful meringue," said Willmouse, remembering.

"Anything to drink?"

"Grenadine."

"The supper things were washed up," said Monsieur Dufour, "so that, of course, we do not absolutely know."

"We can guess," said Inspector Cailleux again and his pale eyes studied Willmouse. "This child knew something."

"What could a child of his age know?"

Inspector Cailleux shrugged. "Children are everywhere, like insects. They can know anything."

"H'm," said Monsieur Dufour thoughtfully. "They say he slept for two days. It must have been strong."

"The drug or the reason?"

"Both," said Monsieur Dufour. "But it was abominable! To drug a child!"

"This was Allen," Inspector Cailleux reminded him. "The little boy is lucky to be alive."

"*Who* are they talking about?" Willmouse whispered more urgently to me.

"You."

"Why?"

"Because they think . . . Eliot . . . put you to sleep."

"*Eliot?*"

"Yes."

"Why? Why?" said Willmouse imperiously to Inspector Cailleux.

"Because, my little man, you knew something he did not want you to tell. It was not a very pleasant thing to do to you, was it?"

"It was silly," said Willmouse. He was wounded. "Why didn't he ask me not to tell? He needn't have put me to sleep. He could have *trusted* me."

"Was this man God to them?" asked Inspector Cailleux. He was getting angry and the questions came fast.

"Why did he send you to bed?"

"I was out late."

"Why were you out late?"

"I had been for my walk."

"Where did you go?"

"Along the river."

"Did you see anything?"

They were coming closer ... like bloodhounds, I thought, and prickled with apprehension. "Did you see anything?" asked Inspector Cailleux peremptorily.

"I saw the barge," said Willmouse.

"What barge?"

"The *Marie France*."

"What was the barge doing?"

"Nothing," said Willmouse truthfully, but Inspector Cailleux was looking deeply into him.

"Do you like barges?" he asked.

"No."

"Then there was something especial about this one? Something you saw perhaps? Perhaps?" rapped out Inspector Cailleux.

"I would rather not talk to you," said Willmouse.

"I am not *playing*," cried Inspector Cailleux and hit the little table with his fist so that it shook. Vicky burst into tears.

"I don't like it," she wailed, "I want Mother."

As if Mother's name had been a touchstone we all began to weep, except Joss, who was still dissociated from us; I was ashamed but the tears were gathering, unbearably heavy and hot, in my eyes. Mother. If only Mother were here for us in this terror! But there was no one, no one for us, and we quailed like little rabbits, chased and cornered, ready to be snared. Helplessly we wept. There was more to come, more shockingness, but we had moved Monsieur Dufour. He protested, "I told you this was not for children."

"Some of them are not children."

We jumped. Mademoiselle Zizi was standing in the doorway. At the sight of her distorted face even Vicky was quelled.

"You are asking them questions," said Mademoiselle Zizi. "Why? You need only ask her." She pointed at Joss. "Ask her what the ladder was doing on the lawn under her window, why the marks of it were on the grass." Madame Corbet had come running after Mademoiselle Zizi, but Mademoiselle Zizi shook her off. "Ask her."

Inspector Cailleux looked at Joss, who had risen like a girl in class. Slowly I rose too, but no one noticed me.

"Is that a child?" said Mademoiselle Zizi, and to Monsieur Dufour, "You have seen her with your own eyes, how she behaved at the dinner. She drove Paul out of his mind. You saw that too. Well, ask her what happened. The ladder was at her window. Elle a couché avec l'un après l'autre."

I did not understand the word 'sleep' used like that, 'sleep with one after the other', nor its import; I was only sure that in some way it was hideous and unjust and I moved nearer to Joss. "She didn't sleep," I said, "she was wide awake. Why, she came to my room and sent me in . . ."

"*You?*" Their eyes all shifted to me.

"Tiens! They begin young in England," said Mademoiselle Zizi.

"Don't be a fool," said Joss curtly to me.

"These little children must go *out*," said Monsieur Dufour, springing up distressed, but Hester and the Littles had already left their yellow satin chairs and come to Joss and me; they did not understand what the talk was about but knew we were threatened and they stood loyally round us.

Once again we seemed small and alone in that French house. Monsieur Dufour was kindly, but he was thinking of Mademoiselle Zizi. Only one person would have defended us—Eliot . . . and he . . . I could not go on. I swallowed, and felt as if the tears were running down my throat.

"So! Two of you," said Mademoiselle Zizi. "And this is what I took into my house."

Your dear house! In that moment of misery I almost said it. Les Oeillets, the gold-green days, the love, to end in this.

It was at that moment I heard a sound in the courtyard outside that made me look up. These were the windows from which Mademoiselle Zizi had so often watched for Eliot, listening for the Rolls. Now I looked out and saw the big gate was shut as it had been on our first night. It had been shut by the police. The sound I had heard was the jangling of the bell.

I do not know how I heard it in the confusion in the room, but it seemed to join on to the bell of that first night; the sound belonged . . . to us? I thought, puzzled.

A gendarme opened the wicket; he spoke for a moment to someone outside and opened the gate.

Inside the salon there was turmoil. The other two policemen had jumped up and Madame Corbet was explaining to them, shouting over our heads while Monsieur Dufour talked to Mademoiselle Zizi as if he were scolding her. Only Inspector Cailleux stayed at his desk, quietly watching.

"Zizi! You haven't a shadow of proof," scolded Monsieur Dufour.

"Haven't I?" She wheeled on him. "Why did I have to put Monsieur Joubert out of the hotel?" Everyone stopped to listen. "They said it was painting!" said Mademoiselle Zizi and she spat the word again, "Painting!"

I had felt Joss quivering, but now happened something so alarming that it burnt out everything else. Joss, dignified, aloof, almost grown-up Joss, crumpled like a little girl. "Mother. I want Mother," she wailed like Vicky.

We stood round her, appalled too. "Help me. Help me," sobbed Joss.

We could not help her. How could we? We barely understood. There was no one to help us now, and soon, soon I should have to . . . Helpless in my tears I looked out of the window and saw that a man had come in through the gate. He was dressed in a grey suit and brown felt hat and was followed by a porter with a handcart and two leather suitcases. There was something very familiar about the man; his small figure looked square and solid in the Frenchness of the courtyard, his skin fresh and pink beside the dark, sallow-skinned gendarme and porter, and there was a wonderful calmness about him. My heart suddenly calmed too. It was Uncle William.

"Uncle William!" The shout I gave filled the little salon. I do not know how we burst out of it, past Mademoiselle Zizi, Madame Corbet and Monsieur Dufour. I think I heard Inspector Cailleux ordering us to sit down, but I was not listening, nor were the others. All of us, even Joss, rushed through the bar into the hall.

Uncle William came in. Joss threw herself into his arms, I had mine round his neck, Vicky and Hester were hugging his legs, Willmouse danced up and down in front of him. Uncle William! Dear, dear, dear Uncle William!

CHAPTER 18

"My name is Bullock."

We had always winced and thought that people must laugh when Uncle William said that, but now nobody laughed, nor did we wince. We kept close behind him; Hester even had a corner of his coat clutched in her hand. "Bullock," and he put down his card on the desk, "of Bullock, Roper and Twiss, Solicitors, Southstone. That is in Sussex, England."

"À votre service, Monsieur," said Inspector Cailleux and introduced the others. "Monsieur Dufour, Monsieur Lemaître, Monsieur Aubry." They bowed. "Madame

Corbet," said Inspector Cailleux; he did not introduce Mademoiselle Zizi.

"You have some trouble?" asked Uncle William after he had shaken hands. "The police . . . ?"

"You have doubtless heard at the station or on your way here of these shocking events," said Inspector Cailleux dryly.

"I have heard nothing. I do not speak French," said Uncle William. His calm flat English voice sounded wonderfully unexcited. "I have come to take my sister—if she can travel—and my nieces and nephew home . . . to England," he added firmly, looking at us.

"You said you wouldn't come and you came!" said Hester, stroking his coat.

"How did you know to come now, just now?" cried Joss, pressed close to him.

"But I was sent for," said Uncle William.

"Sent for?"

Freeing himself from us he said, "This came yesterday," and from his wallet took out a piece of paper and unfolded it; it was a telegram. He read aloud, "Come immediately Hôtel des Oeillets Vieux-Moutiers Marne France your sister in hospital children urgently—repeat urgently—need your help."

"But who sent it?" asked Madame Corbet.

"It isn't signed," said Uncle William.

"Someone must have sent it," said Inspector Cailleux and looked round on us all. I tried to put a surreptitious hand on Hester, but I was too late.

"Eliot, of course," said Hester.

"Eliot!" That came from Joss, Mademoiselle Zizi, Madame Corbett and Inspector Cailleux.

"Yes. He *always* did look after us," said Hester, beaming.

"The fool!" Mademoiselle Zizi's cry rang out as she darted across the room and snatched the telegram from Uncle William. She was crumpling it in her hand, tearing it with her teeth as they caught her. Inspector Cailleux ripped it away and Monsieur Dufour and Madame Corbet struggled to hold her as the little sheet of paper was smoothed out and pieced together on the table.

"Châlons. Eleven twenty-five yesterday morning."

"He was heading for the German border," said Monsieur Dufour.

"Obviously," said Inspector Cailleux and snapped, "Get me Lavalle on the telephone." Then he stopped. "No, wait. Châlons," he said, puzzled. "But Châlons is almost here."

"C'est vingt-et-un kilomètres," said the man in the window.

"Twenty-one kilometres at eleven o'clock yesterday," said Inspector Cailleux.

"He had been at the dinner," reminded Monsieur Dufour.

"But only until about midnight. He had had at least nine or ten hours," said Inspector Cailleux. "I don't understand," but he said it as if in a minute, or minutes, he would understand and he began to pace up and down. Mademoiselle Zizi was quiet now, limp and sobbing against Madame Corbet.

"Could he be walking?" asked Monsieur Dufour.

"With the roads watched?"

"Cross-country?"

"There are *roads* into Châlons," said Inspector Cailleux irritably and he walked up and down. "Somewhere slow, where we would not look for him. Of course not. We are looking everywhere fast. Very clever, Monsieur Allen. Slow, Vieux-Moutiers, Châlons, into Germany."

"Châlons? You mean Châlons-sur-Marne?" said Uncle William in his pleasant voice. "On the Marne?"

"The Marne!" Inspector Cailleux stopped. "The Marne!"

From the river, into our silence, came the hoot of a passing barge.

The River

to
R. de L.P.
in perpetual thanks

Preface

There is a vast difference between a book that is 'vouch-safed', its idea or theme coming of itself into your mind, and a book that comes from searching for a story or plot that fits the idea that is in your mind. *The River* was one of those rare books that are given to you.

Jean Renoir, the great French film director, who made the exquisite film of *The River*, called the book 'a tribute to India and to childhood'; which I suppose it is – to my own childhood, though I never had a small brother who was killed by a cobra.

In my young days all English people living and working in the East, except those who were very poor or very wise, sent their children back to England to be brought up, even though this meant years of separation during which the children were exiles. We, my sister Jon and I, were two small English girls; India was where our father worked, and we lived there until we were left with our grandmother in London, far from our home. Then suddenly, in 1914, we were fetched back, reprieved.

I was only seven but realized, as soon as we were back, how homesick I had been. Jon too. Perhaps the thing we had missed more than anything else was the dust: the feel of the sunbaked Indian dust between sandals and bare toes; that and the smell. It was the honey smell of the fuzz-buzz flowers of thorn trees in the sun, and the smell of open drains and urine, of coconut oil on shining black human hair, of mustard cooking oil and the blue smoke from cowdung used as fuel; it was a smell redolent of the sun, more alive and vivid than anything in the West, to us the smell of India.

In the background of our house at Narayangunj in Bengal – now Bangladesh – there were always three sounds: the regular puff of escaping steam from the Jute Works across the road, puff – wait – puff like the pulse of our days and nights; then, from first daylight until dusk, the cawing of crows in the garden and, all day and most of the night, the tympany of the bazaar: a chatter like sparrows, street cries, a woman wailing, a baby's cry. Sometimes there was a light rhythmic drumming which meant the monkey man was passing: he always had two performing monkeys dressed up as a man and a woman; the servants used to gather round them and not let us see what they were laughing at. There were other intermittent noises: the Jute Works noise of trucks pushed by hand, of presses working, chantings of coolies as they pushed or moved some heavy truck or piece of machinery, of bellows and of iron hitting iron from the forge. River noises came: the whistle of a launch, the deep hoot announcing a steamer. Every now and then there was a near and immediate noise of jarring, which meant the big gates of the house were being rolled open by the gatekeeper; it was always an exciting noise, heralding an arrival; all those noises are still there.

The gates were high and green, made of solid wood for privacy, under an arch of bridal creeper that canopied them with a cloud of green and white. On the garden side was the gate-keeper's lodge, a small cell built into the wall; in the left-hand gate a door was cut through which servants or peons went in and out but, for any of the family, even for a child coming back from a ride on her pony, the full panoply was gone through, the gates rolled open with a rumble that alerted the whole house.

A wide gravelled drive made a half circle round an enormous cork tree whose feathery green reached as high as the roof parapet; in December it burst into a tent of white blossom and had round its foot a bed of amaryllis lilies with red streaked trumpets. I called it my tree. Lawns spread away on either side. On the left was a glimpse of a tennis court with screens of morning glory.

I suppose it was a monstrous house, a great rectangle of pale grey stucco, standing on a high plinth that was hidden by plumbago and a hedge of poinsettias – it has always seemed strange to us that in England, for Christmas, poinsettias are sold singly at large prices. Verandas, stone arched and green shuttered, ran the full length of the two floors, each arch ornamented with white carving. The roof was flat, with a high parapet which was cut into loopholes. Double steps, banked with pots of budding chrysanthemums, led up from the drive.

Narayangunj's river was the Lakya, part of the vast network of the Brahmaputra, and was the only direct way in to the town; a branch line railway ran to Dacca, Bengal's capital – now called Dhaka – eleven miles away and, going to Dacca too, was a road built high on a bund above the jute and rice fields, but these were only side routes: the main traffic was by river.

All my young life was lived on or by Indian rivers and was concerned with tides and weather warnings, with steamers, launches, flats, motor-boats, any kind of boats. Rivers of European countries were pygmies to these Indian rivers; they were often two miles wide, flowing between banks of mud and white sand from which fields stretched flat to the horizon under a weight of sky. If we children grew up with a sense of space in us, it was from the sky.

I left India – at least living there – in 1945, immediately after the Second World War. In my last winter – cold weather as we called it – I was asked to do a report for the Women's Voluntary Services on what British women were doing in the way of war work; derogatory questions had been raised in Parliament. I was told to choose a province, so chose Bengal which I knew best and which allowed me to be in and out of Calcutta where Jon could look after the children. I travelled unobtrusively, wearing every kind of uniform so that people took me for granted; the result was a book, *Bengal Journey*.

As part of the journey I had to go from Dacca to Narayangunj, driving along the road that was utterly familiar to me.

My hostess-to-be at Narayangunj had telephoned early that morning; the manager of one of the Jute Works that spread on both banks of the river had died and was to be buried that morning as is the custom in a hot country – it was April – and, of course, every European in Narayangunj's small community had to drive into Dacca to attend the funeral. As I was booked to leave on the midday steamer for Calcutta it was impossible to postpone my visit and, 'Would you mind,' she asked, 'being received by the babu (Indian clerk) in charge?' Mind! I could not have been more relieved but had no idea of what was waiting for me.

Indians do not change; their clothes and customs are timeless and there was not one Westerner in the little town to disturb this. As I walked through the bazaars and the Jute Works, along the river, past the Club, the bamboo-built church and school, the houses I had known, it was as if I had gone back thirty or more years and was – seven, eight, nine, ten, eleven, twelve – again. Everything was the same: I had lunch on the verandah of one of the houses, waited on by white-clad servants who might have been our own. On the way to the ghat we passed the gates of our house; I could see the top of my cork tree over the gate. A short way up its trunk was a hole, my secret hole where I kept the poems I wrote and showed to no one else but Jon.

For a moment I hesitated. 'Go in. Go in,' the babu urged but I could not bring myself to do that.

Most uncanny of all was the steamer; it was one of my father's double-decked paddle-wheeled steamers – Fa was in the Inland Navigation Company of India – with the first class forward on the upper deck, where I was the only passenger. As the paddle wheels began to turn I stood at the front rail.

Usually, as I knew well, the steamers drew away from the ghat, then turned in a wide circle to go upstream but now, for some reason, the steamer backed. She backed further and further so that I, looking at the town, its banks along the river, its houses, mosques, temples and bathing steps, saw it grow smaller and smaller until it was like looking at it down a telescope, smaller but more and more clear until it was out of sight.

As the steamer turned I went to my cabin and began to write *The River*.

The river was in Bengal, India, but for the purpose of this book, these thoughts, it might as easily have been a river in America, in Europe, in England, France, New Zealand or Timbuctoo, though they do not of course have rivers in Timbuctoo. Its flavour would be different in each; Bogey's cobra would, of course, have been something else and the flavour of the people who lived by the river would be different.

That is what makes a family, the flavour, the family flavour, and no one outside the family, however loved and intimate, can share it. Three people had the same flavour as the child, Harriet, who lived in this garden; were her contemporaries, her kin; Bea was one, the others were Bogey and Victoria. They lived in their house beside the river, in a jute-pressing works near a little Indian town; they had not been sent away out of the tropics because there was a war; this war, the last war, any war, it does not matter which war.

It is strange that the first Latin declension and conjunction should be of love and war:

Bellum	Amo
Bellum	Amas
Bellum	Amat
Belli	Amamus
Bello	Amatis
Bello	Amant

'I can't learn them,' said Harriet. 'Do help me, Bea.

Let's take one each and say them aloud, both at once.'

'Very well. Which will you have?'

'You had better have love,' said Harriet.

In the heat they both had their hair tied up on top of their heads in topknots, but Bea wore a cerise ribbon; the effect of it on her topknot gave her a geisha look that was interesting and becoming. Her eyebrows, as she studied this Latin that it was decreed that they should learn, were like fine aloof question marks.

'Do you *like* Latin, Bea?'

'No, of course I don't, but if I have to learn it,' said Bea, 'it is better to learn it quickly.' She glanced across at Harriet. 'You are always trying to stop things happening, Harriet, and you can't.'

But Harriet still thought, privately, that she could.

It was the doldrums of the afternoon and Bea and Harriet, the older children, had to do their homework, opposite one another, at the dining-room table. It was hot. Outside the garden was filled with hot, heavy, sleepy sun; there was a smell of leaves and grass and of sun on the house stone. Beyond the garden was the sound of the river and from far away came a whoop from Bogey. I wonder what Bogey has found now, thought Harriet, and wriggled. The fan blew on her forehead, but it only blew hot air the polish of the table was sticky and held the skin of her arms, there was a dusty dry feeling of dust between her toes. 'You will get hookworm, Harriet, if you go barefoot,' Nan told her. 'Why do you? Bea doesn't.' Harriet looked now under the table to see. No, Bea's feet were gracefully crossed in their correct sandals.

'You had better get on, Harry,' said Bea. 'You have algebra to do as well, and music, and you haven't learnt your Bible verses yet. Better hurry, Harriet.'

Harriet sighed. Latin, and algebra, and music and other things: eating liver, having an injection, seeing a mad paidog – how did Bea manage to take them all so quietly? How? Harriet sighed. She could not, nowadays, aspire to Bea.

'Nan, why is Bea so different?'

'She always was,' said Nan.

'No, she is changing.'

'She is growing up,' said Nan. 'We all have to, willy-nilly.' Harriet did not much like the sound of that expression, 'willy-nilly'.

'Oh, well!' she said, and sighed again and her mind went off on a rapid Harriet canter of its own, too rapid for stops. Will - I - get - hookworm - you - get - all - kinds - of - worms - in - India - and - diseases - too - there - is - a - leper - in - the - bazaar - no - nose - and - his - fingers - dropping - off - him - if - I - had - no - fingers - I - couldn't - learn - music - could - I - no - March - of - the - Men - of - Harlech. She looked at her own fingers, brown and small and whole, except that one had a nail broken where Bogey had banged it, and one had a scratch new that morning, and two were stained bright yellow from the dye she had been making from the yellow flower of a bush that grew beside the cook-house.

The middle finger of Harriet's right hand had a lump on the side of it; that was her writing lump; she had it because she wrote so much, because she was a writer. 'I am going to be a poet when I grow up,' said Harriet; and she added, after another thought, 'Willy-nilly.' She kept a private diary and a poem book hidden in an old box that also did as a desk in an alcove under the side-stairs, her Secret Hole, though it was not secret at all and there was no need to hide her book because she could not resist reading her poems to everyone who would listen. Sometimes she carried her book pouched in her dress. She was writing a poem now, and, as she began to think of it, her eyes grew misty and comfortable.

*'Saw roses there that comforted her heart
And saw their crimson petals plop apart.'*

'*Plop* apart?' asked Bea, her eyebrows more clear and
more surprised and Harriet blushed. She had not known
she had spoken aloud.

'*Do* get on, Harry.'

'Yes, Bea – *Amo. Amas. Amat* . . . *Bellum* . . . *Belli* . . .
Bello . . .

War and love. How many children, wondered Harriet,
yawning, had had to learn those since – she cast round in
her mind for someone prominent who could have learnt
them – since Julius Cæsar, say, or Pontius Pilate (they
must have learnt them, they were Romans) or even Jesus
– perhaps-if-Jesus-went-to-school. She yawned again and
reached for the Outline of History. Loves-and-Wars, she
thought, flipping over the pages. Xerxes-Alexander-Goths-
and Huns - Arthur - and - Guinevere - RichardtheLionheart -
Marlborough-Kitchener. Love and war, love and hate all
muddled up together. She remembered she had no history
to prepare; it was Bible verses and she shut up the book
and opened Father's old Bible that they used for lessons.
Ever-since-AdamandEve, cantered off Harriet, Cain-Abel-
Jacob LeahandRachel-the-Children of Israeland-all-the-
rest-of-them. Even in stories, even in plays, and she looked
at Bea's elbow holding down the edges of the Shakespeare's
flimsy pages that blew up under the fan. Shylock and Port-
ia-and-RomeoandJuliet-and-Cleopatra. She liked Cleopatra best, but even thinking of Cleopatra she wondered that
no one ever grew tired of it, of all this love and all this war.
Or if they do, she thought, someone starts it all over again.
It is as much life as living, thought Harriet. You are born,
you are a he or a she, and you live until you die . . . Willy-
nilly. Yes. Nan is right. It all *is* willy-nilly, though I think
you could live very well without a war . . . and I suppose

4

without being loved. But I hope I am loved, thought Harriet, as much as Cleopatra, and she thought, I wish I were not so young . . . children don't have loves or wars. She drew circles on her algebra. Or do they? wondered Harriet. Do they . . . of their kind?

A drum began to beat softly in the village behind the house. Harriet sat up. 'Bea. Tonight is Diwali.'

'I know. But if you haven't done your homework,' Bea pointed out, 'you won't be allowed to go.'

Bea loved Diwali night as much as Harriet did, but when she was excited, she managed to contain her excitement as she contained her likes and dislikes. How? Harriet gave her another long look and sank back baffled. 'I thought you had forgotten,' she said.

'How could I forget?' said Bea. 'Listen to the drums.'

All day the drummers had been going round the town and the villages that lay around it. Diwali was the Hindu festival of the Feast of Lights.

There are ritual festivals in every religion throughout the year, and every family keeps those it needs, the Chinese and the Roman Catholics being perhaps the most elaborate in theirs, though the old Russians and the Hindus come close and Tibet has charming holidays of its own. Diwali was a curious festival to find in the keeping of a European family, but in Harriet's, as in every large household in India, there was always someone who had to keep some one of the different festivals as they occurred: Nan was a Catholic; Abdullah, the old butler, was a Mohammedan, and so was Gaffura his assistant; Maila, the bearer, was a Buddhist from the State of Sikkim; the gardeners were Hindu Brahmins, Heaven Born; the sweeper and the Ayah were Hindu Untouchables and Ram Prasad Singh, the gateman, the children's friend, was of the separate sect of Sikh. Now the gardeners were away in the bazaar, buying the little saucer earthenware festival lamps and the wicks and oil to float in them, while Abdullah and Maila were not interested. The children kept Diwali because it is an irresistible festival and no one could live in the country in which it is held and not be touched by it.

Tonight when it is dark, thought Harriet, her eyes anywhere but on her work, Ram Prasad will have bought for us a hundred or two hundred lamps. They are made of earthenware, shaped like hearts or tarts or leaves, and they cost two pies each (a pie is a third of a farthing), and in each we shall put oil and float a wick; then we shall set them all along the roof and at the windows and in rows on the steps and at the gate and over the gate, and we shall light them. Everywhere, on every house, there will be lights, and on the river the boats will have them burning and we shall see them go past, and other lights on rafts will be floated down and the rich Hindus will give feasts and feed the poor and let off fireworks and we shall stay up to dinner to see.

Diwali, to the children, was also the official opening of the winter. The greenfly came, millions of insects that flew around the lights at dusk. The gardeners began to plant out vegetables and flower seeds. There was a coolness in the mornings and evenings, a thicker dew, more mosquitoes. Then Diwali came, and it was winter. Winter, the cold weather. That is the best time of all, thought Harriet with relish. It seemed to her, as she looked forward to it, a pageant of pleasantness. Soon we shall have fires, thought Harriet, and sweet peas. I wonder what we shall do this winter? What will happen? And as people far wiser than Harriet have thought, she answered herself. Nothing. Nothing at all. Nothing ever happens here. And then she asked Bea, across the table, 'Bea. Is Captain John coming tonight?'

Bea raised her head. 'I suppose he is,' said Bea, and she added uncertainly, 'Bother.'

'Yes. Bother,' said Harriet. 'Bother! Bother! Bother!'

*

'We must have a quiet winter this year,' Mother had said. 'The world is too unhappy for anything else. There are hurt men and women, and children dying of hunger . . . '

'Oh, Mother!' said Harriet, wriggling.

'Yes,' said Mother firmly, 'think of Captain John.'

'I don't want to think of Captain John,' said Harriet with a feeling of fixed hard naughtiness. 'Why should there be a Captain John?' she asked angrily. 'Or if there must be, why should he want to come here?'

Captain John had come because he had to try to pick up again the threads of living and of earning his living. He had been a prisoner of war and escaped, only to go for more than a year to hospital. He had been tortured in the prison camp, but he was wounded before he went there. He was a young man, or had been a young man, but now his stiff grey face was any age; he had a stiff body, one leg was amputated at the hip, and he had a heavy artificial one that made him more jerky still. The children were warned to be careful of what they said to him. He eschewed grown-ups, but he seemed to like to come into the nursery. Why does he, wondered Harriet. What does he want? He seemed to want something. To be hungry. For what? At first he liked Victoria best, and this was surprising to Harriet because Victoria treated him in a matter-of-fact, off-hand way, that was shocking.

'You mustn't, Victoria,' Harriet told her. 'Captain John was *so* brave. He stayed there in the battle until his leg was shot off.'

Victoria's brown eyes rested thoughtfully on Captain John. 'Why didn't he stay until the other leg was shot off?' she asked.

But he still seemed to like Victoria best.

'Did Victoria ask him to come tonight?' said Harriet now. 'Or did Mother?'

There was a silence, and then: 'No one asked him,' said Bea. 'He asked me.'

'*Asked* you?' said Harriet. 'But . . . ' She had thought that grown-up people did not ask for things.

'He seemed to want to come,' said Bea.

Harriet stared across the table, but all she could see of Bea's face was her forehead and the withdrawn sealed look of her lids as she studied her book. The shadow of her ribbon made a mark of shadow, like a moth, on her cheek. She had withdrawn even further into herself than usual.

*

Harriet's river was a great slowly flowing mile-wide river between banks of mud and white sand, with fields flat to the horizon, jute fields and rice fields under a blue weight of sky. 'If there is any space in me,' Harriet said, when she was grown up, 'it is from that sky.'

The river emptied itself, through the delta, into the Bay of Bengal, its final sea. There was life in and over its flowing; an indigenous life of fish, of crocodiles and of porpoises that somersaulted in and out of the water, their hides grey and bronze and bubble-blue in the sun; rafts of water hyacinths floated on it and flowered in the spring. There was a traffic life on the river; there were black-funnelled, paddle-wheeled mail steamers that sent waves against the bank and other steamers towing flat jute barges; there were country boats, wicker on wooden hulls, that had eyes painted on their prows and sets of tattered sails to put up in the wind; there were fishing boats, crescents lying in the water, and there were fishermen with baskets, wading in the shallows on skinny black legs, throwing fine small nets that brought up finger-length fishes shining in the mesh. The fish were part of the traffic, and each part was animated by a purpose of its own, and the river bore them all down on its flow.

The small town was sunk in the even tenor of Bengali life, surrounded by fields and villages and this slow river. It had mango groves and water tanks, and one main street with a bazaar, a mosque with a white dome and a temple with pillars and a silver roof, the silver made of hammered-out kerosene tins.

Harriet and the children knew the bazaar intimately; they knew the kite shop where they bought paper kites and sheets of thin exquisite bright paper; they knew the shops where a curious mixture was sold of Indian cigarettes and betel nut, pan, done up in leaf bundles, and coloured pyjama strings and soda water; they knew the grain shops and the spice shops and the sweet shops with their smell of cooking sugar and ghee, and the bangle shops, and the cloth shop where bolts of cloth showed inviting patterns of feather and scallop prints, and the children's dresses, pressed flat like paper dresses, hung and swung from the shop fronts.

There was only one road. It was built high among the fields so that the monsoon floods would not cover it; it went through villages and sprawling bazaars, and over hump-backed bridges, past bullock carts and walking people and an occasional car. It stretched across country, with the flat Bengal plain rolling to the horizon and clumps of villages, built up like the road, in mounds of mango, banana and coconut trees. Soon the bauhinia tress would bud along the road, their flowers white and curved like shells. Now the fields were dry, but each side of the road was water left from the flood that covered the plain in the rains; it showed under the floating patches of water hyacinth, and king-fishers, with a flash of brilliant blue, whirred up and settled on the telegraph wires, showing their russet breasts.

The river came into view from the road, its width showing only a line of the further bank, its near bank broken with buildings and patches of bazaar and high walls and corrugated-iron warehouses and mill chimneys. Small boats, covered in wicker-work cowls, put out from one bank to ferry across to the other. In boats like that the children went fishing for pearls. The pearls were sunset river pearls, but it was the divers, not the children, who found them; the children could not get their hooks to go deep enough; the divers dived naked to the river-bed.

The children lived in the Big House of the Works. The Works were spread away from the bazaar along the river with the firm's houses and gardens on the further side. The life of every family is conditioned by the work of its elders; think of a doctor's house, or a writer's, a musician's or a missionary's. It is necessary for the whole family to live in the conditions that such work brings; for these children it was jute.

The jute grew in the fields; they knew all its processes: from the seed which their father germinated and experimented with at the Government Farm, through its young growth, when they could not ride their ponies across country, to the reaping and steeping in the water along the road, in dykes along the fields, when its stench would hang over the whole land. They saw it come in on country boats, on bullock carts, into the Works and the piles of it lying in the sheds for carding and cleaning and grading, while the great presses went up and down and the bales were tumbled out of them, silky and flaxen with a strong jute smell. They saw it go away to the steamers; the steamers and flats were piled high with it and took it down the river to the mills of Calcutta.

The sound of the Works came over the wall: the noise of trucks running on their tracks, wagons pushed by hand by brown, sweating coolies, of the presses working and of machinery and the sound of bellows and iron on iron from the foundry, and the clang of the weighing points, the shouting of the tally clerks, the bumping down of the bales and always the regular puff of escaping steam, puff-wait-puff; it was like a pulse in the background of the children's lives. In the inner dimness of the press-rooms was the sheen of the press-tubes, of brass locks, going down with the pale shining heaps of jute that came up again as bales. There was a smell there of jute dust and coal, steam and hot oil and human sweat, that was one of the accompanying smells of their childhood, like the smell of cess and incense and frying ghee in the bazaar and of honey from the mustard and radish flowers when they were out in the fields, and in season, the stench of steeping jute. There were thousands of coolies in the Works, though they were as impersonal as ants to the children. (Bogey used to eat ants to make him wise.) In the concrete-built, double-floored offices there were scores of clerks, babus, in white muslin shirts and dhoties; the children used sometimes to go with their mother to visit the babus' wives and they were given coco-nut shredded with sugar and 'sandesh', a toffee stuck with silver paper. The firm had its own fleet of launches, called after Indian birds: the 'Osprey', the 'Hoopoe', the 'Oriole', the 'Cormorant', the 'Snipe'; each had its own crew. There were porters or peons, with yellow turbans and staves to guard the gates.

Beyond the Works was the White House, where the Senior Assistant lived, and the Red House where the Junior Assistants all lived together, and the Little House where the Engineer lived. They stood in their own gardens beside the Big House garden.

Other firms were scattered up and down the river, and to them assistants came, young men from England and Scotland, usually from Scotland, even from Greece, who came out raw and young to learn the trade and ended up as magnates. Later on, they married, and too often, Father said, their wives ended up as magnums.

There were a few other Europeans in the town: a Deputy Commissioner, Mr Marshall, and a doctor, Dr Paget. Once there had been a cantonment, but now all that was left of it was a row of graves in the small European cemetery, where grew trees with flowers like mimosa balls. One grave was of a boy, Piper John Fox, who died nearly two hundred years ago when he was fourteen years old.

Perhaps the place and the life were alien, circumscribed, dull to the grown-ups who lived there; for the children it was their world of home. They lived in the Big House in a big garden on the river with the tall flowering cork tree by their front steps. It was their world, complete. Up to this winter it had been completely happy.

*

Half of Harriet wanted to stay as a child; half wanted to be a grown-up. She often asked, 'What shall I do when I am? What will it be like?' She often asked the others, 'What shall you be when you are grown up?' It was always Harriet who started these discussions. No one else really liked them except Victoria, who was too young to know what she was, even now.

'I shall be a cross red nurse when I grow up,' said Victoria.

'She means a Red Cross Nurse,' said Nan.

What shall I be? thought Harriet, fascinated. There seemed to her to be infinite possibilities. 'I might be a nun,' she said, 'or a missionary perhaps, then I could help people. Or a doctor. It would be wonderful to be a doctor, to save people's lives, and give your own life up.' The vista was exciting. 'Wonderful,' said Harriet. 'Wouldn't you like that, Bea?'

'No,' said Bea. 'I want my life for myself.'

Harriet was too truthful to deny that she did too, and she tore herself away from the thought of being a doctor. 'So many grown-up people seem to be nothing very much,' she said. She was thinking of the people she knew, of Nan and Father and Mother and Dr Paget and Captain John. They are nothing important, thought Harriet, wondering. Why? They did not seem to mind. But I want to be important. I will be. 'Perhaps I shall be a great dancer,' she said aloud, 'or a politician and make speeches.'

'I thought you were going to be a poet,' said Bea.

'Well . . . I am a poet,' said Harriet.

'You will be what you are. You will have to be,' said Nan, who was unconcernedly darning. 'In the end everyone is what they are.'

'But how shall I know?' cried Harriet, chafing.

'You will find out as you grow,' said Nan, running her needle in and out of the sock stretched on her hand. That seemed altogether too slow for Harriet.

'Bea, what will you be? An actress? Or a hospital nurse? Or a doctor? A great doctor? When you are grown up, what will you be?'

'How can I tell till I get there?' asked Bea.

'But say. You must say. You must be something.'

'I shall wait till I am,' said Bea, tolerantly, 'and then be it.'

'That is a funny sort of answer,' said Harriet, disgusted.

'It is rather a good one,' said Nan.

Harriet found her family maddening. Father was too busy, in a general family and office way, to have any special time to spare for Harriet, or for any of them; Mother was busy, too, with the house, the family, the servants, notes and letters and lessons and accounts; and besides, she was having another baby soon and had not to be disturbed. Nan? Well, Nan was Nan, and to Harriet that was like bread, too everyday and too necessary to be regarded, though she was the staff of life. There used to be Bea, but now Bea was different; she had withdrawn from Harriet; she was quiet, altogether elderly and distant, and she had new predilections; for instance, she had made friends with Valerie from across the river, a big, hard girl, whom Harriet disliked and feared, and who switched Bea away with secrets and happenings in which Harriet had no part. She was no longer sure of Bea. Harriet would have liked to play with Bogey. Though he was much younger, she was young, too, in streaks, but Bogey played in his own Bogey way that was not at all Harriet's. Harriet could never leave anything alone, and Bogey liked things to be alive and behave themselves in their own way. For instance, he played with lizards and grass snakes; he played armies with insects. He did not like toy soldiers. 'They are all tin,' he said. 'I play soldiers with n'insecks.'

'But can't you pretend, Boge?' asked Harriet.

'No, I can't,' said Bogey. 'I like live n'insecks best.'

He was a very thin little boy, with thin arms and legs; his hair was cut short and his forehead showed sensitive and lumpy, while his eyes were small and brown and quick and live. He was absorbed in a completely happy and private life of his own, and though he occasionally needed Harriet, it was seldom for long. His best game was 'going-round-the-garden-without-being-seen', and that hid him even from her. He was always being stung or bruised or bitten, but he managed to contain his wounds as Bea did her difficulties. 'You will get into trouble one of these days,' said jealous, discontented Harriet, but he only smiled and she sensed that he preferred to get into his own trouble himself. It was no good. It was just not possible to play with Bogey.

In her loneliness, Harriet was driven to adopt places; there was her cubbyhole under the stairs, and there was a place on the end of the jetty, the landing-stage by the house. Harriet liked to sit on the end of it, her legs hanging down, her back warmed with sun, her ears filled with the cool gurgling of the water against the jetty poles.

'How is it a Secret Hole when it isn't a secret and it isn't a hole?' Valerie asked about the Secret Hole, but it still felt secret to Harriet, though she used the jetty for her more open thoughts. The flowing water helped her thoughts to flow. She had also, though she did not yet understand about this, an affinity with the cork tree. It was her tree, as the brilliant jacaranda trees, the bamboos and the lace tangles of bridal creeper in the garden, belonged to Bea, and the tight Marechal-Neil rosebuds were Victoria's. Why? She did not know, but she liked to go to the cork tree, she liked to look up into it and if she really wanted to hear the river, she went to listen to it there. There it was not too loud, too near, drawing Harriet, drawing her away as it did on the jetty. Under the cork tree, she could hear it running steadily, calmly and with it, always, the puff-steam-puff from the Works.

'It goes on, goes on,' said Harriet, her head against the cork tree. 'I wonder what is going to happen to us?' And by that she meant, of course, 'What is going to happen to me?'

There were ways of telling. Nan used sometimes to play charms with them. She dropped pieces of lead tinfoil into a saucepan of boiling water, and, when they were softened, she lifted them out with a spoon on to a cold plate where they hardened. Whatever shapes they made told your future.

They played this one Sunday morning some three weeks after Diwali when Valerie had come to spend the day. Captain John, too, had limped up the drive after breakfast, and was there, sitting by Nan, his stick propped by his chair.

He is always here, always, thought Harriet crossly. And

so is Valerie. Why should they be? Haven't they homes of their own?

She noticed now that, when Captain John was alone with them, some of the stiffness went out of his face. Sometimes he laughed and his eyes were not unlike Bogey's, except that Bogey's were quick and his had often a curious emptiness; but they were gentle too. Yes, he has nice eyes, Harriet admitted, but I wish he were not so jerky. 'Why is he so jerky?' she had asked Mother irritably. 'Because he was hurt so badly,' said Mother. 'Unbearably hurt.'

Looking at Captain John now in the light of this soft warm morning, as he bent his head down by Victoria's, as Victoria leant against his knee, it was difficult to think of him as being unbearably hurt. Unbearably? questioned Harriet, wrinkling her forehead. What is unbearable? When I caught my nail in the railway carriage door I went mad with pain. Mad. Then why isn't he mad? Why didn't he die? What is it that made him live and not go mad? 'He must be stronger than we think,' said Harriet, looking at Captain John.

She considered him, as he put Victoria carefully away and took the saucepan from Nan, to let Nan have a change and rest. His hands were steady now, and his face had colour from the warmth of the fire. He looked big, yes, almost strong among the children, and his hair, that was dark, patched with white, was attractive. Like a magpie, thought Harriet. Why, he is very good-looking, thought Harriet in surprise.

She knew Nan admired him. 'He is like a young prince,' said Nan.

'A funny kind of a prince!' Harriet had said. 'And he isn't young, Nan.'

'He is, poor boy.'

'Oh Nan!' said Harriet impatiently. 'And why does he come all the time – all the time?'

'Perhaps – we have something he needs,' said Nan.

'What?'

'I don't know. We must pray for him. He will go on when he is ready,' said Nan.

'Go on? Where?' asked Harriet, but Nan did not say. Instead, she added in her admonitory seeing-through-Harriet voice, 'Now you are not to go saying anything to him, Harriet.'

'As if I would,' said Harriet indignantly, but she knew that Nan was right and that probably her curiosity would get the better of her. A young prince, thought Harriet now. She was not quite so sure that Nan was wrong.

'Captain John,' said Valerie, 'will you drop a charm for me?' Valerie, by courtesy of the family to her place as visitor, had been given the first turn. Why then should she have another so soon?

'It is Harriet's turn,' said Captain John crisply, and Harriet heard him, and she knew, warmly, in an instant as she heard this crispness in his voice, that he did not like Valerie either, and did not approve of her. Harriet came closer.

The smell of live charcoal from the brazier filled the veranda with the smell of hot lead from the charms and the smell of warmth in the starch of Nan's apron. Ram Prasad, who was always with the children in all their games, blew up the fire as Captain John dropped a charm for Harriet. The lead melted, ran wide, and he caught it in the spoon and lifted it and dropped it again on the plate, but curiously, the pellet ran together, sizzling, again, and formed itself into a round ball.

'It is round,' said Bogey, 'like a marble.'

'It is a world,' said Victoria. They did not understand her until Nan reminded them of the globe of the world on Father's desk.

'It *is* a world,' said Harriet, taking it in her hand now it had cooled. On its rough surface she imagined she saw seas and lands. 'I wonder what it means?'

'Well, Harriet, are you satisfied? Now you have the whole world?' said Valerie.

Harriet gave her a long straight look.

'It is your turn, Captain John,' she said, wanting to reciprocate. 'Let us make a charm for you. Let us see what you are going to be.'

Valerie nudged her sharply. 'What a silly you are!' she whispered down Harriet's neck. 'You will make him feel awful. How can *he* be anything?'

But – he has to be, thought Harriet. Of course he has to be. He didn't die.

'What do you want to be?' asked the little Victoria, putting her head back to look at him. 'What could you be?'

There was a long silence. No one had any suggestion to make. 'Oh well,' said Victoria, 'I think you had better just stay here with us.'

'Make a charm for Bea,' said Nan.

Bea had a loop, a circle, that made a rough little ring. 'That means you will be loved and married,' said Nan.

Bea took the ring and looked at it by the verandah rail, turning it over and over in her fingers. After Captain John gave the saucepan back to Nan, he stood up and stretched, and limped over to Bea.

'What is the name of those flowers?' he asked Bea, presently.

'Poinsettias,' said Bea, politely.

'They make me realize I am in India,' said Captain John. 'They look so hot and red, even in the rain. And those, those little low pale blue ones on the bushes?'

'Plumbago,' said Bea.

'This is a lovely garden,' he said.

Why, thought Harriet, does he talk to Bea so – earnestly? He was not talking to Bea as if she were a child, but as if she were grown-up. Bea is a little girl, thought Harriet, and why is Bea so polite? There is no need to be so polite to him.

'I am glad you like it,' said Bea.

'I think it is the most beautiful garden I have ever seen,' said Captain John, earnestly.

It was a beautiful garden. The poinsettias grew round the plinth of the house, huge scarlet-fingered flowers with milk sap in their stems. The house was large, square, of grey stucco, with verandas along its double floors and tiers of great green-shuttered windows. It had a flat roof, with a parapet where the children played, and the parapet was carved with huge stone daisies. Can a house, a serious house, be carved with daisies? This was.

Below the poinsettias was the plumbago; it made hedges of nursery pale blue and the flowerbeds it bordered would later be full of the pansies and verbena and mignonette that were now in seed pans in a seed-table made of bamboo. Along the paths were ranged pots of violets that held the dew. Other pots of chrysanthemums were on the verandah and in a double phalanx down the steps. These chrysanthemums had mammoth heads of flowers that were white and yellow and bronze and pink; some of them were larger than the children's heads. Later, in their place, there would be potted petunias.

The lawns rolled away to the river under the trees, but there were flowers, bougainvillaeas, that spread themselves into clumps and up the trees, orange, purple, magenta and cerise, like Bea's hair ribbon; there were Marechal-Neil turrets with their small lemon-yellow roses, and other roses in the rose garden, and bushes of the small white Bengali roses tinged with pink. There were standard hibiscus that were out already in pinks, and creams and yellows and reds, and morning glory and other creepers, on the house, over the porch, along screens, up trees: jasmine and orange-keyed begonias, passion flowers and quisqualis that would flower in January and the spring; now there was only the pink-and-white sandwich creeper out and Bea's bridal creeper over the gate. There were squirrels and lizards in the garden and birds: bulbuls and kingfishers and doves and the magpie robin and sunbirds and tree pies and wagtails and hawks. Birds are little live landmarks and more truthful than flowers; they cannot be transplanted, nor grafted, nor turned blue and pink. The birds were in the flavour of that garden, as the white paddy birds and the vultures were part of the flavour of the fields, and the circling kites and the kingfishers of the river; the garden was full of swallow-tail butterflies bigger than the sunbirds and of Bogey's insects and Bogey's ants; no one really knew the insects except Bogey. At night there were sometimes jackals on the lawn and fireflies, and there was a bush that used to fill the whole house with its scent in the darkness, a bush called Lady-of-the-Night.

Harriet's cork tree stood on the edge of the drive, directly in front of the steps. It was as high as the house. Soon it would bud, then be covered in blossom, and the flowers, when they fell at the end of the winter, would make a circle deep in flowers on the grass. Woodpeckers lived in the cork tree and in season it had Japanese lilies round its foot.

Now Captain John was looking at it. 'And that is a most beautiful tree,' he said.

'It is Harriet's,' Bea told him.

'Harriet's?' He said it as if he were surprised, and Harriet was suddenly oddly shy, and oddly pleased.

'At least, she says it is hers, though I don't know why,' said Bea.

Harriet felt his look bent on herself for a moment, but when she brought herself to look up, she saw that he had forgotten her; he was looking down at Bea and she had a sudden remembrance of him on Diwali night. She had felt him looking at something then, or someone, and she had followed his look and found it on Bea. Why? Why did he look at Bea? Now he was looking at Bea again with that same extreme gentleness and interest. Then Bea, too, looked up and back at him.

'Let me see your ring,' he said.

Bea gave him a curiously startled glance and dropped the ring into his hand from above and walked away to the others.

Nan had made a charm for Victoria. It was scoop shape.

'It is a bucket,' said Victoria.

'Or a thimble,' said Nan.

Nan and Victoria could not have appeared more different. Victoria was very plump, very blonde, built into a beautiful heavy pink and pearl fleshed body with dimples at the joints and fat bracelets at the joins; especially inviting were the backs of her legs and thighs. She shone by contrast with Nan, the old Anglo-Indian, who was thin, small, very dark, with a fine brown skin that was slack and tired now and showed bluish shadows and pouches under her eyes. Her hands were small and thin and busy, and her fingers were wrinkled and pricked at the tips with a lifetime of washing and sewing. Her hair was black and dry and thin and held, each side of her head, by tortoiseshell combs. She wore a striped dress and an apron that had a convent thinness and cleanness. Her eyes were like Victoria's, brown and clear; as her body receded it seemed to leave all her life in her eyes.

Besides their eyes, Nan and Victoria were alike in that, at the moment, they were both perfect. Victoria had reached the stage of completed babyhood; little girls, especially, sometimes linger in this stage for three or four months, and during that time they are quite unconsciously perfect. Victoria had no troubles, she did not trouble anyone, and nor did Nan. Nan had completed her hard womanhood, and she had managed to shed her troubles. She had reclaimed, through living and service, what Victoria had not yet lost.

Then Nan made Bogey's charm.

Sometimes the charms did not act, and now Bogey's refused to coagulate. It ran and spread on the plate and took no shape at all.

'What is the matter with it?' said Harriet. 'How can we tell what it means?'

'It won't tell,' said Nan.

'Put it back and try again, Nan.'

'No,' said Nan. 'If it won't tell, it won't. I am sorry, Bogey.'

'I don't mind,' said Bogey, cheerfully. He picked up the still soft lead and rolled it into a ball like Harriet's and began to play marbles with it.

Harriet left the others and went away. It was Valerie's turn for another charm and she did not want to see Valerie's turn. She went on to the drive and under the cork tree, and looked up at it, thinking of how Captain John had admired it. She herself did not think it was as beautiful as the jacaranda trees, for instance, or even as the peepul tree in the wall by Ram Prasad's house that stood at the gate. 'But I like it,' said Harriet aloud.

She saw a crevice in the trunk low enough for her to reach. Stepping over the lilies, she fitted her charm neatly into it, and the ball rolled down and lay in the five-inch hollow at the bottom. She could reach it with her fingers, but she left it there. That is a safe place, thought Harriet. Now I can find it again. Bogey might play marbles with his charm, but she was sure that hers was an omen.

*

Each year there were nests in the garden. There was always a sunbird's nest in the bougainvillaea that grew up the house wall; a long untidy tear-shaped nest made of fibres and dried leaves with the sunbirds shimmering in and out. Now there was a dove's nest in the creeper above the veranda; you could see her sitting on her nest; she would sit there quiet for hours; her breast was grey, flecked with brown.

'What is she doing?' asked Victoria.

'Brooding,' said Captain John. He spoke often, and very kindly, to Victoria.

He was staying in the house. Mother had made him come over from the Red House so that she and Nan could look after him, because the wound in his good leg had opened and was discharging.

'It can't be very good then,' said Harriet.

'It isn't, but it is the best I have,' said Captain John.

'He shouldn't work here, in this climate,' Harriet heard Father say. 'It is cruelty,' but Captain John managed to work, though he looked ill and frayed and stiff and worn, and he managed to speak kindly to Victoria, though he did lose his temper with the rest of them.

'Brooding?' said Victoria, looking up at the nest. 'Is that brooding?' she said. 'She looks . . . happy.'

'I think she is,' said Captain John, seriously. 'She sits on her nest and she feels the whole world going round her, and she takes everything she wants from the world and puts it into her eggs.'

'You shouldn't tell Victoria things like that,' said Bea. 'She thinks they are true.'

'But they are true,' said Captain John.

'How queer you are,' said Bea. 'You say such queer things,' and Captain John's thin cheek suddenly burnt and he put up his hand to smooth his hair, which was a trick he had to hide his stiffness. His hand was shaking again. Why does he *mind* Bea? thought Harriet. She knew, then, that it was too tiring for him to speak as he wanted to do, to Bea. It was much more restful for him to bark, as he barked to Harriet, 'Blast you, Harry. Take your great hand off my leg. You hurt me.' He would never say that to Bea. 'And he isn't queer,' said Harriet. 'That about the dove was nice.'

'Are we in eggs?' asked Victoria.

'You are,' said Harriet, teasing her. 'Father says you are still in the egg, Victoria.'

It was funny to think that she, Harriet, who was still a child herself, could remember a time when Victoria, standing so large and solid on the veranda beside them, was not. Then there was no Victoria. And there was no gap before, thought Harriet, puzzled. There was no empty place and yet we fitted her in. It was funny, and notable, that families always did fit the babies in. Then she remembered, what she was supposed to know and had been told and still could not yet realize, that soon, in a month or two, or three or was it four, they, the family, were to have another baby themselves.

'Did you know that?' she asked Captain John.

'Know what?'

'How do you expect people to understand what you are talking of, if you go thinking in between?' said Valerie. Bea did not defend Harriet, but looked at her severely too.

Harriet left them.

'Are we in eggs?' Victoria had asked. Fancy asking that, thought Harriet, wandering away, but it would be funny if we were. As she said it, she was frightened. She had too often this feeling of being enclosed, shut in a small shape like a dome, and, if it were an egg, she had no beak to break it. 'How can I get out? I never can get out,' she was just going to say in a panic, and then she remembered that, if she were in an egg, just like the chick, she would grow too big for it and break it. The thing is to grow very quickly, said Harriet to herself, and she said aloud, 'Nan says we change our skin seven times in our lives. Perhaps this is the same idea.'

'That is snakes, not people,' said Bogey. 'Harry, Ram Prasad says there is a cobra under the peepul tree, but you are not to tell. We are going to watch it. Perhaps we shall see it change its skin,' said Bogey.

'Ugh!' said Harriet. She had none of Bogey's freemasonry with insects and reptiles, but in fascinated horror she went with him to the peepul tree. The garden wall was built each side into its trunk, so that it formed part of the wall and half of it was in the garden and half in the road outside. Harriet knew why the cobra, if there were a cobra, had come there. It was because the front part of the tree in the road was a shrine with a whitewashed plinth and the villagers used to put saucers of milk on it with offerings of rice and burnt sugar and curd. Snakes like milk, and Harriet guessed it had come there for that.

She and Bogey squatted on their heels, watching the roots, but nothing stirred. At any moment Harriet expected the horrid bronze-grey lengths of the snake to come flowing out, over, and under, the roots. 'Ugh!' shuddered Harriet, and when at last she tired and stood up, her hands and the backs of her knees where she had folded them were wet. 'I don't want to see it,' she said. 'Bogey. You know I am sure we ought to tell. We are supposed to tell if we see a snake in the garden.'

Bogey had not heard. He was still squatting, still waiting, the whole of him intent on the snake hole. It was not that Bogey was disobedient as much as blithely unaware he had been told. 'Oh well,' said Harriet, 'we haven't seen it yet, and it isn't really in the garden. It is in the peepul tree.'

She went back to the house, and on her way she passed Victoria with her doll. 'I play so beautifully with my baby,' she said to Harriet as Harriet passed. 'She was born again yesterday.'

'You are always having her born,' said Harriet scornfully.

'Why not?' asked Victoria. 'You can be born again and again, can't you?'

It was puzzling. Every time Harriet examined somebody's silly remark, it seemed not to be so silly. 'I don't understand it,' she said, and she wondered who could explain it to her; its surface silliness was such that she doubted if she would find anyone to whom she could make clear what she wanted to ask. Then she made up her mind; she would risk a chance and ask Captain John.

He may swear at me, thought Harriet. He likes Bea, but never mind, he can talk to me for once, thought Harriet. If he laughs at me, he laughs at me. Never mind. And she wavered no more, but went to look for him.

He was leaning on the verandah rail, idling, looking at the sun and the flowers, quiet and dreaming.

'Captain John,' said Harriet, interrupting him, 'I want to talk to you.'

'Must you?' he said lazily.

'Yes, I must; about being born.'

He still did not seem willing. 'Can't you talk to Bea or Nan about that, Harriet? I can't talk about being born.'

'Oh, but you can,' said Harriet, putting a compelling hand on him. 'I don't want to be told anything. I want to talk.'

He looked down at her, his face lazy, not at all stiff.

'Do you know, your eyes have speckles in them, flecks?' he said.

'Like the dove's breast?' asked Harriet.

He looked at her more particularly. 'What dove?'

'The dove on her nest. I liked that – what you said.'

'Did you?' he said, and he seemed pleased. Talking to Harriet he had not changed his lounging, dreaming attitude, and he forgot to smooth his hair and pull his tie straight. He looked down into her eyes lazily without thinking of himself.

'Listen,' said Harriet, and leaning on the rail beside him, she told him of what she was thinking, puzzling over, and it came in words that were unusually clear, almost crystalline. She told him of Victoria's remark and of how it was silly and yet it rang true; of his own remark that Bea said was queer and yet was true too. 'Is everything a bit true then?' asked Harriet.

She could see the peepul tree over the bamboo clumps that hid its lower half, and she wondered idly if the cobra had come out. 'Ugh!' said Harriet again, and moved her shoulders in a shudder while she waited for Captain John to speak.

'My idea,' said Captain John, 'isn't very different from Victoria's, though she didn't mean hers in this way. I have an idea,' said Captain John, his eyes looking now, not at Harriet, but across the rail to the garden, 'that we go on being born again and again because we have to, with each thing that happens to us, each new episode.'

'What is an episode?'

'It really means an incident . . . between two acts.'

'I don't understand.'

'Call it an incident, a happening. With each new happening, perhaps with each person we meet if they are important to us, we must either be born again, or die a little bit; big deaths and little ones, big and little births.'

'I should think it would be better to go on being born, than to die all the time,' said Harriet.

'If we can,' said Captain John, 'but it takes a bit of doing. It is called growing, Harriet, and it is often painful and difficult. On the whole, it is very much easier to die.'

'But you didn't,' said Harriet.

'I just managed not to, but I am no criterion,' said Captain John.

'What is a criterion?' asked Harriet, and before he could answer, she asked, 'Who is it who is important to you, Captain John?'

'Never you mind,' and he stood up and stretched himself. 'Do you think you could leave me alone now like a good girl?'

Harriet went along to the jetty and sat down in her usual place. 'I *wish* he had told me,' she said. She hung her feet down above the water; they were still bare, and she had still, so far, not had hookworm. Wriggling her toes to feel the dust between them, she wondered, all at once, how she, Harriet, appeared to Captain John. Then she wondered, more truthfully, if he ever saw her at all. 'But he said that about my eyes,' argued Harriet. 'Yes, he said they had flecks in them,' but if that were in derision or admiration she did not know. She thought again of the way she had seen him looking at Bea when they lit the lamps for Diwali. They had been on the roof, in the darkness, and the point of light from each lamp lit a circle round itself but was not strong enough to lighten the whole roof darkness. Anyone bending over a lamp was suddenly illumined and Bea, bending to shift the oil round a wick, was lit, her shoulders, her neck, the line of her face, and her hair; she was gilded, and as she moved the oil she looked up at Valerie and laughed at what Valerie was saying. Harriet had noticed that Captain John had stood there, lost, and the oil in the lamp he held ran over the edge on to the floor and Valerie scolded him. 'Yes, he looks at Bea,' said Harriet mournfully.

She wished her big toe could reach the water. The river current gurgled against the poles of the jetty; its traffic floated down and Harriet watched it lazily, while her mind left that part of Captain John's idea and thought of the other. *You are born with each new big thing that happens.* I don't quite understand that, thought Harriet.

A boat floated down laden with bright red pots: then a boat laden with nothing at all; then a launch from up-river; Harriet noted its black funnel, blue-banded, and its white and red hull: From Brentford's, she thought, the 'Sprite'. On its deck sat a large lady dressed in white. Mrs Milligan, Harriet identified her without a flicker of interest. How few, how very, very few people are important, she thought, and lazily she began to think over the people who were important for her. Father-Mother-Bea-Bogey-Victoria. That was automatic, and she did not realize that, as she said their names, she did not think of them at all. Nan? Her hesitation made her think of Nan. No, not Nan, thought Harriet as she watched a police motor boat, with the police flag almost touching the wash at its stern as it went by; the rolling wave behind it presently came in broken rifts to hit the jetty where she was sitting. Anyone else? thought Harriet. Of course, children were not expected to have many people, but however she circumscribed herself, her thoughts came back to the question she wanted to ask. Captain John? asked Harriet at last, and she answered as she had to answer because it was the truth, How can he be important for me? It is Bea he likes. At first we thought it was Victoria, but it is Bea he is interested in.

A porpoise came down, turning slowly over and over in midstream with a beautiful easy armchair rhythmical motion that lulled Harriet. She rubbed her back against the post and picked at her finger lump with her hand. Oh well, thought Harriet comfortably, I shall meet heaps of people when I am older, when I am famous. Heaps of things are going to happen to me.

A whirr and a splash made her jump so that she almost fell off the jetty. A kingfisher had struck from a branch above her. Now it sat on a post with the fish still bending and jerking in its beak. The poor fish had been placidly, happily, swimming and feeding somewhere under the jetty, and then, out of its element, from another, it had been seized and carried off. And swallowed, thought Harriet regretfully, watching it disappear.

I wonder what the other fishes think? thought Harriet, but then, that was the same with any dying; one person was seized and taken away. But what does it feel like if that comes right plumb in the middle of your family? She could not think of it, it seemed impossible and yet she had just seen it happen. Things do happen, she told herself, but she was lulled again with the sound of the river running in her ears. Those were fishes, Harriet told herself comfortably. Only fishes.

There was no sign of the splash. The river ran steadily where it had been. 'There you see ... Anything can happen, anything, and whatever happens the other fishes just go on wriggling and swimming and feeding because they have to,' said Harriet. 'It, the river, has to go on.' Whatever happened, a fish's death, a wreck, storm, sun, the river assimilated it all. The far bank showed as a line across the river, a line of fields, a clump of trees by the temple, and, further away, the walls and roofs and chimney and jetty of Valerie's father's works. I wonder what he thinks about dying; Captain John, not Valerie's father, thought Harriet idly. I wonder if he thinks the same as he thinks about being born, if he really thinks you could die over and over again. Goodness, thought Harriet, I nearly died just now when I nearly fell off the jetty. I would die if I saw that cobra! But what Captain John meant was deeper than that. Harriet suspected that, but her mind was now too lazy, too happy, to explore.

*

Sometimes, in the night, Harriet thought about death. She thought about Father and Mother dying, or Nan, who was really very old; then she would hastily wake Bea to comfort her.

When Ram Prasad's wife died, she was carried on a string bed to the river and put on a pyre and burned. Afterwards her ashes were thrown on the water. Bogey and Harriet went to look, though they knew without being told that Mother would not have allowed them.

'Did you mind it?' Harriet asked Bogey afterwards.

'Mind what?'

'The burning.'

'It looked just like burning to me.'

It had. The pyre was well alight when they arrived, hiding themselves behind a brick kiln on the edge of the burning ghat so that even Ram Prasad should not see them.

'I didn't like the smell,' said Harriet. 'Did you see them throw her ashes in the river?'

'I wasn't looking,' said Bogey, 'there was a frog . . . ' His mind went off on the thought of the frog, but after a while he said, 'No, I didn't mind.'

'Nor did I,' said Harriet. She had not seen the body, only those ashes, and they did not seem to be anything to do with a person who had lived and walked and talked and eaten food and played with her baby and laughed. No, it had been, up to now, birds like the kingfisher, and animals like the livestock of the nursery, guinea-pigs and rabbits and kittens, that had given Harriet her glimpses of birth and death.

Nan said if you were good you died and went to heaven. 'To Paradise.' Mother, not so certainly, half-heartedly, lent some support to that. Nan was quite certain.

'To eternal rest,' said Nan, looking at the swellings her bunions made in her shoes. 'To have wings like the angels,' said Nan, as she toiled upstairs with the washing.

Harriet had seen heaven on the films, but it was a Hindu heaven in an Indian film, Krishna playing his flute in a garden of roses and dancing girls. The Mohammedan heaven? She was not sure about that. She asked Father what Buddhists did when they died; he took down a book and read to her about a drop sliding into the crystal sea and being lost. She asked Mother, and Mother pointed out that Harriet knew already that Jesus rose from the dead; some people, she added, believed that you came back over and over again, to live another life each time. 'A better life,' said Mother.

'Goodness, how good you must be in the end,' said Harriet.

That was the idea, Mother thought, and if you were not good, she went on to say, you came back as something lower.

'Like?'

'An animal. An insect. A flea,' said Mother, smiling.

I should rather like to be a flea, thought Harriet, thinking of herself as a gay acrobatic jumping flea, but Bogey, who did not like to be labelled good or bad, was bored with the idea. 'I should rather have done with it,' said Bogey.

All these thoughts seemed like cracks in the wholeness of Harriet's unconsciousness. It had cracked before, of course, but now she was growing rapaciously.

The winter drew on. Day succeeded day, and ended and went out of sight and was gone. There are such lots of days, thought Harriet, but not more than there are drops of water in the river.

She was on the jetty again. Very often now she went to watch the river. It flowed down in negroid peace, in sun, in green strong water. Harriet, now she was growing from a little girl into a big one, was beginning to sense its peace. 'It comes from a source,' said Harriet, who learnt geography. 'From very far away, from a trickle from a spring, no one knows where exactly, or perhaps they do know; it doesn't matter. It is going to something far bigger than itself, though it, itself, looks big enough. It is going to the sea,' said Harriet, 'and nothing will stop it. Nothing stops days, or rivers,' said Harriet with certainty.

Then the guinea-pig, Bathsheba, died.

The children had several scores of guinea-pigs and they used to play shepherds with them, driving guinea-pig flocks over the lawn. One of the original stock was Bathsheba, an old white guinea-pig, who belonged to Harriet. One day, Harriet found her, lying limp, as if she were asleep, in a corner of the cage. When Harriet picked her up, she did not feel limp, but curiously stiff and resilient and her fur felt hard. 'She is dead, I think,' said Harriet, but she was still not quite sure what dead was. She did not take Bathsheba into Nan or Mother or anyone in the house; she carried her down the garden and out of the gate and into the Red House to find Captain John, but all the assistants were out except one, Mr Corsie, lying ill in bed with dysentery.

'May I come in, Mr Corsie?' asked Harriet.

'Wh't is it ye want?' asked Mr Corsie without enthusiasm. He was feeling ill.

'Please – is this dead?' asked Harriet, offering Bathsheba for inspection.

'Ugh! Take it away, oot o'heer,' cried Mr Corsie.

'*Is* it – ugh?' asked Harriet, doubtfully.

'Dae ye no heer me?' asked Mr Corsie. 'Take it oot. Or I'll tell yeer Pa.'

'But – is it dead?' asked Harriet.

'Daid as a doornail. Take it away. Good Lorrd! It is stinkin'.'

Harriet immediately dropped Bathsheba on the floor.

That night she was worried.

'Bea.'

'Sssh.'

'Bea.'

'What *is* it, Harriet? I am asleep.'

'Bea, when we are dead, do we go . . . like Bathsheba?'

'How did she go?' asked Bea, yawning.

'Stiff. Hard. Stinking,' said Harriet tearfully.

'Yes, I suppose we do,' said Bea, who was sleepy. 'That is called a corpse.'

Harriet shivered, all over her skin, under the bedclothes.

'Bea.'

Silence.

'Bea.'

No answer.

'Bea. *Bea. BEA!*'

'Oh, Harriet! I am asleep, What is it?'

'Bea. I don't want to.'

'Don't want to *what?*'

'Be a corpse.'

'But you are not,' said Bea, practically.

'But I shall be,' said Harriet, and she began to cry.

'Don't you think you could wait till you are,' said Bea. 'I *am* so sleepy, Harriet.' Then as the fact of Harriet's sobs was borne in upon her, she said, more gently, 'Couldn't you wait till the morning, Harry?'

'No. No. I can't,' sobbed Harriet. 'I am frightened, Bea. I can't get the feeling of Bathsheba off my hands. I am frightened, Bea.'

'Don't cry,' said Bea, kindly. She sat up in bed, and by the veranda light Harriet could see her shoulders in her white yoked nightgown, and the fall of her dark hair. 'Don't cry, Harry. It isn't anything to cry about. I am sure it is not.'

The sound of her normal little voice was comforting to Harriet, until she thought that Bea too must die, dark hair, voice and all. 'Then I shall never hear her voice again,' cried Harriet silently, 'and Mother must die, and Nan, and Nan is old and must die quite soon.'

'Why isn't it something to cry about?' cried Harriet bitterly, aloud.

'Oh, Harry. You ask too many questions.'

'Yes, but . . . Don't *you* ever think about dying, Bea?'

'Well, yes I do,' said Bea.

'Then what do you think?' she asked.

'It is hard to know what I think,' said Bea's small voice out of the darkness. 'But I know a few things.'

'Wh-what do you know?' quavered Harriet, and she said suspiciously, 'Nan and Mother and Ram Prasad tell us things about heaven and Jesus and Bhramo, but they don't really know.'

'I think they are all wrong,' said Bea severely. 'Mine are not things like that. They are more simple things.' And she added, as if this had only just occurred to her, 'More sensible things.'

'Wh-what sort of th-things?'

'This,' said Bea. 'When anything, anybody, is dead, like Bathsheba, it is dead. The life, the breath, the . . . the *warm* in it, is gone.'

'Nan calls it the spirit.'

'The spirit then,' said Bea. 'I call it the "warm", but the spirit or the warm is gone.'

'Yes,' said Harriet. 'Yes. It was gone out of Bathsheba.'

'The body is left behind,' said Bea, 'and what happens to it? It goes bad.'

'Don't!' said Harriet, and shuddered.

'You can't keep a body . . . '

'Except mummies and those Rajahs who are pickled in honey,' said Harriet.

'Then I think,' said Bea, and she contradicted herself. 'Then I *know* that it isn't meant to go on. It is useless. The body isn't any use any more.'

'Yes?' said Harriet.

'But the other, the warm, has gone. It doesn't stay and

go bad. So I think,' said Bea, 'that it is of some use. That it has gone to something, somewhere.'

'But where?' asked Harriet. 'Where?'

'You ask too many questions, Harry,' said Bea.

'I wonder what Captain John thinks,' said Harriet in despair.

'Captain *John*?'

'Yes. He would think something,' said Harriet, and her curiosity got the better of her sense, and she said, 'What do you feel like with Captain John, Bea?'

Bea immediately lay down again. Harriet knew she would not tell.

But, as silence settled, Harriet felt obscurely comforted. Why? Bea had not said much, but Harriet felt strengthened. She kept her head under the bedclothes for a little while and then found she was perfectly well able to come out, and she lay calmly, looking through her mosquito net at the starlight that fell dimly between the columns of the verandah, and listening to the puff-wait-puff of steam from the works and the ever-flowing gurgling of the river. I will learn more about it as I grow, she thought comfortably. Living and dying and being born, like Captain John said, she yawned. She naturally supposed that that growing was still a great way off.

She tried to remember the names of the stars as she lay, and she thought how much longer stars and things like trees and rocks went on than people: Mountains and islands and sands, she thought, and man-made things as well; songs and pictures and rare vases and poems. 'Things are the thing,' said Harriet sleepily, and then a thought came like a spear from one of those stars, but real, truthful. It had occurred to her that she, Harriet, might possibly, one day, if she were good enough, have some small part in that. One of my poems might still be alive in, thought Harriet, say, AD 4000. It might. I don't say it will, but it might. I should be like the Chinese poets, she thought dizzily. Or like Keats or Shakespeare, she thought, and she was filled with a sense of her own responsibility. That was a new sensation for Harriet. She was not given to responsibility and it gave her a feeling, more serious, more humble, than she had ever known. 'I must work,' said Harriet earnestly. 'I must work and work and work.' Like Queen Victoria she thought. I will be good. I will be good.

Saw roses wide that comforted her heart

And saw their cr-im-son ... but it was somehow not interesting. She gave a huge yawn, the poem grew fuddled, and she was asleep.

*

Next morning, when she went out before breakfast and stood on the jetty, she wondered what all the fuss had been about. Now she felt she had no need to stand there staring at the river, watching it flow, when it was such a glorious morning in the garden. 'What was I fussing about last night?' she asked. She was filled with such buoyancy of living, of happiness, that she could not stay still any longer; she had to move away, walking up and down the paths, beside the creeper screens, under the turrets of roses, touching the flowers, knocking the dew off them, letting the boughs touch her and spring back, until she came to the cork tree.

It was early. The garden shone. The cold weather light lay on the paths and unfolded across the green of the lawns and through the trees. There was brighter green in the wings of the flycatchers and in the flight of parakeets that flew in front of her and across the river.

Victoria came down the steps. She did not see Harriet. She had some straw under her arm and she was dragging a rug after her. Harriet knew what she was going to do; she was going to make a house. At the moment Victoria was like a snail, she always had a house attached to her somewhere. Now, dragging the rug over the dew and the gravel, she went away round the corner towards the swing.

Harriet had reached the cork tree. By standing very quietly under it, she could hear the woodpeckers tap-tapping on it far above her head. She put her head back and looked through the break in the branches and their canopy to the sky, and as she looked, the clouds, and the grey line with a stone daisy that was the parapet of the house, and the tall tree itself, seemed to tilt gently backwards. That is the world turning, thought Harriet. It gave her a large feeling to see the tilt of the world. Clouds, house, tree, lawns, river, Harriet, were borne slowly backwards as the world turned, but the tree remained upright, steady, rising into the sky, spreading its branches that were coming into bud. Under Harriet's feet, where she stood among the red lilies, its roots went deep into the earth, down down into the pit of the earth. 'I believe,' said Harriet, 'I believe that this is the middle of the world. That I am standing in the middle of the middle of the world, and this tree is that tree, the axis tree, like the one in the story. It goes right through the earth. It goes up and up.'

She put her hand on the tree and she thought she was drawn up into its height as if she were soaring out of the earth. Her ears seemed to sing. She had the feeling of soaring, then she came back to stand at the foot of the tree, her hand on the bark, and she began to write a new poem in her head.

It took her a long time, walking on the lawn, pacing the paths, coming back to the tree, to finish it. She finished it in her head, then she felt for her book that was in the waistband of her dress, and her pencil that she kept in her stocking, and wrote the poem down.

When she looked at it, it did not look like any of her poems. She read it aloud. It did not sound like any of her poems. 'It is not like any poem I ever read,' she said doubtfully. 'It can't be good,' and immediately she had the feeling that it was good. It felt alive, as she did. She felt alive and curiously powerful, and full of what seemed to her a glory.

She glanced round. She could see Victoria's head rising and dipping by the swing, but it was no good reading poems to Victoria. Bea was out riding, she did not know where Bogey was, and every adult was always busy before breakfast. Then, as she stood puzzled under the cork tree, Captain John came limping up the jetty and across the lawn towards her.

'Hallo,' said Captain John.

'Hallo,' said Harriet, considering him.

'I have been across the river.'

'Bea has gone riding,' said Harriet. She looked up at him. 'Captain John,' she said, and stopped.

'Yes?'

'I—' said Harriet slowly, and then easily it tumbled out. 'I have written a poem. It is – either very bad – I expect it is bad, or else it is good. It is so new, I don't know.'

'Show me,' said Captain John, and put out his hand. Harriet gave him the poem and he began to read it.

She had not expected he would read it aloud, quite naturally and unselfconsciously as he was doing, and prickings of acute shyness ran over her until she found that she was soothed, allayed, delighted by the sound of her own words:

'*This tree, my tree, is the pole of the world*' . . .

When he had finished it he looked at Harriet. Then he looked at the poem.

'Did *you* write this?' he asked. 'By yourself?'

Harriet nodded. She could not speak.

'Nobody helped you?'

'Of course not,' said Harriet indignantly.

'But it is good!'

Waves of bright-eyed satisfaction chased through Harriet's every vein. He looked at her as if he had not properly seen her before.

'It – felt good . . . for me,' said Harriet huskily.

'I didn't know you wrote poems.'

'I – I do,' said Harriet. She had to bend her head down. She moved the toe of her shoe along the edge of a root. The silence went on and on. She could hear the woodpeckers again, tap, tap, tap.

'Har-ree!'

That was Bogey.

'Har-ree!' She raised her head.

'He-ah!'

Bogey came chasing round the corner of the house, past Victoria, past the swing.

'Here, Boge. I am here.'

'We are going to make bricks,' announced Bogey. ''n bake them in a n'oven, 'n build a tank for fishes. I have found some lovely mud. It is a little bit smelly, but you needn't mind. Come on, Harry.'

The gate opened and Bea came trotting up the drive on the white pony, Pearl. Bogey ran off and Harriet sped after him.

But when she reached the corner of the house she stopped and turned so fast that the short skirt of her dress whirled round her. She stood in the shadow of the poinsettias and looked back at Bea and Captain John. She saw how Captain John went up and put his hand on the pony's neck and then how Bea let him help her off as if she were a grown-up, not a child. Harriet stood, frowning a little by the poinsettias, then slowly she walked away to look at Bogey's mud.

*

Now Harriet began to think a great deal about Captain John.

What was wrong with him? Something was wrong. There was that emptiness in his eyes. Though he was loosed, among people again, he was not like other people, and he knew it. 'But he was strong enough not to die,' argued Harriet. He was strong enough to bear the unbearable pain, and the prison camp, and to escape, and to live in the hospital through all those operations when no one expected him to live, and to go on working every day with his troublesome wound and the weight of his leg. He could joke about it; he could be kind to Victoria, and in the same way to Nan; he could understand her, Harriet: he had this . . . 'this reverent,' said Harriet, wrinkling her brow to get the exact word, 'this reverent feeling for Bea'; and even someone as young as Harriet could sense he was no common thinker. There was no one she could talk to like Captain John. 'And he *ought* to talk to me,' said Harriet. 'When he talks to me he looks quite strong and rested. He doesn't when he talks to Bea.'

'You can't talk to her, can you?' she asked him.

'No,' he said irritably. 'She is too confoundedly polite.' That was the first time Harriet had ever heard a word against politeness, but she saw immediately that it was true.

But it was not Bea who was wrong with Captain John. It was something in him, himself. 'Or not in him,' she said slowly.

'Leave him alone,' said Nan.

'But I want to *do* something for him.'

'You can pray for him.'

'Oh *Nan!*'

'You can,' said Nan certainly, and then she added, as a warning, 'and, Harriet, you are not to do anything else.'

But Harriet, being Harriet, did, and was snubbed.

She went away with his snub stinging in her, into the

Secret Hole, where she sat down on her box, in the darkest shade. She sat holding her knees in her arms, her face turned down on them, and the stinging passed into a peculiar hurt. 'I – I hate him,' said Harriet, with clenched teeth.

Ayah came presently and found her. 'What is it, Harry Baba? What is it, Harriet Rajah?'

'I have a pain,' said Harriet, she did not know what else to call it.

Ayah began to rub her legs, though the pain, of course, was not in her legs. Harriet had had pains in her legs and arms recently that Nan called 'growing pains'. Now she felt as if she were being stretched to hold this one. This was not exactly a pain, though it hurt. It ached, but it was not like the ache she had had with dysentery, it was not sore, and it was not like toothache, that awful toothache she had when her tooth fell out. Analysing her pain, it began to go away, and she immediately forgot what it had been like.

Every family has its milestones; the first teeth come and the first teeth go; there is the first short hair-cut, the first braces, the first number one shoes, the first birthday in double figures. Events happen, too, which change families and family relations, and sometimes, often, one member is struck at more than another. Now, this feeling of pain, of hurt, had come to Harriet. This winter strange things seemed to be happening to her, eventful things. She felt herself growing and growing as she sat there in the gloom of the Secret Hole.

But soon she had regained her halcyon insouciance.

'Har-ee!'

'He-ah.'

'Get the scissors quick. Ram Prasad says the goldfish should have a worm and here is a worm, Harry. Cut him into bits, quick.'

'Harriet,' said Bogey, as they fed the fish. 'What do you

think, Harry? The cobra comes out into our side of the garden now.'

'*Bogey!*' said Harriet appalled. 'Have you seen it?'

Bogey nodded. His face was illumined.

'Wha – what is it like?'

'It is lovely. It slithers.'

'Ugh!' said Harriet, and she asked, 'How did you make it come?'

'I did what they did. I put down saucers of milk.'

'Ugh!' said Harriet. 'Oh Bogey!' and a quiver of sense, an antenna, lifted and pointed. 'Now I ought to tell Father. It is *in* the garden now.'

'But it is hardly ever in it,' said Bogey, earnestly. 'You can't say it is, Harriet. It lives the other side of the tree. That is where its hole is. It hardly ever comes out. Sometimes I watch for ages n'ages and it doesn't come.'

'Does Ram Prasad know?'

'No,' said Bogey absently. 'I don't *touch* it, Harry.' He added gently to himself so that even Harriet did not hear, his eyes bright and dreaming, 'I only poke it with a little bit of stick.'

Harriet was really too interested in herself to think about the cobra. She was hurt again. She was often hurt now. Things hurt her that would not have hurt her before, that she would have skimmed over without noticing. She was different. She was altogether puzzled, and on the afternoon of the second day she went to talk to Bea.

Bea was reading.

'Bea.'

Bea looked up. Her book was one of those books of Valerie's, *The Girls Own Annual* or *The Rose Book for Girls*, books that Harriet was not addicted to. Harriet liked *The Orange Fairy Book* and *Arabian Nights*. Or did she? Did she like anything? 'Bea,' she said, and Bea looked up but kept her finger on her place to let Harriet know that the interruption was to be only temporary, and Harriet, with Bea in that mood, could not talk about the nebulous things she had come to talk of. She had to think of something else, something important, if only to rivet Bea's attention.

She said, 'I have lumps.'

'Lumps?' asked Bea.

'Yes. On my chest. You know, my two chests, like swellings, and they hurt.'

'Those are your two little new breasts,' said Bea, and went on reading.

'Mine? But . . . I am too young.' Harriet shrank back into her frock. 'I am far too young,' she said, shocked.

'You can't be or they wouldn't come,' said Bea reasonably. 'They don't come until you are ready.'

That was interesting. Harriet looked down, inside her frock, at her chest. Her frock was of blue cotton and the light on her skin was therefore blue as well; her chest no longer had a plain bow; its topography had altered to two soft warm swellings, and in between them the skin was wonderfully tender, fine and silken. 'It is pretty,' said Harriet, looking down inside her frock. 'And my veins *are* blue. It isn't only the light.' That skin, those veins were older than Harriet. They were the sign of a woman. She was visibly growing. Were these signs something only for girls? she wondered, and she tried to think of something male which was a counterpart, a visible growth, like this, and she could only think of stags, of the antlers of a stag. 'I hurt rather like a stag,' she said. 'Like a stag's new antlers hurt. Have you got them, Bea?'

'What? Antlers?'

'Breasts.'

'Yes,' said Bea shortly.

'I never noticed them.'

'You never notice anything that isn't yourself,' said Bea,

which was largely true, though lately Harriet was noticing in this new acute way.

'Bea.'

'Do go away, Harry. I want to read.'

'But I want to talk . . . about you, Bea.'

'I hate talking about me.'

How odd, thought Harriet, who loved above all things to talk about herself.

It was true. Bea had slipped off from Harriet and a space was widening between them. They were still officially 'the big ones', while Bogey and Victoria were 'the little ones', but like most labels, these were not true. Harriet, if she played at all, played with Bogey nowadays, and the truth was, that the completeness went out of their play if Bea played too. 'Not in the doing games,' said Harriet to herself. 'She can still play those: rounders, and flying kites and "animal-mineral-vegetable".' They played rounders on the lawn with the young men from the Red House after a Sunday tea that had plum cake and chocolate tarts; for Harriet it always meant running when she was too full to run, Bogey had a curious inability to grasp what he was doing, Victoria was allowed to play by courtesy, but Bea really played, gracefully and competently. She was good at the game of flying kites too; that was, flying paper kites off the roof with strings glassed with ground glass, when you challenged other unknown kites, crossed strings with them and tried to cut them adrift; your kite wore a bob on its tail for every kite it cut. 'Animal-mineral-vegetable' was agony to Harriet, because she inevitably forgot in the middle and let her mind go off cantering free in questions of its own: What-would-I-feel-like-if-I-were-vegetable-scarlet-flower-flesh-or-if-I-were-silver-or-tin-with-tin-fingers-and-tin-toes-and-little-tin-ears-and-tin-hair? She saw her hair flashing with curls of shining tinfoil and, of course, she lost her place and Father called her a dunce. Bea was never a dunce at this, but she could not play 'being' games any more; being Rowena or a Cavalier, or Arabs or highwaymen or pirates, or even Minnehaha. Bea was still not bad as Minnehaha, not bad, but not really Minnehaha; it seemed she could not be anything but Bea just at present; and now . . . 'Am I going to be like this too?' asked Harriet.

As Bea grew into being only Bea, she grew mysteriously better-looking. She grew beautiful.

'What a beautiful child,' people said when they saw her.

Harriet and Bogey went behind a bush to discuss whether or not they would tell this to Bea.

'We don't want to make her conceited,' said Harriet and she did not know herself why she said that.

'Oh, tell her. Tell her. Tell her,' begged Bogey.

When they told Bea she did not become conceited. She seemed simply to take it as her due and to be unmoved by it, in a way that made Harriet feel breathless.

Now, as Bea was reading, Harriet took a long firm view of her. Over the edge of the bright blue-bound book, Harriet was impressed again by the withdrawn look on Bea's face, by its shape, oval and clear, with the clear modellings of the cheekbones under their soft skin, her straight small nose, and the fine lines of her eyebrows; as she read, looking down, her lashes were spread, fine and curled, along her lids, and her dark hair fell on to her shoulders. Round her neck, on a black ribbon, she was wearing a carved ivory rose, tinted pink; her skin was tinted in exactly the same way, pink on ivory.

Harriet went away and looked at herself in the glass.

'What are you doing, Harriet?' said Mother.

'I am wondering if I am as beautiful as Bea,' said Harriet.

'You have a little face full of character,' said Mother kindly, 'and you have nice eyes and hair.'

That means I am not, thought Harriet. She could see for herself that her face looked pink and commonplace after Bea's; it was speckled with freckles, it had a large nose, green-brown speckly eyes under tawny eyebrows, and something tawny and rampant in her hair. It is more like Bogey's face, thought Harriet. But no, it is not even as nice as Bogey's. Bogey has such dear little bones. He is more like Bea, really. No, mine is nothing, nothing at all, like hers.

'Why do I want to be pretty suddenly?' asked Harriet, and she did not know. Certainly she had never bothered about it before, but then she had never bothered about anything very much. What is the matter with me? thought Harriet. Why do I keep on having these . . . cracks? Why is everything suddenly so funny?

She was unhappy again in rifts, in, as she called them, cracks: for ten minutes, or for a minute only, or for a whole half hour. 'It isn't fair,' said Harriet in a temper, 'for a family not to be the same. To be half ugly and half pretty, to grow up at different times,' complained Harriet. With all she felt, and truly felt, another part of her was watching and found it interesting. She watched herself when she went to brood in the Secret Hole, when she went to sit on the jetty or under the cork tree. 'I give up,' said Harriet crossly, but the other part of her was far too interested to give up.

Meanwhile she was separating from Bea. Bea had passed into a kind of upper society with Valerie or Captain John. Harriet used to overhear them talking; she listened, not to Valerie of course, but to Captain John.

'What is the name of those flowers?' He was always asking Bea the names of flowers. He did not appear to be able to remember any for himself, or to know the commonest flower names. He went on asking them. I believe he likes doing it, thought Harriet, and she marvelled that

Bea never lost patience or let him know she knew he was pretending.

'What is the name of those flowers?'

'Petunias,' said Bea.

He bent down to smell one. 'They remind me of you,' he said to Bea. 'No, you remind me of them, one of those purple ones,' he said, 'or a white one.'

Bea took it with the same calmness, almost with primness, but Harriet was dizzy. They are both behaving like grown-up people, she thought indignantly, or they are both behaving like children. Why? And then Captain John turned and said, 'Why don't you go away and play, Harriet. Don't tag on to me all the time.'

Harriet became scarlet to the tips of her ears. 'I don't . . . tag,' she said in a muffled voice. 'I was only here, that is all,' and she rushed away, up the side stairs to the Secret Hole and cast herself down on the floor. 'I hate him. I hate him,' said Harriet, again, crying into the floor.

Her tears fell into the dust and it mingled with the tears on her face. When she came out Nan said she was not fit to be seen, and made her have her tea in the nursery.

'I warned you,' said Nan.

Harriet hunched her shoulders.

'If I were you,' said Nan, 'I should keep to playing with Bogey.'

'I am too big to play with Bogey,' said Harriet angrily.

'You are too small for Captain John,' said Nan.

*

More and more Harriet was thrust with Bogey, and this meant, usually, being alone. Whatever she started to do with Bogey, he eventually and cheerfully left her alone. After a few minutes, she would look up, and there would be no Bogey.

They were beginning to find that out in lessons. Bogey

had just started lessons. 'He really must learn to read,' said Mother. 'It is disgraceful, at his age, not to be able to read.'

Why had no one taught him to read before? Because he defied them completely. Yet he was not naughty. He was perfectly docile.

'M.A.T. Bogey?'

'Mat.'

'F.A.T. Bogey?'

'Fat.'

'C.A.T. Bogey?'

'Cat.'

'R.A.T. Bogey?'

'Sailor' and Bogey was entirely absent. Nor could they get him back.

'Why did the Ancient Britons find it so hard to make their boats, Bogey?'

'Because they had to make the inside bigger than the outside,' said Bogey gravely, his eyes on the sky.

He was not capable of being made to feel guilty, like Harriet, who knew she dreamed. He simply removed himself, and they were tired of the chase long before he was caught.

'One day you will have to learn to read,' said Harriet. 'Imagine a man who couldn't go to the office, nor sign letters, nor read newspapers.'

'I am not going to be any of those men,' said Bogey. 'I am not ready to learn to read.'

'You can't always do what you like, you know,' said Harriet, who was still feeling sore and angry.

'I can,' said Bogey. 'I always do.' That was true. He always did, and if he found trouble he kept it to himself. Once he fell down the back stairs and broke his front teeth. He never told anyone till Nan saw his swollen lips. Once he set his sock alight when he was cooking on a secret fire. He put out the sock and tied a rag on the burn. He never told. It was of no use. Bogey was no companion. Harriet still needed Bea. She could not, in any ultimate move, do without Bea. Bea still had to be her mentor, her help and her confidante, her guide and her public opinion. She tried to bid for her attention; or now, better than Bea, Captain John.

She painted a picture; it was of a lotus on blue water, and when it was done, looking at it critically, she could see that it was nothing like a lotus, it was more like a pig in bluish mud. She did not show that to Bea. 'I am not a painting person,' said Harriet. 'I am a writer,' and she tried for a little while to recapture the status of the poem she had written under the cork tree; she wrote a book, at least the beginnings of a book, and it kept her happy for some days. Then she showed it to Bea, who had not any great desire to look at it.

And they had four children, read the reluctant Bea, *called Olive, Bice, Emerald and Spinach, all green as grass and slimy.*

'Queer children!' commented Bea.

'This is a book about frogs,' said Harriet huffily.

'Well, you should say so.'

'You are supposed to understand that from reading the book.'

'Well, *I* didn't,' said Bea.

It was no good. This was a thoroughly tiresome time, and Harriet could not do anything with it.

*

It was nearly Christmas. 'It must be a quiet Christmas,' said Mother as she had said about the winter. 'A quiet Christmas, and you must be content with little presents.'

The war again, thought Harriet angrily. She wanted Christmas to have its full panoply, she wanted the right to be happy and excited without this horrible onus of caring about other people, the hungry children, the wounded soldiers, the women left without husbands and fathers. 'And even if there isn't a war, it is just the same,' she said. 'There are always hurt people and starved people, and beaten people and misery.'

'And there are always the people who don't care,' said Bea.

'Well, I care really. I have to,' said Harriet.

'Of course you care,' said Captain John, and he smiled kindly at her. Now Harriet came to think of it, he did not often smile, and when he did . . . Why, he most often smiles at me, thought Harriet dazzled. Not at Bea, nor Victoria; at me, at something I say or do. It is as if he couldn't help smiling then. Yes, I am the one who makes him smile.

'Do you ever feel you want to fight again, Captain John?' asked Valerie.

'No,' said Captain John curtly.

'When I am grown up,' said Harriet, 'I am not going to fight in wars. I am going to fight the people who make wars.'

'Is that any better?' asked Bea. 'Everyone seems to be always fighting and fighting, and it doesn't do any good. If I were a man, I should be one of those people who say they won't fight.'

'I wonder if you would,' said Captain John.

'Why, didn't you?' asked Bea. It was seldom she asked a point-blank question, especially of Captain John, and he answered it with the seriousness it deserved.

'I wanted to . . . but I couldn't trust myself.'

'How – not?' asked Harriet, puzzled, 'if you wanted to.'

'At the last pinch,' said Captain John, 'at the last pinch I think I should have been angry and fought to save myself – and it is no use unless you can go through that last pinch.'

They did not understand.

'But what good does it do?' asked Bea. 'Fighting?'

'Well, that is not the only point,' said Captain John slowly.

'Why not? What other point could there be?'

'It is something,' he said, 'to believe enough to die for that belief. Perhaps it is more than something, perhaps it is everything – to – aspire – to try.'

'Yes,' breathed Harriet. 'Like martyrs.'

'I think the martyrs were stupid,' said Bea. 'I think soldiers are too. Fighting is stupid.'

'Perhaps it is,' said Captain John. 'But perhaps that is neither here nor there. Perhaps the thing is, to believe.'

'And get killed for it?'

'If necessary.'

'I think so,' said Harriet. 'If I were brave enough . . . only I wouldn't be,' she said. 'But I believe in things.'

'Oh you!' said Valerie. 'You will believe in anything.'

'That is better than believing in nothing,' said Captain John.

'Is it?' said Bea.

'Yes.'

'I don't think so,' said Bea.

'I do,' said Captain John.

Harriet stared at them. They were quarrelling.

They had been having tea in the garden, in fact Victoria, who ate inordinately, had still not finished and Nan was pouring out more milk for her. Harriet had left the table early and come to stand under the cork tree, listening to the woodpeckers, while she decided what she would do with the rest of the afternoon. Bea came after her, Captain John came after Bea and Valerie had brought a chair for Captain John. Valerie's fussing and homage annoyed him. It was true it took him ages to lower himself on to the grass, but it is better to let him take ages than to notice him, thought Harriet, and now, he held on to the chair and deliberately let himself down to sit with them on the grass.

Harriet began to build a fence of twigs. Somewhere, in the distance, she could hear Bogey hallooing. Bea sat with her legs curled under her, sitting sideways into her white skirts that were patterned with a pattern of old rose stencillings. Harriet's dress was the same, except that it was patterned with China blue; that difference changed its whole character, it looked merely crisp and fresh, while Bea's . . . 'looks like . . . poetry,' said Harriet. Why are some colours filled with poetry and others not? 'Why can't *I* choose my clothes?' she had said to Mother. 'Why can't I wear what I like?' 'Now Harriet,' began Mother, 'you are very nicely and suitably dressed . . . ' Harriet sighed.

The quarrel was continuing.

'Your ideas are so . . . unsteady,' said Bea to Captain John. Once more they were like two children, or two grown-ups, and that isn't Bea's word, thought Harriet. She learnt that from Father. 'So . . . unsteady,' said Bea.

'Are they?' said Captain John. 'Once they were burningly steady.'

That silenced Bea and moved Harriet. She stopped her play with the twigs and put her hand on his knee. It was the knee of his artificial leg, but he seemed to feel it. 'Won't they ever be again?' asked Harriet.

'No. I don't think they will,' he said, looking down at her hand. It was a little dusty from the twigs, but he did not tell her to take it away.

'I think they will,' said Harriet.

'Valerie,' said Bea getting up, 'come and practise,' and she and Valerie walked away, arm-in-arm, linked together. Presently the not-quite-synchronized sounds of their new duet came down to the garden from upstairs. Harriet looked down at the grass because she knew that Captain John cared. The silence, broken only by the duet, grew too long.

'You shouldn't care,' said Harriet severely, speaking into the grass. 'You are a man and she is a little girl.'

'If I were ninety and she were nine, or the other way round, it would be all the same,' said Captain John. She could hear him breathing.

'Do you – love her?' asked Harriet, digging with her finger in the grass.

'Yes and no,' said Captain John. 'Never mind, Harriet,' and he added, 'There are some things you understand better than Bea,' and he said, speaking lightly, 'We can't change her.'

That was true. Bea would not change. Under her charm and softness she was adamant, and people never guessed how adamant she was because she was resilient. 'I expect you find Harriet the difficult one,' they said to Nan, and Nan shook her head and pursed her lips. With the deadly knowledge that old servants have, Nan could have told a thing or two of Bea, though she never did. 'Bea is by far, far, the most difficult,' was all that Nan would say.

'She knitted more Red Cross scarves than any of us,' said Harriet now, and then she added truthfully, 'But it was because she wanted to be the best at knitting,' but she did not say that aloud because after all Bea was as good a sister as could be expected.

She tilted her head and looked up through the branches of the cork tree to see the clouds moving and the house and tree tilting back against the clouds.

'Funny,' said Harriet to herself. 'The world goes on turning, and it has all these troubles in it.' She looked down the garden to the tea-table, where Victoria still sat. Horrible-wounds-and-milk-and-bread-and-butter-and-loving-and-quarrelling-and-wars. What was a quarrel but a little war?

And there were wars all over the world. They have even come in here, thought Harriet, looking at the big stone house that was her home. But, thought Harriet, this *is* the world.

The sound of playing had stopped and there was no sign of Valerie and Bea. That probably meant they had gone up on the roof; the roof was a favourite place for walking or pacing; its flatness and its four parapets like walls were restful; there you could not see anything but the sky and the hawks circling and a few bright dots of paper kites. If you climbed up on the parapet, of course, you saw the whole wide vista of the land: town-river-boats-trees-works-Ram-Prasad's-little-house-by-the-gate-the-faraway-temple-another-temple-across-the-river, thought Harriet. Climbing up on the parapet was forbidden, but she and Bogey climbed.

Every family has something, when it has left home, that is for it a symbol of home, that, for it, for ever afterwards, brings home back. It may be a glimpse of the dappled flank of a rocking-horse, a certain pattern of curtain, of firelight shining on a brass fender, of light on the rim of a plate; it may be a saying, sweet or sharp, like: '*It will only end in tears.*' '*Do you think I am made of money?*' '*It is six of one and half a dozen of the other*'; it may be a song or a sound; the sound of a lawn-mower, or the swish of water, or of birds singing at dawn; it may be a custom (every family has different customs), or a taste: of a special pudding or burnt treacle tart or dripping toast; or it may be scent or a smell: of flowers, or furniture polish or cooking, toffee or sausages, or saffron bread or onions or boiling jam. These symbols are all that are left of that lost world in our new one. There was no knowing what would remain afterwards of hers for Harriet.

Being European in India, the flavour of Harriet's home was naturally different from most; it was not entirely European, it was not entirely Indian; it was a mixture of both. The house was a large oblong of grey stucco, flat-roofed, its parapet ornamented with those improbable daisies. The river ran past its garden and the tree rose high in front of its serpentine drive.

It was a double-floored house, with long verandahs. The rooms were all high, cavernous, stone-floored and white-washed; shaded by the verandahs, they were always dim, though the end rooms had green-shuttered windows. For nine months of the year electric fans moved the upper air. They did not at first appear the kind of rooms that made a home, but Harriet's home was a peculiarly pleasant place.

On the ground floor was the dining-room, red-floored, pillared, with large pictures in large frames, reproductions of Gainsboroughs, Reynolds and Romneys. The dining-table was oval and capable of taking extra leaves; at night it had an embroidered cloth and pink-shaded candelabra above its bowl of roses or pink sandwich creeper; those candles always woke excitement in Harriet. There was also a barrel, hooped with brass, that had once held salt meat on a sailing ship; now it was used for drinks and the children could just manage to raise the lid and all of them, often, had small secret swigs. There was the high chair that even Victoria had outgrown, and there were Father's silver cups, won by his charger Maxim when he was a younger man in the Bengal Volunteer Horse; there, too, were all the children's christening mugs.

On one side of the dining-room was Father's room; it had his desk, papers, cupboards, his two guns, the telephone and Sally's, his fox-terrier's, basket. At the other end of the house on the ground floor was the double nursery with its battered furniture, the children's own personal bookshelves and small wicker armchairs and the Millais pictures that had been in Mother's nursery. Nan's bed, Bogey's and Victoria's cot were at the back of the room in a row and there was an ironing-board where the iron seemed perpetually heated. Nan's red lamp burnt in front of the holy picture over her chest of drawers; she always kept a sprig of jasmine in her vase. The guinea-pigs' cage, the rocking-horse and the scooters that no one ever touched, were out on the veranda.

Upstairs was Mother's bedroom where she and Father slept and where anything private and serious in the family was discussed: 'talks', and what Mother called 'reasoning' and whippings; temperatures were taken there, the doctor examined throats and chests and ears and stomachs. Harriet, Bogey and Victoria had all been born in that bedroom.

Next door was Harriet's and Bea's room and their two white beds from which they talked at night; next door to that again was the drawing-room.

The drawing-room was always confused for Harriet; there were so many things in it, both objects and happenings, that she could never remember it exactly. It was a large room and one end of it was left almost bare, with its green floor holding only the piano and the music rack and a tiger skin with a snarling head on the wall. The other end of the drawing-room was furnished very thoroughly with chairs and couches, bookcases and a cabinet, a fireseat and, in the centre, a low brass tea-table on carved wooden legs. The tea caddy was tortoiseshell and very old; it stood on the mantelpiece with the Worcester cups and a tiny Dresden china cup that belonged to Bogey. Harriet never knew why it should belong to Bogey. Mother's writing-table held a pile of account books, and notes, and catalogues. There was a sweet-pea chintz on the chairs and real sweet peas in bowls, or else sweet sultans and gypsophila, or else, when it was getting hot, vases of tuberoses. There were small rubbed leather books that were sets of the classics, Scott and Thackeray and Dickens, and there was a scrapbook made for Harriet's grandmother when she was a child. The cabinet held a compendium of games.

The house had three staircases, a main one of dark wood, a side one painted white under which was the Secret Hole, and a back one for the servants which the children were not allowed to use, though Bogey and Harriet used it. Double flights of stone steps led from the downstairs veranda into the garden at the front of the house. The kitchen and the servants' quarters were outside, and there were stables, a washerman's yard, an electric-light-machine shed, a garage, and the porter's, Ram Prasad's, house beside the gate.

'It is more comfortable than anywhere on earth,' Harriet would have said of her home. It had fitted her like her own skin, but just lately she had come to see it more critically and more clearly. 'Is it that I am getting old?' wondered Harriet. 'I am getting old, look at my little breasts. Or is it Valerie and Captain John?' And she added honestly, 'It is something to do with knowing Valerie and Captain John.'

Certainly, since she had known them, everything in the house had been thrown into sharper focus, but then they, particularly Captain John, had coincided in a curious way with her growing up. Had she grown up because of them? She could not tell, but she knew now, for instance, that her parents had not as much money as Valerie's. Her eyes had been opened to contrasts: Valerie's clothes and their own home-made handed-down dresses; Nan and Valerie's travelling governess; Harriet's family had no car, they had only one child's pony. 'When the cradles fill,' said Harriet's father, 'the stables empty.' Of course we do have a lot of children, thought Harriet, but we have no Persian rugs, no wine at dinner, no ice cream, and when we go for picnics we don't have a basket with plates and cups and everything to match. 'Yes. I suppose we are poor,' said Harriet. 'Compared to Valerie . . . we haven't been anywhere, and we don't know anything at all.'

She felt crushed. Captain John raised his head.

'What is the matter, Harry?'

'I was thinking – of us – our family.'

'And what did you think of it?'

'Not very much,' answered Harriet.

'Then I will tell you what I think,' he said. 'I think you are the very best family I have ever known.'

'D-do you?'

'Yes, I do. And don't you forget it,' said Captain John.

Something fell with a small soft plop on Harriet's head. It was a cork-tree flower just breaking into cream petals from its bud.

'Look,' cried Harriet in an excess of happiness. 'Look. That means that it is nearly Christmas. The tree is always in flower for Christmas.' Her face clouded. 'But it can't be as good a Christmas this year,' she said.

'It may be the best you have ever had,' said Captain John.

*

Of the families who keep Christmas, some keep it rather more, some rather less. Harriet's family kept it implicitly.

Besides the cork tree, the chrysanthemums were always out for Christmas; their scent was a part of it, like the smell of the withering fir tree and of hot candle wax and raisins and tangerines. Any of those scents, for ever afterwards, filled Harriet with the brand of quivering excitement she had known as a child at Christmas.

Their Bengali Christmas had its own brand too; it was always perfect weather, the weather of a cool fresh summer day. The day began the night before, as Bogey said, with carols and hanging up stockings; that led to the opening of stockings the next morning and early church in the Masonic

Lodge (the town had no church) where the gardeners gave each person, even children, a bunch of violets wired with ferns. Then the merchants and clerks of the works and the district came to call on Father with baskets of fruit and flowers and vegetables and nuts and whisky and Christmas cakes decorated with white icing, tinsel and pink-paper roses. The servants' children came to see the tree and be given crackers, oranges and four-anna pieces. The young men from the Red House came to lunch and in the evening there was a Christmas tree.

All this happened every year, but there was, besides this, a thread of holiness, a quiet and pomp that seemed to Harriet to have in it the significance of the Wise King's gold. It linked Christmas with something larger than itself, something as large as . . . ? Harriet thought it was a largeness that had something to do with the river, that began as a trickle and ended in the sea. Afterwards she wondered if this feeling in Christmas came from Nan. This year, as the time drew on and there was much less of everything, less buying and hiding and writing and planning, it was there again and it was more pronounced.

Bogey did not want anything for Christmas.

'But you must,' said Harriet. 'You must have something. Mother didn't mean you to have nothing.'

'But I want nothing,' said Bogey obstinately.

'You can't want nothing. You must want something.'

'But I don't. I have what I want.'

'You must want new things,' argued Harriet.

'I don't like new things. I like what I have.'

'What have you?' Bogey did not know. 'You haven't anything. You buried all your soldiers.'

'If I get any more I shall bury those,' said Bogey darkly.

'Pooh! You only like insects and horrid snakes.'

'Harry,' said Bogey, his face changing. 'I have been thinking. You know how the snake-charmers play on their pipe things? Well, I am going to play on my whistle. You know my whistle that Captain John gave me? I am going to play like a charmer on that. My snake might like it.'

This was the season for snake-charmers. This was the time they came walking through the East Bengal towns and villages, black-skinned men with beards, dressed in dark orange clothes. They carried a pole on their shoulders, and from each end of the pole hung down a loop of cloth in which were round shallow baskets that would just hold the coils of a snake. Baskets were piled on baskets, but many of the snakes were great worms, harmless and thick and stupid, not like a cobra with its strong strike and beauty and interesting wickedness. Very often the snake-man would have a mongoose, tied around the neck with a cord, its little red eyes gleaming. The mongoose would be put to stage a fight with a snake. I wish we had a mongoose here, thought Harriet, and he would kill that cobra. 'I don't think you ought to play with it, Bogey,' said Harriet aloud.

'It – doesn't come now. I think it has gone,' said Bogey quickly, but he lied.

The snake-man's pipe was a pipe on a gourd that made a sound like a bagpipe, sinuous and mournful. Bogey's whistle sounded merely hopeful after it.

'Why do you want to whistle if it has gone?' said Harriet sternly.

His eyes flickered. 'Oh . . . just 'cos.'

'If a snake-charmer hears about your snake,' said Harriet, 'he will come and take it away. They are always looking for cobras. You had better take care.'

'I should like to be a snake-charmer,' said Bogey dreamily.

Harriet was tired and cross with her own preparations, which were always elaborate and always caused her family a good deal of tribulation before they were given.

'And what are *you* giving, Victoria?' she asked.

'I?' said Victoria, surprised. 'Nothing.'

'But *Victoria*, you must give people things.'

'Must I?'

'Yes. You can't take things and not give them.'

'But I like taking, not giving,' said Victoria contentedly.

Bea had made a handkerchief for Captain John and hemmed it with even small stitches and competently embroidered his initials in the corner. 'But – I haven't anything nice to give him,' wailed Harriet.

'Why should you give him anything?' said Mother calmly. 'He is more Bea's friend than yours.'

Harriet knew that, but for some reason, to hear Mother say it, filled her with a storm of torment and rage. 'I – I – hate Bea!' she cried, but fortunately Mother had gone out of earshot and Harriet was left to swallow it alone.

All her auguries were for a miserable Christmas, but still that holy quiet persisted, even in her, and beside she had a secret, a secret iron in the fire. She tried to be gloomy about that too, but she could not; the warmth of her secret persisted in the quiet.

Every year Nan made a crib with a set of old German figures of the Nativity. They were of painted wood, older than Nan knew. Harriet could never see them without a great fascination, and now, when they were brought out of their boxes, ten days before Christmas, to stand in their cave of moss and sawdust lit by candles, Harriet's imagination was touched again. In her restlessness and unhappiness they touched her so deeply that a familiar urge rose up in her. 'I am going to write about them,' said Harriet suddenly. 'What shall I write about them? A Carol? A hymn? An Opera,' thought Harriet modestly. 'Or an "Ode to the Three Wise Men"?' But there were so many odes.

There was a blue angel kneeling with a lap full of roses. Her legs and her face were salmon pink, she had a gilt halo with blue in its diadem and she was always the one Harriet remembered best, for the expression of pain and smugness on her face. She looked as if she had a remarkable headache. What is the matter with her? thought Harriet now as she had thought every Christmas. Is she too good? she wondered. Why does she pull that face? And an idea came to her and filled her mind, so that she went straight away into the Secret Hole and wrote down her idea in her book. It took most of the day, but when it was finished and she read it over, she was not surprised as she had been when she read her poem; she was tickled and delighted, as she had thought she would be. 'Good,' said Harriet, biting her pencil. (She bit her pencils so badly that Nan said her inside must be like the floor of a carpenter's shop.) Now, as she remembered to take her pencil out of her mouth, a second idea, an idea of what to do with her idea, came to her, and this was of such dimensions that she was dazzled. 'But – could I?' asked Harriet. 'How could I?' and she looked doubtfully at the pencil-writing in her round handwriting in the book. 'Could I?' and then her face and her voice hardened. 'I could,' said Harriet. 'I shall.'

Captain John was staying with them for Christmas. She went to find Captain John.

'Come into Father's office,' said Harriet to him. 'I want to speak to you.'

He obligingly came, but like Bea, he kept his finger in his book. 'Put your book down,' said Harriet. 'I need you.'

'But—' he said. 'But—' he said again when she had explained.

'It is no use saying "but",' said Harriet firmly, and she began to uncover Father's typewriter that she was forbidden to touch. 'You can type,' she said. 'You said you could. This must catch tomorrow's steamer. And you must write a letter for me too.'

'But – the *Speaker* is a grown-ups' paper,' objected Captain John.

'This is a grown-ups' story,' said Harriet. 'And they do put things like this in at Christmas-time.'

'Yes. But . . . you are far too late. They choose articles for their Christmas number weeks before.'

'They may have kept a little space,' argued Harriet. 'And mine may be so much better than the things they have, that they may put it in after all.'

'That isn't very likely,' said Captain John.

'No, but it is possible,' said Harriet.

He put out his hand for her story as he had for her poem once before. Harriet gave him the book and waited, quiveringly expectant.

'*The Halo that was too Tight*,' read Captain John. He glanced up at Harriet with a twinkle in his eyes and down again. '*An angel complained that her halo was too tight.*' He read on and his lips twitched, and once he laughed.

When he had finished it he did not say anything, except, 'Very well, I will type it for you,' but he gave her shoulder a small squeeze.

'I expect I am a nuisance,' said Harriet humbly.

'Yes. You are,' he said, sitting down to the typewriter.

'I expect you will have to alter the spelling a bit, if you don't mind,' said Harriet happily.

'I expect I will,' said Captain John.

On occasions, very occasionally, things happen as you feel they will, as you feel in your bones they will. Once or twice more in her life, Harriet was to know that calm certainty, that power of will, and have it answered. She was quite right to be certain. There was a surety of touch in that small story; it was small to change, to crystallize and confirm, as it did, Harriet's whole life, but she had known it could not go wrong, and on Christmas morning, when the mail bag was brought in to Father as they were having breakfast, he stopped as he looked over the letters and said, 'Why, Harriet. There is one for you.' Then he looked at it more closely. 'It can't be for her,' he said. 'It is from the *Speaker*. There must be a mistake,' and he was raising his knife to slit it open when Harriet called out in agony, 'But it is for me. Don't open it, Father. It is for me. I . . . I am expecting it.'

Everyone turned to look at her.

Father, still doubtful, handed it to her, and now she learned what facing an inquisition meant; no one spoke; they waited for her to open it. The envelope was buff coloured, addressed in typescript; in its corner was printed, *Speaker Ltd., Speaker House, Calcutta*. The blood began to drum oddly in Harriet's ears. I-expect-I-am-sure-it-is-only-to-say-it-is-no-good-to-send-it-back, she thought rapidly to herself. She wanted to hide the envelope quickly in her hand and rush away with it and open it by herself.

'Go on. Open it, Harriet,' said Father. 'We are dying of curiosity.'

Harriet gave one appealing glance at Mother and opened it. A typed letter and pink cheque form fluttered out.

'*Harriet*! What have you been up to,' said Mother sternly.

'I haven't been up to anything,' said Harriet. 'I – I don't understand what it says.' And she burst into tears.

It was quite true. Father read the letter aloud, and then Captain John came limping in with a paper in his hand. Harriet's story had been there all the time in the folded Christmas edition of the *Speaker* by Father's plate. 'Well. I am absolutely damned!' said Father.

The rest of the day passed in bliss. 'I never want it to end,' said Harriet, and when it had run its full gamut it stayed, still perfect, in her mind. 'It will stay with me for ever,' she said. 'It is my new beginning. Today I have been born again,' said Harriet, 'as Captain John said.'

Father had cut the story out and pasted it into his scrapbook. He showed Harriet what he had written. *Harriet's first published work*, and the date. 'First!' With the feeling of elation there came to Harriet a feeling of responsibility. She had avowed herself. She had signed herself away. It was public now. She was different. With all the glory, she wished she could have kept herself a secret.

That night she could not sleep. She was too excited to sleep. She lay listening to the pulse of the steam escape and to the river; she looked out through the doors, where Mother had left the curtains looped, where the light was clear moon blue. There must be a moon, thought Harriet. I can see branches, but I can't see the top of the tree. I wonder . . . What she wondered she did not say. From Bea's bed there came the sound of a sob. She listened. There came another.

'Bea!'

Instant silence.

'Bea. Are you crying?'

Silence.

'Bea. You are crying.'

No answer.

Harriet left her bed and went across in her nightgown to Bea's. It was cold and Bea made no move to let her in, but she remained sitting on the edge of Bea's bed. It was shaken slightly up and down every second. Bea was crying.

'Are you – feeling sick?'

No answer.

'Is it – because – is it anything to do with today?'

No answer.

'Did anyone get angry with you?'

Only a shake in the bed.

'Is it Valerie?' asked Harriet angrily.

'No.'

'Is it . . . Bea, is it because I wrote the story and you didn't?'

'Of *course* not!'

'Is it – is it anything to do with Captain John?' said Harriet delicately.

Silence and complete stillness.

'What is it about him, Bea?'

'It is – it is—'

'You made up your quarrel, didn't you?'

'It – wasn't a – real – quarrel.'

'Shall I call Mother?' asked Harriet out of her depth.

'N-no. W-we mustn't d-disturb her. You kn-know that.'

'But you can't go on crying,' said Harriet.

Bea made an effort to be quiet. She sat up, but the sobs began again.

'Tell, Bea.'

'He . . . he is . . . going away,' said Bea, in a rush, without any breath.

'Is he?' said Harriet stunned. 'Going away,' and she went on repeating 'Going away. Going away,' till the words felt like two hammers hitting a sore place. 'Ouch!' said Harriet, wincing.

'Yes. He is going away. We sh-shan't see him any more.'

'No,' agreed Harriet. 'Then we shan't.' She sat on the bed feeling more sore, more than ever cold and separated. 'But not yet, Bea,' she said, 'not yet. Not now.'

'No, not yet,' said Bea, but she cried as hard as ever.

'Bea, don't cry so hard. Don't, Bea. He isn't going yet.'

'I am not crying because he is going,' said Bea. 'I am crying because . . . '

'Because?'

'Because *it* is going,' said Bea in another rush.

'It? What "it", Bea?'

'It is all going so quickly,' said Bea. 'Too quickly. It is going far too fast.'

'Mmm,' said Harriet, beginning to understand.

67

'Much too quickly and too fast,' cried Bea. 'It is all changing, and I don't w-want it to change.'

'But it hasn't changed,' said Harriet. As she said that she knew that it was false. How much had changed even since this morning? Everything had changed.

'I like it to stay as it is,' said Bea. 'I don't want this to end, ever. I want it to stay like this always, but it won't.'

'No, it won't.' Harriet had to agree again sadly. There was nothing else for her to do.

'We can't keep it, and today was so l-lovely – happy.' Bea's head went down in her pillow again. 'I want to be like this for ever and ever,' she cried.

So did Harriet. She sat hurt and cold and silent on Bea's bed until Bea put out a hand to her. 'Don't you stay, Harry,' she said. 'There isn't anything we can do, you're c-cold. Your hand feels like a frog.'

Harriet crept, cold and helpless, back to bed, but long after Bea was quiet, she lay awake. She thought Bea was awake too, and this was the first time they had ever lain awake without talking. The day was gone. However they might lie awake and cry or ache, they could not claim it back again. Who was it who had said you could not stop days or rivers? Harriet could hear the river running in the dark, that was not really dark but moonlight. She shivered. In six or seven weeks perhaps he will go away. She tried to make herself believe that, but it did not seem, nor feel, true. What will Bea feel then? wondered Harriet. Will she feel worse than I shall? In books people are happy for ever and for ever. But those books are nonsense. Nothing is for ever and for ever, thought Harriet. It all goes away. But does it? Again she was struck by a doubt. Does it all go, be lost and ended – or in some way do you have it still? Could that be true? 'Is everything a bit true?' she had said to Captain John. Then she lost that hope. No. It is gone, thought Harriet. I didn't notice it before, but now I see. I see it – horribly. Why didn't I see it before? Because I was little? And aloud she said, 'Bea. Are you asleep?'

'No,' said Bea.

'Bea, does it show you are getting old?'

'Does what? I do wish, Harry, you wouldn't think in between the things you say. As Valerie says, how do you expect us to understand?'

Bea was cross, but Harriet persisted.

'What are the signs of getting old – like us?' asked Harriet.

'Lots of things I expect,' answered Bea wearily. 'Do you want to know now?'

'Yes.'

'Growing up, of course—'

'Growing pains?' asked Harriet.

'I suppose so. Learning more. Being more with Mother and less with Nan; not liking playing so much, nor pretending; understanding things more and feeling them longer; wearing liberty bodices; and oh, yes,' said Bea, 'I remember when we came down from Darjeeling this year, finding everything had grown far more little than I expected. When I went away it all seemed so big. When I came back, it was little; and I suppose,' said Bea slowly, 'being friends with Captain John has made me old.'

I am not so far behind all that, thought Harriet to herself.

*

Soon after that conversation with Bea, that talking of growing, Mother sent for them.

'Harriet and Bea. Mother wants to speak to you – in her room.'

'What about?' said Bea instantly and suspicious.

'She didn't tell me,' said Nan smoothly.

'But Nan knows,' said Harriet to Bea. Bea shrugged her shoulders.

It was January. The Christmas holidays were over and life had entered on the second lap of the cold weather. Lessons had begun. The begonia venustra creeper in the garden and along the front of the house was out in orange-keyed flowers. The cork tree had its full spread of blossom. There was, all day long, a smell of honey in the garden and of honey in the fields where the mustard was in flower. It was still cool; there were still cold morning mists that blew over the garden at dawn and gathered on the river. The excitement was all over. Life had settled to its tenor. Harriet's story, with other happenings, had lost its point of interest and been fined down by the passing of the days until now the family took it for granted.

'I want to talk to you,' said Mother. 'I think you are old enough to have this talk with me.'

Harriet, as a matter of fact, was not at all old that morning. She looked down, as she sat, at her brown scratched knees with their sprinkling of golden hairs, and at the shortness of her green-and-white checked gingham dress. The dress bore all the stains and marks of that morning's experiences: papaya-juice-from-breakfast-Prussi-an-blue-from-painting-the-Sea-of-Azov-a-little-torn-hole-from-climbing-trees-a-long-mark-from-falling-down-while-chasing-Bogey-on-the-dewy-lawn.

Mother was looking at the dress too. 'What have you been doing, Harriet?'

Harriet hung her head. 'Playing.'

'A big girl like you! Perhaps you had better not stay,' said Mother. 'Perhaps you are not old enough. I will talk to Bea.'

Bea sat with a stony face, her shoulders hunched. She said nothing.

'Oh, Mother, please let me stay. I am old enough, really I am. It is only sometimes, when I play with Bogey. Mother, let me stay.'

Mother looked at Bea and Bea looked resentfully at the floor. Mother sighed. 'Well,' she said with another glance at Bea, 'perhaps you had better stay.'

Then there was complete silence, with only the regular steam puff from the Works and the steady sound of the river.

'You are getting to be big girls now,' said Mother.

Another silence. Bea sat stiff, withdrawn as far as she could be. Harriet began to be agog.

'Every day you grow a little more,' said Mother.

'Willy-nilly,' said Harriet suddenly.

Bea shot an angry glance at her from under her eyebrows, but Mother smiled. 'Yes, exactly,' she said. 'Willy-nilly. Soon, sooner than we guess perhaps, you will become women.'

'Yes, I suppose we will,' said Harriet.

'I don't know,' said Mother, 'I have never asked you how much you both know about – life.'

'Life?' asked Harriet puzzled.

'Babies being born,' said Bea shortly, breathing through her nose.

'Everything,' said Harriet with certainty.

'Not only babies,' said Mother, and waited. Then she asked, 'You, Bea?'

'A little,' said Bea reluctantly.

'Well—' said Mother. She sighed again. 'We had better begin from the beginning . . . You know it is the women who bear the babies, carry them in their bodies – as I am doing.'

'Yes, Mother,' said Harriet, and she and Bea both averted their eyes from Mother.

'We – women have to make our bodies fit for that,' said Mother. 'Like a temple.'

'A *temple*?' asked Harriet surprised.

'Yes,' said Mother. But still it did not seem quite certain, the idea did not quite fit.

'Because you see, Harriet, the bearing of children, for the man you love, and who loves you, is very precious and sanctified work.'

'Do you love Father?' asked Harriet immediately.

'Yes,' said Mother, 'I am glad to say I do.'

At that small statement, typical of her mother, the conversation became suddenly and intimately true. Harriet felt a surge of love for her. She put her hand on Mother's knee and Mother pressed her hand, but Bea still sat aloof, still as if she were angry.

Harriet was unable to prevent herself from talking, from forcing this on.

'But – having babies, doesn't it hurt – horribly?'

'Yes, it does,' said Mother. 'But nowadays they have so much to help you that you hardly feel the pain, at least, not very much. You needn't be frightened. The doctors are clever.'

'But – suppose there isn't a doctor. Suppose you were caught out in – the jungle – or a desert – or there was a *flood*!' said Harriet.

'Oh *Har-ri-et*! *Do* let Mother go on,' said Bea.

'To get ready this temple . . . ' said Mother, and her voice sounded uncertain again as if she again had been thinking over how to put what she had to say, and was not sure of the result.

'To make it ready, changes happen in your body, when you are beginning to be big girls.'

'I know,' said Harriet, nodding. 'They have happened to me.'

Mother looked surprised and Bea impatient.

'You needn't snort at me. They have,' said Harriet.

'Yes, I expect they have. You are growing, but wait, Harriet,' said Mother. 'Listen.'

'Mother,' broke in Bea, '*must* we talk about this now? Can't we wait till this does happen? And *must* we have Harriet here?' She glared at Harriet as if she hated her.

And Harriet herself suddenly felt that she would prefer to postpone it, though she did not know why.

A sound came from the river, an approaching churning with a regular pulsing of engines. It was the twelve o'clock mail steamer. The noise grew louder as it passed the house, upstream, and then grew fainter; presently there came the sound of waves, its wash slapping against the garden bank. Mother, who had seemed to waver, gathered herself again.

'You can be patient for a few minutes longer,' said Mother. 'I shan't keep you long. It is always better for things to be talked of plainly.'

Bea looked as though she did not agree. 'And,' added Mother dryly as she watched Bea's face, 'it won't do you any harm to hear this from your mother, even if you have been told it by someone else already.'

She means Valerie, thought Harriet. Valerie has told her. Good for you, Mother, thought Harriet, refreshed to find how little of a fool her mother was.

Mother's eyes were resting on Bea's head as she began to talk again. Bea bent her head so that neither of them could see her face and her fingers picked, picked at the wicker stool she sat on. Why was Bea so funny, so resentful? And now Harriet found herself wishing that Mother would not keep them there, keep Bea, at any rate, there, to be talked at against her will.

But Mother talked on calmly and firmly, and soon Harriet forgot to look at Bea. She was listening with all her ears.

Mother's voice went steadily on. Then there was a third silence.

'Well!' said Harriet. 'Well!'

She looked down at herself, and it was true that she was

exactly as before, the same knees, the same hairiness, the dress with the same stains and marks. 'But – I didn't know what I was, what I am, what I am going to be,' said Harriet. For all she knew, had known up to now, she might have been the same as Bogey. Gone, and she thought regretfully of them for a moment, gone were some pleasing vistas she had seen for herself and Bogey; running away to sea and becoming cabin boys; turning into Red Indians, I should have to be a squaw, and I don't like squaws, thought Harriet; being an explorer, No, I suppose women are not really suitable for explorers, thought Harriet, they would be too inconvenient. And every month . . . like the moon and the tides . . . the moon brings tides to the world and the world has to have them . . . it can't help its tides, and no more can I. All at once it seemed exceedingly merciless to the small Harriet, sitting on just such another wicker stool as Bea's in Mother's room.

'I wish I were Bogey,' said Harriet.

'I know,' said Mother. 'I often wanted to be a boy.'

'You?' asked Harriet in surprise. 'You did?'

'Yes I,' said Mother, 'but it is no good, Harry. You are a girl.'

But . . . I don't think it *can* happen to me, thought Harriet, and aloud she said, 'Mother, I don't think it will . . . '

'Will what, Harriet?'

Bea made an impatient movement. 'That is what she always does, thinks, and then expects you to know what she is thinking.' It seemed to help Bea if she attacked Harriet. 'She is a perfect little silly. Can I go, Mother?'

'Bea . . . ' Mother began, but Harriet had to interrupt.

'To me? In *my* body? Are you sure, Mother?'

'I hate bodies,' burst out Bea, 'I want to go.'

'Very well then, go, Bea,' said Mother.

After Bea had gone, Mother sat still, and once again

Harriet heard her sigh, but she herself was too engrossed with herself, with being Harriet, to feel this. 'I don't think,' she said, 'that I can be – quite an ordinary woman, Mother.'

'You will be the same as every woman when your turn comes,' said Mother, 'and so will Bea . . . just as you said, willy-nilly. And now,' she said, 'perhaps you had better go back to your playing.'

'Play!' said Harriet. 'Play! I shall never play again.' But she did. The same day she was chasing Bogey on the lawn again.

*

In the early afternoon, everyone rested. Father snatched an hour before he went back to the office, Mother rested monumental on her bed from two till four; Harriet and Bea read, Bogey was banished to a camp cot in Father's room, while Victoria slept and Nan sat in her chair in the darkened nursery and sewed under the window and sometimes dozed off. It was the servants' siesta time; even the birds were silent; even the lizards lay asleep in the sun.

If, however, Harriet had any pressing business she did not postpone it; she left her book and slipped off her bed and no one was any the wiser. 'I am going to rest in the Secret Hole,' she said to Bea. She was not, but Bea nodded quietly. Then Harriet went downstairs and almost always, as she passed Father's room, Bogey's camp cot was likewise empty.

This was Bogey's supreme time for his adventures, when there was no one to see him or hinder him or even be aware of him. It was the time, too, when the garden was least disturbed, when his insects and his reptile friends were most accessible. Harriet never remembered yet getting up and finding him in bed.

One afternoon, in late February, Harriet needed Bogey. She went downstairs to find him, but of course he was not there. She could not see him in the garden either as she stood on the verandah.

'Bother,' said Harriet, 'I shall have to go out,' and she went on tiptoe to the nursery to fetch her hat.

Nan was asleep. On her lap lay a pair of Victoria's knickers into which she was putting new buttonholes as Victoria grew too fat for the old; she still held her needle and her lips, as she slept, blew gently in and out. Harriet fetched her hat and went out.

She could not see Bogey anywhere. 'He is playing Going-round-the-garden-without-being-seen,' said Harriet annoyed, and she began to follow him over the customary tracks that only she and Bogey knew. The garden was empty, brilliant with sun. Its colour blazed at Harriet. Here, as she went between the plinth of the house and the poinsettias, their flowers, as big as plates, long-fingered, scarlet, looked into her face as she passed; she half expected to see Bogey's face amongst them, Bogey's face screwed up in the sun, under his shock of hair. She crept between the poinsettias and the house just as he crept, but there was no Bogey there. He was not by the morning glory screen trumpeting its blue and purple flowers in the sun, nor under the swinging orange creeper at the house corner. He was not in the bougainvillaea clumps nor anywhere near the rose turrets, nor under the jacaranda trees, nor by the tank. Harriet went into the vegetable garden between the rows of peas and white-flowering beans, and pushed through the tomato bed, malodorous with its yellow flowers, but he was not there. He was not in the stable where Pearl stood looking stupidly out of her stall, half asleep herself. Harriet stopped to pat her, to smell her warmth, but Pearl did not alter her expression at all. She only twitched her ear at a fly.

Bogey was not behind the little midden of manure, nor

in the servants' quarters where Harriet could see forms, stretched out asleep on the string beds, under the trees and the eaves of each hut.

She went behind the hibiscus standards, their flowers hanging pink and scarlet and yellow and cream in lantern shapes with tasselled stamens; she swung them as she passed, but nothing else stirred or shook them. She went where Bogey went, along the drain by the wall behind the bamboos whose pipe stems stood, green and bronze and canary yellow with only the sunlight filtering between them. She went stealthily along expecting Bogey to spring out on her with a cat-call any moment, but the garden was as still and blank as ever. She went into the fern-house and round the goldfish pond. Bogey was not there either.

Out on the open lawn, the sun beat down on the grass that had a haze of its own heat, and sent off a warm dry smell. All the scents of garden mixed with it, but still the scent of the yellow Marechal-Neil roses and of the petunias and of the cork-tree flowers was distinguishable. The lawn, too, was quite empty. The whole garden was empty, and Harriet flung herself down on the grass and looked back up at the house and the tree still making their journey against the sky. Far up the hawks still went round and round in their rings. They made her dizzy. 'I rather wish I had stayed in and had my rest,' said Harriet, yawning. 'I don't know where Bogey is. He plays "Going-round-the-garden" far too well. Probably he is here, quite close to me and laughing,' said Harriet crossly; but no, she had no feeling of Bogey being near and laughing. She had only a feeling of blankness, a complete blank. Blank, thought Harriet aridly, and yawned again. Blank.

All at once she sat up. I believe, she thought. I believe he is waiting for that snake. I believe he is by the peepul tree.

She did not want to go near the peepul tree; even the

thought of the cobra made her spine go cold. 'Ugh!' said Harriet. 'Ugh! I wish he wouldn't. I don't know how he can. I must tell Father. I am going to tell Father,' said Harriet, and she jumped up and dusted the dust of the grass off her hands and knees and elbows.

She went to the gate where the bridal creeper, over now, hung in a tangle of dried green. The gate was open a crack. That meant Ram Prasad was out. His house was empty. Harriet looked in as she passed, and saw his 'lota', his washing-pot, and his lantern and his green tin trunk painted with roses standing neatly under his bed; his coat hung from a peg, his cut-out pictures were pasted on the wall and in the corner, near his earth cooking-oven, were his brass platters, his spoon and his brass drinking cup and his hookah. They were all utterly familiar to Harriet; she had seen them all hundreds of times.

Now she had come to the space round the peepul tree. Here, where the earth was bare because of the peepul roots, there was an empty space like a courtyard edged and screened with bamboos. There was nobody there, not even the cobra; her eyes had looked at once quickly among the roots, under the bamboos, to see a dark heap, a sliding coil. There was nobody, nothing, and then the blankness ran up into the sky, her feet were clamped to the earth; she had seen something else. It was not Bogey; not the snake, but an earthenware saucer of milk lying upset and broken on the ground near a small bamboo stick and, further off, towards the bamboos, on the ground too, Bogey's sun hat was lying by itself. 'He has been bitten,' said Harriet's mind distinctly as she stood there.

It – it came out for the milk and he touched it with a stick and it struck. It struck, and again the blankness ran into the sky into a long pause. Then close to her feet, lying on the ground, she saw Bogey's whistle.

With trembling legs she bent to pick it up, and as she bent, she saw him.

He was lying in the bamboos, only a few yards away, spread starfishwise as if he had flung, or tried to fling, his arms and legs away from him; he was lying on his face, his body drawn up from his arms and legs in a small heap. 'I see,' said that dreadful clearness in Harriet's mind, 'he would do that. Try and hide in the bamboos. He would go off to hide it, not tell – and then when it hurt,' and she knew snake bite was a terrible pain, 'why then, I suppose he couldn't tell. No one would hear him. There was no one near enough to hear.'

She went towards him on shaking legs. 'Bogey,' she said in a voice that was a croak, 'Bogey. Bogey.'

She went nearer, her eyes looking in and out of the bamboos, on the ground, near him, away from him. There was nothing there. Only Bogey on his face.

She looked down on him, at the seat of his shorts, old grey-blue linen, and at his rucked-up shirt that showed his naked back and his spine. His hands were clutched and filled with earth and bamboo bits, and his hair was dirty with them too. He must have rolled about in them, thought Harriet. Her throat grew dryer, her breath hurt, her neck was cold. 'Bogey,' she croaked. 'Bogey—'

There was a rustle in the bamboos behind her, and she jumped so that her skin tingled. It was a bird, a jay. It made a harsh whirring and clapped its wings and flew. Don't they do that when a snake is near, thought Harriet, and now, where she had been cold, she was wet. She bent and took hold of Bogey's foot in its sock and brown shoe and gave it a little pull. 'Bogey,' she tried to say. 'Boge. Bogey. Boge.'

She had not expected Bogey to answer, and he did not answer. He did not move, and she had not expected him to move. The – the warm is gone, thought Harriet. The side of his face she could see was scratched and the skin was blue.

'Blue?' asked Harriet numbly, staring down at him. 'Blue? Why should he be blue?' She went on saying that as she looked and looked and looked. She said it until she heard the gate creak on its hinge. Ram Prasad had come back.

Then she broke the quiet. She screamed louder than the jay. 'Look. Look. Look,' she screamed. 'Ram Prasad! Ram Prasad! *Sarpe*. *Sarpe*. Snake. Snake. Snake.'

*

In India, when anyone dies, it is necessary that they are buried at once, and by sunset of that same day Bogey was lying in the small cemetery where the trees that had honey-balls like mimosa dropped their pollen on the old graves and the new graves, on the short earth mound that was Bogey's, on the stone of the other boy, John Fox, piper, who was fourteen when he died, two hundred years ago.

With the resource that a small far-away town often shows, a coffin was found and made to fit Bogey by the carpenters in the Works. The Works were stopped; the coolies went home, but the clerks gathered in a silent and respectful throng just inside the gate. The firm's small launch, the 'Cormorant', left her moorings and came up to the jetty; from other jetties, up and down the river, other launches put out, and on them were people from the other Works, and flowers from the other gardens. The gardeners knew what ought to be done; without being told they cut all the white flowers, white petunias and roses and candy-tuft and dianthus and gypsophila. In Harriet's garden they sat in the shade making wreaths though no one told them, and they made a cross, too, of yellow roses.

'Why can't I go out? Why can't I go *out*?' whined Victoria.

'Be quiet,' said Harriet.

'Hush,' said Bea.

People, ladies and gentlemen, gathered under the cork tree. Abdullah and Goffura, who also knew what should be done, carried out chairs and trays of tea, but no one of the family came down to speak to anyone; everyone sat or stood talking in low voices while the cork blossom, that was falling, dropped on their heads or into their cups of tea.

'We haven't had any tea,' said Victoria. 'I want some tea.'

'Hush,' said Harriet.

'Be quiet,' said Bea.

Why did all the people come? wondered Harriet. They came as if they had a right to come, as if it were their duty. Now Mr Marshall, who was wearing a grey suit, not whites as he usually did, came and stood talking with a set grave face. They had come for Bogey? Why? 'Why do – they – all come?' Harriet asked Bea.

'It is the custom,' said Bea. 'Bogey has to be buried.'

'Buried?' said Harriet startled.

'Yes. You know that,' said Bea.

Harriet knew. She had always known, but it had not come to her before. When you died, you did not belong to yourself, nor to your family; you belonged to custom, and places and countries and religions; even a small boy like Bogey. Harriet remembered Father telling her about the Registration of Births and Deaths, the birth and death of a citizen. 'Then Bogey was a citizen,' she said aloud.

They huddled under Bea's bookshelf, straining to listen, trying to see and not see.

'I want to go out,' said Victoria. 'Why *can't* I *go out?*'

Then Nan came in.

'Why are you not dressed?' said Nan.

'Dressed?' They stared.

'Yes. You always get dressed for the afternoon?'

'Yes – but – but—'

'You would think no one had ever taught you how to behave,' said Nan. 'Take off that dirty frock, Harriet, and go and wash your face. You too, Bea. Victoria, come here and let me unbutton you.'

'But are we – is – Bogey—'

'Bogey is dressed,' said Nan with dignity. 'The house is full of ladies and gentlemen. We must show them that we – we care for him. You will get dressed and then come with me.'

'Shall we – see him?'

'I don't want to see him,' said Victoria. 'Ayah says he is all black.'

Nan's face folded in on itself suddenly, the lines by her mouth and her eyes folded in, and she shut her lids. Then she picked up the brush and without answering began to brush Victoria's hair. When they were dressed she walked them out on the verandah, between more people who parted and made way for them, and into Father's room. It was very dim, but Nan had lit two candles on the writing-table. There was only Bogey's coffin there heaped up with flowers.

'I don't know what Mother would wish,' said Nan, 'and I cannot ask her, but I think you should *not* see Bogey. You must say goodbye to him here.'

They stood close in the candlelight, in the smell of flowers where again the roses were the strongest. Why again, wondered Harriet. When – in what age had she thought that before? Then Nan took them out into the garden, away from the people, by the river.

The river ran with no noise of steam from the Works. It sounded queer.

Father and Mr Marshall came from the house carrying Bogey in his coffin. They carried him down to the jetty and put him on the deck of the 'Cormorant' and the people followed with flowers, till there was a hill of flowers on the deck. Some of the flowerheads fell off into the river, and were floated down and away. Then the 'Cormorant' cast off from the jetty and backed and turned in a half circle to go upstream, and the other launches, with their people, cast off too, and followed behind. Each launch left a pointed wake in the water.

The river can't close over this, thought Harriet; then she seemed to see again in the water the handful of ashes that had been Ram Prasad's wife, and she remembered how they had been washed, round and round, gently, on the water, before the current took them away.

Now the launches had passed out of sight. The colours in the garden were deepening in late afternoon sunlight; it was nearly evening.

*

Pieces of the next two days broke through to Harriet.

They found and killed the snake, not one but two, two cobras. Harriet saw Ram Prasad stretch them out on the ground when they were dead, one five feet, the other more than four. Bogey had been bitten in the neck, the right side below his cheek, Nan said. 'He was quickly dead,' said Nan.

After the cobras were killed, Harriet began to be sick. She was sick on and off, all those two days. In spite of that there was no respite. There were still things to do. Nan told her to go and find all Bogey's toys. She was packing his things away, out of Mother's sight.

Harriet could not find any toys except an old arrow, thrown down and rusty; she knew where Bogey had buried his soldiers, but she let them stay buried; she found a mud garden under a tree, but you could not pack a mud garden. She wandered round the garden that was the same garden, not changed, not different, but she walked in it not thinking, not touching, merely walking.

There was no clergyman in the town. Mr Marshall had read the service for Bogey. In the evenings, Mr Marshall and Dr Paget came to be with Mother and Father. One evening Mr Marshall stopped to speak to Harriet who sat on the steps looking at the darkness, not thinking, only looking.

'I expect you miss your brother,' said Mr Marshall kindly.

The jackals howled far out on the lawn.

'Well, it is a good thing it wasn't Victoria,' said Harriet.

Mr Marshall seemed slightly taken aback. 'Why?' he asked.

'Victoria is afraid of jackals,' Harriet explained. 'Bogey isn't.'

Nan forgot to pack Bogey's toothbrush. When Harriet was having her bath she saw it still there: Bea, pink; Harriet, green; Bogey, red; Victoria, blue. Harriet stood up in the hot water and took Bogey's down.

'What are you hiding in your hand, Harriet?'

When Harriet showed, Nan turned her back and tidied the towels on the rack.

'You can't keep that, Harriet,' she said.

'No,' Harriet agreed forlornly.

She put her head down on the zinc edge of the bath. Nan stayed by the towels, smoothing them down.

'We don't need to keep things, Harriet.'

'No,' said Harriet, not agreeing; then, as she relinquished the toothbrush, it was true. The less she had of Bogey, the more clearly she saw him.

There began to be shoots of life. Whether they were wanted or not, there were shoots of life.

Father went back to the Works. Mother came downstairs. Harriet heard her ordering the meals again. 'Soup.

Celery soup with cream,' said Mother, 'mutton, mint sauce, peas, the garden peas.'

'Roast potatoes,' said the cook, entering it in Hindi in his notebook. He was an educated cook.

'Then orange baskets,' said Mother, and Harriet found herself chiming in, 'Yes. Can't we have orange baskets too, Mother? For our supper?'

Victoria made herself a new kind of house on the veranda table. She said it was a 'think house'. It was nothing but Victoria herself sitting on the table. 'Where are the walls? The roof? The front door?' demanded Harriet.

'It is a think house,' said Victoria.

'You mean you think it is a house, and it is?'

Victoria nodded.

'But what can you *do* with it?' asked Harriet.

'You can think in it,' said Victoria, with dignity.

Lessons began again. Lessons with Mother, with Father. Eating-sleeping-getting-up-going-to-bed-resting-washing-brushing-and-combing-and-doing-your-teeth-reading-swinging-riding-Pearl-knitting. All the outward things went on. Surprisingly, the inward things began to go on too. Nothing had changed. But everything, Harriet thought, has shrunk. Everyone has shrunk somewhere inside themselves, as if they are hiding and you are afraid to find them because you are afraid of what you may find. Occasionally, you would discover. Mother cutting roses, stooped and picked up a lead Highlander off the path. It was one of Bogey's soldiers that Sally had dug up. Mother went indoors, dropping her scissors and the roses she had picked on the veranda table.

Harriet came into the nursery and there was Nan just as before, making buttonholes for Victoria. Harriet stopped, and her sickness came back again.

'What is it, Harriet?'

'Is is so – horrid – so cruel,' Harriet burst out.

Nan went on with her sewing.

'Going on and on. We go on as if nothing had happened,' wept Harriet.

'No, we don't,' said Nan. 'All we do is to go on. What else are we to do, Harriet?'

'It is as if we had wiped Bogey away. Look at you, making *button*-holes!' wept Harriet.

'What do you think I should do?' asked Nan quietly.

'That is just it,' Harriet could not hold her tears. 'It happens, and then things come round again, begin again, and you can't stop them. They go on happening, whatever happens.'

'Yes, they go on happening,' said Nan, 'over and over again, for everyone, sometime, Harriet.'

Harriet sat down on the floor, and wiped her eyes on the back of her hand. She felt hollowed with her unhappiness, and then, as she sat there, leaning against Nan's chair, another astonishing shoot came up in her mind. 'No,' said Harriet, horrified at herself. 'No. No, I can't. I mustn't. *Write* about this? No. No. I can't,' but it was already forming inside her head, as Nan stitched buttonholes again, and again she heard the sound of her life, the steam puff-wait-puff and the river. It was true; on the surface, even deeper, it was all exactly and evenly the same.

The world goes round.

No, thought Harriet, trying not to listen to herself; it carried her on.

The river runs, the round world spins.

Dawn and lamplight, thought Harriet. *Midnight. Noon.* She shut her eyes and said it over to hear, in the old familiar way, if the words ran. It seemed to her that they ran properly and she went on:

The river runs, the round world spins.
Dawn and lamplight. Midnight. Noon.
Sun follows day. Night, stars and moon.

The customary happiness and suspense and power filled her. She felt lifted again, as if she were rising up. She was ashamed, she tried to crush the words down, but they could not keep down. They insisted on rising.

Sun follows day. Night, stars and moon
. . . the end begins.

'Nan,' said Harriet, shocked.

'Yes, dear?'

'Nan, how can I be happy? How *can* I.'

If surprising things came out of Harriet, no surprises ever came out of Nan.

'It isn't for us to dictate, Harriet.'

'Oh Nan!'

'That is so,' said Nan, snipping her thread. 'If you are happy, you are. You can't make yourself unhappy. We are something, part of something, larger than ourselves, Harriet.'

Harriet was silent, remembering Christmas, and how little she had felt below the stars, remembering Bea and what Bea had said about growing smaller as you grew older, only perhaps Bea meant that this otherness grew larger; she thought suddenly of the fish that the kingfisher had taken out of the river and of the splash it had made and of how the splash had gone and the river, with its other fish, its porpoises, its ships, had gone on running on.

Then what is the good of my writing my poem, thought Harriet, if it is all so big and I am so small? It wouldn't make a mark as big as a – a fly's leg against the whole world. I shan't write anything.

The river runs – it immediately began again.

'I have to go to the Secret Hole, Nan,' said Harriet, jumping up from the floor. 'I have a poem that I have to write down.'

But when she reached the Secret Hole, her box was empty. Her book was not there.

She came downstairs, hurtling down, and there was Valerie reading her book on the lawn.

'What are you doing with my book?' Harriet was scarlet.

'Reading it,' said Valerie, absolutely cool. Bea was standing by as if she did not quite know what Valerie was doing; she made no attempt to stop her reading Harriet's book, and worst of all, Captain John was reading his own book near lying on the grass.

'Give it to me.'

'No, I shan't,' said Valerie, turning over a page. 'I think it is very funny. Listen, Bea: *When I have thoughts they hum. I might have I think a little top in the top of my head—*'

'Bea. Make her give it to me.'

'Valerie. It is Harriet's private book.'

'Yes. I should think so,' said Valerie giggling. 'How could you, Harriet? There are all kinds of things in it. Captain John, here's one about you. There are a great many about you,' and she read out, '*I think that Captain John's face is like one of those plants that you touch . . .*'

'You are not to read it. You are not to,' screamed Harriet, flying at Valerie, but Valerie dodged away, nearer to Captain John, who had lifted his head to listen and look at them.

'*Captain John's face is like one of those plants that if you touch roughly they shrink and close up. I think it is true. Father calls him a "sensitive plant".* Oh, Captain John!' laughed Valerie, and Bea had to laugh too.

'You beast!' screamed Harriet. 'You beastly girl.'

'*I think he is like Antinous whose face you never do forget,*' read Valerie, dodging Harriet. '*Today I am so alive I am glad I am me and am born—*' Valerie ended in a shriek as Harriet tore the book away and pulled her hair.

'Harriet. You mustn't hurt her.'

'She has hurt me,' shouted Harriet, 'the mean sneaking hateful beastly pig. How dare she.'

'I don't want to read your silly diary,' said Valerie, rubbing her shoulder where Harriet had wrenched her. She put back her hair and fastened her tortoiseshell slide that had come undone. Harriet hated her fuzzy brown hair and she hated her face, which looked considerably heated and a little uncomfortable. 'Why be so angry?' said Valerie lightly.

'It was her private book,' said Bea.

'She is quite right to be angry,' said Captain John, who with difficulty had risen from the grass and come to them. 'You had no right to take it, Valerie.' He looked almost as angry as Harriet, and Valerie saw that everyone was against her. She looked hotter than ever and her eyes grew bright with spite.

'I don't see why *Harriet* should be so haughty,' said Valerie, 'when everyone knows it was her fault Bogey died.'

It was said.

There was complete silence in front of the steps, except again, in this pause, the steam puff and the river. Then Harriet turned and ran upstairs.

*

No one had spoken very much to Harriet about the cobra. She knew and they knew, and they knew that she knew. Father had questioned her. Her face and her voice had shown him how guilty and wretched she was, and he did not punish her. 'What,' said his whole attitude as he turned away, 'is the use of punishing now?' and that had twisted Harriet's heart more than any words.

Mother had said nothing either till Harriet had come and stood in front of her. 'Mother – I – I knew about – the – the – cobra – Mother.'

'Yes, Harriet. I know you did,' said Mother.

'Mother – I—'

'It is no use talking about it now,' said Mother.

There had been shocks. Ram Prasad was sent away. 'But why?' demanded Harriet. 'Why? He only knew it was there. *He* didn't know that Bogey—'

'There is no excuse for Ram Prasad. No excuse at all,' said Nan hardly.

Ram Prasad was, later, forgiven and reinstated, but that had given Harriet a glimpse of how people felt. Did they, then, think as hardly of her? She had only, so far, thought hardly of herself. Now Valerie's words burnt into her. *Everyone knows. Everyone knows.*

Harriet lay on her bed, her face turned to the wall.

Nan came in.

'Harriet,' said Nan.

'Please go away.'

'Harriet,' said Nan, 'I think you should get up.'

'I – can't.' Harriet's voice was muffled.

'You will have to get up some time,' said Nan reasonably, 'so I should get up now.'

'I can't, Nan. How can I?'

'With a girl like Valerie,' said Nan, 'a spiteful girl, you have to be very proud. You should not let her see she can hurt you.'

'It isn't only Valerie,' cried Harriet in despair. 'You didn't hear what she said. Oh, Nan, does everyone know? Does everyone say – *that*?'

'I expect they do,' said Nan calmly. 'You have to expect that because it is partly true, Harriet.'

'Yes, but – *who* could have thought—'

'You could have thought,' said Nan. 'You didn't use your sense. You know you didn't, and for that a cruel lesson has been given.' Her voice trembled and she looked with indescribable pity at Harriet, but she went on. 'Very cruel, but perfectly just,' said Nan. 'You can't complain about it. You must not.'

'What am I to do? What can I do?' cried Harriet.

'It is a thing that will have to pass away from you, Harriet.'

'It never will, Nan. Never! Never!'

'Yes, Harriet, it will,' said Nan. 'You have plenty of courage and you are strong. I have faith that it will,' and she pressed Harriet gently on the thigh and said, 'Get up now and face that Valerie.'

She rustled gently out, but Harriet did not get up. She lay on her bed engulfed with misery. All the sounds of the late afternoon came up to her and she could identify each one, but she lay cut off from them all. 'I feel as if I had thorns in my heart,' said Harriet. 'How hard Nan is. How hard,' she said. Now she could not be unhappy for Bogey by himself any more. Mixed with him, irretrievably, was the guilt and indictment, public not private, so that they were not by themselves any more. 'I wish I had died with Bogey,' whispered Harriet.

There was a knock on the shutters behind the curtain.

'Harriet, can I come in?'

'Captain John!' cried Harriet, shrinking in her bed.

'Yes. Can I come in?'

'No. Please no.'

'I am coming in,' said Captain John.

He came in. Made dim by the shadow of the room, he looked large, his movements very jerky. Harriet could not see his face.

'I have brought your book,' he said, and laid it at the foot of her bed.

'Thank you.'

She did not move. She did not want him to see her face.

'Don't you want it?'

Harriet shook her head. 'I won't be doing any writing any more,' she said.

He did not answer that. Instead he said, 'I have come to take you for a walk.'

'Me?' said Harriet.

'Yes. Along by the river. It is beautiful there in the evening. Nan says you can come. Come along, Harriet.'

'But—' Harriet sat up and put her legs down over the edge of the bed, 'don't you want to be with Bea?'

'No,' said Captain John, 'I want to be with you.'

They went downstairs together and out along the drive and past the jetty and along the footpath, that lay beside the river.

The up steamer and the down steamer, the mail steamers, had passed for the day and the river flowed calm and untroubled between its banks. Now under the bank it showed shallows of light, yellow, where the late sun struck down into it; further out the water was deeply green, and beyond, in midstream, it showed only a surface with flat pale colours. On the further bank, a mile across stream, there was a line of unbroken brilliant yellow above a line of white, the mustard fields in flower above the river's edge of sand. The temple showed its roof among the trees and country boats, their sails set square, moved gently down before the current and the wind. Other boats passed, towed upstream by boatmen leaning on long towing lines. A peasant was washing the flanks of his cows in the river above the garden, and on the sand and in the mud lay the halves of empty shells, bleached white, that had baked all day in the hot sun.

'How beautiful it is,' said Harriet. Its beauty penetrated into the heat and the ache of the hollowness inside her. It had a quiet unhurriedness, a time beat that was infinitely soothing to Harriet. 'You can't stop days or rivers,' not stop them, and not hurry them. Her cheeks grew cool and the ferment in her heart grew quieter too, more slow.

She was silent trying to think of it: then, 'I feel better already,' she said sadly.

'Don't you want to feel better?'

'No, I don't,' and she said with the same forlornness, 'I need some time to be unhappy.'

He did not answer, but he bent and took her hand, and holding his hand, she went on walking beside the river, her steps made a little jerky by his. His hand was very comforting to her.

'Soon – you will be going away though – won't you?' said Harriet.

'Yes,' said Captain John.

'What will you do? Do you know?'

'I don't know yet, but something.'

When the sun had gone, they turned and came back. Now the colours had drawn in to tints of themselves in the water and in the sky, but the mustard still showed its brilliant clashing yellow; the last clouds of the sunset hung over the temple. 'They are like cherub's wings,' said Harriet. 'We always call them cherub's wings.'

He made no answer to that.

They heard all the Indian evening sounds, sounds that were alien to him, utterly homely and familiar to Harriet: the gongs beating far off in the temple in the bazaar, the creak and knock of the ferryman's paddle as the ferry came near the bank; the sound of cooking pots being scoured with mud and of a calf bellowing while its mother was milked. There was an evening smell of cooking too, pungent, too raw for their noses with its ghee and garlic and mustard oil; there was the smell of dung fuel burning, and, as they came near the house again, they smelled the cork-tree flowers on the air.

'Those flowers are falling off the tree,' said Captain John.

'It is nearly the end of the cold weather, of the winter then,' said Harriet.

'I must go,' said Captain John, but he did not go. 'Harriet, will you come for another walk with me?' he said.

'Of course. Can we go for a walk when it is dark, and look at the fireflies? I have always wanted to do that,' said Harriet.

'Yes.' He still lingered. Then he said, 'Harry. Put your book back in its place. Promise.'

Harriet nodded.

'I like to think of it back in its place. And I am glad I am in it,' said Captain John.

*

As Harriet came into the nursery, where the lights were already on, Nan and Bea were kneeling on sheets of newspaper spread round Victoria's old basket cot. They were painting it with fresh white paint.

Harriet stood rooted to the threshold, staring.

'Goodness!' she said. 'My goodness!' And she asked startled, 'Is the baby coming then?'

They laughed at her startled face. 'Didn't you think it would?' asked Bea.

Harriet came slowly into the room, still staring.

'There,' said Nan, standing up and cleaning her brush in the jar of turpentine. 'That will be dry tomorrow. It is such excellent enamel,' she said with satisfaction. 'Look, it is nearly dry already.'

Harriet looked at Nan sharply. There was no sign in Nan's face of anything but satisfaction over the excellence of the enamel. 'Nan is like a clock,' said Harriet to herself. 'Every minute she ticks just that minute. Nothing else.' She said it irritably, but she sensed that all the other minutes were in Nan as well, a tremendous aggregate of minutes.

She said slowly, 'Nan, have you seen hundreds of babies born?'

'Not hundreds,' said Nan, 'but many. Very many.'

'And have you seen a great many people die?'

'Don't, Harriet,' said Bea sharply.

'But have you, Nan?'

'A great many, Harriet.'

'I don't understand,' said Harriet more slowly. 'I don't understand how you keep yourself so clear.'

'Don't you?' said Nan, but she did not tell them. 'I must go and see about your suppers,' she said.

After she had gone Harriet was left alone with Bea. Bea was still painting a leg of the cot, working the paint very carefully into the basketwork.

'Captain John has been so nice to me,' said Harriet.

'Has he?' said Bea.

'He took me for a walk.'

'Did he?' said Bea.

'He is – different, Bea.'

'Is he?'

Bea did not seem interested. She painted with small firm even strokes. Harriet could not see her face for her fall of hair.

'Bea,' said Harriet, 'are you unhappy?'

'Well, we all are,' said Bea, without looking up.

Harriet did not think it wise to continue, but she did. She could not go away.

'Does Captain John make you more unhappy, Bea?'

'No,' said Bea shortly.

'What do you do when you are unhappy?' asked Harriet.

'Oh, what a lot of questions you ask, Harriet. What is there to do? I am unhappy, that is all.'

She finished the leg and stood up and began to put her brush away with Nan's.

'I can't believe in this baby,' said Harriet, looking at the cot.

'It will be born all the same.'

'What happens, Bea?'

'Don't you remember when Victoria was born?'

All Harriet could remember was a story she had heard. When Victoria was born the head clerk of the Works, Sett Babu, came to Father and said, 'Sir, I hear you have another little calamity.' That was because Victoria was a girl and a girl to Sett Babu meant a dowry to be given when she was married. 'Do we have to have them?' she asked aloud.

'Have what? Babies?'

'Dowries,' said Harriet, but Bea did not answer.

'I don't see how we can,' said Harriet. 'How can we?'

'What? Have dowries?' asked Bea irritably.

'How can we be expected to have another baby and to like it? That is asking too much,' said Harriet. 'How *can* Mother?'

'If she is, she can. That is the answer,' said Bea. 'Harry, we ought to go and wash for supper.'

Harriet was silent, thinking, and then she said, 'It is too hard to be a person. You don't only have to go on and on. You have to be—' she looked for the word she needed and could not find it. Then, 'You have to be tall as well,' said Harriet.

*

In spite of the sadness and the quiet in the house there began to be a thread of expectation; then a stir.

The nurse came, Sister Silver, and Bea and Harriet were moved out of their room. Harriet went to sleep with Nan and Victoria; Bea went to stay with Valerie.

Then – will Captain John go there – to see her? thought Harriet. 'Won't he come here any more?' said Harriet.

An overwhelming loneliness filled her and the old misunderstood pain. She went again to the Secret Hole and again sat there by her soap-box, with her knees under her chin, brooding. Am I always going to be lonely? thought Harriet, and the right answer seemed to be, Yes, I expect I am.

She had kept her promise and put her book back and now she picked it up, but all the writing in it seemed broken and flat. How silly I was when I wrote it, thought Harriet. Valerie was right. It was all babyish and silly or else crude; the funny bits were not funny; the beautiful bits were too beautiful. 'I hate my writing,' said Harriet.

The day ends, the end begins.

She had not finished the poem. She looked at it. 'Nothing leaves off,' said Harriet crossly. 'But I shall leave off,' and she threw the book back in the box.

*

In the night she did not sleep well. She did not often sleep well now. Her dreams were too intimately concerned with Bogey, with the cobra. That night she woke in her customary cold sweat, and slowly, as she forced open her eyes, she saw that she had not woken to the frightening darkness when everything had long lithe shapes and might, or might not, be sliding, coming, moving, towards her. The light was on, and what had woken her was not a dream, but the sound of heavy treads. They came along the veranda and up the stairs past the nursery, and she heard a commonplace loud and cheerful voice, Dr Paget's voice. She lay and listened to it sleepily; then in a moment she sat up.

'Nan,' she said, 'is it the baby? Is the baby born?'

'Shsh,' said Nan's voice. 'You will wake Victoria.'

'Nan. What is—'

Harriet's voice stopped when she saw what Nan was doing. In front of a hot low brazier, Nan was airing the small clothes Harriet had often seen put away in Mother's trunk; Harriet looked dumbfounded. Washed, ironed and ready, a vest, a flannel nightgown, a coat, a white shawl, were airing there. 'It *is* the baby,' said Harriet in awe. 'The baby is going to come.'

Outside, in the night, a gong struck once.

Harriet listened. One. No more. It was the Works' gong, beaten at the hours. 'It is one o'clock in the middle of the night,' said Harriet. 'Is the baby born?'

'Not yet. Come,' said Nan. 'Get up. As you are awake. You shall help me make some tea.'

'Tea? Now? In the middle of the night?'

In the dining-room the tea things were laid out, sandwiches were cut. Harriet was astounded and Nan laughed at her face as she put on the kettle. 'Whom do you think I first put the kettle on for, here, in the middle of the night?' asked Nan.

'Who?'

'For you, Harriet.'

'For me?'

'Yes. You were born just after I came here.'

'And then – Bogey?'

'Then Bogey.' Nan said his name as if it were the same as anyone else's.

'Nan, you have seen so many babies,' said Harriet. 'Do they always seem new and exciting, like this, to you?'

'Always new,' said Nan, 'and exciting.'

'Every time?'

'Every time.'

Harriet pondered. 'But we don't want another boy, do we?' she said jealously.

'That isn't left to us,' said Nan. 'It won't be another anything. It will be itself.'

Sister Silver came down.

'Is the baby born?' asked Harriet.

'Why isn't that child in bed?' said Sister. 'Nurse, I think we shall want those clothes soon.'

'I am ready,' said Nan. She had poured out a cup of tea before she took up the tray. 'Now, Harriet, here is a cup of tea for you. Can I trust you not to wake Victoria?'

Harriet took her tea and went to sit by the brazier that shed a dim, warm circle of light in the nursery. Even the tea had a different flavour in the middle of the night, dark and strong and hot. It was too hot. She put the cup down and went to look out of the window.

The house was so warm and sheltered, so full of light and hush and life, that it did not know the night. At the window, Harriet met the chill of the early hours. There was no freshness in it yet, the dew had not fallen; the night was still strong. Far away, over and over again, she could hear the jackals howling and the two sounds, always present, always reminding her: puff-wait-puff, and the running of the river.

The strong night scent came to her again from the Lady-of-the-Night; it was heavy, more than ever drenching, in the dark. She did not like it. She shivered.

Usually now all of them in the family would have been asleep, like any sleeping family. She thought of all the families safely and unadventurously asleep and then of how her own was scattered. Only Victoria was in her place. Mother's room was out of bounds, she could not know what was happening to Mother; Father was awake, walking between the veranda and the drawing-room, she had heard him while Nan poured out tea. Bea was across the river and she herself was standing here tied with excitement so that she felt as if she had a knot in her stomach with the coldness of the night blowing on her forehead and the cold howling of the jackals in her ears. And Bogey . . . where was Bogey? The warm of him was gone. It didn't stay – it wasn't made blue by the cobra . . . then where . . . where?

Harriet knew that it would be better, much better, not to think of Bogey now, in the middle of the night.

'If you are cold,' she told herself reasonably, 'why not drink your tea?' She went back to the heater and sat warming herself, her hands cold on the cup, her lips shivering as she drank. She could hear footsteps going backwards and forwards over her head in Mother's room.

Then she decided she would go out on the veranda and wait there. It was nearer. She could hear more clearly there.

The veranda showed her the night and now she saw the stars behind the cork tree, but the tree did not appear to be moving at all. 'But it is,' argued Harriet. 'It is, because it always does.' The scent of the night bush was softened here by the circle of cork-tree flowers, by the thin dew scent of Mother's petunias in the pots.

She is very quiet, thought Harriet. I thought people screamed and shrieked and cried when they had babies. She strained to hear and went to the foot of the stairs. No sound at all. Nothing. She began to walk upstairs.

It was dark on the centre landing, but the upper flight was lit and the lights were on outside Mother's room as well. Harriet kept in the shadow of the banisters. She could hear Father's steps, and cautiously she raised her head to look up. At that moment Sister Silver came out of Mother's room. She had her sleeves rolled, her face looked busy. As Harriet saw her, she saw Harriet.

'What are you doing up here?'

'Is it born?' asked Harriet.

'You go downstairs directly, Miss,' said Sister sharply, and Harriet retreated.

She did not retreat far, about nine steps. There she waited, and presently, when she judged it was safe, she came up again.

Then down the stairs a smell filtered to Harriet. She

sniffed it. She knew it, and she had known what it was going to be. It was chloroform. She knew it from her operation for tonsils. There was no mistaking it. She came a little further up the stairs.

Nan was standing there outside Mother's door, but her back was turned to Harriet.

'Is it born?' That was on Harriet's tongue again when Nan's attitude arrested her.

Nan was standing and waiting for the moment to come. The light showed her thin shoulder blades under the straps of her apron crossed on her back; it showed the combs holding her thin bun of hair, and her old black jacket that she wore under her apron, her print skirts, and slippers. As she stood there, she looked small and quiet and humble to Harriet, who felt she herself had been making something of a clamour. She felt ashamed, but not so ashamed that she went away. 'I couldn't, I couldn't go down now,' argued Harriet. 'Nobody could. Not now.' She stood, trying to emulate Nan in stillness, on the stairs.

Then Nan started, her hands unclasped, and a sound ran through Harriet from her scalp to her feet and from her feet up again.

It was a new sound. First it was a sound like birds chirping; like sparrows in twigs; a twig sound; then it grew; it was broken into hiccoughs: coughs; it was like a little engine starting; it grew again, and it was the baby crying. It was the actual baby crying.

*

There had never been any days as peaceful as those late winter days after the baby was born.

There was no ripple of disturbance in them. Mother lay in bed, and Harriet only saw her to say good morning and good night; Father was away, up-river, on a jute conference; Sister Silver lived apart with the baby and Mother; Bea was still with Valerie; Nan and Victoria were the only two with Harriet, and Nan was never a disturbance, and Victoria never, in any case, made ripples.

Now the days were tinged with heat at midday, cool again at morning and evening. It was almost spring. In the fields the early sowing was finished and the young jute and rice made dark-green and light-green patches over the land. The yellowness of the mustard had dimmed and the first great red pods of the simul, the wild cotton trees, had opened their colour. In the sky, the clouds were soft and puffed as cotton-wool. The sky itself had altered. This was the time of its deepest blue; later the heat took its colour, and later still the monsoon broke and turned it heavy and grey, with intervals that were pale, washed out. Now Harriet, by looking at the sky, knew it was nearly spring.

The sky so attracted her that she opened her money box and took out two annas and asked Ram Prasad to fetch her two new kites from the bazaar. He bought an excellent one, striped red and white with emerald corners, and a second one of plain pink paper. He helped Harriet to pierce the first, and fix it to her glassed string that was wound on a light polished roller made of bamboo with two long handles. Then they went up together on to the roof.

'You launch it,' said Ram Prasad, 'and I will get it up for you.'

'No. I want to get it up myself,' said Harriet.

'You never will. You never can.'

'I can. I shall,' said Harriet. 'Stand out of my way.'

She took the roller on the palms of her hands and allowed plenty of space behind her in which to run back. Ram Prasad took the kite between his fingers and walked with it to the other end of the roof.

Above them the sky waited for the kite. Nothing showed between the grey stone parapet walls, not a tree, not a roof, not a mast, except only the top of the cork tree flowering in its green, and, far up, the specks of the hawks making their circles on the edge of the wind current. 'I am going to send it as high as that,' said Harriet.

'Ready?' called Ram Prasad, holding it up.

'Ready.'

Ram Prasad sent it up in a strong flight. The string pulled taut, Harriet jerked it higher twice, the kite found the wind, rose and jerked away of itself in a short cornerwise dance. Harriet pulled backwards, it rose again, and then suddenly made an arc in the air and fell, dashing itself against the parapet.

'I told you so,' said Ram Prasad.

'Is it broken?'

She stood there while he looked at the torn kite. She kept her lips stiff. She meant to fly that kite. It was important to her that she should, because she had, in true Harriet fashion, made it into an omen. If it flies, I shall fly, is what Harriet had decided.

'It can be mended,' grunted Ram Prasad. As always when they sailed kites, he had brought the second kite up on the roof and with it a pot of flour-and-water paste, a stick with a rag round it and some strips of coloured paper. Squatting on their heels, he and Harriet began to mend the kite; they first patched the torn place, then they weighted the opposite tip with the same amount of paper and paste; they added a blob to the tail to steady it and laid the kite in the sun to dry.

Nowadays Ram Prasad and Harriet were neither of them conversational. While the kite dried Harriet went to lean over the parapet by herself, looking down on the garden as if it were a map in another focus. She saw a small launch tied to the jetty and a pigmy Captain John walking up the drive. She felt herself pause; she looked down on him, held in her thoughts. Then Ram Prasad called her. He held the roller. 'Pick up the kite,' he said, 'and I will get it up for you.'

'No,' said Harriet, 'I shall get it up for myself.'

'You will never do it.'

'Then it shall not be done,' said Harriet.

'If you have husband, poor Godforsaken man,' said Ram Prasad, 'he will need a padlock and a stick.'

'Put it up,' said Harriet, standing ready. She hoped she would get it well up before Captain John found out where they were.

Ram Prasad put it up, clumsily. Harriet stepped back, pulled, and the kite came down flat on the roof in front of her, flat on its back with its string doubled up.

'See how clever you are,' said Ram Prasad.

Harriet did not contradict him. 'Is it broken?' she said.

'No. No thanks to you, thanks to God.'

'Then put it up and more carefully this time.'

Her lips were in a firm straight line as Ram Prasad sent the kite into the sky. Captain John appeared in the stairway.

Harriet jerked her roller, the kite rode up; out of the corner of her eye she saw his eyes follow it. It rode up well, and she brought it up again strongly. Then she let it go a little and it danced away down the current of the wind.

'Bring it up,' said Ram Prasad.

'Leave me alone,' said Harriet.

She brought it up herself, riding straight again, then to the left, to the right, another cornerwise dance off, and a bold fresh flight taking the string. Now it was safe, right up riding the wind, taking the string out, further and further away, higher and higher.

'You do it well,' said Captain John.

'At the third try,' said Ram Prasad. 'Bogey Baba could get it up first time, every time.'

The kite string sang in the wind; it pulled and tugged at

Harriet's hands . . . 'This is me – me – me,' she was singing triumphantly to herself. The string seemed to go up until the kite was among the hawks' rings in the sky.

'Feel it,' she said, and put the roller into Captain John's hands.

It was handing him something that was alive. His arms jerked and his hands had to close quickly to hold it and he had to use his strength on it. She saw his cheeks flush and his eyes grow darker with the excitement of the kite. Soon she saw that he was nearly as moved and as exhilarated as she.

They flew the kite while the afternoon grew later and richer in the world beyond the parapet, until the small clouds took the sunset as they had on the walk by the river. The same sounds, the same smells, came up to them.

Now I have been up here long enough, thought Harriet. I am tired. She began to wind the kite in.

'Are you bringing it down?' he asked regretfully.

'Yes.' She added, 'I always like them to be in before the first star comes.'

'Why?'

'Because it would be fatal for them to be out then,' she said seriously. 'The star would turn them back into paper.'

He did not laugh as she had been half afraid he would. He gravely helped her to wind the string in and the kite came back to them, fluttering, pulling away, getting larger in the dusk until it was over their heads, and Ram Prasad put up his hands and caught it level with his turban, as the last wind sank out of its sides. 'That was not so bad,' said Ram Prasad, 'but not as well done as Bogey Baba could have done it.'

Captain John took Harriet downstairs to ask permission from Nan to go out. 'It is very late,' said Nan, looking at them over her spectacles. 'It is dark.'

'Yes, but we wanted it to be dark. I want to show Captain John the fireflies,' pleaded Harriet.

Nan appeared to be thinking it over. Harriet checked her own arguments, of which she had a torrent ready, and waited too.

'Very well,' said Nan at last. She wisely did not say anything about time, nor bed.

'Shall we say good night to the baby?' asked Harriet.

'Very well,' said Captain John.

The cot was on the veranda, and all they could see in the folds of shawl was the baby's head and face asleep, and her fist doubled up. As they looked, the shawl moved up and down with her breathing.

'Feel how warm she is,' said Harriet.

Captain John held his finger near.

'She is very ugly, isn't she?' said Harriet.

'Look again,' said Captain John.

Harriet looked, at the line of cheek and the forehead where the veins spread, at the tiny mottled lids, like seals or sleeping shells, that showed a line of hairs that were lashes. She saw the nose and the mouth whose corners folded as it slept, and the chin. 'There is a dimple in her chin, like Father's,' she whispered, and Captain John nodded. The lobe of the one ear Harriet could see was laid flat to the head with a glimpse of tender skin behind it, going into the line of the back of the head turned into the shawl. The head was covered with fluff, a down, that was gold too. Harriet looked at the doubled fist, and at the hand and the fingers and the nails. 'I like her nails,' said Harriet. And Mother made her, she thought, finished, complete outside and inside. That was the wonder. This, this like to like. That was the wonder: foals, little horses, to horses; rabbits to rabbits; people to people; all made without a mistake. And without a pattern, thought Harriet, touching the baby's hand. It was always a fresh shock to find it warm, soft and firm, the feel of a real hand . . . Where did Mother . . . what did Mother— she thought. Queer, what people can make: the flight of a kite – and poems – and babies. What a funny power – and I too, one day! thought Harriet, see, how I have grown already.

All at once she said to Captain John, 'Could I go just one minute? There is something I very badly want to write down.'

The minute was half an hour, but when Harriet came out of the Secret Hole, Captain John was waiting quietly for her.

It was nearly dark. They did not walk along the river. 'The villages are interesting at night,' said Harriet, 'and the fireflies are in the village tanks.' They walked away from the Works and the bazaar along the road, where it began to run through the fields and villages. Soon they came to a village. There was a stucco house on the edge of the huts, and, as they passed, a man whose white clothes shone in the darkness stepped through its gateway with a floating oil lamp in his hand. By this house there was an orange tree; it was in blossom like the cork tree, and its flowers glimmered as they passed it, and its scent followed them up the road.

'This is a very smelly time of year, isn't it?' said Harriet.

'You mean scented,' corrected Captain John.

'Yes. All the flowers smell,' said Harriet.

Here was a village tank, a sheet of water with a black shine, with the fireflies they had come to see along its bank and under its trees. Now they came to the huts built of earth, mud-walled with reed and bamboo roofs; every doorway, as they passed, was lit and showed a still life of figures or of things, lit and quiet. Here, on the earth floor, was a block of wood with a hollow in it, and a handful of spices and a pestle. 'That is where they grind spices for curry,'

Harriet interpreted. By the block on the floor were chilis, bright red in the lamplight, and behind them on the wall hung a wicker scoop. 'That is for separating the husks from their rice,' said Harriet. Here a woman in a cotton cloth crouched down on her ankles, while she turned the stone handmill for grinding grain to flour; with her other hand she threw in the grain, and on her turning arm her silver bangle caught and lost the light. Two old men, next door, sat by the bamboo pole that held the roof up and shared a waterpipe, passing it from one to another politely. Here a mother sat and oiled another baby, her own baby, in her lap; the baby had a girdle of silver bells round its waist. There were sounds too of a tap, a goat bleating, of bullock-cart wheels in the road, of a passing bicycle's bell.

They went further, to another village and another, and then turned to come back. When they came to the first village again, some of the doorways were already dark, and the mother was singing to her baby, a song that was ineffably sleepy and low with only half cadences of notes.

'That is like Nan sings to our baby,' said Harriet. 'Nan sings like that.' The other woman was still grinding, the old men were still smoking and no one put the spices away.

From the stucco house, as they passed it, came music, a flute, cymbals, the interpitched grasshopper-playing of a sitar, and a drum. As they came nearer, a man's voice began to sing.

'What is he singing?' asked Captain John.

Harriet listened, but she could not make out the words. 'It will be about Radha and Krishna, I expect, and their love. They are always singing about that. Or else about Ajunta and his wars. It is always love and war,' she said.

Now they had come back to the house again, and they went in at the gate and up the drive, where the cork tree stood in its complete wheel of fallen flowers. Its branches were quite bare.

'So the winter is over,' said Harriet, as they stood under it.

The drum gave two throbs, a beat, and was still. 'It has done, for tonight,' said Harriet. 'Do you remember Diwali, Captain John? There were drums there too.'

'Diwali?'

'The Feast of Lights.' He nodded. 'Funny,' said Harriet. 'We talked about living, and being born and dying, and we didn't now then about ... Bogey ... nor the baby really ... nor anything ...' And she said under her breath, 'Bellum ... Belli ... Bello ... Bello ... Amamus ... Amatis ... Amant. I was doing those then.' How young I was, thought Harriet. Now how I have grown, and she said aloud to Captain John, 'Are you any different?'

'I think I am,' said Captain John.

'Because you have decided to go?' asked Harriet.

'Partly, perhaps.'

Harriet nodded. 'That is what Nan used to say. "Leave him. He will go on when he is ready." I used to wonder what was wrong with you,' she said candidly. 'You hadn't died ... but ...'

'I wasn't alive?' he suggested.

'You hadn't come alive,' said Harriet, and she said, 'You were like the baby ... you had to be born. ... You were quite right when you said that,' said Harriet. 'I died a bit ... with Bogey. I died much more when Valerie said that to me ... for a long time I didn't come alive ... not the whole afternoon!' she said.

'You are alive now, Harriet.'

'Yes, and so are you ...'

She had a sudden excess of happiness as she had had that other morning, long ago.

'Look at my tree,' she said. 'Do you see it turning ... Up in the stars? Sometimes,' she said, remembering that morning, 'I write poems that are taller than I am.'

Captain John brought his eyes down and looked at her. 'I thought you were not going to write any more.'

'That was—' but Harriet did not say what it was.

'You can't help it, can you?' said Captain John. 'And what is this one? A story? A poem?'

'It is a poem.'

'And I have to read it, don't I, Harriet?'

'It is too dark to read,' said Harriet.

'Well, say it to me then,' said Captain John.

'It is good enough to say,' said Harriet. 'Really it is. This one is good. You will enjoy it. You will really. I wrote it after my other poem. It is much older.'

'I see,' said Captain John.

'This is it,' said Harriet, and she said it aloud:

'The day ends. The end begins . . . '

'Hm!' said Captain John, when she had finished. 'You will be a real writer one day, Harriet.'

'Oh, yes,' said Harriet. 'I shall be very great and very very famous.'

He did not say anything to that and she ran her hand up and down the tree's smooth bark. The woodpeckers, of course, had gone to bed. 'Does everyone have one?' she asked.

'Have what? A poem?'

'No, a tree.'

'Not everyone finds theirs so soon,' said Captain John. 'You are lucky, Harriet. That is where I am going,' he said more firmly. 'I am going to look for mine.'

A launch, as it passed on the river, gave a mournful little hoot that sounded like an owl. A real owl hooted a minute after.

'I must go,' said Captain John.

'It is so dark you can hear the river,' said Harriet. She meant 'quiet', but dark was better. 'Time to go? Oh, no!'

but that tag of remembrance came in her mind. When had she said it? You can't stop days or rivers?

Captain John smoothed his hair with his hand, smiled once more at Harriet, and went.

'But . . . you haven't said goodbye to me,' she called, caught unawares, in dismay, but he did not answer and limped steadily away until his footsteps died in the distance, and she knew he had reached the Red House.

Slowly she turned the edge of the thick carpeted wheel of flowers over in the grass with her foot; over and over and over.

'Tomorrow we shall have to sweep these up,' said Harriet. 'They don't smell nice when they wither.'

She remembered something she had forgotten all these days and weeks and months. She stepped over the old lily shoots up to the tree and put her hand down into the hollow she had found, all that time before. Cold, sticky from dew and tree-mould, her charm was still there.

My world, thought Harriet. She was pleased to have it again, but she thought regretfully, I have it still, but I never found out what it meant.

Holding it in her hand she went slowly across the drive and up the steps and into the house.

'Puff-wait-puff' sounded the escape steam from the Works, and the water ran calmly in the river.

Elizabeth Jane Howard
Special Limited Edition
The Long View/The Sea Change £4.99
Two beautiful stories for the price of one!

Loyalty . . . Passion . . . Discovery . . .

Elizabeth Jane Howard, bestselling author of The Cazalet Chronicle, dissects love, marriage and relationships in two revealing – and wonderfully entertaining – full length novels.

THE LONG VIEW

Elizabeth Jane Howard's acclaimed fictional portrait of a contemporary marriage – ingeniously constructed to give a very real view of the shifting relationship between two people.

'If artistry lies in heightened awareness, this is it' *The Times*

THE SEA CHANGE

A classic story of compulsion – deftly unravelling the complex interactions between two men and two women whose lives become entangled in London, New York, and finally on a remote and mysterious Greek island.

'Beautifully written and richly perceptive' *Daily Telegraph*

Clare Francis
Special Limited Edition
Requiem/Wolf Winter £5.99
The best of Clare Francis, in two classic thrillers.

'Magnificent . . . move over Frederick Forsyth and Hammond Innes'
Sunday Telegraph

REQUIEM
The death of an innocent child leads to outcry about the environmental
vandalism of an American petro-chemical giant. A reclusive rock star and a
Green activist team up to stalk the enemy – but no one could foresee the
terror to come . . .

'Plenty of action, and more than enough murderous surprises' *Independent*

WOLF WINTER
In the deadly chill of the Cold War, two Norwegians are gunned down after
straying into Soviet wilderness – killings that will bind three people together
in a web of treachery and passion . . .

'The spy thriller has rarely been better done' *New York Times*

James Herriot

Special Limited Edition £7.99

**Every Living Thing/If Only They Could Talk/
It Shouldn't Happen to a Vet/Let Sleeping Vets Lie**

Four bestsellers in one great value volume!

For more than 25 years, James Herriot captivated millions of readers and television viewers with tales of the triumphs, disasters, pride and sometimes heartache that filled his life as a vet in the Yorkshire Dales.

Included here is the story that launched a legend, James Herriot's very first book *If Only They Could Talk*. Also included are his second and third books, *It Shouldn't Happen to a Vet* and *Let Sleeping Vets Lie* – and his last, unforgettable bestseller, *Every Living Thing*.

'Enormous pleasure . . . the stories can be read and re-read' *Sunday Times*

'After an evening among his tales, anyone with as much as a dog or a budgerigar will feel they should move to Darrowby at once' *Yorkshire Post*

'It is a pleasure to be in James Herriot's company' *Observer*

All Pan Books are available at your local bookshop or newsagent, or can be ordered direct from the publisher. Indicate the number of copies required and fill in the form below.

Send to: Macmillan General Books C.S.
               Book Service By Post
               PO Box 29, Douglas I-O-M
               IM99 1BQ

or phone: 01624 675137, quoting title, author and credit card number.

or fax: 01624 670923, quoting title, author, and credit card number.

Please enclose a remittance* to the value of the cover price plus 75 pence per book for post and packing. Overseas customers please allow £1.00 per copy for post and packing.

*Payment may be made in sterling by UK personal cheque, Eurocheque, postal order, sterling draft or international money order, made payable to Book Service By Post.

Alternatively by Access/Visa/MasterCard

Card No.

Expiry Date

Signature

Applicable only in the UK and BFPO addresses.

While every effort is made to keep prices low, it is sometimes necessary to increase prices at short notice. Pan Books reserve the right to show on covers and charge new retail prices which may differ from those advertised in the text or elsewhere.

NAME AND ADDRESS IN BLOCK CAPITAL LETTERS PLEASE

Name

Address

3/95

Please allow 28 days for delivery.
Please tick box if you do not wish to receive any additional information. ☐